EMPIRES OF BRONZE

# THE SHADOW OF TROY

by Gordon Doherty

www.gordondoherty.co.uk

First Edition

Also by Gordon Doherty:

**THE LEGIONARY SERIES**

1. LEGIONARY (2011)
2. VIPER OF THE NORTH (2012)
3. LAND OF THE SACRED FIRE (2013)
4. THE SCOURGE OF THRACIA (2015)
5. GODS & EMPERORS (2015)
6. EMPIRE OF SHADES (2017)
7. THE BLOOD ROAD (2018)
8. DARK EAGLE (2020)

**THE STRATEGOS TRILOGY**

1. BORN IN THE BORDERLANDS (2011)
2. RISE OF THE GOLDEN HEART (2013)
3. ISLAND IN THE STORM (2014)

**THE EMPIRES OF BRONZE SERIES**

1. SON OF ISHTAR (2019)
2. DAWN OF WAR (2020)
3. THUNDER AT KADESH (2020)
4. THE CRIMSON THRONE (2021)
5. THE SHADOW OF TROY (2021)
6. THE DARK EARTH (2022)

**THE RISE OF EMPERORS SERIES**

1. SONS OF ROME (2020)
2. MASTERS OF ROME (2021)
3. GODS OF ROME (2021)

*UXORI MEAE CARISSIMAE*

# THE GREAT POWERS OF THE LATE BRONZE AGE (CIRCA 1258 BC)

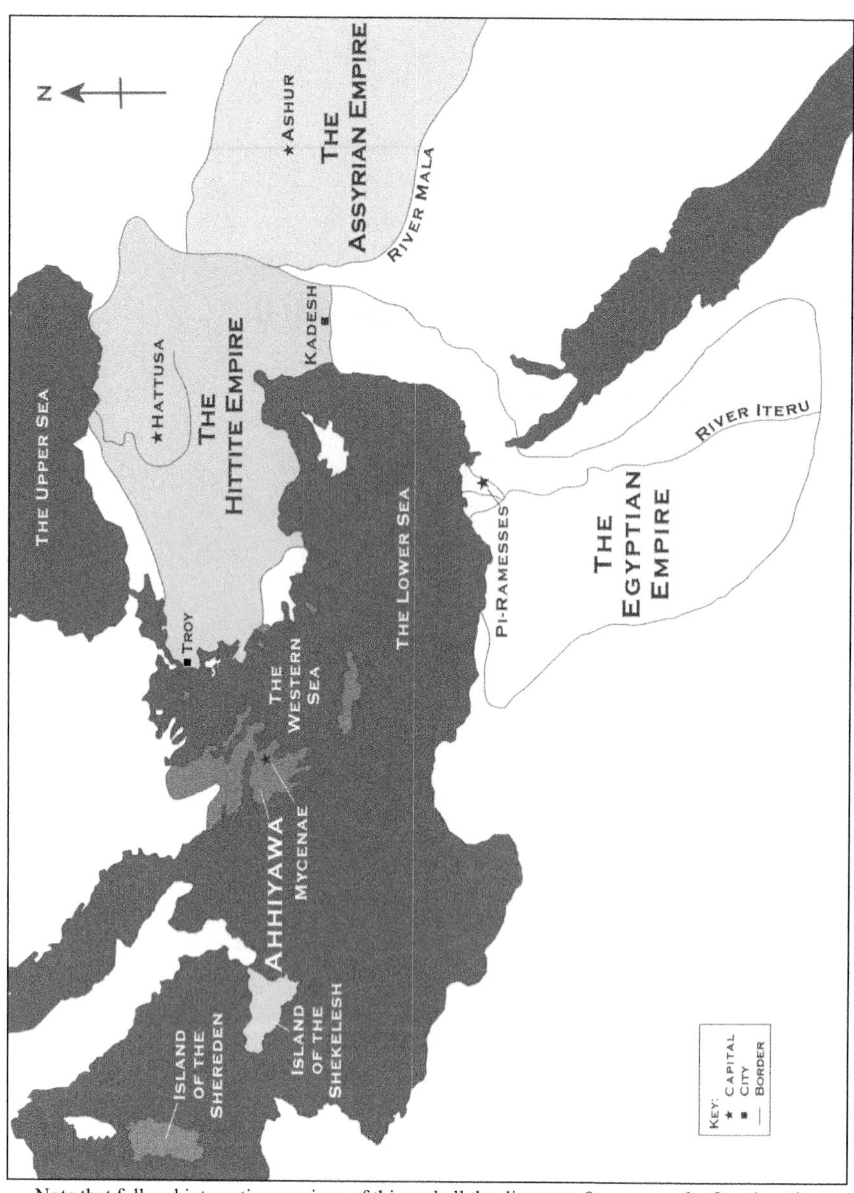


Note that full and interactive versions of this and all the diagrams & maps can be found on the 'Empires of Bronze' section of my website, www.gordondoherty.co.uk

# THE KINGDOMS OF THE WESTERN SEA

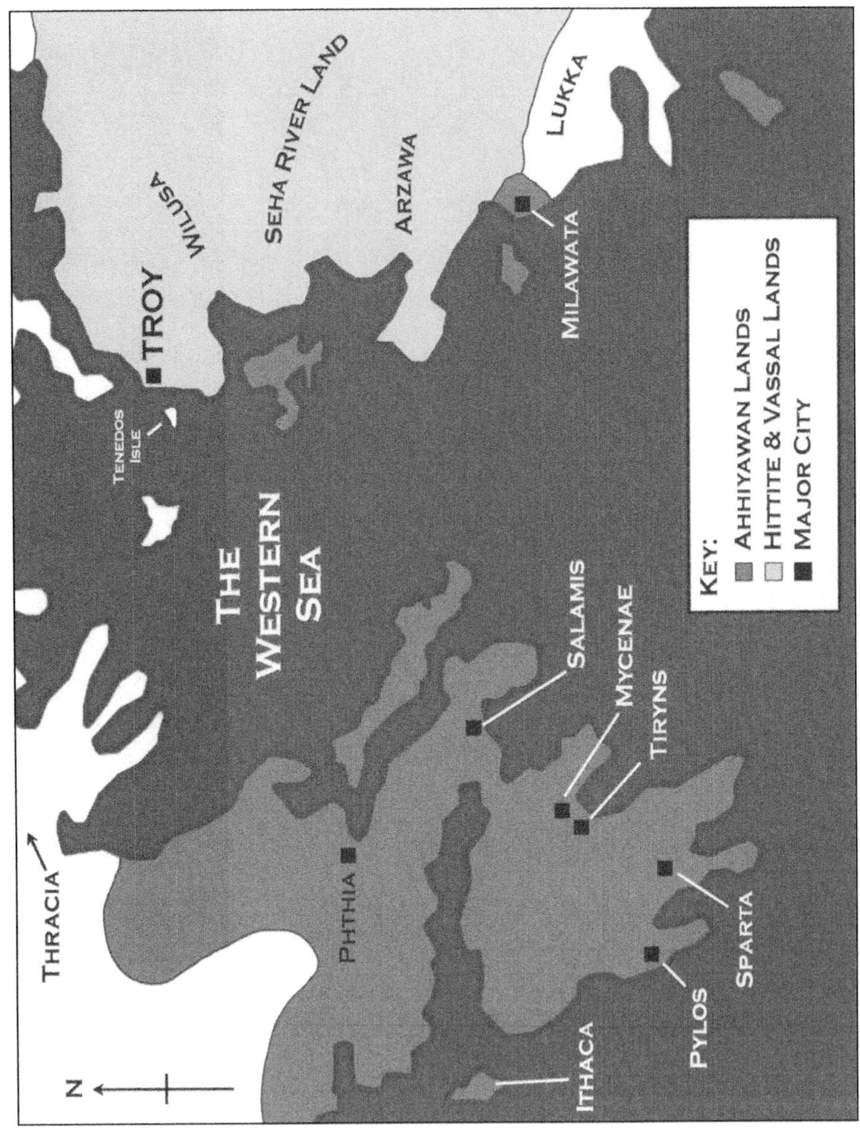

# THE SCAMANDER PLAIN

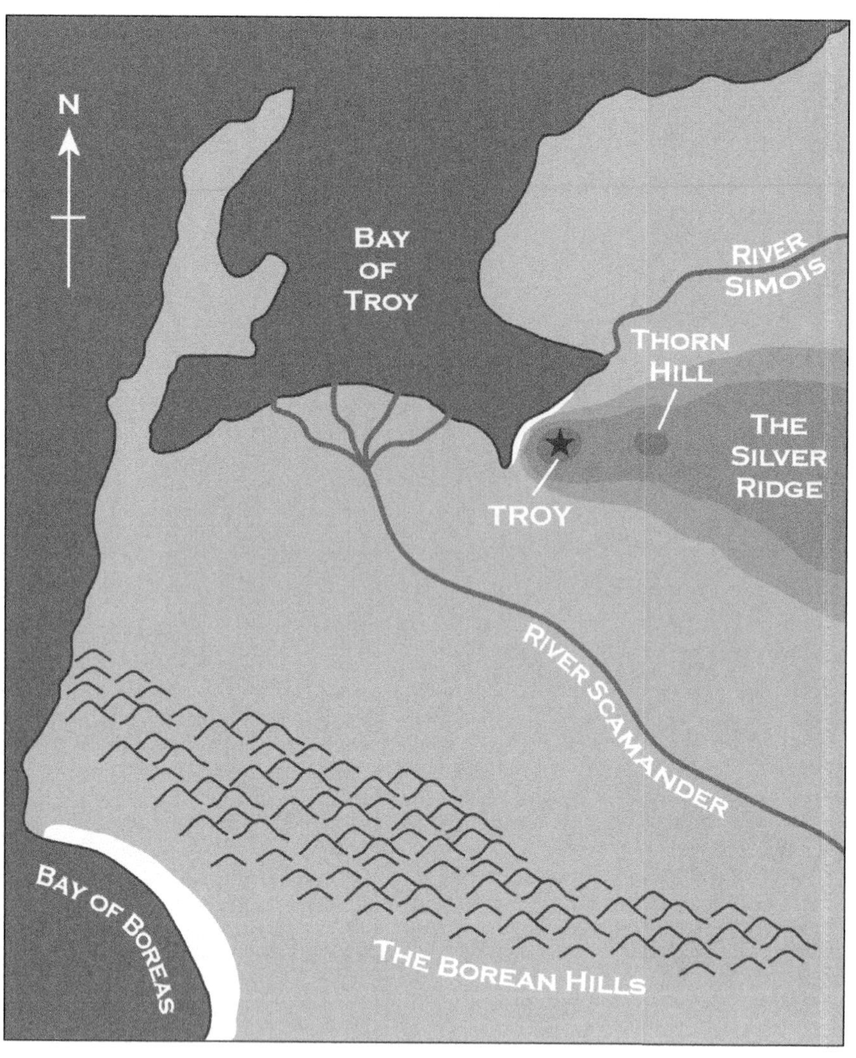

# THE CITY OF TROY

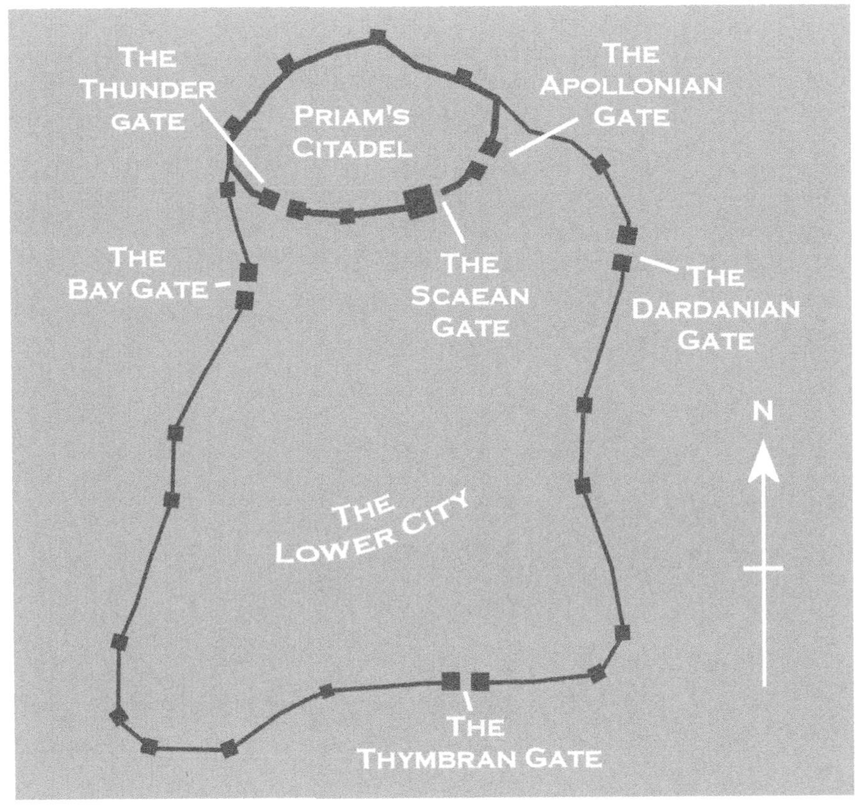

# PROLOGUE

## A LION IN THE GRASS
## WINTER 1262 BC

'Faster!' yelled Troilus, gripping the sorrel-red stallion's neck and leaning forward in the saddle. As the steed burst into a gallop along the frost-jewelled Silver Ridge, the morning wind roared in his ears. His mop of tawny curls snapped behind him like a banner, the coldness stung his lips and nostrils and brought tears to his eyes. He sucked in a breath and tasted the earthy, sweet scent of the Scamander plain. '*Faster!*' he cried again, his young voice shrill. 'Yes… faster than the arrows of Apollo!'

Hooves thundered up by his side. Polyxena flashed him a devious grin. 'But not as fast as me, Brother,' she cackled, then with a '*Ya!*' drove her steed on ahead towards the low winter sun, dazzling on the eastern horizon.

Troilus exploded with an indignant cry that broke down into laughter. 'Ya,' he geed his horse on after his sister. With the stallion's every stride, he felt a tap-tapping on his bare chest of the wolf's-tooth necklace the strange easterner had given him years ago. *Take this,* the towering warrior had said, *and always remember that you are a Prince of Troy*. It made him feel like a man, like his older brothers. A hero!

After a time, the siblings dropped into a canter and ranged together, side by side. They slowed to a walk, picked their way down from the Silver Ridge and onto the frost-sheathed river plain. Curlews trilled in the air around them as they entered this sea of grass and winter wheat, the icy tips of the tallest stalks brushing against their ankles.

He gazed southwards, across the dips where mist lay in thickly-whipped folds, picking out a distant smudge of marble, gleaming in the morning light. The Shrine of Apollo, perched on a knoll where the Thymbran stream bled into the River Scamander. He patted the sack hanging from his saddle: grapes and small pots of honey. The yearly ritual had always been carried out this way: a prince and a princess of Troy would travel alone to take a winter offering to the ancient shrine. His father, his brothers, the priests – *everyone* – had said that it was too dangerous this year, that it could not be done… but Troilus knew that it could. A tingle of excitement scurried across his skin. He clutched the wolf's-tooth necklace again: this was his time, at last. After all, the seers claimed that he would one day be Troy's hero: *when he reaches his twentieth summer, Apollo will grant immortality to Troy.* So why wait seven more years to become that hero? Why not now?

He glanced at Polyxena from the corner of his eye. She wore a look that summed up the way he felt: devious, excited. Nobody had seen the two slipping out of the Dardanian Gate that morning at the change of the guard. They would be done with this offering and back to announce the heroic deed before anyone had even noticed.

When a crow cawed suddenly, Polyxena yelped. Fear fizzed in Troilus' gut. Both slowed. He thought of their older sister Cassandra and the visions she had spoken of, so different to the other seers.

*A lion stalks the plain near the Thymbran track, mane and face stained red with blood, meat hanging from his fangs.*

Troilus gulped a few times, then gritted his teeth, eyes combing the way ahead, ears hearing every whisper and crackle from the long grass. He loved his sister, but not her gloomy divinations. In any case, Chryses the Priest had dismissed her mutterings, as he always did. He sat tall in the saddle, fighting away his fears. *No lions here,* he thought. With a click of the tongue, he bade the two horses onwards.

The gentle burble of the Thymbran stream rose from just ahead. Troilus lifted a hand to shade his eyes, regarding the stream's meandering path towards the shrine. He noticed Polyxena fussing over her steed.

'We should water the horses here before we go on,' she said softly.

Troilus patted his stallion's neck – damp with sweat from the recent gallop. The waters were always the sweetest and purest here at the edge of the plain, especially in these winter moons. 'Aye,' he agreed.

They slid from their saddles and thudded onto the hard ground. It became softer near the stream, dampness seeping between their bare toes. At the water's edge, the two horses drank. Troilus gazed into the waters, spotting cobalt fish darting around under the surface.

'The way the stream sparkles in the morning light,' Polyxena sighed, 'it makes me think that there is still magic in this land.'

Troilus half-smiled. 'They cannot rob us of that,' he said. 'They may plague our countryside like locusts… but they cannot take away the magic of the soil, the air, the rivers.'

'Can they not?' Polyxena answered. 'What use is magic out here when we live out our lives trapped inside Troy's walls?'

Troilus threw out his hands. 'Trapped? Not today. Today, we are free to roam.'

'So too are the Ahhiyawans.'

Troilus snorted. 'The plain is empty. I see no smoke of their plunder nor hear the ugly yap of their tongues.' He had stolen those very words from one of Hektor's recent rallying speeches to the allies, but she didn't need to know that. Regardless, he thought, she was right. Life had never been the same since the Ahhiyawans came. Six years ago their black boats had sliced across the Western Sea, churning onto Trojan sand like axe blades. Six years during which the air had carried a constant odour of pyre smoke.

He squinted and looked to the east and the highlands there. Some way far beyond lay the mightiest empire in the world. Troy's best hope. As a boy, he had seen them come from that horizon – tall, fierce-looking, their long dark hair tagged with amulets and animal teeth. It was their famous leader who had bequeathed him the wolf's fang necklace.

'The Hittites are not coming,' Polyxena said quietly, reading his thoughts.

His nose wrinkled. 'They are delayed, that is all.'

'Delayed?' Polyxena scoffed. 'In the six years since we called to them for help, they could have marched to our aid and back ten times over.'

Troilus gulped. It felt as if he was trying to swallow a stone. 'Have faith in our oath of alliance. Troy has called for help. The Hittite Army *will* come.'

But Polyxena was not listening. Instead, her eyes darted, tracking a wagtail as it sped from a spot in the rushes downstream. 'We should move on,' she said. 'Something doesn't feel right.'

Troilus glared at her, annoyed that she had barely listened to him. 'Very well, to the shrine,' he grumped, leading his horse from the stream. 'But you'll see. The Hittites *will* come. Twenty thousand strong. When they do, they will trample the Ahhiyawans like twigs, drive them back into the sea like-' The words stuck in his throat as if a hand had gripped his neck. What was that noise?

A rapid crackle of breaking reeds.

His head snapped round and his eyes latched onto the shuddering stalks… and at the thing in there, ploughing towards them. His heart pulsed as he saw what it was.

The nightmare. The bane of Troy and her armies.

'A… Achilles,' Polyxena shrieked.

'Ride,' Troilus half-croaked, half-screamed.

First, he bundled Polyxena onto her saddle, then slapped the beast's rump, sending it off at a mad gallop. Next, he vaulted onto his own horse, yanking on the reins and jabbing one heel into its flank. '*Ya!*' he screamed.

The horse bolted and Troilus clung on. Glancing in his wake he saw the enemy champion: bare footed for speed, wearing just his helm and kilt, he moved like a great cat. *Like a lion.* This one had slain more Trojans than any other of the Ahhiyawans. Always, men said, he left his opponents looking ungainly and slow-witted. *Not this time,* he mouthed, seeing Achilles fall back and slip from view, beaten for speed.

He looked ahead, seeing Polyxena at the shrine, dismounted and seeking the protection of Apollo. He yanked the reins to steer his horse there also. *Safety*, he thought as he sped closer, *sanctuary*. For no man, Ahhiyawan or Trojan, would dare desecrate a shrine to the Sun God.

At just that moment, the mist in the nearest dip puckered and swirled. Achilles lunged back into view, running almost level with his horse. With a *zing*, the killer's sword was free of its sheath.

Troilus knew he was barely capable of fumbling his own sword free, let alone fighting with it. Crazed, he lifted his baldric over his head and tossed it away, shedding the weight in hope of a dash more speed. Next, he pulled on the sack hanging from the saddle, letting fall the offerings of grapes and honey intended for the shrine. The grapes pattered and the honey urns smashed in his wake. Lighter… faster?

The answer came in the form of a violent jolt as his head snapped backwards, his flowing curls seized by the leaping Achilles. He uttered a choked cry, falling from the saddle. The stallion rode on while he and Achilles came crashing down in a heap, tumbling along the frosty ground.

Achilles rose to his feet, yanking Troilus up by the hair again, onto his knees, then rested the edge of his long, straight sword against the base of his neck.

Troilus' eyes rolled up at the Ahhiyawan champion. His mouth flooded with words – pleas for his life, threats, inhuman screams of fear.

Achilles' cerulean eyes drank in Troilus' features, recognising them. A group of less impressive Ahhiyawans emerged from the mist and wheat, eyeing the champion's prize. 'It *is* him. It is Prince Troilus,' said one.

Achilles smiled thinly. 'No twentieth summer for you, Son of Priam… and no immortality for Troy.'

The sword sliced through Troilus neck. In his last whispers of life, he heard Polyxena's scream and felt his head being hoisted high like a trophy. The last thing he saw was the lesser Ahhiyawans falling upon his decapitated body, clawing at his possessions to take as their prize.

# PART 1
# SPRING 1258 BC

FOUR YEARS LATER...

# CHAPTER 1

## AN OLD DEBT

A lone ox wagon swayed through a windswept land of pale terracotta hills spotted with shrubs and boulders. The two Hittite soldiers clinging to the wagon's sides watched the track ahead vigilantly. All was desolate. Just as the sun turned deep red and began to cast long shadows across the countryside, one soldier's battle-scarred face slackened, his eyes widening. He held up and shook his spear towards a spot on the horizon where a soaring tor of limestone rose into view, silhouetted by the setting sun. 'It is the Vulture Peak. We are here.'

The wagon slowed by the trackside and the soldiers hopped down, followed by the driver. And then the final passenger alighted, his long silver hair framing a weathered, fox-like face and odd eyes – one hazel, one smoke-grey. Hattu, Great King of the Hittites, folded his green cloak over one shoulder and strode to a knoll overlooking the sweeping plain between them and the jagged mountain. He crouched as he studied the windswept grasslands, bare all the way to the north. Everything was silent bar a gentle moan of wind, the cicada song and, somewhere in the unseen distance, a lone elephant trumpeting.

The driver dropped to his haunches beside him, his copper hoop earrings jostling as he regarded the plain also. 'There's nobody here,' Dagon rumbled through thin lips, flexing one hand – weary from holding the reins for so long – and running the other through his shock of white hair. 'They were supposed to rendezvous with us here.'

The two soldiers joined them. 'Perhaps they are delayed, *Labarna?* The bridges in the north have fallen into disrepair, after all,' said beanpole Zupili. 'Maybe they had to trek upriver and find another way across?'

Hattu shook his head slowly.

'The light has not yet faded,' suggested the broad-faced Bulhapa. 'They might still arrive before dark.'

Hattu shook his head again. 'If one thousand of our soldiers were anywhere near, we would see their dust rising in the sky. I see nothing. Not even a-' His next breath caught in his throat. His grey eye ached, and at last he *did* see something out there. Movement. An eagle, circling low. The great bird was tracking something moving through the grass – not a thousand Hittite soldiers. Just one. Staggering. White tunic stained dark red. A moment later the others saw it too. In a flurry of scraping and thumping boots, Bulhapa and Zupili ran to the injured man, catching him as he fell to his knees. Hattu and Dagon arrived a moment later.

Hattu knelt, sweeping the injured man's long dark hair away from his face. 'Captain Tazili?' he said, recognising the young officer. The man groaned in reply. Hattu glanced over the slash that ran from his shoulder to his abdomen, and at the white bone and iridescent organ peeking from within. A fatal wound. He thumbed the stopper from his drinking skin and held it to the dying man's parched lips, comforting him with a drink. 'What happened?'

'The Azzi warbands ambushed us at,' he stopped, clutching his wound, his face contorting, 'at the canyon of the four winds. We had assured the people of Zalpa that they were gone and-' another convulsion '-and we thought they were. But they were waiting for us. It was a massacre. I am the only one left.'

Hattu gulped slowly, feeling as if he had just swallowed darkness. It had taken years to raise the Hittite Empire from its knees, to find and train those thousand men. The first seeds of a reborn army, he had proclaimed. Dashed, gone, ruined once more. A bloody hand touched his shin.

'Take me home, *Labarna?*' Captain Tazili begged, his face turning grey. 'Take me home to see my wife and sons at Hattusa?'

Hattu took Tazili's hands in both of his. 'They are waiting for you,' he said softly, looking along the track whence their wagon had come, into the haze of distance. 'Go to them,' he said quietly. Tazili slid away with a weak sigh. Hattu stayed by his side for a time, thinking. Eventually, he looked up at the two guards. 'Gather brush and wood, prepare a pyre.' The two set off to do as bid.

As Hattu stood, the eagle that had spotted the wounded soldier silently glided down onto his shoulder. For ten years Andor had been his companion, throughout the ruinous civil war and ever since. He fed her a scrap of salted venison as his mind began to rake over this latest disaster.

'What now?' asked Dagon.

Hattu eyed his oldest friend. The two of them – he the King and High General of the Hittite Empire and Dagon the legendary Chariot Master – were without an army or a single chariot. He looked west towards Troy, then back east towards Hattusa. His gaze lingered there longest.

When he closed his eyes, he could almost taste Queen Puduhepa's farewell kiss on his lips, see his adopted son Kurunta's firm left-fisted salute, feel little Ruhepa's sapling embrace. He took from his purse the small wooden goat his daughter had given him on that day of parting. There was something invaluably charming about its irregularity. One horn was huge and the other small and apologetic, and the beast sported something of a deranged smile.

'By all the Gods, I want to turn round and go home too,' Dagon said, thumbing at the silver horse pendant on his necklace – a precious keepsake from his wife, Nirni. 'My heart aches to be with my family. But I feel it as you do,' he continued. 'I know that our debt to Troy can no longer lie unsettled. It is as if the Gods are pushing us there.'

A crackling of twigs sounded as the two guards hoisted Tazili's body onto the small pile of wood then lit the kindling. In unison, they droned a song of the Dark Earth and all poured a splash of wine on the edges of the fire. As Hattu gazed into the flames, he thought of his previous visit to Troy, before the civil war. 'We once promised King Priam an army. We don't have even a single company of men to take to his aid. And so, so *few* we leave behind to guard Hattusa.'

'Queen Puduhepa and Kurunta are wise and resourceful,' said Dagon. 'They will marshal the city militia to keep the capital safe in our absence. They will ration the dwindling crop wisely and fairly.'

Hattu smiled, imagining the pair bickering as always. Dagon was right. They would keep the city safe. They would not let the people go hungry. Something about the light changed then, a dark shadow spilling across the land as the fiery sun began to slide behind the Vulture Peak. It made Hattu think about another one back there at Hattusa. Tall, dark, troubling. His smile faded.

Dagon read him – as always – like a clay tablet. Planting a hand on Hattu's shoulder he said: 'And *he* will do his part also.'

'Will he?' Hattu grunted, rolling his eyes towards Dagon.

The Chariot Master shrugged unconvincingly, betraying his own private misgivings.

Hattu looked across the land, and eventually his gaze returned to that track whence they had come. Darkening, deserted. Yet for some reason he felt as if he was being watched. How close were those raiding Azzi, he wondered? 'Come on, old friend. Let us be on our way to a safe campsite.'

***

Under the looming night shadow of Vulture Peak, Hattu lay awake. He was tired, but every time he neared the edges of sleep, Bulhapa, lying nearby, would twitch and mutter the names of past lovers, jolting him awake. He cast an envious eye at Dagon, sleeping like a dead man on the other side of the low, flickering campfire.

So he sat up and stoked at the embers, enjoying the scent of charred beer-bread still floating in the hot air. He cast his eye across the night: the elms hemming their campsite seemed silvery in the moonlight, writhing every so often in the night breeze. Zupili stood watch near a small brook, sipping slowly from his water skin. And then there was the mountain.

Up on the dark tip stood a Hittite turret – a lone tower like those that studded Hattusa's walls. The structure had once served as a beacon tower for relaying messages from Troy to Hattusa and vice versa. Ten years ago during the civil war, the garrison had been slaughtered and never replaced. Now, it was nothing but a broken tooth, a symbol of his empire's failure. For no Trojan signal had ever reached Hattusa. Indeed, he had only heard about the trouble at Troy via the lips of a passing merchant, and that was two full years after the Ahhiyawans had landed on Troy's shores. The war there had since raged on ever since. Ten whole years now.

He stared into the fire's last, cherry-red ember. Gradually, his head dipped forward and he drifted into a slumber. Soon, the slumber became a dream.

*His chest rose and fell in slow, controlled breaths as he circled his rival. Drums rattled in a rapid rhythm from the darkness all around him – unseen demons dictating the pace of this dance. It was a familiar feeling, twin swords in hand, body primed to dodge or spring in attack. But what was not familiar, and most troubling, was his opponent. King Priam, spry and strong, matched his every pace, wore a green-eyed leonine glower, held a spear and sword of his own. This was not right; the Trojans and Hittites were allies, always had been. Up above, in the blackness, he heard the beating of giant wings. Ishtar was circling, watching. 'Why are we doing this?' Hattu called up to the Goddess.*

*When she did not answer, he returned his gaze to Priam. 'Comrade?' he said.*

*Priam responded with an animal twitch of his upper lip. 'No more of your slippery words, King Hattu. I should have known. I should have seen it coming.'*

*'Seen what? I don't understand?'*

*Priam's shoulders jolted with dry laughter, as he pointed at Hattu's weapons. 'You did not seem so puzzled moments ago when you took up swords against me.'*

*Hattu, disgusted with the insinuation, threw down his twin blades. 'I know I am dreaming. I know this is not real.'*

*'Like the dreams you once told me of?' Priam snarled. 'Of Ishtar, of the desert of graves at Kadesh? Of the famine all across your empire? Of you seizing the Hittite throne for yourself? They all came very horribly true, did they not?'*

*Hattu bridled at this. 'You are like a brother to me, Priam, but do not dare throw my failings back at me like knives.'*

*'What happens next in Ishtar's song? Eh, Great King of the Hittites? What happens next?' Priam's every word was a hiss, dripping with accusation.*

*Hattu made a cage of his teeth. 'Remember, King Priam of Troy... vassal of the Hittite throne... remember your place. It is not wise to bend our friendship like this.'*

*Behind Priam, Ishtar descended gently, her great wings folding away, her towering form swaying and talons clacking as she strode up behind the Trojan King. She raised her arms and – as if he were a puppet, attached to her by twines – he raised his arms too. Her lips parted to reveal her fangs and when she sang in her throaty burr, Priam sang too in perfect mortal harmony.*

*'A burning east, a desert of graves,*
*A grim harvest, a heartland of wraiths,*

*The Son of Ishtar, will seize the Grey Throne,*
*A heart so pure, will turn to stone,'*

*The Goddess and Priam paused in unison to suck in full breaths...*

*'The west will dim, with black boats' hulls,*
*Trojan heroes, mere carrion for gulls,*
*And the time will come, as all times must,*
*When the world will shake, and fall to DUST!'*

*Ishtar grinned and fell silent, letting her arms rest. Priam's arms dropped and he once again held his weapons at the ready. 'Is this not simply the latest leg of your journey through life, King Hattu? Everywhere you tread, you leave death in your wake. Now you are coming to Troy. Coming to save us... or so you say.' Priam's face pinched and spittle puffed from his lips as he spoke: 'Here to destroy us, I suspect.'*

*Hattu took a moment to control his anger. It would do him no good here, he realised. It was like swallowing a glowing coal, but he managed it. 'Friend, why do you say these things?' he reasoned, stepping towards Priam.*

*'Because it will come to be as it always does. The great Hattu is here and brings his black curse to my land. To kill me and my countrymen.'*

*Hattu held his gaze. 'Remember all we have shared in the past. You know me, Priam. Our fathers were like siblings and so are we.' He walked between Priam's spear and sword, and the Trojan King could not bring himself to resist. Hattu planted his hands on Priam's shoulders reassuringly. Priam's face softened and a hint of the old smile appeared.*

*With a sudden jolt, it changed horribly.*

*Priam shuddered again, and a thin red runnel of blood ran from his lips, striping his chin.*

*Appalled, Hattu shook him by the shoulders. 'My friend, what is wrong?' It took a moment for Hattu to realise that he was not holding Priam's shoulders, but the twin hilts of his iron swords that he was sure he had thrown down moments ago. Eyes growing wide as moons, he pulled his shaking fingers from them, sickened at the sight of the weapons lodged hilt-deep in Priam's shoulders. Trembling, blood now pattering down around him, Priam sank to his knees, eyes misting with death. He crunched onto his side, stone dead.*

*'No…' Hattu croaked, looking from Priam's body, punctured by his swords, then to Ishtar, receding into the darkness again, smiling still. 'No!'*

Like a drowning man, he swam up from the deep swamp of sleep, clawing, desperate, and woke with a start, gasping. It took a few moments to realise where he was – still sitting by the fire. He looked around as if certain the Goddess was here in the world of the wakened too. His heart pounded for a while before he felt safe again.

Regardless, there was no chance of getting back to sleep now. For one there was the Goddess' nightmare, and then there was Bulhapa: the sleeping soldier was now in the full throes of a dream-orgy by the look of it – squeezing at imaginary breasts and gurgling in pleasure. So Hattu gazed up at Vulture Peak for a time. The mountains were calling him again.

He rose, threw on his cloak and left the camp, giving Zupili a nod as he went. Outside of the weak bubble of warmth around the fire, the night air was cold, every breath of wind bracing. He glanced back along the road they had travelled, into the inky blackness of distance. For a moment he had that odd feeling again, as if there were eyes in that well of darkness, staring back at him. He shook his head. *Nothing out there but swaying trees,* he reassured himself. On he went. As he walked, his joints complained, knees fiery hot, shins aching, ankles clicking like rocks. Fifty-six summers, he had known. Gods, he thought, some mornings it felt like five hundred.

When he reached the base of the mountain, he glared up at the peak. A tamarisk tree swayed in the stronger winds up there like the taunting ghost of youth. Hattu shot it a menacing look and grinned… then set his hands to the rock. Cold, dry. Perfect. He crouched to pat his palms in the terracotta dust, all the while looking up to scan the moonlit face of stone for holds. Andor glided over to land on a ledge some way up and settled there to watch him. With a thrust of power from his right leg, he reached up and caught the first handhold, then pressed his left foot onto a crimp, then reached for the next handhold. It was as if he was in the palm of Sarruma the Mountain God, his aches forgotten, his every upwards motion strong and well-executed. The breeze soon became a squall, casting his silvery hair to one side. His mind fell into the rhythm of it all, through old climbing mantras, each like the beat of a drum. Eventually, he did not have to think at all.

Thus, his mind drifted back to home and the troubles there. First, there was the wavering loyalty of the Hittite vassals. Many of these minor kingdoms – vital buffer states around the heartlands – no longer attended the yearly gathering to renew their oath of loyalty to the Grey Throne, nor even sent a message of apology for their absence. Then there was Assyria, the mighty eastern empire who had sent no envoy and offered no gift to recognise Hattu's ascension. When Hattu closed his eyes he could still see the one thing the Assyrian king *had* sent him. A tablet, etched with a bold message: *I delivered you no gift, I put no envoy on the road to your city, because you are not worthy. You are but a substitute for the true Great King of your lands whom you dislodged.* And that was the third and most troubling matter. Urhi-Teshub: whom Hattu had ousted from the Hittite throne. He had spared his nephew's life and granted him comfortable exile. But Urhi-Teshub had since broken free. Rumours were thick and varied – that he was gathering an army to reclaim his throne, that he was trapped in an Egyptian desert oasis, that he had sailed to the far west to establish a great kingdom there. A ghost, stalking his every thought.

Suddenly, the drumbeat of the climb stuttered. One foot scraped and slid, and his arms tensed. He found himself hanging, hearing his own yelp as if it had come from another. He was nearly halfway up, he realised, eyeing the mocking tamarisk and the crumbled turret. The rest of the way was sheer and almost smooth. His legs were burning. So much easier to retreat back down to the ground. But he knew it was fatal for a climber to let doubt claw into the mind, and so he set off again. As he went, he shook his head downwards once to cast away beads of sweat. For a moment, he halted, staring below. Had something moved down there? Was there another climber on this dark mountain? He saw Andor in flight now, sweeping past in a strange pattern – the way she did when hunting or during battle. Something had caught the eagle's attentions.

As the biting wind whistled around him, he shook his head again to clear his mind and carried on upwards. His thoughts returned to the empire. Not enough grain to feed the families. Too few families to provide men and women to work the fields or to repopulate the army. A paucity of tin and a relentless drought. The futile pacifying and wooing of vassals. The intensifying earth tremors. The rising threat of Assyria. His head began to spin again, until he thought of the one good thing he had achieved in all that time.

The Silver Peace. A lasting truce with Egypt – the colossal empire of the southern sands. It had been talked about since the Battle of Kadesh. Pharaoh Ramesses and he were not friends, but they had developed a certain affinity at the close of that terrible clash, both talking of their wishes never to fight such a war again. Puduhepa and Kurunta had directed the talks that had finally seen the vow committed to clay and silver. In truth it was more of a defensive alliance than a mere truce: should the Assyrians attempt to invade Hittite lands, Ramesses would be oath-bound to raise his armies against them. *Thus, the empire is secure,* he told himself over and over as he clambered on upwards. *Now, it is all about Troy.*

His ankles felt numb, and the shaking in his legs grew quite unsettling. More, the icy wind battered at him, determined to fight against his ascent. Yet there were only a few handholds to go and he would be at the top – a chance to rest. Just before he propelled himself up onto the last stretch, he glanced down to check his footing was good. It was. Even better, he could see clearly now that there was no other climber on this rock face. His mind had been playing tricks. *Up, up, up,* he willed himself, getting ready to launch up and reach for the summit's edge. He thrust upwards with his right leg… only for the ledge upon which his toes were perched to shear away.

It felt as if someone had replaced his bones with tallow. He clawed uselessly at thin air, falling away from the rock face, weightless, within sight of the summit he would never reach. His dreams and fears smashed together like waves in his mind. Andor shrieked nearby, helpless to save him.

*To fall, to die!*

A hand shot out and grabbed him by the forearm. He jolted, grabbing this hand with his other. His ears pounded with blood as the dark figure hauled him up onto the grassy summit. Hattu, gasping, rose from all fours. His lips moved to thank the stranger, then froze like the rest of him. This was no stranger! The black tunic, the doeskin boots, upturned at the toe, the black chin length hair held back by a red headband. The eyes – like silver studs.

'*You!*' Hattu rasped, his hair streaming across his face in the high wind. It was his worst nightmare arisen and alive.

***

Zupili scratched at his buttocks, eyeing the brightening band of blue on the eastern horizon. Dawn wasn't far off and he had been itching madly all night – ever since he had emptied his bowels on the far side of the brook and used that strange fuzzy leaf to clean up. He remembered Bulhapa's jibes about it earlier, and considered picking some more of the leaves and placing them into his comrade's sleeping blankets. Every so often he glanced up at the Vulture Peak. King Hattu must have reached the top, presumably – nowhere to be seen on the face now. The *Labarna* was wont to such things. Some said he only ever knew peace on the mountain. For Zupili, the whole trip had felt odd: being out here in these estranged vassal lands should have been unnerving. Yet all the time he had been unafraid. Why? Because the *Labarna* was with them on the wagon. The Sun himself, appointed by the Storm God. Now that King Hattu was away on the mountain, it felt different. The shadows in the trees began to writhe oddly. The embers of the fire snapped and crackled in a way that set his nerves on edge. The brook behind him whispered and chattered as if in conspiracy…

Just then, a crazy patter of galloping feet sounded from the far side of the brook. Zupili swung round. The elms across the water shivered and he stared at the spot… before a shape burst clear. A bald, grubby, kilted Egyptian, bounding across the stream on all-fours coming directly for Zupili, spray leaping up all around him.

Zupili shrieked, bringing his spear round and stumbling backwards.

The aged Egyptian skidded to a halt a pace away. Settling on his gnarled haunches, he smoothed at his tuft-beard with overgrown fingernails as if considering some vital matter. 'Very good. You passed the test.'

'Who… wha… Sirtaya?' Zupili croaked.

Dagon and Bulhapa, awake and scrambling to their feet, rushed over, snatching up sword and spear. 'What's wrong?' Dagon slowed first, sighing. 'Sirtaya? What are you doing here?'

Sirtaya shook himself like a dog, spray hitting all three camp members. 'I'm on a very important mission.'

'I had him reconnoitre your camp, and test the guard system,' said a young voice.

All looked round to see King Hattu, returned from the mountain, with Andor on his shoulder. But it was not Hattu who had spoken. By his side walked Prince Tudhaliya, Hattu's son and heir.

***

Zupili and Bulhapa sank to one knee, heads bowed, left fists raised in salute to their returning king and his heir. Sirtaya also. Dagon stared at the royal pair, stunned. Hattu nodded to him. *Give us a moment, old friend.*

Understanding, Dagon waved the others up and had them set about preparing the wagon for the coming day. 'Come, we will eat cold porridge on the road.'

Hattu turned his back on the others, screening off Tudha. 'You followed us?' he growled.

'Your gratitude is most welcome, Father,' Tudha replied.

Hattu glared at him. The face of a boy, the shoulders of a man. At fifteen summers, he was both. More, he was *Tuhkanti* of the Hittite Empire, the king in waiting. One day men would call him *Labarna,* and he would have untold power in his hands. The thought terrified Hattu. 'You should not be here. *Cannot* be here.'

'Yet I am. Were I not, you would be lying at the base of the mountain right now, a bag of skin and smashed bones. I was below you at first. You looked down and saw me. But I skirted round the mountain and climbed to the peak long before you even got close to it. Even if you hadn't slipped near the top you'd never have made it back down without me. Your legs groan like the hinges of old bronze gates these days.'

'You have learned nothing, apparently,' Hattu raged back. 'Not least that a King and his heir should not both be abroad in the same place. What if we were to be ambushed here?'

Tudha gazed off around the camp confidently. 'Then the ambushers would die. You would have to return my sword to me first, of course.'

Hattu peered down his nose at his heir. His voice fell to a snake's whisper. 'After what you did?'

Tudha shook his head slowly, bitterly, taking a step back, jabbing a finger towards his father. 'I gave you victory at Hatenzuwa.'

Hattu's pounding heart began to slow, dreadful memories of the previous summer rushing back to him. 'Still, you do not see. It was not about the victory; it was about how you won.'

Dawn spread the first feathery tips of her golden wings above the eastern horizon, striping the land in pale light. Hattu thought of the days of Tudha's first years in his and Pudu's arms. Then of his boyhood – so much time Hattu had invested in training him, honing him, preparing him for greatness. But from the moment he was first set loose on his own… Hattu's happy memories crumbled.

The oxen lowed and moaned as Bulhapa and Zupili stepped up onto the wagon's side platforms. Sirtaya climbed onto the vehicle's open back while Dagon settled on the driver's berth. 'We're all set to go,' the Chariot Master called to Hattu. 'But I must warn you, these two oxen seem to have developed rampant flatulence.' He cast a sidelong look at Sirtaya, busy scratching his nether-regions. 'At least, I think it is the oxen.'

Hattu gazed west, then slid his eyes back down the eastern track one more time, towards Hattusa. Home.

'We are only days from our destination. Too far from Hattusa now to turn back,' Tudha said, reading his thoughts. 'By your own logic you can't send me back alone – not with so many bandits abroad.'

Hattu's head pounded with indecision. Tudha was right. Maddeningly so.

'I left word with my guards back at Hattusa,' the prince said. 'They will have told Mother by now that I left of my own designs. She will not have to fret for me.'

Hattu's teeth ground. '*Tuhkanti*… do you understand exactly where we are headed?'

Tudha's silver eyes glinted like jewels. 'To Troy. To the greatest war ever waged – so the rumours say.' He held out one hand. 'Give me my iron sword, Father. It is only right.'

Hattu stepped towards the wagon, pulling a leather bag from the back. He strapped on his own leather crossbands, the hilts of his twin blades jutting from behind his shoulders. The swords were as impressive as the day Jaru had forged them. Sharper and harder than any bronze, almost immune to notching. They were two of only a handful made by old Jaru, before the civil war, crafted not of bronze but of good iron. They were even more precious now that the Royal Metalsmith was gone, and all that remained of his secrets was a tablet detailing a method that so far no other Hittite smith could repeat. He reached into the bag again, watching Tudha. The young man's eyes grew wide, hungry, fixed on Hattu's hand as it moved towards the other iron blade in there… then passed across it to instead take out a clay tablet and a reed stylus. He offered the scribal tools to Tudha.

'You will learn as I did to observe, to study and to record. Only once you understand war fully, truly, will I trust you with a royal sword again. Besides, the stylus is a greater weapon than any blade. Wars have been averted, won and lost with its single stroke.'

Tudha's lips rippled, betraying a flash of white teeth. He snatched the writing gear and barged past Hattu, vaulting onto the wagon to sit beside Sirtaya.

***

Whips lashed on sweating, bleeding backs. A train of roped-together Lukkan men and women trudged across the docks of Milawata and onto the slaver ship, heads bowed, sobbing and whimpering.

Sheltering from the noon sun under a tavern awning, a finely-dressed man watched on as he finished a meal of goose and wine. 'Put them in the bowels of the boat,' Mardukal said. His voice, like the sound of a snake sliding over shingle, didn't even come close to penetrating the noisy babble of agitated voices that filled the seething wharf. But it didn't have to. A rat-like man by his side nodded and carried the message to the slave handlers, who barked and brayed the captives down into the dark interior of the boat, where infections ran rife and rats chewed at the wounds of sleeping men.

Mardukal dipped a white cloth into a bowl of rose-scented water and cleaned his hands and mouth, then smoothed at his pale-blue mantle. His mane and beard of tight, oiled curls and his Assyrian silks marked him out as a special presence in this slave-market city, and he enjoyed the way people looked at him: in awe, afraid.

'General, the slaves will fetch a good price when we sell them on… but…'

Mardukal swung his eyes round to pin his burly, bald bodyguard. 'But?'

The bodyguard smiled weakly. 'We… we were not sent here to trade slaves.'

'No, we were sent here to wait,' Mardukal said. 'So while we wait, we might as well make a profit.'

'But the troops grow restless,' the bodyguard said. 'They will kill each other if they remain cooped up here for much longer.' He laughed as if this was a joke, but it was not.

Mardukal followed his darting glance towards the waterside, where sixty Assyrian warships bobbed, moored and serried. His troops sat on the decks and the dockside, drinking, bartering and whoring with the locals. There had been fights and disputes, but that was common when soldiers were confined to towns.

'Forget the soldiers and their brawn and bronze. The greatest weapon – in this city, in this land – is up here,' Mardukal tapped his temple. 'For I am Mardukal, the Leveller of Cities. And right now one of the finest cities in the world is under siege. But the besiegers are clumsy and poorly-skilled at breaking walls. It can only be a matter of time before they accept our king's generous offer and invite me to the siege.' His lips curved like a hunter's bow. 'For Troy will fall, and I will be there to make it so.'

# CHAPTER 2

## A CITY OF SHIPS

The Hittite wagon arrived in a country of forested granite ridges and green vales. Unlike the windswept highlands across which they had journeyed, this land was calm, still and serene, the air sweetened with the scent of jasmine and broom. The rutted old track descended and they were soon riding along the banks of a river, fringed with rushes and pink-blossomed tamarisk trees that overhung the waters as if looking at their reflections in the yellow-brown surface.

Hattu glanced over his shoulder. Bulhapa and Zupili, perched on the wagon sides, were watchful as always. Sirtaya was like a puppy on its first day outdoors, spellbound, eyes like glass orbs, drinking in the sight of a dragonfly hovering above the water, at a heron gliding along the banks, his ears pricking up at the drumming of every woodpecker. And Tudha… Tudha was glaring right back at him.

Hattu noticed the clay tablet lying on the wagon floor, unmarked. 'Make note: we have reached the land of-'

'Wilusa,' Tudha snapped, finishing his sentence, snatching up the tablet and tapping out the information onto it. 'And that is the River Scamander,' he added, writing that too.

'I thought this was the first time you had been to these parts?' Dagon said, glancing at the prince, one eyebrow arched.

'It is.'

'Then how do you know these things?'

Tudha shrugged one shoulder. 'From your lips, Chariot Master,' he replied.

'The tales I tell around the feasting fires at Hattusa?' Dagon laughed. 'How do you know I am telling the truth? Most of those stories are warped beyond fact.'

'Because that,' Tudha flicked a finger to the south, where a massif rose in the ethereal haze, green sloped, the peak capped in dazzling snow, 'is clearly Mount Ida.' He then confidently jabbed the finger ahead. 'And that is the White Shrine of the Thymbran Apollo. Unmistakable.'

Hattu and Dagon twisted their heads forward again to see the landmark rising into view: a small but striking white-stone temple perched by the riverside.

'These fields are the Thymbran Meadows,' Tudha continued, jotting down the fact. 'The farmers here are friends of Troy. No?'

Tudha's tone was goading but Hattu ignored him, for his senses had sharpened on something else. His eyes combed the lands. Deserted. Every time he had journeyed to Troy before, he had been greeted here by Thymbran priests singing from the shrine rooftop, and escorted for the rest of the way to Priam's city by a troop of Trojan soldiers who garrisoned and protected the place. Today, the shrine was deserted and looked shabby and forgotten. Nearby, where manicured farm plots had once stood, was a huge overgrown expanse of wild flax, dazzling blue and green.

'What happened here?' Dagon said in a breathy whisper so only Hattu would hear.

'War,' Tudha replied, sliding up behind the driver's bench. 'That is why you are here. That is why you need me here also. That is why I must have my sword.'

Hattu ignored his heir again, and tried to rid his mind of what had happened during the rebellion at Hatenzuwa. Yet try as he might, he could not shake off the abiding image. The forest shrine, silent. The old wooden door, ajar. The darkness within. He blinked, hard, refusing to let the memories lead him any further.

Soon, the mirage of heat and dust motes ahead thinned, revealing a vast, sweeping flatland. The Scamander wound across this, sparkling like a vein of liquid silver until it met with the western horizon. A long ridge of hoary rock and green grass hemmed the plain in the north. 'The Silver Ridge,' Dagon muttered, then glanced to the south, where a range of low, brown earth fells marked the opposite end of the huge river plain. 'The Borean Hills.'

Hattu shielded his eyes, staring at the distant end of the Silver Ridge – a stony bluff, shaped like the prow of a ship riding high above the plain. Up there sat Troy, capital of Wilusa, a hunkering lion of a city. Its acropolis the lion's head, the sprawling lower city the lion's body. All looked intact. Below it lay a calm bay that shone like a bronze mirror.

'There is… no siege?' Tudha remarked, scanning the plain around the city. As bare and deserted as the parts they had come through to get here.

'Well there's no blockade, at least,' Hattu corrected him. 'But a siege can take many forms.'

A scratching sounded. All looked to Sirtaya, whose talon fingernails were scraping at his tuft beard. The Egyptian's demeanour had changed. His nose was wrinkled in disgust. 'I smell… death,' he whispered.

It hit Hattu and the others an instant later: the stink of drying blood – of soil and metal and decay – and the hum of insects. Hattu saw a frenzy of black flies buzzing near the trackside ahead, clustered over a corpse. The wild dogs and great cats had scavenged most of the body, leaving a yawning, flytrap-like cage of ribs. Andor shrieked – she no longer touched carrion, but the sensory explosion of it all had her agitated, head and neck flat, staring at the body. 'Stop here and wait,' Hattu said to Dagon.

He hopped down from the wagon and approached the cadaver, his hunter's eyes watching for movement anywhere nearby. But there was no sign of men here, apart from these dire remains of one. He crouched by the body, holding his breath. Taking a branch from a nearby bush, he prodded at the remains until they partly rolled over, revealing a sticky mess of blood not yet dried, and the staring, lifeless face, caved-in on one side from a spear wound. Hattu's heart plunged. It was Pandarus, The famous archer-king of Zeleia, ally and protectorate of Troy.

He glanced around, and as his eyes adjusted to the heat haze, he spotted more clouds of insects hovering over many more broken shapes of men. Carrion crows too, pecking at the remains. The ground was riddled with corpses.

He backstepped to the wagon, never taking his eyes off the plain. 'A battle was fought here – yesterday, going by the state of the fallen.' Tracing a hand across the plain towards the Borean Hills, he jabbed a finger towards the horizon there. 'They came from over there,' he said.

'They?' Tudha asked.

'The Ahhiyawans,' Dagon answered for Hattu.

'The Ahhiyawans carry out a "siege" from beyond the horizon?' Tudha laughed. 'Then they are fools, for we are free to enter Troy.'

Hattu looked at his heir sideways. 'Do not be overconfident. It is wise to wait until you have taken the honey before kicking the hive. The ways of war here are very different to those in our heartlands.'

'But we came to save Troy,' Tudha protested, throwing a hand towards the city. 'The way to Troy is clear,'

'No,' Hattu said calmly, gazing at that southern ridge. 'If we are to save Troy, then first we must understand her enemy.'

***

As they trekked up the Borean Hills, Dagon fidgeted with his slack, ringless earlobes. With every step, he shuffled and scratched at the old Masan tunic that they had found aboard the wagon – a blue and distinctly un-Hittite robe that hung to the ankle. 'Itchy bloody thing,' he mumbled. 'Worst of it is my bladder is suddenly full, and I've no idea how to hoist this thing out of the way to get at the necessary parts.'

Hattu chuckled. He too wore such a garment. All his Hittite trappings – his upturned-toe boots, green cloak and kilt – had been left back at the wagon with Tudha, Sirtaya, Andor and the two guards. Likewise, he wore no trinkets in his hair, nor his leather bracer etched with Hittite hieroglyphs. His swords also were back at the wagon.

'In the name of-' Dagon grumbled, scratching madly again. 'Who wore these things last?'

'We are traders, old friend. As traders we might get into the Ahhiyawan camp. As Hittites we most certainly will not.'

Dagon nodded along with every word like a bored child. 'All well and good. But how come you got the smooth tunic, while I got the one riddled with bloody lice and flea-' he stopped dead.

Hattu did likewise, suddenly alert, hearing a panting noise nearby. 'Sentries?' he whispered.

They both scanned the dry grass covering the approach to the brow of the range. No sign of sentries, but… a head sticking from the earth, twitching and grimacing, spitting and snarling. A man buried to his neck.

'Water, please,' the man begged.

Dagon and Hattu both stared at the head, the thin, untidy beard ringing the snarling mouth, the eyes like inky dots. 'Piya-maradu?' they hissed in unison.

Hattu's mind reeled. This was the very bastard who had started stirring up the trouble all those years ago, spreading false messages amongst the western vassals, whipping up hatred against Troy – opening the door for his Ahhiyawan paymasters to finally get a foothold in this land. The pair rose and stepped over to glare down at the wretch.

'It seems the rat has become caught in his own trap?' Dagon said with a grin in his voice.

Hattu noticed how the rogue's balding head was coated in insect bites and crusted skin from constant exposure to the sun. 'The Ahhiyawans did this to you?' he asked.

Piya-maradu's jaw fell agape as he stared up at Hattu's odd eyes. 'King Hattu?' he gasped in recognition.

Hattu felt a sudden burst of anxiety. He was known the world over for his odd eyes. No disguise would be adequate were it not to cover his eyes. How could he have been so inattentive?

'It *is* you! Set me free,' Piya-maradu whispered on. 'I know I had a few run-ins with your father and your brother, I accept that, but-'

'Run-ins?' Hattu raged, sinking to one knee beside Piya-maradu. 'You have plundered and murdered across the edges of my empire for generations.'

Piya-maradu winced. 'Let's leave old differences in the past, aye? Dig me free and together we can flee the wrath of Agamemnon.' He nudged his head towards the brow of the hills as he said this.

*Agamemnon,* thought Hattu, glancing to the hilly crest. So far the Great King of Ahhiyawa had been but a name mentioned – often – in the Hittite court. A foreign leader from a foreign land. 'I thought you were his servant?'

Piya-maradu's face wrinkled into an angry ball. 'I was no mere *servant!* I was in league with him. I roused the nearby tribes against Troy as he asked. My reward? He came with his many fleets and took my soldiery from me, subsuming them into his own forces and reducing me to the role of a... a... '

'A useless prick?' Dagon guessed.

Piya-maradu glared up at him. 'What?' he rasped, indignant.

'Whatever your new role was, it seems you disappointed him,' Hattu mused.

Piya-maradu gurned. 'He may or may not have caught me loading one of his silver shields and a hoard of jewels into a sack one night. Anyway, don't be fools, turn around, you will find nothing good beyond these hills. Now will you *please* give me a drink of water?'

'Unfortunately for you, dog, we are not here to run from this Agamemnon. We come in guises, to see for ourselves what his force looks like.'

A sparkle appeared in Piya-maradu's eyes. 'Then I will shout to his sentries,' he yelled. 'They stand just beyond the brow. Here!' he yelled in that direction. 'Hittite spies are he-*garumph.*' His rising diatribe ended when Hattu rose and side footed a mass of brown earth into his mouth. He packed the dirt in tight, rendering Piya-maradu mute and irate. Next, he tore a strip from his robe and fashioned an eye bandage from it, covering his smoke-grey eye. 'For once I have something to thank you for,' he grumbled. For added authenticity, he used a thorn to prick the pad of his thumb and pressed it against the area covering his eye, the crimson stain blossoming out like a flower.

Hattu and Dagon looked towards the brow of the hills, now hearing faint noises from the other side. They were about to set off that way again when Hattu had an idea. 'You said your bladder was full?'

Dagon shrugged. 'Always. One of the joys of getting old.'

Hattu smirked. 'Then give Piya-maradu there a drink, will you?'

'With pleasure,' Dagon grinned, setting his feet and hitching up his long robe.

Piya-maradu's eyes widened and a muffled scream sounded uselessly behind his plugged mouth.

***

Reaching the crest of the brown hills was like walking into another world. A stiff, salty sea wind hit them, casting their hair and robes backwards as they set eyes upon the Western Sea, sparkling like silver cloth, speckled with foamy white peaks and striped with progressively deeper shades of blue. Gulls and cormorants screamed and circled, drawing their eyes in to the shore below the hills. The far side of this low range was not brown earth but sand and marram grass, bent by the breeze. The sands ran down into a long sickle-shaped bay. Hattu froze, staring at the dark mass near the shoreline. Boats. Hundreds of them. The timbers sealed with shining black resin.

He heard Ishtar sing in the chambers of his head.

*The West will dim with black boats' hulls,*

*Trojan heroes, mere carrion for gulls...*

The ships were arrayed in three huge ranks: one with their prows partially in the water; one where the boats had been dragged further up the beach; and a final front rank furthest from the shore, the hulls on chocks or deeply embedded in the sand. The decks of these ships were covered with tents. Bowmen patrolled the rails and sat on the spars, bare-chested and gleaming with sweat. Thousands more men – like ants at this distance – scuttled and hurried in the grid of lanes between the ships. Huts and lean-tos hemmed these makeshift streets. Spears jutted from the sand holding limp cloths embroidered with heraldic lions, boars, griffins, bulls and bears.

Even closer to Hattu and Dagon, about an arrow shot from the base of these hills, a stripe of industry was underway. Men busied themselves digging, throwing the sand up into a rampart that faced the hills and walled off the ship camp. Along the top of this sandy rampart, men affixed wooden pickets and wicker screens to make battlements. Scout archers patrolled the walkway behind finished sections of this stockade. Locrians, Hattu surmised, recognising their distinctive chequered kilts. One man stood around near the works, pointing and directing. He was clearly of a superior class going by his showy helm – made of bronze with huge, menacing spirals of the same metal stretching out either side, fitted with strips of fluttering horsehair dyed red and black.

He combed his gaze over the vast ship camp again, this time noticing some men splashing in the surf, washing. There was one fellow much further out – where the sea changed from pale turquoise to cobalt. He was swimming gracefully on his back. Nearby, dolphins played, one even swimming on its back like him.

'Look,' Dagon whispered, batting Hattu on the chest, drawing his attentions back to dry land. He followed Dagon's finger to one of the 'lanes' between the ships. Men lay in rows, groaning. 'Soldiers injured in yesterday's clash?'

Suddenly, a string of jagged syllables erupted and bronze flashed from the top of the sand wall. The bronze-clad overseer there was staring up at them, stiff with alarm. Under his orders, a knot of Locrian scout archers came lolloping up the slope towards Hattu and Dagon while many other Ahhiyawans were scrambling for their weapons.

Hattu's heart pumped. He hadn't meant to halt like this. 'Move to meet them,' he hissed to Dagon. 'Not too fast, not too slow. Look bored. Show them that we are nothing but Masan traders, coming to see if the Ahhiyawans need anything.'

The two trudged downhill, palms open, their bare feet sinking into the hot sand. Hattu heard the gaggle of the Locrian bowmen as they came closer. The tongue was a tricky one to understand, but his childhood tutor, old Ruba, had taught him the core of their language.

One of the bowmen squinted at the pair. 'They are not Trojan,' he called back downhill, his gold teeth glinting. Another of them sprinted to the top of the hills and scanned the Scamander plain. 'They are alone. It is no attack,' he shouted back also. At this, the bronze commander called off the alarm. Hattu's pulse slowed a little.

Yet the lead bowman was not satisfied. He walked in a predator's crouch, circling them, bow half-drawn. 'What do you want?' he said with a sneer.

'We come to trade,' Hattu said in the Ahhiyawan tongue, holding up a leather sack of bits and pieces they had hastily gathered together from the wagon.

The bowmen sneered and squinted at the sack. 'Why would we need your rubbish?'

Dagon held up his bag, while mimicking putting on a bandage and nodding towards the laid-out injured men. 'Medicines, herbs,' Hattu explained.

The three seemed to understand this, and their demeanour changed. One shrugged, relaxed his bow and swished it down the slope, ushering them that way. 'Go, go,' he said.

The escort three left them as they entered the camp through one of the narrow gaps in the nearly-complete sand wall. The smell of the place hit them like a slap – a stink of sweat and sheepskin, barely disguised by the odour of pine from the ship's timbers. Hattu quickly gauged that there were two classes of warriors: a thousands-strong underclass of soldiers in simple leather kilts and hats, and a bronze elite – men crowned with helms of white boar tusk or polished metal, some decorated with long ivory horns or rings of bright feathers. They glittered with white greaves, painted armour, animal pelts, shining cloaks, ribbons and tassels. The only thing these choice types had in common was their beards, short, curled and with no hair on the upper lip. One of these elites – a young mountain of muscle with his hair in braids – sat in the shade at the entrance to a hut, chewing on a hunk of juicy boar meat. A slave rubbed oil into his shoulders and another buffed his shield – a disc of bronze and leather, adorned with the face of a cyclops. The exterior of the hut was studded with distinctive helmets and breastplates and even purple cloaks. Trojan battle gear, he realised – trophies stripped from the bodies of the slain.

They ambled into the grid of lanes. Here, herds of stolen goats bleated, bells tinkling, Gulls shrieked and strutted along the ships' rails, hoping for scraps of food. A cluster of the lower-grade fighters sat in the shade of the boats. Spartans, he realised, seeing the golden bull head emblem painted on some of their shields. They played games with polished pebbles and glugged on drinking skins or chewed on what looked like blood sausage. One groped at a gaudily-painted prostitute sitting on his lap. Nearby a musician played a whistling tune on a set of *syrinx* pipes while another man hopped and sprang in a circle, singing:

*'Proud Prince Paris stepped up to fight,*
*with an ugly Trojan sneer.*
*King Menelaus took him on,*
*and launched his golden spear.*
*It flew with all of Ares' rage,*
*And halved proud Paris' shield.*
*So Paris shat his princely kilt,*
*and sprinted from the field!'*

All the groups of men rose in a throaty chorus of laughter at this.

Others shared stories of battle: 'Priam's famous fifty children become fewer and fewer every time we make battle,' one boasted. 'How many has he left?'

A third group seemed less confident, their voices heavy with angst. 'We need Achilles back. Invincible Achilles.'

'They say he was raised on lions' gizzards and eagles' beaks.'

'He was trained by Chiron the centaur.'

'Imagine how we might fare were he to come back to the fold? Achilles, the Widower of the Streets, is unkillable, descended from the Gods. Our lion!'

Hattu wracked his mind, thinking back over the tablets that he had exchanged with the Ahhiyawan states in times past. Achilles was a name unknown to him.

One of this group lowered his voice. 'We must pray to the Gods that he *does* return for the next battle. My master says that if Achilles will not fight then neither will he.' His voice fell even quieter. 'He says he will put our boats to sea one night and leave this war behind.'

They came to the shore and walked along the waterline, following a ragged stripe of washed-up seaweed and stone anchor blocks marked with reliefs of octopuses and leaping fish. Groups of women – captured Trojan women, Hattu realised – sat in half-naked huddles, roped together, leered at by the soldiers guarding them. They sang and wept, every so often cut off by spittle-flecked threats. Groups of them were being driven at spearpoint onto ships at the waterline, destined for a life of slavery in Ahhiyawa. Grain sacks were heaped in a mighty stack – high as a building – a short way up from the shoreline, where they had been unloaded by supply boats.

'Some three hundred warships in total,' Hattu surmised. 'I'd guess each holds roughly the same as a Ugaritic galley. So…' he began the mental arithmetic.

'Thirteen… fourteen thousand men?' Dagon worked it out first, suddenly a little hoarse.

'Aye, but not too many steeds,' Hattu reasoned, spotting just a few small paddocks of nickering war horses, and only a handful of chariots resting here and there – vehicles that looked somewhat rudimentary.

Suddenly, a great roar sounded from the waves. Hattu swung on his heel. His heart leapt into his mouth as a black galley came churning from the waters and onto the shore like a god's harrow, driving up great folds of wet sand. The prow was cutting right towards him and he could only clumsily elbow Dagon clear and stagger back himself. The ship ground to a halt a hand's-width from his nose. A man leapt down from the ship's rail and crunched into a patch of shingle, landing in a crouch. The man's head swept around like a predator's, his eyes greedy. Hattu stared at the fellow, at his apparel – the kilt, the bronze helm, horned, with a small disc on a stalk rising from the crown. The trident strapped to his bare back…

'The Sherden,' Hattu and Dagon whispered in unison.

Dozens more like this dropped down. They carried sacks rattling with loot, and their fingernails were dark with dried blood. An elite from the ship camp appeared before them. The first Sherden tossed down his sack before the officer. 'More silver from the islands for Aga-mem-non, Lord of all *Ah-hee-yaaa-wa,*' he said, contorting his mouth to speak the word that was obviously foreign and fairly new to him. The other Sherden dropped their sacks of loot beside the first.

The officer eyed the booty and nodded briskly. 'The *Wanax* will review your tribute later. If it is deemed enough, then you can keep your berth here at the camp.'

The lead Sherden bowed obsequiously, backing away. Once the Ahhiyawan officer had turned his back, the man's expression changed completely – back to a look of pure, rapine greed. His eyes darted around like a thief's… then slid round to stare at Hattu, and narrowed.

Hattu twisted away quickly, nudging Dagon. 'Keep moving,' he hissed. They headed quickly on up the shoreline.

'What are the Ahhiyawans thinking – inviting Sherden into their army?' Dagon whispered.

Hattu tensed. Memories of his people's ruinous interactions with those pirates from the distant west scudded across his mind like particles of hot sand. He saw in his mind's eye the long-dead face of the wretched Sherden adventurer, Volca, who had almost brought the Hittite world to ruin.

'Not just Sherden,' Dagon added, discreetly gesturing to a point further up the beach. There, three more of those stocky galleys rested. Around them, ankle deep in the shallows, stood spearmen with bronze skullcaps and trailing cloth aventails. 'Shekelesh too. They and the Sherden are the scum of the seas.'

They passed a group of men sanding down planks of wood with sharkskin and another lot hammering together a new hut. The wind changed then, and a stench of decay hit them hard. Not just sweat and cattle, but rotting flesh, vomit, effluent. Dagon, gagging, lifted the collar of his itchy robe up to cover his nose and mouth. 'Gods, that is worse than the stink on the river plain back there.'

Hattu was close to retching, and then he spotted the source of the smell: the row of men lying by one ship – the stricken ones they had seen from the hills. They bore no battle injuries or bloodstained bandages. Yet each of them was pale, gleaming with sweat and shivering. Some sported boils and patches of flesh that were black with rot.

'Plague,' Dagon said with a haunted whisper.

They slowed, seeing a healer moving slowly from man to man, sponging water on their foreheads, talking softly to them. Every so often, he would shrug or throw his hands to the skies in exasperation.

'He has nothing to treat them with,' Hattu guessed.

Dagon slowed a little, clutching the haircloth sack. 'Sagewort works well on fever,' he said. 'But… these people are the enemies of Troy,' he mused, looking at Hattu for approval.

Hattu chewed on the matter for a moment. 'It is never wrong to help a sick man. And… you might see or hear something of interest. Go, be swift. I will wait here for you.'

Dagon approached the healer, using hand signals in lieu of words to communicate. The healer's face quickly lit up when Dagon presented the small pouch of sagewort, and the two went about grinding some up to prepare a potion.

Alone, Hattu glanced discreetly up and down the shoreline. Troy's enemy was strong indeed. He began to wonder how Priam's small force could possibly have held out against this multitude for so long. So perplexed was he that he didn't notice a man rising from the waves, slick with water, until he was right by his side.

'Welcome to the Bay of Boreas, stranger,' said the man, wrapping a cloth around his waist.

Hattu jolted. The fellow's long tawny hair was slicked back with seawater, droplets of which glistened in his deeply-furrowed brow and short beard. He was stocky and small, with the build of a boxer and deep-set eyes. He lifted a rough woollen cloak from the sand and wrapped it around his shoulders, then tugged a tatty old traveller's cap onto his head. A lesser fighter, Hattu suspected.

The stranger sat on an anchor block to pull on his sandals. 'Keep your distance from those fellows,' he said, glancing at the men being treated by Dagon and the Ahhiyawan healer. 'So many like them, coughing blood, shaking, unable to hold food or water.'

'So it *is* plague?' Hattu asked.

'I would say so,' the man answered. 'It started with the dogs and mules. Soon, it moved onto the men. So many have died here from the illness and at the edge of Trojan swords that we have had to burn our dead as the Trojans do – for there is not enough space in this land to bury all those who have fallen.' He nodded towards a black stain much further down the beach – a heap of charred bones and ashes. Sucking in a deep, dissatisfied breath, he looked Hattu up and down. 'So who are you?'

'My friend and I are peddlers from Masa,' Hattu answered.

'Hmm,' the man replied. 'Why come to the scene of a great war? Why not head south to the city of Milawata – the slave market there is never short of noblemen willing to part with their silver. Though I use the term 'noble' lightly.'

Hattu smiled despite himself. 'The markets of Milawata may well be lucrative. But there is no greater bazaar than that of war. Tell me, is it as they say? Is this war really all over a woman?'

The man's eyes grew hooded. 'If you believe that then you are not as cunning as you look.'

There was a moment of silence. The fellow's gaze was searching inside Hattu. Just like that Sherden leader…

'Odysseus,' a voice called out.

Hattu turned to see who had shouted: the young elite Hattu had seen earlier with the braided hair sitting by the trophy-studded hut. His shoulder-rub was finished, and now the warrior busied himself by sharpening his sword. 'Odysseus,' he called again, to someone near Hattu. *Odysseus?* Hattu thought, having heard the name mentioned in his court, *Odysseus of Ithaca... the Island King.* Hattu glanced around, wondering if he could spot this Odysseus amongst the glittering elites. He eyed one of them, unfeasibly handsome, clanking along in a suit of bronze. *Yes*, Hattu thought, *this must be Odysseus of Ithaca.*

But it was the scruffy swimmer who had been speaking to Hattu who replied. 'Ah, Diomedes,' he called back to the braid-haired one. 'The surf is smooth, the swim invigorating – you should have come with me.'

Braid-haired Diomedes laughed, a deep and booming sound like drumbeats echoing in a grand hall. 'While you were frolicking with dolphins, I was whetting my swords. I'd say my blades will help kill more Trojan than your dolphins will.' A smattering of nearby men laughed at this.

'King Odysseus?' Hattu said, taking a step away from the fellow beside him and bowing as a peddler should. 'You should have told me. I would have paid you the respect you deserve.'

Odysseus shrugged and offered an uneven smile. 'Sometimes it is fun to pretend we are something we are not, eh?'

Hattu felt the Ithacan King's deep-set eyes boring into him again, studying the makeshift eye bandage. This short hour he had spent in the Ahhiyawan camp now began to feel like a year.

Odysseus chuckled, breaking the spell. 'Come, walk with me.' They set off on a slow meander. 'What caused the war, you ask? Some say it began with Helen eloping from Sparta with Prince Paris of Troy. Others might suggest there was another reason.'

'Troy and her golden houses sparkle brightly and catch many an eye,' Hattu mused.

Odysseus looked suddenly serious. 'Agamemnon did not come for gold, either. He has plenty of that back in his palace at Mycenae.'

'Then why is he here?'

Odysseus' gaze grew distant. 'Oaths – sworn in good faith, broken by strangers. A madness that pulled him and all of us down into a boiling pit. Sometimes I look across this bay and realise that ten summers have passed since we landed here. I wonder at those moments if this is truly a campaign of conquest, or if we in fact died on the way and this is some infernal cage the Gods have built for our shades.'

Hattu looked over the city of ships with him. 'So many soldiers together. I have never seen the likes before,' he lied skilfully.

'Hmm,' Odysseus said. 'Yet not enough to win the war, despite the fact that Troy has but one champion – Hektor – while we have many.' He waved towards an older man, balding with flowing white hair and a bony torso weighed down by an armless cuirass emblazoned with a prowling griffin. 'Nestor, King of sandy Pylos brought twenty ships and one thousand men.' Arrayed before the older king stood a brigade of warriors wearing bright feather headdresses. Odysseus gestured this way and that as he strolled on past other groups. 'The King of Crete mustered twelve hundred soldiers. The Locrian King summoned five hundred.'

*Thock-thock,* the sound of arrows batting against timber sounded. Hattu and Odysseus entered a small plaza of sorts in a gap between the ships. Here, a ring of men drank wine and rumbled in amusement and awe as they watched a practice duel. Six fighters of little distinction, each clutching sword and spear, circled carefully around a shaggy-haired monster of a man with dark slashes for eyebrows, muscles gleaming like polished stone. He held a huge staff and a mighty shield. Tucked inside the protection of the shield was a smaller man with a bow and tipless arrows. Every so often, this archer would emerge from behind his giant companion's shield and shoot a shaft low at one of the six. *Thrum!* One of the circling six, a scrawny fellow, dropped his shield low to deflect the missile. *Thock!* The shaft bounced harmlessly away. But in the same instant, the giant one swept his staff round, the end connecting sweetly with the scrawny one's exposed face. With a shower of blood and teeth, the scrawny one fell flat on his back, unconscious.

'Mighty Ajax, Lord of Salamis, and his brother, Teucer the bowman,' said Odysseus. 'Twelve ships and more than six hundred men.'

They came back to the point where he and Odysseus had met. The Ithacan gestured to the braid-haired champion. 'And that, as you heard, is the famous Diomedes, Lord of Tiryns.'

Hattu regarded the young warrior king. He was the fittest and most impressive looking of the elites he had seen so far. 'So is this the greatest fighter on these shores?'

'Diomedes? No,' Odysseus shook his head. 'He is incredible, but he – *no one* – can outshine Achilles.'

Hattu followed Odysseus' eyes to a tent, open on the sea-facing side, the flaps pinned by two staffs bearing black-boar pennants. In it sat a bare-chested young man with fair curls tucked behind his ears, hunched over a board game of some sort, chin resting in his hands like a bored child. His harsh gash of a mouth and his snub nose gave him an angry look. Resting beside him on a wooden frame was the most splendid suit of armour: A gilded helm and a moulded cuirass of bronze decorated with roundels of silver and chevrons of gold.

'They say Achilles was raised on lion's gizzards-'

'-and eagle's beaks,' Hattu finished for him.

Odysseus grinned. 'Well he is a northman – they'll eat anything,' he roared at his own joke. His humour quickly faded though. 'He is faster than any fighter I have ever seen before. In these long years of war he and his Myrmidons – a lethal corps – have ranged far and wide, widowing the streets of the Trojan-allied villages and islands.'

Hattu cocked an eyebrow. 'He looks rather harmless right now.'

'Ah, and that is due to one of the flaws of our Great King. Agamemnon has many strengths, but his jealousy undermines them all. He and Achilles are in dispute, you see. Achilles took a Trojan woman captive. Briseis is her name. The men in the camp gossiped about her beauty – a match for Helen, they claimed. Agamemnon heard this and,' he stopped and slowly shook his head, 'just *had* to have her for himself. Thus, Achilles – our battle lion – now refuses to fight.' Odysseus gazed over all those he had pointed out.

A brutish voice interrupted. 'What riddles are you telling this stranger, Island King?'

Hattu twisted to see Ajax the giant, his staff – tipped with blood – resting on one shoulder and his tower shield strapped to his back like a turtle's shell.

'None more perplexing than the riddle of your unmatched strength,' Odysseus smiled.

The oily charm worked. Ajax smiled almost boyishly, proud but embarrassed at once. 'Well, I'll have to take him from you,' the giant asked in a more affable tone. 'Great King Agamemnon asked us to show all newcomers to his hut.' He said this with a nod towards the largest shack, the doorway draped with a black cloth embroidered with a golden lioness.

Hattu noticed the cluster of armed men with Ajax. This was clearly not a request.

# CHAPTER 3

## LORD OF MYCENAE

Agamemnon stroked the arms of his throne – solid gold inlaid with pebbles of blue glass. A fine thing, and a reminder of his airy and majestic Hall of Lions back in Mycenae. So different to this cramped and stuffy hut, he groused inwardly. Worst of all was the squabbling of his gathered *kerosia* within the confined space. He glanced over the gaggle of bickering kings, champions and elders sourly as they shouted at and heckled one another in a ceaseless wail of discord. But they had to be tolerated. As one smirking advisor often reminded him: *This alliance of Ahhiyawan city-states is a fragile one. Your magnificent throne is not what binds them to you. Instead, your power is like a worn old stool, and each of the kings are its legs. Without their support you would not be Wanax, leader of this expedition to Troy.* The belittling image of the stool always stood his hackles proud.

This latest daily gathering had begun with one man speaking at a time, then calmly handing the golden speaker's sceptre to the next. Now they were grabbing at the thing and screaming in one another's faces. When a younger man dared try to shout down one of the older ones, the elder swung the sceptre at the fellow, bashing him on the skull. The young one staggered away, groaning.

'Still the Trojans hold us at bay. *Still* we failed to take and hold the River Scamander,' a man with a turnip-shaped head pronounced.

'What are you yapping about?' screamed another. 'We slew many of Priam's soldiers yesterday. The Gods are with us.'

'Three hundred and seventeen of our men died in yesterday's battle,' rasped a third. 'The same number again lie injured. The victory was Troy's!'

'The plague has killed twice as many in this last moon,' argued another. 'Use your wits – the disease is our real enemy now. Apollo shows his favour for Troy by raining his poisoned arrows upon us.'

A fifth voice cut through all the rest: 'Gods or otherwise, if we had Achilles in our ranks yesterday, we would have broken the Trojans, taken the river *and* driven them right back against their city walls.'

Agamemnon looked up to see who had said this, smelling a metal stink of dried blood. Kalchas the augur waddled to the fore. Wearing a leather cuirass and with his white beard gathered into two long, thick braids, he looked more like a warrior than a prophet. Then again, battle was where he operated – scavenging behind the main press, running his fingers through the entrails and burst skulls to divine that which was to come. His blood-encrusted fingernails were a testament to his methods. Kalchas was staring through all of the squabbling men, right at him. Agamemnon felt pinned to his throne, as if the man had a strange power. It had been the same on the day before the fleet had set sail for Troy, at the shores of Aulis, when he had convinced Agamemnon to do the unthinkable. Somewhere deep within, he wept the name that had haunted him since: *Iphigenia…*

'*Wanax,*' Kalchas said, the word like the snap of a whip. 'We *need* Achilles and his Myrmidons. Briseis *must* be given back to him. Else all this, all of these ten long years and everything you sacrificed to come here will have been for nothing.'

*Everything you sacrificed.* The words echoed long in Agamemnon's ears. He stared at the priest for a time, then turned to one of the few silent men in the hut. Menelaus, the red-haired King of Sparta, holding his dark, long-horned helm underarm. The man cuckolded by Paris of Troy. 'What say you, Brother?' he boomed.

On hearing their *Wanax* speak at last, all fell silent, looking to Agamemnon then to his sibling.

Menelaus – silent since yesterday's battle when his sword had been a whisker's width from Paris' neck – momentarily blushed at the sudden attention. Without wine in his veins and away from the madness of battle, he was as shy as a tortoise hiding in its shell. His lips twitched nervously and finally he replied. 'Kalchas is right. We must give the girl back. I want Helen to pay for what she has done. I want revenge on Paris. To do these things we need Achilles. We *need* our war lion.' Short, clipped bursts. That was how Menelaus communicated. Uncomfortable with speaking, he would say just enough to get his message across and no more. It was a surprisingly effective contribution. All eyes now drifted back to the throne.

Agamemnon imagined what it would mean to give the girl back. People would say that Achilles, surly and aggressive, had bullied him, the supposed *Wanax* of the expedition, into submission. How long before the next challenge? And what chance of that challenger backing down, in the knowledge that he had folded so readily to Achilles?

'*Wanax,*' Kalchas ventured once more. 'I implore you.'

Agamemnon snatched a cup from the table beside the throne and threw back a mouthful of wine. 'Never,' he said with a rolling burr. Kalchas, reading his Great King's mood, quarter-bowed and sunk back into the crowd. The others all erupted in a fresh bout of squabbling, hands raised, fingers wagging, tongues flapping. He noticed a few more of his council entering the hut. Old Nestor, mighty Ajax, young Diomedes and sly Odysseus. There was a stranger with Odysseus: a tall fellow with long, silver hair and a swarthy, fox-like face, striped with a grubby eyepatch.

Nestor approached the throne, snatching the sceptre from one of the bickering lot. '*Wanax,* if I may bring something new to the table?' he asked, his voice like the hinges of a rusty gate.

'Please,' Agamemnon drawled.

'Every time we have pressed the Trojans in battle, they have always repelled us back across the Scamander plain. Not once in these ten summers have we even reached or scratched the shell of stone that is their city.'

'Finer walls even than Tiryns,' big Ajax mumbled. Diomedes the Tirynean King shot him a sour look.

'We outnumber the Trojans,' Nestor went on, 'but not enough to overwhelm them. Not yet, at least.'

Agamemnon slid his head a little to one side, widening his stronger eye in the way he unconsciously did when hearing something of interest.

'A boat arrived this morning,' Nestor continued. 'Its cargo was a messenger and a tablet… from Assyria.'

Agamemnon felt an instant revulsion at the name of that eastern power. Equally, many in the hut sighed and grumbled.

Nestor raised his hands for silence. 'The Assyrians are no friends of ours. But King Shalmaneser has heard about our investment of Priam's city. He feels that if he can help precipitate the fall of Troy, then this will further grind Troy's overlords – the Hittite Empire – into the dirt. For him, that would be a good thing.'

The murmuring voices rose again, this time with a timbre of interest.

'King Shalmaneser offers you two brigades of royal macemen, two of spearmen and a wing of archers, plus a fleet of two hundred chariots. All led by Mardukal the siege master. It is no trick, for that force has arrived on a flotilla of warships at Milawata, our southern port city. They are moored there, awaiting our response.'

The murmuring faded in a gasp.

'Three thousand elite footmen. That would swell our army hugely, *Wanax,*' Nestor appealed. 'And a chariot school that would dwarf our own and match Troy's. More, if we can finally bring our army to the foot of Troy's walls then what better man to show us how to break them apart than Mardukal?'

Agamemnon felt the expectant stares of his council like the tips of hot pins on his skin. His teeth ground, and everyone heard it.

'I beg of you, *Wanax,*' said Nestor. 'Let me reply to King Shalmaneser. Let his soldiers come here, so we can unleash them upon Troy. A swift end to this long war would be a fine thing.'

Agamemnon's left knee began bouncing in irritation. 'What then? Do you think Shalmaneser will simply recall Mardukal and his troops? No. Assyria will claim the triumph as theirs. I will not share the conquest of Troy with anyone. It has to be mine. It *has* to be.' His heart began to pound as he saw in his mind's-eye images of Aulis on that last day before the war. 'Give the messenger a gift for Shalmaneser – one of the silver rhytons we plundered from Lesbos – then send him away with a rejection.' He finished with an obdurate look that made old Nestor flinch. The Pylian King backed away with a bow.

The weasel-like King of Locris plucked the sceptre from Nestor's hands and spoke next. 'There is another option, *Wanax*. Our friend within Troy's walls, perhaps it is time to-'

'Silence,' big Ajax grunted, cutting him off. 'We have foreign ears present.'

Agamemnon leant forward on his throne, his eyes sharpening on the tall stranger beside Odysseus.

***

*A friend of the Ahhiyawans within Troy's walls?* The words tumbled into Hattu's ears. Before he had a moment to consider them, the Ahhiyawans before and around him parted with a clatter of leather and bronze, opening up a short corridor to the throne, flanked by two chariot elites who stood guard, gurning, tall and straight as their spears.

Agamemnon was younger than Hattu had imagined, chiselled with a dimpled, beardless chin and jet-black tresses of oiled hair, one lock curled on his forehead, the rest swept back and hanging in a thick cascade behind his shoulders. He wore a tasselled leopard pelt kilt. Hattu could smell a perfume of pine resin emanating from him, stark against the odour of unwashed nether regions elsewhere in the shack. Agamemnon stared back at him, head dipped menacingly. 'Who… and what… are you?'

'I am a travelling peddler, *Wanax*. Here to provide you with whatever you might need.'

Agamemnon looked him up and down a few times. 'Need? An explanation, perhaps. In the early years of this war, traders flocked to our camp. They would come to buy and sell wool, ingots, gems, spices, wine. But soon the war became fraught, resources stretched. Now, ships stay in port, merchants remain at home.' His top lip quirked in disdain. 'We have not had a trader here for over five years…' one of his eyes narrowed, 'then you arrived.'

Hattu's mind flooded with ideas and explanations – all felt flimsy at best. At last, like the glint of a precious metal in the sunlight, he thought of something… *the* most precious metal. 'None who came here before, nor any of those who have stayed away since, would have been in possession of what I can offer. Weapons.'

Agamemnon sucked his cheeks in and slumped back on his throne, resting his chin on one palm. 'Oh?' he said dismissively, glancing around the shields and crossed spears fixed to his hut walls.

Hattu's lips twitched at one end. 'Weapons… of iron.'

Agamemnon arched one disdainful eyebrow. He made a noise in his throat, somewhere between a grunt and a laugh. 'Take him away,' he said with a lazy swish of the hand, gazing outside through the doorway, 'beat him and throw him outside the camp.'

The two guards moved for him.

'… *good* iron,' Hattu added.

Agamemnon's eyes snapped back round. He perched forward on the throne, snapping his fingers to still his guards. All around Hattu, faces fell agape. After a pregnant silence, Agamemnon clapped his hands. The council is over. Everyone, leave me.'

The place drained, the council members helped on their way by the two elite guards.

Alone with Hattu, Agamemnon looked over him again. 'Nobody knows the secret of *good* iron. It is an impossibility. A myth.'

Hattu simply smiled. If it was to be a game of bluff, then he was well-practiced. 'I dare not contest the assertions of a Great King. Thank you for your time, *Wanax,*' he quarter-bowed. 'Now, I will take my leave.' He turned to depart.

'Wait.'

Hattu slowed and halted, turning back to the Ahhiyawan King.

'How many such weapons?'

'Racks filled with swords and spears,' he lied. 'Hundreds of them. Enough to help win you this war.'

Agamemnon licked his lips. 'What do you ask in return? Silver? Spice?'

'I have no need for such things. I would gladly give you the blades for free.'

Agamemnon looked at Hattu askance for a moment, then rocked on his throne, laughter pealing freely. 'You have been out in the sun too long, my friend.'

'All I want to know is that I am giving this gift to the right side in this war.'

Agamemnon's laughter stuttered to a halt. 'The right side?' he said, leaning forward again. 'What do you know of war, Peddlar?'

*Too much,* Hattu thought. 'On my way here, on the plain before Troy, I saw shells of men, cages of ribs and armies of flies. I heard rumours that this conflict was started by one woman, and waged by the Ahhiyawan Great King, hungry to extend his territory.'

Agamemnon slapped a hand on the arm of his throne. 'Ha!' he forced a laugh that was terse and dripping with fury. Hattu knew he had riled the king: enough to elicit information, hopefully. 'And did they tell you about the Trojan ships, confiscating huge tolls from our grain fleets that sail to and from the Hellespont strait? The northerly winds blow all vessels either here into the Bay of Boreas or into the Bay of Troy. Like two webs with Priam's city crouching on the edge like the hungry spider. Meanwhile the harvests of Ahhiyawa – meagre at the best of times – grow dangerously light with every passing year of this damned drought.'

Hattu felt an unexpected flicker of sympathy. The story was the same all across Hittite lands. A world drying up, the parched crust cracking with every earth tremor.

'These weapons… give them to me,' Agamemnon demanded, 'and I will finish this war before the summer is out.'

Hattu spread his palms. 'I do not carry such precious goods with me – I'm sure you understand. I will take leave of your camp, and return with the weapons tomorrow,' he lied.

'I will provide an escort for you,' Agamemnon said, eyes growing hooded.

Hattu smiled, masking his frustration. 'That would not be good. At my hideout, I have a band of archers who have sworn to shoot on sight anyone they see approaching, unless it is me alone.' He slid his satchel from his shoulder and left it on the floor, the simple goods within partly-visible. 'Keep my belongings as assurance.'

Agamemnon scowled at the satchel then scrutinised him for a time, before flicking his fingers towards the hut door. 'Go, and return here by dawn… or I will have my dogs track you down.'

Hattu, head full of the things he had heard and seen, bowed and turned towards the hut door. In his way stood two of Agamemnon's bodyguards, spears crossed, granite faces glowering at him. They slid their spears apart to let him leave, but before he could do so, a scrawny figure entered. The Sherden who had watched him closely on the shoreline. 'Do not let him go, *Wa-nax,*' he said in that awkward accent. 'He is a Hitt-ite!'

Hattu's blood ran cold.

Agamemnon's lips peeled back to reveal clenched teeth and gums. 'A Hittite?'

'I heard them talking in the Hittite tongue, I have seen their like before. I know it, *Wa-nax,* I do!' the Sherden gushed like a child trying to impress its parent.

'I know many tongues,' Hattu waved a dismissive hand. 'That does not mean that I am-'

'You are a spy,' Agamemnon hissed. 'A *Hittite* spy for Troy. How many of your kind are there here?' he said, his face growing ashen. 'Where are your armies?'

*If only,* Hattu thought, *if only the four ancient divisions of the Hittite Empire were here, then this war would be over in days.*

'I am a mere peddler,' Hattu persisted.

'After he came into the camp, the archers advanced to the brow of the hills, *Wanax,*' one of the guards advised. 'There are no signs of a new army in the vicinity.'

Agamemnon drummed his fingers on his bottom lip. 'Whoever you are, you have heard too much in this hut. Perhaps you are a Hittite, perhaps not. At dawn tomorrow, when we advance to fight the Trojans again, you will come with us… and you will be impaled on the hills as a pre-battle sacrifice.' He clicked his fingers. 'Seize him, bind him in the prisoner tents, then prepare a stake.'

The guards' hands slapped down on Hattu's shoulders.

***

The burly pair bundled Hattu inside a filthy tent, shoved him to sitting then bound him to the central poplar-trunk pole. The place was pitch black, so thick were the hides, and stank of sweat. The guard pair left with a burst of coarse laughter. His head swam in the silence that ensued. What a fool, to think he could wander into the heart of the enemy lair and go undetected. *When you were younger, sharper, perhaps,* he berated himself.

What hope now?

It came like a flash of lightning. 'Dagon,' he whispered to himself. His friend was still in the camp. He would surely have noticed that something was wrong, find a way to help him escape.

'Yes?' came a totally unexpected reply from the other side of the pole.

Hattu cranked his head around, his eyes rolled to their edges in order to peer into the darkness behind him. 'Dagon?' he said again, this time as a question.

'Unfortunately, yes. I made the mistake of muttering a Hittite prayer for one of their sick men, and the healer heard me, worked out that I was not in fact a Masan trader. My reward for treating their feverish soldiers? A massive sharpened stake up the arse tomorrow, apparently. Wonder if we'll get some breakfast first?'

The two sighed deeply in unintended harmony.

'Well, this could have gone better,' Hattu mused. It was almost comically bad, even without the grim spectre of impalement at dawn. But then he thought of the others, back with the wagon. 'We told them we would be back by noon,' he whispered.

'We also told them to stay hidden,' Dagon replied.

'Sirtaya, Bulhapa and Zupili might do as we commanded. But my heir?'

'Aye, well,' Dagon started. 'These ropes feel old. Perhaps we can work our way free?'

Together, they twisted and pulled in an effort to free themselves. Time rolled past. Beads of sweat ran down Hattu's face and torso in the suffocating heat of the tent. The more he and Dagon struggled against the ropes, the tighter they became.

'It's no use,' Dagon said, panting with effort.

Outside, the slow, careful rasp of a carpenter's saw began, along with muffled words in the Ahhiyawan tongue. Hattu picked up a few of these – 'make those stakes sharp', 'thick as masts', and 'leave the splinters in' were three phrases that did not fill him with confidence. A short while later the rasping outside ended with the thick clunk of sawn stakes hitting the ground.

Hattu and Dagon fell into an exhausted silence, heads lolling, eyelids closing over. The only hint of respite came when a very slight breeze passed across them and a strange flicker of light flashed within the tent. Hattu blinked his eyes fully open, staring at the tent entrance. Still shut. All was still dark. *Strange*, he thought, wondering if he had dreamt the breeze and the light.

'Perhaps we could volunteer some false information,' Dagon croaked from behind him. 'Call on the guards, tell them we have something vital for Agamemnon.'

'I tried that ploy already,' said Hattu, 'pretending that we had a cache of good iron blades hidden nearby.'

'But the guards standing watch outside the tent are grunts. They won't know what went on between you and him, will they? We can tell them anything. Anything that convinces them to untie us and take us to him. once these ropes are off, we have a chance, at least. We can make a break for it.'

Hattu laughed bitterly. 'I don't know about you, my old friend, but we are so deep inside this bay camp that I think they could cut me into one thousand pieces before I made it to the edge.' He fell silent and sighed. 'But you are right. What other options do we have?'

'Ready?' Dagon said.

'Ready,' Hattu replied, sucking in a full breath as Dagon did the same.

Just as the word *guards* rolled onto his tongue, a hand clamped over his lips, and a cold edge of bronze rested against his neck.

'Not a wise idea, traveller,' a nasal voice spoke in his ear. 'If you want to keep your blood in your veins, if you want to escape the sharp stakes they have prepared for you, then you will not utter a word.'

Hattu's eyes darted. Even though they had been in here for some time, he still could not discern much in the darkness. He realised Dagon had also failed to call to the guards as planned. Before he could even comprehend what was happening, he felt the cold bronze leave his neck, brush his forearms, felt the ropes binding his wrists strain, then snap and fall loose. The hand moved away from his mouth.

Backing away from the pole, he eyed the darkness where his rescuer must be. Flints sparked, then a bubble of pale light appeared, growing weakly on the wick of a tallow candle, uplighting the menacing face of Achilles.

'You?' Hattu whispered. 'You're freeing us? Why?'

Achilles' top lip twitched in disdain. 'Not for you, or your friend,' he replied.

Hattu saw now that Dagon too had been freed by another man with Achilles, older and weathered.

'I do this only to teach my so-called *Wanax* a lesson.'

'For taking the *namra* woman from you?' Hattu realised, thinking of the captured Trojan woman Briseis.

'*Namra?*' Achilles snorted with mirthless laughter.

Hattu groaned inwardly, annoyed that he had let slip the Hittite word for war-captive.'

'So it is true what they say,' Achilles rumbled, 'the Hittites *have* arrived?'

Hattu said nothing more.

'Well here we call the prisoner women *toroja*,' Achilles said. 'Taking Briseis from me was just Agamemnon's latest affront. I will have her back,' he hissed, his face contorting in a way that made him look bestial. 'Nobody offends me and lives to tell the tale. I will have my *revenge*!'

The venom of his words, the hatred in his eyes, turned Hattu's blood cold.

He gestured towards his older companion who had cut Dagon free. 'Patroklos will guide you from the camp and set you on your way to Troy,' he said as if the name of the city was poisonous. The older man handed Dagon and Hattu each a hooded cloak, then lifted the concealed flap at the rear of the tent through which they had sneaked inside, gesturing for them both to follow.

'By freeing you, I undermine Agamemnon's efforts,' Achilles hissed to them. 'But make no mistake, once he has begged for my forgiveness, or once his head rolls at my feet – whichever happens first – then my prayers will turn to your death. I am destined for glory at Troy. Nobody will stand in my way.'

Hattu tilted his head to one side in a mixed gesture of pity and gratitude, before following Patroklos outside.

The glare of the sun was blinding at first, but the heavy, grubby cloak hoods helped with that. Like Dagon, he kept his head down, watching the muscle-knotted calves and chapped heels of Patroklos, seeing the passing shapes of many Ahhiyawan warriors, animals and roped lines of war captives taken from nearby villages. He knew not where Patroklos was leading them, and for one terrible moment wondered if this escape was all a cruel joke, and that they would reach their destination and he would draw down his hood to see that they had been led to the stakes. He imagined Agamemnon waiting, grinning and eager to watch their deaths.

But the crash of waves and the clatter and chatter of the camp faded. The ground underfoot changed from sand to earth, and the hum of bees and insects rose. 'Draw down your hoods. You are safe now,' Patroklos said, his voice deep and soft.

Gingerly, Hattu did so, he and Dagon sharing a look, then both gazing around the narrow and overgrown trench valley he had led them to – a way through the Borean Hills. 'Follow the route through and you will be safely back onto the Scamander plain,' he said.

Hattu searched his pale eyes, seeing the lines of age spreading from the corners. Unlike Achilles, Patroklos seemed genuinely pleased to be helping them. 'You seem like an experienced warrior. Why do you follow that young man?'

He smiled a little, the lines beside his eyes being joined by many more on his cheeks and forehead. 'Because Achilles is the greatest of the Myrmidons.' He winked and flashed a full smile now. 'Although I taught him everything he knows. How to hunt, how to lead, how to fight.'

Hattu saw before him now an avuncular, overly-modest man. 'Then why do they not speak of *you* as the greatest – as the "lion of battle"?' he asked.

Patroklos' face twitched then in a weaker smile. 'Because I am not a true warrior. My blood is common and I am merely his attendant.'

'But if you taught him to be the leader that he is, then you too could surely be a fine commander in your own right?'

Patroklos shook his head. 'Not for me… not for me. You see, when I was first assigned to mentor Achilles, he was a delightful student. Merry, full of life, besotted by nature, beguiled by the ancient songs. All too soon, he grew into Achilles the warrior. Men are too easily bewitched by their own legends… he has gone too far, seen too much, done things he should not have. He can hear noises, ones that others cannot. He says it is the screams and shouts of the fallen – the shades who have followed him from his many battles of the past.'

Hattu felt an unexpected chord being plucked within him – a sad note of empathy. For a fleeting moment, he heard and saw the atrocities from Gargamis, Kadesh, and from the war for the Hittite throne.

Patroklos' face was hanging now, adding another ten summers of age to him. 'Since we came here, it has been worse. He sits awake at night, rocking, with his hands over his ears. He says that the Scamander spirits whisper to him. It is a hard thing for me, to be able to mentor and comfort him in all matters… all but those dark things. The Gods foretold that he would know glory here at Troy. Sometimes my people speak of death in battle as the greatest glory.' His eyes misted a little. 'Part of me thinks this might be best for him… the only way he might find peace.'

A silence stretched, Patroklos staring into space, Hattu digesting the wisdom of this stranger.

Patroklos looked past Hattu then, into the undergrowth. 'The young man in the bushes there, with his bow trained on my neck, he is your protégé, yes? He has the same look as you.'

Hattu recoiled, confused, then turned to the wall of greenery. Within it, two silver-stud eyes glinted behind a stretched warbow. '*Tuhkanti*, no!' he said stepping across Patroklos to shield him.

Tudha's draw arm shook for a time, before he gently relaxed the weapon. Nearby, a hacking and swishing of branches sounded. Sirtaya came loping through from another direction, followed by Bulhapa and Zupili, leaves and twigs stuck in their long hair. 'Master Hattu, he gave us the slip,' Sirtaya panted. 'One minute we were filling our drinking skins at the rushes by the river, the next he was gone, Bulhapa's bow too.'

'I told you to stay by the river,' Hattu raged as Tudha emerged from his screen of foliage.

'The Gods told me you were in trouble,' Tudha replied.

'Pithy words, foolish actions... once again,' Hattu spat, snatching the bow from him and handing it back to the red-faced Bulhapa.

There was a silence then, as Hattu realised he and his party were surrounding Patroklos, and Patroklos understood that he was encircled. Tentatively, Bulhapa and Zupili levelled their spears, looking to Hattu for direction.

Hattu gently swished one hand downwards and both retracted their weapons, stepping aside to open a way back through the vale for Patroklos. 'Tell Achilles that I will not forget his gesture in freeing us, regardless of his motives.'

Patroklos backed away towards the camp. 'He meant what he said. His thoughts will soon turn to your downfall. Thus I, as his servant, must seek the same also.' With that, he slipped into the undergrowth and was gone.

Hattu watched the spot where he had been, then slowly turned to look north, towards the valley's end, the sweltering plain and the high city overlooking it all.

# CHAPTER 4

## GOLDEN TROY

They emerged onto the plain and trekked north through the mid-afternoon heat, so fierce that the air in the middle-distance danced like liquid silver. Having reclaimed their wagon, Dagon drove while the others walked alongside. Hattu, once again dressed in Hittite boots, kilt and cloak, buckled on his leather crossbands as he walked, the weight of the twin swords on his back reassuring. He noticed Tudha eyeing the iron blades enviously.

'Describe it again,' the young man said as if he had not been admiring the swords. 'A spy… an enemy planted within Troy's walls? Or a traitor – a disenchanted Trojan?'

Hattu ground his teeth behind closed lips, regretting his decision to describe his findings to the group. 'I didn't hear enough to be sure, *Tuhkanti*.'

With a haughty look, Tudha raised his clay tablet and wagged his reed stylus. 'You asked me to record everything of interest. Surely this matter needs to be marked on the clay?' His tone was goading, again. 'Is that not what a good scribe would do?'

'A skilled scribe knows that some matters are not for the clay,' Hattu burred, sliding his eyes round to glare at his heir. 'Just as a soldier should know that his job...' as he spoke, memories of the aftermath at Hatenzuwa rose in his mind's eye, '… is not all about killing.'

Tudha's face twisted with hurt and anger. He slid his tablet and stylus away and walked on in silence.

Hattu turned his attentions to the mighty city ahead.

Troy.

The lower city, ringed by a collar of walls, spread out like a great tongue, stretching down the Silver Ridge's gentle slope and onto the plain. Above it all, the citadel dazzled in the sunlight, the defences soaring like sheets of bronze, tipped with rows of mud-clay merlons that looked like jagged teeth. Catching sight of the royal palace made him think of the dream, of he and Priam in a duel. Such a cruel dream. *But only a dream,* he tried to reassure himself.

From somewhere deep within, the Goddess Ishtar hissed in reply: *Hittites should always heed their dreams...*

A breeze picked up, warm and balmy. Goat bells tinkled, and Hattu spotted a few thin herds being grazed on the grassy slopes of the Silver Ridge, the herdsmen sticking close to the city walls. Women crouched by the few rock streams further along the ridge, washing garments and drawing water. Teams of men and boys foraged in the bushes along the ridge top. All of these small groups shot looks at Hattu and his party of five approaching.

They came to the Thymbran Gate – the southernmost entrance to the lower city. It lay open. A marker of confidence, perhaps, Hattu mused. In ten years of struggle, the Ahhiyawans had indeed not even managed to scratch Troy's walls, by the look of things.

From up on the Thymbran Gatehouse walkway, two glints of bronze caught his eye. Purple-cloaked Guardians: the elite corps of the Trojan Army, unbearded in the Hittite fashion, with long hair knotted loosely at the nape of the neck.

'Halt!' one Guardian yelled. The other up there winked behind a fully-stretched bow, trained on Hattu. Hattu stopped on the spot, the others following suit. The cicada song grew intense and the archer guard's arm began to tremble at full draw.

Just then, another figure strode out from the gate tower: a Guardian too, but draped in a wolfskin, a bronze browband holding back his long curls, his heavy jaw shadowed with silvery stubble. This one planted his hands on the curves of the mud-brick crenelations and screwed his eyes up, examining Hattu carefully.

'Dolon?' Hattu croaked, recognising the veteran Trojan warrior. Memories flashed through his mind from Kadesh, where he and Dolon had fought side by side in that frenzied desert war. The man now wore the purple-painted breastplate reserved for the Commander of the Guardians.

Dolon's face brightened with a smile. '*Labarna?*' he gasped. The other sentries nearby rose, necks lengthening, faces suddenly wide in interest. '*Labarna?*' they echoed in an eerie susurrus. Dolon pushed the archer guard's bow down. 'Come, come,' he called, waving Hattu and his party forward.

They passed through the tunnel-like gatehouse and onto the paved Scaean Way, a wide, rising street hemmed with flat-roofed houses. Sheltered on all sides, the air here was still and stifling. As Dagon parked the wagon, Hattu looked uphill towards the citadel. Above the stout defences, high halls soared, the architraves banded in bronze and silver, supported by columns of speckled blue and green marble. A golden acropolis, just as he remembered it. But these lower city wards around him were different: a warren of plainness where once there had been beauty; shabby buildings instead of proud family homes. None of the thriving street markets of the past, he realised, recalling the flashes of colour, cheerful cries of merchants and their exotic goods: ostrich eggs, hippo teeth, peacocks, vials of toad sweat and much more. Now, dust lay piled up in drifts at the corners. Tents and lean-to shacks fringed the way – rudimentary shelters for countryfolk who had fled into the city for protection, he realised, seeing Thymbran families in one such tent, grubby and sullen. The war might not have scratched the walls, but its claws had found their way inside nonetheless.

He noticed a rising burble of voices from the doorways and rooftops, where faces appeared and stared. A hunched, hoary old soothsayer emerged onto one rooftop, rattling a staff and proclaiming: 'The Great King of the Hittites has arrived. The *Labarna* is here.' Another lifted a triton shell to his lips and blew long, haunting notes. Crowds began to gather around them, many voices yammering in excitement: 'The Hittites have come! Their armies are here at last?'

Hattu gulped. What to say?

A soft voice floated over it all. 'King Hattu?'

Hattu glanced around, recognising the voice. An owl-faced older man shuffled through the crowds with the aid of a cane, impeccably dressed in the old Trojan style with a long white robe embroidered with purple ducks. A pack of greyhounds followed him, leaping, tails wagging. 'Is it really you?' he said, his winged brows rising, his face filling with pleasure.

'Antenor,' Hattu said, recognising the elder. In times past, Antenor had accompanied Trojan embassies on their annual visits to Hattusa. Back then, he had been black haired and fleshy. Now, he was lined, his short hair and beard white as the snow atop Mount Ida.

The hounds pranced around Hattu, sniffing and licking his hands.

Antenor took one of Hattu's hands in both of his and clasped it firmly with a quarter-bow. 'By Apollo it is good to see you.' He looked past Hattu, through the gate and off across the plain, his mouth twisting in thought. 'May I ask where the Hittite divisions are camped? There are some approaches that would be more favourable than others and it would be wise not to follow the Scamander path directly, because…'

Hattu held up a hand to interrupt, and whispered: 'There are no others, my friend.'

Antenor glanced at the five with Hattu, and his face changed, deep lines of worry spreading across his forehead. 'Ah…'

'I come to advise, and to fight, even though I am but one man,' Hattu explained quietly. 'I bring the Hittite Chariot Master too, and he can give counsel to and ride with the Trojan wing.'

Just then, a Trojan who had climbed onto a high roof to look out over the countryside called out. 'There… there is no army out there.'

The babbling voices changed then, from excitement to confusion and concern.

'I will explain all this to King Priam,' said Hattu to Antenor. 'Where is he?'

'Praying,' Antenor said, twisting to gaze up at the citadel. 'Come, I will escort you to him.'

Antenor's cane clicked as they went, the greyhounds and a gaggle of citizens tagging along in their wake – gossiping about the absence of the Hittite army. They passed more warrens of run-down homes. Women sat in the doorways, carding flax and weaving mats, hands never ceasing to work while their eyes followed the newcomers' every step. On the flat roofs, men worked wood and leather and children laid out grapes to dry in the sun, but every single one of them watched the procession. One slave boy following them, overly-engrossed, tripped and dropped the clay jar he was carrying. The jar smashed and the oil it contained rolled down the slope like a glistening tongue extending. The lad fell, first onto his knees, helplessly skidding through the oil and past Hattu, then tumbling onto his buttocks before enduring the rest of the slide downhill with the indignity of his kilt riding up round his torso. Young women at the street side covered their mouths, tittering. Dagon helped the boy to his feet. 'Not to worry, lad,' he said. 'It could be worse.'

'How?' the boy wailed.

Dagon shrugged. 'Fair point.'

As they climbed the way and ascended towards the citadel, the hot breeze hit them once more: the famous Wind of Wilusa, always blowing southwards. Hattu glanced along yet another shanty lane. 'The war has been cruel,' he said quietly.

'Crueller than you could imagine,' Antenor agreed.

'How have the people managed to live through ten years of this?'

Antenor gazed up at the citadel. 'I cannot speak for the others. I know only my own thoughts. Before all this, when I was young, I was a merchant. Happy times, when I simply made the best of what I had. I've tried to think that way throughout this war. It has been tricky. But now you are here. You, the hero Troy has been waiting for.'

'Is it heroic to put out the fire I started?' Hattu answered. 'Had I not waged war against my nephew, the Hittite armies might have been here, and ten years sooner.'

'Do not dwell upon it, *Labarna.* Sometimes the winds guide us in the strangest of ways,' Antenor said with a reassuring smile as the breeze whistled a sombre tune. 'And while you are here, you will stay with me at my villa, I hope?' One of the dogs licked his hand as if to sweeten the offer.

Hattu nodded in gratitude. 'Thank you, friend.'

The hot wind grew stronger, sparring with them as they climbed the steep final section of the wide avenue towards the citadel's Scaean Gate – the thick wood planks black and shiny with age and studded with bronze rivets. Unlike the other gates in the city, this one sported not two sturdy flanking towers, but one colossal one on the left hand side – a hawk's nest rising as high as the city summit itself. Against the tower's base rested five huge tablets, each etched with a prediction. Oddly, the first of these lay broken, violently.

'The prophecies of protection… what happened?' Hattu said, crouching by the broken one.

'King Priam will explain,' Antenor said. He called up to the roof of the great tower. The sound of straining ropes and clunking cogs arose from behind the gates as they parted.

On the other side of the gate lay a different world of sumptuous villas, temples and halls. There were quince and fig orchards, burbling fountains of porphyry and hanging gardens from which birds trilled in gentle song. The war's claws had clearly not reached these high wards, Hattu realised as he walked. A different class of Trojan dwelled here: by the fountains sat jewelled women with oiled skin; in the doorways and on the rooftops stood men with expertly-groomed hair and purple-edged gowns that seemed to shine like liquid, chatting and laughing. Up on a palatial balcony, one fellow with a golden headband and a shock of receding brown curls stood. He was glaring down upon the incoming party, unsmiling. Hattu squinted to discern who it was. Just then, a slave girl wearing a lotus flower crown hurried over to him. She bore a tray of foaming wooden beer cups. Like the others, Hattu thanked her, took one and sucked on the reed straw. The cool, malty brew thankfully washed the dust from his throat. When he looked up at the balcony again, the unsmiling man had vanished into the shade of his home.

In any case, his attentions were quickly grabbed by a shimmer of metal from the city's flat summit. A fine one-storeyed temple, crowned with a statue of a kneeling, golden archer, silver bow drawn towards the sky. The Trojan Sun God, known to some as Apollo, others as Lyarri. As the party passed this wonder, Hattu noticed a woman in the temple doorway, staring at him.

'Princess Cassandra,' Hattu whispered, recognising her. He and her had spoken once before, briefly, but long enough to share with one another the dreams the Gods subjected them to.

Her face turned sour. 'I prayed that Apollo was wrong, and that you would not come,' she said.

'What do you mean?'

'How could you?' she said as they passed, tears rolling down her cheeks. Two temple lackeys known as the Servants of Apollo emerged to flank her, then guided her inside.

'What did she mean?' he asked. 'Is she still held in that temple like a prisoner, even after all these years?'

'Troy is full of seers, King Hattu,' Antenor said. 'Enough to drive a man mad. Now come, we should not delay.'

The elder hurried on, leading them to another shrine that rose like a cliff, faced in all colours of marble slabs. Two Guardians flanked the entrance, the doors pinned open by bronze bolts fashioned like arrows. This great sanctuary was known as the Palladium, home to the famous idol of Pallas Athena, the Trojan Goddess of War and Wisdom. Antenor halted here. 'King Priam is inside,' he said quietly. 'Though he is… not quite himself.'

Somewhat unnerved by the elder's grim tone and the deprivations he had seen in the lower city, Hattu twisted to Dagon, Sirtaya, Tudha and the two soldiers. 'Wait in the shade,' he said, pointing over to a colonnade upon the roof of which Andor had already decided to perch.

'And I mean *wait,*' he demanded, directing his words and a fiery look at Tudha.

The wind dropped away as he entered the Palladium. The space inside the high-ceilinged temple was dark and blissfully cool, the walls of lime-plaster painted in swirls of deep ochre and sea blue. Cones of musky incense smoked away on wall burners, and sandalwood crackled on a low hearth. But the centrepiece of the shrine was the silver altar upon which the Palladium idol rested. Such a simple, small statue of wood that meant so much to the Trojan people, Hattu thought. The ultimate guarantee of divine protection. Garlands and recent offerings of figs and wine lay around the altar. A frail priest knelt before it all, thin white hair trailing down his back. 'Bless the stone, the clay, the streets of this city. Guard Troy's children, mighty Athena, I implore you to watch over them.'

Hattu waited for the old priest finish to his incantation before he spoke, but the fellow repeated the same lines over and over without a pause for breath. 'Pardon my interruption,' he said finally, his words echoing around the temple. 'I am looking for King Priam.'

The kneeling one stopped chanting, falling utterly still as if struck by an invisible spear. Unsteadily, he rose and turned slowly to face Hattu.

Hattu stared at the hollow rack of a man. 'Majesty?' he croaked, for it was Priam, no doubt. When last they had met the King of Troy had been strong-shouldered, brown-haired, full of vigour. This one before him was aged, drawn, gaunt, old before his time, but those green eyes were unmistakeable. 'I have come to honour the oath of my empire,' Hattu continued.

Deathly silence reigned for a time. Then…

'For ten years, I have waited,' Priam said in a long, low burr.

Hattu nodded slowly. How to explain all that had gone on in that time?

Priam's haggard face flared as if he was boiling from within. '*TEN YEARS!*' his cry reverberated around the Palladium and felt as if it might have shaken the entire Scamander plain. With a sudden jolt of energy, he strode for Hattu, shaking with anger. Hattu did not flinch and Priam halted before him, a good head shorter, chest heaving with rapid breaths. 'Your oath lies shattered.'

'No, Majesty. I am here.'

Priam's eyes grew distant and his lips parted as he recited words that sent a shiver up Hattu's spine – the very words of his dead brother: 'I, Muwa, Great King of the Hittites, swear to you, Priam of Troy, under the eyes of the Gods, that the four mighty Divisions of the Hittite Empire will, at your request, turn to and march upon the west. We will drive the Ahhiyawans from the land or to their knees.' The fog cleared from his eyes. He stabbed a finger out in the direction of the Scaean Tower. 'Ten years ago we rang the great beacon bell. For ten years, I have waited. For ten years, I have mourned the loss of my kinsfolk, my children.' His face spasmed with grief. 'Do you know what they did to my dear son, Troilus?'

Hattu thought of the youthful Trojan Prince he had met once before, and of the wolf's tooth he had given the lad. In return, the affable youth had given him a small bronze key – a token of friendship that Hattu had carried in his purse ever since.

'They cut off his head and desecrated his body,' he said in a tumble of words and sobs. 'He was only a boy. They danced and feasted that night, claiming that the first of Troy's five sacred prophecies of protection had been broken.'

Hattu closed his eyes, understanding why one of the five tablets by the Scaean Tower had been smashed. The Trojans were honour-bound to destroy the writings of any prophecy should it become an impossibility.

It took Priam a time to straighten up and compose himself. 'Throughout those ten years, I watched the eastern horizons, awaiting sight of the Hittite army. For ten years those horizons have remained bare.' He glanced to the doorway and the runner boy outside. '*Now*, I hear whispers rising that you come before me with, with… with a party of just five… *five!* And you claim that your oath is fulfilled?'

Hattu saw just how deep the wells of sadness in Priam's eyes were. Without a further thought, he dipped to one knee, took Priam's hand and kissed it. 'My empire is a broken husk. My capital, Hattusa, relies on desperate, temporary defences. The Fields of Bronze have been forsaken and the barracks there lie in ruin. I bring all that I can. Forgive me.'

Priam gazed down at him, lost, gawping in incredulity. 'You are the Great King of the Hittites,' he said, pulling his hand away. 'Great Kings do not kneel before their vassals or beg apology.'

'No,' said Hattu, 'but friends do.'

A sandalwood branch snapped in the hearth. Tears shone in Priam's eyes and he sagged, sobbing.

Hattu rose. 'Know that were there any other way, I would have been here long ago, with the forces my brother promised you. But think not of the past. Think of now, of the fact I am here, and that I can help guide Troy in this struggle. You know my strengths, and you know that one good general is worth ten thousand troops. I have heard exorbitant rumours of this war. But I want you to tell me… tell me what happened here.'

The King of Troy gulped away his tears and led Hattu in a slow walk around the cool hall of the Palladium. 'First they took the Bay of Boreas,' Priam said. 'There was a ferocious battle. Hektor was sure we could rebuff them there, but back then he was not familiar with the Ahhiyawan ways of war. Their ships cut onto the sand and they sprung on our half-prepared defences like jackals. Next, my advisors claimed that they would starve, if we were to bring our herds and grain into the city and set light to the fields. But they simply called upon supply shipments from the Ahhiyawan islands and mainland. And when the deeper seas were rough and they could not do so, they ravaged Wilusa's coastal islands and the outlying towns – none with good walls like Troy's. Thebes-under-Plakos, Lesbos, Lyrnessus... all razed to dust. The twin forts in the south too – now but black heaps of rubble, the garrisons butchered. They fell upon my northern stud farm in the first year of the war, stole every steed there – even though they have not one decent charioteer amongst their ranks.'

'We underestimated their determination,' said a new voice, clipped and dry.

Hattu looked up to see a group coming in through the temple doorway. The one who had spoken was that unsmiling fellow with the receding curls who had glowered so coldly at Hattu on the way in. His eyes, the colour of mud, were like creatures peering out from underneath rocks.

'Ah, Deiphobus,' Priam said. For all the world the words sounded like they were spoken through gritted teeth.

*Prince Deiphobus*, Hattu mused, recognising him now. Priam and Hekabe's third son, outranked only by Hektor and Paris. He was bulky and tall compared to the last time Hattu had seen him when he was a slip of a lad in the last years of boyhood. With him were an odd pair Hattu had seen before but never spoken with: Old Chryses, the High Priest of Apollo, bald as an egg, face like a winter's apple, shuffling and grossly overweight; Laocoon, the tall, dark-bearded Priest of Poseidon, clutching his ceremonial staff – topped with a *hippocampus*, a creature with the head and torso of a steed and the tail of a fish.

'We made the mistake of thinking they would have a certain way of war. A code.' Unsmiling Deiphobus continued.

Chryses raised a hand and extended a chubby finger towards Hattu. 'You Hittites begin every war with two tablets, do you not?' he asked, his voice tremulous. 'One with an offer of peace and one detailing what will happen to your enemy should they persist with their antagonism. Well the Ahhiyawans gave us no such choice.'

'Well, there was the delegation,' Laocoon mused. 'But look how *that* ended! They don't want Helen, they want Troy. They want utter and complete obliteration of this ancient place.'

'In any case,' Priam threw back at them, 'had they offered terms, I would not have given Helen back.'

'Paris and Helen do not even lie together these days,' Deiphobus argued. 'Their affair is spent. She means nothing to Troy.'

'Were I to allow her to go to the Ahhiyawans, it would be seen as a sign of weakness. All kings have to maintain at least an illusion of strength.' Priam swooshed a hand towards the door. 'Now leave us. I must speak with the *Labarna* alone. There will be a feast of welcome tonight where all can celebrate the arrival of our great ally.'

The trio turned to leave. Deiphobus halted, twisting back, his face carefully expressionless. 'Will the *Labarna* be requiring bread and wine to feed his army too?'

'I said… leave us.' Priam hissed, glaring at his son and the priests until they departed.

Priam waited until they were alone before speaking again. 'The Ahhiyawans have not the might or nous to build a siege line around our city, but thanks to their constant marauding, they have a stranglehold on us nonetheless. The trade ships that once crowded here now stay away. The roads too used to be clogged with merchant wagons. Now they take long, circuitous detours to avoid the countryside of Wilusa. We have lost more than three-quarters of the income we once knew. How can we fix this, *Labarna?*'

Hattu chewed over this for a time. 'The enemy army is one matter, and I will get to that. But there is a deeper, darker danger. I have heard a rumour. Talk of an enemy presence within Troy.'

Priam smiled sadly. 'I have suspected as much for some time. Ever since the start of the war, battles have swung suddenly and strangely in our enemy's favour. In the winter our springhouse was polluted with a dead dog's body – weighted down in a sack of rocks so it was hard to spot. For fourteen days we were without clean water. Thank the cold north winds for bringing frost and snow to keep our cups full. And then there was…little Troilus,' he stopped, taking a shuddering breath. 'Somebody told the enemy that he was going out into the countryside that day. The Ahhiyawans were waiting for him. There *is* a rogue amongst us.'

'I will keep one eye open at all times, Majesty,' Hattu vowed. 'If it helps,' he said quietly, 'you may like to know that one rogue has been wiped from this war: Piya-maradu – the bastard who kindled this fire – lies buried to his neck at the enemy camp.'

Priam snorted with a pale echo of humour. 'This mess was not Piya-maradu's doing. He was but one of many servants of Agamemnon. Agamemnon possessed a swollen navy for many years before this war started. He was waiting for the tiniest crumb of encouragement… and then Paris gave it to him when he took Helen from the halls of Sparta.'

'I know now this war was not about a woman,' Hattu asked, 'but she is here still, yes?'

Priam nodded sombrely. 'Helen watches on as, one by one, my children die,' he said flatly. 'Think not of her, King Hattu, for she will not win us this war. Think instead of those who can… who *will.* Prince Hektor is at the northeastern bastion, by the Apollonian Gate. Go, speak with him.'

***

The hot north wind chopped and sparred as Hattu climbed the last few steps, and when he emerged onto the walkway it hit him like a dragon's breath, casting his hair back like a battle pennant. The bastion jutted from the citadel mound like a ship's prow, dominating the nearby Apollonian Gate.

Hattu moved to its V-shaped point, planting his hands on the hot clay of the bastion edge, taking it all in. The outlook was incredible – a perfect vista of the Western Sea, the wooded hills of Tenedos Isle sharp and clear in the foreground and the more far-off isles hazy blue in the distance. More, he had an almost bird's-eye view of the Bay of Troy immediately below. The sheltered oval of water was still and glassy, apart from where the Scamander and its sister river, the Simois, flowed into it in smooth, banded ripples. Yet just as Priam had described, there were no merchant ships. No ships at all, apart from a few war galleys roped up and disused near the wooden wharf, some partially submerged and rotting. During his previous trips to Troy this bay had been permanently crammed with a traffic of trade cogs. He glanced around the gleaming and opulent citadel, then the shabby lower city. It was clear how the shortfall in trade income had been bridged. There was but one notable spot in those dilapidated wards: a small shrine to Apollo built into the slope. The pillared stone entrance gaped like an open mouth, waters from the spring deep within Troy's tell gushing forth into clay channels that ran down into the watering troughs around the city. The traitor who poisoned those waters clearly knew the city well.

When he turned to look east along the spine of the Silver Ridge, the breath caught in his lungs. Out there, a hill rose proud of the ridge, the gentle slopes thick with a tangle of hornbeam and vines. On the spacious and flat summit, a village of military tents was arrayed, spotted with colours and movement. The army and allies of Troy, Hattu realised. The hairs on his neck stood proud – this was quite a force.

At the camp's centre, staffs stood planted in the earth here and there, topped with the twin bulls, Serris and Hurris, sacred to Trojan and Hittite alike. Commander Dolon was out there now, inspecting the block of Trojan Guardians – some seven hundred, maybe eight hundred of them. A few hundred black-kilted Dardanian archers worked nearby, waxing bowstrings and fletching arrows.

Further out from this central area, he spotted a large force of men in shuddering headdresses of ostrich feathers. 'The Lukkans are here?' he whispered to himself boyishly, seeing some of them practice-sparring with one another. Ancient and loyal allies of Troy and of the Hittite Empire. Wolf warriors, some called them, so fierce and loyal were they in battle. A tall fellow in a yellow cloak strode amongst them, scrutinising and encouraging as he went. He wore a simple circlet with a single peacock feather rising from the brow. *Sarpedon!* Hattu mouthed, thrilled to see the Lukkan King, another of his close comrades from the Kadesh war. A hero. The Lukkan people even claimed he was the Son of the Thunder God.

He tracked Sarpedon's path through the tents until the Lukkan halted to clasp forearms with another man. This one was clearly not a Lukkan – he was swarthier and wore nothing but a cloth headdress and a hide cuirass – not a stitch of clothing below the waist. 'Masturi,' Hattu laughed, his gaze darting until he spotted Masturi's contingent of five hundred or so, likewise without loincloths or kilts. These men of the Seha Riverland had been there too at Kadesh. Now they were here to aid Troy. Hattu's heart swelled. This was no lost cause, he realised. Odysseus' words *"Troy has but one champion"* now seemed wildly inaccurate.

He swept his eyes over the patchwork of others – most of them Hittite vassals: a clutch of bald-headed bowmen from the River Axios. Thymbran spearmen, distinguished by their silver headbands. Karkisans, expert archers, wearing wide-brimmed straw hats. Shooting on a practice range were the remaining Zeleian archers of poor King Pandarus. There were some five hundred swordsmen from Percote. The militia of Ascania, the men of Cyzicus. Adrestians, Ciconians and more, all mixing, preparing food, honing weapons, repairing shields. He saw chiefs and commanders of some of the various tribes come together in a circle to slaughter a goat kid. Each dipped a sword or spear into the blood and held the reddened weapons high, blades interleaved.

'A wordless, solemn oath of allegiance… to the death,' a voice spoke beside Hattu.

The figure beside him, robed in immaculate white, clunked a bright battle helmet onto the parapet, plumed with a coiled whip of leather and a trailing purple tail. Hattu recognised it instantly: the Helm of Troy. King Priam had worn it at Kadesh, as the High Commander of the Trojan forces. Now it belonged to his eldest son and heir… Hektor.

He was unmistakable, even fourteen years on since Hattu had last set eyes upon him. He had been a precocious talent, gaining legendary status in his adolescence by leading men to impossible victories. But Hektor was a youth no more, with lines of experience at the sides of his eyes, and a certain dryness of expression on his weatherbeaten face. His long dark curls, knotted loosely at the nape of his neck, shuddered in the breeze.

'I am honoured to have you here, *Labarna*,' he said with an earnest nod. 'I trust Queen Puduhepa fares well?'

Hattu felt a sharp twist in his chest. *Gods, how I miss her*. 'She rules at Hattusa in my absence.'

'They say Prince Tudha is here too? When last you were here he was but a baby! I trust he has grown strong and wise like his father?'

Hattu smiled a mask of a smile. 'Aye,' he lied.

Hektor issued a poignant sigh. 'Much has changed since your previous visit. You must meet my wife, Andromache,' he pointed over to the palace. There, on a balcony, a swan of a woman sat with a child at her bosom. 'Little Astyanax was born in the winter, on a morning when the Scamander froze over. We both pray for the day to come when peace arrives and we can bathe him in the shallows. Gods, let this damned war end.'

'That is why I am here,' Hattu said. 'Alas, with no regiments.' He watched Hektor carefully, anticipating a dry response to this like that of Deiphobus, or an angry one like Priam's.

'I hear my father rather vented his frustrations at you?' Hektor said calmly. 'I hope you took no offence?'

'I understand entirely. There was not a passing day when I did not dwell on my empire's neglected oath.'

Hektor planted one foot onto the crenel, resting an elbow upon the knee, studying the horizon. 'My father is desperate for allies. At first, only local tribes, bands of mercenaries and showers of peasants arrived. Next came Sarpedon and Masturi – real men of war with armies of substance and strength. Their tents might dominate the Thorn Hill,' he gestured to the allied encampment and shook his head, 'yet they are still not enough. Word has been cast wide to the other major powers who might help us. To the Thracians across the strait. To the Elamites, far, far to the east, way beyond even your realm. Even to the Amazons, wherever they might now roam.'

'How many spears and bows do you have out there right now?' Hattu asked.

'Since the outset of the war we have arrayed ourselves and fought in five battalions. Just shy of eight thousand men in total.'

'So the Ahhiyawans outnumber you, nearly two to one.'

'They have outnumbered us for ten years. Yet look at our walls. Unscathed,' Hektor replied. He turned and walked along the parapet, running his palm along the undulating merlons as he went, coming to the edge that looked back over the city and the great Scamander plain to the south. 'Yes, they seized the Bay of Boreas, they have laid waste to the outlying villages, and many times they have come from their beach camp and driven across the plain. Yes, they have more than once pushed us back almost to Troy's walls, but always we have repelled them. Not once have they even scratched these mighty defences.'

Hattu had always admired the expert architecture of the place. Envied it even. But there was one stretch of the city walls that had always snagged his eye: on the western side ran a section with older and less expertly-fitted masonry. It was like a boil on a fine face. His attentions returned to the Thorn Hill camp on the Silver Ridge, drawn there by movement. Small groups were now moving slowly down the ridge's southern slopes onto the plain. They were carrying stretchers and hide sleds. He saw a group of Zeleians moving towards the location of King Pandarus' corpse. Collecting the dead, he realised. He noticed tiny, ant-like groups of men emerging over the Borean Hills in the south. Ahhiyawans doing likewise.

'We have this single day of truce to collect and honour our dead,' Hektor said. 'The pyres will burn brightly tonight.

'Yesterday's battle was costly?'

Hektor nodded sombrely. 'It was the worst thus far. Yet it began with an honourable proposition.' He gestured to the Scaean Tower. The rooftop was dominated by a giant bronze beacon bell, but beside it sat a lone figure, bare-chested and wearing soft-looking eastern-style trousers, his long, sun-bleached curls hanging around his face. He was caressing a lyre. Over the constant growl of the warm wind, Hattu heard the soft notes of a lonely tune. 'Paris was a reckless boy. He stole away from Sparta with Helen not because he loved or lusted for her, but because he thought that with such a beautiful and powerful woman as his bride it might make him a finer prince. He still has that rashness in him, but over the years of the war he has come to understand just how dark a cloud he has dragged over our city. He blames himself for our young brother Troilus' death and languishes in despair most days.'

'Ah, yes,' Hattu sighed, absently touching his purse, feeling the key within. 'I was saddened to hear of Troilus' fate.'

'Because it means one of the prophecies of protection is gone?'

Hattu recoiled slightly at the odd assumption. 'Because he was your brother. Because he was a pleasant lad.'

Hektor's face hardened. 'Hmm. The people care only that the prophecy is no more. Still, four others remain: the prediction that horses of faraway Thracia will come here, drink and rest by the Scamander side – another guarantee of Troy's safety. There is the presence of the Palladium, of course, and as long as that remains in the city, then Athena will shield us from danger. And the city's oldest soothsayer proclaimed that as long as the son of Achilles did not join the war, Troy would come to no harm. Finally, there is me,' he smiled wanly. 'I have a duty to remain alive, for as long as I do, Troy will be safe.'

Hattu nodded along. He gazed over at Paris again, noticing the dark black bruise on the prince's neck. 'Your brother does more than mope, by the looks of it. That is a battle wound, no?'

'Of sorts. Yesterday, he went against my father's wishes and offered to fight King Menelaus in a duel to decide who would have Helen,' Hektor smiled weakly, 'and to prove to the armies that he is not just a cowardly bowman.'

Hattu recalled the mocking song he had heard in the Ahhiyawan shore camp.

'He fought well at first but… but Menelaus smashed away his shield and beat him to the ground. He grabbed him by his helmet plume and began dragging him into the watching enemy lines, choking him on his own chinstrap.' He laughed sourly. 'Sometimes I wonder if the Gods use us as their playthings, for at that moment, the scudding north wind turned eastwards, sending a billowing dust cloud across the battlefield. It came, blinding and stinging, then it was gone. When the air turned clear again, Paris had vanished. Some said the Gods spirited him away to safety behind Troy's walls. I, however, saw him fleeing through the dust, face white with terror as he slipped inside the city. The Ahhiyawans cared only that he had broken the duel pact, and exploded in outrage. We clashed with everything we had. The fighting was fervid,' Hektor shook his head. 'Last night there were discussions here in the citadel halls – that we should return Helen anyway… as if that might end the war!' he laughed sourly. 'Paris argued vociferously against the proposal and demanded that he be put in charge of a battalion tomorrow in order to redeem himself.' He patted a fist upon the merlons. 'But there should be no battle tomorrow. For we should not have collapsed as we did yesterday. I still don't understand it. My best men were on our right yet they gave way.'

Hattu gazed over the many commanders down in the allied camp. It made him wonder again about the mention of an Ahhiyawan agent planted within Troy. Perhaps not within Troy's walls, he mused, gazing over the camp. A military man would have the ultimate range for interference. In a large army like this, it would be easy for a trained spy to melt into the ranks, hide away in a tent – to sabotage or muddle orders during battle and to enter the city without challenge to carry out sabotage there too – like the poisoning of the well that Priam had mentioned. 'How much do you trust your commanders?'

Hektor looked at him askance. 'Paris, Deiphobus, Scamandrios? Utterly. They are my brothers, after all.'

Hattu nodded. 'And the allies? How do you feel about them?'

Hektor frowned and smiled at the same time. 'The soldiers down there are comrades of ancient family lines. You know this too, surely...' his smile grew wryer. 'Ah, I see. You have heard about the rumours. About the enemy spy somewhere amongst us? Not in my army... not in my army.'

Hattu sighed in apparent agreement. Privately, he decided that he would evaluate the soldiery for himself – tomorrow's mooted battle would allow him to watch for signs of sabotage. 'So what now, Prince of Troy? I am here, and although I am a Great King, you must employ me as if I were any other ally. I may not offer one thousand swords, but I have many years' experience in warfare, so too does Chariot Master Dagon. We understand the dance of battle, and how to trip the enemy.'

'You will be a welcome addition to my officer corps, *Labarna*,' Hektor said, 'and our chariot general was killed yesterday, so what better replacement than the legendary Dagon of Hattusa?' He sighed. 'If only we had replacements for all of the fallen. We lost many good men yesterday. Too many,' Hektor sighed.

'So too did the Ahhiyawans,' Hattu replied. 'Three hundred and seventeen dead, a similar number injured.'

Hektor cocked an eyebrow. 'You counted the corpses on your way here?' he said with a snort of bemusement.

'No, but we heard the figures for ourselves when we infiltrated the enemy camp earlier today.'

Hektor looked at him as if a wasp had just flown from his mouth. 'What?'

'We came perilously close to being spitted and used as battle sacrifices. It was worth it though: all is not well in Agamemnon's ranks. The best of his warrior kings, Achilles, helped us escape – merely to rile Agamemnon.'

Now Hektor took a step back. 'Achilles? Never. The man is a beast. He lives only to slay us Trojans and our friends.'

Hattu shrugged. 'He certainly made it clear that once he was finished arm-wrestling with Agamemnon, that would be his priority. For now, however, it seems that he has laid down his weapons in protest over a captured Trojan woman.'

Hektor's eyes darted. 'That would explain why Achilles was not at yesterday's battle,' he whispered to himself.

'He won't be at tomorrow's either, as things stand,' Hattu agreed.

'If this is true then Apollo shines upon us,' Hektor enthused.

'Quite,' said Hattu. 'More, with Achilles abstaining from battle, some of the Ahhiyawans seem doubtful of the whole war effort. There was even talk amongst some factions of sailing for home.'

Hektor's eyes sparkled. 'Their spirit is breaking at last?' he said in a breathy whisper.

'Not entirely,' Hattu cautioned. 'There are plenty who remain steadfast. It seems to be Odysseus and the man-mountain Ajax who serve as tentpoles for Agamemnon's army. The young Tirynean King Diomedes too, and the old one, Nestor of Pylos. They have built a sand rampart to fortify their beach camp – hardly the act of an army ready to flee.'

Hektor nodded slowly, his optimism tempered. 'What else did you see? Do they still suffer the plague?'

'Aye,' he answered. 'It is a constant bane, from what I saw and heard.'

'Ha,' Hektor grunted. 'The fever of the river plain and the lower grounds – it is one of our greatest defences. The first lords of Troy knew this, and that was why they built their city up here where the wind is fresh and the air clean all year round.'

'Walling themselves into the bay will only worsen the matter,' Hattu agreed.

Hektor chewed his bottom lip, nodding away to himself. 'You know something? I can feel it in my blood,' he shook one fist, grinning, 'a telling victory over the invader is near.' He batted the merlons. 'But that is for tomorrow, when we take to the battlefield once more. First, you should rest after your long journey, and look forward to the feast tonight – a celebration in honour of the fallen. Then, come dawn, we will line up side by side, King Hattu, as it was always meant to be. To save Troy, aye?' he smiled.

***

The figure watched the Crown Prince of Troy and the King of the Hittites talking. For so long, the sight of the two together had been equally feared by the Ahhiyawans and desired by the Trojans. Neither had expected the Hittite lord to arrive like this, with nothing but a beggar's band in tow. The mighty Hittite Army was not coming. The figure smiled. It had all been rumour until now. Now rumour was fact.

What an interesting development, the figure mused. It would offer King Agamemnon many new possibilities, each like a key that might finally unlock Troy.

# CHAPTER 5

## BATTLE'S EVE

A fat, waxing moon rose over Troy, so large and sharp that every detail could be seen on its pale crust. In the balmy night heat, Tudha strode through the citadel gardens, shooting the Trojan Guardians imperious looks. He was proud of his height – taller even than most Hittites his age – and he liked the way the Trojans looked up at him with a glint of awe in their eyes. Even better when the women did so. He noticed two of them – handmaidens for King Priam and Queen Hekabe, glancing at him coquettishly as he passed. Both wore open-fronted gowns, breasts on display. Feeling his throat soften and his loins swell, he broke into something of a dutiful strut. Then…

*Shrieeek!*

He yelped, shambled and tripped. The two young women vanished in fits of giggles, and then Andor landed on his shoulder with another completely unnecessary shriek. He stared at the bird, exasperated. 'You're lucky that cooked eagle is not a delicacy in these parts,' he seethed. But he could not stay angry with her for long. He came to a magnificent sphinx monument, carved from pale-blue marble. Planting himself on a bench nearby, he brought out a strip of salted tunny he had taken from the evening feast at King Priam's table and fed it to Andor. She tore up the morsel – letting her gratitude go unspoken, as always. He eyed the blue sphinx, and as he sometimes did, let his mind's eye drift to a future where Hattusa would be grand once more. Not just repaired of the ruinous damage from the civil war, but expanded to cover the sweeping hills southeast of the current city. He had drawn diagrams of how it might be, even building models with wooden blocks. Father had always chastised him for both. *Our Empire is disintegrating, we have no army, and you dream of building grand monuments?* The memory only drove him to greater imaginings than ever.

He envisioned a great gateway, with sphinxes for gateposts. Grinning, he drew out his stylus and tablet, wetted the surface with a few fingertips of water from the nearest water channel, and began to jot down his ideas. No sooner had he started writing than he realised it had been of his own volition. He set the tablet and stylus down as if both were poisoned. *I have served my years in the scribal school,* he complained inwardly. He glanced back to the palace and the megaron hall where the feast was still ongoing.

In the stripes of torchlight and shadow within, men raised and clacked cups together, their laughter pealing. Mouthwatering aromas of spiced meat wafted on the night breeze. He could see his father sitting in there too, brooding and silent, aloof. *You gave me my iron sword, told me I was a man, entrusted me to quell the uprising in the north. And I did! Now you take the blade away as if I am a child again?* He stared at his father, teeth grinding. 'Why won't you trust me?' he said quietly.

'He sees too much of himself in you,' said a voice, close by.

Tudha started, head switching round. On a low wall opposite the sphinx, a man was perched like a crow. How long had he been there? An archer, Tudha guessed, seeing the bow strapped to the fellow's back. The man slid down from the wall and strolled towards him, tucking his hair – sleek and dark like a hawk's wing – behind his ears.

'Who are you?'

'Someone who understands that look you wear,' he smiled. 'A boy on the outside, always looking in. Never quite good enough. Not sure why.'

It was as if the strange archer had reached inside Tudha's chest and stroked his heart with a feather. He laughed once, a sad sound.

The stranger sat alongside Tudha, the moonlight picking out his profile, clean and sharp. 'They say it was the same between him and his sire.'

'Aye, it was, or so the stories go,' Tudha said. He then cocked his head to one side, regarding the man. 'You seem to know a lot about my father.'

'I am Aeneas, Prince of Dardania, nephew of King Priam.'

Tudha rocked backwards, suddenly quite awestruck. 'You fought beside my father at Kadesh. The greatest war ever waged!'

Aeneas smiled weakly. 'There was nothing great about it.' He took an arrow from his quiver and rotated it on its shaft slowly, stroking the green mallard fletching, his black thumb ring glistening in the torchlight. 'At Kadesh, I tossed my old bow on one of the many pyres, because I was sure there could never be another war as terrible as that one.' He looked up at the night sky, now flickering strangely as the pyres of the dead began to rise in flames out on the plain. 'I was wrong.' He sighed deeply. 'At least that horrible conflict cleared my mind, showed me something: that I had spent my youth – wasted it – ruminating over my father's preference for my brothers, and his fawning over Priam's sons. My cousin Hektor was always the impossible ideal,' he said. 'If only I had ignored it all and put my energies into bettering myself. Think about that, Prince Tudhaliya. You are the heir to the Hittite Empire. The second most powerful being alive, and still you doubt yourself and fret over your father's esteem for you. Forget all that. Just be the best you can be. Do what *you* know is the right thing. Do not seek the judgement of others – untrustworthy is the man who makes choices to please another. Be your *own* man. He will respect you and trust you all the more for that.'

Tudha dipped his head a little to hide his boyish smile. Why was it that a few sentences from a virtual stranger felt so much more heartfelt than anything his father had ever said to him? 'I tried that once,' he said. 'Back at Hattusa, many thought the dark shadow of Urhi-Teshub the usurper was long gone. And it was… until last summer. North of our capital, in the Upper Lands, lies a great forested region known as Hatenzuwa. It was one of the last reliable outlands of our fragile empire – like a torch in the night, a reminder we were not alone, a symbol of hope. One day, that torch blew out. An uprising, led by one of Urhi-Teshub's old generals – a man who had hidden his identity all that time – had consumed the place. It was my fourteenth summer, my time.'

'The uprising was quelled,' Aeneas guessed confidently, 'else you Hittites would not be here.'

'The struggle was won,' Tudha confirmed. 'I, however, was deemed a failure. Father took my sword from me that day, and has kept it from me since.'

'I know things are precarious for you Hittites, but I hope there is more than one spare sword? Take up another. Do not allow anyone to tell you that your victories are defeats.'

Tudha shook his head. 'It was not just any sword. It was a blade of iron… *good* iron.' Aeneas' eyes widened in interest. 'One of only six ever made. Father wears two, Dagon the Chariot Master has one, my cousin Kurunta has another. Even the Kaskan Lord, Grax, was granted one.'

'Where is yours?'

Tudha flicked a finger towards the hall, where Sirtaya was now performing some feat of acrobatics for the amusement of the rest. 'Sirtaya keeps it. I love that old wretch and I have no gripe with him – he does only what my father demands of him. The iron swords are great weapons, but that is less important than what they really mean. Each blade is a symbol, granted only to those my Father trusts.' Tudha glared into the palace, seeing his father sitting there still, sober and silent. 'But you are right… I will not be told my victories are defeats, that up is down. I will be my own man,' he muttered quietly. His thoughts moved to the last hours of light, and the things he had overheard Hattu and Dagon muttering about before the feast.

'I see a glint in your eyes,' Aeneas said.

Tudha grinned. 'Have you heard the rumours about an enemy spy?'

Aeneas rolled his eyes. 'Gods, yes. The shadow amongst us.'

Tudha felt a faint shiver pass across him at the Dardanian's tone. 'Father and Dagon believe the culprit might be hiding out in the ranks of the army.'

'Evidently you disagree.'

Tudha looked around. 'It's this place – a rising warren of lanes and streets. Perfect for this "Shadow" to lurk within.' He shrugged. 'Father insists that when the army steps onto the plain tomorrow, I am not to be part of it. My job will be to record the battle on clay. Well, if I am to be left behind in these streets when the action starts… then I'll use the time wisely. I'll see what I can find.'

Aeneas stopped rolling the arrow in his hands, looking Tudha firmly in the eye. 'Be careful, lad. Spy or otherwise, Troy's streets can be dangerous.'

'So can I,' Tudha replied with a grin. 'As the rebel general at Hatenzuwa would tell you… if he were still alive!'

Aeneas laughed, rising. 'Until we meet again,' he said, swaggering towards the Scaean Gate.

***

'Again!' Laocoon the priest yelped, teeth and lips shining with wine, his words bouncing around the sumptuous megaron hall – a cavern of lush purple drapes and bright pillars.

Sirtaya once more scampered towards the wall and – like a spider, scurried almost halfway up it, before thrusting backwards, turning head over heels and landing on his feet. Another explosion of hilarity erupted, hands slapping the table, knives and plates and cups rattling.

Dagon shot Hattu a look of boredom and disdain. Hattu half-cocked an eyebrow in agreement. As always on the night before battle, he had eaten a small meal of bread, yoghurt and honey, topped with sesame seeds. A combination that would keep him light on his feet but energised. And not a drop of wine. For he had come to this feast in expectation of finer-grained talks about battle tactics tomorrow, and wider discussions about allies yet to arrive. Yet for all that their world was falling apart, the Trojan elite in this hall seemed happy to pickle their brains and hoot at Sirtaya's makeshift gymnastics. Even Sirtaya – usually tireless in his strange frolicking – sighed when they demanded more. Was the Egyptian getting a fraction slower these days? Hattu couldn't tell for sure.

At least, he thought, it was not the military commanders softening their minds like this – for Hektor, Paris and the other princely sons had taken their leave so they might rest before tomorrow. Hattu thought it best to stay longer so as not to offend their hosts. Of those remaining the priests, Laocoon and Chryses, were the worst, stuffing their mouths with goose meat and bread to soak up the great quantities of unwatered wine already consumed. The noblemen were a close second, their behaviour distinctly ignoble. As for the rulers of Troy, they were mute. Queen Hekabe sat slumped in her chair, her hands limp in the fingers of Antenor the elder, who massaged her palms tenderly and soberly. Since last Hattu had been at Troy, Hekabe had lost her good looks and gone fully grey. She wore a sad, submissive expression. Her at least, Hattu could forgive for escaping into a drunken pit, for she had lost many sons and daughters in this intractable war. Priam should have been at the table head, setting the example, but he was instead standing by the hall's inner door, insisting to Commander Dolon and a troop of Guardians that no lamentations for the dead were allowed tonight lest the enemy hear and take heart from it. There was a madness in his eyes, his hands visibly shaking as he chopped one into the palm of the other to underline his demands. A moment later, Priam gesticulated in frustration and led Dolon and his men outside.

Time ground past, and those at the table got more and more drunk. Hattu felt his jaw working, his patience crumbling. Something odd happened then. He noticed the vibrations first in the souls of his feet, then in his palms – resting on the table. He leaned back from the table, staring at the plates and cups, shuddering and jangling where they sat. He had felt the ground shake like this all too frequently back in the Hittite heartlands. Tremors that began like this but grew and grew, some capable of reducing forts and turrets to rubble. All around the table fell mercifully quiet, looking up and around as if the Gods were in the eaves.

'At ease, *Labarna,*' Laocoon said with an easy manner. He extended one hand, palm down as if controlling the invisible force of the quake. 'It is but a small shiver in the earth. They come and go quickly in these parts. It is merely the passing hoofbeats of Poseidon's horses.'

Indeed, the vibrations ended without any damage.

'More frequent this year than I remember,' Chryses added, 'but Troy's walls were built to withstand anything.' He grabbed and lifted a cup, saluting Laocoon. 'To Poseidon!'

'To Poseidon!' others echoed.

Laocoon gracefully accepted the acclaim as if he were the God of the Sea and Horses in human guise… then filled and drained a fresh cup of wine, before slurring the first words of some old song.

Hattu sighed as the drunken babble rose once again, many of those present singing along. It was old Antenor who cracked first, rising and bowing as he made his excuses, rolling his eyes at Hattu as he left. Taking the elder's lead, Hattu rose too. He addressed Queen Hekabe with a gentle voice and a half-bow: 'Excuse us, Majesty. We must take our leave and rest. After all, tomorrow promises to be an important day.'

The measured and respectful tone seemed to cut through the air like a knife, showing up the behaviour of the inebriates. Hattu felt their powerful glares on his back as he swept his green cloak across his shoulders and walked from the palace with Dagon and Sirtaya in tow.

'Well I've never been so entertained since that time a horse kicked me in the balls,' Dagon said flatly as soon as they stepped outside.

'At least the rest of us enjoyed that,' Hattu mused, thinking of long-lost comrades – big Tanku and Kisna the bowman – broken with laughter at Dagon's misfortune.

Another hoot of laughter sailed from the megaron behind them. 'They drink until they have the minds of children,' Sirtaya scoffed. 'Simpletons, fools… entertained so easil-' he halted in his diatribe when a mouse scurried past. His eyes grew wide as plates, and he scampered after it. Hattu and Dagon watched him go, bemused at the irony.

'So,' Hattu sighed, 'tomorrow.'

'I've briefed the Trojan chariot teams on what I expect from them,' Dagon said. 'At first the captains seemed uneasy at taking direction from me, but – by Tarhunda – they know now that I will not accept any grousing or hesitation.'

'Until tomorrow,' Hattu said. The pair embraced and parted.

Dagon had asked for quarters near the royal stables, Tudha at the archer compound and Sirtaya, Bulhapa and Zupili in the Scaean Barracks. Hattu trudged towards his billet at Antenor's villa, seeing the glow of a tallow candle from within. His body was weary and heavy, ready for sleep. But his mind crackled and fizzed with thoughts. The idea of fighting a war without his Hittite Divisions was a worry. How would the Trojans and their allies respond to his commands? In what way would they make battle? Then there was the spy. To survive the fray one had to be utterly confident, like a dancer, one's comrades all part of the same troupe. But to know that any of the men by your side could be that traitor… this "Shadow" the people spoke of… it set his thoughts whizzing again.

Knowing he would not sleep like this, he turned towards the Scaean Tower, climbed its many steps and emerged onto its high rooftop. He traced a hand around the cold metal of the great bronze beacon bell, circling the thing, wondering what might have been had he arrived much sooner than this. He spotted Paris' lyre – a pretty thing made of tortoiseshell – lying atop of a pile of coloured cushions, the kind of sight that made one feel calm and at home. Finally, he stepped over to the tower's outer edge. Gazing down across the lower city, he spotted Aeneas, the Dardanian Prince, walking through the streets. He seemed to be heading towards the Apollonian springhouse. Interesting, Hattu thought, that a relative of Priam would choose to wander those poorly-lit parts at night.

Finally, he lifted his gaze to the Scamander plain. Many hundreds of pyres now glowed out there, the flames licking high and turning the night sky the colour of dried blood. Trojan dead burned on this side of the river and enemy corpses blazed on the far side. A distant wail rose from the Ahhiyawan mourners, but the Trojan crowds were silent, as Priam had commanded.

He could not smell the smoke – Gods bless the northerly Wind of Wilusa – but there was something else in the air. A sweet scent of rose petals. For a moment he was back in Hattusa and in Pudu's arms… but then the scent changed, tinged with notes of anise and sage. A click-clacking sounded behind him. He turned to see a woman approaching, striding across the wooden walkway that linked the Scaean tower top to the palace. The oiled skin of her face – the colour of honey – seemed to glow in the light of the distant flames, and her hair shone like runnels of amber. Tassels hung from the sleeves of her white silk gown, and a thick belt cinched just below her breasts made her look tall and curvaceous at once. Not seeing Hattu and thinking the tower top was deserted, she breezed across and halted at the tower's outer edge with a long, slow sigh, her smoky eyes hooded and lost in thought.

He knew who she was without asking. He had seen her once before, as a girl, in a very different time. 'Come to see what you have created?' he said.

Helen blinked, only now realising he was here. Her brow creased as she studied his face for a moment. 'Ah, King Hattu,' she said with a tune of disdain, now looking him up and down as if he was diseased. 'So it is true: the Hittites have arrived at last. A few less of you than were expected, I hear?' Her nose wrinkled a little as she eyed his sloping features and darker skin. 'They say that your kind live on mountains and chew on the bones of wolves.'

'All true. Though I do prefer a nice stew,' Hattu said, deadpan. He wagged a finger at the pyres. 'Now tell me why you are up here to watch these corpse fires. They fought and died over you, did they not? I assume you mourn both Trojan and Ahhiyawan equally?'

She turned her back on him, gazing out at the flames again. 'Do not presume to know me, King Hattu.' The words were sent like arrows.

It seemed that she was done with the conversation. She remained like that, shunning him, taking from a pouch on her belt a small silver bracelet – too small for an adult – and feeding it carefully through the pads of her thumb and forefinger, as if counting the delicate links.

'Just tell me one thing,' he tried again. 'Were you to walk from this city tonight and return to Menelaus' side… could the war end?'

She stopped toying with the bracelet. 'I think we both know the answer to that.'

'Very well, you cannot bring it to a close,' Hattu ceded. 'But,' he stepped a little closer to her, clenching a fist and shaking it as if seizing an invisible spear, 'you had the power to prevent its beginning.'

She swivelled towards him, face pinched, her dark blue eyes glaring. 'What do you want me to say?'

'I want to understand this war I am about to join. To do so, I must understand you. Was it worth it? The hand of a young and pretty Trojan Prince, in exchange for all this?'

'No,' she laughed. A laugh that sounded more like a shiver.

'So why did you come away with him? Tell me, please.'

She snorted and looked away. 'Didn't you hear? It was a great love, ordained by the Gods of Troy. When first we met, my tongue was frozen silent and stiff in his presence. When he touched me, a pale flame seeped under my skin. I could not see nor hear anything but him. So long ago…' When she looked at Hattu again, she was smiling coldly. 'Paris and I have not shared a bed in many summers. Since I saw him for what he really is: Petulant, entitled, needy, vain, weak-minded yet sly.'

Hattu withdrew slightly, unnerved by the sight of her gums as she spoke, each word like a dagger. She was a beauty, yes, but there was ugliness under that veil of skin. 'So this all started for nothing. Nothing but a meaningless fling.'

'Many things start out with great ambition and hope and turn out to be meaningless, King Hattu. Including your arrival here. Do you know how many allied "heroes" have turned up at Troy's gates since the Ahhiyawans landed? Count the ash stains out on the plain, that will give you an idea.'

'What about your marriage to Menelaus,' Hattu said. 'Was that meaningless too? Is that what you do: enchant men and ride the wave of passion for a few moons before becoming bored and disinterested in the wreckage you have created?'

She gave him a withering stare. 'As soon as I blossomed, I was used to secure a marriage alliance. I, the daughter of the king and heir to the Spartan throne, was offered up like a prize heifer to the headstrong champions of Ahhiyawa. They came to my father's palace at Sparta and hopped like peacocks, shooting their bows and wrestling to prove their worth. Charm, wit, manners – all were measured.'

'And Menelaus won?' Hattu said, trying to disguise the note of disbelief in his voice.

She read him easily. 'Menelaus brought with him the coffers of the House of Atreus. To my father, that was more important than my welfare. But I showed him in the end.'

Hattu saw something in her eyes, a spark of defiance. 'You brought it with you, didn't you? You brought the treasure of Menelaus with you.'

She shook her head slowly. 'I brought the treasure of *Sparta* with me. For it was mine before Menelaus added his paltry contribution. For I was Queen of Sparta and I *chose* him to be my king. Anyway, I needed a gift for the Trojans, so that they might accept my arrival and not send me straight back. In any case, it matters not. And to answer your question: no, neither Paris nor the treasure was worth ten years of this. More, the treasure of Sparta is gone, doled out to the brigands and hired spears who have flocked to their deaths under Troy's colours.'

Hattu sighed. *What a mess,* he thought. *What an intractable, horrible mess.* 'Before I set to battle tomorrow, is there anything – anything at all – that you can tell me that might mean less widows and wailing mothers tomorrow evening?'

'Every night up here in the darkness,' she replied, 'I look out over the land and ask the Gods and the spirits the very same question. Every night, they remain silent.'

# CHAPTER 6

## RED SCAMANDER

Hattu slept a blessedly dreamless sleep, waking shortly before dawn in the same position in which he had lain down. For a moment he forgot where he was, and enjoyed the warm comfort of the clean, soft bed and its heavy blankets. The air smelt of pine and freshly-laundered linen. He peeled one eye open, looking around the quiet, dark bedroom: a plush chamber of wooden panels, decorated with strange things: an elephant's tusk gilded with Babylonian gold; a crocodile skin from Egypt; a painted Libyan hunting bow; a Mitannian chariot wheel. Not market trinkets, but unique pieces. During his merchant days, old Antenor had travelled far and wide, Hattu realised.

Just then, one of the heavy 'blankets' stretched and sighed, the greyhound flopping its sleepy head down near Hattu's, licking his nose once by way of morning greeting before drifting off into a doze again. Hattu let his eyelids slide shut too. It was blissful, but those few moments were all too short, for the darkness was soon spoiled by a shaft of pale light, creeping in through the shutters. Dawn was almost here on this momentous day.

As he slid regretfully from the bed and threw on his kilt and boots, a high-pitched wail from a triton shell echoed across Troy, and a burble of voices arose. Padding through the villa and taking care not to wake the snoring Antenor, he passed the scullery and the elder's impressive collection of herbs and potions, carefully organised on a wall of shelves, then climbed the ladders onto the roof. The dawn chill was bracing, the sky sullen with clouds, the air pregnant with energy. A light rain had fallen overnight, and the scent of damp earth swirled in the warm breeze.

The rooftop was the elder's favourite spot for relaxing, apparently, and it was certainly appointed for leisure: a trestle table, a few stools and a hammock were set out up here. He took a fig from a covered bowl and poured himself a cup of water. Andor glided down to land beside him as he ate slowly, eyeing the land. The Trojan troops had not left their Thorn Hill camp yet. The river plain, grey under a flotilla of dark clouds, was empty. So too the Borean Hills at the opposite end of the flatland – no sign of the enemy. Far in the distance, a thunderhead flickered over the snow-capped massif of Mount Ida, veins of brilliant white stabbing across the sacred peak, low rumbles of discontent rolling across the heavens.

Four more short bursts pealed from a triton shell, up on the Thorn Hill. Hattu turned to watch as, like a lava flow, the forces of Troy poured from the camp on the ridgetop and rumbled downhill. They came with a clatter of metal and wood and a drumming of boots, slowing and arraying themselves in a patchwork line immediately beside the city, facing south across the Scamander plain. As they gathered, the storm near Ida growled again, louder this time.

Closeness of thunder was a powerful portent, Hattu knew. Were this his army to command, he would tell them it was a good sign – a direct message from Tarhunda the Storm God, a guarantee of victory. But the Trojans had their own way of reading such signs. Even from here, he could see their unease: those already formed up were quiet, lips in thin lines, eyes wrought with worry as they beheld the lightning. Those still coming down from the ridge camp halted in their step as the distant thunder sounded, staring out over the empty Scamander plain as if invisible monsters waited there. An ill mood that would quickly spread, Hattu knew. Indeed, for the first time in many years, he felt deep, dark reservations about stepping onto the battlefield himself. *You're old and slow! You have no army of your own!* He set down his cup and took out the small goat idol little Ruhepa had given him, running the pad of his thumb over it, thinking of her and of Pudu.

Just then, old Antenor emerged from the roof hatch, struggling up the last few rungs of the ladder to join him. 'You should have woken me,' he chirped, 'Help yourself to figs and… oh, I see you already have,' he chuckled. 'Well, I did tell you to treat the place as if it were your own-' he fell silent when he noticed Hattu's doubtful demeanour. Then he glanced over the Trojan forces, shrinking somewhat at the sound of the thunder. 'Ah. It does not bode well when one's troops cower before battle, eh? Well do not worry, King Hattu. Watch,' the elder said with a wry smile. He pointed up towards the ridgetop and repeated in a breathy whisper: '*Watch.*'

Hattu frowned. The Thorn Hill camp had drained of men. There were no more to come. Then he spotted a lone figure, crowned in a bright helm, striding downhill from there. The masses clanked and clattered, stepping apart to create a corridor for this one man as if they were water and he the prow of a ship.

It was Hektor, Hattu realised, the trailing purple plume of the Helm of Troy flowing in his wake. He strode through the front ranks and turned to face his army. He said nothing for a moment, simply pacing to and fro, staring at the faces of his charges. Finally, he stopped, planting his feet wide apart, eyes sweeping.

'Yesterday was long and weary, was it not?'

Nervous looks, a few nods and mumbles of agreement.

'Yes, we did not have to fight and endure the stresses of battle. But we had to gather and burn our fallen brothers, all the while unable to punish those who took them from us.'

The arrayed soldiers of Troy shuffled, some turning their faces skywards and issuing words of farewell to their fallen comrades.

'That single day felt like a year for me. I woke this morning, burning inside with the light of Apollo. Then I heard the roar of the Thunder God.' He turned his hands to the sky, the painted scales of his bronze vest blinking in the grey light as he called out the many names of the deity. 'Zeus! Tarhunda! Indra! Ninurta!'

Men rumbled, each hearing and repeating whichever name they used for the God of Thunder.

'Do you know what he said to me?'

A smattering of voices and hoarse shouts, begging to know. Hattu stared, feeling every hair on his back and neck rise. This was Hektor of Troy at his finest: legendary, god-like.

*Zing!* Hektor drew his sword, sliding his shield round from his shoulder. *Boom!* He struck the shield boss with the blade's hilt. 'He said: Trojans! The day has come to rid this land of the Ahhiyawan locusts. Hear me as I don my armour and take up my thunderbolts and spears. I am coming to war beside you, children of Troy. With me walks mighty Apollo, Lord of the Silver Bow. Are you ready to march by our sides? Are you?'

The serried army of Troy gawped for an instant and then exploded in a zealous fervour, every weapon rising and jabbing into the air, many drumming their blades and bludgeons on their shields to make a thunder of their own. The effect was stirring, the noise rolling out across the plain like a reply to the distant storm. Hattu felt his confidence soar skywards.

With a gentle chuckle, old Antenor patted Hattu's shoulder. 'Now, I shall leave the business of battle to the men who know how to hold a sword.' he said. 'Speaking of which…'

Hattu heard the ladders creaking. From the corner of his eye, he saw Tudha arise onto the rooftop, and Sirtaya too – albeit a little stiffly – each carrying parts of Hattu's armour from the rooms below.

'Father,' Tudha said. 'It is time.'

Without reply, Hattu took the bronze jacket from his heir's arms and slid it over his shoulders, the cold metal heavy and reassuring. Next, Sirtaya helped him to buckle on his thick leather belt, into which he slipped a bronze knife.

He noticed Sirtaya rubbing at the small of his back, then spotted the necklace of mouse tails the Egyptian wore. 'The rodents tired you out last night?' he asked.

Sirtaya smiled languidly. 'I suppose they did, yes.'

Next, he strapped across his chest the leather crossbands and his twin iron swords, and then pinned on his green cloak. He reached up to scoop up his hair, knotting it tightly at the crown. Sirtaya quickly weaved the loose locks hanging from the temples into braids. The old pre-battle rituals needed no instruction. Finally, Tudha handed him his tall bronze helm and Sirtaya waited to give him his spear and slim-waisted leather shield.

As he tied the chinstrap of his helmet, he glanced over his shoulder into the city, seeing Dagon and the Trojan chariots arraying themselves at the stables. A panoply of silver and juddering purple plumage, horses and men draped in bronze scale. Dagon saw him and raised a left fist in salute. Hattu returned the gesture. *See you in the field soon, old friend,* he mouthed.

Hattu turned to his heir. For the first time he noticed that Tudha was wearing a leather Trojan cuirass and a bronze headband. Assuming that he would be going to battle? 'I told you last evening that you will not be fighting today. Yet your job is just as vital as mine: watch from these walls, safe like Priam and Hekabe. See how the fray unfolds – as Andor would, from on high. Record everything you see on a clay slab. Later, we will compare observations.'

'It will be so,' Tudha said with a respectful quarter bow.

This was new, Hattu thought. New and impressive. Patience and deference – two things he had rarely seen from his heir. Yet neither was enough to temper the horrible memories of what he had done. Irredeemable crimes. He watched his heir for a few moments longer, saddened at this truth, then clicked his tongue.

Andor hopped onto his shoulder with a flare of her wings, before he stepped down from the rooftop and made his way from the city. Outside Troy, he strode across the front of the Trojan Army, Bulhapa and Zupili speeding over to flank him in their leather war gear. Rumours had spread through the Thorn Hill camp of his arrival yesterday, but now the many faces – setting eyes on him for real – fell agape. 'The whispers are true. He *is* here. The *Labarna!* The Great King of the Hittites! The Sun! The Emperor!' groups gasped. 'King Hattu!' one lot bellowed and many others echoed. Some dropped to one knee in reverence, offering a raised left fist Hittite salute. Other groups, however, muttered and frowned at the empty space in his wake – the space where the Hittite army should have been. Hattu regarded them all with an emotionless glare. It was a king's duty to ride above emotion. In any case, one of those saluting or scrutinising him, he was sure, was a spy. In what was to come, he would be watching closely.

'King Hattu,' Hektor said, turning to him, beaming, then beckoning a select few others close: Prince Paris and two other royal sons who were experienced in battle command – the scowling Deiphobus and youthful Scamandrios; Sarpedon of Lukka too – who flashed Hattu a brotherly smile. In a tight huddle, they listened to Hektor's plan.

'I will lead our central battalion with Commander Dolon and the Guardians. Paris, you will command the second battalion – that is the Thymbrans and the Ciconians – and march on my immediate left. Deiphobus, you take control of the Percotians and Cyzicans on our left flank.'

The others nodded. Hattu watched the brown Borean Hills across the plain. Still no sign of the enemy.

'King Hattu,' Hektor's voice interrupted his thoughts. 'I need you to lead the fourth battalion on my right hand side – the Ascanian warbands and the men of the Seha Riverland.'

Hattu glanced at the two groups, each several hundred strong. 'As you wish,' he said calmly, pleased – firstly because Masturi, King of the Seha Riverland, was the kind of warrior-king anyone would want by their side, and secondly because the near-central position of the fourth battalion meant he would be well-placed to watch for any treacherous activity amongst the Trojan ranks. But in truth he felt irked by some of Hektor's other placements – knowing certain vassal bands well enough to understand that they might be better positioned on the opposite end of the line, or nearer the front. But these were minor matters. A clear plan was most important. He glanced at the Borean Hills again. Still no sign of Agamemnon's war machine.

'Sarpedon, your Lukkans are our strongest contingent and will anchor our right flank as the fifth battalion. Give Captain Glaucus a small reserve and have him shadow our advance. Prince Scamandrios, you will lead the archer brigades in a screen to our rear and…'

'Cousin?' another voice interrupted. Prince Aeneas paced over to join the conference. He shot Hattu a warm look, saluting him in the Hittite way before returning his attentions to Hektor. 'Cousin, what would you have me do with my Dardanians? If you join us with other archer nations, I can orchestrate great volleys of arrows and-'

Hektor chopped a hand for silence. 'Get back to your men, Aeneas,' he said tersely. 'Prince Scamandrios is the archer commander today and he will direct you and your Dardanians as he sees fit.'

Hattu maintained his mask of equanimity, but inside, he winced. Aeneas, hero of Kadesh, several years Hektor's senior, nephew of Priam, Prince of Dardania – dismissed like an over-enthusiastic boy.

Just then, Andor flared her wings, twisting round on Hattu's shoulder and shrieking across the plain. All those with Hattu and Hektor fell silent, heads twisting slowly to stare at the Borean Hills. Nothing there… then light winked on metal somewhere on the brow.

'The Ahhiyawans come to battle,' men whispered.

The whispers grew thicker and louder as – like a great bird unfolding its wings – the single glint of light in the distance became many. Within moments the enemy dominated the hills. A faint bleating sailed across the Scamander plain and then ended abruptly as the Ahhiyawan priests slaughtered a lamb to their Gods.

Hektor sped up in his instructions, chopping hands, pointing. All of a sudden they were done. Paris and the other princes sped off to organise their respective commands. The Trojans and their allies swarmed and shifted like flocks of birds as they got into position. Hattu called over the men of his battalion. The Ascanians hurried to him, their chieftain clanking in a unique suit of solid bronze that made him look like a turtle, just his nose and eyes peeking out of the top and his arms and shins from the sides and bottom. An awkward suit of armour, but one that allowed him to dispense with a shield and instead carry two spears. Masturi brought over his Seha Riverlanders – every single one of them bare from the waist down, pricks and balls bouncing as they jogged.

'Gods, it is good to see you, *Labarna*,' Masturi said, falling into place beside Hattu.

Very soon, the forces of Troy were in an ordered front of spearmen and swordsmen arrayed in five battalions, with a dense bank of archers to the rear. A fine sight.

It was at just that moment that a thought struck Hattu: Dagon and the chariot teams were still inside Troy, at the stables. Surely this was an oversight. In the triad of archer, soldier and chariot, that final one was not just important, it was vital. It was a soldier's job to engage the enemy, an archer's to harry… and a charioteer's to destroy. Especially against these Ahhiyawans – predominantly spearmen and swordsmen – the archers and the chariots were Troy's special weapons.

'Prince Hektor,' he called across the battle front. 'Dagon is waiting for the signal to bring the chariots from the city. Does he know what position to take up? On which flank will he be riding with the Trojan wing? I would recommend the right.'

Hektor, taking his place front and centre of the Trojan line, did not look at Hattu. Instead, he said flatly: 'We will field no chariotry today.'

'What?' Hattu spluttered.

'The rain overnight will have turned the plain to mud. The wheels would sink into ruts and render the war-cars slow and unwieldy. This will be a battle of footsoldiers only.'

'Prince Hektor, this is a mistake,' Hattu said, pacing along the front, closer, to keep his voice as low as possible lest the men hear. 'The plain yesterday was cracked and pale, so dry it was. The rain last night was but a short mizzle. The ground is good for chariotry. Trust me, I have judged enough battles to know.'

Hektor's head swung to him, his expression dark. 'And you think I haven't? I have judged and directed ten years of battles on this very plain to keep the enemy at bay,' he said, making no effort to keep his voice low.

Many heads swung back and forth, astounded by this exchange between the two legends at the front of their battle lines. Up on the Scaean Tower, the small shapes of King Priam and Queen Hekabe, Helen and Andromache stared down at this and spat in disbelief.

Hattu swallowed his anger as best he could. 'Prince Hektor, I implore y-'

Just then, a groan of enemy horns crawled across the plain, along with a storm of guttural roars. The great wall of Ahhiyawan soldiers broke forward, spilling down the Borean Hills and onto the plain.

'They're coming,' a Trojan commander wailed.

'Advance!' Hektor roared. 'Cross the Scamander before they reach it. Hold those far banks.'

Trojan triton shells keened, deafening. Scores of musicians raised pipes to their lips and filled their lungs, sending up a skirling song of war. Many thousands of allied voices roared in support, and the entire mass of them moved off at a steady jog down the lower part of the Silver Ridge slope.

Hattu, mind reeling, shrugged one shoulder to set Andor to flight, then hurried back across the front to retake his place in the advance.

'No chariots?' Masturi said, reading the look on Hattu's face. 'Many commanders have learned the hard way how stubborn Hektor is. I've come to accept his faults and appreciate his strengths. He is the champion of Troy – faster and stronger than any other warrior in our ranks. Some say he is even stronger than Achilles.'

'No one man can outweigh the advantage of a chariot wing.' Hattu replied. '*You* know this.'

'And no man can teach Hektor,' Masturi smiled wryly.

Hattu shook his head. It made no sense. 'When he was younger, he was painstaking in his battle tactics. He'd never make a mistake like this. They used to say he had the mind of a grizzled old general.'

'He did,' Masturi replied. 'Not many know this, but back then he leaned heavily on a veteran commander – a brilliant soldier who had lost his sight. He shared his tent with this blind fellow, taking prompts from him: tactical guidance, ruses and more. When the old dog died, Hektor was left with a reputation he has since struggled to justify.'

Hattu's capricious confidence shifted once more. As they spilled from the slopes and onto the plain, he glanced down to see the flat ground was indeed still cracked and barely moistened by the night rain. *Ideal* for a chariot charge. He felt steam build inside him.

They came to the Scamander ford and surged across with a fury of foam and splashing. Chill jets of water leapt up Hattu's legs and soaked his boots and the hem of his green cloak. Up onto the far banks they surged, spreading out and halting there to meet the Ahhiyawan charge.

Hattu beheld the rampant Ahhiyawan mass coming for them. So many soldiers. Their armour clattered and clicked, the sound like locust legs rubbing together. He spotted the champions amongst them: big Ajax roaring as he ran, his archer brother Teucer with him. Menelaus of Sparta looked like a nightmarish bull, the long, white horns on his helm pointing forth. Odysseus the Island King was there too, his island warriors braying and waving their axes, spears and hammers. His eyes flashed along their lines once, twice, again. No black boar shields. So no Achilles, at least. He almost laughed at such a modest crumb of solace.

The ground shivered as the two sides drew closer, closer. Two hundred paces apart. Bulhapa and Zupili pressed shoulder-to-shoulder with Hattu.

One hundred strides away.

Perfect killing range for an archer, Hattu knew.

'Archers of Troy!' Hektor boomed. 'Raise your bows.'

*Yes,* Hattu cried inwardly. The bowmen of Troy and her allies in these parts were amongst the finest in the world.

Ninety strides.

The rear ranks of the Guardians stretched their bows skywards.

'Archers!' Sarpedon bellowed, his Lukkan bowmen following suit.

Eighty strides.

'Archers!' Hattu cried. Masturi and those with bows within the Seha Riverlanders did so too. But the metal-clad Ascanian leader and his men – despite many of them carrying bows, did not react. 'Draw your bows!' he compelled them urgently. The metal-shelled leader frowned, looking at Hattu's mouth as if he had just vomited liquid silver. Hattu flicked his head to look over one shoulder then the other, seeing that the dense bank of archers behind the infantry front were in a similar state of confusion. Some had their bows nocked and raised, others only seemed to understand this was required when they saw the others doing it.

Seventy paces.

'Loose!' Hektor cried.

What should have been a sky-darkening rain of nearly four thousand arrows was in fact a pathetic and poorly-distributed light shower. At most, a few dozen Ahhiyawans fell, caught in the eye or neck as they gawped up at the arrow hail. Hattu cursed inwardly. First the chariots, wilfully withheld and now the archers, marshalled with shambolic confusion. The Trojans' twin-strengths, squandered.

That was when he saw telltale whorls of dust rising behind the enemy infantry front, heard drumming hooves and piercing whinnies, the jangle of bells. Bulhapa's broad, battle-scarred face gawped. '*Labarna,* is that-'

'Enemy chariots,' Hattu snarled, finishing the sentence.

At just that moment, Agamemnon's war-car surged through and ahead of the enemy infantry charge – the Great King wearing a lion hood and banded armour and his team of brightly-caparisoned horses braying. Sliding out either side of him came the chariots of Diomedes and old feather-crowned Nestor. Behind them, these three kings' elite charioteers fanned out in a skein – a combined squadron of thirty. Agamemnon spotted Hattu. 'You?' he howled over the din of the charge.

'Ares walks,' Old Nestor spluttered, 'the escaped peddler from yesterday!'

'He is no peddler. He is King Hattusili,' Agamemnon snarled at Nestor.

'And just as our friend reported, he has only a pair of Hittite soldiers with him.' Diomedes roared with laughter. 'So much for the mighty Hittite Army!'

Hattu's ears twitched. *Our friend? The Shadow?* No time to think on the matter, for the enemy warlords cracked their whips in unison and unleashed a combined cry '*Yaaa!*'

The gap vanished rapidly. Sixty paces. Fifty. Forty. Thirty. Twenty.

'Spears, level!' Prince Hektor cried.

'Spears, level!' Hattu echoed the command, he, Bulhapa and Zupili bringing up their shields like interlocking tiles and training their spears. On their right, Masturi had his Seha Riverlanders did likewise, adjoining with the trio. But on his left the Ascanians simply stood in a swaying, disordered mass, holding short swords and cudgels – a hopeless defence against a chariot strike. Likewise many of the other allies. Only Hektor and his Guardians and Sarpedon and his Lukkans presented a solid spear wall. '*Spears!*' Hattu cried again, desperate. As the Ahhiyawan chariot front surged to within strides, Hattu saw the whites of their steeds' eyes and the red wetness at the backs of the yelling charioteers' throats. He realised he had never been this close to meeting an enemy chariot charge in battle in such a disordered state. He had seen plenty of foes ruined by it though.

'*Yaaa!*' Agamemnon roared gleefully, guiding his chariotry towards Hattu and the weak spot of the Ascanians.

Hattu's mouth dried to sand and his stomach twisted like a sack of snakes. He clung to his shield and spear just as the Ahhiyawan war-cars slammed against what should have been a Trojan wall.

*Bang!*

His world turned upon its head. The breath leapt from his lungs as he tumbled backwards, his shield almost caving in, Agamemnon's spear streaking down to stab into the earth a finger's-width from where he landed.

Shadows, dust, chaos.

Cruel slashes of light shone down to reveal Zupili falling under the enemy king's chariot wheel, his body and head crushed before the chariot ploughed on into the allied masses. He heard Ascanians behind him roar and scream, bodies punctured by charioteer's javelins or burst under wheels. He had no sooner struggled to his feet than a chorus of roars washed over him, and the wall of Ahhiyawan infantry rushing in the wake of the chariots slammed into the Trojan lines.

With a deafening clatter of shields and scream of swords meeting, he found himself flailing backwards, he and Bulhapa almost surrounded. Cretan spear elites drove at him, shrieking, shouldering, stabbing. Hattu ducked back from one such, spearing the foe up through the soft tissue under the jaw, the tip raking through his grimacing teeth, severing the tongue then bursting out of the skull just behind the hairline. The man's wild expression faded into an eternal, emotionless gaze, his eyes crying blood as death's dark cloud closed around him. Hattu pulled his spear back, a shower of blood and brain matter soaking him as the man's face collapsed. The warm, stinking mess ran in runnels down across his lips, forcing him to taste it. Ishtar hissed in his mind: *Drink the wine of battle, King Hattu. A toast to what lies ahead...*

He launched a frenzied series of blocks and slashes and so too did Bulhapa by his side, but it was not enough to halt the enemy push. Stumbling backwards over fallen Ascanians and Seha Riverlanders, Hattu felt the splashing coldness of the river shallows underfoot again.

'Hold the riverbanks,' he heard Hektor howl from somewhere nearby. His tone was wrought with worry. As Hattu blocked with his half-ruined shield and parried with his spear, he saw something through the forest of enemy warriors. Something wretched. The enemy augur, Kalchas, crouched by the ripped-open body of a Riverlander. The man was wet with blood to his elbows as he raked around inside the torn carcass, pulling free entrails and organs, holding them to his face to smell the steaming morsels, blood dripping down his braided beard, eyes rolling back in their sockets. What kind of warfare was this?

'The kidney pulses strongly,' Kalchas keened, standing tall, holding the dead man's organ aloft so blood rained down upon him. 'Victory awaits!'

The Ahhiyawans exploded in a new and fierce roar, drums and pipes blaring as they surged at the Trojans with even more intensity. More Cretans hacked down at Hattu's tattered shield. No chance to take his eye from the relentless attackers, let alone carry out his plan to watch for traitorous behaviour in the Trojan ranks. Just then, one of the Cretans sliced the tip from his spear and thrust for his throat.

'*Labarna!*' Bulhapa cried, leaping in to beat the lunging Cretan away, saving Hattu… only for an axe to split the brave warrior's body, ripping through his leather cuirass, tunic, flesh and bone as if all were tallow – shoulder to gut. Bulhapa's riven body fell, spilling all manner of filthy and glistening organs and tubes.

Stunned, Hattu realised he was now truly alone. The last Hittite in the Trojan ranks. A red-bearded Cretan seized upon his tattered shield, wrenching it aside, opening it like a door to give two brutish others a chance to strike him in the chest. Hattu strained to pull his shield back to himself, but Red-beard was a strong one and he could not. The two coming for him raised sickle swords, arms straining as they tensed to slash down at him.

At the last, Masturi's broad-headed spear sped through the air and sliced through the red-bearded foe's arm. Hattu's shield snapped back into place over his torso in the flash before the two attackers' sickle swords bit into the rim of the leather screen. Hattu thrust his head forward into the face of one Cretan, caving in the man's nose and cheek. He shoved forward on his ruined shield, throwing it at the second to unbalance the man. In the breath of respite this gave him, he reached up and snatched free his twin iron blades.

This was the moment – just a trice – when those fighting nearby seemed to sense something change. Hattu roared with all the frustration of the day so far, bringing the two dark-silver blades together around the second attacker's neck. The man's head leapt free of his body like the contents of a squeezed boil. Thick gouts of blood pulsed from the neck stump and spattered on all nearby. Hattu pirouetted on the ball of one foot through the raining mess then lunged in an overhead strike towards the next foe – a giant Cretan. The giant grinned, raising his shield high to block the attack. Deftly, Hattu pulled out of the overhead feint and brought his second iron blade slicing across the man's exposed belly – ripping leather armour, skin and muscle. The giant's face changed, falling in despair as his bowels scurried free of the horrible tear, splattering into the already bloody shallows underfoot. As the giant fell onto his knees, Hattu planted a foot on his shoulder and used it to leap into the path of the Cretan King himself. The man's boar tusk helm – supposedly a symbol of his courage – slipped down over his eyes. He held up his bronze sword in defence, and Hattu struck down upon it with all his might, the iron shearing the copper-heavy bronze weapon. Dozens nearby saw this, and gawped. The Cretan King staggered backwards, sliding the helmet upwards to see again, then blanching at the sight of the towering, blood-masked Hittite King stalking in to finish him. He and his Cretans parted, scampering away in fear, a move disguised as 'looking for another opponent'.

Finding himself in a rare pocket of space where the Cretans had been, Hattu swung this way and that, dazed, seeing not two lines of battle locked together like warring serpents – for that was what he was used to – but a mass, a confused, bloody mass of Trojan and foe. Men locked in single combat instead of trying to hold some sort of front, archers loosing individually without any sort of coordinating voice. Men drowning one another in the river shallows, red ribbons of blood running through the waters. Slingshot sped through the chaos, catching men's heads, dashing out brains. Hattu saw one Ahhiyawan slinger pick off a Dardanian captain like this, then dance a jig, crowing the victim's name as if that was his part in the war eternalised. He heard a metallic drumming, and spotted the Ascanian chieftain, assailed on all sides by horned Spartans and feather-tiara'd Pylians raining blows on his clumsy bronze suit. Clumsy but effective, Hattu now saw, as the fellow weathered this storm and fought back, slaying each of his attackers as they tired.

'Help!' a cry rang out from the right. Hattu stretched on his aching legs to see who was shouting. The cry had come from Sarpedon. The Lukkans – Troy's strongest and staunchest ally – had been pinned back against the banks at a section where the river ran deep. Driven into the waters by the enemy, they were slipping and sliding in the muddy shallows. Worse, the rearmost men were up to their necks in the strong current, gasping and gurgling to stay above water, their armour like anchors. They were on the edge of capitulation. Were they to be slain, the battle would turn hard upon the remaining Trojans.

Hattu glanced this way and that. Every Trojan soldier nearby the

Lukkans was entangled in combat. Worse, he couldn't see any of the major commanders – no Hektor, no Aeneas, no Paris, no Deiphobus. Realising it was down to him, he cried out for his men 'Fourth battalion!' But his soldiers were scattered amongst this chaos, swords and spears locked with enemy troops. Only Masturi and a small band of Riverlanders were close by.

Hattu eyed the route from here to the beset Lukkans – a jagged path paved with broken bodies and twitching, cleaved men, with walls of whirling axes and jabbing spears. 'With me,' he barked to Masturi, then plunged into this corridor of bronze and death.

***

Tudha watched from Troy's lower city battlements, breath locked in his lungs, heart pumping, Sirtaya by his side. The clay slab he held was marked with the initial formation of the Trojan forces, but – rapt – he had not made a single imprint since the first clash of weapons. The Trojan army had advanced confidently but met the enemy terribly, ceding ground and succumbing to penetrating charges all over the place. Now the Ahhiyawans had the Lukkan allies pinned at a deep section of the river, and the rest of the Trojan forces were beginning to bend out of shape. In the broiling mass of battle, he could see nothing but blurs of bronze, milling arms and bright spouts of red. No sign of Hattu, no flash of his green cloak or distinctive iron blades. A cold thought struck him.

'What if he has… fallen?' A wretched whorl of emotion began to spin within him.

'No,' said Sirtaya, 'look.'

Tudha followed the Egyptian's pointing talon, seeing Andor out there, gliding through the bruised sky above the clash, watching. That meant Father was alive, the eagle tracking him as always. The tightening within slackened, to be replaced by that ever-present void of regret, of loneliness. What did it matter if his father survived today? He hated Tudha for what had happened last year. Now Tudha began to hate himself for it all too.

The words of Aeneas from the previous evening halted his fall into self-pity. *You are the second most powerful being alive, and still you doubt yourself and fret over your father's esteem for you. Forget all that. Just be the best you can be. Do what you know is the right thing.*

'The Shadow,' he muttered to himself, twisting to glance back over the city, eyes raking the streets. Where to begin looking? Terse shouts arose from the chariot stables, snapping his attentions there.

Dagon and the Trojan chariot elites were locked in an argument. Dagon was mounted on one battle-car, reins in hand, but the Trojan spearman who was to be his accompanying warrior was refusing to board. The other two hundred crews stood beside their chariots likewise, arms folded, jaws stubbornly jutting.

'Don't you hear that?' Dagon bellowed at them. 'That's the sound of your countrymen dying out there. You can change that. You!'

'We were told to stay in the city,' one of the elites complained to Dagon. 'Prince Hektor commanded us to abstain from battle today. You are a legendary figure in these parts, Master Dagon, but you cannot command us to disobey the Crown Prince of Troy.'

'Gods,' Sirtaya groaned. 'this is not good.'

Tudha could not disagree. He looked over the stables again. There were a trio of spare chariots – two recently crafted and one mended. A reckless fantasy arose: he wondered for a moment if he and Sirtaya might steal down into the chariot stables, hitch horses to and leap aboard one, ride down to the Thymbran Gate and… his plan crumbled when he saw the thick metal-strapped locking bar in place on those gates, secured there by a long chain and bronze lock.

The captain of the gatehouse watch, a man with a stork's neck, stood on the gate walkway, the keys dangling from his belt. Trojan citizens buzzed around near the gates, shouting up to the Guardians to ask how the battle was going. Some wandered up onto the walls to look, before being chased back down and away by the stork-necked captain and his men. At one point even Helen and Andromache ventured down from the Scaean Tower and onto those battlements, the priests Chryses and Laocoon too, as if being closer to the fray might allow them to control it somehow.

Just then, a noise rose from the plain, cutting through the solid wall of screaming and clattering. A panting and pattering of feet, coming closer. Tudha swung to look: a small party had broken from the struggle. The princes, Hektor, Paris and Deiphobus, Aeneas too, with a small bloodied group of Guardians and allies in tow. The stork-necked captain atop the Thymbran Gatehouse bawled for the hatch door to be opened, allowing the princes and their men inside where they strapped double quivers of fresh arrows to their backs and replaced bent weapons, before sprinting back outside and to the fray.

Tudha watched their return to battle, and then noticed Andor suddenly twisting and speeding low. *Now* he spotted his father in the fray, beneath his faithful eagle: he was running through the midst of the struggle with Masturi and a bunch of Riverlanders, spray from the river shallows flying up as he fought his way through towards the doomed Lukkans.

***

Hattu dodged a thrown spear then slashed out to block an axe strike, the iron sword biting into and bending the bronze axe and taking barely a notch itself. Masturi launched his spear into the face of a Mycenaean then Hattu scissored his swords across the chest of a Locrian. As the man fell into the shallows, a clear path opened up to the embattled Lukkans. Now Hattu saw that it was the Pylians pinning them at the edge of the river's deep section and driving them into the strong currents with a crescent of jabbing spears. The aged Pylian king, Nestor, rode his chariot in careful arcs nearby – directing his footsoldiers in their efforts. Every so often he took up a throwing spear, aimed and launched it into the Lukkan mass. His latest one pierced the forehead of the man by Sarpedon's side. As the dead man sank back into the deep waters and faded under the surface, drifting downstream, Sarpedon roared as if it was he who had been struck – pain stricken, bereft.

'Break their line, relieve the pressure,' Hattu cried to Masturi and his men, then charged at the Pylian entrapment. Nestor was alert to the danger though, and his clipped shout brought a full score of his men swinging round to meet Hattu's charge with a row of spears. Masturi and his men traded blows with their lances and Hattu sliced at the enemy spearheads with his swords, but the Pylians were holding firm, marshalled by one handsome, grinning man in their centre. Hattu made to lunge for this one, only for a Pylian spear to rip down his arm, sending him backwards with a pained roar. One of Masturi's men tried next, only to be speared through the throat.

Bleeding, aching, Hattu realised these men were like a jacket of armour, the handsome officer the strongest scale. Impervious to head-on attacks, their flanks blocked by other clusters of combat. So he looked skywards and whistled.

Andor shrieked, swooping, talons extending. One moment the handsome one was smirking darkly, the next, his helm was gone and so were his eyes – just red sockets remaining, blood and eye-matter drooling down his talon-slashed face. Andor shot skywards again as quickly as she had swooped, carrying the man's helmet. She dropped this from a height, the helm falling and braining another, hatless soldier of Pylos near the blinded officer. As these two foundered, falling, the others stumbled and staggered backwards, levelled spears swinging askew.

'Now!' Hattu and Masturi roared.

They and their small knot of men barrelled over the enemy twenty then plunged into the riverside girdle of Pylians, breaching the press and joining the beset Lukkan mass within. Hattu splashed into the waters, knee-deep, to press his shoulder to Sarpedon's. The Lukkan leader twisted to him as if he was a threat, raising his red, wet sword, snarling face striped with dirt and blood. The warrior-mien evaporated as soon as he saw who was beside him. 'King Hattu,' he panted. His face changed again. 'You should not have come into this press. We are outnumbered and surrounded.'

With the flat of one sword, Hattu whacked away a flying spear coming for Sarpedon. 'Reminds me of the last time we met,' he growled through a battle-rictus. 'Anyway, I did not come alone. Masturi is here too with a few scores of Riverlanders. Let's use them.'

Sarpedon howled with manic laughter. The sound seemed to unnerve the Pylians, while the Lukkans took heart from it, surging from the muddy shallows and deeper waters against the belt of attackers. The new momentum and extra numbers were enough to tilt the balance of weight, sending Pylians toppling and flailing. Handfuls of them began to break, then the entire force of them – realising the Lukkans would not be an easy kill – dissolved into the wider melee. Lukkan cries of victory split the air as they stumbled from the currents and safely onto the churned banks.

Hattu almost cried out with them, but caught the breath in his throat. His grey eye ached and latched onto the chariot squadron scything along the riverside, churning over allies, coming right for him and the Lukkan mass. Agamemnon led, hair whirling in his wake, his stallions' teeth gritted and eyes bulging white. Flanking him was the young powerhouse, Diomedes. Nestor and his war-cars fell in to join this surge. All hoisted javelins and bows.

Hattu's heart froze, remembering the havoc the enemy chariots had wreaked at the onset of battle. He sheathed his blades and snatched up a lance and shield from a dead man. 'Spears!' he cried out desperately, remembering the shambolic attempt at a spear line earlier. But unlike earlier, every single man around him – Riverlanders and Lukkans – heard and heeded the order. All spears swung forth, all men gathered in a front, shoulder-to-shoulder, feet planted wide, heels dug into the bloody mire, braced. As it should have been in the opening moments of the battle.

'Loose!' Diomedes bawled. A score of enemy javelins whizzed forth with all the power of the throwers' arms and the speed of the chariots. A few Lukkan screams rang out and puffs of red stained the air. But the shields took the brunt of it and the front held firm. Yet on Agamemnon and his fellow kings hurtled.

Hattu stared the enemy *Wanax* dead in the eye. 'For Troy!' he bellowed along with Sarpedon and Masturi, unmoving.

Strides away, Agamemnon's horses reared up, refusing the charge onto this wall of sharp speartips. The rest of the chariot surge slowed into a tangle of confusion, each battle-car veering in a different direction, some crashing into one another.

A trice later, Hektor and a wedge of Trojan Guardians burst across the Scamander ford, bearing fresh swords and spears. Aeneas and his Dardanians too, bristling with replenished quivers of arrows. They rushed the slowed enemy chariots from the side. 'For Troy!' Hektor howled the ongoing cry, vaulting over the shuddering body of a Pylian soldier whom he had just decapitated, then hurling his spear at a chariot. The lance took the jaw clean off of the charioteer and the man fell to the floor of the vehicle, the reins still clutched in his spasming hands. The horses panicked, the chariot crashed onto its side, throwing the crew of warrior and his jawless driver like pebbles across the fray. They landed somewhere amongst the Seha Riverlanders, who turned upon them with a frenzy of milling sword arms. The careening chariot hit a rock, bucked, spun in the air once, then came plummeting down into the Scamander with an explosion of foam and spray. Now Hektor launched his second lance. The missile came speeding across Agamemnon's face – and would have shaved off his moustache had he sported one. Agamemnon wailed, staring at the javelin as it sped on past him to plunge down between the black shoulder blades of one of King Nestor's cantering chariot stallions.

The beast's cry was terrible, wet with a vomit of blood. It fell – stone dead – crunching gracelessly onto its head, churning up dirt and blood-clotted earth in a stinking shower. Only the skill of Nestor's driver in swiftly slitting the reins prevented them from suffering a similar fate to the wrecked chariot of moments ago.

Hattu's eyes widened, seeing the remaining chariots – slowed to a trundle now… vulnerable. 'At them!' he roared.

'Death to the Ahhiyawans!' Hektor cried.

'For our Trojan brothers!' Sarpedon boomed.

Several other Trojan allies, seeing this chance, swarmed at the enemy vehicles, surrounding them, pulling charioteers down and slaughtering them. Nestor's footsoldiers and Diomedes' men too tried to form a shielding ring around the three kings. Hattu launched his spear then drew his swords and waved men with him as they slammed against the enemy. He barged and shouldered, hacking at enemy shields, smashing relentlessly.

On and on it went. The many allied death screams of moments ago now became Ahhiyawan wails and final cries. Hattu saw Agamemnon bawling for more and more reinforcements to come to their rescue, while Glaucus brought the Lukkan reserves splashing across the river to press home the Trojan advantage.

Only Diomedes seemed to have any heart left for battle. The young warrior king had his driver break their chariot out of the swell and round in a lone charge towards Trojan backs, hoisted a fresh spear and took aim at Hektor. 'Death to Troy!' he screamed. A swell of his Tirynean soldiers near him began to roar in support.

At just that moment, the bruised sky issued an ear-splitting *crack* of thunder, directly overhead. A shuddering thorn of lightning struck down and burst against the high bronze helm of Diomedes' charioteer. The light was blinding, the man's cry almost swallowed by the subsequent thunder.

In the aftermath, the stricken chariot slowed and the din of the fray suddenly faded, men staring at the sight of the lightning-struck charioteer – or what was left of him. The skin of his face rose in a thousand blisters and blood wept from his swollen eyes and nostrils. Diomedes, gawping at his half-melted charioteer, dropped his unthrown spear and stumbled backwards out of the chariot – the cabin flickering with flame, the steeds rearing up in terror. The stilled horses of Agamemnon and Nestor too began braying in panic.

Hattu stared, seeing through the horror, spotting the opportunity, stepped up onto a small mound of corpses and raised both iron swords high, striking them together to send a shower of sparks into the air. 'The God of Thunder has entered the fray. Soldiers of Ahhiyawa, look upon his power… and despair!'

The Ahhiyawan masses saw all this – a charioteer melting like a candle; Diomedes, their young champion, abandoning his weapon, struck dumb with fear; the Emperor of the Hittites, conjuring light from his blades – and the effect was momentous. They broke out in a panicked chorus of wails and prayers. Tranches of them backed away from the centre of the fray, Agamemnon the first of the chariots to turn tail with them. Soon, they were falling away like a wave receding from a beach. They began to break back towards the Borean Hills. The Trojans howled in delight, raising and shaking their weapons, drumming them on their shields.

Hattu stumbled down from the corpse mound and staggered over to Hektor, celebrating with his men. 'Prince Hektor,' he panted, pointing after the fleeing Ahhiyawan masses, 'call for the chariots. You have seen for yourself that the ground is good. Bring them to the field and they will catch the enemy before they can flee back to their beach camp.'

Hektor, staring after the departing foe, shook his head slowly. 'No. This chance to save our country was carved out by the men on the field here and now. By their hand the day will be won.'

'If the enemy fall back behind the sand wall I told you about then we have no chance,' Hattu protested, 'for spears and swords will be useless against that rampart. We will lose hundreds to their rain of slingshot and arrows.'

Hektor was already turning away, ignoring his argument.

Hattu burned with frustration inside. He seized the crown prince's shoulder, turning him face to face once more. 'One signal to the chariot wing is all it will take,' he said before Hektor could complain. 'If the move succeeds, you will be an even greater hero. If it fails, *I* will take responsibility.'

Hektor's top lip twitched in annoyance and he shrugged off Hattu's hand. 'Very well, do it,' he snapped, then turned away again, raised his sword and shield overhead and beat one against the other like a war drum. 'After them,' he cried urging the infantry on after the fleeing enemy. 'Onwards, to victory!'

As the Trojan masses surged after the retreating Ahhiyawans, Hattu ran against the flow, seeking out any Trojan officer with a signal horn. The chariots had to come swiftly, he knew, or many of these battle-maddened Trojans would be rushing to their deaths at the foot of that sand wall. He saw a Guardian with an officer's plume and a triton shell dangling from his belt. He grappled with the man and took the triton, then blew three times, staring back at Troy.

*Be swift, Dagon, old friend!*

***

Whenever Tudha dared to blink, he saw the ghostly scars of lightning in the momentary blackness. In the long stretches between, he watched the incredible turnaround: despite their lesser numbers, the Trojan army was winning. In a bullhorn formation, they were sweeping the Ahhiyawans back from whence they had come. The enemy were half fleeing, half engaged in a fighting retreat. Voices all around Tudha murmured and rose in hope, for now hundreds of citizens had gathered on the battlements to watch. Even the stork-necked Guardian commander at the Thymbran Gate had given up trying to shoo them away.

From that mass of warring men, three clear notes rose, low then high. Tudha's eyes sharpened on the source of the signal. He saw his father there in the midst of it all like a rock in a river, standing facing Troy while all other Trojans chased after the fleeing Ahhiyawans. A pause, then the same signal again.

'The call for the chariots,' Sirtaya said throatily, shaking with nerves. The voices near them rose in an excited prattle now. 'The chariots are to ride. The enemy are in disarray. Victory is near!'

From behind Sirtaya and Tudha, Dagon's voice cracked like a whip, and this time there was no complaint. With a clatter of wheels and hooves on flagstones and the snap of some two hundred lashes, the Trojan chariot wing funnelled out of the chariot stables and down the Scaean Way towards the Thymbran Gate.

'Open the gates,' Dagon yelled.

The stork-necked captain jolted, realising the onus was upon him. He weaved his way through the many peasants on the gatehouse walkway, then flitted down the stairs – flailing halfway when the arm of his white tunic caught on a nail.

'Hurry up man!' cried another chariot elite as the war-cars gathered at the locked gates, slowing and stopping.

The captain tripped and rolled down a handful of stairs – much to the amusement of a few of those he had been berating earlier – then sprang up, red-faced, and loped over to the locking bar. 'May Apollo be with you,' he said, shooting looks over his shoulder to the massed, stationary chariots. 'Bring me the helm of an Ahhiyawan, will yo-' he fell silent, his hand patting his belt. Tudha stared at the spot where the man's keys had been a short while earlier. The captain turned bone-white.

'Open the *fucking* gates!' Dagon thundered just as lightning scudded across the sky.

'The keys. I… I had them a moment ago. I… they were here a moment ago. I…'

Dagon leapt down from the chariot, shoved the captain out of the way and seized the padlock – heavy as an altar stone. The chain too was thick as a man's arm. Tudha knew even from here that no axe could break through it. Indeed, that was the point of it. 'Find. The. Keys,' he seethed.

The stork-necked captain shambled up onto the gatehouse walkway again, babbling and pleading with the people up there to move out of his way as he fell to all-fours and frantically searched the paved walkway for the missing keys. Just then a lesser sentry appeared from the gatehouse tower's ground level doorway, shaking. 'The second key is gone from the strongbox too. It was there this morning.'

Now Dagon turned white too. He swung round to face the waiting chariotry. 'Back,' he said. 'back uphill. To another gate. Which is closest?'

'The Dardanian Gate,' said the warrior aboard Dagon's chariot. 'But the streets to reach it are narrow – like lanes in places. We will have to walk the chariots through in single file. It will take us an age.'

'We could reach the Bay Gate more quickly for the streets are wide there,' said another, pointing to the western end of the city, 'but the chariots would founder badly on the slope outside.'

Dagon's eyes flicked one way then the other. 'Make for the Dardanian Gate,' he bellowed, stamping up onto his chariot again. Tudha watched the shambolic attempts to turn a chariot wing about face from a standstill in the limited space before the gates. Men cursed and shouted. One lashed his whip above his horses, only to catch the driver of another chariot on the back of the neck. The horses sensed their crews panicking and began rearing up, whinnying. One vehicle toppled over and this set a few other horse teams bolting down lanes. All the while Dagon barked and howled to try to regain a crumb of control. The first of the chariots to set off towards the Dardanian Gate fared little better, halted by market stalls in the way, broken wagons blocking the corners, strings of washed garments hanging out to dry like webs. The chariots would take hours to depart the city that way.

Shaken, Tudha turned back to the battle. At least the Trojan army was still winning, pushing the enemy up the slopes of the Borean Hills now. Soon it spilled onto the brow of the range, where weapons flashed against the backdrop of the roiling sky. He rose a little, neck lengthening as the melee slipped over the hills… gone. His heart seemed to fall still at that moment. Along the walls either side of him, the amassed citizens whispered amongst themselves, peering at the distant hills as if their quietness might allow them to see through the range. Even the royals were here now on the lower walls: King Priam, Queen Hekabe and the elites, faces wrought with hope and terror. The priests, Laocoon and Chryses, watched with moon-like eyes. Hektor's wife Andromache, cradling baby Astyanax, shook with emotion. Old Antenor comforted her and the babe. Helen watched, staring and emotionless, fidgeting with that silver bead bracelet of hers.

'And so the enemy are driven back onto their beach camp,' Sirtaya said, standing beside him.

'The camp? But the sand wall? Father said it is too tall and stout to be stormed by infantry alone. He has no ladders or siege equipment. What is he thinking?'

'This is not Master Hattu's army,' Sirtaya replied.

He and Sirtaya watched the line of the Borean Hills obsessively. Every puff of sand or smoke rising from beyond setting his nerves on edge. It was not until nearly dusk when true movement appeared up there again. The Trojan Army, backstepping. An ordered retreat. Horns blared and voices cried, the sounds partly drowned out by the Wind of Wilusa. Tudha watched them draw back from the hills and to the Scamander's southern side. Ahhiyawans gave chase in packs here and there, striking in places only to be repelled. As the shadows grew long, the attacks stopped and the Ahhiyawans melted back beyond the hills to the shore. Trojan and allied standards and totems were planted along the river's southern banks in a long stripe. Men began to erect tents, to gather wood for fires and to establish a watch perimeter. He saw his father out there – silver hair and green cloak distinct amongst the rest.

A boy messenger riding on a blue-dun mare came galloping over the Scamander ford towards the city, almost choking as he relayed the words given to him. 'Prince Hektor dealt a heavy blow to the invader today, pushing them all the way back to their city of ships, stopped only by a stubborn rampart of sand. The Army of Troy is to camp on the far side of the river tonight. For tomorrow, the assault will be renewed… and the war won!'

Behind and all around Tudha, those watching on the walls and towers exploded with joy and cheering. Old men danced jigs and women kissed strangers. Dogs yapped and sprang and children screamed in delight.

But Tudha was not for celebrating. His mind flashed, piecing together the battle. 'Father called upon the chariots because he knows they were the only hope of catching the enemy before they fell in behind that sand wall.' A thrill of realisation crept through him. Slowly, he twisted to look along the walls towards the Thymbran Gate once more.

His gaze became a fisherman's net, trawling over the many hundreds celebrating on and near the gatehouse battlements. The stork-necked guard captain was sobbing now, the gate still locked tight. Two sets of keys, lost in the same hour of need. *Not lost*, he realised with a second frisson of understanding.

Priam swished his hands this way and that, making demands of his servants for wagons to be readied to take him and Queen Hekabe to this new river camp. He bid his nobles, advisors and clergy to ready their wagons too. The chariot wing, only now fully outside the city, began to canter towards the new camp. Dagon barked at some of them to wait behind to escort the royals and elites.

Tudha looked to Sirtaya. 'Father said I should stay safe – like Priam and Hekabe.'

Sirtaya stroked his tuft beard. 'He did, but-'

'So we should head out to the river camp also.'

'I'm not sure that is what your father meant, Master Tud-'

But Tudha was already on his way down to the coach house by the Thymbran Gate.

Sirtaya sighed and trudged after him.

# CHAPTER 7

## NIGHT SHADOWS

That night, the southern banks of the Scamander glowed with the light of ten thousand torches. Near the central stretch of the long camp, a great fire blazed, pipes blared, voices rose and fell in rich laughter and chatter, and priestesses sang songs of Wilusan lore.

Through it all, Hektor held court, striding to and fro in front of a dense circle of onlookers, his clean purple cloak and washed curls of hair swooshing behind him every time he turned. 'It was a momentous triumph! Menelaus, Odysseus and Diomedes – three of the enemy's strongest – were all injured. Lightly, yes, but enough to send them scampering back to their beach lair. And Achilles – their so-called battle lion – sulks like an old tomcat. We drove them all the way back onto the sands. Only their crude stockade and the failing light forced us to relent and fall back here.' he proclaimed, raising his silver cup aloft, wine dribbling over the edge, the crowds roaring in support. 'So tonight, let the Ahhiyawans hear us,' he encouraged them, cupping one hand to the side of his mouth and directing his words at the Borean Hills and the bay hidden beyond. 'Let them lie with open eyes and tired minds. Let them dread the coming dawn. For tonight we hold this camp, so that tomorrow, we may drive home a complete and final *victory!*' Every soul present exploded in a fervour of cheering.

Having washed in the shallows, Hattu now sat on a rock by the Scamander, some way from the crowds. His damp hair hung down his bare back – the skin decorated with bruises and cuts from the fray. He ran a hand up and down each leg, from knee to shin. The joints were aching badly. Tomorrow they would be white-hot with pain. With military matters back in the Hittite heartlands, he could plan for days of recovery between spells of action. Here, he was a slave to the winds of this foreign war. With a sigh, he took up his iron swords and began sharpening them with slow, deliberate strokes of his whetstone. Hektor continued with a new homily, and every word offended Hattu's ears. No mention of the shambolic organisation and near capitulation. No reflection on the puzzling decision to leave the chariots of Troy unused. Or the chaos that had apparently unfolded when he finally did agree to call for them. All disastrous knots in a tangled rope of a battle that had cost him the two warriors he had brought with him. Bulhapa and Zupili's bodies would likely never be identified in the churn of carrion. 'May Tarhunda's lightning illuminate your path through the Dark Earth,' he burred quietly in a private farewell to the pair.

Dagon swaggered over, picking at a hot loaf. His face was pinched with annoyance. 'Hektor, Hektor – the *great* Hektor,' he muttered.

'Keep those words inside, old friend, as difficult as it may be,' Hattu said quietly. 'Remember that he is like a demigod to the people of Troy, and vital to their morale. Grousing about him openly will help neither them nor us.'

Dagon swung a heavy hand towards the chariot wing, now arrayed neatly at one end of the camp, steeds picketed and cropping at silage. 'We were ready, in armour, the horses caparisoned, the reins and yokes tied and tethered, all morning,' he rumbled, tossing a piece of bread into the river shallows, eliciting a grouchy croak from an unseen toad and the shrill piping of an oystercatcher.

'You should have been on the plain from the first light of dawn,' Hattu agreed. 'We needed you.'

'I could hear the battle's ebb and flow. So could the horses. They were pawing at the ground and snorting.' Dagon glowered over towards Hektor. 'Why did he keep us at bay like that? And when we did finally get the call, the organisation at the Thymbran Gate was shambolic.'

'They still haven't found the keys?' asked Hattu.

Dagon shook his head, dejected. 'What does it matter now. The day is done.'

'I don't know what Hektor was thinking,' Hattu sighed, finally giving letting loose his own frustrations. It was as Masturi had described: Hektor was a skilled and charismatic hound of battle, but he was no tactical genius. 'Most battles have a pattern, but in this one…'

'The pattern was a mess,' a new voice finished for him, a shape emerging from the darkness.

Hattu's heart leapt as the shape took form in the light of the nearest torch. '*Tuhkanti*?' he croaked.

'I watched five battalions blunder forward and act as if they were strangers to one another,' Tudha continued, coming closer. 'Thank the Gods that the enemy – apart from a few elite bands – attacked like mindless brutes also.'

Hattu stabbed his swords down into the riverside silt and stood tall. 'I told you to stay in the city. I told Sirtaya to keep you there.'

'I challenged Sirtaya to try and stop me,' Tudha replied, halting before his father.

In the background, the Egyptian appeared, shrugging apologetically. 'I shielded him all the way here at least, Master Hattu.' As he spoke he glanced into the river shallows, pinpointing the croaking toad. A glint of interest shone in his eyes.

Hattu sighed heavily, face dark with anger, and opened his mouth to berate Tudha.

'Before you list my failures, Father, you must listen to me,' Tudha said first.

Hattu's nose wrinkled at the disrespectful words. 'So the patience and wisdom you showed before battle, when you calmly took up tablet and stylus – that was all a mask, eh?'

'About the Thymbran Gate keys,' Tudha continued as if Hattu hadn't spoken.

'The lost keys?' Dagon said.

'The keys were not lost, they were stolen,' Tudha replied to Dagon, then swivelled his eyes back to Hattu. 'You thought the traitor was in the army. I thought he might be in the city. Well today proved me right.'

'That is what matters to you, isn't it?' Hattu drawled. 'Not what you did or why, but that you were right.'

Tudha broadened, his face souring. 'This is not Hatenzuwa, Father. This is Troy. And today this "Shadow" robbed Troy's armies the chance of outright victory.'

Hattu rocked back a little. 'How can you be sure the keys were stolen?'

'*Both* sets of keys went missing at the same time. At the vital moment during the battle when the gates had to be opened. That is not misfortune. That is treachery.'

Hattu tapped one foot in thought. 'Maybe… maybe'

'Maybe?' Tudha said, his face twisting. 'Ah, I understand. You do not trust me. Not before, not now. When, Father?'

Hattu stared at him. Memories flickered through his mind of the forest shrine at Hatenzuwa. The old timber doors. The darkness… the *horror* that lay inside. *How could you. How?* He wondered. Before he could reply, a deep lowing sounded.

The group looked over to the central fire. Hektor, homily complete, stepped back as the priests, Laocoon and Chryses, led an aurochs bull into the centre of the crowd. A dozen Servants of Apollo followed, garlanded and droning a sacred song as they walked in circles around the terrified animal. Laocoon raised his ceremonial hippocampus staff and began to wail in well-practiced verse. He carefully sheared a forelock from the bull's brow, causing it to instinctively tilt its head up in fright. With a fat hand, Chryses reached around the animal's exposed neck with a sickle and slid it quickly back towards himself. The lowing changed into a horrible sucking and groaning noise. Chryses closed his eyes, smiling euphorically as the blood spurted over his chubby face and golden sun tiara, pulsing down his white smock. The giant creature's front legs gave way and it fell, chin first, then its back legs wobbled and collapsed. Laocoon, arms outstretched to the sky, cried out words of veneration to Poseidon.

Having witnessed enough death for one day, Hattu turned his gaze away, and looked over the crowds instead: King Priam was there with Queen Hekabe, seated on a wooden dais, flanked by Commander Dolon and quartets of Guardians. On a step, Andromache suckled baby Astyanax. The youngest of the royal children, Princess Polyxena and the two boy princes, Polydorus and Polites, sat around the babe, pulling faces and making animal noises, causing little Astyanax to giggle and stick out his little pink tongue in attempts to imitate them. The sight was far more inspiring than that of a dying bull. For the first time since dawn, Hattu allowed himself to think of Pudu, of Ruhepa and Kurunta, of home. He drew Ruhepa's goat idol from his purse and stroked it fondly, a sad pang passing through his chest.

He noticed Helen there at the royal bench too, seated beside Paris but leaning away from him, toying with that silver bracelet of hers while he plucked a gentle tune on his lyre. On the far side of the flames stood the nobles and their families. Priam's elders too, all lightly-flecked with the blood of the bull – apart from Antenor, who had hopped back like an old mother, lifting the hem of his robes to protect them from the spray. Then he noticed Deiphobus. He was watching the dissection of the bull.

Yet Hattu had the distinct feeling that, a heartbeat before, the man had been staring at him. Unnerved, Hattu looked away, only to meet the direct glare of Princess Cassandra. Either side of her sat two templefolk, hands positioned close so they could seize her if needs be. She stared at him for an age. Finally, her lips moved, and she repeated those cold words she had uttered at him on his day of arrival at Troy.

*How could you?*

A cold shiver passed through Hattu.

Suddenly, with a splish-splash of feet and hands, Sirtaya barrelled into the river, startling the toad and sending the oystercatcher nearby flapping away in panic. The Egyptian leapt for the two creatures, missed and tumbled gracelessly to a halt before Hattu and Dagon. 'Trojan toads and birds appear to be faster than those in the Hittite lands,' he grumped, dusting at his scraped shoulders, wheezing a little.

Dagon munched on a piece of bread, arching an eyebrow mischievously. 'Ah, of course: the famously fleet-footed frogs of Wilusa. Nothing to do with you getting old, is it?'

Sirtaya shot Dagon a sour look. 'You wouldn't be saying that had I caught the fat toad and you were right now eating it with me.'

Dagon looked nonplussed. 'No, I would instead be saying "why am I eating toad?".'

Hattu smiled. These glib exchanges always made him smile. It made him think of another companion: Andor had left him at the end of battle and had not returned since. Worried, he looked up into the grey silk of night cloud. It took him a time to spot her, gliding up there. He recognised the way she was banking left and right, fighting against the zephyrs to stay in the same spot. It was how she flew whenever she spotted some disturbance. The odd thing was she was facing north, towards Troy and beyond. A creeping sense of unease came over him.

Just then, from the dull glow of Troy, a fire arrow sailed up.

Dagon's head twitched up, staring at it and seeing Andor at the same time. 'Danger?'

The chanting and chatter from the heart of the great Trojan camp faded away to nothing, then pockets of uneasy jabbering started, all faces pale in the torchlight as they stared up at the blazing missile. Hattu gazed at the spot on the plain below the arrow. Its dim orange bubble of light betrayed almost nothing. Then… his eyes narrowed. *Movement?* As the arrow descended further, he saw it more clearly now: an army, between Troy and the camp, approaching the camp's supposed safe edge, veering towards the river ford. Hattu began to rise from his spot, dread crawling across his skin like insects, plucking his swords from the silt. The Trojan crowds began to break up and yammer in alarm.

'How did they get around behind us?' Dagon croaked, going for his weapons too.

Hektor stepped forth, between them all and the falling fire arrow. He climbed atop a boulder on the Scamander side, spreading his hands wide. 'Fear not, families of Troy. Those that march in the night are the men of Thracia, here to answer our call, to swell our forces, to *guarantee* our final victory tomorrow.'

Hattu remained half-risen, like a drinking deer unsure whether to run or remain by a waterside. He stared at the mass of men streaming closer. Soldiers in peaked cloth caps, clad in leather shells, he realised. Spearmen. Not Ahhiyawans, certainly. A herd of seventy horses too – white stallions with night-black manes. Striking creatures. Chariots too, packed on the backs of wagons. Their thickly-bearded leader crossed the river ford and came before Priam's plinth, falling to one knee.

'King Rhesus?' Priam uttered as if he had seen a dead man walking. 'We heard that your realm had collapsed. When you did not respond to our calls for help we were sure it must be true.'

Rhesus' face grew stony. 'Aye, the earth tremors brought my hall to the ground.' He beat a fist against his armoured chest and grinned. 'But the Thracian spirit is stronger than any masonry. I bring six hundred fresh and eager soldiers to Troy's side, Majesty,' he proclaimed, throwing out an arm. 'Born and trained on the hills and plains of the north. No hardier a fighter will your enemy have faced.'

Hattu's mind raced. The army of Thracia. More specifically, their steeds… it brought the words of one of the five prophecies of protection to his lips, which moved soundlessly: *The horses of faraway Thracia will drink and rest by the Scamander side, guaranteeing Troy's safety.*

Evidently, all here knew what this meant, as the Trojan crowds erupted in a gleeful chorus of cheering and celebration.

Hektor moved over beside the Trojan royal bench. 'Rise, King Rhesus. Tomorrow, you will play a part in a victory that will echo through eternity.'

More joyous roars. Cups were raised and wine and barley beer sloshed, and the pipes struck up once more in a gay rhythm.

Hektor, beaming, cast his eyes around the central fire and began issuing new orders. First, he sent Commander Dolon and a squadron of

Guardians off towards the Borean Hills to scout the enemy camp in preparation for the next day's attack. Next, he spoke one by one to the officers of the Trojan and allied armies. Soon he approached Hattu and Dagon. '*Labarna.* If I may summon you? Before my men pickle their minds too much, we must have a council of war.'

***

The Trojan and allied command gathered in a ring near the river. Within this circle, Hektor knelt on one knee outlining the plan for tomorrow in finer detail using the age-old implements of a general – a twig and a patch of dry earth to draw upon. As Hattu watched, he could not help but think of the blunders of battle he had witnessed in the day just gone, and worry that there were more to come. He itched within to take charge. As Great King of the Hittite Empire and overlord of Troy, he had every right to do so. But the lingering guilt of his late arrival with no army in tow weighed heavily on his thoughts. Equally, he knew it could do more harm than good if he were to bluntly commandeer what had for ten summers been Hektor's war. Beside him, Dagon tapped one foot, equally frustrated.

'From what we saw today, the enemy have completed their beach rampart.' Hektor drew a line in the earth, then marked the shape of a few beached ships behind it to indicate the Ahhiyawan camp. 'But they are pinned there. So tomorrow, the onus is upon us to assault that stockade.' Murmurs of support broke out all around the watchers.

An instinctive need to speak, to point out the flaw in this thinking, pulsed through Hattu. He remained silent for a moment, letting the murmurs fade, selecting his words so they would not undermine Hektor too much. 'I would advise against attacking them tomorrow.'

Hektor looked up, taken aback. 'You have something else planned?' A few men laughed nervously, but most noticed the Trojan Prince's clipped tone.

Hattu let a moment pass before replying. 'Yesterday, I explained to you that I overheard some of their soldiery sharing their fears and talking of sailing away from the war. Then, the balance was too delicate. But today's reverse will have compounded those doubts, tilted the balance. If there is one maxim that has held good in every war I have ever fought, it is that one should never interrupt an enemy when he is minded to withdraw. So do not attack tomorrow. Instead, hold this line, block off their routes inland and deny them their usual plunder and forage. Give them a day or two to stew in their misgivings. In a few mornings' time we might wake to see them setting sail, abandoning the war, all without any further loss of life.'

A few men muttered in interest, others doubtfully.

Hektor smiled for a moment, then shook his head. 'We attack tomorrow, *Labarna,*' he said with a god-like confidence, then returned to his map.

Hattu felt a spike of indignation, but suppressed the instinctive urge to berate Hektor. *I am here to advise, not to command,* he reminded himself.

On the Trojan Crown Prince dictated. 'We will advance at first light. Our archers will take up elevated positions on the far slopes of the Borean Hills, using the marram grass as cover, and showering arrows upon the sand wall defenders,' Hektor said, tracing the lie of the hills in the dirt, parallel to the line of the sand wall, making dots along the southern edge of the range to denote archer spots. 'Likewise, the five infantry battalions will advance and wait just behind the brow of the range.'

Another bell pealed in Hattu's mind. 'Will the battalions be of the same composition as today?' he asked.

Hektor blinked and issued a terse sigh. 'Yes,' he said quickly, giving Hattu no more than a quick glance before returning to his dirt map. 'Once in position, we-'

'They will be much stronger if they are reorganised,' Hattu interrupted.

Hektor rested his elbows on his knees and looked up. 'King Hattu, this is not the time to gut and reshape our army. An army that almost clinched victory today.'

'And almost crumbled to a crippling defeat,' Hattu said, 'because of one critical weakness.'

Hektor sucked in a long breath through his nostrils. 'Enlighten us.'

'It was the weakness that plagued you the day before I arrived when your right wing collapsed. The same weakness that has no doubt been present in many battles of this war before that.'

'The enemy spy?' one officer said, eyes darting around suspiciously.

'The Shadow,' whispered another.

Hattu shook his head. 'I thought so too, when I heard of the grievous turns in the recent clashes. My eyes were keen today, but I saw no traitor at work. Instead it was my ears that discovered the problem.' He turned to meet the eyes of all. 'Language,' he said in the Hittite tongue. All those gathered around Hektor understood. But when he said it again, loud enough for the lesser officers and soldiers milling around nearby to hear, it was different. A few of these ones frowned, others cocked an ear, not entirely sure what he had said. Only a handful seemed to have understood the word.

'Perhaps we will speak of this later, after tomorrow's attack,' Hektor said, drawing confidence from the apparent lack of interest in Hattu's point.

'By then it might be too late,' Hattu countered. 'I watched your homily to the massed army this morning, on the Silver Ridge. The men stood tall and cheered just at the sight of you, but do you realise many of them understood barely a word you said?'

'What?' Hektor snapped. 'Nonsense!'

'They were roused by your mere presence, but it was only when you repeated the name of the Thunder God in each of the common tongues that they *understood*. In the depths of battle, men need to understand what their general wants them to do.'

'You think this army has been following me all these years without understanding my-'

'Language,' Hattu cut in resonantly, then repeated the word in Luwian, Nesite, Hurrian and a few of the Island tongues old Ruba had taught him many years ago. The faces of all nearby changed like a passing wave, each of them understanding at least one of the tongues.

Hektor saw this, his nostrils flaring in frustration.

'When I led the Ascanians today, they did not understand my Luwian tongue,' Hattu said. 'When I later fell in with the Lukkans, they did. The first bout was a disaster, the second was what turned the key of victory. I urge you: reorganise the battalions, so each consists of men who understand one of the common tongues. It is a lesson we Hittites learned the hard way a long time ago. Had we not, we would have lost at Kadesh and many other clashes down through the years.'

'I will think upon it, King Hattu,' Hektor muttered, then returned to his dirt map. He marked the central spot on the sand wall line – the gate. 'Now… with our five battalions poised in the hills, the fifth will emerge and attack the gatehouse in their stockade.'

'Those gates are rudimentary, Majesty, but stout enough,' Dagon said. 'We will need siege equipment.'

'Quite,' Hektor said, more patiently seeing that it was not Hattu who had interrupted him this time. 'That is why we will take a ram. When the gates are broken,' with his fingertips, he brushed through the sand wall, tracing a furrow towards and around the ships, 'we will flood into the camp, and we will put their boats to the flame. Next, we will-'

A warning bell again tolled inside Hattu's mind. 'Prince Hektor,' he said.

Hektor looked up, somewhat taken aback at being interrupted yet again. Hattu realised he was not used to the experience. 'Yes, Great King?'

'If the objective is to rid your land of the Ahhiyawans, then burning their ships is not the answer. For then they will have no means of escape, no option but to fight for their lives.' He searched Hektor's eyes, trying to find a crumb of empathy. 'In the past I have made the mistake of trapping opponents in a corner. Even the most dejected and worn-down of foes caught like this will fight with a renewed and unnatural ferocity until death comes.' Hektor's jaw began to work, and his eyes grew distant, as if thinking it over. So on Hattu went: 'We must leave one door open to them: the sea, and their boats… the chance to escape back to their homes. They surely will seize it.'

Sarpedon, Masturi and Aeneas – all well-versed in working under Hattu – nodded slowly, seeing wisdom in the plan. Hektor's princely brothers, Paris, Scamandrios, and even sulking Deiphobus seemed to be in agreement too. All began to chatter and murmur in positive tones.

Hektor noticed this, and the thoughtful look in his eyes faded. He glanced around at them darkly. 'You sound like the elders. One thousand years from now, what will people say when they speak of us? Eh? That we, the children of Troy, behaved like cowards, too afraid to seize victory in the true sense? That we chose to chase our enemy away because we were too meek to finish them? Is that a story you would be proud to tell your grandchildren?'

Aeneas answered. 'If it meant that we lived to sire and regale those grandchildren, then my pride would be overflowing,' he said calmly.

Hektor chuckled grimly, his head hanging and shaking from side to side. Hattu realised he was in danger of alienating this hero. A legendary leader of men, if not – as the day's events had demonstrated – a great tactician. He adopted a conciliatory tone. 'There is no hiding from the reality of the things I suggest. It is the war of the flea – the grim and ignoble struggle that the dog cannot beat. Fight with poisons, deadly insects, plague garments, psychological tricks. It is the means by which I took the Hittite Empire from the hand of a murderous usurper, and by which I have held our realm together in the years since, despite a critical lack of manpower and supplies.'

Hektor continued to shake his head. 'I mean no disrespect, Great King. But I thought you were better than that.' Those in the command circle sucked in tense breaths. 'They told me you were a lion, yet you talk of fleas?'

Hattu remained expressionless, tall, staring. *They told me you were the scion of Troy, stronger and wiser than any of your forefathers.*

'I will *not* fight this "war of the flea",' concluded Hektor, rising to stand tall. 'We will win this struggle in the way it was foretold by Apollo. With bronze and valour. We will drive at and into the enemy camp tomorrow and reduce it to ashes.' Many of the commanders were whipped up with enthusiasm by his sheer magnetism.

Hattu maintained his composure but could only see disaster ahead with this plan. One last hope came to him. 'You have made up your mind about how we will attack them. Also that you will not countenance waiting a few days to see if they will retreat. But have you considered bringing the attack *forward*?' He looked around all of the men. 'Rise not at dawn but *before* the sun pierces the night. Advance in darkness. There are valley paths through the Borean Hills as you will know – thick with vegetation,' he said, thinking of the vale Patroklos had led them through to escape the camp. 'We could use those to approach unseen, to advance right up to their bay camp before they have even stirred from sleep.'

The watching men rumbled in new interest at this.

The muscles at the corners of Hektor's jaw bunched. 'Thank you for your suggestion, Great King,' he said. 'Tomorrow, we attack the camp of ships.' He let a tense silence pass, before adding: 'At dawn. Not before dawn. *At* dawn, as the ancient code of battle demands. And we will destroy the enemy to the last man, burn their boats, cleanse this land of their foul presence.' He drew his sword and stabbed it into the earth, rising, looking round his commanders. 'Who stands with me?'

'Aye,' each cried as they were sworn to.

Hektor stared at Hattu, the only one not to have spoken.

Hattu calmly nodded, once. 'Always. As our oath states.'

***

Odysseus, head pounding, grouchy, crept through a tight valley in the Borean Hills. Dressed in black like his young comrade Diomedes, they were invisible in the moonless night. The pair were not exactly friends, but were well-used to working together, and that was why they had been chosen by Kalchas the augur for this mission.

As they wove through the leafy vale, all Odysseus could think about was how satisfying it would be to hold the garrulous Kalchas by the throat and dunk his head in the beach camp's stinking latrine pits, over and over. Just about every word the man had ever spoken had resulted in ill-consequence. The atrocity that had happened on the shores of Aulis before the fleet had come here had been Kalchas' doing. The twists and turns of the war ever since always seemed to be tied into the seer's nonsense. Now tonight, after the thumping defeat just gone, a scout had spotted the arrival at the Trojan camp of the Thracian King. It had been Kalchas' utterances on the beach that had seen Odysseus and Diomedes sent out like this when they should have been resting their bodies and nursing their light wounds.

*It is the next of the five divine prophecies that shelter Troy. If the horses of Thracia come to rest and drink by the Scamander, the city will be blessed with immortality.* Face uplit by the fire, Kalchas had raised a hand, bone and tooth bracelets clacking, one finger – nail encrusted with dried blood – pointing at Odysseus and Diomedes. *Go forth, steal those northern beasts before they can fill their bellies and sleep!*

The other kings had howled in support, sand spraying up as they danced, beef-brained Ajax thumping his towering shield like a drum. Odysseus knew there was no chance of reasoning with them. In any case, these crumbs of morale were becoming ever more vital in such days of plague and inner strife.

*Kwok!* A night heron cried out in the dark as it streaked over the heads of the two men. Diomedes grinned, his teeth like a crescent moon in the darkness. 'The bird flies along our path, Island King. A good sign.'

Odysseus eyed his young companion sideways. 'A good sign for me will be steam rising from a pot of bubbling stew back at my hut. My feet are sore, my crotch is damp with stinking sweat and my head is aching with tiredness and too much sun.'

'Serves you right for swimming with the dolphins in the morning – no wonder you are cooked like a lobster. Especially with that bald patch at the back of your head.'

'What?' Odysseus snapped, shocked.

'Nothing,' Diomedes grinned again.

Odysseus glanced enviously at Diomedes' scalp and the thick braids of hair sprouting there, and made a mental note to check his own hirsuteness with a polished mirror later. They roved on, passing a dark hole in the earth. The wretch, Piya-maradu, had been buried to his neck there, sentenced to death for stealing. Scouts had brought word earlier in the evening that somehow the man had managed to worm his way free of his grave. A horrible creature, was Piya-maradu, but a survivor nonetheless.

Just then, he noticed the echo of the valley sides fading away as they emerged onto the Scamander plain. Some way ahead stood the Trojan camp, a glittering stripe of torchlight stark against the moonless night. The camp hugged the Scamander's near banks like a serpent. After ten years of this war – ten years during which neither side could claim the river plain fully as their own – this felt like a massive reversal of fortunes. A new Trojan frontier, closer to the beach camp. Pushing towards victory. It turned his thoughts to the wavering morale, and to what arrows were left in the Ahhiyawan quiver. The greatest one by far was Achilles, the talisman of the war so far.

In the aftermath of the day just gone, having seen his beach camp surrounded, Agamemnon had offered to return Briseis the war-bride to the sulking Achilles. Not only that, he had granted him a wagonload of treasure too.

Achilles had turned it down.

'Achilles,' Odysseus rumbled, imagining giving the stubborn champion a good slapping around the face, or at least asking Achilles' closest comrade and battle-tutor Patroklos to do it. 'Do you think he'll go through with it?' he asked Diomedes.

Diomedes half-smiled. 'He behaves like a child. To reject Agamemnon's offer is one thing, but to claim he is done with this war and set to sail home in the morning? That is like my nephew back in Tiryns: I once asked him to clear away his wooden toys and come to eat with the family. In a fit of pique, he smashed his toys against the wall, destroying them. He claimed it was *my* fault for making him angry. Perhaps, come morning – after a night of rest – Achilles will not be so irrational.' He rolled his muscular shoulders. 'And if he does leave, so be it. *I* will take on his mantle as the greatest Trojan-slayer.'

'Hmm,' Odysseus replied, unconvinced. Before leaving to come on this mission, he had seen Achilles and his elite Myrmidons packing up their possessions. What a blow it would be to the morale of the Ahhiyawan confederation were they to witness the black boar sails of their champion's fleet shrinking into the western horizon. What man could watch that and not think of their own home... *Home*, Odysseus thought, his heart melting at the memory of his bed in Ithaca, of Penelope's bare buttocks and back pressed against him, of the softness of her neck against his lips, the warmth of her skin. *Soon,* he prayed. Especially given the worrying reports that continued to be spread by the captains of supply ships – tales of unrest back in the homelands, of large bands of foreign brigands, of severe drought and savage earth tremors. It all brought his thoughts back to the infernal question: how to end this damned war decisively? There was one answer, one glittering option, so far unused. 'The Assyrians – had we called upon them – would have swung the balance of the day just gone.'

Diomedes shrugged. 'Agamemnon was right though; they'd just as soon cut our throats while we slept as they would help break Troy. In fact, no: cutting our throats would be too quick. They'd probably peel us of our skin. They love to torture before they kill. Anyway, there's no point mulling over that, for the Assyrian fleet will be long gone from the port of Milawata by now.'

'Not quite,' Odysseus winked. 'I convinced Nestor to leave that door ajar. I had him give the messenger on the boat a silver rhyton as a gift for King Shalmaneser, just as Agamemnon demanded... but I also gave him a bag of silver rings for Mardukal.'

A notch of confusion appeared between Diomedes' eyebrows.

'The Assyrian army has sailed back home, but Mardukal remains in Milawata,' Odysseus explained. 'The offer of soldiers was a tempting one, but Mardukal was the greatest part of it. We'll need his nous to crack open the stony shell of Troy.'

Diomedes cocked an eyebrow. 'He's *still* at Milawata? That place is a seething slave market and a warren of brothels. His cock'll have rotted off by now,' he chuckled grimly, then sighed, flinging a hand out ahead at the long Trojan camp. 'What does it matter anyway? The opportunity to bring siege weapons to the walls of Troy has passed – that camp is the new line of war.'

Odysseus did not answer. All his attentions were on the tall grass ahead. The stalks there were moving. Something was coming in the opposite direction, from the Trojan camp. In the meagre light it was hard to tell, but it looked like… a wolf? No, Odysseus realised: it was a man draped in a wolfskin cloak.

He met Diomedes' eye, and both shared a nod. Cat-like, the pair came round to flank the moving thing. They mouthed together: *Ready... now!*

Odysseus seized the man by the shoulders.

Diomedes clamped a hand over the man's mouth. 'This is the end of the war for you, Trojan scum.'

It was no ordinary man, Odysseus realised, seeing the craggy face of the veteran. 'Commander Dolon of the Guardians?' he whispered in the Trojan tongue, crouching before him as Diomedes took him in a wrestler's lock, one bulky arm around his throat and another twisting an arm up his back.

'Men!' Dolon croaked to the grasses nearby. A trio of Trojan Guardians rose from the stalks, brandishing swords and spears. But in the same breath, a band of Ithacan axemen and black-helmed Tirynean spearmen rose a short way behind Odysseus, launching a volley of spears, killing the Guardians.

As he saw his men fall, gurgling, moaning, Dolon's eyes grew wide with anger and horror. 'Release me,' he rasped. 'Fight me!'

'Tell us where the Thracians are within the Trojan camp, and the rota of the watch,' said Odysseus. 'Tell us, and you can go on your way.'

'Never.'

Diomedes, quick as a striking snake, snatched the blade from Dolon's belt and held it to his neck, grabbing his hair with the other hand. 'Talk, or I will slice off your head.'

'You will never let me go, for I will simply return to my camp and have the watch changed and doubled.'

'You make a fair point,' Odysseus shrugged. 'Very well. Tell us about your camp, and I guarantee your safety within ours.'

'Imprisonment on your mosquito-infested bay of dried-out boats? Pah, I'd rather die.'

Odysseus leaned in, seeing the telltale sparkle in Dolon's eyes. A glint of fear. 'You truly wish to feel a blade sawing through your neck, the sound of sinews snapping and stretching and your throat tubes popping? You have a choice… and you would *choose* that?'

Dolon gulped. Odysseus knew he had done enough. He softened his voice. 'You have a wife and son, I believe.'

Dolon nodded.

'You are our prisoner now, but you can be with them again.'

'How? Either Troy's army will overwhelm you on the beach camp, and in desperation your kind will slit my throat along with the other prisoners, or Agamemnon's horde will somehow turn the tide against Troy and butcher my loved ones.'

Odysseus shook his head slowly. 'There are ways in war, order to the taking of cities. Codes and signs that commanders know and follow – even against bitter enemies. Trust me. If… *when* Troy falls, I will see to it that your home is spared and that your family survives. Now tell us where the Thracians are. We mean only to steal their horses.'

Dolon's eyes grew wet now. He gulped several times before speaking. 'The Thracians,' he paused, a tear escaping, 'are near the western end. The watch at that section is in disorder while men bring tents and firewood and rearrange supply heaps.'

'You chose wisely, Dolon of Troy,' Odysseus smiled. Before the words had fully left his lips, a burst of crimson spattered across his face. With a sharp intake of breath, he sank back, appalled at the sight of the snarling Diomedes pulling and sawing with the blade at Dolon's neck. The Trojan commander's eyes rolled in their sockets and he thrashed with his arms and legs – fiercely at first, then with more feeble spasms. With a *snap*, his head came free.

Odysseus stared at his blood-spotted comrade. 'Why?'

'One less prisoner to feed, said Diomedes, stripping Dolon's body of the bloody wolfskin, taking it for himself. 'And when Troy falls, it means we don't have to bother ourselves with picking out and sparing his family. They can suffer with all the others.'

Odysseus rose to standing, wondering if there was any way he might apologise to Dolon's spirit. He looked at Diomedes again. 'You and I work well together, young Lord of Tiryns, but we are very, very different.'

Diomedes cast him a sideways glower. 'Why – because I killed a Trojan tonight? How many have you slain in these ten years, hmm?'

Odysseus sighed. The sad truth was that Diomedes was utterly wrong and absolutely right.

They scurried on towards the Trojan camp, soon hearing the pipes and chatter from within, seeing the many soldiers sitting around their cooking fires. Civilians too had come from the city of Troy, it seemed. He wondered if Dolon's family were in the camp. If they had wished him well before he set off on his scouting mission.

'Down,' Diomedes hissed.

Odysseus, shaken from his thoughts, dropped to one knee behind an oleander bush. He saw what Diomedes had seen and what Dolon had confessed: the Thracians, unarmoured, clattering around trying to set up beds and tents for the night. Their herd was tethered near the camp's edge.

Diomedes tensed, ready to rise and lead the strike, but Odysseus halted him.

'Wait,' said the Ithacan King. 'Look.' Diomedes began to grumble, but stopped when he saw a troop of one hundred feather-helmed Lukkans, jogging over to take up places around the Thracian camp works, their eyes scouring the darkness of the countryside.

Odysseus looked back over his shoulder to the spot in the darkness where their team of sixty soldiers crouched. Thirty Ithacans and thirty Tiryneans. Turning back to the Trojan camp again, he glanced left and right along the broad line of tents, until he spotted the one figure that made the difference, standing by one of the many celebration fires. 'Luckily, our friend will soon deal with that Lukkan watch,' he said. He cupped his hands around his mouth and issued an owl's hoot.

The figure in the Trojan camp suddenly twitched, looking out in his direction, before leaving the fireside and fading into a darker area of the camp.

'Remember,' Odysseus said as they waited. 'We take the horses and run. That is all that was asked of us.'

Diomedes made some grunting noise and grinned.

***

Tudha sat slumped on a pile of grain sacks in a dark corner of the camp, far from the celebrations and the engineers busy sawing to make a battering ram. Belly full of fatty boar meat, he tossed strips of what was left on the bone across the thin grass clearing before him. Time after time, Andor swooped down and caught the piece before it landed then glided away to some dark recess to devour it. The next piece he aimed carefully, lobbing it a little higher to see if he could fool her. A green-feathered arrow sped out of the darkness, pinning the meat to a wagon.

'In the name of the Moon God!' Tudha yelped, sitting bolt upright.

Laughter echoed from the shadows under an awning. Aeneas emerged, Andor on his shoulder, chirruping in amusement too.

'Working together?' Tudha grumbled, though he was unable to stop a smile spreading across his face. He slumped back on the grain sacks.

'You are tired of the feasting?' Aeneas asked him.

'I don't understand it. In the Hittite heartlands, we don't celebrate until we have achieved a full victory,' he replied.

Aeneas tilted his head to one side. 'Prince Hektor insisted that, so close to the Ahhiyawan camp, we should send up sounds of gaiety. I'm not sure I would have ordered the same were I in his position. Likewise, I don't think he and your father see eye to eye.'

'Father doesn't like Hektor… and doesn't trust me.'

'This, again?' Aeneas said.

Tudha shrugged. He explained his theory about the Thymbran Gate keys. Aeneas nodded along. 'I saw the crowds around the gatehouse when I came in with the others for fresh arrows. Thousands were there. It could have been any one of them.'

'At least you entertain my theory instead of dismissing it,' Tudha replied. He shook his head and gestured back to the feasting fire. 'But yes, my father does not make friends easily. Comrades, aye. Devotees, yes. But friends to him are things from his childhood. Dagon is a true companion of his – people liken Father and him to the legendary Gilgamesh and Enkidu – but he is the last of them. All the rest are dead. Dead to the blades and poisons of his enemies.'

'It teaches us does it not?' Aeneas said. 'To value our loved ones while they are with us.'

'That look on your face,' Tudha smiled. 'Who are you thinking of?'

'My father, though he is old now. My wife Kreousa – she is a daughter of Priam. And our lad,' he grinned now, 'he is only a babe. I love them all dearly. Sometimes I question my wisdom in bringing them here to Troy.' He fell silent for a time, his eyes growing misty. 'But back when I was your age, it was Yanos and Ki. Brothers, sons of a leather tanner in Dardania. I cared not that they were sons of a worker, and they minded not that I was a prince. In high summer, we would go to Mount Ida. There is a spot where the streams become waterfalls, toppling into a pool as blue as a maiden's eyes. The cliffs are smooth and pale as cream. We'd hunt for rabbit, cook and eat it there, then take turns to leap from the cliff and into the pool. I'll never forget the sense of boundless energy, of pure joy. In winter, we'd go there to slide across the ice.' He laughed and shook his head, staring up at the night sky. 'The strange thing is, I don't remember ever feeling the cold back then.'

'Are Yanos and Ki in Troy also? Or did they remain back in Dardania?' Tudha asked.

Aeneas blinked and turned away, gazing out over the Scamander plain. 'They marched to Kadesh with me. Never came back,' was all he could say, forcing the words past a lump in his throat.

Tudha had seen the few remaining Hittite veterans of Kadesh behave like this. They spoke in that same, strangled way. He had learned that it was best to listen and let the gaps of silence pass uninterrupted.

A gentle, balmy breeze swept along the Scamander, bringing with it continued noises of celebration from the central part of the camp. Aeneas sat beside Tudha on the grain sacks with a sigh, his eyes bright, if red-rimmed. 'Once again, young Hittite friend, the elites of Troy feast and laugh, while we sit in the dark fringes.'

Tudha played with his thumbs.

'What about you?' the Dardanian asked. 'You must have good friends back in Hattusa?'

Tudha half-smiled. 'My closest friend is here. Sirtaya.'

Aeneas arched an eyebrow. 'The old Egyptian? He is… not exactly the kind of friend I would expect a young Hittite to have.'

Tudha laughed. 'He is warm and wise. Like me, he has made mistakes, but he does not dwell on them. He thinks only of the future, of good things to come. Some of the happiest days of my boyhood were spent with him, walking the banks of the Ambar River, talking, joking, telling tall tales. He taught me much with those tales – quite the teacher, even if he doesn't realise it.'

Still Aeneas looked perplexed. 'What about the other young Hittites – you would surely have more in common with them?'

Tudha shook his head slowly. 'Boys and girls avoided me – avoided my father really. You see, when I was not with Sirtaya, I was always with him. If I tried to wander he would demand my presence. Some say he was desperate to make up for his failings with Kurunta in that respect. He was never there for my half-brother, and so chaining me to his side meant I would not turn wayward as Kurunta once did.' He let out a sad laugh. 'Thus, I spent my youth in the chariot with him, by his side on the military fields and at his talks in the royal court. Learning to use the spear, the reins and the stylus in every hour of every day. From the off I was to be his successor, had to live up to his every reputation. I am his heir, but he…' he smiled tightly, 'sometimes I think he has forgotten that I am also his son. No walks in the countryside, no hunting expeditions,' he shook his head, 'we never talk like… like this.'

Aeneas beheld him with the strangest gaze – even sadder than he had looked when talking about Yanos and Ki. 'When this wretched war is over, we should take to the hills of this country, catch rabbit…'

'…leap from the cliffs?' Tudha recoiled, horrified. 'I am a climber, not a faller!'

Aeneas rocked with laughter. 'Perhaps not then, though we could admire the view.' He took from his belt a short piece of planed wood, bent in the middle, and gave it to Tudha. 'I could show you how to use this: it's an Egyptian throwing stick, brought back from Kadesh. Lethal as an arrow. Bring Sirtaya too, he could no doubt show us *both* how to use it properly.'

Tudha weighed the stick, admiring the painted patterns of scorpions and gazelle on the polished wood. 'A weapon of war,' he said quietly. 'My father would not approve.'

Aeneas took a cagey breath. 'May I ask… what did you do, at this rebellion in Hatenzuwa? Fall asleep on watch? Desert?'

Tudha smiled with one edge of his mouth. 'Those are the crimes of a spearman. I was the commander of the imperial force sent there.'

Now Aeneas rocked backwards, astonished.

'Yes, at fourteen summers. I told you, I was measured against my father in my every action. At a similar age, he spearheaded the conquest of the Lost North alongside his brother, Muwa. It elevated him to a level where people spoke of him as a god. So when the Hatenzuwan task force was picked, it had to be me who led.'

'So… your father chose you to do this?'

'Wholeheartedly,' Tudha answered. 'It would vindicate all of the training he had put me through. He sent me into those rebellious forest lands to quash that uprising.' He shrugged. 'And that's exactly what I did.'

Aeneas licked his lips nervously. 'But… how did you do it?'

Tudha felt the inquiry sink into his chest, prod at his heart, ask questions he dared not ask himself. 'There… there was a shrine, in the heart of the woods…'

He stopped, hearing an odd noise.

'Something wrong?' Aeneas asked.

Tudha, frowning, heard it again: behind him, out on the plain. An owl hooting. Something about it was… unusual. He was well-trained in the handling of birds, owls amongst them, so he was familiar with the calls of those night hunters. When Andor settled low, neck stretched and eyes keenly trained in the direction of the sound, he knew there was something going on.

'Tudha?' Aeneas asked.

Tudha planted a finger to his lips and turned on the grain sacks, onto his knees to peer out over the southern half of the plain, like a bird spotter in a hide. It was too damned dark to see a thing, other than the slight change in the blackness where the Borean Hills met the night sky. He and Aeneas scanned the darkness for what felt like an age, each cursing inwardly at every shriek of laughter or high-pitched buzz from the pipes. Tudha's heart, bouncing along like a stallion's trot, slowed eventually. No more owl calls. 'I'm sorry,' he said, sighing. 'It was nothi-'

A splash sounded, somewhere behind him – in the Scamander. Tudha swung round to look that way, past Aeneas. 'What was that?'

Aeneas grabbed his forearm as if demanding new silence. 'I don't know, but look.' He was staring neither out at the southern stretch of the plain from where the owl sound had risen, nor to the north where the splash had come from, but along the line of the camp. There, a short way from their spot, the tents of King Rhesus had finally been pitched, and the Thracian men – weary from a long march – had retired. But the contingent of one hundred Lukkans posted to watch the southern edge of their encampment were peeling away, through the camp, spears levelled as they moved towards the sound of the splash – near the ford. Tudha's heart pounded again. 'Something's not right.'

Andor hopped onto his shoulder as he and Aeneas rose, edging past small fires where people drank and sang, around webs of tent ropes and past crates and tethered horses. Closer now, they saw the Lukkans. All but a few had pulled over to the Scamander-side, peering north, heads sweeping side to side as they scoured the ford and the far banks, their crowns of feathers juddering as they did so. 'Who goes there?' one called out, over and over. The Lukkan men edged out into the shallows, spears braced.

Just then, Andor chirped. Tudha saw how she was staring back at the southern edge of the camp. He twisted to look back that way. Movement. There, coming in from the night, trudged a few soldiers, headed straight for the Thracian area. He spotted the wolfskin hood worn by the lead soldier, and the Guardian armour of those with him. 'It is Dolon's patrol,' he said with a sigh of relief. The few Lukkans left standing watch there moved to welcome him back. Tudha and Aeneas approached as well.

That was when Tudha spotted something odd. It was as if Dolon had sprouted another head higher, broader too. As the leader of the incoming party set foot across the threshold of the camp, he cast off the wolf hood and cloak to reveal a tumble of braids and a savage grin.

'It is Diomedes,' Aeneas croaked, throwing an arm across Tudha to halt him.

Tudha now saw the others for what they were. Not Guardians but Ahhiyawans in Trojan armour. Tiryneans and Ithacans. They and Diomedes ran the few Lukkan sentries through.

'Enemy in the camp!' Tudha cried. Only four men, he thought. Then, suddenly, dozens more in enemy garb rose from the grass and surged to join their kinsmen. With an explosion of guttural roars, the attackers flooded around the tents of King Rhesus, slashing and hacking through the leathers, bursts of blood erupting inside those shelters. They kicked over crates and tipped wagons, cleaved the skulls of Thracians who stuck their heads out of the tents in confusion, and tossed torches onto tents still packed with men. Tudha saw the stocky Odysseus slash through the leather straps tethering Rhesus' horses to a picket, leading them back off into the night, running, waving his Ithacan axemen away with him.

The horses were gone, but Diomedes and his Tiryneans were not done yet. King Rhesus staggered from his pavilion, his night robes trailing, his long hair unkempt, his face hanging in distress. An instant later his head was spinning free of his body. The body stumbled a few steps then collapsed, leaking black blood and bodily humours. Standing where he had been was Diomedes, his sword wet with the Thracian King's blood, face twisted in a battle-frenzy. He spotted Aeneas and Tudha and grinned like a jackal. Stomping forward, he swished his blade before him to shake off the blood. A group of soldiers hurried to join him.

Aeneas fumbled with his bow, loosing an arrow which whacked into the shoulder of one of the Tiryneans. That was all he could do with the weapon, as the enemy rushed into close range. He stepped before Tudha, shoving him. 'Run,' he yelled, pulling his sword free, ready to face the enemy alone.

'Never,' Tudha snarled and staggered forward to Aeneas' side, grabbing a spear from a stack. Diomedes came at him, feinting to duck under Aeneas' defensive strike, then bringing his sword down for Tudha's head. Tudha threw up his spear to block. The strength of the strike bit deep into the spear shaft, sending Tudha down onto one knee. Weapons locked like that, the King of Tiryns drove downwards, forcing his blade towards Tudha's throat. A battle of strength... and one that Tudha began to turn, rising again, shaking with effort. But the other Tiryneans were rushing in to support their king.

What happened next was like a storm rising from behind him. He saw a flash of green and twin flickers of iron, as Hattu surged forth and battered Diomedes away in a frenzy of sword strikes. Dagon lashed his chariot whip at another attacker, striking the man's eyes out. Sarpedon of Lukka launched a spear that sailed for one of Diomedes' men, taking him through the mouth and bursting from the back of the skull. Masturi cleaved the shoulder of another. Behind them came a mass of Trojan soldiery from all allied nations. The enemy warriors fled in panic, speeding off into the night faster than they had arrived.

Shaking, Tudha let his spear sag, angered that his father had thought he needed saving. As commanders and kings and officials arrived at the scene babbling in confusion and panic, Hattu approached, eyes trained on the half-bitten spear he held, glaring at the weapon darkly. 'You found trouble again?'

'Trouble found me,' Tudha growled in reply. 'And I needed no help.' He half expected a cutting response, but instead his father grasped out for balance, panting. Tudha dropped his spear and caught him. He was quivering, breathless from the brief effort. With a groan of pain and a wince, he stooped to rub at his legs. The *Labarna*, the Sun incarnate, was ailing like an old man.

'What were you doing in this part of the camp?' Hattu said between gasps, the tone accusatory.

'Someone here helped the raiders,' Tudha whispered in reply.

Hattu looked at him, face pale with fatigue as he straightened to stand tall. 'What? What did you see?'

'Nothing. We *saw* nothing, but Aeneas and I heard it. Someone within the camp drew the Lukkan guards away.' He searched his father's eyes, seeking his trust. 'Think about it. The traitor was in the city today to steal the keys. That same person is here tonight. Only the elites and nobles of Troy came from the city to be at the camp tonight. Thus, this "Shadow" *must* be one of them.'

With Hattu, he looked around the faces of the rich-born men and women of Troy. Those whom Troy had given everything; one who sought to see her fall.

***

The Thracian soldiers wept openly. They gathered around the cadavers, washing them and whispering to them. Tudha found and gave Dolon's bloody wolf cloak to the young Trojan spearman, Eumedes, who collapsed to his knees, sobbing for his dead father. Hattu, giddy and aching, stood amongst it all, angry that the watch had been so easily deceived, unsettled by the sight of the chopped-through tethers where the snow-white horses of Thracia had been, and by the meaning of their capture. Priam arrived in his nightshirt, wringing his hands through his hair, muttering to himself. Eventually, he waved madly at a stonemason. 'Ride back to the city at once. Take a hammer to the second tablet by the Scaean Tower.'

People yammered in distress. Soon all the talk turned to the three prophecies of protection that remained: the survival of Hektor, the son of Achilles, and the Palladium.

A stomping of feet sounded. Hektor pounded into view, his face twisted with rage. 'Did you catch them?' he snapped at Hattu.

Hattu glowered back at him. 'No. but we drove them off.'

Hektor glanced at those near Hattu with the barest of acknowledgements, saw the grieving Eumedes, then shouted to Paris: 'Brother, you are now Commander of the Guardians. Organise a group of five scouts. Send them out at once to be sure the enemy have retreated, then have them hunker down on the Borean Hills to watch the beach camp and ensure there are no more raids.'

Paris stretched a little taller at this, clearly proud of the station. 'Yes, Brother,' he said, before setting off across the camp to carry out his first task in the post.

Hektor returned his fiery glare to Hattu, then swept it around all who had gathered at the Thracian encampment. 'How did this happen?' he snarled. '*How?*'

'Because,' Hattu replied calmly, 'it appears that the Ahhiyawans had help from within our camp.' He said nothing about Tudha's deduction – still treating the logic of his wayward heir like a hot coal. 'They, Prince Hektor, appear unconcerned with how people will remember their victory, only that they achieve it. They, Majesty, chose to attack during the hours of darkness. They, Heir of Troy, fight the war of the flea.'

Sarpedon, Masturi, Glaucus and a band of Trojan noblemen arrayed near Hattu, rumbling in agreement. The Trojan princes, Deiphobus and Scamandrios, seemed won over too.

'It is not too late to change our plans for tomorrow,' Hattu pressed.

Hektor glared at Hattu, then at his council of command… before waving a dismissive hand and stomping off into the night.

'Give him time, *Labarna*,' said Glaucus. 'I have seen him like this before. He reacts hotly, but sometimes comes round to the thinking of others later. He may yet see sense.'

Hattu stared after Hektor. 'Pray to the Gods of Lukka that he does. Otherwise, tomorrow will be a dark, dark day.'

# CHAPTER 8

## CRIMSON SAND

*Hattu drifted through the black halls of sleep, weightless, restful... for a time.*

*And then he heard a rising hubbub of chaos: swords, shouting, beating hooves. The darkness receded and he realised he was gripped in Ishtar's talons as the goddess glided over a roiling land. It was a grim parody of the day just gone. The dream-Scamander splitting the plain was red and opaque, and the banks were writhing with combat. He saw Kalchas pouring blood from the neck of a severed Trojan head into a goblet and gulping the lot down. Diomedes too, drowning Trojans in the shallows. Ajax, battering men to death with his staff as if they were ants. It was a disaster. Then came Agamemnon and his chariots, pulled by skeleton horses, driven by horned beasts. 'More blood!' the enemy Wanax cried.*

*'Set me down,' Hattu cried, straining and struggling helplessly in Ishtar's cage of talons.*

*'Why, what could you possibly do?' she drawled. 'You are but one man.'*

*Of all the Trojans down there, only Hektor fared well, spinning and lunging in his suit of painted bronze, his bright helm flashing as he made kill after kill. But his one-man assault left the Trojan battalions without leadership, drifting and confused – their flanks exposed and ripped raw by Agamemnon's war-cars. The ragged remains of each unit were then set upon by the other enemy kings. 'You know me well enough,' he snarled at the Goddess. 'You know I can save some of these men.'*

*'As I thought,' she said. Suddenly, her talons sprang open, and Hattu fell like a stone.*

*He landed upon a pile of corpses, rolling across the wet bodies and scrambling to his feet. Only now he realised that he was weaponless and without armour. Sharp blades milled and whooshed through the air, hair's-widths away from his skin. He dodged and ducked frantically, shooting evil looks up to the winged Goddess still circling the sky. 'Why?' he roared up at her.*

*Just then, a Trojan staggered over to him, limping and bruised. 'Take it,' the man gasped, thrusting a heap of bronze and leather at Hattu. Armour.*

*Hattu grabbed the heap and pulled it on quickly without a second thought. He strapped on the helm last, feeling suddenly secure and strong, then took up shield and spear and began beating back the nearby attackers. 'Battalions, come round,' he bellowed. 'Join flanks!'*

*With a crunching of boots and clatter of bronze the tattered remains of each group began to do so. It was not too late to avert disaster, he realised. That was when he heard the shouting.*

*'Help me!' Hektor cried.*

*Hattu pinpointed the crown prince immediately. He was by the red Scamander side, naked, being held by two horned demons, while Diomedes and Ajax swirled their weapons, ready to slice him in half. Too far away to be saved. Too late.*

*'Where is my armour?' Hektor wailed hopelessly.*

*It was then that Hattu saw the dull reflection of himself in a nearby Trojan's shield... dressed in Hektor's painted scale and bright battle helmet.*

*'Help me!' Hektor cried as Ajax and Diomedes swung their weapons down at him. 'Help m-aargh!'*

Hattu woke with a start, sweating, heart pounding. He sat up in his bed, confused and horrified by the dream. A glance around the tent confirmed that it was still night, blackness reigning outside. Just as his heart began to slow, he heard something out there, creeping, coming closer. *The Shadow?*

He saw the outline of a stranger, saw the tent flap opening... and reached for his swords.

Sirtaya popped his head in through the flap, grinning innocently, a new necklace of what looked like toad bones and oystercatcher feathers hanging around his collar. 'Your advice sunk in at last, Master Hattu.'

'What?' Hattu croaked.

Sirtaya planted a tray with a fresh loaf and a pot of water by the bedside. 'Prince Hektor has agreed to your plans to rearrange the battalions. He also relented on destroying the enemy, and has declared that we will instead push them to their boats and force them to take to the waves as you suggested we should.'

Hattu sighed deeply in relief. Both concessions were like heavy weights lifting from his shoulders.

'He also agrees to a night attack,' Sirtaya added. 'The army is to be ready one hour before dawn.'

Hattu nodded, wondering if he might find a few hours of dream-free sleep before then. 'How long till dawn?'

'Er, one hour,' Sirtaya said with an apologetic shrug.

Hattu groaned, seeing beyond his Egyptian friend the ranks of the five battalions forming quietly in the near-darkness. It was time to rise. With a groan of pain, he slipped from the warm pocket of his bedding, reaching for his kilt and boots, drinking from the water pot and chewing on a mouthful of bread as he dressed. 'Take my heir back to Troy, you hear me? The *Tuhkanti* and the *Labarna* cannot both be risked in battle.'

'It has already been arranged, Master Hattu. All the other non-fighting elites are to take wagons back to the city immediately.'

'That will be all, friend. Now go,' Hattu said, buckling on his bronze armour.

***

The five battalions of Troy moved quickly and quietly through the pre-dawn blackness, spicing the air with a scent of leather and oil. Hattu, leading the fourth, cast a look across the force – their armour glinting like beetles' backs in the light of the sickle moon, the units organised carefully this time so each would understand one another and each had a commander that could understand and translate an order given in any of the main tongues. Even better, Dagon and the chariot wing waited near the river campsite, ready for the moment when the enemy camp was breached and its long shores were opened up to allow those war cars to charge into the fray.

With a crunch of bracken, the battalions moved into the Borean Hills, each sticking to a vale or low pass. Hattu saw a Thracian up ahead, crouching beside the body of an Ahhiyawan watchman. The neck of the corpse shone wet and black, opened before the man could shout in warning.

Soon, the *snap* of bracken became a *shush* of marram grass as they emerged onto the bay side of the hills, the night sea wind furrowing their hair and plumage. Hattu crouched like the others behind rocks, knolls and screens of grass. He swept his eyes along the bay before them, taking in the strange brightness of the sand in the moonlight, the dark mass that was the city of ships and the oily sheen of the dark sea beyond. The grid of lanes between the beached ships was quiet, beaded with torchlight and a handful of strolling sentries and those guarding roped-together prisoners of war. The sand wall was complete, the parapet watch strong – composed of several hundred Locrian bowmen. But they strolled to and fro lazily, wearily, unaware of the military mass observing them.

He glanced along the kneeling Trojan front to Hektor. Their eyes met, and Hektor nodded his approval.

Hattu glanced back over his shoulder. 'Bowmen, forward,' he whispered. Silently, Aeneas led the archer wing onto the downward slope of the hills – a perfect vantage point. There the bowmen of Troy, Dardania, Lukka and Karkisa all sank to one knee. Aeneas mimicked drawing a bow – a silent gesture that relied on no knowledge of tongues. In perfect unison, the many archers of Troy stretched their bows likewise.

***

The men of the Locrian watch padded along the high sand battlements, swapping wine skins and bawdy jokes. Marcion swigged his share then passed it on. 'I'd better not have too much or I'll be soft by the time I get back to my blankets,' he said, glancing down to the Locrian area of the bay. The beached ship's timbers were dry and cracked and he was sick of the black flies that patrolled the air there. But the Trojan bitch he had captured on a recent raid was there, roped to a stake, and she made the nights more enjoyable. He imagined what he would do to her tonight, scratching at a plague boil as he did so. 'One more drink and it'll be time for the next watch,' he murmured to himself, raising the skin to his lips. Something popped, and wetness soaked his bare torso. He glanced at the drinking skin, confused by the arrow that had pierced it. He turned to his nearest comrade to ask what was going on, but that one stood like a pole, another arrow quivering in his eye socket. Marcion heard a hiss from the night sky and looked up to see hundreds more bronze beaked arrows whooshing down. One ripped off his genitals, sending the pain of the

Gods through him in the instant before another smashed through his throat lump and destroyed his windpipe before he could scream. Sliding down the inside of the sand wall, he saw scores of his fellow Locrians fall like this, peppered with Trojan arrows.

***

A train of wagons rumbled north, taking the king and queen and the elites back to Troy. Sirtaya leaned from the side of one vehicle, his long neck twisted so he could look back towards the Borean Hills. The broad front of Troy's army had some time ago vanished through the clefts in the range like fingers ruffling through hair. Just then, the skies above the hills glinted, as if a flock of shiny-feathered birds were speeding across the night sky. Sirtaya's eyes widened like moons as he realised it was a storm of arrows – the start of the attack. 'It has begun,' he said over his shoulder, into the wagon where Tudha sat.

Not looking away from the direction of battle, the Egyptian toyed anxiously with his new necklace of toad bones and feathers. In days past he would have pressed his case to be part of the Trojan force, to fight alongside Master Hattu or at least to serve as a battle runner. But these days were different. In the moons since winter, he had laboured somewhat to do things he could previously do without breaking sweat. It was as if he wore bands of metal on his limbs, slowing and tiring him. He was getting old, just like Hattu! And that infernal ache in his belly – how many days had it persisted now? Regardless of his ageing body, his mind was still young, and fighting every step of the way.

'Your father will finish this today,' he said to Tudha. 'His plans last night were as intricate as those that won him all his victories past.' Sirtaya bit his lip, realising that this kind of talk would likely stoke Tudha's ire, stoke some sour comment about his victory at Hatenzuwa and how nobody spoke of it in the same way. But for once there was no retort. 'By agreeing to this night strike, Hektor has seen sense at last.'

Sirtaya sighed and slipped back inside the wagon window to sit by the Hittite Prince. Tudha kept his head down, his cloak hood up. Sirtaya frowned, used to Tudha's moods, but not this level of disinterest in such a crucial battle. 'Master Tudha!' he snapped, angry and forgetting that he was talking to the heir to the Hittite Empire. He pulled down the hood, mouth shaping to berate him further, then halted, stunned.

The slave stared back at him, doe-eyed and grinning with guilt. 'The

*Tuhkanti* commanded me to take his place,' the boy mumbled. 'He said he had to go.'

Sirtaya's heart leapt into his mouth. 'What? You? Then where…'

He clambered half out of the wagon window again, staring back at the hills, the clouds of arrows flying above and the rising shouts of battle. 'Master Tudha, what have you done!'

***

As the arrow storm thinned, Hattu swept his gaze along the sand wall parapet. The sentries had been wiped out entirely and with little commotion. And from within the enemy camp? Nothing. Utter silence.

Rising from his haunches, Hattu twisted to his battalion – Sarpedon and Masturi both waiting for the call with eager eyes. 'Forward,' he waved madly. They charged out from the Borean Hills. In their midst a team of fifty of Masturi's Seha Riverlanders carried a huge pine trunk, carved to a point, on a cradle of leather straps. The device was rudimentary, Hattu knew, but it was all they could craft in the limited time since last night, and it would surely be enough to smash in the sand wall's crude gates. Surely? They reached the point near the foot of the hills where earth became sand and pounded out across the bay towards the sand gate.

He glanced up at the parapet every few steps, seeing nothing, nothing… then finally, a few new faces rose there, gawping down at the battalion. One gormless-looking Spartan's face twisted in horror, his mouth contorting into a wide circle: 'Troy attacks!' he screamed.

'Move,' Hattu yelled now, all cause for hush gone. But they could only move as fast as the shuffling, sweating ram bearers they were assigned to protect.

Within a breath, horns were blaring inside the sand camp and bells clanged. Raised voices pealed out from every spot within. An instant later and a new wall of faces appeared up on the stockade, bristling with javelins, bows, whirling slings and rocks, all taking aim at the approaching battalion.

*Now, Aeneas... NOW!* Hattu willed the call to come.

From back at the hills, another hissing and dense cloud of shafts sped over Hattu's head and hammered into these new defenders, piercing eye-sockets, throats and chests, punching them back from view. Aeneas had read the danger.

Closer they ran towards the sand wall gate. But only for a fresh wave of defenders to appear at the parapets, and this time they were clad in bronze or bearing shields. The next arrow volley from Aeneas' archers clanked down and zinged from the enemy shells. In the breath that followed, the defenders raised their own javelins and bows and slings, taking aim at the approaching ram battalion.

'Shields up,' Hattu bawled. With a clatter of leather and bronze screens, they formed a roof over themselves and the ram carriers. He heard the rapid, echoing breaths of them all under the makeshift shelter. As they moved closer, deep *thumps* sounded all around him as the bombardment began. His own shield juddered and jolted as all sorts of heavy objects were tossed down upon them. Spears pierced through the shield roof, inviting in fingers of weak moonlight. One man screamed. Hattu glanced back to see a spear sinking through the man's shield and shoulder. With a gout of blood, he fell away, but the others quickly reorganised to close the gap. A ram-bearing Riverlander near Hattu jerked violently as a stone axe hurtled in through one gap and cracked open his bare head like an egg. The man babbled in tongues, blood pumping from his ears and nose, and them whumped, face-first onto the sand. Hattu grabbed the leather strap the man had been supporting. Dozens more of the battalion fell like this before they reached the rough-hewn timbers of the sand wall gate.

Here, the ram squadron slowed. 'Heave!' Hattu, Masturi and Sarpedon growled. With bulging triceps and flexing torsos, Hattu and the ram handlers brought the leather cradle and the log back… then swooshed it forth again. His whole body juddered as the tip crashed against the gate timbers, sending a grievous crack up and down the planks. Even better, it came with the stark *crunch* of a horizontal locking bar on the inside breaking. A low wail of dismay sounded from up on the sand wall parapets, while the Trojan masses watching from the safety of the ridge slope exploded in cheers.

'Heave!' Hattu called again. His shoulders ached and trembled as he helped swing the ram again. He saw the faces of the others, eyes screwed shut, grimacing with effort, sweat rivulets darting across their faces.

Now he heard the dull rumble of voices from above, heard the *thump* of descending feet and a gruff and urgent Ahhiyawan voice. 'At them!'

Hattu glanced out from the edge of the shield roof to see men streaming down the steep slope of the sand wall. A sally over the parapet, he realised, from both sides of the gate. A huge force. He and the ram crew could not bring their weapons to bear, nor could those holding their shields overhead.

*Crunch!* the ram battered into the gates again, and the timbers sagged inwards. Just one more strike…

'Kill them all!' the gruff Ahhiyawan voice howled, the thumping feet descending closer.

Hattu knew he had to act, to drop the ram and draw his spear or swords… but then the gate would remain unbroken and the attack would have failed before it had truly started.

'Battalions of Troy,' Hektor cried from the Borean Hills, 'charge!'

Just as Hattu had advocated, the officers each relayed the command in different tongues. The other four battalions and Aeneas' archer wing came flooding down onto the beach in a massive wave of bronze and leather, intercepting the sallying enemy. He saw flashes of Trojans running at foes, their swords smashing away enemy blades. Invading soldiers folded over belly strikes, hands spun free of wrists and blood spurted freely. Within moments the enemy sally force was obliterated.

*Crunch!* The ram pounded again – this time right through the gates, sending them flying inwards. Hattu dropped the biting leather straps. As the ram thumped into the ground, he gawped at the sight of big Ajax and his Army of Salamians hurrying towards the broken gates carrying planks and logs intended to bolster them.

'At them!' Hattu screamed. From behind, Masturi and Sarpedon echoed his cry. Hektor, Paris and every other Trojan commander added their voice to the refrain as the entire Trojan Army now surged forward through the broken gates. In response, pockets of Ahhiyawans powered from the shore and the ships towards the gates, intent on damming the breach.

Hattu shortened his strides as he sensed Ajax – the greatest of the defenders – loping directly for him. *Whoosh!* went the giant's staff, nearly knocking Hattu's helm from his head as he ducked. He dived sideways to miss the follow-up swipe of Ajax's towering shield, then tossed his spear at the colossus. The lance whacked hard against Ajax's breastplate but did not pierce it, yet it sent him stumbling backwards. That tiny reversal was like a single piece of straw falling loose from a dam, and a river bursting through. As the first rays of dawn streaked over the bay, the Trojans barged past and slew the first enemy defenders, then pushed on into the heart of the Ahhiyawan beach camp, flooding into the maze of alleys between the black-hulled ships. Half-prepared enemy warriors swung round in shock, bawling at their charges to defend the precious boats. Diomedes burst from the shell of captured armour that was his hut, head sweeping to and fro, eyes wide with horror as he snatched up his cyclops shield. Up on the prows of their beached ships, Menelaus, old Nestor and Odysseus howled along the bay camp, calling men to this position and that.

'With me,' Hattu cried, forging through the chaos, the men of his battalion coming with him. *Clang!* a bronze enemy hammer pounded on a Riverlander's shield, blasting him away. *Riiip!* a Lukkan's stomach was torn open by a hooked pole.

A familiar war scream tore across the mass of helmets and slashing weapons like a streak of lightning. Hattu saw Diomedes' hurtling spear before he saw the champion. It came flashing at Hattu's face like a bolt of lightning. He cranked his head to one side with nothing to spare, and the lance sped on into the shield of one of Masturi's men in the ranks behind. 'Next time, Hittite, I will have your head and your helm to decorate my hut,' Diomedes foamed as the press of battle carried the two away from one another. Masturi and his Riverlanders too were pulled away from Hattu's battalion – becoming entangled with the Cretans.

In the next instant, a Tirynean soldier burst through the chaos and came barrelling at Hattu, sword drawn and swinging. The blade clattered against Hattu's helm. Dazed, he saw the man's follow-up neck-slash at the last moment and leaned back, the tip passing a finger's-width from his jugular, then rammed his spear up and under the bare armpit of the Tirynean swordsman. The spearhead cracked and crunched deep, mashing one lung and bursting his heart. He pulled the lance free in a shower of black gristle, growling through an animal rictus, swinging the weapon round to pierce another man through the neck. Quickly he found himself in that black whirling void that he knew all too well, where his body grew numb and his mind aflame with the animal will to survive and to protect those standing with him at all and any cost.

He and Sarpedon parried and blocked, leapt and feinted, cutting down attackers, and all the way his battalion was whittled away or drawn into pockets of fighting here and there. Soon he, Sarpedon and the small pack of Lukkans left with them tumbled out of the battle at its far edge. They had reached the shore side of the bay camp, the sea wind prowling strongly here.

'We are ready to charge in again, just give the word,' Sarpedon panted, swinging to face the press, swaying on his feet, steam rising from his sweat and blood soaked body.

'No,' Hattu answered. 'Wait.' He spotted the mound of grain sacks nearby, and clambered up to its summit to take in the shape of the battle. The struggle was horrendous and evenly-balanced, a seething mess of blood and metal, glittering in the rising sun, sand and blood spray rising in bursts. He saw Kalchas the augur once more holding aloft bloodied Trojan organs, the blood showering him, Sherden pirates savaging the bodies for armour and any remaining valuables. Trojan Guardians too, falling upon the healers' tents, swords swinging down upon the helpless plague victims in there. One held up a boil-riddled severed head and danced a jig as if it was a worthy war trophy. If the battle continued like this it would be like his taking of Hattusa – when both his army and that of his murderous nephew had been whittled away to almost nothing. A fool's victory. This had to end. Now.

The crash of huge breakers sounded like a call from the Mother Goddess, reminding him what he had to do. The waves glittered as they rose then foamed down upon the shore. A low tide, he realised. A broad stripe of bare sand running along the waterline… and the gatehouse, smashed wide open and undefended, with broad tracks looping round from there to the shoreline. A perfect run for chariots to herd the Ahhiyawans towards the waves, towards their boats. His every hackle stood proud with hope.

He pulled the triton shell from his belt, held it to his lips and blew. As the last of three short, high notes pealed above the noise of combat, he stared back at the Borean Hills, willing his oldest comrade to come to battle.

'Ha!' Sarpedon barked. 'It is that time, eh? Time for the ground to rumble?'

'Aye,' Hattu burred. 'And now we must return to the fray.'

'But where, *Labarna?*' Sarpedon asked, eyeing the edges of battle, seeking a place to engage.

Hattu scanned the action too. There were a dozen points of weakness he knew he should go to support. Hektor against the soldiers of Ajax, Paris in his struggles with the Pylians. But then his eyes snagged on something right in the middle of the battling masses. Mycenaeans, hacking at a small group of Trojans, and coming to finish the job was their king and the *Wanax* of the enemy expedition, Agamemnon, standing tall in his chariot, lion hooded, spear hoisted and ready to throw.

Amongst the beset Trojans he saw one. A young warrior with a blood-red headband, silver eyes wide as he locked swords with a Mycenaean veteran. Hattu's heart fell into his boots.

*Tudha?*

***

As the three notes of the Trojan horn struck through the sky, Tudha staggered round in a tight circle, deafened by the clash and clatter all around him, lips wet with another man's blood, the bronze sword in his hand notched and bent. The Trojan Guardian he had been fighting alongside suddenly dropped his arms to his side. Tudha snatched a look at the man's face, only to see nothing there but a hacked through neck stump, vomiting blood. The man's severed head thumped into the gory sand and rolled across the ground before him, tongue jutting, eyes bulging. The bald Mycenaean killer roared in triumph, shaking his dripping sword aloft then pacing towards Tudha, who jinked away from the man's strike, then parried the next, being driven back. His every second step was a splash into a pool of spilled bowels or a crunch across a hacked-apart cadaver. Spurts of entrails, blood and saliva leapt past and over him and the stink was overpowering. Swords whooshed past him like sudden gusts and arrows hummed overhead like bees. He was alone now, cut off from his group.

In those moments before first light when they had been crouching in the hills, the men of Deiphobus' battalion had been so nervous and focused that they had not noticed him sneak up to join their rear ranks. He had felt invincible during that charge down onto the bay with them, his whole body shuddering with hubris as he cried out with them. As they poured through the gate and into the enemy camp, Aeneas' words had echoed in his mind: *You are the heir to the Hittite Empire. The second most powerful being alive.* It felt as if he had lightning in his veins. This would be the day when all here would see that he was no mere scribe, when he would consign the events of last summer to the pits. Then, like a veil dropping, he had seen that temptress, battle, for what she really was. The warriors of Mycenae had burst from a lane of ships and rushed the battalion's flanks. The Trojans were butchered in their hundreds before they could even turn their spears on their attackers, and the nightmare of blood and screaming had intensified with every heartbeat since.

The bald Mycenaean hacked and swished at him again. Tudha realised the man was not trying to kill him… he was trying to herd him. A whinny sounded from behind, and the sand shivered underfoot. He swung on the ball of one foot to see the thrashing, speeding mass of Agamemnon's war chariot coming right for him, the *Wanax'* face wide with glee, spear hoisted and trained on him.

Unbalanced, arms wide and flailing, Tudha knew he was as good as dead. The past flashed before him like a lightning strike. Boldest of all was the memories from Hatenzuwa. The truth would die with him, he realised, bracing…

…and then a man hammered into his flank. He and the other went tumbling through bloody sand, leaving Agamemnon's spear to rip through the empty space in which he had been standing.

'I suspect you are a good warrior, Prince Tudha. But try not to take on half of the Ahhiyawan Army at once next time, hmm?'

Tudha shook his head to clear it, seeing his saviour: Aeneas. The Dardanian Prince hauled him to his feet. Tudha glanced around: no other Trojan or ally was close. 'Where are your archers?'

'I don't know. Once we flooded inside the gates all order fell away.' His eyes widened, staring beyond Tudha. 'Be ready!'

Tudha twisted to see Agamemnon wheeling round, a new spear raised, his chariot flanked by six more. 'Time to bleed, Hittite boy…'

'Move!' Aeneas screamed.

But Tudha shook him off, setting his feet wide apart, dipping his head like a bull set to charge. This time, he was ready.

'Tudha, are you mad?' Aeneas yelled. He paced towards Tudha, set on pulling him away again, only for a Sherden to block his path, brandishing a trident.

Tudha felt the bay shudder under him, heard the blood hammer in his ears and fastened his eyes on Agamemnon. The horses pounded closer until Tudha could feel the spray of their saliva and the wet sand thrown up by their hooves. The enemy warlord screamed in delight, throwing his spear with all his strength. Now Tudha moved, swivelling on one heel to dodge the throw and pirouette clear of the chariot horses' hooves, into the gap between that vehicle and the one flanking it. Still in the same spinning motion, he grasped the lip of that flanking chariot's side and tensed his body, letting the vehicle lift him from the ground and swing right round and into the cabin. With a jerk of his sword arm, he rammed the hilt against the chariot driver's temple. The man fell like a sack of stones from the back of the war-car, the reins flailing loose. The stunned warrior gawped at the driver's plight, then clumsily swished his spear up, the tip streaking across Tudha's face from chin to forehead. Tudha roared in pain, batted the spear away, then headbutted the stunned warrior, smashing in the man's nose and sending him toppling away too. He grabbed the loose reins and tugged on the rightmost, bringing the chariot veering in sharply towards Agamemnon's until the wheels bumped. Both chariots jounced and splinters flew. Agamemnon, stunned, let out a high-pitched wail, reaching for his sheathed sword. Tudha slashed across the small gap, bringing his blunted bronze blade down to strike the enemy leader on the forearm, biting into the flesh.

White with shock, the Great King shrieked, staring at Tudha then at the wound and the sheets of blood pulsing from it. 'Take me back to my ship!' he demanded to his driver with a tremulous cry. The royal chariot peeled away and the other chariots of Mycenae followed like starlings.

Tudha's captured war-car limped badly thanks to a damaged wheel. He turned sharply back towards the beset Aeneas then tugged hard on both reins, bringing it to a halt, then leapt down into the bloody sand, using his momentum to drive his bent, blunt bronze sword down between the shoulder blades of the trident-wielding Sherden.

The pirate fell in a series of bloody spasms, revealing Aeneas. The pair found themselves in a pocket of respite left behind by the departure of the Mycenaean chariotry.

Aeneas stared at Tudha, whose face was half red with blood from the spear wound. 'You saved me. You... you nearly slew the enemy leader... alone. You leapt aboard a speeding chariot!'

'It is not new. I did as much in the winning of the war at Hatenzuwa.'

Aeneas recoiled in confusion. '*That* is what your father resents you for?'

Tudha smiled with one side of his mouth and shook his head. 'There were many things I did at Hatenzuwa. That was just one of them.'

The eye of calm evaporated then, as dark shadows fell across the pair.

'The nephew of Priam... and *you*, the Hittite boy-prince,' Diomedes purred, stalking over with his spear resting on his shoulder, a crew of his Tiryneans with him, all steaming with blood. 'Your head should already have been split by my sword last night.'

Tudha and Aeneas braced.

'You can have all the armour, Diomedes,' said Ajax, arriving on their other side with a squadron of Salamians, 'so long as *I* get the Hittite boy's head. Agamemnon will pay well for both.'

Now Tudha and Aeneas pressed together, back to back, bent weapons raised.

'Very well,' Diomedes smirked, then roared, 'tear them apart!'

The enemies around them exploded in a raucous cry. But they planted no more than a foot forward when the sand underfoot began to shudder and a snapping of whips sounded. All halted, looking up, suspecting that their *Wanax* had come back to the fray. Tudha knew better, seeing over their heads to the north, to the Borean Hills: a tide of bronze and leather, of thrashing manes and hooves, spilling over the hills and down through the sand wall gates and into the bay camp. Nearly three hundred chariots – the wing of Troy and the allied squadrons of Lukka. A horn sounded from the lead chariot and the war-cars came slicing round the edge of the bay camp and streaking along the shoreline, spreading into a narrow V like a skein of geese. Tudha saw Dagon driving the lead vehicle, wet with spray from the breakers.

'Loose!' Dagon cried, meeting Tudha's eye and double-taking. Three hundred javelins sailed from the battle-cars, plunging into the backs and flanks and chests of the Ahhiyawan soldiery around Tudha and Aeneas. Men screamed and fell. Like a knife the chariots plunged into the corridor of space this created in the swell of fighting bodies. The chariot warriors now sliced, stabbed and bludgeoning the enemy from the sides of their cars. Ahhiyawans spun away, faces and necks ripped, heads crushed. The rest scattered back from this deadly charge like deer from a wolf pack.

Dagon peeled away from his fleet – his warrior crumpled and broken by an axe strike to the shoulder. He slowed near Tudha and Aeneas. 'Prince Tudha?' he panted as he helped the stricken warrior down onto the sand. 'What in the name of Tarhunda are you doing here?'

'What I was born to do. What I one day will have to do,' he replied, the bloodsoaked half of his face bending upwards in a fierce rictus. 'Let me ride with you, as we did at Hatenzuwa.' Dagon's mouth shaped to protest, but Tudha continued before he could: 'The battle turns, let us finish it.'

Packs of Aeneas' archers gathered around them, driving away enemy soldiers who tried to close in with short, deadly volleys. 'The young prince is right, Chariot Master,' said Aeneas. 'The fray tilts, look!

The enemy *Wanax* has fled from the battle and the rest of them are losing their nerve.'

Dagon saw what they were seeing: the Ahhiyawans, falling back into the lanes between the ships, shouting in panic, heads switching to and fro in search of the missing Agamemnon.

'It is just as father wanted. We have them penned in to their beached boats. Now we just need to herd them to the sea.'

'Get onboard,' Dagon said flatly.

Tudha took the wounded warrior's sword and clambered into the cabin. 'Until tonight, at the victory feast,' he said to Aeneas with a stony confidence.

Aeneas flashed him a parting grin. 'May Apollo ride with you, friend.'

Dagon lashed his whip high above the traces and the chariot jerked into life, coming round to re-take its place at the head of the roving chariot wing and to lead them onto the shoreside, spray thrown up by the wheels ballooning into an iridescent mist in their wake. They came face to face with a band of Locrians who were speeding along the sands in the opposite direction, intent on escaping into the grasslands at the end of the bay. The Locrians shrieked in fright, skidding and stumbling when they saw the fearsome chariot wing hurtling towards them.

'Loose!' Dagon called out, conjuring another rain of missiles. Tudha – without a spear, tossed the throwing stick Aeneas had given him. The spears sped into the Locrians, felling many and driving the rest back towards the city of beached boats. The throwing stick spun madly, clipping one man on the back of the head, knocking him out cold and intensifying the panic. As they passed the fallen man, Tudha hung expertly from the side of the cabin to snatch the stick up. The Locrians fled back to and clustered around the ships, brandishing spears in a desperate defence. The sea wind whipped at Tudha's curls as Dagon drove the chariots at full-tilt for these horrified soldiers. 'Ready,' Tudha cried this time to the chariots behind, who each took up a fresh javelin. 'And…' At the last moment, Dagon wheeled away from the panicked Locrians, '…turn!' The chariot wing glided round in his wake, javelins unthrown.

'Get on your cursed ships,' Tudha screamed at them over his shoulder, 'or die.'

The war-cars of Troy circled there, driving back any groups who tried to break away from the beached boats. Group after group tried to sally and were driven back. Soon, Tudha heard something. Hammers knocking at wood. He saw it now too – on the stripe of boats nearest the waterline: Ahhiyawans, battering away the semi-rotten chocks holding their boats upright on the beach; others had tossed away their weapons and now dragged madly on ropes, trying to tug their boats towards the shallows, the keels grinding and ploughing up thick folds of damp sand.

Tudha's eyes widened. 'It's working.'

'It's their only way out now,' said Dagon, head cranked forward like a hawk tracking prey, twisting slowly as they circled again.

One Cretan ship reached the surf and the prow began to rise with the swell, a churn of white water and disturbed sand belching out around it. The men shinned up the ropes and clambered aboard as the boat broke free of the sands. Further up the bay, men straining to pull another ship were nearly at the waves. Another six were on the move like this just beyond.

He and Dagon exchanged looks of hope. After ten years… the enemies of Troy were on the run at last.

At that moment, a cry echoed across the bay. 'Chariots of Troy – destroy them!'

Tudha and Dagon's heads snapped round. 'Hektor?'

The Crown Prince of Troy, rampaging through the swell of the infantry battle with the Guardians, coated in blood, bawled to the shoreside again. 'Don't let them escape – kill them all!'

Tudha's blood ran cold. Behind him, the hooves of the many Trojan chariots accelerated, breaking from the circular path they had been beating until now, speeding in a direct line up the shore towards the boats being dragged for the waves.

'Come back!' Dagon screamed after them. Only the chariots of Lukka remained with him and Tudha. The rest were deaf to Dagon's pleas, thundering for the nearest of the escaping boats.

The Cretan men hauling that vessel caught wind of the chariot charge. Their faces turned to and gawped at the Trojan war-cars. First one man threw down his rope and ran, then every other followed. They sprinted back from the waves like reluctant swimmers, speeding back into the city of ships for shelter. The unsupported vessel groaned in complaint, before crashing down on its side in a thunderous boom of collapsing timbers, shredded planks flying and sand rising in a bloated cloud.

The men dragging the other ships, halfway towards the waters, all heard this calamitous din, all turned and saw the chariot wing speeding along the bay and spearing down the terrified Cretans like fish. 'I come to settle our debt, you dogs,' one Trojan nobleman screamed from his chariot as he lopped off a Cretan's head: 'Ten summers of slaughter, repaid with the edge of my sword.' Scores more enemy soldiers fell. Now more groups abandoned their efforts, dropped their ropes and ran back towards the city of ships.

'No,' Dagon croaked.

One vessel that had made it partly into the waves came crashing down on its side. The prow, already in the water, thunderclapped into the shallows, sending up a huge geyser of foam.

'*No!*' Dagon croaked, hoarse.

Tudha's face drained of colour as every single Ahhiyawan rope-crew fled like this, the escape to the waves snuffed out, their one way out closed. 'Never interrupt your enemy when he is in the process of withdrawing,' he said quietly, repeating his father's mantra.

Dagon slowed the chariot, stunned, and he and Tudha watched from a distance as the rest of the wing now plunged into the city of ships, spearing into the backs of those fleeing into the lanes. The enemy warriors locked in combat with Hektor's men saw this and now took to desperately scrambling up the sides of their boats, being hauled up by the arms and dragged over the rails onto the decks. They gathered around the lips of their vessels, using them like forts, throwing down rocks and spears as if at sea and trying to ward off sharks.

Amidst it all, Tudha saw Nestor of Pylos, beset on all sides by Lukkan warriors, his chariotry being torn down around him. Everywhere, Ahhiyawan champions vanished in spurts of blood. From the midst of it all, Prince Hektor, crusted in the gore of the slain, howled: 'Where are you, Agamemnon? Too cowardly to fight me in person?'

From up on the deck of a Salamian ship – panicked defenders bristling at the rails – Ajax swung his staff down at the Trojans trying to climb aboard, braining one and smashing the spine of another. Diomedes too slashed wildly to defend his Tirynean flagship.

The Trojan masses – albeit slightly fewer in number – dominated the lanes between the ships now. They swarmed up and down, raining arrows and javelins up onto the boats, clambering up ladders and ropes to storm the decks, others rocking the ships in attempts to pitch them over.

Tudha could sense it just as he had sensed the last turns of the battle to quell the rebellion at Hatenzuwa. 'We're winning,' he said.

'Aye,' said Dagon, setting his reins down. 'but not in the way your father wanted.'

***

While the battle raged all round the outer lanes of the city of ships, the centre was akin to the eye of a storm, the lanes empty.

Agamemnon shuffled on his splendid throne, awkward and uncomfortable in full armour, his lion hood hanging limp over one knee. The stink of blood permeated his shady hut, and the clash and clatter of battle nearby came and went in echoing, distorted waves. He winced as a healer cleaned his forearm cut, packed it with terebinth resin to cleanse it and then smeared it with sheep's fat to seal the lesion, before dressing it in a strip of white linen. He stared at the shaking limb, his mind flashing with memories of the Hittite boy-prince who had beaten his chariot crews and so nearly slain him. The Hittites were known as creatures of great skill… but that young man was almost preternatural.

He looked up: Odysseus and Patroklos were there too, watching anxiously as the sounds of battle outside drifted closer to the hut. Apart from these three, only a handful of his guards were here, and two slaves bearing a freshly-resharpened sword.

'Your blade is honed as you commanded, *Wanax*,' they bowed, offering him the weapon. 'Ready for you to return to battle.'

Agamemnon glanced to the hut's open door and the brightness out there. His retinue of chariot elites stood in a ring, backs to the hut, spears trained on the empty space around it and in particular at the two ends of this empty 'lane'. How long before the marauding Trojan mass would spill into view and swamp this lane too. What then, he fretted – a desperate last stand aboard the decks of his flagship?

Just then, a guttural roar bounced through the air outside. 'Where are you, Agamemnon? Too cowardly to fight me in person?' Hektor's challenge shuddered through the hut, shaking Agamemnon to his marrow. Hektor, the great hero of Troy. Some claimed he wore an invisible suit of armour, granted to him by Apollo himself.

*I too am a great warrior,* he told himself. The best in Mycenae – as he had proven when he had stormed the Lion's Hall and seized that kingdom for himself, throwing from the throne the dog who had usurped his father. He stared again at the proffered sword. The thought of having to answer Hektor's call turned his guts to liquid. He was tired, and the wound had caused him to lose a fair amount of blood. To go out there and face the enemy champion-prince? The stinking heat, the many eyes upon him, everything to lose. Grasping and ungrasping the arms of his throne, he muttered to himself over and over. *You can do this. You must do this. Think of all you have given up just to be here, with the prize of Troy in reach.*

Yet he imagined at that moment the opposite: Hektor's blade driving down through his collarbone. The feeling of the cold bronze slicing down through his organs. The humiliation and the pain. This new wave of fear turned his thoughts again. 'We cannot put to sea?' he asked.

Odysseus looked at him with an arched eyebrow. 'Did you not hear the thunder, *Wanax?* The Trojans have slain the crews of the ships which tried, and those boats lie broken on the shores. Worse, they have pulled down the sand bastion gates and sections of that rampart. They have us penned here like goats.'

Just then, a new cry reverberated around the hut. Hektor again: 'Bring fire. Burn the ships. Burn them all and every Ahhiyawan within to ashes!'

Now Agamemnon's fears multiplied. He gripped the arms of his throne tightly. Death by fire had always been his greatest fear. Ever since childhood, when he had crawled into a smith's kiln to play and fallen asleep in the cold, soft ashes. The smith had come in, unawares, and loaded the kiln with kindling, then set it ablaze. The cage of flames had stolen the breath from his lungs, the heat had bitten and stung at him fiercely. Only when he was blind with pain and panic had the smith realised, smashed the kiln open and saved him.

A heartbeat later, an Ahhiyawan swell of terror rose. One common cry rose louder than the rest: 'We need Achilles!'

Agamemnon, Odysseus and Patroklos all shared a look.

'The answer is clear to me,' said Patroklos. He stabbed a finger towards the hut's dark northern wall. 'Four ship's lengths from here, on the far edge of our camp, the Myrmidons sit idle. Five hundred of the best warriors in all Ahhiyawa. Twenty five chariots. All chosen men. Chosen by Achilles. Achilles, descended from the Gods, the man who has won us how many Trojan heads? He who cannot be killed? How many towns and their loot of grain has he taken? How many battles has he turned for us?'

Agamemnon's hackles stood on end. 'I did everything to bring him back to the fold,' he growled. 'Everything except bend my knee to him. I offered him the return of his war bride, treasure too!'

'He came here for glory. Do not deny him,' Patroklos protested. 'Let me go to him.'

'If he will not listen to his *Wanax,* why would he listen to you, his underling?' Agamemnon scowled.

Patroklos laughed, exuding confidence. 'Even after all these years, you still do not realise that Achilles respects men, not titles. We share our food, our prizes, our grief, we lie together with our slaves. He and I know a bond that I doubt you share with anyone.'

Odysseus' eyes slid towards Patroklos. 'Be careful, old friend.'

'On the edge of death for every man here, what is there to be afraid of?' Patroklos replied, then appealed again to Agamemnon. 'So what is it to be, *Wanax?* Either you sit here and prepare to burn…'

Agamemnon gulped, a bead of sweat speeding down his face.

'… or you take up your sword and step outside to face Hektor…'

Just then the shouts and hollers and smashing of battle rose in sonorous waves, and the milling shadows of the fray bent around the end of this lane of ships. Agamemnon felt the urge to vomit.

'…or you let me do as I ask.'

Agamemnon disguised a trembling lip with one ring-encrusted hand. With the other, resting on the top of a white, blood-streaked greave, he flicked a forefinger. 'Go.'

# CHAPTER 9

## THE LION WAKES

In the midst of battle, Hattu's head pulsed with thirst and exhaustion. '*Tuhkanti*?' he yelled again, elbowing allies out of the way, blocking, slashing, frantically looking for his heir. How many hours of this horror had passed since he had spotted him in the middle of the fray? Had it been his eyes playing tricks? Maybe it was another soldier he had mistaken for his heir? No, it could not have been – no other footsoldier present in this land could have blown apart Agamemnon's chariot charge like that.

With a great cry of triumph, the Trojan Guardians sent a crimson-hulled Ithacan ship toppling over, crashing into the one nearest, wrecking both and pulverising many aboard each. One man fell on fangs of snapped timbers, the sharp points piercing him from groin to throat. Another landed on the sand then took the mast of the falling ship full on the crown, the heavy log dashing his head and crumpling his body. Those who rolled or scrambled free of the chaos – many helpless and without swords – were speared to death by the rampant Guardians.

'What are you doing? Let them flee,' he croaked, horror-struck, watching as they mowed down any who tried to escape, seeing the boats lying toppled over near the shore – it made no sense. This was not the plan. Hektor had agreed to drive the enemy to sea, not to trap and obliterate them on the sand. Yet the Trojan infantry mobbed around the boats, rocking and hacking, while the Trojan chariots sped in a pattern of corralling loops around the city of ships, showering the boats' decks with arrows and then, whenever any of the Ahhiyawans tried to descend into a lane to counterattack, they would gallop down that lane, slicing them down.

'*Labarna*,' Sarpedon panted, stabbing his blade into the ground, bending double, his handsome face creased with the effort to draw breath. Hattu lent him an arm of support. 'What is this?' the Lukkan panted. 'We were supposed to drive off the enemy of Troy. Not to pin them here and butcher every last one of th-.'

'Bring fire,' Hektor's voice thundered across the fight. 'Burn the ships. Burn them all and every Ahhiyawan aboard to ashes!'

Hattu and Sarpedon froze, gawping, the words blowing away the earlier plan completely. Just then, a knot of elite Trojan archers touched their pitch-soaked arrows to a burning brazier. 'Are you mad?' Hattu snarled, shoving down the bows of two of them.

'Prince Hektor calls for the enemy ships to be burned,' said one, just as blazing arrows whizzed from the bows of the others, streaking into the dry timbers of the nearest boat. Hattu watched in horror as the vessel took light and quickly became a wall of flames. Black smoke bulged across the blue sky.

'We have been at Troy since the second year of the war,' Sarpedon snarled at the Trojan bowmen. 'But we did not come here for this.'

Hattu glanced beyond the Lukkan King to see that his soldiers, dripping red from the push of battle, now stood back, chests heaving, looking on stonily, their bows stowed on their shoulders. Same too with Masturi and his Seha Riverlanders – all refusing to launch fire arrows.

The grinding of chariot wheels right behind him brought Hattu round on one heel, swords raised to fight this strike. But he froze like that, seeing the war-car and the two on board. 'Dagon… and *you?*' He dropped both blades and seized Tudha by the collar, pulling him nose to nose, eyes darting over the deep vertical slash running down his heir's face. 'Why are you here?' he seethed. 'You are the *Tuhkanti*. You and I cannot be in battle at the same time. If we were both struck down it would be disastrous for the Hittite realm.'

Tudha held his stare. 'For the realm?' he growled. 'That is all you care about, isn't it?'

'While *you* care only for the smell of blood!' Hattu snarled.

Still Tudha stared back at him, silent and composed.

'Hattu,' Dagon intervened, stepping between the pair. 'Tudha turned the tide of this battle. Had he not arrived, then-'

'I saw his reckless leap at the enemy battle-cars,' Hattu rasped, shoving Tudha away as if he was ablaze. 'But I am more interested in Troy's chariots. Why are they running down the enemy who are trying to flee? Why did you not hold them back?'

'I led them into the fray today, but they turned at the first sound of Hektor's commands to them.'

Hattu twisted this way and that, seeing the seething cauldron of fighting around the ships now. The Ahhiyawans trapped in a fight to the death.

Somewhere above, an eagle shrieked. Many heads shot up.

'Andor?' Hattu whispered, seeing his eagle swooping and rising a short way north of the epicentre of battle.

'An omen,' many Trojan voices babbled. 'An *eradi.* A sign from the Gods. The battle is about to be won!'

But Hattu, Dagon and Tudha alone knew what Andor's flight pattern meant. Trouble was stirring.

Hattu's gaze fell like a lump of lead to the patch of ground below Andor, at a distant edge of the beach camp. There, the weltering heat haze hovering above the sand seemed to bulge and mutate for a moment… before a great host of soldiery burst through it, as if emerging from another realm. Fresh and unstained, they came with a huge roar: spearmen in burnished dark shells of bronze, single white horns rising from the brows of their helms. From the spear of one fluttered a cloth emblazoned with a black boar. Now every Trojan voice changed, dropping into low, tight tones. 'The Myrmidons? Apollo, spare us!' Blazing a trail at their head came a compact squadron of white chariots, led by a man in a glorious golden helm and a jacket of silver-chased armour. Hattu squinted, unblinking, knowing where he had seen that armour before... on that first day here.

'Achilles!' the Trojan masses now wailed. 'Achilles fights!'

Hattu felt a horrible shiver at the sudden change of mood. In that moment the press of Trojan soldiers all around the Ahhiyawan ships slackened. They backstepped, ceding ground, their noose of spears around the city of ships loosening. 'No,' he shouted across the ranks of Guardians and allies as they backed away. 'This is worse even than the slaughter. To let victory slip away after all that has gone on today? So many deaths will mean nothing, *nothing!*'

But they were deaf to him. Achilles bawled and brayed, steering them with his voice right into one lane where a clutch of Trojan Guardians were rocking an enemy boat. The Myrmidons exploded like shards of a dropped urn, springing and leaping, hacking Troy's weary elites down. At this, the Ahhiyawans marooned on their ship-forts exploded with unbridled joy, crowding at the rails, staring in delight.

'Achilles fights!' they roared. Diomedes, Ajax and Nestor leapt down from their decks and returned to battle, thousands of their men coming with them.

From nowhere, Hattu jolted, seized by a pair of hands. Hektor shook him, eyes maddened. 'You said Achilles was not fighting.' The words dripped with blame.

Hattu stared down his nose, ignoring the gross breach of decorum in manhandling a Great King like this. 'I also said we should be cautious, that we should leave the enemy with at least one route of retreat – a plan to which you agreed. And then you closed that door. *You* roused Achilles to battle.'

Then, disaster. The Trojan chariot wing came blazing out from behind one row of ships, unaware of this sudden twist of events. Achilles' and his squadron of war-cars hammered into their flanks, making kindling of dozens, running horses and men through. A bunch of the Myrmidon footsoldiers sprang onto the rest of the slowing, disoriented war-cars, wrestling and slashing at the crews. Now Diomedes and Ajax stalked forward with their wall of warriors towards the Trojan infantry swell.

The Trojan archers now backed away, the Guardians too.

'Stand your ground,' Sarpedon screamed at them. 'If I, an outlander, can stand firm to protect Trojan soil then so must you Trojans!'

Hattu pressed up beside his old comrade in a show of unity. 'Get back into line!' he roared.

'For your city,' Sarpedon bawled, 'for your people, get back int-*hargh!*' he juddered as a javelin punched through his throat, casting him backwards like a toy and showering all nearby in blood.

Hattu stared through the red puff of mizzle by his side where Sarpedon had been, then down at his broken body. Sarpedon of Lukka, Son of Thunder, hero of Kadesh, staunch ally of the Hittite Empire since Hattu's youth. Dead.

'My lord!' Captain Glaucus wailed in a strangled cry, rushing over to and falling to his knees beside his slain king. 'Help me lift his body. He cannot be left on the sand like this.'

But Hattu sensed danger. His eyes slid round to find the spear thrower: Achilles, thundering this way on his dazzling chariot, already taking up his next javelin. Now the Trojan Guardians and allies nearby began to scatter, their nerves failing them.

Achilles led his chariots into Sarpedon's Lukkan host, trampling and beheading. Their arrows and thrown lances whacked and bounced from Achilles' armour – there was little of his skin exposed, just his forearms and his thin, determined mouth. Quickly the Lukkans too were sent running in fright. Hattu found himself stranded with the kneeling, bereft Glaucus and the corpse of Sarpedon.

'Come back. Help me carry his body!' Glaucus appealed again to the retreating wall of allies. 'Help me fight to keep his body. He came here to stand with you,' he appealed to the Guardians. 'You owe him this much at least.'

Hattu, seeing scores of Myrmidons closing in around him and Glaucus, threw up his shield. This was a battle he could not win, he knew. In that breath, Dagon and Tudha arrived at his side, breaking back from the retreating masses. Finally Hektor came too, bringing a small knot of Guardians. All stood back to back and held up their swords and lances like the spines of a threatened porcupine. The Myrmidons came surging for them. Hattu spread his feet to meet their attack. The first of them struck hard, the parry jarring Hattu's body. The next almost caught him off guard. The blows came like rain, and he felt his strength failing him, heard the death screams of others in the defensive knot. Through it all, he saw Achilles' chariot, gliding around the small pocket of resistance. Watching Hektor, waiting…

Spry as a cat, the enemy champion leapt from the moving war-car, landing and half-rolling, lunging up towards the unaware Hektor, hurling his third javelin at the Trojan Crown Prince's back. Hattu, body screaming in protest, lunged out from the small knot of resistance and launched one of his swords through the air. The blade whirred, slicing through the wooden shaft of Achilles' thrown spear, sending the tip fishtailing off to one side harmlessly.

Achilles swung towards Hattu, now adrift of the small defensive knot, alone, sand blowing between the pair. 'You,' he hissed. 'That was a grave mistake. My lance could have ended the war.' His next move was like a lightning-flash: a burst of speed towards Hattu, a feint left then a duck and finally a spring and a sword slash at his flank. Hattu could only down swipe his remaining sword weakly, but it was not enough to stop the enemy's blade from clanging against his bronze scales, dislodging one, sending a pulse of pain though his ribs.

Like a dancer, Achilles stalked around him on the balls of his feet. With an almost animal shudder, he sidestepped left and right in rapid succession, before lunging low, for Hattu's belly. Hattu melted back, but knew at that moment that this man was too fast, too strong. Fresh too, and brimming with belief. Trying to second-guess his movements was like trying to pin a wave in the sand. The blood pounded in his ears, and he began to see spots at the edges of his vision. His ankles – his *damned* ankles – felt like broken glass, grinding with every movement.

Achilles raised his sword level again, swaying on his hips like a cat ready to pounce. He sprang forth, his blade coming round for Hattu's neck. Hattu, even as he raised his own blade to block, knew the response was too slow and weak, and there were no scales on his neck to save him this time. Time became a blur of memories and dreams.

*Clang!*

Achilles barrelled past him, off-balance, his weapon spinning away into the fray. Confused, Hattu stared at the iron sword that had appeared before his face to block the enemy champion's strike, saving him. Hattu's own sword that he had thrown a moment ago. Holding it: Tudha.

Just then a small wave of Trojans ran forth from the retreat to reinforce the defence of Sarpedon's body – enough to drive back the Myrmidon assault. Some flooded around Hattu too, protecting him and Tudha. Achilles, grimacing, his sword hand shaking from the trauma of Tudha's block, backed away, stunned. In the moment of respite, Hattu stared at his heir and the iron blade in his hand. An image that had haunted his thoughts ever since Hatenzuwa. 'Give me the sword, *Tuhkanti*.'

Tudha flipped the iron sword to catch it by the blade, offering the handle to Hattu. 'Take it. I used it only to save you, Father.'

Hattu took the sword, searching his heir's eyes, seeing images of that forest shrine at Hatenzuwa, the old wooden door… the horrors beyond.

'Back,' Hektor roared, snapping Hattu from his thoughts. The crown prince was helping the detached group to hoist Sarpedon's body.

'Back!' echoed Glaucus.

They backstepped rapidly through a toppled section of the camp's sand wall, catching up with the main retreat outside. All the way the Ahhiyawan horde shadowed them, and the Trojans in turn kept the horde at bay with a picket of spears. When one Myrmidon dared break forward in an attempt to strike at Hektor, Tudha lanced him in the chest. When another bare-headed one tried the same, Andor swooped and ripped off the man's scalp.

In one defensive mass, the Trojans backstepped through the Borean

Hills. Exhausted commanders barked out in the many tongues needed to ensure all stayed in position and marched in time. On they went, across the Scamander plain. A grim place in the powerful afternoon heat. The only shade came from the vultures gliding above. All the way, the Ahhiyawan host tracked them, loosing the occasional arrow or sling stone, most of which whacked against the allied shields. The Trojan chariot wing, battered and thinned as it was, formed a mobile screen of sorts, complementing the rearguard action, ensuring the enemy dared not force another full attack.

Stumbling, suddenly numb and cold to his knees, Hattu vaguely realised they were fording the Scamander and backing towards the city itself. Now he realised that Tudha and Dagon were supporting him with an arm each. Someone held a water skin to his lips. He drank deeply, then took an offered ball of sesame and honey. It gave him a sudden burst of vigour. With another round of splashing shortly after, the Ahhiyawans crossed the river in careful pursuit. Trojan soldiers sighed in sad prayers to the Scamander Spirit. From behind, priests and women on Troy's walls wailed at the sight of their half-broken army and the enemy closing in on their city.

Around him, Hattu heard princes and commanders trying to assure their men. 'They will not scratch Troy's walls. Athena favours us.'

As if in reply, a fat dust cloud spewed up behind the Ahhiyawan line. The Trojan oaths became murmurs of confusion… and then the enemy line parted, and once more Achilles cantered to the fore at the head of his chariot squadron. The Ahhiyawans exploded in joy, and broke into a jog, coming forth with him, now closing in on the retreat. The Trojan soldiers and those watching from the walls cried out in fear.

'Open the gates, let our soldiers inside the city,' King Priam cried from the citadel's high wards.

The Thymbran Gates whined on their hinges, the wood groaning. 'Inside!' Antenor cried urgently. Like a pond draining, the dusty, battered, bleeding rags of the Trojan Army funnelled into Troy's lower city. Paris and Hektor waved in the bruised chariotry. As Achilles and the Ahhiyawan wall of warriors prowled closer and closer, Hattu, Masturi, Dagon and a screen of allied kings and champions formed a shielding rear line, blocking the path to the open gates. Hattu glanced up at the battlements: no defensive volleys from Trojan archers on the walls or turrets, for all had been in the field. 'Inside,' he shouted over his shoulder to the rest, backing in with them, his line like a stopper in a drinking skin. 'Hurry!'

Just as the shadow of the Thymbran Gatehouse began to creep over them, Achilles held his sword aloft and screamed some guttural, wordless sound. At once, the enemy line surged into a run towards the open gates. Hattu felt suddenly shot through with that burst of fire that comes when a man knows he is in mortal danger. First, Ajax the giant came barrelling forth. The metal-shelled Ascanian chieftain moved to intercept him, only for Ajax's giant staff to crush him – his solid armour shell and his ribs – against the foot of Troy's walls. Next, Achilles sprung once more from his chariot, ducking a sword-swipe from the Chieftain of Percote, slashing the man's hamstrings then driving his sword down into the back of his neck.

Hattu parried and blocked madly as the Myrmidons assailed him. Dagon used a shield and a spear to fend off Menelaus, and Tudha fought by his other side expertly, felling three Myrmidons and a horned Spartan clubman. Allies too fell in gouts of blood before the open gates, but the defensive line held good. A few more backsteps and they might be able to swing the gates shut and lock them. But Achilles – where was Achilles?

Hattu saw him in the way one spots a bird in the sky even when they are not looking upwards. With a crazed scrabbling noise, Achilles was running at the curtain wall right next to the gates – the battlements above undefended – and clawing up the plaster and stonework like a spider. Now the beetling slope of the walls was the city's enemy, allowing him to rise almost to the parapet. But at the last, he slid down again, his grip failing him. Once more he tried this, his fingers bleeding with effort. Next, he demanded a rope from one of his Myrmidons.

Hattu's blood turned to ice as Achilles tossed the looped end up and perfectly caught the triangular tip of one of the mud-plaster merlons. 'With me,' he cried to his Myrmidons, before planting a foot on the wall and beginning to walk up. The few watching women and old men up there scattered, screaming. Queen Hekabe shrieked, demanding soldiers come to this section of the battlements or that someone throw her a sword to cut the rope. Knowing that if Achilles and the Myrmidons spilled inside the lower city, a massacre would ensue, Hattu sank back from the defensive line at the gate, edging along behind that embattled rank, shouting at Lukkan soldiers to come with him. They forced their way out of the scrum at the gates. Hattu launched one of his swords at Achilles' climbing rope, the blade whirring and slicing the cord. Achilles plummeted and fell on his back with a *whump!* The dozen or so Myrmidons waiting to climb up after him helped him to his feet, then all rushed to meet Hattu and the Lukkan fighters. The Myrmidons clashed with the Lukkans, and Achilles came straight for Hattu, as Hattu knew he would. Achilles was fast and strong, far better in both aspects than Hattu. It would take something else to defeat this monster of battle.

Achilles sprinted for him, his hips moving with leonine grace, spear and sword in either hand. Whichever side he struck with, it would be too swift and it would be lethal, Hattu knew. He raised his lone sword carefully, not to block or parry or counterstrike, but at an angle, the flat facing the afternoon sun. Achilles sprang – both weapons swung back to strike and kill for sure – and then Hattu's blade flashed with sunlight, casting a dazzling reflection onto Achilles' face. Hattu sidestepped as Achilles swished his blade and lance through fresh air, then fell in a tumble to his knees, blinded, startled, both weapons falling and clattering away. More, Hattu realised something else – a secret revealed by that bright reflection that illuminated the thin face slot in Achilles' helm.

This was *not* Achilles.

'Patroklos?' he panted, pressing his iron sword to the man's neck before he could rise from his knees.

The older companion of Achilles glanced at his Myrmidons – locked in combat with the men of Lukka and unable to come to his aid. Next, he looked up along the iron blade and into Hattu's eyes. His face was red, his neck pulsing with veins.

'Why have you taken Achilles' armour?' Hattu snapped, eyes suddenly darting around in suspicion. Was the real Achilles already climbing another section of the wall?

'My young master remains in the Bay of Boreas,' Patroklos answered. 'He was set on sailing home this morning until the disturbance of your attack.'

The words hit Hattu like a stone between the eyes: Achilles, the enemy talisman, was not even here. He was set on leaving this land anyway. Had the Trojans not attacked this morning and triggered this bloody, horrible day, the Ahhiyawans would have suffered the blow of seeing their battle champion and his boats and elite soldiers vanishing across the sea. Surely the rest would soon have followed.

Patroklos grabbed the metal of Hattu's sword, pressing the edge tighter against his own neck. 'Do it. Kill me!' he hissed.

'What?' Hattu almost recoiled.

His eyes were wild, filled with tears. 'Achilles wants us to sail home tomorrow instead. Yet the Gods foretold that he was to find glory here at Troy. Glory and then death. Peace from the demons that torment him. How can that happen if he leaves?' he wept. 'Kill me so he will stay and have his glory, so he will have his peace… for vengeance is the only thing that will keep him here.'

From above, Hattu heard braying and chanting from Trojan onlookers on the battlements and felt a rain of spittle land around 'Achilles'. 'Slice off his head!' screamed Laocoon the Priest, pointing his hippocampus staff like a spear. 'Cut out his heart,' snarled Chryses, his spare chins shuddering. King Priam was with Hekabe now, and both stared austerely down their noses at the scene, in tacit demands for the slaying of 'Achilles'.

'Do it,' Patroklos hissed again.

Hattu's face twisted in a furious snarl. He swept his sword back… then planted a foot on the kneeling Patroklos' chest and kicked him away.

Patroklos, rising, wept. 'Why won't you kill me? Why? Wh-'

A thunderous rumble sounded from somewhere behind the embattled Thymbran Gate. Hattu knew the sound even before he turned to the source. His eyes locked onto the gate skirmish. 'Split!' Hektor's hoarse cry pealed from within the lower city The thin line of defenders at the gate pulled away, as if capitulating. The enemy surged into the space momentarily, before they were thrown back out like toys smashed from a table by an angry child's hand. Ox-sized Cretans, scrawny Sherden, Myrmidons and Spartans alike, tossed in the air by and crushed under the wheels of Hektor's chariot. Paris came after him, then another dozen of the Trojan wing – those least-damaged in the battle at the ships. Having pierced the skin of the attackers at the gate, they came arcing round along the base of the walls towards Hattu, towards 'Achilles'. Hektor, bronze helm gleaming, face bent in a snarl, hoisted a spear, training it on what he thought was the Ahhiyawan talisman.

'Hektor, no!' Hattu cried, stumbling in an effort to put himself in the way. But he was not fast enough. Hektor's spear flew true and fast, the purple ribbons tied to it fluttering madly as the tip crashed through Patroklos' neck. The old companion of Achilles swayed where he stood, then collapsed, writhing in his own blood.

Hektor leapt down from the chariot, a rictus smile on his face as he crouched by his kill, to take the famous helmet of Achilles for himself.

The moment he did so and the truth was revealed, his face fell like a flag at the end of a storm.

'Prince Hektor, what have you done?' Hattu whispered. Hektor turned to him, suddenly looking like a lost boy.

Patroklos' bloody hand seized Hektor weakly by the collar of his armour. 'You too will die, Hektor of Troy, and it will be at Achilles' hand,' he gurgled, before sighing into death.

Footsteps thudded up behind them. Hattu swung to see a mass of Ahhiyawans stampeding to avenge Patroklos, eyes red with hatred. Hattu lurched to grab his second sword, still lying by the heap of cut rope. Big Ajax's tower shield came swooshing round, crushing his helm and sending a spray of white sparks through his mind.

All was dark as the darkest night.

# CHAPTER 10

## DUEL OF LEGENDS

*The darkness lasted for what felt like an eternity. It was a restless void, with sounds of distress coming and going in waves, swells of nausea, and a great sense of unease. When the sounds of turmoil receded, he found himself kneeling in a grey well of light, with inky nothingness looming all around.*

*'Plague, treachery, slaughter,' Ishtar whispered from the darkness.*

*Her two lions emerged into the twilight shroud between the light and the darkness, patrolling slowly in circles, growling lazily as they went.*

*'It is not the Troy you once knew, is it?' She paced into the light now too, giant and graceful, almost weightless in her movements. 'And what of Troy's heroes? Many lie on the plain and the bay, do they not, as a feast for the gulls? Just as I foretold. Why?'*

*'Because they gave their lives to protect their home,' Hattu answered.*

*She shook her head slowly, smirking. 'Because of Hektor's folly. Hektor! The greatest of Troy's soldiers,' she boomed theatrically. 'What chaos he wreaked out there on the sands! If only he had listened to you…'*

*'Troy stands,' Hattu replied, 'that is all that matters.'*

*'…the invaders might now have been halfway across the sea, gone. If only it was you at the helm, Troy's army might not have been bludgeoned back across the Scamander plain and chased behind its gates. If only it was you,' she repeated one more time, crouching before him, grinning, her tongue tracing the tips of her fangs. 'You and not Hektor.'*

*She placed before him a pile of armour and a bright helm. Hektor's battle gear.*

*It resurrected memories of that last dream of the blood Scamander, of an unarmoured Hektor slain by its banks. He stepped back from the armour as if it was poisonous. 'Prince Hektor has many faults, but he is also the spirit of Troy. He is the figurehead holding the army and people together. They look to him as their king more than they do his withered father. As long as the people see him at the head of the defence, they will never give up hope. They will continue to fight, to sacrifice what little they have, to drive off the invaders and put things right here.'*

*'Fine and noble words, King Hattu,' Ishtar purred. 'But I am not sure you speak from your heart. Thus, I come to offer you a choice. A choice of life or death, just as I once offered your father on the night of your birth.'*

*Hattu felt ice snaking through his veins. Legions of dark visions rose around him. Father, broken by his choice. Mother, dead on the birthing stool. The birth curse. The tragedies that followed.*

*'I place in your hands, right now, the fate of the Crown Prince of Troy,' Ishtar said.*

*'What?' Hattu rasped.*

*'Hektor can live, but the rest of the war will be fought out under his reckless leadership. Or he can die, and another might rise to take his place, to do things as they should be done, to lead... and to win.'*

*Hattu smiled a wretched smile at her. 'I will not choose from your poisoned fruits.'*

*'Your father said the same thing, at first. Yet your mother died that night, and all so you might live.'*

*Hattu's defences collapsed. A great invisible hand of emotion swamped him. 'I... will... not... choose,' he repeated with difficulty, his head dropping.*

*Ishtar placed a long finger under his chin, tilting his head up. She stared deep into his eyes, and Hattu felt her inside his mind, inhaling his thoughts, her snake-tongue tasting his heart. 'You already have,' she said, rising and backing away into the blackness.*

*Hattu stared at her fading form. 'What? No! I did not choose. I did not!'*

'I did not… I… I did not,' he croaked.

'Save your strength,' Antenor muttered. At the same time, a cool rag touched his brow, and rivulets of chill water streaked across his face, pulling him up from the blackness. He cracked open his eyelids only to wince at the bright, harsh light. A pain struck through his head like a lance, and he made an animal noise, sinking back into what felt like luxurious bedding. 'The wound will heal, but you need to rest.'

*Wound?* Hattu thought. Then, like a lightning-flash, he remembered the great dark shadow of Ajax's tower shield swinging towards him. 'My battle helm-'

'Is ruined,' Antenor replied. 'But it saved your life, so say Masturi and Glaucus. It was they who rescued you and brought you in yesterday, after the enemy were driven off from their attack on the Thymbran Gate.'

Hattu opened his eyes again, this time braving the bright light of midday – though everything was still a blur. '*Yesterday?*' he exclaimed, trying to sit up. His mind flashed with parts of the battle at the ships: the chaos, the burning boats… Tudha leaping like a panther, making fools of Agamemnon and his best charioteers. *He turned the battle, like a key in a lock,* he thought. Then a horrible thought crackled through his aching head: Tudha was defending the gate with him before Ajax knocked him unconscious. 'The *Tuhkanti*. The *Tuhkanti*. Is he-'

'You mean… your son?' Antenor said, bemused. 'He is well. So are the others in your party. Chariot Master Dagon twisted a knee in the gate defence, but he will mend, and is being tended to by Sirtaya the Egyptian.'

A wave of cool relief washed over him. Until he remembered…

'Sarpedon,' he said quietly, gulping deeply to hold back the swelling sadness in his throat. Memories flitted across his mind – of the years in which Sarpedon and his faithful Lukkans had marched with the Hittite Army. The wine shared around the campfires at night, men broken with laughter as they swapped tales, soldiers who became brothers, the raucous festivals in the Lukka lands for Sarpedon's wedding, Hattu's naming of the Lukkan lord's child.

'His body was washed and honoured by Glaucus and his bodyguards,' explained Antenor. 'They touched the flame to his funeral fire and pronounced that his spirit would be carried south to the faraway Lukkan meadows by Sleep and Death. I did not quite understand that last part.'

Hattu smiled the saddest of smiles then. 'Those were the names of his old chariot stallions. He always said he was destined to die in battle.'

Antenor handed him a cup, from which gentle curls of steam rose. 'Mountain tea,' the elder grinned, 'brewed from the stems of a root that grows on Mount Ida's lower slopes. All the goodness of the mountain flows down through those soils. It'll ease your pain and lift your mood too.'

Hattu took the cup, sipping. It was strong and earthy. Pleasantly warm and comforting. One of Antenor's old hounds appeared at the bedside then and nuzzled his free hand.

'Now close your eyes, *Labarna*,' Antenor said gently. 'You have been unconscious for over a day, but you have been fitful in that time. You need proper sleep.'

Sleep, Hattu mused. It made him think of that menacing dream. What had Ishtar seen in his heart?

Just then, a sound arose, floating in on the hot air from the shutters – open with bright blue sky beyond. A sound distant, but drawing closer, and most unwelcome. The metal chatter and feral howl of men in combat. Now he sat bolt upright, swinging his legs from the bed. 'What is this?' he croaked.

'You must rest,' Antenor protested. A trio of his hounds whined in agreement.

Hobbling, realising he was naked, Hattu stumbled over to snatch a loose Trojan robe hanging by his bedside, throwing it on. Barefoot, he clambered up the ladder and onto the villa roof, high enough to give him a view down over the lower city and the Scamander plain. The roof was stinging hot on the pads of his feet and the noon sun prickled on his skin. His grey hair floated gently in the hot breeze as he stared at the mass of men and bronze out there on the river plain. It was as if yesterday's battle had never ceased, as if he had simply taken leave from it while the rest fought on. The fray swayed one way and then the next, leaving behind stains of red and shells of men and metal. A frenzy of shuddering feather headdresses, gleaming armoured coats, purple cloaks, helms of leather, tusk and bronze.

A Trojan Guardian standing watch on an adjacent balcony saw Hattu and saluted in the Hittite way. 'It is good to see you well, *Labarna*.'

'How long have they been fighting?'

'All day. The Ahhiyawans camped last night near the Scamander and attacked at dawn. The struggle to hold them back from Troy's walls has raged all morning.

Hattu watched, captivated by the dreadful sight of the two forces. He spotted Agamemnon and Nestor in what remained of their chariot fleets, ploughing into Trojan allies and breaking lines of defence. Hektor, dressed in the captured gold and silver armour of Achilles, led the chariots of Troy – now less than half of the number fielded yesterday – racing and fighting in a constant effort to intercept and engage the Ahhiyawan war-cars. But there was something wrong, he thought, his eyes darting. 'Where are the others?' he said, unable to make sense of the noticeably reduced soldiery on either side. Thousands were missing, it seemed – and far more were absent for the Trojans than for the enemy.

The Guardian seemed perplexed. 'That… that is everyone, *Labarna.* Almost every soldier left for Troy and for the invader.'

'Do not fear,' Antenor added quickly, climbing the ladder and emerging from the roof hatch. 'Your lad is not out there. He has been held back as a reserve.'

He spotted something then: A warrior in dark silver armour – *wondrous* armour. He moved like a cheetah, sprinting from foe to foe, slashing down Trojan noblemen and Guardians without taking so much as a breath between kills. Despite the new and wonderful shell of metal, there was no doubt in his mind who was inside. 'Achilles fights,' Hattu said quietly. It all flooded back to him then. Patroklos' bloody final words: *You too will die, Hektor of Troy, and it will be at Achilles' hand.*

'Aye,' said the Guardian on the balcony. 'At dusk last night, the horses dragged Patroklos' chariot back towards the enemy camp. Soon after, when we were collecting our dead and preparing our pyres, we heard a scream from beyond the Borean Hills. A terrible, deep, animal noise. He appeared on the hills, alone, staring at our city. At the onset of battle this morning, he proclaimed that this would be the day that Hektor died on his sword.

A weeping rose from nearby. Andromache, up on the Scaean Tower, a short way from this balcony and with a cruelly perfect view of the battlefield. She held baby Astyanax to her bosom tightly, pacing up and down, daring to watch for a few moments only to wheel away again in distress. Queen Hekabe stood with King Priam, their hands tightly locked as if trying to preserve some sacred bond.

Hattu, feeling their distress, watched Achilles work: spinning, hacking. The Chieftain of Thymbra, already limping, put up a good defence, only for Achilles to drop to his haunches and slash clean through the man's shin. The Thymbran Chief fell, screaming, blood pulsing from the stump. When a Trojan Guardian staggered to the edge of the fray, clutching a bloodied arm, Achilles pounced, slicing off his head. Now Hattu leaned a little against the balustrade, spotting something: the way Achilles worked on those edges of battle, never delving into its midst. More, every man he killed was sporting some kind of wound already. This warrior was a pale copy of Patroklos. An imitator.

From the fray, a voice pealed: 'There are too many of them. Fall back!' Masturi howled to his men. The Lukkans, now under Glaucus' command, receded too. Hattu saw why: Agamemnon's chariot wing had turned the chaotic Trojan flank, and was now coming round on their rear.

'Back!' Prince Deiphobus echoed Masturi's cry.

Within moments, the stubborn battle became a rout, the Trojans once again fleeing back to the city, the Ahhiyawans giving chase, slaying hundreds as they ran. A groan sounded as the Thymbran Gates swung open and the Trojans retreated inside. King Priam, Queen Hekabe and Andromache descended from the Scaean Tower and hurried to those gates.

Barefoot, Hattu hobbled and winced his way down through the villa, ignoring Antenor's protests. 'King Hattu, have you taken leave of your senses?' the elder almost choked on his drink, one of his hounds howling as if to reinforce the argument. 'You should be resting!' but Hattu shuffled on outside, leaving the citadel, joining the hurried procession down to the Thymbran Gate.

'King Hattu?' Priam gawped. 'Antenor said you would be unconscious for days?'

'I must speak to Hektor,' Hattu croaked. 'He must not fight any longer today, not even in screening this retreat.'

'What? Why?'

Hattu considered explaining the dream and Ishtar's dark choice of futures, but now wasn't the time. 'You have lost enough sons in this war already, Majesty. Do you need any other reason?'

As they came to the Thymbran Gatehouse, Hattu caught a sickening waft of sweat and blood. Priam, Hekabe and Andromache climbed onto the gatehouse walkway, Priam for once sounding almost martial as he barked at a troop of archers there, compelling them to send volleys of covering arrows at the Ahhiyawan host. Hattu remained at ground level, shouldering past the exhausted troops making their way in. He passed shaking men lying in heaps, moments from death. One sat muttering to himself with a horrid cleft in his skull, bare brain showing, still with a shard of axe bronze embedded in the soft matter. Many more still flooded in while a screen of men shielded the retreat just like yesterday. A furious press of Ahhiyawan soldiers vied to get in behind.

'Where is Prince Hektor?' Hattu shouted over the din. All shook their heads, too tired to speak. Hattu's fears began to rise like a cold spike.

'King Hattu?' replied Hektor himself, striding in, his gold and silver shell blinding. 'By the Gods we missed you on the field today. We so nearly had them. So nearly.'

Hattu shook his head. 'Why did you attack so soon after yesterday's reverse? With so many injured? You should have used the defences, let them throw themselves against the high walls.'

'Brother,' Paris interrupted, 'it matters not that we had a brief advantage. They pulverised us in the end. Nearly half of my battalion perished out there today.'

'The second battalion is gone entirely,' Prince Deiphobus gasped. 'Many of the Guardians were slain out there too. More lie dead than stand alive.'

'So too the fifth,' said Prince Scamandrios, prizing off his leather helm, dripping with sweat, and casting it across the street angrily.

Hattu's skin crept. Troy could not suffer such losses and hope to turn this war. The Guardians in particular, for they were the small but hardy core of Troy's army. Had they really been whittled down so badly?

One soldier hobbled over to Hektor, weeping. 'Majesty… I didn't know.'

Hektor frowned at the bloodied soldier. An injured captain of the Guardians. 'Stand up, man. What are you talking about?'

'He looked like a grown man in the armour and so I didn't question him.'

'Who?'

'Prince Polydorus,' the soldier choked. 'He disguised himself and joined my squadron. Achilles cut him down.'

Hekabe, hearing this, pitched to her knees and emitted a high-pitched wail. Hattu stared, thinking of the boy prince, just nine summers old. Princess Polyxena immediately pulled Polites – even younger than the slain Polydorus – to her bosom, covering his ears. Hektor's face paled.

'Close the gates,' Trojan soldiers roared. The ropes strained and the gates began to swing shut, and the small bank of Trojan archers on the gatehouse parapet launched another volley, forcing the Ahhiyawans back, buying a precious moment to allow the defensive screen to slip inside too.

With a *boom*, the locking bar slammed into place behind the gates. Hektor stiffened. The distressed babble of the streets near the gate faded.

'The enemy lines draw back,' an archer commander reported from the walls. 'All but… all but one.'

Hattu looked up, seeing the fear on the archer's face.

'Hektor,' the cry sailed over Troy's streets. 'Hektor of Troy!'

'It is Achilles,' the archer croaked.

'Achilles,' the Trojans on the streets whispered in an eerie echo.

'Hektor: I challenge you. I demand revenge for my fallen comrade, Patroklos. Come from behind your walls and fight me. Let no other man cast a weapon. Just my sword and yours.'

Troy fell so silent that the whistle of the famous northerly wind could be heard.

Hektor's face sagged.

'Ignore him,' Hattu said, taking Hektor by the shoulders now. 'They have no siege machinery, and so his only weapons are his words. You and your people are safe here behind the walls.'

Hektor said nothing, glancing up at the gatehouse walkway, seeing Andromache up there, looking back down at him. Just as Pudu could read Hattu's eyes like a tablet, Andromache saw what Hektor was thinking. Slowly, her head began to shake. 'No… no, no, *no*' she said, her voice breaking down into a wail.

'I must,' he said quietly, but in the silence, all heard.

Andromache came flitting down the steps with baby Astyanax, her purple gown flowing. She threw herself at Hektor, imploring him. '*No!*'

'Remember the prophecies of protection,' Hattu argued. 'If you go out there you risk your life and one of those precious chances for Troy. You have a choice, Prince Hektor. Choose to live today so you may fight tomorrow.'

'Choice?' he said, pulling Andromache into his embrace, kissing her brow and Astyanax' head, then looking over the shattered, stained masses of the Trojan Army. 'There is no choice. The beast out there killed my brother today, just as he murdered Troilus. For ten years, they have called him the greatest fighter of all Ahhiyawa. For those same ten years my people have championed me as the greatest warrior of Troy. He and I have clashed briefly in battle, but never to a finish. Now, we must. For if I defeat him it will crush the spirits of the Ahhiyawans.'

'Think carefully, Prince of Troy,' Hattu warned in a quiet murmur.

Hektor leaned in to murmur back: 'I envy you, King Hattu. You have an eagle's mind. Battle to you looks like a tapestry – clear in shape and meaning. You can read it and understand how it works. You know when you will win and when you will not. To me it is a blur of coloured threads, a rush of emotions, a thing I have somehow been able to dominate without understanding why. The people of Troy respect me because I can stir them with my words, and because I have blustered my way through many battles to conjure an illusion of invincibility. Now look around you, see the faces of my people – already they doubt me for this terrible defeat today. Were I to reject Achilles' challenge, they would lose all respect for me.' He leaned in even closer, voice dropping to a whisper so only Hattu could hear. 'What then, eh? My surviving brothers would jostle and jockey to supplant me and one another as my father's favoured son. The nobles and priests already hover near his throne like hawks. That none have tried to seize power for themselves is down to my standing and nothing else. You know all too well the disaster that comes with a war of succession, do you not?'

Hattu beheld Andromache and baby Astyanax, heartsick for both, but knew that – at least this time – Hektor was right. He eyed the Trojan Crown Prince, garbed in that wondrous armour captured from Patroklos the previous day. Strong… but heavy. His mind began to work. 'You *can* defeat him,' he said.

For once Hektor did not rebuff him, nodding for Hattu to go on.

'Today is the first time I have ever watched Achilles fight from afar. He is not the warrior they speak of. Patroklos, his mentor, was fast and skilled and excelled in the heart of battle. Achilles is just as swift and strong, but he operates on the fringes, preying on injured men, racking up many kills without ever facing a true challenge.' He looked Hektor up and down. 'And you… you are fast too, yes?'

'The swiftest runner in Troy,' Hektor said proudly.

'Then take off that armour. It will only slow you down. Achilles has been running around the edges of battle all day. So make him run more – dodge, weave, retreat from his attacks. He will eventually tire.'

'*Run* from him?' Hektor croaked.

'The war of the flea, remember?' Hattu said authoritatively. 'Nobody will care how you win this bout, only that you do.'

Fire flared in Hektor's eyes, that bullish defiance returning. 'Bring me a fresh spear and shield,' he said to a nearby Guardian, turning away from Hattu, his armour still firmly strapped in place.

Hattu sighed inwardly. Hekabe, up on the gatehouse, fell to her knees, weeping, opening her robes to bare one withered breast at her boy. 'Not you, Hektor. Show respect to your mother, who suckled you and loved you. Do not put me through this!' But Hektor was deaf to her. Priam stared, distraught, realising that his eldest son, his heir and the champion of Troy, the hope of the people, was to face the monster, Achilles, at last.

Hektor embraced his brother Paris, took a water skin offered by a lowly slave and drank a deep draught from it, then handed it to Hattu. He cast one more valedictory look around Troy's streets, and finally to his wife and babe. Andromache crumpled with grief. Hattu caught her as she fell, supporting her and the wailing Astyanax.

***

Slowly, Hattu guided Andromache up to the gatehouse where the royalty of Troy watched. Dagon was there, Andor perched on his shoulder, Tudha and Sirtaya too, all rapt by the goings-on outside the walls. Hattu eyed Tudha sideways. The ugly cut to his face had been stitched, giving him a mean look. They had not spoken since the midst of yesterday's fray. He wondered then why, when he had woken a short while ago he had felt so worried about his heir, yet here – beside him – he felt a coldness, a tendency to disapprove, to dislike, even. He answered his own question inwardly: *Because of the shrine... because of what he did!* With a low grumble, he planted his hands on the hot parapets, and set his attentions on the coming duel.

The cicada song grew shrill as, in the wide no-man's land between the city walls and the Ahhiyawan mass, Hektor and Achilles paced to within a spear's throw of one another. They then took to strutting slowly in a circle, each staring at the other, each a gleaming god. Like Hektor, Achilles carried spear, shield and a sheathed sword. The skin on their forearms and necks glistened with sweat and streaks of blood from the battle so far.

*Run*, Hattu hissed inwardly. *For once, at this most important of times, heed my advice.*

'It is time for me to show everyone what you are, Hektor of Troy,'

Achilles snarled. 'A lumbering fool. Patroklos' spirit waits for you on the far banks of the Styx, and his blades are sharp.'

'He wore your armour that day.' Hektor batted his chest. 'This armour. When my spear met his flesh I thought it was you I had slain.'

'Ha!' Achilles boomed. 'I thought I heard the Gods laugh!' He waved his spear dismissively. 'Before I came here, they talked of you as a hero. Now I know what you really are. A murderer.'

'A murderer?' Hektor seethed. 'And what were you when you slaughtered my brother Troilus at the shrine, when you cut down young Polydorus today? What were you when you razed every village on Lesbos? When you raped the women of Thebes-under-Plakos and had your men pound the heads of the children against that city's walls? When you set ablaze the simple farm homes of the countryfolk of Wilusa…' he rattled his fist against his chest again, 'of *my country!*'

'Your country?' Achilles scoffed, spitting into the dust, looking around. 'Open your eyes, Trojan Prince, this land is yours no longer.' He pointed with his spear towards the city. 'Troy's king and people quiver like frightened sheep within that stone pen.'

'While you hover like flies on our fields, homeless, hopeless and frantic after ten years of failure to even trouble our walls.'

'Enough of your bleating, sheep of Troy,' Achilles snarled. 'It is time for me to strike you down and avenge Patroklos. Take up your spear, and prepare to breathe your last.'

Hektor raised his spear and so did Achilles. 'Let us fight, then,' he said as their circling footsteps quickened, heavy armour clanking, 'but first, an oath: whoever wins must treat the other's body with respect – just as I allowed Patroklos' body to be taken back to you. If there is any thread of nobility left in either of us, we will do this.'

Achilles smirked. 'There can be no pact between sheep and lions!' With that, he fell into a crouch.

Hattu felt a stark shiver, recognising his cat-like poise from the battle. *Run!* he screamed inwardly at Hektor.

With a puff of dust, Achilles burst forward, using his sudden momentum to launch his spear at Hektor. Hektor, caught on his heels, arched his back crazily to avoid it, the lance scraping his chin. Now Hektor came upright, hurling his spear at the still charging Achilles. Hektor's lance scored through the heat. Achilles' face changed then. Panic, Hattu realised. All at Troy's battlements craned forward, breath bated, as the spear plunged towards Achilles' chest.

*Clang!* Achilles swatted Hektor's spear aside with his shield. At the same time, with a *zing!* he tore his sword from its sheath. Hektor, again wrong-footed, stumbled crazily backwards, pulling out his own sword.

*No,* Hattu seethed. *Tire him first, then fight him!*

Yet Hektor was still deaf and stubborn to Hattu's advice. He brought his sword up, ready to meet Achilles' blade. The Ahhiyawans roared in anticipation. Many of those watching from the walls of Troy sank away in grim despair. But Hattu saw something: Hektor was on the balls of his feet, ready not to fight but to dodge. As Achilles' blade came down at an angle for his neck, Hektor bounded to one side. Achilles' fierce strike slashed through the air where he had been. Hektor met Achilles' eyes for a moment, then glanced up to the wall, to Hattu. With a stroke of his sword, he slit the leather straps of his splendid armour. The chest shell fell away in two halves. In the same motion he plucked his helm from his head and cast it aside.

And then he ran. Fast as a deer, legs a blur, arms pumping.

The Ahhiyawan masses thundered in protest and whistled and howled in derision.

King Priam's face crumpled in confusion.

'Interesting,' said Antenor, one eyebrow arching.

'He's fleeing?' Laocoon said, his voice dripping with despair.

'You always were a plain thinker, Priest. Hektor knows what he is doing. Have faith in him,' Queen Hekabe said, shooting a look at Hattu.

Achilles, shaking with rage, took a moment to digest what was happening. Then he too burst into that cheetah-like sprint of his, pounding the footsteps of Hektor's path. He sliced his own armour away as he went, shedding its weight and catching up steadily. Andor watched the chase intently, her head twitching round in tiny increments as Hektor bent north towards the Silver Ridge, following the route of the lower city walls. The wails of the Trojan people rose and rose as the gap slimmed to almost nothing. Yet as soon as Hektor planted a foot on the Silver Ridge's lower slopes, the balance changed. Hektor picked a path expertly, hopping over divots and tussocks, jumping across a stream and clambering up squat faces of rock like a spider. Achilles, robbed of good flat sprinting ground, stumbled and foundered, confronted by tangles of gorse or sliding on scree.

'When he was a boy, he would compete in foot races around the city,' said Queen Hekabe, sidling up near Hattu. 'He knows the route so well, he could run it blind.' She pressed a hand on his. 'I know it was you who urged him to use this to his advantage. Thank you for driving some sense into him.'

Hattu tried to smile, but could barely rip his gaze away from the chase. The running pair vanished up onto the Silver Ridge's brow, sliding out of sight behind Troy's high citadel. The Ahhiyawan mass rumbled in confusion, hope, bemusement. Hattu's heart pounded. 'What is up there?'

'A goat's path – treacherous even for goats,' Hekabe said. 'Do not fear. Watch,' she added, pointing him to the far side of the citadel, where the walls ran down from the section overlooking the Bay of Troy and joined with the lower city defences on that side. Time seemed to stick. Hattu could not breathe. With a puff of dust and a glint of sweating skin, Hektor appeared there, hopping and springing down the ridge on that western side of the city, past the Bay Gate, a windswept old fig tree and that weak stretch of walls, descending towards the Scamander plain once more, his loose ponytail swinging with every leap. Behind him by a good thirty paces, Achilles' laboured, skittering and sliding gracelessly. Hektor came round past the Thymbran Gate, completing a full circuit of Troy. Here Achilles – back on good, even ground – quickly closed, only for Hektor to once more speed up onto the slope in a second lap of Troy. Once again Achilles lumbered, ranted and cursed, his every utterance making him look more and more like a beaten man. Hattu began to feel relief and hope seep into his veins.

'If Hektor wins this bout, if he slays Achilles…' Dagon whispered.

'The Ahhiyawans' spirits will be broken,' Sirtaya finished for him.

'The champion will lie dead soon enough,' Tudha said.

All three meant the same thing, but the unintentional ambiguity of Tudha's statement wormed into Hattu's blossoming confidence. At the same time, Hektor came streaking back down on Troy's western side, supported by a gulls' chorus. The Trojans on the walls began to cheer now, realising what their hero-prince was doing – not fleeing, but blowing away the myth of Achilles' unrivalled speed and strength. The priests and seers chanted and cast their arms in the air, pointing at the gulls as if they were each an omen of luck. Women sang and men roared in support. In contrast, the Ahhiyawans were silent, stunned at the sight of Achilles lagging some way behind Hektor, tripping and bowling head over heels down the last stretch of the slope.

But Hattu noticed something else. Hektor's strong, confident stride had changed. He missed a step, landing badly, his ankle almost turning.

His pace had dropped off. The cheering from Troy's walls began to fade now. Up the Silver Ridge Hektor went for a third lap of Troy. Except this time he was shaky, weak. Achilles did not lose ground this time.

Hattu's eyes narrowed. He saw the same look on Hekabe's face.

'Something's wrong. My boy can run around our city a dozen times, even at the end of a hard day.'

Hattu looked to the sky. It was hot, but not as hot as it could get in these parts. The battle so far this day had no doubt been hard, but so much as to rob Hektor of his strength so quickly?

When he came round on the western side again, he looked as pale as milk. Now it was he who slid to one knee and tumbled down a section of the slope, bumping clumsily against the fig tree and shambling down onto the plain. He rose, but only to lope crazily forward like a drunk man. Achilles came scrambling down the slope then sprang into his graceful sprint again. The gap shrank in heartbeats.

Hattu felt sickness swell in his belly. Hekabe clasped his hand once more, her other holding Priam's. Andromache made a choking sound. Andor shrieked in alarm.

Prince Hektor, hearing the footsteps behind him, swung round, bringing up his sword. *Clang!* Achilles' blade met his. Hektor reeled away, struggling to find his footing, even his balance. *Clang! Clang! Clang!* Achilles came at him, weaving and hacking. *Whoosh!* Hektor's sword flew from his grip, spinning through the air and landing near the Ahhiyawan lines.

Now the Crown Prince of Troy had just his leather shield. Achilles drove at him, battering at the screen, shredding it to strips. When the blade lodged deep in the shield and Achilles could not free it, Hattu's heart fell still. A chance? Prince Hektor strived and strained to pull with the shield and take Achilles' sword with it. Yet he had not the strength, his head rolling weakly on his neck as if it weighed as much as an anchor.

In the end it was Achilles who wrenched his sword back and brought Hektor's shield with it. With a confident flick of his arm, he tossed the two entangled pieces away, dropped low to snatch up his earlier-thrown spear from the dust, then strode towards the backstepping Hektor.

Hekabe shook madly now as her son staggered weaponless before Achilles.

Andromache gagged as if choking on the sight.

'No... no,' Priam croaked.

Achilles sprang like a lion, thrusting his lance underhand, upwards and into Hektor's gullet. A spurt of dark crimson leapt from the back of Hektor's neck as the speartip poked through, the thick droplets of redness spattering in the dust behind him. Hektor spasmed on Achilles' lance, and the Ahhiyawan champion's words rang clear across the plain. 'Patroklos is avenged.' He wrenched his spear back, and Hektor's body crumpled to the ground. 'Your remains, foolish Prince of Troy, will be given to the dogs.'

Shrill cries of horror rang out all along the walls. Priam, Hekabe and Andromache were struck dumb with shock. Achilles called for his chariot, then knelt by Hektor's body with a bronze dagger. Hattu's eyes widened in horror. 'Guards, take Prince Hektor's family away,' he demanded. A group of Guardians ushered them from the battlements, mercifully before Achilles proceeded to pierce the flesh of Hektor's ankles and feed a rope through those bloody holes, tying the other end to the back of his chariot. He boarded and, with a crack of the whip, the chariot jerked to life and wheeled round, away from Troy, Hektor's corpse trundling through the pale dust in its wake.

Hattu watched, numb, as the Ahhiyawan masses parted to allow a corridor for their victorious talisman to pass through, Troy's slain champion in tow. From the corridor's edges, men speared and spat at the dragged body, Diomedes and Ajax amongst them.

Agamemnon watched Achilles go then turned to Troy, eyeing the closed gates and the stout defences. Finally, he boomed: 'Battle is over for today, King Priam, and I am victorious. This plain and your sacred river are now firmly mine,' He tossed a spear into the dust, where it quivered. 'I grant you amnesty only to gather your many, *many*, dead. Pray that they burn slowly, for when the funerals are over, my army will march again... and this time, it will be to make war with your walls. The end is near for Troy. Can you hear me, King Priam? The end is near!'

# CHAPTER 11

## THE HELM OF TROY

The third of the five prophecy tablets was smashed at dusk on the day of Hektor's death. For the next seven days, the Scamander plain glowed with pyres that painted the night sky amber. King Priam – for so long insistent that his Trojans should hide their grief – now wailed openly from the highest parts of Troy, a discordant, elegiac song of a broken king.

Hattu, head still aching from his wound, sat up on the Thymbran Gate defences, carefully whetting his iron blades, sparks dancing. Beside him lay a tray with a fresh loaf, a pot of honey and a vase of wine – fare reserved for the citadel elites. He had touched not a morsel.

Close to the city defences – for the Scamander plain was lost to the enemy now – the priests Laocoon and Chryses led a train of lamenting citizens around the Trojan pyres. Hundreds of them. The five battalions of Troy were in tatters. In the days since the last ruinous battle, men had stopped using the term battalion, and instead referred to the patchy force left with much less grand terms like 'squadrons' and 'companies'.

Down on the plain, on the near and far banks of the river, myriad Ahhiyawan fires flickered likewise. None was brighter than the blaze up on the Borean Hills – the funeral fire of Patroklos. From around that mountainous inferno strange noises sailed out into the night – whistling, cheering, raucous applause, the sounds clashing with the wails and plaintive song elsewhere. Around the flames he caught flashes of movement: the silhouettes of men boxing, running and leaping, of horses speeding, of axes being thrown at painted boards.

'They are holding games in Patroklos' honour,' reported the kilted Trojan scout he had sent out earlier. 'It is Agamemnon's measure to appease Achilles and convince him to stay and help see out Troy's capture. Achilles is red-eyed with grief and rage. I watched from the bushes as he took twelve Trojan prisoners and had them tied to the pyre timbers before setting the torch to the wood himself. Meanwhile, Hektor's body lies out by his tent like a rag.'

'Thank you, that will be all,' Hattu said, giving the man his food tray. 'Take this to your family.' The scout's belly rumbled and he bowed in gratitude then left, heading back down from the battlements to his lower city home.

King Priam's wails rose again in an unsettling crescendo. Hattu turned away from the sound, and gazed down at the dusty earth outside the city, criss-crossed with chariot tracks. There, every day since the clash of the two champions, Achilles had ridden his chariot in a macabre display, trailing Hektor's decomposing body around in his wake, the corpse bouncing and breaking on rocks and divots like the hearts of his family who had to endure this spectacle.

*It shouldn't have been this way*, he thought. *No matter what Ishtar saw inside my heart, Hektor should not have lost.*

He glanced over to the far corner of the gatehouse battlements, where Sirtaya and Andor were perched next to one another, watching the funeral fires silently. The Egyptian seemed scrawnier than usual today, Hattu thought. Perhaps it was his distaste for Trojan food – and his preference for catching and eating vermin. He noticed something else: his ears were twitching, and his palms were planted on the defences as if he was communing with them.

Hattu opened his mouth to ask Sirtaya what was wrong. The Egyptian seemed to sense this and held up a talon-finger for silence. Hattu watched, bemused, as the Egyptian closed his eyes. It happened so gradually: the battlements began to shiver gently… then firmly. Rattling noises sounded from the turret guardrooms, and the sound of a smashing plate rang out. Sentries all along the walls looked to and fro, worried. Horses within the city began pawing at the ground skittishly. It faded quickly.

It reminded Hattu of how the priests had described it. 'Poseidon's horses walk,' he said quietly.

Sirtaya grinned and twisted his head to look at Hattu. 'Walk? No, that was a trot. Stronger than the last.' His face twisted strangely then, in a way that aged him dramatically. 'Even at Hattusa, have you ever known the tremors to come so frequently as they seem to here?'

Hattu cocked his head a little. The earth tremors had been infrequent during his youth, but with every passing year they had become more and more numerous. Still, two quakes in the same moon was a rare thing. Yet here it was different: it had been barely ten days since that tremor during the evening feast on the day of his arrival at Troy. 'What do you make of it, old friend?' he asked with a sense of unease – for Sirtaya was adept at reading the heartbeat of the earth.'

'Nothing good,' Sirtaya replied. 'I never told you how I learned how to sense the tremors and read the patterns, did I?'

'It was in the Well of Silence,' Hattu replied.

Sirtaya nodded. 'Aye… aye, but long before you were thrown in there, years before we became friends. There was a prisoner next to me – an ancient goat of a man – who taught me how. He said there were two types of tremors: passing ones and mighty ones, and that instances of each should be respected and feared. But those quakes were isolated heartbeats. The ones to be truly dreaded were those that came again and again like the pounding of a smith's hammer, faster and faster, stronger with every strike.'

Hattu now felt positively cold.

Sirtaya's eyes misted with memory. 'The rivers will boil,' he said, voice hissing like wind through the branches of a dead tree, 'the birds will scatter. The herds will lie down… and the cities of men will fall.' For dramatic effect, Andor threw her head up and shrieked skywards.

Hattu drew his cloak around himself as if it were winter.

'Of course,' Sirtaya said with a grin, 'the old goat also used to chew his own toes, so maybe he was exaggerating about it all.'

'Maybe,' Hattu said with a weak smile. 'Maybe…'

Footsteps approached from the chariot stables then padded up the gatehouse stairs. Dagon arrived by his side carrying a cup of foaming barley beer, massaging his right shoulder and cracking his joints. With a sigh, he sat down, guided the straw to his mouth and drained the cup in one draught. Another sigh. He looked along the line of the battlements and wagged a finger. 'The Dardanian Prince and Tudha seem to have struck up a friendship,' he said.

Hattu looked that way. Tudha sat at the nearest turret. The copper sutures had been removed from his face wound and there was no danger of infection now, but it hurt to see his heir marked like that. Aeneas was with him, the Dardanian Prince showing Tudha how to fletch arrows in the Trojan way. He used the black ring on his thumb – fixed with a tiny shaving blade on the outside – to whittle away imperfections on the shaft, and the inlaid whetstone on the inside to sharpen the bronze head.

'Aye, they have many similarities. Perhaps Aeneas will teach him some temperance. I have seen signs that my heir is learning from him. It can only be a good thing to foster new bonds between our empire and Troy. When this war is over, we'll need to tie together whatever threads are left.'

'Perhaps you will return Tudha's iron sword to him soon?' Dagon asked.

Hattu said nothing. He looked along the dark hump of the Silver Ridge, eyeing the shadows of the Thorn Hill that had until now been the campsite for Troy's Army. So many had fallen on the day of Hektor's death that they could not afford to remain encamped in the open like that, lest the Ahhiyawans strike from the plain at night. Thus, the tattered remains of Troy's Army – less than four thousand men at the last muster call – had withdrawn into the city, taking billet in the houses of men already fallen. He gazed over the lower city, seeing Lukkans and Seha Riverlanders eating gruel with families on the flat roofs of the many houses. He thought of that short-lived optimism when Troy's Army had been replete and stationed proudly on the southern banks of the Scamander, one careful move away from squeezing the enemy from the land like the putrid contents of a boil. A victory that should have been, but never came to be. It made him think of Hektor's death again.

He tucked his swords in his shoulder sheaths, rose and strolled over to the turret where Tudha and Aeneas worked. 'You were right,' he said flatly, climbing onto the square roof space.

Tudha stopped shaving the arrow he was working on and looked up. Their eyes met.

'About the traitor,' Hattu explained quietly. With a jab of a finger up towards the citadel, he added: 'It's someone up there. One of the elites, just as you said it was.'

Tudha nodded gently. Dagon sighed in agreement. Aeneas' eyes widened. Sirtaya and Andor cocked their heads round in unison. 'You didn't believe me when I told you that at the river camp. Why now?' Tudha asked.

'Because the same person was responsible for what happened to Hektor,' Hattu said, unclasping from his belt the simple drinking skin that the dead prince had swigged from moments before the duel. 'He was poisoned. That was why he lost his strength and footing so swiftly.'

'Poisoned?' Tudha whispered, coming closer.

'With the oil of crushed oleander petals. The skin was laced with it,' he explained.

'Who gave him the water?' Aeneas asked, coming close enough to whisper also, sitting against the parapet.

Hattu thought of the shapeless one who had given Hektor the skin inside the Thymbran Gate. 'A slave. A ghost of a man. So unremarkable I cannot put a face to the memory of him,' he said, sighing in annoyance. 'The only thing I can remember is that he wore a clean, fresh robe. There are few slaves in the lower city, and none of them wear anything more than rags.'

'Then the slave's master is the Shadow,' Dagon said, looking up towards the citadel.

'How do we flush the culprit out?' Sirtaya mused, scratching behind one ear madly.

'Gather the elites together,' Tudha suggested. 'See if we can spot the slave and who he serves.'

Dagon sighed. 'Priam has insisted that there are to be no feasts, no ceremonies… not while Hektor's body lies in Achilles' camp.'

'And Hektor's funeral is the one thing that would bring together every elite in Troy,' Aeneas said. 'Yet it cannot happen. Achilles will not give up my cousin's body.'

Hattu looked the Dardanian in the eye. 'It will happen, my friend. For you, for Priam and Hekabe and for Andromache. I will find a way. I may need your help,' he said, a tumble of ideas passing through his mind.

'You will have it,' Aeneas smiled, standing.

Hattu smiled back. 'I will call on you soon.'

Tudha watched this exchange jealously. With a grumble, he upped and left.

Hattu watched him go. 'Perhaps we should call it a night,' he said to the others.

The group dispersed, Dagon and Sirtaya heading to the acropolis to turn in, Aeneas tending to some other business of his. Hattu strolled the lower city streets, quiet and hot. He glared up at the high citadel and its hundreds of shady doorways and windows – like staring eye sockets in a pile of skulls. *Where are you?* he mouthed as if it might coax the traitor out.

Something caught his eye then, a man walking alone in the lower city's western ward – conspicuous given the emptiness of the streets at this hour. He recognised the graceful swagger. Aeneas, heading towards the Apollonian springhouse. *Praying will not expose the spy, comrade,* Hattu half-smiled. There were few others: a skulking merchant near the old market. A man lingering on his rooftop long past the time when people normally did so. A woman, glaring from her window.

A strange prickling sensation rose on his neck then. A patter of soft feet sounded behind him, running… followed by the skittering and skating of claws. Coming for him, fast. Hattu swung on his heel, just as the dog leapt for him and slurped at his face. Two others circled his legs, yapping, tails beating against him softly.

'Come, you rascals, come,' old Antenor sang adoringly, waving his cane at the dogs. The hounds skipped back to the elder's side.

'It is dangerous to walk the streets of the city after night curfew,' Hattu said, wiping his face.

Antenor swiped a limp hand through the air. 'Pah! On the nights when the pyres burn there is no curfew. Who can sleep, anyway?'

Hattu looked around the dusty avenue they were in. 'Of all places in Troy, why while away sleepless hours here?'

Antenor smiled slyly. 'Come on, King Hattu, you and I should both right now be slumbering at my villa. Let us not dance around the open secret. There is a rotten apple in this stony basket. Darkness is a time when it is so hard to see, yet there is so much to be seen. We're out here for the same reason…'

'If you're looking for clues about the traitor, then you're looking in the wrong place,' Hattu said. 'Hektor was poisoned by someone from the citadel.'

Antenor's face sagged.

Hattu took the drinking skin from his belt. 'A slave handed Hektor this before the duel with Achilles. A citadel slave.'

Antenor took the skin and rotated it, eyes wide. At first he seemed set to argue, until he sniffed the mouth of the skin. 'Oleander,' he said. His face grew a little sadder. 'Who would do such a thing?' he muttered to himself. His eyes lit up again, and he beckoned his hounds, holding the skin out towards them. Tails and ears proud they sniffed madly at it, but quickly lost interest. 'Whoever did it left no scent marker,' the elder sighed.

Hattu was about to take the skin back, when Antenor edged away, towards a torch fixed in a wall socket, holding the thing up towards the light.

'Hmm,' the elder said, his face like that of an inquisitive bird.

'What?'

'Sometimes the eye alone is not enough to spot the clues.' He held the skin in a variety of different positions. 'I have a few potions at my house, picked up years ago in the Alasiyan markets. Potions that leather tanners stopped using generations ago. Potion... that might reveal this skin's secrets. But that is for tomorrow. Come, let us return to the villa. I will brew some mountain tea to help us sleep.' One of the dogs stood on its hind legs and whined at Antenor. 'And you can help me feed these rascals.'

***

On the twelfth day after Hektor's death, Hattu crouched in the shade of a giant boulder southwest of Troy. The cicadas buzzed fervidly, and his green cloak stuck to his bare back with sweat. A tang of old woodsmoke permeated the hot air. He stretched his neck to peek carefully around the boulder's edge, looking south.

The plain there was swarming with Ahhiyawans. They came in long trains, carrying supplies and arms down from the Borean Hills and across the Scamander ford, each king and his army setting up tents and huts in what was to be a permanent new camp. As he watched them work, the noon heat and insect buzz grew soporific, and there was a moment where he felt his eyelids slide over.

That was when the grinding of chariot wheels sounded.

Hattu blinked his eyes wide open, sucked in a breath and pulled back from the boulder's edge, pressing flat against the rock.

Achilles' chariot burst past his hiding place, the black boar standard aboard rapping in the wind of the ride. Bouncing behind it was the flayed, broken sack of Hektor's corpse, hair and skin trailing in ribbons. Achilles sped along the course of Troy's lower city walls, staring up at the defences. The archers up there did not shoot. They had tried in the days gone past but Achilles was clever enough to stay clear of their range.

'Look upon your mother city, foolish Hektor,' Achilles raged, shaking his spear towards Troy. 'Ha, perhaps you could, if only you had eyes!'

During the first few days of this spectacle, the other Ahhiyawans at work on establishing the new siege camp had set down their tools and burdens to watch, cheering and braying in support. Gradually, their enthusiasm had dimmed. Hattu risked another peek south: now, just a few watched on, and most wore looks of pity at this gory daily ritual. He saw Odysseus amongst them, head bowed like a parent watching a son's disgrace, before turning away and vanishing into the camp.

Patiently, he waited for Achilles to reach Troy's eastern limits, then – as with every day before – turn back to follow his own ruts towards Troy's western edge this time. Hattu ducked down, eyes watchful. Achilles rode closer, screaming curses. Now, Hattu crept forward a little, watching the enemy champion's course. The stallions sped down into a slight depression. A hollow, obscured from his fellow Ahhiyawans.

Silently, he lifted a small rock, aimed and threw. It flew out and whacked one of Achilles' two black horses on the muzzle. The beast reared up in shock. Achilles yanked on his reins in fright, and the chariot came to an inelegant halt near Hattu's hiding place.

Achilles thumped down onto the dust and stomped round to examine his steed's wound. 'A scrape and no more,' he grumbled, stalking back round. Just as he was about to remount his chariot, Hattu emerged from behind the boulder.

Achilles stopped dead. 'You!' His eyes flicked to the south, and the hollow's edge screening him from his allies, and finally to Hattu's sword hilts.

'I did not come to fight you, Achilles,' Hattu said, palms empty and upturned.

'It makes no difference whether you put up a fight or not. I would kill you, and you know this.'

Hattu cocked an eyebrow. 'Perhaps. But I am not injured or tired like those you tend to choose as opponents,' he countered.

Achilles went for his spear, resting in the chariot cabin. Hattu simply smiled, and from behind him, Prince Aeneas appeared near the boulder, bow nocked and trained on the enemy champion. Now Hattu whistled and in a blink, Andor streaked down and snatched the spear from Achilles' reach.

'You would not dare harm me,' he seethed, his snub nose wrinkling. 'I am the shining son of Peleus – descended from the Gods!'

Hattu gently raised his hand. Aeneas stretched his bow a little further.

Achilles' lips peeled back to reveal his yellowing teeth. 'Kill me then. But know this: when the bards sing of our victory, they will sing my name the loudest. There will be no place in that great verse for you, Hittite, or the pathetic group you brought to the war with you.'

'As I said, I did not come to fight you,' Hattu repeated, flicking his fingers again, downwards this time. Aeneas lowered his weapon just a fraction, but never took his eyes from Achilles. 'Nor did I come to this war for fame or glory like you. I have travelled that road before, reached its end and found only desolation – the phantom of glory gone to dance on another horizon.' He gestured at Hektor's discoloured, bloated corpse. This close, Hattu could smell the soft and purulent flesh, see the maggots writhing within. 'You bring Hektor's body to this plain every day… to humiliate him?'

'I will never tire of it.'

'Are you sure? That is but a rotting shell you drag behind your war-car. You can pull it around all day, but it will never blush or weep or beg for mercy. The only man I see suffering here is you.'

Achilles recoiled, his angry frown deepening. 'I wear not a single scratch from this war. Suffering is for others, not the divine Achilles.'

'The deepest scars are invisible,' Hattu replied. 'It must have hurt you terribly to discover that Patroklos had taken your war gear that day and gone to fight?'

Achilles' face twisted awkwardly. 'Not as much as when they brought back his body.' He snatched a hidden spear from his battle-cabin in a lightning-fast move. The point came up for Hattu's neck and quivered there. Only Hattu's raised hand kept Aeneas from loosing.

Achilles stared into Hattu's eyes. 'Patroklos did not steal my armour that day,' he said in a choked snarl. His chest rose and fell a few times before he spoke again. 'I gave it to him. I told him to lead the Myrmidons. The whole time I had only one thought in my head: of the victory celebrations later that night, and how I would have Patroklos – still disguised as me – demand Agamemnon's gratitude… of how Agamemnon would duly oblige in front of all the kings and lords. Then, *then* I would reveal the ruse. Patroklos would throw off his helmet and all would roar in laughter at the "great" Agamemnon, kneeling before a mere companion warrior.' He paused again and air escaped his lips in a tight, pained sound. He was shaking now, and at last he lowered his spear. 'Never once did I consider that Patroklos might die. I put my pride and a petty feud with Agamemnon before the welfare of my oldest and closest companion.'

'Patroklos meant a lot to you,' Hattu said.

'Everything,' Achilles said in a quick gasp. 'I staged foot races, boxing matches and contests of strength around his burial mound. Not enough. Nothing will ever be enough. He showed me how to run, how to fight, how to hunt, how to live!' Achilles' lips moved, but he could not speak anymore. The redness in his face now lined his eyes.

'Up on Troy's towers, Priam suffers too,' said Hattu.

'You expect me to have sympathy for the King of Troy?' Achilles said, steadier now. 'The greedy lord who imposes an outlandish levy on my ships? Do you know that before war broke out, he had his navy – that pathetic flotilla – sink six of my grain ships on their way back from the Hidden Sea. Four score sailors and enough wheat to feed my people through winter, condemned to the deepest waters because we had not enough silver to pay his toll.'

Hattu thought of the finery in Priam's palace again, and the hollow cheeks of the citizens. Had Priam ordered the sinking of the Ahhiyawan grain boats, or was it some mean officer going too far? He pushed the disturbing imagery away, and held Achilles' gaze. 'We all have our flaws, Achilles. But no parent deserves… this.'

Achilles ran his fingers through his fair hair, as if wringing dark thoughts from his head.

'Patroklos told me how you were destined for glory here at Troy...'

'I am,' Achilles said, proud and confident.

'…and that glory and death often come together,' Hattu finished.

A strange look passed across Achilles' face now.

'Hektor killed Patroklos in battle, as he would any other enemy soldier, as would you, or I,' Hattu continued. 'When he faced you, he offered you a pact for the victor to respect the loser's body. A pact which you rejected. Your blood was hot then. So think on it again now. Release his carcass, and I promise you that if you do perish during this war then I will fulfil the pact and see that your body is treated well too.'

Achilles looked back at Hektor's corpse quietly.

'What if it was your body there, roped to the back of a Trojan chariot?' Hattu asked.

'Then I would feel nothing, care not at all,' he muttered, 'just as you said of Hektor's corpse.'

'And what if it was your father, up on those towers, watching. What would he feel, seeing his boy treated like this?'

Achilles' eyes turned shiny then. 'What does he mean to you, Hittite? I will not give *you* his body.'

'I don't expect you to, here, like this. But what if his father came to you?'

Achilles' face bent in a frown, eyes darting past Hattu's shoulders to the boulder. 'Priam is here too?'

Hattu shook his head slowly. 'Would you do the right thing, if he were?'

Achilles' dropped his head, staring at the dust. 'If Priam were to come to me – come to my hut, pay me due respect… and speak to me as you have. Perhaps.'

***

Hattu watched Achilles' chariot trundling away. 'Go, head back to Troy,' he asked Aeneas. 'I will stay out here for a time. I want to reconnoitre this new camp of theirs a little more closely.'

Aeneas nodded.

'And check on my heir, will you?' Hattu added. Tudha had been sour in his farewell earlier. In truth he was renowned for his stealth and skill on missions such as this. Not enough, Hattu thought, to erase the memories of what he had done when last he had been trusted. 'For me.'

'I planned to talk with him regardless,' Aeneas smiled. 'I enjoy his company.'

As the Dardanian prince departed back towards the city, Hattu crept further from it, following a shallow gully – the bed of a dried up stream – to where it met the banks of the Scamander. Here, he crawled on his belly through the rushes, staying in the shade of spreading oaks. Soon he had a perfect view of the back end of the enemy camp. His teeth ground when he saw how well patrolled it was. Soon he noticed something else: a small bundle at the river's edge a stone's toss upstream. He crept closer towards it: a cloak of some sort, with the hilt of a knife or sword jutting from it.

'Ah, King Hattu,' a voice chirped.

Hattu almost leapt from his skin, shooting up to his feet.

Odysseus rose from behind a screen of rushes, pushing a stopper into the mouth of the water skin he had been filling.

Hattu glanced at the bundle and the knife hilt; it lay halfway between the pair. He shifted his weight onto the balls of his feet.

'I know what you're thinking,' Odysseus said calmly. 'You would undoubtedly slay me… *if* you got to the knife first. But you would not. I have watched you in battle. You are like an old ship: you can move well, but not fast. Your fighting days are almost over.' He took a swift step towards the river's edge and reached down to take the knife. It was blunt and rounded at the end. 'Besides,' he grinned, 'unless you wanted to smear fat on bread for me, there's not a lot you could do with this thing.'

'I didn't come here to fight,' Hattu said, relaxing a fraction.

'I know. I've been watching you all day. I saw you with Achilles.'

'You saw us… and you didn't call to your soldiers?'

'Why would I? I hoped you would somehow help him see sense. It takes a brave man to reason with that lion – so rampant with grief and anger. I admire you for it. I had to face him in the hours immediately after he learned of Patroklos' death – and it was hard enough for me, one of his allies.' Odysseus calmly sat cross-legged under the oak and gestured for Hattu to do the same. 'Now, will you join me? The shade is pleasant here – ideal for a drink and a bite to eat?'

Hattu looked over his shoulder: the enemy camp was suitably distant still, and this spot was well-screened from it. Cautiously, he crossed his legs to sit opposite.

Odysseus tossed Hattu the knife and the cloak.

Watchful, Hattu unravelled the cloak to find a small loaf and a pot of what smelt like boar fat.

'Never waste any part of an animal,' Odysseus said. 'It makes no sense to kill a creature just to harvest the piece you want and throw the rest away.'

Hattu cracked the bread in half and spread the fat upon it, handing Odysseus the other half. 'It makes less sense to kill men in a war like this. Every death so far has been meaningless.'

Odysseus arched an eyebrow. 'There were many deaths that day you broke down our sand gates and had us pinned on the decks of our beached boats. You were not shy in swinging your impressive swords,' he said somewhat smugly, then crunched into his portion of the stale loaf.

Hattu eyed his own bread, hungry but hesitant. 'I wanted to drive you onto your boats and into the sea, not massacre you. It was Hektor's madness that twisted that day into a hopeless massacre. In any case, I could say the same of you. Slaughtering King Rhesus of Thracia in his bed? Beheading Commander Dolon when he was merely scouting? Hardly the acts of brave men.'

Odysseus stopped chewing. 'Men?' He shook his head slowly,

sadly. 'Here on this plain we are hounds of war, and war makes all hounds snarl. In any case, you cannot tar me with those acts. Diomedes slew Dolon. I cannot control him, for he is a king in his own right, lord of a kingdom far more powerful than my own. As for King Rhesus, killing him was never our plan. Diomedes and I were tasked merely to steal his horse herd. That is what I did. I was long gone from that night raid before I heard that Diomedes had slaughtered Rhesus.'

At something of an impasse, both men fell silent. Hattu at last took a bite of his bread, finding it surprisingly enjoyable, the boar fat salty and flavoursome.

'I sailed here only to honour an oath,' Odysseus said. 'As soon as it is fulfilled, I will return to my island and lie with my wife, then go hunting with my son.' He gazed off to the west and fell silent.

'Your integrity is impressive,' said Hattu. 'But you could right now set sail back to your island, could you not? Is this oath really more important than your family?'

The Ithacan King's gaze remained on the west. 'The oath arose back when Helen chose Menelaus as her husband. I convinced the rejected suitors – the kings arrayed here with him – to swear upon the blood of a slain stallion, to uphold Helen's choice and defend it against any who tried to break her and Menelaus apart. I did this because I saw in their eyes envy, cinders of malice. I did it to bond them, to avoid a great war.'

Hattu gazed across the pyre-stained Scamander plain. 'That worked out well.'

'This is certainly not what I intended to happen.' Odysseus smiled in that lop-sided way of his, face weary. 'Still, you see that I, as the proposer of the oath, cannot abandon it. Not until Troy has fallen.' He sighed deeply. 'Anyway, you speak of family. You didn't tell me your boy was here too? It takes a brave father to bring his son to war.'

'My heir was not supposed to be here. He is reckless… dangerous.'

'When you attacked our camp of ships, he was deadly,' Odysseus countered, one eyebrow rising. 'He made a fair fool of our mighty *Wanax*.'

'Hmm,' Hattu grunted.

'You were unimpressed?'

Hattu shook his head slowly. 'I did not say that. Killing soldiers in battle is one thing…' Again he thought back to the end of the previous summer. The northlands lying in ashes. The woods of Hatenzuwa a suppurating tomb. All that, he could accept, for he had asked his heir to quell the rebellion and that is what Tudha had done. But the rest of it…

He noticed Odysseus' eyes reading him in the way a scribe might eye a clay slab. 'Have you told him?' the Ithacan king asked. 'That you were impressed by his feats at the shore?'

Hattu shook his head gently.

'Then you should. It is the things a father does *not* say that shape a child's weaknesses and worries. Those things stay with you for life. Gods, I know only too well from my own boyhood.'

Hattu remembered Tudha as a baby in his arms. The toddler he had hugged in the nights when the civil war was swinging firmly against him. The boy had been his reason to carry on… back then. Time had changed everything. He thought of the stony hall in the ancient shrine at the heart of the woods. The bloody handprints on the door. The stink of death from within.

A sacred place. Desecrated.

He shivered again. Seeking a change of subject, he looked around. 'So here we are, locked into this war until Troy falls or we all die.' He noticed how Odysseus' gaze again drifted to the western horizon, the sea. A familiar twist of concern passed across his face. A look Hattu recognised from the mirror. 'There is something else,' he deduced. 'You do not simply yearn for your loved ones… you fear for them.'

Odysseus arched one eyebrow. 'How the face speaks even when the tongue is still,' he laughed sadly. 'I came from Ithaca with a few hundred farmer-soldiers. I left enough men back on my island to tend to the herds and fields and watch the shores for pirates. But by all the Gods, there is something out there that no army could possibly repel. Something creeping eastwards. Towards my homelands, towards yours.'

Hattu felt a stark shiver crawling up his back.

'Far to the west, beyond Ahhiyawa and as far away again, things have changed,' Odysseus explained. 'One day, not long before this war, an amber trader on his way back from those parts put in at my docks as always. Usually he would stay overnight. We would eat lamb and drink wine while he grew ruddy-faced and regaled us all with tales of debauchery and far-fetched adventure in those mysterious parts. But this time, he stumbled off the boat ashen-faced, wasn't interested in food or wine, didn't even try to barter at my market – he just wanted to take water and set off again and get as far eastwards as he could. I insisted that he tell me what had shaken him so.' Odysseus paused, gulping slowly. 'He spoke of barren lands, a drought more savage even than the one that had beset Ahhiyawa. Earthquakes too, and revolts. Multitudes of tribes had upped and left their ancient villages, he claimed, and had set sail aboard huge fleets in search of new homes. Others I have spoken too – wool merchants from Thracia – talk of more great hordes roving overland across the northern floodplains. All of this… all rumbling steadily eastwards.' Now he turned to the crescent camp and flicked a finger towards it, glowering at two groups in particular. 'Those cutthroats, the Sherden and the Shekelesh – they are the outriders of that storm. Agamemnon does not see it. To him, they are cheap blades for hire. One day, they might be the ruin of him.'

Hattu felt deep, powerful waves of unease pass up through his body. 'Put aside the oath, put aside family, put aside everything…' He leaned forward and held up one hand, forefinger and thumb pinched as if presenting some tiny jewel to Odysseus, looking the Island king in the eyes. 'Does your *Wanax* understand the magnitude of this game he plays?'

Odysseus cocked his head a little to one side.

Hattu sighed gently, nodding to himself. 'I thought not. And so I will explain.' He took a deep breath and gestured to the countryside around them. 'Hittite kings have, for centuries, woven a delicate political fabric here in Wilusa. The city of Troy has always been the lynchpin of these parts. If you Ahhiyawans pursue Troy's fall doggedly, *if* you somehow achieve that goal, then you must at least understand the consequences.' He picked up a dry twig, snapping it in three and making a little tepee in the earth. 'There are three great empires in this world. My realm, that of the Assyrians and of the Egyptians. Whatever our ambitions might be or might have been, we are interdependent on one another. Together, we bring stability.' He removed his fingers from the tepee, which remained upright. 'Think of the merchant ships that brought tin to make you that knife, flax to craft your tunic, the gemstones in your wife's earlobes back on Ithaca, the spices on your food… that trade exists only while the powers remain balanced. It would only take one power to tumble,' he pulled one piece of twig away and the other two fell, 'and the whole lot would collapse.' He looked up to see if the Island King was following. He certainly was. '*If* you break Troy, it would damage my empire gravely. If my empire founders, you would not win our lands, you would unleash chaos. You would stoke uprisings, give rise to one thousand petty warlords, bring about a world of brigands. Imagine the trouble in the far west, and the desolation here at Troy… now multiply it all one thousand fold.' He watched Odysseus' face grow pale. 'I urge you, Island King, turn away from this war. Do the *right* thing.'

Odysseus laughed. 'I am but a minor king amongst many, all beholden to the oath.'

Hattu held his bright gaze. 'No, you have a choice. You could be the first king to set sail for home, the example for many more. I know some have thought about it already.'

Odysseus smiled and opened his mouth to reply, when a rustling of dry grass sounded from nearby. Hattu glanced over his shoulder, seeing two Spartan scouts stalking this way. He rose cautiously, shooting Odysseus a look: had this had been the Island King's ruse all along – to distract and delay Hattu here while these guards crept up?

'Go,' Odysseus hissed.

'You would help me escape capture?'

'It wouldn't be the first time an Ahhiyawan had done so,' Odysseus said. 'Achilles helped you escape from the beach camp, remember?'

'You saw us, didn't you?'

Odysseus smiled thinly. 'I see everything.'

Hattu backed into the dry stream gully, looking back once. 'The siege of Troy is a dangerous game, Island King,' he said, 'and you are part of it.'

'Then you had best hurry back inside the walls,' Odysseus whispered after him. 'For I fear the game is about to grow horns.'

***

Back in Troy, Hattu trudged up to the citadel, the whole strange encounter with Odysseus spinning in his head. He reached Antenor's villa, stepping into the pleasantly cool shadows of the scullery where the dogs had sensibly retreated to some hours ago. His mouth felt gummy and unpleasant, and his head throbbed. He realised he hadn't taken water all morning. An easy mistake to make.

The curtain of laced sea shells clanked and clinked. 'Ah, *Labarna,*' Antenor said, appearing and planting a filled jug – frosted with condensation – and a cup before him.

'Thank you. I could build a temple for you, my friend,' he croaked, then poured and guzzled two cups in single draughts, the coldness exhilarating. At first he thought it was merely water, then he realised it was Antenor's favourite drink. 'Mountain tea,' Hattu smiled, pouring himself a third cup.

'Always!' Antenor cackled, pouring himself a cup and beckoning Hattu into the low-ceilinged, wooden sitting area – as gloriously cool as a cave in the Hittite heartlands. Hattu crumpled down into a pile of cushions, sighing.

The elder too rubbed at his lower back and groaned, then whumped down rather gracelessly. Two hounds came speeding over then leaping in competition for the coveted spot on Antenor's lap. One, over-enthusiastic, overshot and crashed into his stacked pile of Elamite wooden bowls. Antenor hooted with laughter and the second hound howled in triumph, before taking the prize spot on his lap. Hattu chuckled, sipping on the dark herbal brew. It was bitter and strong – with a sharp kick too. The hotness of it brought a gentle and cooling sweat to his skin.

Antenor supped his own cup and let out a long, decadent sigh, then tapped a small clay plate of honeycomb on the trestle table between them. 'To sweeten your tea, if you so desire,' he said.

*Honey*, Hattu thought. The citadel gardens sported dozens of hives. It sparked an idea, of how the city defences might be bolstered. But that was for later. He added some of the amber honey to his tea, then rubbed at his knees and ankles, wondering if there was any healer in Troy that could douse the fire in there. The disgraced hound came over to nuzzle at his hands. He stroked the beast's long, thin snout and rubbed its ears.

'I saw Dagon a short while ago,' Antenor said. 'You went outside to bargain with Achilles, I hear?'

'He will return Hektor's body. I am sure of it.'

'That is no mean feat, *Labarna,*' Antenor cooed. He held up a finger. 'And neither… was this.' He reached behind the cushions and produced the drinking skin Hattu had given him. It looked different, weathered and pale around the neck.

'You've… half-ruined the skin?' Hattu said glibly.

'No,' Antenor scowled. 'Look!' He thrust the neck of the skin before Hattu's face.

'What did you do to it?'

'I steeped it in unwatered wine overnight thinking it might reveal some sign of wear – giving a clue to which side the skin was most often worn on the belt or suchlike. A broad measure to at least rule out some suspects. But I didn't expect *this*.' He tapped the skin's neck area. The leather was marked in a crude spiral.

'Is that a design?'

Antenor shook his head like one of his dogs. 'At first I thought so too, but it's too rough. It's a stress marking. See the definite edge there? See the distinctive pattern? I'm not sure what it tells us, but it's a clue, definitely,' he said, his old face boyish.

Hattu scrutinised the marking, intrigued.

***

Bats rapped across the full, flaring moon. A wagon and a small escort party of six Trojan Guardians snaked back across the plain from the enemy's new and almost-complete camp, entered the city and rode uphill to arrive at the citadel. There, people waited in solemn masses around a tall stack of acacia and sandalwood. The Guardians helped King Priam down from the wagon, then the priests of Troy lifted a cloth-covered stretcher from the back of the vehicle. Hattu watched as they washed and dressed Hektor's mutilated body. The Wind of Wilusa mercifully carried off the stench of decay, and the owl-light masked the grievous lesions and putrid humps on his skin. Laocoon proclaimed it a gift from Apollo that his body was 'fresh' even after all this time. A lie, albeit a well-meant one.

Despite the state of the body, Hekabe and a shaking Andromache insisted on helping the priests, bathing the skin and combing his hair.

'My dearest, truest boy,' Hekabe said in a strangled whisper as she washed his face with a perfumed oil. 'May Apollo, Lord of the Silver Bow, protect you now as he did in life,' her words choked off into a sob. Antenor the elder knelt with her, taking her against his shoulder and soothing her. His hounds howled mournfully behind him.

Andromache knelt by Hektor's other side, cradling her husband's head, speaking to him in soft tones that wavered sharply with grief every so often. 'In spring we were three, you little Astyanax and me. We dreamt of a future beyond this war, of growing withered and old, of being by one another's sides and at peace in our final days, together. That future crumbles to nothing. For now I am a widow. Astyanax will never know his father. People have said throughout all of this that Troy's fate and yours were entwined. My love, tell me, tell me this is not the end? I shake at the thought of what it might mean for our boy if it is. Tell me?' she wept, fixated on Hektor's face as if it might actually speak. A group of templefolk eased her away so that the final preparations might take place.

Hattu found himself thinking of the five prophecies of protection and the two that remained. Right here, now, seeing the dead warrior-prince beside his pyre, Hattu would gladly have traded those last two things and all of his gripes about Hektor's leadership of the Trojan Army just to bring the city's hero back to life.

Hektor was dressed in his armour and his sword was laid beside him so that it might journey with its master to the beyond. Finally his senior brothers Paris, Deiphobus and Scamandrios lifted the stretcher and placed him on the pyre. Paris lifted and kissed Hektor's hand then stepped back, red-eyed. He took a few deep breaths then delivered a soaring eulogy, eyes meeting those of every other present, then turning up to the star-strewn sky. Hekabe, on her knees, wept as Priam whispered some last words to his boy, then tossed a torch on the heap. To the rising song of the priests, the body of Hektor, Breaker of Horses, turned to ash, blown by the Spirits of the Air and the Wind God into the sky above Troy.

Andromache sobbed uncontrollably. Hattu gazed at her, heartsick, thinking of Pudu and little Ruhepa back at Hattusa. How many times had he put them through the terror of wondering whether he would ever come home? *This will be my last war,* he swore, there and then.

Hekabe did not rise from her knees. She stared, dead-eyed, into the flames.

Cassandra watched on from the opposite side of the fire. She seemed listless and clearly full of the temple potion that the priests fed her to dull her mind and quiet her tongue. But then her eyes slid up and round to meet his. She said nothing, but Hattu heard in his mind an echo of her wintry greeting: *How could you?*

Unnerved, he looked away. He spotted Aeneas watching on, pensive, Tudha offering him a comforting hand on the shoulder. Sirtaya crouched by the pyre, looking up and around in that strange way of his, as if he could hear the earth and the sky lamenting too.

Many of those gathered muttered and glared at Helen. Accusatory looks, terse whispers.

Helen's eyes darted, and suddenly she exploded: 'Hektor! Dearest to me of all Paris' brothers,' she cried towards the crackling fire and the outline of the dead hero. 'I would die on these flames if it would bring you back, if it could spirit me back to the day I came to Troy's shores and brought such misery upon her people.' She looked around the gathered ones. 'Aye, that's right. I wished for none of this. You who shrink away from me as if I were the plague walking. You who speak of me as if it were I who put the spears through the hearts of your fallen husbands, fathers and sons. Throughout it all, only Hektor and Paris stood up for me, and you, Majesty,' she said to King Priam. 'The rest of you, If you resent me so, then throw me into the fire. See what good it will do for Troy!'

Paris stepped over to her, shielding her in an embrace, whispering to her, calming her. A short time passed with no more words, then Paris, eyes bloodshot, came to stand beside Hattu and Dagon. 'Father says the Ahhiyawans have agreed to twelve more days of truce. Tomorrow, when the flames have settled, the priests will pick his bones from the ashes, wash them in wine, then wrap them in the Trojan purple.' He pointed to a spot up on the Silver Ridge, near Thorn Hill, where a number of small humps were visible against the darkening sky. 'They will be put in a golden chest and buried in a barrow, up there, with the other legends of our country.'

'It is only fitting,' Hattu said.

As the flames roared on, Hattu used the edges of his eyes to observe the gathered elites: the glittering royal line of Troy, the garrulous priests, the elders, the nobles. United in grief. Yet one here was a fine actor. He rolled his eyes towards Dagon, who wore the same look. *Which is the traitor? Who is the Shadow of Troy?* The one who had poisoned the springhouse well, who had betrayed young Prince Troilus to the enemy, who had thwarted the chariot support by stealing the gatehouse keys, who had poisoned Prince Hektor. Yet, damn it all, no sign of that slave. That faceless, forgettable slave who had handed Hektor the drinking skin.

'Hektor, my love,' Andromache sobbed, falling onto all-fours and reaching out towards the flames. The priests had to drag her back. 'Let me cast myself upon the pyre with him!' she protested. 'He was our champion, our future king… and now he is gone, like most of his army,' Andromache cried on, struggling against the priests. 'What hope is there for Troy now?' The cry was echoed in many forms by the mourners.

After a time, Hattu realised that all eyes had fallen upon him, and that King Priam had shuffled over to his side. The King of Troy was now offering him something in outstretched, shaking hands. Hektor's bright battle helmet. The Helm of Troy. 'They said when this war began that Hektor would defend Troy until you came with your armies to win it,

*Labarna.* You came with no army, but now you have one. I, as King of Troy, appoint you High Commander of her Army. I give to you this ancient battle-helm, and the walls of my city. Troy's fate rests with you, King Hattu.'

Hattu's mouth turned dry. Lost for words, he took the helmet – heavy and cold. The sea of eyes around him were unblinking. Most were awestruck. But the sons of Priam: Paris, Deiphobus and Scamandrios, stared at the helmet jealously.

A tense silence stretched.

Aeneas broke it, stepping over beside Hattu, bowing. 'It will be an honour to serve under your command, *Labarna*,' he said, then lifted a funereal wine skin from a rack, twisted at the neck to pull out the stopper then drank a deep draught, then held it aloft. 'And so it will be an honour for us all!' he proclaimed.

This shook the Trojan mourners from their stunned silence. They exploded in a sonorous chorus of vows and praise, lifting their drinks also.

Hattu fastened on the Helm of Troy, weighty and solid, the purple plume hanging to the small of his back. Aeneas handed him the wine skin, then stepped back. Hattu took a sip, the enormity of what had just happened starting to sink in. When he made to take another sip, he paused, the neck of the drinking skin a hand's-width from his face. The leather was marked with the pale, irregular spiral just like the one that poisoned Hektor. The marks were fresh, new. He glanced to his side, to Aeneas… to his strange fletching ring. His heart pounded. *You?*

# PART 2
# SUMMER 1258 BC

# CHAPTER 12

## BESIEGED

The late morning sun sizzled the land of Wilusa. The Scamander plain, not so long ago freckled with flowers and carpeted with grass, was now a dry brown husk of baked mud and ashes, pocked with boot and hoof prints and wheel tracks. The last few brackish pools were clouded with flies. Dominating the northern side of the parched river plain was a great crescent of Ahhiyawan huts and tents, jutting with stacked spears and war staffs. For now the invaders had completed this partial siege line around Troy's lower town, enveloping the entire southern side of the city. Every few days the tips of bright sails could be seen drifting behind the brow of the Borean Hills, coming in to the old shore camp – new ships arriving to unload fresh fighters for Agamemnon's army. There were Ahhiyawan mainlanders, islanders, more Sherden and Shekelesh and other piratical clans – all come to see if the rumours were true and that the golden city of Troy was indeed on the cusp of capitulating, and if they could grab a piece of the loot for themselves. From the countryside in the east too, roving bands of brigands emerged from the woods and valleys and traipsed in to bend the knee before the Mycenaean warlord.

Two bull-horned Spartan sentries greeted the latest band, one slapping at flies on his neck every few moments, the other scratching madly at weeping plague boils on his face. They guided the newcomers towards the open-air plinth beside Agamemnon's hut. Here, the *Wanax* sat in sweat-soaked skins and robes to receive the leaders of these rabbles. Each bowed, scraped and gave offering to him. With each show of deference, Agamemnon glanced over at Achilles' tent. The talisman was back in the game of war, but he would not upstage his *Wanax,* Agamemnon avowed.

'The new camp is complete. The men grow restless,' old Nestor said from the cluster of advisors arrayed before the plinth, his bald pate shining in the sun. 'What now, my lord?'

'At last we have Troy's walls before us, the remains of her armies caged inside,' Ajax burred, face pinched in discomfort at the heat. 'Let's break open this shell.'

The kings and elite warriors nearby rumbled in agreement.

Agamemnon nodded, noting a few prominent empty spaces amongst his council. A fair few of them had succumbed to the plague. Some, he would miss, others not so much. His thoughts returned to the matter in hand: the stony shell that needed to be smashed. It reminded him of the city wars that usually dogged the kingdoms of Ahhiyawa. The fine gates of many a palace had shaken and collapsed under the pounding of bronze-capped timber. He flicked a finger towards a group of men in tunics. Not soldiers but engineers, their master craftsman Epeius standing to the fore, meaty arms folded. 'Begin work on a squadron of battering rams. Take what men you need into the forest to fell trees.' Next, he called to a soot-coated fellow tapping away over an anvil. 'Smith! Smelt the finest bronze. Tanner, I want leather screens, strong and well-stitched.'

With every order he issued, the council of kings rose in swells of agreement. Yet he sensed the absence of one supporting voice. 'You have something to say, Odysseus,' he said wearily.

Odysseus cast a lasting look at the long southern stretch of Troy's lower city defences, studded with towers. The battlements were heavily patrolled and a stripe of industry was going on along immediately outside the city. 'The walls speak for me. Finer defences even than mighty Tiryns.'

'Why does everyone keep saying that?' Diomedes growled. 'Pick on someone else's city.'

'If we're to break through those ramparts of stone,' Odysseus continued, 'those thick gates, and then the even hardier citadel walls at the apex of the city, we need rams the likes of which Ahhiyawans cannot build.'

Agamemnon's face soured. 'A less than useful observation, Island King.'

'One I made the moment we first set foot ashore on these lands,' Odysseus answered. 'That was why I took it upon myself to retain the services of... Mardukal.'

The council hissed and gasped like a forest brushed by a sudden gust. 'Mardukal? The Assyrian? We sent him away in spring!' they jabbered.

Agamemnon stretched taller in his throne, sucking in a sharp breath through his nostrils. 'What have you done, Island King?'

'*Wanax,*' Odysseus quarter-bowed towards the plinth. 'I used my own silver to pay him to remain in Milawata. For I knew this moment would come.'

Agamemnon felt the prickling heat of the sun on his face. As if the nearby presence of Achilles –the "lion" of the army – wasn't emasculating enough, now this shepherd from the tatty island of Ithaca had gone behind his back. The final insult was that Odysseus had done it all to arrange for an Assyrian – an *Assyrian!* – to parade onto this hard won plain then steal his crown as Troy's would-be conqueror. 'Then…you…wasted your…silver,' he hissed through a cage of teeth.

'*Wanax,* allow me to expla-'

'Troy will fall to Ahhiyawa, and Ahhiyawa alone,' Agamemnon barked.

Odysseus' lips grew thin, his deep-set eyes glinting. He nodded in a way that suggested he disagreed completely, then backed away.

Agamemnon glared at all the faces staring at him. Kings, soldiers, craftsmen, slaves. *Don't they remember?* He raged inwardly, staring at Kalchas the augur in particular. *Don't they remember what I gave up to have this chance?* He licked his lips, thinking of the potion Kalchas had started making for him. A drink that made one forget. Perhaps they had all been drinking it too? He made plans then to guzzle another skinful of the stuff tonight. *Why wait until tonight?* he reasoned. He shot to his feet and waved his hands at them all as if scaring away crows. 'To work! Build me the rams that will break apart Troy!'

***

Along the top of the Silver Ridge, yet another band of warriors arrived, emerging from the heat haze. Their leader stopped and planted a foot on a small rock, lifting a hand to shield her eyes from the noonday glare. The sunlight glistened on her leather vest and sweat-beaded flesh. The long tassels hanging from her helm's crest clacked and swung as she regarded the land ahead: the stony hulk of Troy at the distant end of the ridge, framed by the foam-flecked sea; and down in the lowland plains to the south, the mass of Ahhiyawan soldiery.

'It seems the rumours were true, my Queen,' said the lithe warrior nearest. 'Agamemnon is close to victory. Close to unlocking Troy's gold.'

The queen smiled a sickle smile, her eyes dark with malintent. 'Then we are not too late.'

'It looks like a squalid struggle,' the warrior remarked. 'Do we really wish to join this war, or go home?'

The Queen's lips quirked. 'It is a long way home, and I am too thirsty to make decisions. Let us choose in the old way.' Stepping over to a small tumulus topped with a semi-crumbled marble block, she twisted to look back over the train of twelve hundred pale-skinned female warriors with her, and the slave women leading a small herd of livestock. 'Bring forth a sacrifice.'

A slave girl brought the lamb to the spot and slit the creature's neck, then looked up at the queen for approval, smiling sweetly. But the ceremony was not complete. Instead, a priestess – naked, her shaved head streaked with paints – walked up behind the girl and seized her hair. The girl squealed and struggled but the priestess was oblivious, chanting in an ancient tongue, her eyes rolling in their sockets, and then she sliced the girl's throat. The slave girl bucked and shuddered, falling to her knees as blood sheeted from the wound, her and the lamb twitching their last.

Even before the girl sighed in death, the priestess set to work sawing at her belly, throwing aside her entrails and pulling free her organs. The liver she placed on the stone ruins, then knelt before it, watching as it trembled with the final pulses of life, reading its movements. 'Look to the skies,' the priestess proclaimed. 'There, you will find the answer.'

The many heads of the women scanned the dome of pale blue, seeing nothing but a single fish skeleton of cloud up there. Then, an eagle shrieked.

The Queen's mean smile widened as she saw the great bird soaring along the ridge towards Troy. 'War it is,' she drawled.

***

Hattu stared up to the sky, hearing Andor's cry. *What's wrong, girl?* he mouthed. He could not see where she was, so bright was the day. After a time, he turned his attentions back to the job in hand: In the stripe of shade immediately outside the lower city walls, teams of men worked, bare-backed and sweating, shoulders hunched, spades biting into the dirt. All along that southern approach, they scooped away the earth to create a sweeping ditch.

Hattu walked slowly to and fro along the edge of the ditch works, examining the depth and the width. It was his first initiative as high commander. When finished, the trench would be as good as an outer wall, blocking any approach from the Scamander plain. There would be only three narrow causeways, one at each of the lower city entrances: the Dardanian Gate on the eastern side, the Thymbran Gate here on the southern edge, and the Bay Gate on the western side, overlooking the Bay of Troy. An enemy attack would have to funnel across these tight spaces and suffer a raking storm of arrows and slingshot from the gatehouse towers.

Overlooking the works on the lower city battlements, Trojan archers stood watch every twenty paces or so. In truth many of the bowmen were in fact boys, hastily trained to replace some of the huge number of losses in the last clash. Same too with the spear infantry – old men and young lads wearing badly-fitting suits of armour to swell the decimated allied and Trojan forces as best they could.

He spotted a team of men struggling to break through rocks in the line of the ditch, their faces twisted with frustration. Grabbing a spare pick from a bucket, he dropped down into the earthen furrow alongside the labourers and added his strength to the effort. Dirt and dust flew as they struck away, until the rock cracked in half and then crumbled into pieces. The men beamed now, one swearing at the broken rock triumphantly. Climbing back out of the ditch, he walked along its edge once more.

'Digging is not toil. Did Hektor not say it was honourable to fight for your country? Well, fights come in many forms. Today these spades and picks are your swords and this ditch may save more Trojan lives than one thousand fresh Guardians.'

Up and down he paced, every so often peering through the searing heat haze towards the Ahhiyawan crescent camp, hearing the buzz of saws. *Siege weaponry?* he guessed. It had become a race against time.

'Sirtaya will tell us for sure what they're building,' Dagon said as if reading his thoughts. The Chariot Master stood nearby, hands on hips, his thick hoop earrings swinging as he scanned the enemy camp like a hawk.

Hattu gazed into the heat once more, concerned for the Egyptian. He had been gone on his spying mission for over an hour.

'He'll see what's going on, and we'll be ready to deal with it,' Dagon said with a calm conviction.

Hattu eyed his friend sideways. 'The last time you sounded so confident was the day you brought "special" wine from the *arzana* house,' he said with a cocked eyebrow, remembering the night a few years ago in Hattusa.

'It *was* special,' Dagon said, indignant. 'In a way.'

'Special? I woke up in the animal pens, in a bloody water trough, with a litter of piglets snuffling at my face,' Hattu chuckled. 'It'd have been useful if you had told me you got it from a Wise Woman, and that it was crammed full of toadstool juice.'

'Aye, what a concoction, eh? The Wise Woman said it'd help with my bad shoulder. Gods, by the time we were done I had forgotten I even had shoulders. Nirni says I came home gibbering to myself. Apparently I tried to climb into a cupboard as if it was another room and refused to come out. She left me there, snoring in the cupboard, twisted like a prawn. And the next day, urgh… it felt like I was wearing a heated, shrunken helmet.' He shrugged and chuckled.

Hattu and he shared a moment of silence, thinking of home and of their loved ones. They heard voices carrying on the warm breeze, and turned their eyes up to see Aeneas and Tudha arriving at the battlements, keeping the archer watch in check. Tudha's face wound was now a straight line of white scar tissue, running down his forehead, cheek and chin. And then there was Aeneas…

Until recently, Hattu had considered Aeneas a brother. Now, the mere presence of the Dardanian made him deeply uneasy. He thought of the drinking skin and the peculiar markings on the neck. The fletching ring Aeneas wore on his thumb was unique and matched the markings perfectly.

'I don't feel comfortable about this,' Dagon said quietly. 'Aeneas was with us in the darkest moments at Kadesh.'

'That was a long time ago,' said Hattu. 'He was a young man then, and the sixteen summers since are more than enough to change any man.'

'Why would he poison Hektor,' Dagon said in a whisper, 'let alone all those other things the traitor is supposed to have done?'

'My heir told me of an old rivalry that burns within Aeneas. He feels the royal family of Troy do not treat him with the respect he deserves,' Hattu said.

'Tudha still knows nothing of our theory, or our plan?' Dagon asked.

'Nothing. It must stay that way.' A stampeding of bare feet sounded. Hattu and Dagon looked along the trench. 'Speaking of our plan…'

There came Sirtaya, loping back from his spying mission, face pale with fear and excitement as he looked up at Hattu and Dagon. 'I sneaked right up to the perimeter, Master Hattu. I overheard the discussion of Agamemnon and his council. They mean to construct nine battering rams. Forty sets of ladders too,' he said.

'Rams. I knew it,' Dagon grunted, then spat into the dirt.

'So many?' Hattu said, staring at the enemy camp again then glancing nervously along the incomplete ditch works. 'More water,' he called to the boys sitting at the drinking trough just inside the Thymbran Gate. 'Ask the clerk at the citadel storehouse for emergency rations of honey and bread too.'

He glanced up at the battlements once more, at Aeneas, then turned back to Sirtaya. 'Anything else?'

'No Master Hattu. nothing. Nothing at all.'

Hattu gave him a prompting look. 'Nothing? Are you sure?'

Sirtaya looked confused for a moment until at last he smiled, understanding. 'Ah, yes. There is good news too. I also managed to reconnoitre the camp via the rear,' he said with a louder voice. 'The watch pattern there is complacent. I think they assume that they are safe from that direction. A select team of soldiers could creep in that way, right up to Agamemnon's hut! The other kings' shacks too. Imagine it, Master Hattu, you could slice off the head of this invasion army in one stealthy swoop.'

'You'd need quick men, quick of foot and of mind,' Dagon mused. 'Go at night. No armour, mud on the faces.'

Hattu stroked his chin, mulling the idea over… all the while watching Aeneas from the corner of his eye. He and Tudha were listening. A moment later they peeled away from the walls and emerged from the Thymbran Gate.

'Did I hear correctly, Father?' Tudha said. 'You must make me part of this squadron. You know I am an expert at such raids.'

Hattu glanced at his heir. *At slaying the defenceless?* he thought bitterly.

A shadow fell across them both. 'You'll need an archer, yes?' Aeneas grinned.

Hattu's head twisted slowly to the Dardanian Prince, holding his dark gaze carefully for a moment before replying. 'Most likely.' He eyed the heat mirage between the trench works and the enemy camp for a while, then spoke again. 'I will decide upon the members of the raid party during this afternoon. We will strike this evening. Now go back to your duties, as I must attend to mine.'

Tudha and Aeneas left them, returning to their wall patrol, while Hattu and Dagon pointed along the ditch works, directing the diggers.

'Do you think it worked?' Dagon said quietly from one corner of his mouth.

'Time will tell,' Hattu replied. 'We'll know by the end of toda-'

A scrabbling sound interrupted him. He glanced down. Sirtaya, halfway through trying to clamber from the ditch, winced and fell, landing on his back like an upside-down spider on the trench floor. Hattu and Dagon began to laugh as they usually did at the Egyptian's overly-energetic antics, but when Sirtaya clutched his stomach and groaned, both caught the laughter in their throats.

'Sirtaya?' Hattu said.

The Egyptian's face was screwed up, a weak groan coming from behind his cage of foul teeth. 'I… I am fine, Master Hattu. Must have been something I ate,' he said, his face melting back into a sheepish grin. With a shake of the head, he clambered free of the trench, catching Hattu's offered hand for support. Off he scampered inside the Thymbran Gates, calling up to Tudha about some striped butterfly he had seen on his spying mission.

Hattu stared at the spot Sirtaya had been.

'Something wrong?' Dagon said.

'In all the years I have known Sirtaya, he has never once accepted my help like that, as if he always saw it as a sign of weakness.'

A moment of silence passed, then Dagon planted a hand on Hattu's shoulder. 'And how are your joints these days?'

Hattu shot his friend a sour look. 'Perfectly good,' he lied.

'I used to say the same about the hinges on the old gate back at the stables in Hattusa… until the gate fell off,' Dagon replied with a tune of mischief. 'Time laughs at us all,' he finished with a sigh.

But Hattu wasn't listening, for up on the battlements Tudha strode… alone. 'Aeneas is on the move,' he whispered.

Dagon's eyes grew hooded as he saw it too.

'With me,' Hattu said.

The pair headed inside the city, past the weary masses working to thrash every last grain from their thin sheaves of wheat and millet.

'Wait,' Hattu said, placing an arm across Dagon's chest to halt him. Up ahead, Aeneas had stopped to chat with a baker. The fellow had but a few small loaves on display, and the Dardanian Prince bought one of these with what looked like a silver ring – a generous overpayment. The baker grinned after him as he set off again. Hattu and Dagon waited a few moments before moving off in his wake. Any time Aeneas turned around, they used the crowds as a screen, turned in at stalls or stooped to pet passing goats. Higher up in the city, the streets were less congested. When he went through the open Scaean Gate and into the citadel, Hattu and Dagon waited a moment before slipping inside too, then hid behind the blue sphinx, watching as Aeneas entered the royal palace.

'Did you see the look on his face?' Dagon mused. 'Eyes narrow, always looking over his shoulder.'

'All he's done so far is go to the palace,' Hattu said. 'That's where his father, his boy and his wife are. There's no crime in that.'

But when Aeneas emerged, he looked even more shifty. He carried a sack under one arm too, the knuckles of that hand white. Once the Dardanian had passed their hiding spot and left the citadel again, Hattu and Dagon peeled away from the sphinx, shadowing his route once more. As they went, Hattu spotted old Antenor and his dogs, watching from the porch of the elder's villa. The old fellow had a weary look on his face.

'Is it as we thought?' the elder asked.

Hattu nodded sadly. 'We know nothing for certain yet, but he took the bait.'

Back outside the citadel, they followed Aeneas down through the lower city's western wards. A warren of lanes and alleys split by a single wide avenue. They passed stale-smelling taverns, weaved around washing troughs and pushed through forests of clothing hanging out on lines to dry. The two halted by the side of a wood turner's workshop where the air was sweet with the scent of sawn pine. Here, they peered round the corner: across the lane, the Prince of Dardania climbed the marble steps towards the Apollonian springhouse – the place Hattu had seen him go a few times before at odd hours, always alone. Except this time Hattu knew why. He watched as Aeneas slipped between the bright door pillars, vanishing into the darkness within.

Hattu looked up to the citadel walls. Antenor was up there now, having watched their progress carefully. He looked years older than moments ago, his eyes hanging on the springhouse doorway. He and Hattu had enjoyed their usual pot of mountain tea that morning, chatting about Hattusa and Troy, sharing tales of families and fond memories. They had watched in amusement as one of Antenor's hounds had approached a sleeping Andor on the villa balcony, only for the eagle to wake and flare her wings with a fierce shriek, sending the dog skating and scraping in fright – straight into the side of a table where it lay whimpering and ashamed, a lump forming on its head. But the talk had turned – as it had to – towards the matter in both men's minds. The elder's words echoed in Hattu's thoughts. *In the springhouse shrine there is a door. A door that leads outside the city.*

It had been Antenor's idea to plant a false piece of information about a proposed raid on the enemy camp. Sirtaya had played his part brilliantly, Dagon had done his bit too. Aeneas, apparently, had bought every word of it… and now he was on his way to warn the Ahhiyawans. Aeneas, Prince of Dardania, hero of Kadesh, was the Shadow of Troy.

His heart felt like a lump of stone, and he could not bring himself to continue the pursuit, to confirm the horrible truth. *Why, Aeneas? Why?*

Dagon sensed his hesitation. 'We have to do this, Hattu. Aeneas was here during the times of sabotaged embassies, of poisoned wells, of young Prince Troilus' ambush. He came back from battle and was in the city in the moments before the Thymbran Gates keys vanished, penning me and the chariots inside. That night at the river camp, he was there with Tudha when the Lukkan sentries were lured away. Tudha didn't see who tossed the stones in the river to draw their attentions. And that skin,' he pointed at the drinking vessel clipped to Hattu's belt, 'is his. The markings prove it.'

Hattu gulped down his reluctance. 'Come on,' he said, 'we have to be quick.'

They hurried up the steps and into the shrine, slowing to a careful creep inside. It was dark and musty, the space filled with a burbling gossip of running water. Hattu's eyes quickly adjusted to the darkness. Unlike the fine façade, the walls and ceiling were of rough-cut bedrock, damp and jagged. The floor was tiled red, and an altar stood at the end, draped with offerings of garlands, cups of wine and grain. It was only now he noticed how the waters gushing up from below were yellowish – the same colour as the Scamander. Something about this made him feel uneasy, but he couldn't put his finger on exactly what. He shook his head to clear it of the matter, for there was a more important one at hand.

Looking around, it seemed as if there was nothing more to the springhouse than this chamber, but then they heard Aeneas' footsteps echoed, fading, somewhere beyond the altar. The pair crept past the offerings and peered along the narrow corridor that stretched out to the left. At its end, a thick timber door clicked shut and a key clunked in the lock from the opposite side. They waited, listening to the fading of footsteps beyond.

Hattu beheld the locked door, Antenor's words again echoing in his mind: *In the springhouse shrine there is a door. A door that leads outside the city. A locked door for which only the royal elites of Troy possess a key.*

From his purse, he produced a key of his own. The key of Troilus. Hattu hadn't realised the significance of the gift, thinking it a symbolic token and no more, but when he had shown it to Antenor this morning – while the old man was mid-way through some rambling plan about how they might pinch Prince Scamandrios' key while he was bathing – the elder's jaw had dropped and he had rocked with bemused laughter.

Sliding the key and turning, the lock clicked again, and the door creaked open. They saw before them a set of crudely-hewn rock steps, winding down through Troy's mound into total darkness.

The air was cool and still as a tomb as they descended. Cooler, quieter… until a waft of warm, salt-tinged air hit him, blowing his hair backwards. At the same time he heard the cawing of gulls and the gentle wash of the tide. Ahead, he saw brightness: a cave mouth, draped with a curtain of wet vines. Hattu eyed the pale sand and foaming waters outside, bright in the noon light.

As they stepped outside, the full northerly sea breeze hit them and the damp sand gave gently under their soft leather boots. Cormorants honked and chattered in welcome from their nests above the cave mouth. 'The Bay of Troy,' Hattu said quietly, eyeing the vast natural harbour up close for once: the sweeping sickle of sand was dotted with patches of reedy swamp to the south, and the old harbour lined the north, the timbers warped and half-rotten. The handful of cogs and warships moored there looked even sorrier this close: three lay sunken in the silt, the decks submerged. Behind them, the gnarly bluff end of the Silver Ridge soared, with the back end of Troy's citadel towering at its edge.

'Look,' said Dagon.

Hattu followed his friend's pointing finger, seeing the telltale bootprints in the sand leading north, past the wharf and vanishing around the base of the bluff.

They crept around the bluff's base, leaving the sands to arrive on the grassy flats north of the Silver Ridge. The meadow ahead was freckled with yellow asphodels. An oak dell lined its edge. But no sign of Aeneas? They each sank to one knee like waiting hunters, watching, breathing slowly, tasting the scent of wild rosemary riding on the summer breeze. Then… one of the low-hanging oak branches shuddered slightly, disturbed. Hattu and Dagon shared a glance, then crept across the meadow and into that shady canopy of trees. It was cool and quiet inside, apart from the swishing of bracken and the gentle crackle of fallen branches underfoot. Soon, Hattu heard the sibilant hiss of something up ahead, saw a clearing in the trees, a sparkle of light. The River Simois. There, standing by the banks of Troy's boggy northern river, Aeneas waited. The pair dropped to their bellies behind a screen of ferns to observe.

'This is where he meets Agamemnon's men to pass on information,' Dagon deduced in a whisper.

Hattu glanced around. Indeed, the spot was well hidden from Troy by the trees and the ridge. They watched and waited… and waited and waited. Soon, the sun crawled past its zenith. Lying like that on the rough forest floor, Hattu's body began to ache, and a wasp began a campaign of terror against Dagon, constantly buzzing around his head, Dagon swiping and whispering curses at it. Aeneas too seemed to be growing impatient, looking up and downriver.

'What's happening here?' Dagon grumbled. 'Where's this Ahhiyawan contact of his?'

'He's watching the river,' Hattu said. 'We're waiting on a boat from upstream.'

'A boat? Upstream? That doesn't make sense. Why would the Ahhiyawans come to him that way?'

Hattu made to reply, but noticed Aeneas' eyes grow hooded. He *was* watching the river… but his *hunter's* eyes were on the ferns. He saw the Dardanian Prince's arm muscles twitch. 'Oh fu-'

Before Hattu could finish, Aeneas swung round, in one motion pulling his bow from his back and fixing an arrow to the string, falling onto one knee and aiming expertly towards the ferns. 'Come out, you bastards. I could shoot a dozen of you before you reach me.'

Hattu took a deep breath and rose to his feet.

'*Labarna?*' Aeneas croaked, lowering his bow. 'I… I didn't realise it was you. Dagon, you too?'

'Expecting someone else, were you?' Dagon replied, rising beside Hattu.

A sudden pallor of guilt came over the Dardanian's face. 'How did you know?'

'That doesn't matter,' said Hattu.

'What are you going to do?'

Hattu hadn't planned for this. He had expected a struggle, swords, blood. 'That depends on what you say next.'

Aeneas set down the sack he carried, tugging it open to reveal the silver rings inside. 'I came to meet the boats from Dardania,' he said. 'This is *not* Priam's silver,' he added quickly. 'It is the silver of Dardania. When the war started I brought it here and added it to Priam's strongroom for safekeeping. But not all of my people came with me to shelter behind Troy's walls. Some families chose to stay in the Dardanian woods and meadows. It was not my place to command them to come with me. In fact I admired them for their courage in staying behind – to brave whatever the war brought and to continue to live off the berries and crop of the land.'

Hattu paced over slowly, eyeing the silver rings, listening.

'Two summers in, I heard word that the Ahhiyawans had raided my lands, burnt the fields, taken away many women and the cattle and slaughtered dozens of men. Every year they return to raid anew. My people have taken to hiding in caves now. They are desperate, but determined not to abandon their lands. Without their farms they can only hope to buy food from the boats that pass in the north. To buy food they need silver.'

'Why didn't you just explain to Priam?' Hattu asked.

Aeneas smiled tightly, shaking his head. 'Come, now, *Labarna.* You have seen how it is in Troy. The lower city can be stripped of its fineries, but wealth is not to be taken out of the citadel.'

'So where are these boats?' asked Hattu, looking upriver.

Aeneas shrugged. 'That's what I don't understand. I saw the usual signal – a boil of grey hawks flying across the city, it's the same every time they come. But this time they are not here.' His face sagged. 'They must have been attacked upstream,' he sighed. 'Twice before this happened. The last time I only realised what had happened when one of the bodies floated past this spot, Ahhiyawan arrows jutting from the back.' He dipped his head, pinching his nose between thumb and forefinger.

Hattu and Dagon looked at one another, suspicions fading.

The Dardanian Prince looked up then. 'Wait, what did you *think* I was doing here?' he spluttered.

Hattu unclipped the drinking skin from his belt, tossing it to Aeneas.

The Dardanian Prince caught it, confused. 'I am not thirsty… and it is empty?'

'See the markings on the neck? They were made by your fletching ring.'

Aeneas eyed the skin markings and the ring. His eyebrows lifted, bemused. 'Ah… yes.'

'That is the skin that was used to poison Hektor.'

Aeneas' face paled to a sickly white. 'Apollo's bow. You think it was me?'

'Are you denying the marks were made by your ring?'

Aeneas glanced at the evidence again. 'I cannot, for it is clear they were.' He looked Hattu straight in the eye. 'But I did not poison my cousin. There were times when I wished him ill – times when he was paraded around the streets of Dardania in my chariot, worshipped like a god when I hoped he would fall and skin his chin like a buffoon – but never *this!*' he said, throwing the drinking skin down as if it had turned into a snake. 'Someone must have stolen my ring.'

'He's telling the truth, Father,' said Tudha, coming round through the grass from the other side of Troy.

All heads swung round to see the young Hittite Prince, Andor on his shoulder.

'I've watched him doing this before. I followed him outside once, witnessed him giving the bags of silver to the river skiffs from the north.'

Dagon cocked an eyebrow. Hattu sighed. Aeneas laughed. 'Gods… let that be enough?' he said.

Hattu stepped towards him and hugged him tightly. 'Forgive me, comrade. I had to be sure. You understand that, yes?'

Aeneas and he parted, the Dardanian prince nodding.

Tudha stepped closer too. 'If you had simply included me in this ruse of yours, Father, I could have cleared it all up before it came to this. You still think it is dangerous to trust me. With every day that passes, it becomes more dangerous that you do not.'

***

Hattu and Aeneas sat by the banks of the Simois, drinking fresh water and watching the mayflies floating over the lazy currents. Tudha and Dagon explored nearby, sending Andor after rabbits. Every so often, Tudha would toss the throwing stick to startle a rabbit from its hiding spot. Oddly though, Andor seemed agitated. Hattu couldn't help but remember her cry from earlier at the ditch works.

Aeneas glanced over his shoulder, towards the bay and the bluff-end of the ridge where the vine-draped cave entrance. 'There have been nights where I have considered coming to the springhouse, bringing my family… leaving and never coming back.'

'Yet here you are still, after ten years,' Hattu consoled him. 'I understand why you might think of it. The thought of escape scampers across my mind every hour of every day. Indeed just being out here is a relief.'

Aeneas flashed him a look of gratitude. The pair watched as Dagon, loping after Andor, stubbed his toe on a hidden rock and exploded in a string of Hittite curses. 'Don't tell him this, but Dagon reminds me of my father,' he chuckled. 'Always grousing!'

Hattu smiled. 'He prides himself on his complaints.'

'Your boy, he is quite something. For his age he cuts an impressive figure: strong, fleet-footed, quick-witted… strongly-principled too.'

'Aye, he is a precocious one,' Hattu agreed.

'He worships the ground you tread upon,' Aeneas said quietly. 'His greatest wish is for you to hold him in esteem of some sort.'

Hattu looked away.

'What…' Aeneas started, 'what happened at this rebellion in the woods?'

'Ah, Hatenzuwa. How much did he tell you?'

Aeneas shook his head. Not much, but I can tell there is something in there, something unsaid, that hurts him deeply.

Hattu laughed coldly. 'What he did hurt others much more deeply and truly.'

Aeneas frowned. 'Tell me. A smouldering coal on a man's tongue does him no good. Spit it out.'

Hattu spent a time in silence, the words rising through his throat but jarring in there. To say it aloud would be like letting a demon loose. He stared at the Simois' surface, but all the time saw that stone shrine in the forest, the old wooden door, saw his hand reaching towards it, pushing it open, heard the throaty creak of the timbers. He closed his eyes.

'My cousin Zanduhepa lived in those woods. She was a Priestess of the Forest. She and her templefolk lived a frugal life there, offering daily libations to the oldest trees, and sending woodcutters on down the wrong tracks so they would not use their axes on the sacred oaks. Travellers were welcome to stay in the dene by the shrine, or when the snows and rains fell, inside the shrine itself. Zanduhepa would always have root soup bubbling away in a cauldron in there, and enough bowls to feed one hundred passers-by.' He stretched his fingers and clenched them into fists as he spoke. 'And then… the rebellion rose from the heart of those woods.'

'Zanduhepa was part of it?'

Hattu shook his head. 'She would never have betrayed me. Even if she had…' he saw his hand moving towards the old door again. He could not bring himself to say any more.

Aeneas' brow slowly crumpled into a frown. 'I… I will not press you, *Labarna*. But I will say something that I am sure you already know: war is a horned beast, one that drives people to do things they normally would not. Some of the things I have done in the heat of battle… I have never told Kreousa, my father or my boy. Nobody. Only the Gods know my shame.'

Hattu's mind flashed with memories of things done, horrors that could not be forgiven. Ishtar shrieked with laughter from the caverns of memory. The only defence was that they had been carried out in the heat of war. *If only Tudha's crimes had been in the midst of the fray,* he thought, remembering the peaceful shrine, far from any of the rebellion battlegrounds.

'Look upon the good things he has done,' Aeneas continued.

Hattu plucked a strand of grass and began tying it into a loop. He tried as best as he could to feign a brighter mood. 'You and my heir seem to have formed a bond.'

'Effortlessly. I can ramble to him about any subject in a way I cannot do with any other fellow in all Wilusa. He listens, and I know he is listening, for when he replies, he rambles on in turn, but always – *always* – comes back to whatever point I was making with a wise counterpoint of his own. There is none of that tedious underlying rivalry that usually sours relationships between men. I've seen him talking with others around the city in the same way. Men young and old, women too, youngsters likewise. He is set on finding out who the traitor was, just to prove himself to you.'

'Yet still we do not know,' Hattu said, now picking at a dry reed. He stared at Aeneas for a while, noting how the Dardanian could not meet his gaze. 'You are innocent, Aeneas, as I hoped you would be. But you *do* know something, don't you?'

Aeneas smiled sadly. 'I would have told you before now, but like you, I wanted to be sure.'

Hattu's skin prickled in anticipation.

'All this time we've been hunting for this "Shadow", this Ahhiyawan spy…' the Dardanian mused. 'What about the only Ahhiyawan in Troy?'

A shiver raced over Hattu's skin. 'Helen…'

Aeneas smiled apologetically. 'There's a slave who works as a messenger in the city and a forager in the countryside. I've watched him when he gathers. Every day he goes to the same spot on the ridge. The same damned spot, even though the bushes there are bare of berries. Every evening he comes through the citadel's Thunder Gate and to the Fountain of Poseidon. He just sits there, watching the fountain waters. I thought for a time that it might just be his way. You know – to relax. But then I noticed that a while after the fellow has left, Helen goes to the same bench by the fountain… every night. One night, I watched and saw her crouching beside a bush next to the fountain. She was rummaging in the roots there, and she lifted something out and tucked it away in her gown. Her eyes were like a fox's, looking around warily to be sure nobody had noticed.'

Hattu saw it all in his mind's eye. He batted a hand upon his knee. 'The Ahhiyawans are passing messages into the city. Planting them at the forage bush. This fellow brings them inside. Helen picks them up. *Helen.*'

'And she was present at all of the sabotage and poisonings we have endured,' Aeneas added.

Hattu's eyes rolled downwards, saddened, but not surprised. 'This slave, what does he look like?'

Aeneas jolted with a humourless, single laugh. 'Every time I see him I try to imprint his features in my mind. An image, or even just words. Every time the description fades within moments. He is the most plain, indistinguishable man I have ever seen.'

Hattu laughed wretchedly. 'The slave… the one who gave Hektor the drinking skin.'

Just then Andor shrieked in that urgent way again, abandoning the rabbit hunt. Jolted by the sound, Hattu watched as she sped up and over the woods, on to the other side of the Silver Ridge, then banked and wheeled over one spot in particular somewhere on the Scamander plain. The abruptness of her departure startled all. A pang of fright passed through Hattu. Suddenly, he realised how exposed they were, out here, a good way from Troy's nearest gate. What if the Ahhiyawans who had intercepted the Dardanian boat upstream were roving close to this spot? Or if one of the incoming bands of brigands was coming this way?

'Trouble,' Dagon hissed to the sitting pair, not that they needed telling. Both rose.

'The Dardanian Gate is closest,' said Aeneas, waving the others with him.

The four sped like deer away from the Simois, back through the woods, across the meadow, then up the Silver Ridge's northern side. Hattu's thighs burned with the uphill effort, and Dagon groaned and panted all the way, while Aeneas and Tudha sped with more youthful grace. Beyond the ridge's brow, they heard Andor shrieking louder and louder. The tips of Troy's walls bobbed into view, and then when they crested the ridge, Hattu saw for himself what Andor had spotted. Spartans on the Scamander plan, crawling through the tall, dry grass towards the Dardanian Gate. For a heartbeat, he felt utter relief, for the Spartans clearly carried no siege equipment, and could not hope to penetrate those stout gates with swords and axes alone. But when he glanced at the gates he almost choked: they were pinned open with dirt upcast from the trench works. The band of archers patrolling the gatehouse walkway was thin and unawares. He called down to them: 'Watchmen! The enemy attack!'

At the same time, the Spartan trumpets pierced the air, masking his cry. King Menelaus rose from the dry grass, his bronze helm like living flame, the bull horns glaring white. His Spartan Army rose with him. Some eight hundred men, sprinting towards the Dardanian Gates.

Hattu, Dagon, Tudha and Aeneas, closer to the gate than the enemy, thundered down the ridge's southern slope, dust and blades of dry grass flying up behind them, yelling at the trench diggers. 'Defend the gates!'

The sweating, startled workers yelped and scrambled out of the trench, taking up spades as weapons, shaking with fatigue from their work and blinking in horror at the Spartan charge coming for them. The gatehouse archers blew on triton shells to alert the rest of Troy. Some men tried to use their hands to scoop away the dirt pinning the gates open. But it was too late, Hattu knew. He and his small band fell in with the diggers, knowing this was a hopeless fight. They could not win against Menelaus' hundreds. All they could do was slow down the fall of the Dardanian Gate and hope those inside Troy could repel the enemy after that. He squinted, sweat half-blinding him, seeing the attackers fall into a wedge as they raced across the final stretch of ground towards him and his half-prepared defensive rabble.

And then: disaster.

A streaming second band of attackers flooded down from the Silver Ridge with cat-like speed, coming for the open gates too. Two talons of attack! He sensed his ill-prepared men slipping backwards, petrified, felt himself compelled to do likewise. The second band arrowed towards Menelaus' Spartans, set to join them. They were tall-helmed, bearing bows, clubs and swords. These two forces would flood the lower city and tear Troy down from within. He braced himself for this final fight. Thirty paces away, fifteen…

In that single splinter of time, Hattu realised all was not as it seemed. Instead of converging with Menelaus and his men, the newcomers from the ridge instead slammed into the Spartan flanks with terrifying shrieks. They bowled men over, pulverising heads, slicing off limbs and shooting warriors through from close distance. They moved like dancers, weaving and bobbing, leaping and cutting, driving the Spartans away. Menelaus himself wailed, stumbling round in a tight circle, seeing his men being slaughtered all around him, his speedy run for the Dardanian Gate crushed.

'Come,' Hattu yelled to his small band. They loped over and piled into the fray, Hattu's swords flashing as he slashed the belly of one Spartan and parried away a second. Dagon sliced the hand from one Spartan axeman. Andor swooped low to pluck the helm from Menelaus' bodyguard, and Tudha brained the man with a short-range toss of his throwing stick. He snatched up the stick again, then swung round to train it on Menelaus. Menelaus' face paled. Behind Tudha, the diggers came, spades swinging, smashing heads and breaking bones. The attack ended as swiftly as it had begun, with Menelaus and the surviving two-thirds of his army breaking in terror, speeding back into the southern heat haze towards the Ahhiyawan crescent camp.

Hattu, panting, legs pulsing with pain, bent double to catch his breath, trying to snatch looks at these strange warriors who had saved Troy. Now he saw them clearly: they wore strange leather cuirasses. It was only then he noticed the lead warrior's striking features. A woman. All of them were women, he realised. Could it be? He had only ever heard of them from Hittite lore of his grandfather's generation.

Their leader crouched beside a dead Spartan then rose and strode a few steps in the retreating Menelaus' wake, holding aloft a dripping, crimson mass in her hands. The dead man's heart, he realised. She emitted another of those blood-curdling shrieks. Tightening her fingers into a tight, shaking fist, the Spartan heart she held erupted in spurts and strings of matter through the gaps.

When she was done, she stepped before Hattu. They were matched in height – unusual even for men to be as tall as him. Respectfully, he quarter-bowed. 'Your intervention was vital. I am Hattusili, Great King of the Hittites.'

Her blood-striped face contorted into a wicked grin. 'The *Labarna* is here? Then it truly must be the great war the rumours talked of.'

'There is little greatness here,' he replied, hesitating when he realised he did not know her name.

'I am Penthesilea,' she said. 'My people have an ancient bond with Troy, and we come to serve in her defence.'

Hattu, both unsettled by Penthesilea's appearance and euphoric about her words, swung towards Troy. Reinforcements had just reached the Dardanian battlements. Many citizens had arrived on the walls too, looking out in confusion and fear. Up on the citadel's high towers and roofs, a windswept Priam and Hekabe looked down, their princely sons and councillors with them.

Aeneas beheld the women warriors with a look of utter delight. 'People of Troy, rejoice,' he cried, his voice carried by the Wind of Wilusa across the city, 'for the Queen of the Amazons and her famous warriors are here.'

# CHAPTER 13

## THE DEAD OF NIGHT

News spread around the Wilusan countryside about the arrival of the mighty Amazons. This brought more allied bands to Troy. All these were small groups in comparison, but every single soul was welcome, each adding a spear or bow to the thin defence force. Some came in the shadow of night, travelling along the Silver Ridge as the Amazons had done. Others arrived by sea, landing at the Bay of Troy and hiking up the steep and short western path to the city's Bay Gate. More still came from the north, via Dardania.

At a feast held shortly after her arrival, Hattu was seated beside Penthesilea. He found her to be cold and abrupt to the point of insulting. But when they shared a krater of wine, she softened a fraction.

'Out there,' she explained to him, her lips shining with wine, one finger pointing along the Silver Ridge to a small tumulus out there, the crumbled marble block atop it glowing dimly in the reflection of the torchlight from the city, 'my ancestor, Myrine, lies buried. Many generations ago, she married into the Trojan line. On her death bed she vowed that our people would come to Troy's aid in the city's time of need.'

'So you came to honour an old oath?' Hattu said with a half-smile, understanding her a little more, and why the presence of the Amazons was so meaningful to the Trojans and their near neighbours.

He and the Amazon Queen spent the next few days in talks, he laying out his existing plans and she adding to or altering them. They sat in the cool recesses of the Scaean Barracks, cross-legged on woven mat, gazing over the tray of sand between them. It was criss-crossed with lines, marking out Troy's walls, and dotted with polished, coloured pebbles, each representing a body of soldiers. Hattu placed stones at key parts of the walls.

'The trench is vital,' he explained. 'It will sap the energy from any assault, and double the effectiveness of the wall defences. The enemy will be forced to attack across the three causeways before the lower city gatehouses,' he tapped the blocky outlines in the sand either side of the Thymbran Gate, 'where the archers on the towers will annihilate them.'

'For how long?'

Hattu looked up from the sand tray. Her tone was direct and clipped.

'How long before there is a breach, a ruse,' she continued. 'Or before a Trojan throws open the gates? I have inspected the grain silos. They rumble like hollow drums. How long will a hungry mother let her baby starve before her mind turns to ending the siege and pleading for the invader's mercy?'

Hattu sighed and looked to the slot window and the golden sun outside. High summer, lingering like a cloud. How long before the snowy season came and a cessation of hostilities with it?'

'Winter will not chase them away,' Penthesilea said, reading his thoughts. 'Ten years, they have been here.'

Hattu nodded sadly.

'We should attack their camp. Take the fight back to them,' Penthesilea insisted.

'We do not have the numbers to face them in the field again, even with the welcome addition of your army, my Queen.'

'There is more than one way to fight,' she punched her fist gently into her palm as she spoke. 'You say the enemy bask in comfort, certain that victory is only a matter of time. Then let us break apart that confidence, piece by piece.'

'The war of the flea?' Hattu half-smiled. It was refreshing to hear another talk like this, after Hektor's stubborn refusal to entertain such tactics.

Over the next moon, Penthesilea led three night strikes. Every time, she insisted on selecting and leading the small squads. Her selflessness impressed Hattu more than her fine armour and weapons. On the cusp of the first sortie, she stood in the pale moonlight by the Bay Gate, her face half sheathed in darkness. 'I am here to fight for Troy. If I die trying, then it will be a good death, and may my heir be more successful,' she said.

Hattu offered her a clenched fist salute as she stole down the rocky slope with her chosen warriors. Soon after, a crazed whinnying broke out from the Ahhiyawan crescent camp, followed by a stampede of horses. The enemy herds ran wild, tethers cut, haunches lashed by Amazon whips. He watched as a naked Diomedes staggered around in the torchlight like a fool, trying to calm and catch his prized steeds. Agamemnon too, drunk and caterwauling as his stallions ran amok, trampling his supply tents. No Ahhiyawan died that night, but neither did any sleep. Penthesilea and her team returned near dawn, grinning. The first tile had fallen from the solid roof of enemy confidence.

Six days later and during the last hour before dawn, the Amazon Queen and Hattu took one of the few seaworthy Trojan warships out of the Bay of Troy and round the headland, sails and masts down so none in the crescent camp would spot them. They glided south under power of oar, hugging the rocky coastline, then turned into the Bay of Boreas not long after sunrise. The city of enemy ships – now just a bridgehead – was manned only by a few hundred men, who guarded the boats and the latest supplies brought in from the islands. As before, sacks of wheat and dried fruit lay like a rampart near the shore. The nearest watchman – more of a clerk, busy cataloguing the provender – looked up the incoming craft, confused as to why its oars were moving rapidly, why it was speeding for the shore. When he realised it was a Trojan ship, he dropped his tablet and stylus, mouth wobbling in shock, eyes fixed on the duo at the prow: the Great King of the Hittites and the Queen of the Amazons, holding hands.

Hattu stared dead ahead at the waterfront as the boat ploughed directly towards the sands. 'Now,' he drawled. Penthesilea struck flint over the pitch-soaked torch they both held in their joined hands. As it whooshed alight, the sparse crew of Trojans behind them dropped their oars and leapt overboard, clambering onto a skiff being towed behind the warship and slitting the tow rope.

A spear's throw from the shore, Hattu and Penthesilea dropped the blazing torch. As it fell towards the decks, they each sprang for the ship's rail and jumped overboard too. Behind them, the resin-soaked deck went up in a wall of flames. Hattu plunged underwater, deaf and blind to it all for a moment before surfacing near the skiff, where he and Penthesilea were dragged aboard. As they rowed back out of the enemy bay, they watched the unmanned, speeding and blazing ship crunch up onto the sands, ploughing into the mountain of grain sacks. The clerk squealed, rolling away as the whole lot was swallowed by the blaze too. Another tile had fallen.

Fourteen nights passed before she struck again. This time, she took her ten best Amazons out directly towards the crescent camp in the broad light of noon, striding without a jot of fear. The enemy – the many thousands of them – dropped their spoons and cups in shock, then hilarity. 'The bitch means to charge us head on with ten of her whores,' Ajax roared, rocking with amusement. Agamemnon – sucking on a wine skin as he often seemed to be these days – waved a lazy hand towards his Locrian bowmen. 'Shower them with arrows,' he slurred.

'Daughters of Ares,' Penthesilea screamed. She and her ten dropped into wide-footed stances, snatching haircloth sacks from their belts, each bringing them overhead and whirring them like slings. 'Loose!' They let fly the sacks. The unready Locrian bowmen, Agamemnon, Ajax and every other gawped, watching the flight of the things, bemused. The sacks landed in different parts of the camp, the contents spraying across the ground. Agamemnon frowned, his wine-reddened face straining to see what was happening. Screams arose, then big Ajax staggered past, keening with pain, clutching at one hip and swiping over his shoulder with his other hand. Scorpions clung to his skin – black, shining stings pulsing. All around Ajax others rolled and flapped, beset by the venomous arachnids. The scorpions marauded across the camp, scurrying and stinging. Men tripped and fell back onto smouldering fires, some clambered onto hut roofs, mad with fright.

'*Seize* them!' Agamemnon howled.

A mass of Ahhiyawans surged towards Penthesilea. She and her troop turned and fled for the ridge and melted into the woods beyond. There, screams arose as Ahhiyawans blundered into pit-traps or were crushed under rolling logs set up earlier. Dusting her hands, Penthesilea swaggered back towards Troy like a leopard. She flashed a smile up at Hattu on the walls. 'The roof is close to collapse, *Labarna.*'

Hattu rocked back from his vantage point, a strange noise toppling from his lips. Laughter. For the first time since Hektor's funeral, he felt a sense of hope.

***

One fiercely-hot day, Tudha sat with Prince Aeneas atop a turret at the Dardanian Gate. While they crafted new arrows, Andor perched on the parapet's edge watching the goings-on outside the city and Sirtaya lay in a corner, curled up in a ball and snoring. Bees and insects hummed and a smell of burning sandalwood floated from one of the lower city temples, sweetening the hot air. He glanced down to the parched earth outside: the trench shielding the city's southern approaches was complete – vitally, before the Ahhiyawans had stopped sawing and hammering at their siege machinery. There were sounds of Trojan industry too: Dagon, overseeing a team of chariot engineers at the stables, instructing them in how to build a small squadron of the famous 'Destroyers' – the heavy three man war-cars that had been the difference against the Egyptians at Kadesh. Like this the two forces worked, readying for a new and final clash.

Tudha held his finished arrow up, looking down the shaft for straightness, checking the green duck blue-green, white-tipped mallard fletchings for position and the bronze tip for sharpness. Satisfied, he handed it to Aeneas.

'I have plenty of my own,' Aeneas said, gesturing towards the small bucket of shafts he had made so far that day.

'Consider it a token of friendship,' said Tudha. 'I'm not sure if my father apologised for suspecting you, but even if he did, I want you to have this.'

Aeneas smiled, taking the arrow. 'That's the difference between you and him, right there.'

Tudha smiled earnestly. 'Whatever happens between the Hittite Empire and Troy, between Ahhiyawa and Egypt and Assyria and all the states of this world. We, Prince of Dardania, shall remain friends.'

Aeneas tucked the arrow inside his quiver. 'Friends.'

The pair carried on working new arrows quietly to the rhythm of Sirtaya's snoring. The plop of each finished arrow into a bucket was most soothing – a sense of hope, of growing strength, of building towards victory. Things had felt like that since Penthesilea's arrival.

Suddenly, as if the Gods had grown bored of waiting for battle, a boom of war drums rumbled across the heavens. Tudha looked up, his skin crawling. Sentries rushed to the walls, taking up spears and bows. Penthesilea and the Amazons braced, teeth bared, eyes like hunting cats. All eyes twitched this way and that as they regarded the Ahhiyawan camp, waiting for the enemy to emerge in a great front from the blistering heat haze there.

Instead, a flock of waxwings scattered from the trees up on the Silver Ridge. All heads swung that way. A broad column of charcoal-skinned men emerged from the treeline, striding along the ridge's spine, towards Troy, their leopardskin cloaks fluttering. Tudha rose on his tiptoes, counting their glinting spears. Two thousand strong at least, he reckoned. Their leader wore just a loincloth, a cape embroidered in silver thread, and a headdress of rising golden spikes. 'I am King Memnon of Elam,' the leader hailed the city defences with huge eyes and a winning smile, 'nephew of King Priam. I bring the Sons of the Dawn to Troy's aid.' There was a moment of stunned silence before, with a burst of rapturous cheering and pipe music, the Dardanian Gates were thrown open and this welcome contingent streamed inside. The Ahhiyawans saw all of this, but Troy's archers were posted densely along the walls near that gate, and they dared not try to rush the Elamites.

Tudha took his clay tablet and reed stylus from his satchel and began furiously tapping out a description of this latest allied army, looking down from the walls every so often at the marching column to pick out some extra detail. As the Elamites trooped through the streets, the desperate people of Troy brightened, stoked with another fresh wave of hope. 'I am told the Queen of the Amazons is here, and the *Labarna* too?' Memnon called to the onlookers. 'Truly, the Gods must favour Troy for it to be so.'

A frisson of awe and excitement passed from Tudha's toes to his scalp. 'With an army like this, we can turn this war on its head,' he said.

Aeneas smiled wryly. 'With the Amazons and the Elamites on our side, we have maybe three thousand fresh spears, young friend. Still way too few to even countenance a foray out onto the plain. Especially as the Ahhiyawans have drawn in maybe twice that number of reinforcements. Not that numbers guarantee anything anyway.'

'True,' said Tudha. 'All it takes to win or lose a war is one man. A weak soldier who runs away and leaves a gap in his regiment's shield line. A headstrong general who sends his best men into a trap. Or the shadow that stalks Troy's streets,' Tudha said. 'Just one man…'

'Who said it is a man?' Aeneas said quietly.

Tudha sat a little taller, eyebrows rising as he followed Aeneas' gaze to the high palace. A lone, amber-haired beauty stood on the rooftop veranda there, gazing over the city. 'Helen?'

'Your father didn't tell you?'

'Of course he didn't,' Tudha sighed.

'The theory is plausible. We just need to prove it,' Aeneas said. The Dardanian Prince then went on to explain to Tudha about the exchange of messages and the slave. 'I have tried to follow him to the Fountain of Poseidon and every time he gives me the slip. I tried waiting in the shadows near the fountain then after he had been and gone I dig under the bushes… but there is nothing there. He knows when he is being followed or watched.'

Tudha's eyelids grew hooded as he eyed Troy's streets, zig-zagging up towards the citadel.

'You wear that same look as your father,' Aeneas said. 'Like a fox eyeing the chicken coop.'

Tudha smiled. 'No, the fox is inside the coop. We two and every other in here are part of the brood.'

Aeneas sighed. 'And how are us chickens meant to catch a fox?'

Tudha gazed slowly around Troy, seeing no answers. There was something about the heat, however, and the smell of high summer, that reminded him of his childhood forays into the countryside with Sirtaya. The Egyptian was inhumanly nimble, capable of scampering up cliff faces like a cat, creeping through dry grass without a sound, wading into rivers without a splash. 'Perhaps we need a jackal,' he said. 'An Egyptian jackal.'

At that moment, Sirtaya, as if hearing his name, grumbled and rolled over, muttering in his sleep, scratched at his ear and curled up in a ball again.

***

All the next day, Hattu and Dagon oversaw a parade formation of the Amazons and Elamites through the lower city, then an archery and spear-throwing contest between them and the Trojan soldiers and other allies near the Springhouse. Citizens lined the nearby streets and rooftops cheering and applauding. Penthesilea proved unbeatable in almost every round, much to Aeneas' chagrin – especially when it came to sharp-shooting.

The archer prince climbed the steps to the rooftop from which Hattu watched, sweating, laughing. 'I swear she has stolen her arrows from a god!'

'Or maybe it's the cup of wine you had beforehand?' Dagon said with a hint of a wry grin.

'Ah, yes, speaking of which,' he said, pouring himself a fresh cup and mixing it with water on a table near the roof's edge. He gulped it down and sighed in satisfaction. 'Now, *Labarna*, I had something to run past you. A plan.' He looked around to check none except Hattu and

Dagon were near enough to hear. 'A means of catching the traitor.'

Hattu listened to the idea, and quickly realised that it was not Aeneas' plan but Tudha's. A few choice words and turns of phrase about Sirtaya were what gave it away. Clearly the two had conspired carefully to get his approval. He did not let on. 'I will consider the matter,' he said, while privately deciding to avoid the proposal. Like all of Tudha's initiatives, he worried what dark consequences it might hold. More importantly, Sirtaya – the key player in the plan – was still carrying some ailment.

At sunset, Hattu retired to Antenor's villa. The elder cooked a meal of oat porridge and honey which they enjoyed together with the usual pot of mountain tea. Full and drowsy, Hattu then retreated to his bedchamber and lay down to rest, followed by a selection of hounds. Infused with confidence, sleep came swiftly.

*His mind drained of thought and he was weightless. Sinking deeper and deeper into a hall of darkness. Silent, still, free of threat. He felt his body relax in this world of slumber, knowing that troubles for once could not find him here. Nor could the Goddess. This was a sanctuary within himself. A place of peace. Of solitude.*

*But he was not alone.*

*At first he felt just a creeping chill on his skin. Next, he saw faint grey coils of breath, heard a spluttering, and the slow clop of hooves. From the blackness, a pair of eyes peeled open. Eyes as red as sunset, bent in anger.*

*The walls of confidence around him disintegrated and his fears flooded in. What was this? He backed away through the darkness from the thing, yet with a slow, ominous clop… clop… clop it followed.*

*'Why are you trying to get away, King Hattu?' whispered a voice right behind him.*

*He swung round to the voice, struck through with fright. Ishtar knelt there, smiling and staring past him towards the hidden monster.*

*'What is it?'*

*'It is the future,' she replied. 'Something which no man can escape.'*

*'I will write my own future,' he said confidently, looking from Ishtar to the shadowed beast then back up at her again.*

*She turned her great head down towards him, the smile fading into a cold, soulless glower. 'Will you indeed?' she growled.*

Hattu woke with a burst of breath, the soft bedding tangled around him. He could still see the outline of the giant Goddess looming over him. The dream visions always took a few moments to fade from his eyes. But – his heart pounded anew – this was no illusion. There *was* someone standing over his bed.

Frozen for that instant of realisation, he stared at the silhouette, then rolled clear of the bed, clattering down onto the floorboards at the far side and rising in a somewhat ungainly stance, naked and holding a half-melted tallow candle towards the stranger as if it were a sword.

Blinking, his eyes adjusting, he saw that it was a woman, draped in a frayed black gown, a crown of decaying lotus flowers on her head. The dogs lay slumbering around the floor. They hadn't even so much as whimpered. It was as if she had cast a spell on them.

He took and struck flint, lighting the candle. The pale bubble of light grew to reveal her: hands hanging by her sides, face long and sagging like one exhausted from a long journey. Her cheeks were wet with tears. 'Princess Cassandra?' he croaked, throwing on his cloak then stepping round towards her. 'What is wrong?'

When he reached out to guide her by the shoulders towards an Egyptian wicker chair, she flinched, her eyes snapping onto his face, her lips wriggling like growling dog's. 'Stay away from me,' she murmured as if it were he who had crept into her bedchamber.

Hattu looked around the room. *His* room, and shrugged. 'I… look, what are you doing here in the dead of night?'

She smiled coldly now. 'You mean why am I not locked away inside the Temple of Apollo? I know Troy better than most, King Hattu. I play along with my temple imprisonment most of the time, but I can find my way in and out when I need to.'

'Why tonight?'

'At first I could not sleep. I kept seeing it over and over again. My brother sliding from the blade of Achilles. Do you know that, while Hektor was still alive, the Gods showed me that vision time and time again in my dreams? Always, they foreshadowed it with something else.' Her eyes darkened. 'You, King Hattu. Your arrival… then Hektor's death. Every time, that is how it plays out: you, then tragedy.'

He realised now that is what she had meant on the day of his arrival with her first words to him: *How could you?* His head shook from side to side. 'I had nothing to do with Hektor's death. You must believe me. *Someone* did,' he said, his mind flashing with Aeneas' theory about

Helen, 'and I will prove it and bring them to answer for it.'

'Ah, yes, our saviour,' Cassandra drawled. 'How heroic.'

Hattu bristled at this. 'So you came to mock me? Very well. Say whatever you need to say and be gone.'

'I came,' she snarled, 'because when I did finally fall asleep tonight, the Gods showed me something new. Something I do not understand. I hoped you might grasp what I could not. Your Ishtar talks to you just as Apollo whispers to me, after all.'

Hattu cocked his head slightly to one side. 'Go on.'

'I saw a great shadow, looming over our city,' she gulped. 'A wretched thing, with eyes of blood, a tongue of bronze and a mane of fire. A giant stallion of war that some great dark spirit might ride. Around its hooves, Troy lay in ruins.'

Hattu's skin crept as he recalled his own dream – the sound of the clopping hooves, those horrible red eyes staring at him from the darkness. It wasn't identical but… 'I think I saw it too.'

'So what does it *mean?*'

Hattu held out upturned palms. 'Ishtar toys with me as Apollo does with you.

Fresh tears began streaking down her cheeks. 'I feel it in my chest: a crushing sense of despair. No matter what I say or do, I cannot change the dreadful futures I am shown. No one believes me. I saw young Troilus' death; I saw Paris and Helen arriving here from Sparta. Each time I was ridiculed. Both things came to pass, just like Hektor's demise did… just like this horrible new vision surely will.'

Tentatively, he approached her again. This time, she did not flinch. Squeezing her shoulder gently, he said: 'I believe you. We Hittites are always taught to heed our dreams. But I also believe Troy can still win this war. Is there a city of greater unity in the world?'

She dabbed at her face with a rag. 'You speak of Troy as it once was, King Hattu. Times have changed. The unity crumbles. Since you were appointed as High Commander, my brothers have struggled to contain their jealousy. They have always jockeyed for our father's favour, but not like this. Deiphobus has become moodier than ever, contrary about everything. Scamandrios' every word is laced with venom. And Paris… he has become guarded and terse – suspicious that everyone in Troy thinks poorly of him. My cousin Aeneas once respected my father utterly, yet now he follows orders with a stony look in his eyes. The nobles meet in whispering cabals at night, the priests use their hoarded fortunes to buy their templefolk's loyalty and muscle.'

Hattu dropped his gaze to the floorboards, struggling to find words of reply. Everything she had said was right: he had noticed it in his every visit to the palace for Priam's councils. The suspicious looks between factions, the thinly-veiled insults in every speech, and plenty of dark glances in his direction. When he looked up again. Cassandra was gone. He moved to the villa's threshold, seeing her drifting silently across the citadel grounds, feeling her unease infecting him, eroding his earlier confidence.

From the corner of one eye, he noticed the first winks of dawn on the horizon. No more sleep tonight, he realised, sighing in frustration. Just as he was about to turn back inside, he noticed another figure on the move. Hooded and cloaked, yet there was no mistaking her height and graceful movement. Helen, gliding up the stairs towards the palace. At this time of night, there was only one place she could have been. His eyes drifted to the winding street that led to the Fountain of Poseidon. Aeneas had been trying for several nights now to track the slave who was bringing messages in for her. Every night, the man had outfoxed him. So again tonight, it seemed. He curled a fist into a ball and batted it against the door frame. The greatest danger to Troy was not dream-creatures or besiegers or squabbling elites. It was the one trouble that underpinned them all: the Shadow. How long before the shadow struck again and blew away all of the newfound confidence completely?

Reluctantly, he turned his mind to Aeneas – or rather Tudha's – plan.

***

The day passed – hotter than ever – and night came again. A pan of rich, fresh milk bubbled gently over a flame, the comforting scent of cinnamon rising in steamy ribbons. Theron stirred carefully, eager to ensure the mixture did not develop a skin. He licked his pale lips, his insipid eyes devoid of emotion as he ladled some into a cup and drank. The hot, creamy mixture coated his tongue and glided down his throat, splashing into his hollow belly. He sighed, gazing at the polished bronze mirror on the far side of his slave room. A blank, unremarkable face stared back at him. Heavy eyes that carried no trace of emotion. Mousy brown hair neither long nor short. No scars, no kink in the nose, a chin that was there without being big or small. His mother, after too much wine, had often mocked him for this.

*I always wanted a handsome, strong son. Instead, I get this – a grey spectre of a man, devoid of charisma. It'd be better if you were ugly or lame. When Kessiya came by the other day, I saw you sitting in the corner of the room, staring at her, drooling at the sight of her bare breasts. She was here for over an hour, remember? Well I saw her the next day at the water troughs. I apologised for your behaviour. You know what she said? 'I didn't even notice that he was there.'*

Tears stung behind his eyes, but they would not come. For tears meant emotion, character, distinction. The Gods had gifted him none of those things, and so the remembered humiliation flared and smouldered away inside him while his grey, forgettable face stared emotionlessly into the mirror.

'Perhaps if I polish you more I will truly be able to see myself – with all my quirks and charm,' he asked the mirror. Nobody replied. He beheld the small tablet he had picked up at the forage bushes near the Silver Ridge today. If he delivered it on time, maybe his master would give him some good polish and buffing cloths?

He slid the tablet into the pouch on his belt and slipped outside into the moonless night, silent on his bare feet. As he moved through the citadel districts, his ears picked up the faint whistle of people snoring inside houses, the grumble of a hungry man's belly a few streets away, and the slurp of a cat licking its nether parts on a windowsill across the way. But no scraping of boots this time. The Dardanian Prince had tracked him nearly a dozen times. Each time, Theron had calmly given him the slip. At last, he had given up, it seemed.

Up ahead, the Fountain of Poseidon rose into view, cold and dark in the moonless night.

***

Standing in the arch of a porticoed veranda on the palace hill, Hattu gazed down across the citadel streets. The trees in the quince orchard swayed in a quiet susurrus, the leaves shining like silvery daggers in the soft, lustrous starlight. The Fountain of Poseidon was infuriatingly hidden from view by the orchard on two sides and the gold-painted wall of Apollo's Temple on the other. A perfect blind spot, and that was most probably why it was being used to exchange messages. It all rested on Tudha's idea now. Saying yes to the plan had felt like tearing a barb from his skin. *But this is not Hatenzuwa,* he told himself. *The plan here is good and clear. Tonight, we will catch the Shadow of Troy at work.*

He heard the gentle padding of bare feet and edged back behind a pillar, the painted stone cold even through his cloak. He saw her now. She wore a hood and dark robes, but the sound of her fineries and tassels clacking underneath gave her away. Just as he had been doing moments ago, she looked down upon the street leading to the fountain, transfixed, waiting.

'There's nothing of interest for you there,' he said, stepping out, 'not yet.'

Helen jolted, taking a step back from the veranda's edge. 'You were watching me?'

'No, I was watching the approaches to the fountain. So were you. Why?'

'I don't like your tone. King or not, you should address me – a Princess of Troy and wife of Priam's heir no less – with respect.'

'I respect Troy and Priam's throne,' Hattu replied, 'and that's why I am here tonight. To catch the Shadow.'

Her face curled up like a scrunched robe. 'The spy… you think it's me? You suspect *me*?'

'An Ahhiyawan inside Troy's walls. Erstwhile wife of one of the enemy leaders.'

'Is that it? Notions, theories? They said you were clever, King Hattu,' Helen hissed. 'But any fool knows not to confront a suspect until they have proof.'

'Oh I have proof. It's on its way right now…' Hattu said calmly, glancing down towards the streets again.

Her confident glare began to falter.

***

Sirtaya crept like a squirrel along the flat rooftops of Troy's citadel villas, edging around the dome ovens up there, still hot from recent use, weaving deftly past stacks of tripod urns and across the ladders laid like bridges between the rooftops of different houses. There was no moon. That was key, Master Tudha had insisted: it meant he could track anyone acting suspiciously from on high without fear of his shadow giving him away. Tudha and Prince Aeneas had showered him with all manner of compliments about his skills of stealth.

He turned his eyes down towards the citadel streets – seemingly deserted during this time of night curfew. They were stripes of blackness, the buildings shapeless blocks. But Sirtaya's eyes, for more than thirty years starved of good light in the Well of Silence, saw through the darkness. He saw the ripples in the black, felt the movement down there. There *was* someone moving. He tracked the figure carefully while moving like a spider in time with this other. The person glanced up at the night sky at one point, and Sirtaya fell still. For a moment, he wondered if it was a person at all, or merely a painting on the streetside wall – so bland and flat were the features. It was a citadel slave, right enough, he realised, going by the man's robe. Heading uphill to the Fountain of Poseidon too – just as Master Tudha had explained. On Sirtaya went in silent pursuit, leaping from this rooftop to the next and edging along that one. *Sirtaya, the champion of Troy,* he fantasised as he went. *He who caught the Shadow!* They would shower him with gifts. Maybe even bring him mice to eat!

When the slave passed a row of lesser nobles' houses, Sirtaya slowed to a crawl, feeling a rising sensation in his abdomen. It was warm and soft at first, then it became jagged, and finally like a lance of fire. He crumpled to his knees, eyes shut, teeth gritted, clutching his stomach. The pain passed, but not before a rotten burst of metallic bile had risen all the way into his mouth. Back in the spring, this had happened to him only every few days, and he had disguised it well – making himself an excuse to go off into a lane or a dark storeroom to ride out the pain. Now? Now it was coming at least five times a day. In between the fits he felt so tired and heavy-limbed. How could Sirtaya of Memphis be floored by nothing other than a sore belly? He seethed at himself. Spitting and cursing in Egyptian, he crawled onto all-fours again. 'I will have my mice!' he groaned, eyes sweeping the street below. But where was the slave?

***

Hattu watched Sirtaya's squirrel-like silhouette, creeping across the rooftops, and the slave he was tracking. When the Egyptian suffered a turn of some sort, Hattu's heart climbed into his throat. *Old friend?* The slave slipped from sight and the plan crumbled before him.

Seeing this, Helen relaxed. 'This is pointless,' she sighed. She leant on the veranda balustrade, drumming her slender fingers confidently.

'What exactly were you expecting to find here anyway?'

Just then, the slave re-emerged from the fountain area. Helen saw this and suddenly seemed to stiffen again. A moment later, a recovered Sirtaya dropped down onto the street and confronted the slave, brandishing a knife, driving him back towards the bushes by the fountain. Hattu shot a sideways look at Helen. Her brief confidence was gone now. *Got you*, he realised.

'I am not in cahoots with Agamemnon or my old husband,' she hissed.

'Really? You spoke of proof before,' Hattu said. 'Well, proof is on its way.' He said this as Sirtaya and the slave re-emerged into view. The Egyptian guided the slave – now grubby-handed and holding the tablet he had moments ago buried – towards the veranda stairs.

'I'll show you proof of what this is all about.' She took from her robes a small silver bracelet – the one she was always fidgeting with – and rattled it before his face. 'This belonged to my daughter, Hermione. She remains in Sparta where I left her.'

Hattu's eyes narrowed. 'What?'

'That's right,' Helen said. 'I abandoned my only girl to come here and indulge my passions with Paris. What a fine mother I am, eh? The Trojans and the Ahhiyawans alike call me a bitch, a war-maker, a whore. Let them, as long as Hermione is not harmed.'

Hattu eyed her. 'Your daughter is back in Ahhiyawan lands? I'd say that makes a fine reason for you to collaborate with the besiegers, so you might return home with them to her side.'

'You'd think so, wouldn't you?' she smiled tightly. She tilted her head skywards and gazed up into the star-speckled blackness. 'After I eloped, my mother went down to the River Eurotas one morning. Her slaves left her there, humming a tune, steeping her feet. When they returned she was gone. They found her body downriver. An old man said she had simply walked into the currents midriver until the waters flowed into her mouth, choosing death over the shame I had cast upon her.' She glanced at Hattu. 'So as you can imagine, the people of Sparta would be less than pleased to see me.' She took a few breaths before continuing. 'For the first few years of this war I would go to the Scaean turret to scour the battlefield in search of my brothers, Castor and Pollux, amongst Menelaus' Spartan band. For yes they might have convinced me to come away from Troy. One day Agamemnon came before the walls and addressed me – while battle raged around him – and told me that both had been slain and lay cold and dead under Spartan soil. Now he tells me that my daughter despises me, and waits eagerly to spit in my face should I ever return.' She walked slowly along the edge of the veranda, tracing a finger along the balustrade. 'So you can see that I have little wish to return to the Ahhiyawan fold, or to go "home".'

'Your girl, your mother, your brothers,' Hattu said, 'why did you forsake them? Why did you elope with Paris? He is not a great man. Troy is not a paradise – certainly not now. Please, tell me why?'

She smiled sadly. 'Throughout my childhood in Sparta, I was mocked for being the cursed daughter of a swan – our thunder god, Zeus, in animal form. As soon as I began to reach womanhood, I was pushed into a loveless marriage to Menelaus, slyly arranged by his war-hungry brother. Life as a Spartan Queen may sound grand but it is harsh and cold. I had no friends, not even my mother. My brothers were so often gone on expeditions, and Hermione… Gods I tried, but she and I never had the bond I hoped we might. I have never been happy in my life apart from that heady time when first Paris and I met. I cannot explain it, just as one can rarely explain their mistakes. It happened, and I have been paying for it with every moment and every breath since.'

She took a while before speaking again. Enfolding the silver bracelet in her delicate fingers, she slid it away. 'I *have* had messages sent to me privately by the warrior kings out there in the enemy camp. Brought to me by the slave down there.' She nodded towards Sirtaya and the slave, climbing up the steps now.

Hattu's ears pricked up.

'But they are simply threats. Messages telling me about my mother's death, telling me to stay in Troy so that the war will keep flowing, or they will have a troop of soldiers despatched back to Sparta to kill Hermione. They have not asked me to sabotage Troy's defences, nor have I ever considered doing so. They do not want me back, King Hattu. They want only fire for Troy.' She looked with weary eyes towards the city's highest turret, her voice reedy and high. 'And you asked me several moons ago why I spend so many nights upon the Scaean Tower? It is the tallest place in Troy. I go there now not to seek my brothers but to join them. All it would take would be a single step from the parapet's edge and I would be free.' Her chin quivered and tears shone in her eyes. 'But unlike my mother, I am not brave enough to seize that kind of freedom.'

Hattu dipped his head. He knew now that his suspicions had been wrong, even before Sirtaya scampered up the remaining veranda stairs and handed him the slave's tablet. He read the markings. Another threat on Hermione's life. 'I apologise, Majesty,' he said quietly to Helen. 'I trust you understand that I must suspect everyone at this time.'

She nodded quietly, gulping.

Hattu glanced down at the slave, waiting halfway up the steps. He realised something else now: the slave – the one who had handed Hektor the poisoned skin – was not Helen's. 'Who is your master?' he demanded.

'I have no master,' the man replied calmly. 'I am a citadel slave, and I serve any and all who ask me to serve them.'

'Who compels you to bring these messages to the princess?' Hattu snapped, exasperated.

The slave's shapeless, grey face remained devoid of emotion. 'If I tell you, will you give me a bright mirror? One in which I can truly see myself?'

Hattu, confused, stared into his soulless eyes. 'As... as you wish.'

The slave smiled as if Hattu had just granted him a suit of gold. As he opened his mouth to answer Hattu's question, none of the small group noticed the faint glow that appeared overhead, until the fire arrow plunged down between the man's shoulder blades. The slave, agog, fell before Hattu's feet, choking on his own blood. He, Helen and Sirtaya gawped, all looking through the blackness whence the fire arrow had come. The western end of the citadel – bathed in blackness.

'Who's over there?' Sirtaya hissed.

Hattu stared that way too, looking for the assassin, seeing only dark outlines of buildings. But another question arose in his mind. *Why use a fire arrow?* He sensed something then, his flesh creeping. He turned slowly, noticing that the watch on the lower city defences were in transition. A short moment of weakness down there. His eyes ached as he stared at the darkness beyond the city.

*What if it was not just a killing strike? What if it was also...* at that moment, he saw how the blackness outside the city shifted and changed. Movement. Masses and masses of movement, coming for Troy.

*... a signal flare!*

'To the walls!' he yelled. 'The Ahhiyawans attack!'

# CHAPTER 14

## AT THE GATES OF TROY

Bells clanged, whistles blew and boots pounded on the streets. Hattu sped down from his meeting with Helen and into the palace guardroom, grabbing his swordbelts and Hektor's helm – no time for armour. Skating and skidding across the marble outside, he nearly crashed into Prince Paris. Remarkably, he was already armoured in full. The other princely sons of Priam emerged from their bed chambers too, slaves helping them with their scale jackets and bringing weapons. King Priam and Hekabe shuffled around in their nightshirts, faces sagging with confusion, Prince Scamandrios trying to reassure them.

The Trojan Guardians scrambled from their guard billets, ready to escort the princes and Hattu to the walls. As they hurried down the Scaean Way, more shouts and clipped commands rose all around them, and trains of torchlight snaked from the various billet houses of lower Troy: Memnon and his Elamites, Penthesilea and her Amazons, Glaucus and the remnant Lukkans, Masturi and the Seha Riverlanders – all streaming to man the walls.

Hattu eyed the plain outside – still nothing but inchoate shapes in the darkness there, coming closer. 'It may be night, this may be a surprise strike,' he boomed to the princes as they went, 'but nothing else has changed. We each know which section of the walls we have to defend. The plans we discussed remain sound. Stick to them and we will see this attack off.'

'*Labarna,*' the princes vowed, all parting like the fingers of a splayed out hand, towards different parts of the defences.

'Let me fight alongside you, Master Hattu,' Sirtaya rasped, gambolling next to him.

'No, old companion. Stay clear of the walls. I need your keen eyes: find a high spot and watch for any unexpected incursions.'

'As you wish, Master Hattu,' he said, bowing and backing away, coughing then scrambling up onto a tannery rooftop and perching there like a crow, head switching this way and that.

Hattu sped up the stone staircase onto the long stretch of walls abutting the Thymbran Gatehouse. Still the plain outside offered nothing but swirling shadows, much closer now.

'Give me light,' he demanded. Aeneas, posted there, raised one arm high. The Trojan archers and the Dardanian bowmen under his command nocked blazing arrows and cocked their bows skywards. 'Loose!' he roared, chopping his hand down. A flock of fiery shafts sped high above the plain, illuminating the grim scar of the trench, then the dry grasses... then the rumbling mass of incoming Ahhiyawan soldiery – a sea of plumes, horns, spears and axes. Every single one of Agamemnon's soldiers. Their advantage of surprise gone, they now shrieked and howled, banging weapons on shields, blowing on pipes and battering drums. At some barked command, the front splintered into three huge contingents like the prongs of a trident, one angling towards the western Bay Gate and the weaker walls there, one bending east towards the Dardanian Gate and the central prong coming right for Hattu at the Thymbran Gate. Each prong of men carried ladders. Worse, each contingent was led by a trio of rams. Sturdy-looking, thickly-capped in bronze and swaying on solid wooden wheels, the carriers sheltered by a hide tent roof. As the Trojan fire arrows faded and fell somewhere behind the advancing enemy, the plain darkened again and Hattu's mind whirled.

'Prince Aeneas, direct all your fire missiles at the battering rams. Forget about the soldiers. The rams are the biggest danger.'

'Yes, *Labarna,*' Aeneas replied.

He saw Tudha with Aeneas' men. His heir stepped forward, extending a palm. 'Give me my sword, Father.'

Hattu hesitated for just a heartbeat, and Tudha pounced on it.

'You *know* I am one of the most skilled warriors here. Troy needs me.' His silver eyes grew glassy, boyish almost, searching Hattu's.

Hattu glanced to the tannery roof. Sirtaya bore the sack with Tudha's iron sword. It would be so easy to call the Egyptian over. But then he remembered the shrine. The blood-soaked shrine. 'You have a bow, *Tuhkanti.* Stand with the archers and stay clear of any melee fighting,' he said. As he turned away, he sensed Tudha slump behind him. But now was not the time to agonise over the matter; for now, Troy stood on the brink of disaster.

*Thrum, whoosh!* the night sky turned molten orange again as Aeneas' men loosed a blazing volley at the battering ram squadron coming for the Thymbran Gate. The arrows whacked into the hide tent of the foremost ram and quivered there, flickering away gently but not setting the leather alight. The men under the hide canopy jeered and whistled, flicking hand gestures towards the archers and picking up speed as they came to the causeway bridging the ditch, only strides from the gates.

Hattu's top lip twitched. 'Throw,' he said in a low burr.

A trio of Aeneas' men hurled small clay pots down at the ram. Two missed, smashing on the earth, the black filth inside spraying across the ground. The third struck the apex of the ram's leather roof, the black resin bursting across the thing, meeting the flickering arrows embedded there. With a *whoosh!* the entire ram became a giant torch. The Ahhiyawans wailed and screamed, scrambling out from the hide shelter. Some men were too slow, and flailed blindly, engulfed in flames. Hattu's nose wrinkled at the stink of burning hair and flesh. *I had almost forgotten what you were capable of,* Ishtar whispered in his ear.

Behind the Ahhiyawan mass, Hattu now spotted the enemy chariots, wheeling carefully to and fro behind the infantry front like herders, watching, waiting for the defences to fall. On one vehicle stood Agamemnon, uplit by the fires and given inhuman shape by his lion hood and its fluttering mane. 'Forward, you dogs – smash those gates!' the enemy warlord howled with a wine slur. The two remaining rams in the squadron coming for the Thymbran Gates picked up speed. The first rocked across the causeway before Aeneas could order another volley of fire arrows. Hattu gripped the battlements, peering over at the thing. *No,* he panicked. But the men pushing the thing were clumsy. One wheel was too close to the causeway's edge. It slid down, taking part of the earthen crossing with it. The men inside wailed as the whole thing tipped upside down and into the trench like an upended tortoise, the ram crew floundering and slipping as they tried to climb out.

'Loose!' Aeneas barked. A volley of arrows hammered into the struggling men, ending their fight.

But Hattu did not wait to see their fate, for in those few breaths, the third ram had rocked right up to the Thymbran Gates. The archers began to light new fire arrows.

'No!' Hattu and Aeneas cried in unison. 'It's too close. If that thing goes up in flames, so too will the gates,' Hattu explained.

*Boom!* the ram pounded against the gate timbers, shaking the walkway. An untold number of Ahhiyawans now rushed to get behind the thing and add their weight to each swing.

*Boom!*

'Archers, back,' Hattu cried. The bowmen atop the gatehouse walkway, unable to use their fire arrows, peeled away.

'Men of the Seha Riverland,' Hattu bawled, waving them into place instead.

Masturi stepped up to the parapet, swarthy face etched with a malevolent grin, a score of his kiltless men arriving with him. With grunts and groans they heaved steaming copper cauldrons to the wall's edge. 'Time for a bath, you stinking whoresons!' Masturi roared, tipping his cauldron over. The rest followed suit. A dozen loads of boiling oil plummeted down onto the roof of the ram, sizzling, fizzing, gushing through every seam. Terrible screams arose and the roof disintegrated. The men inside fell to their knees, arms raised in horror as their flesh slid off, clutching faces that bubbled grotesquely as the skin boiled away. The next load of boiling oil hit them directly. This deluge took the scalp clean away from one man's head, leaving a clean white dome of skull.

The din of battle ebbed for just a trice as the Ahhiyawan masses stared in horror. A short way back from the gates, Ajax was the first to shake himself from this stupor. He whirled his staff overhead. 'Attack!' he screamed at his Salamians and others nearby. 'The ram is not yet broken. Take up the tethers and break those gates.'

Likewise, Diomedes unleashed a wolf-like howl and drummed his spear against his cyclops shield to rouse his Tiryneans.

With a harsh explosion of battle screams, the Ahhiyawan soldiery flooded forward across the causeway.

'Archers – at their infantry. With everything!' Hattu bawled. Aeneas echoed the cry, his bowmen returning to the parapet's edge.

*Thrum!* the massed archers unloaded a withering volley at the rushing crescent of warriors. Shafts whacked into cuirasses, zinged from helms, skated from shields and punched into flesh with a chorus of wet, fatty thuds. The Ahhiyawan marksmen sent sporadic volleys back, arrows skating off the merlons of Troy with puffs of dust or striking down Trojan archers. A sling bullet hammered through a Dardanian archer's head as if it were made of tallow. The man screamed, rivulets of dark blood sputtering down across his nose and cheeks, before he folded outwards over the parapet and plunged, skidding lifelessly down the slight slope of the walls and rolling into the trench.

Ajax and his lot reached the gates first. He had some of his Salamians make a roof of shields while he and the rest took up the ram. *Boom!* it crashed once more. Then *rat-tat-tat* as dozens more began hacking at the gates with their axes.

Hattu stared down, horrified. No barricade could withstand this forever. The reserves of hot oil were spent. 'Hives!' he cried.

Three men crouching behind the parapet rose to hurl down pale lumpy orbs. These hit the attacker's raised shields and exploded in clouds of dust. All of a sudden the night air shook with an intense buzzing as swarms of bees, enraged, shot out in every direction from the ruins of their hives and clouded around the attackers. Men screamed, stung all over their faces and arms, dropping their shields or swatting madly and disrupting the efforts at the gates.

During the momentary relief this gave, he noticed that Diomedes and many hundreds of enemy soldiers had peeled away. They were loping along the ditch edge, moving out of range of the gateway defenders.

Hattu grasped the parapet, staring, tracking their position.

'Here!' Diomedes boomed, waving towards a dark, unmanned section of the walls. He halted by the ditch's edge, milling an arm. 'Cross here. The ditch is not so deep.' Hundreds scrambled down into the trench, eager to be first up and at the foot of the walls. That was when it happened. Hattu's top lip twitched in an animal smile as the light, loose layer of earth along the trench floor sank under the enemy feet to reveal the true depth and the floor of sharpened stakes. The noise was horrific – a wet, tearing, splashing sound and the grinding of gristle and snapping of tendons, all accompanied by shrieks of agony. Diomedes backstepped, aghast at the broken mess of bloody men skewered down there. 'Use the ladders to bridge the trench,' he snarled to the rest of his men.

His Tiryneans did so, throwing the ladders down and walking edgily across, coming to the unmanned walls at last. Sherden and Cretan warriors hurried to join them, sensing that a breakthrough was imminent. 'And... up!' Diomedes bawled. Every second ladder swung up now, clacking into place along the bare battlements. 'Take the walls!'

Hattu watched. The ditch's hidden stakes had thinned and slowed the enemy. now it was time for the next gambit. 'Sons of the Dawn... rise!' he boomed.

With an other-worldly, trilling howl, Memnon and his Elamites rose from where they had been crouched behind the merlons, their broad-headed spears sweeping out, almost cutting the highest ladder-climbers in half. Some used poles to shove at one ladder, straining to push it away from the walls until vertical. Now, studded with climbing men, the ladder overbalanced, crashing down into the spike-floored ditch. Screams and death curses rang out. Undeterred , more and more men flooded up the other ladders, vaulting the merlons and lunging into combat with the Elamite warriors. Just as the enemy began to outnumber the Elamites up there, a triton shell moaned, and from the doors in the two nearest wall turrets, Penthesilea and the Amazons burst out onto the walkway, spearing into the attackers' flanks, barging many over the edge. Yet more attackers still streamed up the ladders. Soon, the wall top was broiling with combat, the mud-plaster defences stained with streaks of running blood as torn defenders and attackers pitched over the edges.

Hattu barked commands in every direction as he strode to and fro on the Thymbran Gatehouse. When he glanced west, towards the Bay Gate and the weak section of walls, his heart soared when he saw that the trio of rams headed there had foundered, unable to ascend the rocky slope towards those old gates. But here at his station, Ajax and his men were close to breaking through the Thymbran Gates. *Boom!* went the ram again, along with the rattle of axes.

'Father!'

He swung on his heel. Tudha was pointing madly eastwards, at the Dardanian Gate.

The final three rams were approaching that gatehouse unharmed, the defenders up there pinned behind the merlons by a savage rain of arrows and slingshot.

'The fire pots did not work there. The bowmen are outnumbered, trapped, and so the gates will fall to those rams, and so too might this gate,' Tudha shouted to be heard over the din.

*Boom!* went Ajax's ram again on the gates right here, shaking them both.

'Once you taught me the art of defending a siege,' Tudha continued. 'When the lion attacks head on, you must steal around behind it and swipe away its hind legs.' He turned to look back into Troy's lower city, and the quiet stableyard, then returned his confident glare to Hattu.

'Trust me, Father. One day every Hittite will have to.'

The words were like a boxer's flurry of expert blows, knocking aside any argument Hattu might have before he could even muster it to his lips.

***

Agamemnon cantered to and fro at the rear of the three-pronged Ahhiyawan surge, watching the assault, the bells on his two white chariot steeds jangling as he went. First he rode to the faltering charge near Troy's western Bay Gate, then across the rear of the infantry press at the Thymbran Gate, begging those timbers to capitulate to Ajax's ram and axes, and for Diomedes and his force to break the stalemate on the walls. King Hattu had vanished from those walls, he noticed. Where was he? He imagined the Hittite King lying in a smashed heap, riddled with arrows. On he went to the Dardanian Gate on Troy's eastern side. The three rams there were rocking confidently closer to the gates. Even better, the Locrian bowmen were pinning the Trojan defenders on the parapet with volley after expert volley. His brother Menelaus waited with his Spartans, spears and shields in hand, ready to rush the gates as soon as they were smashed open. Agamemnon snarled some animal noise of support at them, clenching and shaking his fist, before wheeling back to Ajax's central attack on the Thymbran Gates.

Slowing there, some way back from the fray, he eyed the sombre warrior-king standing in reserve. Achilles and his Myrmidons were like grave markers, so still and silent they stood. 'Looks like you won't be needed tonight after all,' Agamemnon said with a smug sigh. 'When they talk of Troy's fall, few will remember those who stood back and watched.'

'Like you?' Achilles snorted.

Agamemnon blanched momentarily. 'Me? I, I…' he flicked his head around, then gestured towards the gate battles. 'I'm directing the armies of Ahhiyawa.'

'Really?' said Achilles. 'Is that what you call your wine-fuelled howling?'

'Look,' Agamemnon seethed, stabbing a finger towards the embattled gates, 'Troy is falling, here, now… and you will play no part in it. Tonight, your legend dies. Tonight, you will be forgotte…'

His words trailed off as he heard a groan of timber. His head snapped round to the east, eyes narrowing on the Dardanian Gate. *The rams are set to swing!* he assumed…

…wrongly.

For the gates there were swinging open. His jaw slackened as from within Troy's streets, a stream of shapes sallied forth, dust pulsing up. Wood, flashing bronze, blurred wheels, cracking whips, thrashing manes and whinnying steeds. They spilled around both sides of the lead ram approaching that gate and slaughtered the escort soldiers, then made short work of the other two rams also. 'Trojan chariots,' he croaked as the vehicles sped on out towards Menelaus' position. 'I thought we had smashed them all at the beach camp?' He looked over his shoulder to the second reserve of his own chariotry. 'Nestor: go, help my brother to blast away that Trojan sally.'

Laughter crackled through the night air. Agamemnon twisted back to the Myrmidons. 'Something amuses you, Achilles?'

Achilles smirked. 'The chariots of Troy are one thing. Those things… are a different prospect entirely.'

Agamemnon turned back to the speeding sally, peering at the modest-sized wing of war-cars hurtling this way. Some fifty or so twin-manned Trojan chariots – all they had left. But leading them, eighteen or so hulking masses of muscular steed and solid wood packed with not two but three crewmen. They slammed through Menelaus' unprepared Spartan footsoldiers, sending men spraying in every direction.

'*Wanax,*' Nestor croaked, cantering forward. 'We must not engage, for those are no ordinary chariots. They are Hittite Destroyers… the battle-cars that turned the deserts of Kadesh into a mighty grave. They will shred our vehicles.'

'They're not interested in you or your chariots,' said Achilles. 'See how they move in a staggered line? They are coming to streak across the rear of Diomedes' infantry pressing at the ditch. Right now I'd say they'll make many a widow tonight. It looks like it might be a famous defeat for you tonight…*Wanax.* You will forever be remembered as the fool who held Achilles in reserve.'

Throat tightening as if an invisible murderer's hand was clamped there, Agamemnon squawked to Achilles. 'Forward. Stop those chariots!'

***

The lead Destroyer hurtled forth, jolting across potholes and over small rocks, the three men on board spotted with Spartan blood, faces set in rictuses. The hot night wind screamed in Hattu's ears, the huge shield on his arm straining like a sail whenever it caught the wind. 'Ya!' Dagon cried, whirling and cracking his whip above the two yellow-dun mares. Tudha stood with them, feet planted apart in an expert charioteer's stance, lance held two-handed, eyes fixed on the Tiryneans of Diomedes clustered around the trench and waiting to cross the bridge of ladders and join the assault up on the battlements.

They rocketed in at an oblique angle, coming along the rear ranks of Diomedes' soldiers, all taken by surprise, turning and fumbling to bring their weapons to bear. 'Ready?' Hattu screamed, holding his shield around Tudha like a protective arm. Tudha roared something unintelligible, bracing his legs as he trained his lance, Hattu using his body weight to support his heir.

*Bang! Bang! Bang!* The lance rat-tatted through enemy shields and ribs, blood spurting, men spinning away, torn open. The impact sent Tudha and Hattu jolting, sharp pains shuddering through their joints with every kill. Behind them, the metallic thunder of the other Destroyers rattled out again in an endless din, mimicking the expert example of the lead vehicle. Next, from the lighter Trojan war-cars came the whistle and hum of speeding, short-range arrows and a rain of thrown javelins. It caused chaos. Ahhiyawans pushed and shoved to get back from the chariot strike, knocking over others, sending hundreds of those waiting to cross the bridge of ladders falling into the trench, crunching down on the stakes. Half of the ladder bridges gave way and collapsed in too.

The chariot wing reached the end of Diomedes' lot, then sped on for Ajax's mass at the Thymbran Gate. 'Charge,' Hattu roared, his grey hair streaked red and streaming behind him.

The Destroyers fell into a skein formation and this time came at a more direct angle towards the enemy masses. The rearmost Salamian warriors glanced over their shoulders, faces growing wide with shock, men scattering and running, others frozen with fright. One Sherden vanished under the horses' hooves with a *whump*, and the lead Destroyer jolted over the body, a sickening gush of red bursting out from under the wheels, leaving the man halved, top half crawling, somehow still clinging to life. Hattu drew one iron sword now, slashing out with it from the chariot's sides, striking the jaw from one Salamian's face, leaving his tongue wildly lolling down his neck, and then swiping with his shield, breaking the nose of another. Tudha speared out in the brief gaps in between, puncturing chests and throats, while Dagon guided the horses in a murderous trample over those directly in front. The skein behind them did the same, carving through the mass like a hot knife. They arced round and burst clear, and Hattu glanced back to see the remaining men with Ajax now scattering away from the gates in fright, fleeing into the darkness of the plain, the ram abandoned. Only Ajax himself and a few hardy teams of axemen continued to hack away at the battered gates.

'One more charge!' Tudha cried over the wind of the ride and the din of battle. 'One more charge and we can bring down that giant.'

Hattu saw that Tudha was right. The enemy colossus was vulnerable.

At the very same moment, screams rang out behind him. He glanced over his shoulder and his blood iced: like wolves, the Myrmidons burst from the blackness of night, lunging at and toppling and boarding the other battle-cars in his wing. Some vehicles drove wildly askew, drivers slain, others crashed. Over thirty of the Trojan vehicles, swept away. Seven Destroyers met this same fate. Achilles leapt into the cabin of one Destroyer whose crew was already injured, the shield bearer's arm hanging by a sinew. He elbowed the shield-bearer out of the vehicle, ran the warrior through then stood straight and yanked the driver's head back by the hair, before slicing his throat and seizing the reins for himself.

Dagon squeezed one rein to guide their Destroyer round towards the Myrmidons, but Hattu clasped his hand. 'No, old friend,' he said, suddenly fearful of their position, out on the plain with just a few war-cars left, the enemy all around them.

'One more charge!' Tudha raged again.

'Enough!' Hattu roared at him like a bear. 'Take us back into Troy.'

With a nod, Dagon swerved free, only three other chariots escaping with them. They sped wide and away from Troy, then came back round towards the Dardanian Gates. As he went Hattu glanced over his shoulder and saw Achilles grinning horribly up at Troy's defences. The enemy champion then brayed at his Myrmidons and – like wolves on the hunt – they sped towards Diomedes' half-crippled ladder assault. The hairs on Hattu's neck rose like needles as he watched the Myrmidons speed deftly across the last remaining ladders bridging the ditch, then up those balanced against the walls. They sprung over the parapet and in a blur, flooded the battlements. Blood spurted and swords flashed in the torchlight. Elamites and Amazons fell in their droves. Achilles preyed on the edges of it all, hacking down the injured and weary. Seeing the turn in the struggle for the walls, Ajax and his men now abandoned the Thymbran Gate assault and rushed to join the effort there.

Hattu's heart hammered, knowing that wall section was about to be overrun. There was no reserve. Nothing bar a small watch up on the citadel.

'Faster! Get us inside the city,' he rasped. 'Or Troy may not see the morning.'

***

Up on the tannery rooftop, Sirtaya winced with pain, clutching his abdomen. Every part of him felt like fire now, and he wanted so much to roll onto his side, close his eyes and scream. But he would not, for he could not let Master Hattu down: *I need your keen eyes: watch for any unexpected incursions.*

And so he watched the battle at the walls change: one moment the enemy assault seemed to have been broken, the next it had burst into life again. First the Amazons and Elamites had fought the attackers fiercely. Andor swooped to and fro up there as well, scoring the faces of and snatching weapons from the attackers. But then the Myrmidons had arrived, clambering up and onto the walls to turn the tide, slashing guts and elbowing Trojan defenders from the walkway – a death drop to the street below. Achilles danced and weaved like an acrobat, rushing at the Amazon fighters already tangled in battle with his men, stabbing them in the back and spearing them in the flank.

'Fight me. Fight me face to face, you coward,' Penthesilea seethed, rushing the enemy talisman. When he slashed at her, she slid onto one knee expertly, ducking the strike, then struck for his back. Her blade bent against his fine armour. He whooshed round and swiped low at her, only for the Amazon Queen to leap over the cut. She raised her shield, picked up a dropped spear and held it level over the rim, approaching him like a stalking leopard. But another Myrmidon grappled her from behind, wrenching her arms back, exposing her midriff to Achilles. Achilles did not waste the opportunity, ramming his sword up and under her leather armour. 'My, you are a beauty,' he rumbled. 'In another life, perhaps I would have taken you as a war bride.' With a twist of the blade and a hollow groan, her guts toppled out. So fell the Queen of the Amazons.

Memnon and the Elamites battled heroically against a team of

Tiryneans, cutting down man after man. Eventually, he was up against Diomedes. The pair locked swords, muscled bodies shaking and straining. Memnon, despite a disadvantage in size and weight, drove the mighty Diomedes to one knee. 'So it ends for you, Lord of Tiryns,' he snarled, drawing his sword back to strike. When the blade was at full stretch, Achilles' spear appeared from nowhere and rammed into his armpit. Shuddering, Memnon fell from the walls. His Elamites wailed in dismay, and the Myrmidons began to overwhelm them, some speeding down the steps into Troy's lower city.

'Every man to the Thymbran wards!' cried Prince Scamandrios, seeing the breach and waving his troops there from the Bay Gate area. Prince Deiphobus came with Glaucus and the Lukkans and the thin reserve of Karkisan archers sped to the spot too. They tried to cage the breach by forming a semi-circle around the bottom of the wall stairs, but the enemy push down those stairs was strong.

Sirtaya noticed something then: Achilles was not part of the fray anymore. His eyes darted in confusion. Had the invincible, divine Achilles, fallen? The foolish thought evaporated when he saw the champion again, creeping along the parapet to come to the next stairwell. Light on his feet, Achilles sped down and came at the backs of the defensive semi-circle, slashing their hamstrings and slicing their throats. Any time a man turned to face him, he would dart away, using his speed to find the nearest Trojan with back turned or bearing injury, killing in the way a street thief would murder his victims.

'King Hattu was right,' Sirtaya hissed to nobody. 'He is not a champion lion. He is a scavenger, a rat.'

With a roar, the Ahhiyawans burst through the corral of Trojan allies and further on into the lower city streets. Sirtaya's heart jumped into his mouth as he saw them flooding past his rooftop perch. Achilles led one group towards the Scaean Way – the unguarded arterial road to the citadel. With a shaking hand, Sirtaya reached for Tudha's iron sword. He had never before used the thing, only guarded it. Weak and shaken with pain, he scampered across the timber walkway spanning this roof and the nearest, tracking the great Achilles. Meanwhile, other groups sped off in different directions, howling in triumph as they kicked down doors to houses and storerooms, set upon terrified families and threw down votive statues.

It seemed like it was over, like Troy was doomed… and then he heard the rattle of hooves and wheels. King Hattu, Dagon and Tudha sped through the streets at the head of the small band of returning chariots, blazing into one group of these raiders, knocking them aside like toys, driving others back, containing them. All but Achilles and his small band, who were deep inside the lower city now. Sirtaya ignored everything but the enemy champion, eyes fixed on him as he moved from rooftop to rooftop, swinging on washing lines, clambering across ledges, his body screaming in protest with every movement now. The chaotic sounds of battle faded a little as they headed further into Troy, higher and higher. As he scurried along one wooden ledge, he glanced up at the citadel. The Scaean Gate had not been closed and King Priam and Queen Hekabe stood up on the towers there, guarded only by a thin force. *I have to get ahead, to warn them,* he realised. Yet he was breathless – too breathless to shout. He moved to the wooden ledge at the edge of this rooftop and eyed the one across the lane – a horn hung there, and he could blow a note of alarm that those on the citadel would understand. He reckoned he could make the jump, even though his head was pounding and his stomach blazed with pain. He pushed down into his legs, ready to spring… then heard a terrible *crunch* as the wooden ledge fell away under his heels. Falling in a shower of timber and dust, he landed on his back, banging his head on the ground. Clothes, a washing line and an urn crashed down beside him. He croaked weakly. Nothing left. Not even the power to climb onto all fours.

Before he could clear his head, footsteps rattled up the street and halted before him. Achilles peered down at him. 'What is this?' he scoffed. 'A mutant?' He stalked round Sirtaya. 'Worse – an Egyptian!'

'You cannot pass,' Sirtaya croaked, rising on one shaking elbow, holding his sword up weakly.

Achilles brayed with laughter, casually flicking his spear flat at Sirtaya's hand, knocking the iron sword from his grasp and taking it for himself, then kicking Sirtaya's supporting elbow away as if taking down a tent. 'I think you'll find that I can. Troy has been breached at last. The city will be pillaged and burnt tonight.' With that, he stalked on up the Scaean Way.

'Wait,' said one of the Myrmidons. 'This wretch is the Hittite King's companion. I have seen them together when watching the city.'

Achilles halted, pacing back down to Sirtaya. 'Well, there is still time for me to face and defeat the mighty King Hattu tonight,' he said, crouching by Sirtaya. There was a madness in his eyes – a fire. 'But in case someone else robs me of that honour, then this creature's head will be a consolation of sorts…' he seized Sirtaya's tuft beard, tilting his head back, and lined the iron blade up against his neck, taking just a short backswing.

Sirtaya smirked up at Achilles… then gouged his talons into the bare spot behind his left greave. Achilles' face spasmed in shock. Sirtaya ran his talons right through, feeling the skin popping, then grabbed hold of the taut tendon in there, braced his arm and yanked backwards. The tendon snapped free with a wash of dark blood. Mouth agape in a shrill scream, Achilles crumpled, dropping the iron sword and clutching at his haemorrhaging ankle in horror. The Myrmidons too were stunned. Sirtaya rose, body pounding with a sudden surge of battle blood, snatching his iron sword back and eyeing the Myrmidons like a one-man army.

The lead Myrmidon's face twisted in a snarl. 'Kill him!'

The elite warriors had not even planted one foot forward in a rush to slay Sirtaya, when they juddered to a halt as if a God had seized them where they stood. Spearheads burst through their chests and throats. With wet groans, they fell, revealing Prince Paris and a knot of Trojan Guardians. Only one Myrmidon escaped, fleeing back down the avenue whence he had come.

Achilles clambered backwards on his elbows and good foot, dragging the ruined foot in a trail of slick blood. Sirtaya held his iron blade at the Ahhiyawan champion's throat as he went. 'Not so fast now, eh?' the Egyptian smiled. 'Now you are the wounded man – like those upon whom you prey.'

'No,' Paris said. 'Stand aside.'

Sirtaya turned to Paris, bowing. 'Yes, Majesty.'

Paris stood over Achilles, taking up his bow, nocking and drawing, the arrow tip an arm's-length from the grounded enemy talisman. 'Perhaps if I bring your body to my father, he might admit that it should have been me leading tonight's defence.'

'You?' Achilles rasped. 'You think you can kill me?' He laughed. 'Then you are a fool. I am descended from Zeus! I am the greatest warrior alive.'

'I can fix that,' Paris said flatly, loosing his bow. The arrow whizzed into Achilles' right eye, sending his head shooting back. His whole armoured body clunked to the ground like a stone. 'It appears that this demigod was in fact mortal.'

Glaucus arrived on the scene, panting, his Lukkan armour streaked with battle-filth. His eyes grew like moons when he saw Achilles' body, the arrow in the eye, the bleeding ankle tendon hanging loose like red rope. 'Achilles has fallen? Apollo is with us! How, how did you manage to beat him, Prince Paris?'

Paris darted a cautionary look at Sirtaya, then raised his voice so all would hear. 'He was fast but not fast enough. I ripped his ankle tendon with my first arrow, then killed him with my second.' As all around whispered in awe, Paris muttered something to his Guardians, who picked the body up by the wrists and ankles, then began to carry it up the Scaean Way, towards the citadel.

'Where are you taking him?' Glaucus asked.

Paris looked over his shoulder. 'To pierce his other heel then hang him from the citadel walls. He did worse to my brother.'

Glaucus recoiled, then strode forward. 'You must not, Majesty. King Hattu made a pact with Achilles that his body would not be dishonoured.'

'I will have my battle trophy and all in Troy will see it,' Paris snapped, carrying on uphill. 'No longer will people speak of Prince Paris the cowardly bowman. My father too will see that when Hektor died he should have entrusted me with the Helm of Troy.'

'Think about what you're doing!' Glaucus raged. Sirtaya watched, alarmed, as the Lukkan strode between two of the Guardians carrying the corpse, then tried to pull the body from them. The body fell to the ground and a blur of swearing, grunting and shoving ensued.

***

The street hemming the beset section of walls was a writhing mass of warring soldiers. Hattu jumped down from the slowing Destroyer and smashed a mace – taken from a dead Locrian – into the face of Ajax. The giant roared, his nose exploding and a shower of teeth flying. His brother, Teucer, vengefully nocked his bow, only for Andor to come streaking down to tear the weapon from his hands. Dagon took a cut to the shoulder as he lashed his whip across the face of Diomedes, sending him flailing, while Tudha slashed aside the lion-emblazoned shield of a Mycenaean then ran the man through. Up on the battlements, Kalchas the enemy augur crouched beside Penthesilea's body, rummaging elbow-deep in her entrails before Masturi ran at him. But more and more enemy soldiers piled over the ladders and onto the taken battlements. The allies were exhausted, Hattu realised, seeing that there were just a few hundred men here to defend this spot. 'We're going to have to withdraw up towards the citadel,' he growled.

'Hattu, if they trap us in the citadel… it's over,' Dagon panted back.

At just that moment, a Myrmidon came flailing down the Scaean Way, screaming: 'Achilles had been slain!'

All heads – allied and enemy – swung to the shout. The effect was instantaneous: The confidence of the Ahhiyawans seemed to evaporate. Brandished swords were drawn back and shields were held up in defence instead. Cretans, Spartans, Locrians, Tiryneans all looked this way and that for direction. But with Ajax half-blinded and choking on his own blood, and Diomedes being driven gracelessly off the battlements – down the ladders in a clumsy half-fall, there was no commanding voice to shout in reply. When some men began to flee back over the walls, many others followed. In a few moments, the Ahhiyawans were on the run.

It was like two dogs exhausted from a fight pulling apart – skin ripped, ears hanging off, eyes gouged. The Ahhiyawans withdrew to their crescent camp, while the Trojans reformed on the battlements to be sure it was not a false retreat. Hattu gazed over the wreckage: corpses lay on the battlements, arms dangling, dripping blood, some draped over the merlons like wet washing; the ditch and the lower city streets were carpeted with bodies, Memnon amongst them, spine jutting from the top of his back from his fall. Hattu spotted Prince Deiphobus nearby, gazing in a stupor at it all. 'Stay here, Majesty,' he said. 'Marshall the wall sentries. I will be back soon.'

Deiphobus nodded slowly, absently.

Hattu headed uphill from where the screaming Myrmidon had come. Soon he arrived at the scene of the slain Achilles. Part of him had not believed the shouts until he saw the body. Patroklos' final words echoed through his head: *Glory and then death. Peace from the demons that torment him.* His gaze drifted from the arrow jutting from the dead champion's eye to the grievous wound to his ankle.

Prince Paris stood over the corpse with a small contingent of Guardians. With a clank of armour, another small wing of these elite sentries came down the slope, flanking King Priam, Queen Hekabe and old Antenor. The priests too: the tall, striding Laocoon and the fat, shuffling Chryses.

'The attack has been thwarted, Father,' Paris reported.

Priam halted, gazing downhill at the many slain, then at the finely-armoured body before him. 'And the legend of Achilles ends here,' he said.

'Thanks to Prince Paris,' a Guardian officer boomed. 'Tore Achilles' leg with one arrow then killed him with the second.' Paris stared into the distance heroically.

Hattu eyed the body again: the torn ankle tendon was no arrow wound. He glanced at Sirtaya's blood-smeared talons. There was more to this than met the eye. He looked again at Sirtaya. The Egyptian was breathing hard, paler than usual and blue-tinged around the lips – yet he bore no wounds. There was something else too: an odd expression on Sirtaya's face. 'Something wrong, old friend?'

He coughed a few times, shaking, then gave Hattu another one of those looks, his eyes darting towards the dark street-side. There was nothing there, Hattu was sure. Confused, he made a note to speak to Sirtaya later, privately.

His thoughts turned to that chat with Achilles outside Troy, and the pact. 'We should return the body to his soldiers.'

'Why?' Paris said. 'He dragged my brother's corpse behind his chariot for days.'

'Yet he relented in the end. What would be gained in repeating Achilles' mistake?'

Paris' face pinched, and then he clapped his hands in instruction to the Guardians with him. 'I have spoken. His body is to be hung from the citadel walls – by the heels.'

Hattu stepped before the body. 'Do the right thing, Prince of Troy. Do as your brother wished should be done had he beaten Achilles that day.'

The Trojan Guardians hesitated, sharing nervous looks. 'Step aside, King Hattu,' said Paris, rocking on the balls of his feet to gain a little height. 'This is Troy, my father's city. One day it will be mine.'

Tudha and Dagon arrived on the scene, flanking Hattu. Andor shrieked, gliding down to land on Hattu's shoulder. Masturi trudged uphill from the walls, his bloody face sagging in exhaustion. 'What's going on here?'

'Achilles' body is to be returned to his people,' Hattu said calmly. Scores more Seha Riverlanders appeared around Masturi. Lukkans too. Now the Trojan Guardians – so few in comparison – seemed rooted to the spot. Paris and Hattu's gazes were like knives, both refusing to look away.

Priam intervened. 'King Hattu is High Commander of the Army of Troy. Matters of battle are his to adjudicate. Step aside, my son.'

The body was lifted and taken down to the gate area to be delivered onto the plain so the Ahhiyawans might collect it. Paris bristled, before turning away with a swish of his cloak and stomping uphill. As relieved chatter broke out around him, Hattu finally sighed and allowed the rock-hard tension in his muscles to seep away. He noticed something else then. At the streetside – the light of a nearby torch now fell upon the spot Sirtaya had been furtively gesturing towards. Another body lay there. Many voices muttered in confusion, seeing it too.

Hattu knelt beside the corpse, rolling it over. 'Glaucus?' The Lukkan captain's face was grey and locked in shock, his armour pierced at the chest, the hole stained red. A dagger wound. Hattu's heart plunged into his boots. *How many age-old comrades must fall? How many?*

All the Lukkans who had gathered at the scene erupted in cries of woe, some falling to their knees, others kneeling beside the corpse and rocking, stammering words of prayer, tear-streaked.

'He was Achilles' final victim,' one of the Guardians said.

'Master Hattu,' Sirtaya croaked, tugging on Hattu's sleeve.

When Hattu turned to him, he seemed like he was about to say more, but instead, he broke down into a coughing fit. It grew intense, the Egyptian hacking madly. He fell to his knees, bringing a filthy rag to his lips, coughing and shuddering. Hattu saw dark blossoms of blood spotting upon it. A moment later, he slumped onto his side and fell slack.

'Sirtaya?' Hattu cried.

# CHAPTER 15

## A CAGE OF FEAR

A moon passed. Dog-hot days of waiting and watching, evenings of desperate prayers and libations around the Palladium altar, and nights quiet as death. The two armies licked their wounds, carefully studying one another. Increasingly, however, it was not two mighty bears facing off, but the wounded deer of Troy trapped by the Wolves of Ahhiyawa.

Hattu walked the streets with Andor on his shoulder, his tunic sticking to his back with sweat, pressed there by his sword crossbands. The sentries up on the battlements shimmered in the infernal heat. They were, out of necessity these days, a mishmash – the remaining few Lukkans, a smattering of Amazons, the last of Masturi's Seha Riverlanders, a handful of Elamites, and the last hundred or so of the Trojan Guardians. As for the chariotry, only three Destroyers and two Trojan vehicles remained. The Army of Troy was in a sorry state.

He glanced northwards along the Silver Ridge, to the new town of tents and huts perched up on Thorn Hill. The enemy had established this second, smaller camp there, where the Trojan allies had once been ensconced. It was Agamemnon's means of blocking any more reinforcements who tried to approach Troy along that elevated pass. In truth, Hattu knew, there were no more allies coming. The war had sucked in every sympathetic and mercenary force near and far like a whirlpool, then devoured them here on this infernal plain. The devotion of the allied commanders who were here had been steadily unravelling since Hektor's death. The arrival of Penthesilea and Memnon had improved matters for a time, but the death of both had sent morale plummeting once again.

More, by capturing the Thorn Hill camp, the enemy could also now block any Trojan attempts to forage. Two hundred Thymbrans had tried… and their heads had been tossed over the walls a short while later. This development more than anything else could prove disastrous, he knew. For famine – that brutal champion of war – had arrived.

Bony hounds lay in the shade by the roadside, pestered by clouds of flies. Families sat slumped in their doorways or under dirty rooftop awnings, their eyes sliding to track him, too tired to speak or move, their hollow faces betraying their hunger. Famished old men sat around the edges of taverns, sipping on barley beer to numb the cravings for food. There were no plump grape bunches laid out to dry now, no venison hanging in the shady storerooms to cure. The pit jars within the houses lay empty of grain, the resin-sealed tops long-since removed and the contents consumed. When the hot breeze blew over these, the vessels sang in a mournful groan. His own belly gurgled in sympathy, and he ran his dry tongue over his gummy lips.

He came to the Thymbran Gate area. The gate itself was buckled and dented, but unbreached. The dead from the night battle had long since been cleared, anointed and put to the pyre. But the cracks in the streets here were still tainted with dried blood, and the walls were scarred, the merlons broken like a mouth of bad teeth. Denied access to Troy's twin rivers, there was no good mud-clay with which they could repair the damage.

With these deprivations all round, Hattu had waited for Priam's response. How might the King of Troy rally his ailing people? So he had watched in disbelief when the Guardians descended from the citadel not to help fairly distribute what food there was or to relieve the tired lower city watch, but to strip what little of value there was left down here. Copper was bent and twisted from the doors of homes, every remaining scrap of silver chasing was ripped from votive fonts and shrines, and family homes had been turned over to levy every gem and scrap of precious substance. All this was so Priam might fill a war purse with which to entice new allies to come to Troy's aid. Hattu had appealed to him that the effort was likely to be futile, tactfully sharing his thoughts that all and any reinforcements that might come were already here, but Priam was adamant.

With the sea the only way in which to get word to potential reinforcements, the booty was halved and stored upon two of the ocean worthy galleys lying idle in the Bay of Troy. They set off one day. That night, a thunderstorm had crackled out at sea, giving rise to a strong swell. The next morning, the Trojans woke to the sight of washed-up shreds of timber and dead sailors lay strewn along the Bay of Troy, bringing deep lamentations from the school of priests and the widows of the dead sailors.

All these memories tossed and churned in his mind and he began to feel light-headed in the heat. Worse, his ankles were throbbing with pain, even though he had only been walking for a short time.

A burst of insincere laughter rippled across the summer sky, punctuated by the clack of silver wine cups. Hattu glanced up towards the citadel, seeing the glimmer of golden architraves up there, untouched. While the heirlooms and precious keepsakes of simple families had been requisitioned to fill the treasure boats, the citadel had given nothing. More laughter and a snort of hilarity echoed from those high halls. He spotted Masturi and Aeneas and a handful of officers making their way slowly up the Scaean Way towards the acropolis. Soon, Priam's Royal Council was to gather, and he and the remaining allied commanders were expected to attend. Hattu knew he should head there now, but did not. There was something else, far more important, he had to attend to first.

He cut uphill towards a Trojan home set upon a rocky terrace. Putting Andor to flight, he stepped onto the home's stone porch. The view of the Scamander plain was good from here, and so he sat on a bench under the semi-shade of a vine canopy, the sensation of weight coming off of his feet as pleasant as steeping his legs in a cool bath. With a relieved sigh, he slid off his boots and the joyous sensation multiplied.

Tilting his head back, he noticed a curious gecko watching him from within the vines that had grown over the wall behind the bench. He eyed the creature, wishing for a moment that he and it could swap places. *To care only for basking in the sun and eating flies,* he mused. As if it suddenly reckoned his tongue was about to shoot out and catch it, the beast scampered off into the vine leaves. Quickly, he spotted why the creature had really run off: a trio of striped grey kittens, bounding towards the bench, one tumbling over the other, and the third biting at the two's tails. They frolicked around his feet, their soft warm fur pleasant against his aching shins. One grappled his leather boot and began biting the upturned toe, eyes wide and wild, ears back, while cycling madly against the sole with its back paws. Hattu reached down to tickle the kitten's tummy. He realised he was smiling. What a welcome distraction.

He heard a low moan from inside the home. One of the injured men. The healer couple who lived here, Kelenus and Tekka, had taken in four

Elamite soldiers badly-wounded in the night battle. Two had died, but at least under the soft haze of poppy sap. They had also taken Sirtaya in. They had washed and tended to the ailing old Egyptian as if he was one of their own children. The couple had lost their only son in the fourth year of the war, in a headlong charge at Hektor's behest – a tactic typical of the dead prince. Their kindness, their story, and this wretchedly hot month of inaction, had made him think long and deeply about everything.

He rummaged in his purse with one hand – knuckles chapped, fingernails ragged – to bring out the small wooden goat figurine given to him by Ruhepa. *Mighty Tarhunda, Lord of the Storm, watch over her and Pudu for me,* he mouthed, almost overwhelmed by the thought of how far away they were and how long he had been gone from them… that given Troy's virtual encirclement he might now never get back to them.

The kittens suddenly scattered as the door creaked open. Kelenus stepped out, his skin beaded with sweat and his forehead wrinkled with worry. He rested his hands on his wide hips, muttering quietly to himself before finally noticing that Hattu was there. '*Labarna,*' he said in a reverent whisper.

Hattu smiled. 'How goes it?'

As he said this, a gentle breeze blew and the door creaked open a little more behind Kelenus, revealing the sight of one of the Elamites on a makeshift cot. The warrior's coal-dark skin shone with sweat, face wracked with pain. The wound to his thigh was grievous, and the stink of maggoty meat wafted from the shady room. Kelenus' wife, stocky and red-faced like him, bathed and wiped at the mass of scab around the wound, but when pressure brought forth a runnel of bright-yellow pus, she sighed and shook her head. Placing a towel under the thigh, she worked a section of the scab with a scalpel, then took the loose part between her fingers and used it to rip the whole thing free. The Elamite spasmed in pain, but the removal allowed the suppurating wound to ooze pus freely, the mess draining onto the towel. The healer's wife then began applying a honey-soaked poultice to the wound.

Kelenus smiled sadly. 'Were Tekka and I better-trained healers, perhaps we might have saved more of these men.'

'Without your care, they would all have died,' Hattu replied, thinking of the Elamite he had seen at the temple ward earlier that day – alive and well, albeit hobbling on a crutch with one leg amputated at the knee. 'How is…' he gulped, feeling like he was standing on a cliff edge, not wanting to ask the question. 'How is Sirtaya?'

Kelenus could not look at him.

Hattu looked inside the shady home again, seeing the bed beyond the groaning Elamite. There Sirtaya lay, still and shrivelled, robbed of his innocent charm and boundless energy. Kelenus had discovered a canker deep in the Egyptian's guts. Every so often, he would contort slowly, weakly, one hand rising and clenching the air before him. 'He has remained unconscious?'

Kelenus smiled sadly. 'He was awake for a spell. Yesterday, not long after you were here to check on him. The kittens sprang up onto the bed, nuzzling him and playing with his fingers and attacking his tuft beard. Monstrous creatures, he called them.' His smile grew true now. 'Then from the other room we heard him naming each of them after the Gods of Egypt. "I shall call you Horus, and you Ra",' he said, affecting Sirtaya's accent. 'When we looked in next they were asleep on and around him, purring madly, and he was stroking each of them and kissing their heads.'

Hattu found himself smiling like a boy, wishing he had been there to see it.

'And,' Kelenus said, frowning. 'And… there was something else. He still has something he wishes to say, but only to you, King Hattu.'

Hattu's ears pricked up. He had visited every day since Sirtaya had been here, but hadn't been lucky enough to catch the Egyptian on the few times he had woken from his feverish slumber. Every time, Kelenus said, he croaked some urgent need to see Hattu, to tell him something.

A weak groan sounded from inside the house. Hattu looked round, hoping it might be Sirtaya rousing. But it was the poor wounded Elamite again. Sirtaya remained lost in a feverish oblivion.

'The poppy sap. If you need any more for him, you must tell me.'

Kelenus began shaking his head.

'I will venture outside the city to get it personally,' Hattu insisted. 'I will find a way to sneak past the Ahhiyawan besiegers out there.'

'There is no need,' Kelenus said. 'The sap… it does not make him comfortable anymore.'

Hattu felt a hard stone rising through his throat, pushing wetness to his eyes. He rested his elbows on his knees and let his head droop. His long silver hair fell around his face like a privacy veil, and he felt the invisible armour he at all times wore falling off in chunks. A boyish half-sob escaped his lips.

'You are a good man, King Hattu,' Kelenus said. 'I have never known a king to talk to ordinary people – people like me – as if they were equals.'

Hattu took a moment, breathing to control his emotions, sat back, gazing down over the streets, the walls and the sweating sentries. 'We are equals, are we not? Chickens in the same coop, my heir calls us? Your fate and mine will be shared.'

'Indeed. It will soon come to an end, I fear,' Kelenus said quietly. 'Almost all of Troy's heroes – Prince Hektor, Sarpedon, Memnon, Penthesilea, Commander Dolon – are gone. Countless noblemen and warriors too.'

Hattu's eyes scanned the main Ahhiyawan encampment out there on the plain, the clouds of plague flies visible even from here. 'Likewise, Achilles and Patroklos are now nothing but ash. Thousands upon thousands of their fighters whose names we never knew are no more.' He thought of something both encouraging and terrible he had heard. 'A scout told me this morning that Ajax too is now dead, not slain by a Trojan sword, but by his own hand.'

Kelenus' eyes bulged. 'That brute? Why did he do it?'

Hattu shook his head. 'Quarrelling in the enemy camp, apparently. Once Achilles' funeral games were complete, his fine armour was up for grabs. The Ithacan, Odysseus, outsmarted Ajax to win it for himself. Ajax wept and wept, leaving the camp to wander alone. The scout says he slaughtered a herd of wild sheep before falling upon his own blade.'

'Because of a suit of armour?' Kelenus croaked.

Hattu thought of the things war did to a man. The invisible scars. The immortal memories that danced like fire through one's mind many years after the swords had swung. He stared out across the Scamander plain, turning the wooden goat in his fingers. 'They say that Odysseus won the armour not as a trophy for himself, but as a gift – a means of enticing Achilles' son, Neoptolemus, across the sea and to join the war.'

Kelenus' face sagged. 'N… Neoptolemus is here?'

Hattu nodded slowly. 'It seems he wears Achilles' magnificent suit of gold and silver now, ready to lead the Myrmidons in his father's place.'

Kelenus sighed in despair.

It had been the weakest of the five prophecies, for no Trojan was capable of preventing the young warrior's arrival here. Still, it was the fourth to have been whittled away. The news had not been shared widely yet, but the fourth tablet at the foot of the Scaean Tower was due to be smashed tonight, and then all in Troy would know. After that, only one would remain. Still, Hattu thought, the final prophecy was surely the strongest. The Palladium statue was in place in the high heart of Troy. Untouchable.

'In the ten years this war has raged,' said Kelenus, 'there must be many sons of fallen fathers who have taken up the spear in the name of vengeance. Is that not a wretched cycle?'

Hattu said nothing. The question needed no reply. It made him think of Tudha. Of the chances that he and his heir would perish here in Troy. The thought brought a clamour of voices into his head, a discordant panic. Such a dazzling display his heir had given on that night of the enemy attack. He was everything he claimed to be, faster and stronger than Hattu at the same age. Dangerously perceptive and almost preternatural in his reactions. *Still,* he thought of the leather bag and Tudha's iron sword inside it, *still I fear what you might become.*

'Your son has been round here every day, usually soon after sunrise,' Kelenus said, as if he had overheard Hattu's thoughts. 'He sits with Sirtaya, talks to him.'

'Talks?'

'Well, it is rather one-sided, but yes, he speaks of things he thinks the Egyptian might like to hear, deep in his slumber.' Kelenus paused for a time. 'I never once tried to listen in, but in the quiet of the early mornings it is impossible not to hear.'

'What does he say?'

'He speaks of the things he and the Egyptian did in his boyhood days: walking the river near Hattusa, fishing, gathering polished stones from the stream beds, silly stories, legends.' Kelenus played with his fingers. 'He… he didn't have many other friends when he was a boy, did he?'

Hattu shook his head slowly. 'He was born to be my successor. It was his duty to learn from me and mine to teach him.'

'You have taught him well, from what I have seen and heard. The people of Troy talk of Tudha in the way the enemy once exalted Achilles.'

Hattu smiled thinly, gazing across the sweltering heat towards the earthen barrow under which the Ahhiyawans had buried their talisman. They sat in silence for a time, each man's eyes narrowed against the glare of the afternoon. One of the kittens gingerly popped its head around the corner of a stone water cistern, sniffing the air.

'These terrors were born to the pounce of cats we looked after here,' Kelenus said with a tune of fondness in his voice. 'Cats who used to prowl out there on the Scamander plain, hunting mice, basking in the sun. When the Ahhiyawans came, they grew terrified of the strange sights, smells and noises. They never went out again. These kittens were born into that. They have no desire to go beyond the city walls. This is their world. Born into a cage of fear.' He wiped the film of sweat from his upper lip. 'And it is not just that outside which is to be feared,' Kelenus added.

'What do you mean?' Hattu said, suddenly uncomfortable. 'The Shadow?'

He shook his head sadly. 'It happened last moon. From the walls, I saw an Ahhiyawan boy – born into their camp as my kittens were to Troy. He was playing, splashing in the Scamander. His arms were stumps, stopping before the elbow. I wondered if it was the blight out there that had claimed his limbs. *But the plague does not eat the flesh,* I muttered to myself, thinking I was alone. One of the Guardians on the wall near me… laughed. He said it had been his doing. He and another had been out scouting and had happened across the boy playing upriver. They had asked the boy to hold out his hands. They told him they were going to cut off his arms, and that it would be good for him… because just like blades of grass, they would grow back stronger.' Kelenus stopped talking and cupped a hand over his mouth, shaking his head.

Hattu followed the dark look Kelenus cast across the city to the Guardian on the nearest tower. A broad-chinned ox of a soldier, chatting breezily with a bare-breasted servant woman, hooting with laughter at his own jokes. He had heard the man's name a few times. Skorpios.

'It is not the only such tale I have heard,' said Kelenus, 'I hear that our Guardians butchered the enemy plague victims on their stretchers at the Bay of Boreas? And that Prince Paris wanted to dangle the corpse of Achilles from the roof of Troy's sacred hall?'

Hattu realised that Kelenus was hoping he might be able to explain those stories away. He could not.

The healer sighed. 'When the Ahhiyawans came, we looked upon them as wretched serpents, sliding from the sea. Then evil wolves, roving across our river plain to battle our noble young champions. Finally, they were vultures, prizing armour from the bodies of our fallen.' He held out his open hands in exasperation. 'But think of the things you have seen, of what I have just told you. How much more of this can there be before we realise we are becoming vultures like them, this husk city and that plague-ridden camp out there the cadavers upon which we feed?'

Hattu nodded gently, blown away by the profound words, troubled that he could find no way of refuting the theory. 'I came here to end this war, and that is what I will do,' he said, affecting a confidence he did not feel. 'Troy will know peace and nobility again.' He stood, hoping to end the conversation on a note of optimism.

'Every night, I pray that Apollo will make it so,' Kelenus said, rising with him.

Hattu glancing into the shady interior of the house. 'I should go. But before I do…'

Kelenus nodded, understanding, guiding Hattu inside.

When Hattu came to Sirtaya's bedside, the Egyptian was asleep and free of pain for the moment at least. But Hattu could see all too well how the disease had ravaged him. Once, he and Dagon had theorised that Sirtaya might be trapped in his thirtieth summer, ageless. Now, he looked like the oldest man Hattu had ever seen. With a shiver and a weak moan, Sirtaya shuffled in his bed. Hattu squeezed his hand and lent down to kiss his forehead. 'Rest easy, my old companion,' he whispered. Like a faithful sentry, one of the kittens hopped up onto the bed, gave Hattu a "ferocious" hiss, then nestled itself inside the crook of Sirtaya's arm and began purring, licking his skin.

***

Compared to the dusty, dilapidated lower city, the royal megaron was almost unearthly in contrast. Long fingers of late afternoon sunshine stretched in from the open end, gleaming on the cool marble floors, the bright pillars, the pure-bronze and silver shields mounted on walls striped with long purple drapes. Camphor wax candles sweetened the air, and the aroma of juicy, fatty goodness wafted from the hunks of roast lamb at the centre of the table, bringing water to the mouth.

Priam sat at the head of the table, his eyes vacant, the delicate silver circlet of Troy resting on his head like a crown of stone. Queen Hekabe sat by his side, eyes equally distant, face drawn. Antenor and the elders sat nearest, with the princes next, then the priests. The noblemen and few allied commanders left occupied the far end of the table with Hattu, who sat with his head bowed, mulling over his impossible promise to Kelenus.

*I came here to end this war, and that is what I will do...*

'... and now Achilles is nothing but ashes and bones,' Paris continued his summary of matters, pacing near the head of the table. 'The remaining Ahhiyawans perish to the plague that stalks the Scamander plain. All the while, Troy's walls remain unbreached.' He twisted towards Helen, seated near the unlit hearth, giving her an unctuous half-bow. She replied with a distant, haunted stare. Paris was oblivious to this. He looked up and around all those at the table. 'We may not possess the numbers to win this war on the battlefield, but time is on our side.' The priests and most of the elders raised and clacked their silver cups at this. The Guardians bumped the hafts of their spears on the marble floors in support. Prince Deiphobus, face bent in the opposite of a smile, applauded, but his eyes were laden with jealousy.

Hattu turned his head slowly upwards to stare at the heir of Troy. A storm of cutting words rose in his throat, but it was Aeneas who spoke first.

'With respect, Majesties,' the Dardanian Prince said, addressing Priam and Paris, 'hunger will defeat us before plague ruins the enemy.'

'Hunger?' Laocoon threw a caustic look at the Prince of Dardania. 'There is still the grain store here on the citadel.' He waved his hippocampus staff across the fare on the table. 'Open your eyes, man, we will not starve!'

'No, *we* probably will not,' Aeneas said, his voice dripping with scorn. 'But what about the lower city? The silos there are hollow. Time is *not* on the side of the families there. The masses who once enjoyed thick stews of milk and meat now cook grass and tough inedible roots in water. They are starving. Three score died of hunger in the western quarter. That was yesterday alone.' He now cast his hands at the succulent food on the table too. 'But that matters not, apparently, as long as we have stores enough to comfortably feed the greedy mouths of those who live up here?'

Laocoon sneered. 'Your wife is one of those greedy mouths. A daughter of the king and queen, no less. She, your boy and your doddering old father enjoy homes on this high, royal ward. You should be grateful.'

'Grateful? I brought the Dardanian archers here to fight for Troy. Troy is not this citadel. Nor is it this city. It is this land, its people. What is Troy without Trojans?'

'Do not presume to tell me of my own land,' Laocoon growled. 'I have seen many more summers than you.'

'Then you should be wiser for it,' Aeneas chuckled mirthlessly. '*Should* be.'

Laocoon's lips rippled, betraying glimpses of his caged teeth. 'You rest too readily on your bloodline, Prince of Dardania. Nephew of King Priam you may be, but I am our Majesty's High Priest of Poseidon, and disrespect is not to be shown to me or any other in this hall.'

Aeneas stood, his chair screeching back. 'Then perhaps I should leave, and return once I have found some respect for you.' he gestured towards the open end of the hall and the hazy ghost of Mount Ida, far to the southeast. 'Were we not surrounded by the enemy I would travel to and scour the slopes of the mountain for it, but I suspect it is like your honour,' he leant across the table, pounding a fist down. Cups bounced and wobbled and all eyes stared at the Dardanian Prince, who hissed: 'A myth!'

Laocoon's face twisted. 'How *dare* you?' he raged, rising too, his fellow priest, Chryses, rising with him. Likewise, the Trojan Princes and Guardians clustered by the priests' sides, planting hands on their sword hilts.

At this, the nobles and allies around Aeneas shot to their feet in support of the Dardanian. Every other rose in a clamour, and the hall trembled with a cacophony of shouts and recriminations, oaths and threats. Unlike most of the fiery elders, Antenor waddled around the table, planting hands on shoulders, trying to be heard above the din. 'Stay calm, friends,' he pleaded. 'We here are our Majesty's eyes and ears. Shouting will blind and deafen us.' But the advisor's soft words didn't stand a chance against the quarrelling others. He and Hattu had shared many discussions now, always over a pot of mountain tea, and one thing had become abundantly clear: the elder too was at his wit's end about the in-fighting.

Hattu's head throbbed – the din was worse than a flock of gulls fighting over fish scraps. No, not gulls… vultures. The imagery brought him back to his promise to Kelenus. He realised now that there was only one hope of ending this war. Rising slowly, his tall frame blocked out the sunlight and cast a dominant shadow along the table. The squabbling faded and all turned to look at him.

'Look at yourselves,' he drawled. 'Ready to draw bronze on one another. Is this your answer to the disaster that has befallen Troy?'

Nobody answered. A few gulped.

'*Is it?*' he stormed. Still nobody answered.

'It is you who should be answering that question?' Laocoon ventured, trembling slightly, folding his arms, his face puckering in defiance.

'Aye,' Chryses agreed with a waver in his voice. 'It is *you* who carries a reputation as a master of war, King Hattu. Well you have been in possession of Hektor's helmet and the high command for long enough and still the situation has not improved. I say you should unveil to us your great plan to turn things around, or hand over the command to another.'

'Aye,' another priest rumbled in agreement, emboldened by the nearness of the Trojan Guardians.

Prince Paris moved to stand behind Priam's chair, planting one hand on his father's shoulder, staring at Hattu. 'Make your case then, Great King of the Hittites.'

Hattu stepped away from his seat and began pacing around the table, all heads turning to watch him as he went. 'We cannot attack the enemy on the field for it would be futile. They are too numerous and strong. Equally their many spears cannot break our sturdy defences. Thus, we find ourselves at an impasse. One which will suck Troy and her besiegers down into a pit of depravity and desolation.'

'What nonsense is this?' Paris scoffed.

Hattu squinted at the crown prince. 'Nonsense? They came here to seize women and families, to ship them away to their rocky coastal kingdoms to spin their coarse wool for them. They came here to strip your houses of electrum and silver. They came to take for themselves the toll of passing trade ships. Now look outside. Look!' he cast a hand to the open end of the hall, across the sloping streets of the lower city. 'How many shiploads of women have been taken off to Ahhiyawa? How many men lie dead or as ashes? The families are ill with hunger. The great trade fairs? They are no more. The passing merchant fleets? They are gone. For years now they have sailed wide of Troy. The world has moved on in that time – they will not be back. There is no electrum and silver,' he paused to shoot Priam a testing glare, 'apart from the fineries that remain up on this citadel.'

Priam, still silent, looked up now with a haunted look, like a fish realising it has just bitten down on a hook and is being dragged up to the surface.

'Be careful, *Labarna*,' Chryses the Priest burred, edging closer to Priam's side. 'Remember where you are.'

Hattu pinned him with a gaze of fire. 'By all the Gods I know exactly where I am. I remember what Troy once was. And every morning I wake and look over this city to be reminded of what it has become. This war has reduced her to a husk.'

Stunned looks all round.

'So if this war is to end,' he met every set of eyes, 'then you must accept that victory… is an illusion.'

Gasps erupted.

'For what victory could there be now, after all that has gone on? Even if we could somehow overcome them, even if *they* overran us. What would the winner truly gain? It would be like becoming the champion tick on the body of a dying dog.'

He halted near Priam. 'The winds of war have slowed to a whimper, Majesty. It is time to do what should have happened long, long ago. It is time to open talks with the Ahhiyawans before any more lives are churned into the dust, before the war destroys everything and everyone.'

Silence.

Priam looked up at Hattu.

Paris stared at Hattu also… and then exploded with bitter laughter. The two priests and some of the lesser Trojan Princes joined in. 'Talk?' he cooed. 'We waited for ten years for you to come with twenty thousand bronze blades. Then you arrived with a boy, a twisted Egyptian and a worn-out charioteer… and your plan was to beat the enemy not with bronze… but with your flapping gums?'

Another explosion of sarcastic laughter.

'My father was wrong to entrust you with Hektor's sacred helmet,' Paris added with a humourless glare. The laughter rose to new heights.

Hattu waited until the laughter faded, disappointing those near the crown prince who had expected him to react angrily. 'Diplomacy is the only way left,' he said calmly. 'Majesty,' he said, turning his gaze upon the silent King Priam. 'You must see it as well. The war has lost all meaning now.'

Priam stared into space.

Prince Paris stared at Hattu, then at his father, his head switching back and forth between the two like an irate younger brother of two siblings who were talking over his head.

Masturi spoke up from amongst the allied generals. 'Majesty, I agree with King Hattu. Queen Penthesilea was one of our last great hopes. She has come, she has fallen and only a handful of Amazon warriors remain. If this war is to continue, I see nothing ahead but more graves… until eventually Troy herself becomes one giant ossuary pit.'

Priam's eyes rolled over Masturi, regarding the Lord of the Seha Riverland in a strange, listless way – the way a dying pet watches the world moving on around it.

Another nobleman piped up now: 'King Memnon is dead too and his Elamites have been whittled down to mere hundreds. The army is threadbare at best. It is time to talk.'

'Nonsense,' Chryses the Priest snorted, the skin on his bald head wrinkling. 'Did you not see the boatloads of treasure our king sent out in search of new allies?'

'I saw the wreckage on the shores,' the nobleman replied.

'A prow and a few oars. So one boat sank. Poseidon saw that the black-hearted captain meant to flee and keep the treasure for himself!' Laocoon proclaimed, bumping the base of his staff on the floor three times, rousing a chorus of support. 'The other ship will sail far and bring fresh troops to our aid.'

'Who is left and how long dare we wait?' Masturi countered. 'What is there to be lost by opening talks?'

'Our reputation,' Paris scoffed. 'Anyway, talks would be useless… for they would not understand your Riverland babble.'

At this, several near Paris hooted and snorted sycophantically, while those around Masturi erupted in anger. In moments, all in the room were pressed against the table's edges again, fingers pointing, hands swishing angrily, faces reddening and spittle spraying from their braying mouths in a cacophonous din.

Hattu rested his palms on the table's edge and let his head droop. Antenor, hoarse with ineffective words of reason, slumped onto a seat and groaned, rolling his eyes in Hattu's direction.

The sound of a chair screeching cut through it all like a knife. King Priam was standing at last. Hattu looked up as the clamour faded away. *Speak, King of Troy… speak the wisdom your sons cannot.*

'They killed my boys,' he said quietly. His distant, glassy eyes slid across all the faces and came to a rest on Hattu. 'I am sorry, old friend. But there will be no talks. There *can* be no talks. It would be to spit on the ashes of my dead sons were I to allow this.'

Hattu's spirits plunged into his boots.

Paris grinned smugly. Chryses' fat face creased with a triumphant smile. Laocoon smirked with his eyes. Deiphobus looked on, calculating and quiet.

'I respect only the Gods more than you, King Hattu,' Priam continued. 'But I did not give you Hektor's helm so that you could surrender to the enemy. I cannot have a mood for parley circulating and building momentum. I certainly will not have anyone approaching our enemy for discussions. Thus, Troy must become like a turtle's shell.' He turned to Paris. 'Triple the watch on every gate. Collect the Springhouse passage keys from all who possess them and surrender them along with your own to my strongroom. None may leave. Anyone who attempts to step outside the city walls is an enemy of Troy,' he said, turning towards the hall door. He paused for a moment, looking back over his shoulder. 'Anyone.'

Hattu stared, stunned.

Paris smiled affably and bowed towards his departing father's back. 'I will see to it at once, Majesty.'

'The council is over,' Laocoon snapped, dashing his staff butt on the ground.

With a rumble of feet and tense whispers, the attendees slipped outside, into the light of the coming dusk. Paris stood at the door and, one by one, his royal brothers handed their keys to him. Aeneas too.

Outside, the Guardians were already being arranged into new teams to oversee the external gates and watch the streets for any attempting to escape. At first Hattu had thought the elite warriors to be majestic and exemplary. Maybe the generations of them he had fought alongside were. But amongst those left, he had witnessed some slaying sick and unarmed men in battle, and there was Skorpios, the one who had cut off the enemy boy's arms. They had mocked his ideas of peace talks back there in the megaron and he knew they would not be brought to reason. Beyond the city walls, the Ahhiyawan camp stretched like a mocking smile, unreachable.

'Fools,' Aeneas seethed, walking by Hattu's side. 'They've just sealed their own grave.'

'One we will share,' Masturi added dryly. 'There is no way out of this city now.'

Hattu felt the small weight in his purse. The key of Troilus. 'Not necessarily. There is still one last chance to reach and talk with our enemy.'

Aeneas and Masturi glanced sideways at him. When Hattu guided them over to a quiet spot and furtively showed them the key in his palm, their eyes widened. Yet he sighed and curled his fingers over the key again. 'Still, it means nothing unless we have something we can offer the Ahhiyawans.'

Aeneas' eyes grew hooded. 'Perhaps I can help with that,' he said with a sly smile.

# CHAPTER 16

## IPHIGENIA'S WEDDING

In the last hour of darkness, the moon cast a ghostly sheen across Troy's lower city. All was striped in pale silver and shadow or spotted with the occasional puddle of weak orange torchlight. Hattu moved fast, hugging the shadows. The streets were deserted thanks to the night curfew, and so he made good progress. Then…

*Crunch, crunch, crunch.*

Marching boots.

He fell still in a dark corner, breath caged as a pair of Guardians patrolled towards him. This had become the duty of the Guardians, thanks to King Priam's recent decree. While the allies manned the curtain walls, these elites policed the streets and the main gates. Last night, two starving young men had been caught trying to creep outside via the hatch entrance in the Dardanian Gate. Paris had ordered them flogged raw and thrown back into their homes. No one, no matter how desperate, could leave Troy.

The patrol passed and he let the held breath spill from his lungs. On he went through the shadows. Soon, he reached the western quarter. His eyes slid up to the Apollonian springhouse, the bright red and yellow door columns ghostly grey at this hour. Two Guardians stood watch there too. He waited, watching, for an age. They were like statues, unblinking.

At last, a pebble skittered down the street nearby. Both heads swung to the sound. Next came whispering and then the padding of feet from that direction. The two Guardians looked at one another, then one called out: 'who goes there?'

Suddenly, the padding feet broke into a rapid patter.

The two Guardians burst into a run, clanking towards the noise.

*Thank you, Dagon,* Hattu mouthed in the direction of the distraction, then stole across the street and flitted up the steps and into the springhouse. He passed the altar and came to the door at the end of the rear corridor, then slid the key of Troilus into the lock.

By the time he had descended the rocky stairs within and arrived at the vine-draped cave entrance to the Bay of Troy, dawn had broken, throwing pink ribbons of light across the dome of virgin blue sky. He walked out onto the sand – dry and powdery from the low tide. Dolphins were at play in the calm waters, leaping over the semi-submerged prow of a dilapidated Trojan warship. He looked south, along a tapering arm of the bluff that ran all the way to the reedy swamps on the far end of the sickle bay – a perfect screen behind which he could creep close to the Ahhiyawan crescent camp. All he could see of it from here was the tips of a few tents, the dawn casting long fingers of light between them.

He crept closer, crouching to stay hidden behind the rocky scarp. The bay narrowed as he went. The waves, whispering along the strand, soaked him to his ankles in waters shockingly cold. An old rag, washed up on the shore, tangled around his feet and he had to kick it off. A few paces further on and he could see a little more of the enemy tents and shacks. Soldiers too – the dawn-silhouetted outlines of Locrian archers patrolling the camp perimeter. The madness of his plan seemed to swell and grow horns as he edged closer. What to say? How to pacify the enemy sentries and convince them he was here to talk peace with Agamemnon? Taking a deep breath, eyes closed, he summoned a few words of the Ahhiyawan tongue – a greeting to use with the sentries. His heart pounded in his ears, and he readied to rise to his full height, to stand and announce his presence.

'I wouldn't do that if I were you,' an Ahhiyawan voice said from behind him.

Hattu swung round with a jolt of fright.

Odysseus waded from the freezing water like a fish that had just sprouted legs, his naked body glistening wet. Out in the bay behind him, the dolphins leapt and twisted, clicking and squeaking as if trying to coax him back in to swim with them for longer. The King of Ithaca stooped to pick up the 'rag' Hattu had kicked away a moment ago and wrapped it around his waist, before unceremoniously covering each nostril with the tip of a forefinger to blow snot from the other. Sweeping his hair back from his face, he grinned. 'You come to hand yourself over? To switch allegiance?'

'I came to offer Agamemnon a chance to end this war peaceably,' said Hattu.

'I told you before, the time for talks passed long ago,' Odysseus said. 'It cannot end until Troy has fallen.'

'If your *Wanax* hears me out today, this war could be over tomorrow,' Hattu countered. 'You could be sailing home the day after.'

Odysseus offered a weak, lop-sided smile. 'I have had a strange dream in recent nights,' he said, stooping to pick up a long woollen cloak wedged between two rocks. 'Of just that – sailing home. The voyage begins with singing and relief, men bright with joy. Then… the sea opens in a yawning chasm. A black well that swallows my ships and laughs as it does so, drinking us into its belly – a land of unforgivable crimes, insufferable torment, unthinkable monsters.'

Hattu looked out to the sea then back inland to the Scamander flats. 'No monsters could be worse than the things you have seen on the plain of Troy over these last ten summers. Perhaps it is those memories that will plague your journey home.' He tapped his temple. 'I know that the things I have seen in my few moons here will stay with me forever.'

Odysseus and he shared a strange look then. A look that needed no words.

Hattu took a deep breath. 'See sense, Island King. Troy will not fall. After ten years of attack, the city's walls stand firm. Your fleet of battering rams barely scraped the defences. Troy has plentiful water and food,' he lied.

'So too do we,' Odysseus countered.

There was something about the shape of his eyes that told Hattu he might be bluffing as well. He gestured towards the lowland crescent camp. 'What about the fever? How many has it claimed now?'

Odysseus' lips moved as if to issue a quickfire rebuttal, but his forehead grew rutted with lines. 'Let us dispense with our desperate lies, eh?' He sighed deeply and shook his head. 'The plague is rampant within our camp, just as hunger rampages through Troy's streets.'

'As things stand, you will remain camped out on the Scamander plain for years to come. So too will your children,' said Hattu. 'Is that what you want? Generations born into starvation and sickness? A few words from me to your *Wanax* might prevent that.'

'I wish that you could end this with your words, *Labarna*,' Odysseus said. 'To be gone from this plague camp forever, and to be where my heart longs to be: at home. You will have seen in this last moon, new boats arriving?'

'Fresh soldiers,' Hattu guessed.

'Aye, but they bring troubling news. The outlying towns beyond the great mountains of Ahhiyawa have been overwhelmed.'

Hattu's eyes narrowed. 'The western peoples you spoke of… the roving fleets and rootless hordes?'

Odysseus nodded gently. 'So you see, King Hattu, we are now stuck on the horns of dilemma: a need to return to and defend our home cities from that creeping storm, to defend the wider world from it – for I remember what you said about the delicate balance of powers. But we cannot leave. Agamemnon *will* not leave until we have cracked open the shell of Troy.'

'Trust in me, Island King… give me an audience with him. Let me try to change his mind.'

'The last time you entered his hut, he decided to have you impaled.'

'A lot has changed in the moons since.'

The waves lapped nearby like a heartbeat until, finally, Odysseus looked away. He beckoned Hattu. 'Come, I will take you to him.'

Hattu hesitated.

'I guarantee your safety within the camp.' Odysseus reassured him. Scratching his beard, he handed the woollen cloak to Hattu. 'But just to be on the safe side, wear this, and raise the hood.'

As they walked on up the bay, Hattu sensed Odysseus eyeing him sideways. 'Your boy, Tudhaliya, continues to impress. He is some fighter. He was the eagle's beak of that chariot charge which ruptured our night attack. The men of my camp rumble about him in envy and fear.'

'Hmm,' Hattu shrugged as if the matter was of no interest.

'As I thought,' Odysseus said, a hint of smugness in his voice. 'There is still some rancour between you and him, isn't there? I have seen the way you both are in battle: supreme, but rarely together. And on the parapets of Troy, gesticulating, bristling at one another.'

'The matter does not concern you,' Hattu said.

'So there *is* a matter,' Odysseus concluded.

Hattu eyed him sidelong, distrusting.

Odysseus laughed. 'I was asking only as a father. Before I set sail from Ithaca I struggled to control my boy, Telemachus, and he was but an infant.'

'It is no trivial dispute,' Hattu offered. He eyed Odysseus again. So much the Ithacan had shared with him that he wondered if – for the first time in moons – he might be able to speak of the matter… to purge his mind of the built-up angst, for a time at least. 'There was a rebellion near the Hittite heartlands,' he began hesitantly.

Odysseus nodded as they walked.

'I entrusted my heir to stamp out the uprising with what limited soldiery we had. He defeated the rebels, and I visited shortly after to assess the aftermath. There was a shrine in the heart of those forested lands. My cousin lived there. I went there because I wanted to be sure that she was safe.' He closed his eyes, seeing the stony temple once again, his hand moving towards the bloodied wooden door, the door swinging inwards… the stink of death. His thoughts began to whirl around him, growing dark and real.

*The walls encrusted with half-dried gore, the buzz of flies.*

*The priestesses strewn in ripped, bloody ribbons.*

*The death scream written on sweet Zanduhepa's face.*

'They…. they…they had been slaughtered,' he stammered.

*The dead baby in her arms.*

'All of them… dead.'

*The dull thud of his footsteps, stumbling away from the place.*

*The shrine a tomb.*

*His heir, a slayer of women and infants.*

'Easy, easy,' Odysseus said. 'I genuinely do not seek to trouble you.'

Hattu halted for a moment, breathing to regain his composure. 'The memories haunt me every day. Bad seeds often sprout from the Hittite royal line. The last one to do so nearly destroyed our empire completely. I have tried so hard to train my heir to be noble and proper in all his actions, yet I cannot help but dread that he might be the darkest seed yet.'

'Think of something else,' Odysseus advised. 'Your friend, the Egyptian. How is he?'

Hattu looked at him askance. How could Odysseus know about Sirtaya's illness?

'I watch Troy's defences every day,' Odysseus explained. 'In the spring, I saw you pacing the battlements like a crow. He was with you always, like a faithful shadow. I have not seen him for some time.'

Hattu's throat thickened. 'A canker grows in his belly.'

'Ah, I am sorry, my clumsy words again,' Odysseus said quietly. 'Is he suffering?'

Hattu half-nodded, looking away.

'The juice of the poppy can help with cankers,' Odysseus said.

'Not anymore,' Hattu croaked. 'His time is near.'

'I am sorry for you and for him,' Odysseus said solemnly. 'But I suppose as things stand, we are all set to die on this disease-ridden plain.'

'No. Trust me, Island King. The dying can stop, today,' Hattu said as they came round the scarp end and approached the crescent camp. He set eyes upon Agamemnon's hut. 'All I need is a short time alone with your *Wanax*. I can talk the most stubborn men around.'

'Oh, I do trust that you can,' Odysseus said. 'And Agamemnon is very stubborn. But there is more to it than that. His tale is a dark and twisted one. A tangle that cannot be undone.'

***

Odysseus led Hattu through the enemy sentry line and into the sea of tents and huts. None challenged the Ithacan King or the hooded stranger he led. The pair entered the royal hut and waited at the rear as the members of the kerosia debated. The shack was similar to the one Hattu had been in at the Bay of Boreas… but smaller, more squalid. The gathering was thin – many faces that had been in the hut that previous time were missing now, and a fair few of those still here were gaunt, riddled with suppurating bites and sores. Kalchas the armoured augur cut a bedraggled figure, his bronze garb dull and his beard matted in tangles of sweat and dried blood. Agamemnon sat slumped on his splendid throne – itself dulled and stained with smoke and grease – eyes pouchy, face bloated and red with wine, chin resting in the palm of one hand. He was almost unrecognisable from the trim, gleaming warlord Hattu had stood before in the spring. The two leather-armoured guards either side of the throne were streaked with sweat, lips blistered with thirst and malnutrition, eyes swinging between the group arguing before the throne.

'My men have spent days and nights crafting new rams. And you say it was all for nothing?' raged the King of Crete.

'We sent rams and every soldier at the walls the last time, and we could not break through,' countered old Nestor of Pylos.

'Then we had only nine rams,' argued a young one Hattu had not seen before. 'This time, we have *thirty!*'

'Thirty rams sound impressive, but only one at a time will be able to traverse each of the narrow causeways leading to their three outer gates,' Nestor replied calmly. 'All while their fire devices and missiles pelt down on us, just as it was during our night attack. Their defences are too strong, our rams are too weak. It is as simple as that.'

'Ah, the words of a wise old warrior,' the young one hissed. 'Or a coward, afraid to seize the moment?'

Hattu, head shrouded by the hood, peered at the young one sideways. Red-haired, snub-nosed, cradling a familiar golden helm. Achilles' helm. Hattu shivered, realising this was the dead man's son, Neoptolemus.

'Troy's defences may be strong, but their regiments are perilously threadbare. That is if we can trust the latest information from our...' Neoptolemus continued, '*friend* inside the city.'

All of Hattu's senses pricked up. *The Shadow?* Since his chat with Helen, the trail had gone worryingly cold.

'Friend?' Menelaus barked, then spat on the floor. 'I think not!'

Hattu saw something in the Spartan King's face. Not mere dislike. Pure malice. A hatred of this spy. Who amongst the population of Troy could Menelaus despise so fervidly? His mind swam, recalling that night when he had tried to entrap Helen. Had she deceived him? Was she the Shadow after all? Who else but her could Menelaus hate quite so much? And then it hit him like a hammer tolling upon a bell.

The Trojan who had cuckolded the Spartan King.

Paris.

Paris... who had been there when the Thymbran Gate keys had gone missing, when the river camp had been attacked. Paris, who was inexplicably awake, armed and ready that night of the enemy attack. Had he been the one to shoot and silence Theron the slave... the slave who had given Hektor the poisoned water skin? It could not be. It was a dark logic. The new Crown Prince of Troy was the Shadow? Arranging his own city's downfall? Murdering his own brother? Not just Hektor, he realised, but Troilus too. His mind chattered with past conversations – first Priam's suspicions: *Somebody told the enemy that Troilus was going out into the countryside that day*, then Hektor's words: *Paris blames himself for Troilus' death.*

How could it be? But it made perfect sense now why Paris – if he really had all this time been working against Troy – would be so against talks. His thoughts began to swarm like angry wasps. What horrible web of lies had he walked into?

More exchanges between the Ahhiyawans flew over his head, before Agamemnon sighed deeply, then sat upright on his chair. He took a deep draught of wine from a dented silver cup, then swished a hand. 'Leave,' he slurred. The two leather-armoured guards stepped forth like herders, ushering the council towards the hut door. Hattu, head dipped, lost in his own conclusions, looked up, feeling suddenly exposed.

Odysseus planted a hand on his shoulder. 'This one stays,' he said confidently.

The guards eyed Hattu then herded past him.

'This is your chance. Use it well,' Odysseus whispered, and then was gone too.

The hide door flap slid shut, leaving just a few shafts of pale morning light inside the hot, gloomy shed. Hattu squeezed his eyes and fists tight to clear his head of everything except this chance. Calmness came upon him like a golden mantle. He stepped forward, approaching the throne.

Agamemnon seemed to think he was alone until Hattu stepped through one of those sun rays. He jolted, sucking in a breath as if to shout angrily at this one who had not heeded his command to leave. At the same moment, Hattu shed his borrowed cloak.

'King Hattu?' he croaked, his face warping in drunken confusion.

Hattu quickly extended his arms to the sides, palms upturned. 'I am unarmed. I come to propose something that King Priam is too proud to offer. A chance to bring this war to a close.'

Agamemnon sagged, the full breath seeping away in a long, heavy sigh. 'King Hattu,' he said again, this time disdainfully. 'Victor of the Kadesh War, Lord of the North, Son of Ishtar,' he rocked gently with an unsettling mirth. 'Such a fine reputation you have. Yet even you cannot end this conflict. It is mine to finish… whatever the cost.'

'Open your eyes,' Hattu said calmly, 'set down your wine cup and step outside. Look upon the hill of Troy. Is that husk of a city worth the lives of so many of your kinsmen?'

'It is worth everything,' Agamemnon slurred. The wine krater gurgled as he poured himself a fresh cup and took a deep drink from it. 'Some fights simply must be fought. Like the one I waged to win my throne at Mycenae. A war to drive out the pretender – a cur named Aegisthus – who had stolen it from my father.' He smiled devilishly at Hattu. 'Not so dissimilar, are we, Hittite? Throne-stealers, both of us.'

Hattu shuffled in discomfort, memories of Urhi-Teshub tumbling down the steps of the throne room at Hattusa flashing behind his eyes. With a grunt, he shook the memories away. 'Then you should know that thrones are most at risk when the king is absent. You and the other lords here and all of your armies have been gone from Ahhiyawa for ten years. They say that a great swell of tribes moves towards your lands from the far west and north.' He saw a change in Agamemnon's face, knew he had hit a nerve. *Good,* he thought, leaning closer, clutching the air with a fist as if seizing the point. 'Pirates, diaspora from faraway fallen kingdoms, brigands, opportunists… all pouring towards your weakly-guarded cities and empty palaces. Heaving fleets, slicing across the waves. Hordes, roving down through the mountain passes.'

Agamemnon's top lip twitched. 'Pah! The wretched lot you speak of is nought but a disorganised rabble, moving in circles far from our homelands. We have recruited the best of them as soldiers,' he gestured through the hut walls in the vague direction of the Sherden and Shekelesh tents. 'We are their masters. The rest? They will never trouble the Ahhiyawan cities – certainly not mine! You have never been to Mycenae, have you? It is set high on a mountaintop, an impregnable fortress of stone overlooking the green vale of the Argolid. The palace guards I left behind are more than capable of fending off attacks by grubby bandits. And if their boats dare to approach my shores, then the Watchmen of the Coast will rain fire upon them. I am not afraid.'

The barest upwards inflection at the end of his sentence betrayed a sliver of doubt. Hattu leaned a little closer. 'What about the families back in Mycenae, close enough to hear the sounds of the approaching troubles? Can you speak for them?'

Agamemnon's nostrils flared. He slapped a hand on one arm of his throne. 'Enough!' he slurred. 'You came here unarmed, bleating about ending the war. Tell me what you have in mind before I have you dragged outside and stoned.'

Hattu let a few moments of silence pass to avoid sounding panicked or hurried. 'Send your best negotiator to the city gates. Priam is stubborn, but if you were to make the first move, I am certain that he would welcome terms at this time. You could make so much more from an agreement than you ever would were you to grind Troy into the dust. Think of yourself on the waves, sailing for home, Troy's tribute stowed on board, a profitable truce arranged between her and Ahhiyawa. You could be back in your halls before winter, your troops could once again patrol your lands – instead of relying on the skeleton watch you left behind. Ahhiyawa would be strong once more, a shield against these western masses. Troy could even be an ally. Two towers of strength, side by side.'

Agamemnon issued a bark of a laugh. 'Allies? After all you have seen here?'

Hattu did not blink or look away. 'At Kadesh, the Egyptians and we Hittites fought like jackals. It was a torrid, animal time. Yet now, years later, Pharaoh and I have struck words of peace on a tablet of silver. His empire and mine have learned to live like brothers. It would not be easy, but this could happen here too. For the sake of your homes, for the sake of your families…' he paused for effect, 'set down your swords and talk.'

Agamemnon smiled sadly. 'The very reason I came here was to save my family. Did you know that, King Hattu?'

Hattu's mind rolled back to that earlier chat with Odysseus under the oak tree by the Scamander. 'You came to honour the vow made between you and all the other kings – to protect your brother's marriage to Helen.'

Agamemnon shook his head slowly, wryly. 'The oath was not for Helen and Menelaus; it was for unity. Odysseus' idea was that the oath would serve like a rope, allowing us to stand together, united. But within a year, the twines began to fray. It started with the drought, you see. It was beginning to thin our lands of crop and pasture. This drove some of the city kings – those golden champions who strut around this camp – to look enviously around them at the neighbouring estates. It does not take much to bring the city kingdoms of Ahhiyawa to loggerheads. There is a saying in my land: how do you get a Spartan, a Tirynean and a Pylian to agree? Ask them if there is trouble ahead.'

'They were spoiling for war; a ruinous internal war, city against city. They would have killed each other, and no doubt marched upon my palace at Mycenae to cut me down too. I do not relish the idea of death by the sword, but I like to think that if it happens, I will die bravely. But my wife and daughter... do you know how us Ahhiyawans treat the wives and young of an overthrown king?' The look on Agamemnon's face was suggestion enough. 'The oath alone was not sufficient. So I had to find another way to bind the kings in unity, to find a stronger rope, a common cause. All the while trade ships stopped by at my ports talking of Troy, *glorious* Troy,' he cast his arms around mockingly, 'pride of the east, with its golden houses and roads of marble, great storehouses brimming with grain, immeasurable herds and endless pastures.' He shrugged. 'When you Hittites – Troy's great protector – fell into civil war and your empire shrank away to the nub it has become, Troy was left like a prize goose, standing proud and alone here on this shore. What was I supposed to do?'

A horrible tingle crept through Hattu. 'Since I arrived here people have told me you had been waiting, hungry for conflict with Troy for many years. But it is worse than that, isn't it? You did not simply wait for the chance of war… you… you *created* the opportunity.'

Agamemnon looked up through a sheen of despair. 'My grandfather died on Crete, and so it was my duty as his eldest grandson to attend his funeral. I could have gone alone. Instead I called upon Menelaus to join me.'

Hattu saw the pieces of the past come together in his mind. His stomach turned as a picture began to form. 'During Paris' visit to Sparta… when he and Helen eloped?'

Agamemnon nodded, eyes concealed by a forefinger and thumb. 'I lured my brother away, leaving his Queen alone with the handsome Trojan Prince. I knew what would happen… wanted it to happen. But, may Hestia forgive me, it was a minor transgression in comparison to…'

Hattu stepped forward. 'To what? What else did you do?' he spread his arms wide as if to encompass the land of Troy. 'What could possibly be worse than *this*?'

Agamemnon sobbed, head bowed. Just when Hattu thought he was lost to drunken sorrow, he threw himself upright against the throne's back, his head tilting as if he was staring up through the cobwebbed hut ceiling and off into the sky. 'My daughter was born on a winter's day. One of those bitter winters that gnaw to one's marrow. The palace of Mycenae was cloaked in snow and the guards stood in shivering knots around braziers. Misery and coldness all around. But when the obstetricians and maids delivered Iphigenia from Clytemnestra's womb and brought from her that first breath and sweet, sweet cry of life, I fell to my knees and sobbed with joy. I kissed my wife's hand, thanking her for carrying the girl. We cradled the babe together for days, watching the snow falling outside, the hearth crackling by our bed. Despite the troubles creeping into our lands, I had never in my life known such happiness. When my girl was old enough, I taught her to ride on the Argolid fields, to hunt deer in the mountain woods. I took her to sea to visit the islands near Mycenae's shores. She would collect rose petals, dry and press them, then later use them to make bright garlands. One day, she and I stood on the palace balcony while her older sister leant at the balustrade, judging noblemen, champions and princes who wrestled and raced in the field below, all vying to win her favour and become her husband. Iphigenia squeezed my hand. I remember her looking up at me, telling me how one day it would be her, choosing a husband like this, set to be a Princess, even the Queen, of Mycenae.'

Hattu felt a terrible twist in the offing, seeing Agamemnon's face tense up every so often in distraught grimaces.

'Time passed. Ten years ago, when the armies were gathered at the port of Aulis, I beheld them all: the many tents and piled spears and bows, the horses and the countless ships waiting in and around the harbour. Blades of battle ready to be turned not upon each other but upon Troy, our common enemy where Helen had been taken away to. I told myself over and over again that I had orchestrated it all for Clytemnestra and young Iphigenia, for their safety and for the safety of my land.' He pinched his bottom lip as if trying to stop his head from shaking side to side. 'Damn the infernal wind, for there was none – not a breath to carry my ships to Troy. Moons slid past with the armies clustered there. A madness grew amongst them, and they began to fight amongst themselves – the very thing I had been trying to prevent! Nights became a thing of dread for me. Sitting awake, eyes wide, mind whirring over the details. But no matter how much I planned, I could not plan for the quietness of the wind and the deadness of the sea. Sleep became a distant memory for me over that time.'

He looked up, eyes now glassy with tears. 'Do you know what kind of madness that brings upon a man, King Hattu? I knew nothing of time or reason. All shape and sense became a blur. All that mattered was getting my fleet onto the waves. The war with Troy *had* to begin lest another break out right there in Aulis and rage instead across Ahhiyawa as I had always feared.' He began circling one finger around the top of his cup. 'It was old Kalchas the priest who convinced me that I had to look to the Gods for that elusive wind. Because... I owed them something.'

'You see, on one of those deer hunts with Iphigenia, I had shot a deer. I only realised after I had killed the thing that I had accidentally stumbled into a sacred grove of Artemis and spilled the beast's blood there. The Goddess of the Hunt was furious with me, Kalchas explained, and it was she who had stolen the wind from the sky. If I was to win her favour again, then I needed to pay her tribute. A wedding, Kalchas described it as. He even convinced Odysseus of it, despatching him to summon the bride. Not just any bride… this was to be the bride of Achilles.' He gulped a few times as if swallowing a bitter medicine, then continued. 'Iphigenia came to Aulis on a hot, still day. I can see her now, seated atop a polished carriage, draped in a soft marriage gown, her skin sparkling with oil, one of those pressed garlands in her hair and the priests showering her with petals. Soldiers lined the way from the dockside, cheering and whistling in support. The people of Aulis too came with bread and wine. Musicians played sweet melodies on their lyres. Who would not want to be present to witness her joining with Achilles, the greatest warrior in all Ahhiyawa?' The circling finger stopped. 'I can see it all still, but no part more starkly than the moment the carriage rolled around a bend to arrive at a low hillock. The moment her sweet face fell as she set eyes upon the sacrificial altar up there.'

Hattu felt a swelling sickness in his belly.

'Achilles was not even there. Kalchas persuaded me to use his name like a lure, to feed her that dream of a wedding that she had always harboured. To make it easier for her… and for me. That was the madness I endured in those days.' His breathing became rapid and deep and he could not continue for a time. Tears sped down his face. 'Diomedes and Ajax helped the priests to control her and splay her flat, face down, upon the altar. Her cries to them and over and over to me felt like wayward arrows, hissing down around me but never striking, never breaking my shell of sleepless stupor. Finally, Kalchas cranked her head back, then sliced her throat open. He called out to the Goddess of the Hunt as she bled out, and I remember feeling some great sense of hope. I looked up and around with all my soldiers. We felt it in the moments after she died… a tickle of wind in the air at last!'

'It became a breeze and then a stiff squall, rocking the many boats in the water. The war was afoot! The soldiers of Ahhiyawa would spend their wrath upon Troy. Our homelands would go unspoiled. And best of all our loved ones would be spared the danger of war at home. Our loved ones… *my* loved ones... my darling Clytemnestra and little Iphigenia…' a hysterical yelp escaped his lips and he trembled. 'The… the sheer absurdity of what I had done did not settle upon me until we were here. So much so that I was sure it had all been a bleak dream. I asked Kalchas about the waking visions and night terrors I had experienced over the previous moons. He explained them to me as best he could… but not the dream of Iphigenia's sacrifice. "That, *Wanax,*" he said, "was not a dream".'

Agamemnon sagged, spent of tears. 'That was how the madness was. The nightmare has haunted me ever since.'

Hattu let a time pass as Agamemnon's breathing slowed to normal again. After taking more time to play with his words, he finally spoke. 'Some nightmares never end,' he said, the faces of dead loved ones bursting across his mind: Atiya, Muwa, Ruba, Tanku, Kurunta, Kisna, Jaru, Colta, Danuhepa, Sargis… he closed his eyes tightly until the chant of names halted. 'But see through your grief, *Wanax*. It is clouding your mind just as much as that madness during those windless days at Aulis. For ten years, the warriors of Ahhiyawa have suffered and perished on these shores. Were you to return to your homeland now, would there even be enough men left for the earlier tensions you spoke of to rekindle?'

'Return to my homeland?' Agamemnon blinked, the last of his tears rolling away. 'That cannot happen until Troy is ash.'

'Do you come for a prize of ashes or gold?' Hattu said.

Agamemnon's eyes changed.

'That's right,' said Hattu. 'There is still gold in Troy. Under the acropolis mound, Priam stores a hoard of it.' Hattu said. It felt like a cold betrayal. But that was the thing Aeneas had gifted him: the truth about what Priam kept in the palace strongroom. Cups, beads, circlets, armour of precious metal, rings, bracelets, silver bullion – a sizeable stack of personal wealth, all hidden away. 'It could be yours in exchange for a treaty of truce.' He and Aeneas hadn't planned exactly how they might convince Priam to agree to this, but that would be the next struggle on their hands. First, he had to get the hook into Agamemnon's mouth.

Yet the warlord beheld him with an absurd scowl. 'Did you not hear my story? What price my dear daughter's life, but the utter conquest of this city and its preening eastern princes? Eternal glory in Iphigenia's honour is the prize I must have, not gold. Nothing else matters to me now. Nothing else will shut out the memory of her final cries to me. Troy must burn.'

Hattu saw the molten determination in Agamemnon's eyes, and felt a crumpling sense of utter defeat. This had been his great hope, and now it lay dashed on the rocks like the Trojan treasure boat wrecked in the storm. He tried to control his anger as he spoke: 'Then for the sake of the greater world, Agamemnon of Mycenae, if you somehow manage to burn Troy, then I hope that you are prepared to take on her mantle, to weather the troubles from the west as she has done for over four hundred years.'

Agamemnon leaned forward in his throne. 'I don't know how you got into this hut or this camp, but you took a great risk. With a clap of my hands, I could have you peeled or halved.' He let a moment pass, smirking a little. 'But I will not, for your visit here has given me great encouragement that Troy is ailing. The *Labarna* of the Hittites, Troy's greatest ally, begging before the *Wanax* of Ahhiyawa? Go back inside her walls, King Hattu, or if you are as shrewd as I think you are then break for the east instead, back to your distant home before Troy falls… and fall she will.'

Watchfully, Hattu stooped to pick up his cloak and threw it on again, raising the hood. Without bowing, he backed out of the hide door flap. Squinting in the bright light of day, he saw the Ahhiyawan tribes and warrior elites practising swordplay and archery, some riding their chariots in a frenzy simply to conjure up roars of support from their people. Gaunt, diseased and grubby they may be, but the appetite for Trojan blood had not waned.

Odysseus emerged from the shadows near another hut, chewing on a grass stalk. 'Follow me,' he said quietly.

They walked back to the end of the crescent camp and onto the Bay of Troy where the tide was rising with a calm *shush* of waves.

'Talking was no use?' Odysseus asked.

Hattu replied with a shake of the head. 'I think you knew it was futile from the start.'

Odysseus let out a great sigh.

'I thank you for letting me try,' said Hattu. 'Your *Wanax's* tale is a sorry one indeed. He is dying from within from an invisible pain. Drowning himself in wine will not help. Believe me, I have tried that.'

'It is not just wine,' Odysseus said. 'Nepenthe, we call it, a potion that makes a fool of the mind so one might escape his own memories for a time.' He clicked his fingers. 'Speaking of potions: while you were in talks, I remembered something. Back when I was a child, my uncle suffered from a canker of the gut just like your Egyptian friend. The healers on Ithaca made him a mixture. While it did not save him, it granted him relief from the pain in a way the poppies could not. The potion is not easy to make, but I believe the root grows here as it does on my island. I'm sure I saw it sprouting from the rocks at the southern end of the bay.' He twisted and peered back that way, drumming his fingers on his lips. 'I will check for certain during tomorrow's swim.'

'You would help me like this?' Hattu asked.

Odysseus shrugged. 'You came here to try to help us all. It only seems fair.'

They came to the concealed cave entrance, draped with wet vines. 'So what now?' Hattu asked.

'Now, like you, I will do what I must to bring this war to a close,' Odysseus replied. 'You have seen that our *Wanax* is only half-fit to lead us. Thus I will try to steer him as best I can. The end must come. I will aim to make it as swift and bloodless as possible.'

'A noble intent,' Hattu said, backing inside the cave and resolving at once to have the entrance blocked up immediately. Just before he turned his back on Odysseus, he noticed the fierce glimmer of determination in the man's eyes, and felt a streak of unease pass through him. Something told him that the war was about to take a sharp and unpleasant twist. 'I warn you though: your Ahhiyawan Gods could pound at these walls and they would not break.'

As Hattu flitted up the stone-steps within, Odysseus called in his wake: 'You and I both know, King Hattu, that it is men and not Gods who break walls.'

# CHAPTER 17

## GODS & MEN

Two days passed. On the third day, Odysseus rose just before dawn as always. He heard the chattering and clicking of the dolphins from the nearby Bay of Troy, but he ignored them and forewent his morning swim for the first time in years. Instead, he ate a breakfast of thin porridge at his hut door, watching as a small trickle of northern herders and farmers appeared over the dawn-streaked crest of the Silver Ridge. They drove goats and sheep and oxen towards Troy's Dardanian Gate. A squadron of Locrians from the secondary camp up on Thorn Hill spotted them late and tried to intercept, but they only managed to loose a few volleys of arrows before the incoming herders slipped through the hatch door and inside the safety of Troy's walls. A short time later, a few members of the group were allowed back outside again, to retrieve a knot of rogue sheep stubbornly cropping at the grass. Incoming groups like this had been spotted over the last few days, Dardanians and other peoples from the north who had finally given up their lands in the face of constant raiding by the besiegers, coming to Troy in the hope that the mother city might protect them. He sighed for a moment, setting his bowl down, thinking of the troubles at home once more. What if his people were in danger like this? *That's why I must do this,* he assured himself.

Retreating inside his hut again, he picked up his bronze shield and set about buffing it madly with a piece of leather. It came up bright and showed his distinctive blocky features like a mirror. Curling up a fist, he then punched himself square in the centre of the face. A snap of nose cartilage and a pulse of blood marked the strike. Blinking, he eyed his flat, bent nose and sighed, unsatisfied. Next, he took up his dagger, turned it hilt-first towards one eye and rammed the blunt handle against the edge of the eye socket. A few yelps of pain later, he held up the shield again and admired the puffy, misshapen visage staring back at him, wiping off the dribbles of blood. *Perfect.*

A short while later, the sun fully risen, he met with Diomedes at the Thorn Hill camp. The usually-preened young King of Tiryns had combed out his braids to leave his hair in a wiry mess, and a few days of growth on his upper lip gave him a full beard like some of the nomads in these parts. Both wore shabby robes and went barefoot as they trekked north of Troy towards a small cypress wood. Diomedes scratched at his crotch every so often, then swished the crook he held. 'How am I supposed to split skulls with this?'

'Today is not about splitting skulls or letting blood,' Odysseus said.

'Yet you did a good job of breaking your own head,' Diomedes said with a grin.

'I mean it. Do not let me down,' Odysseus growled.

'I will not. But this plan of yours had better be worth it, Island King.'

'Trust me,' Odysseus said.

'Words are cheap,' Diomedes winked.

'Then have this,' Odysseus said, pulling a solid silver ring from his pouch and giving it to Diomedes. 'If my plan fails, you can keep it.'

Diomedes' bottom lip curled and he tucked the ring in his own pouch, bet accepted.

A short while later, they waited on their haunches just inside the treeline of the wood, the shade cool, the air scented with the smoky scent of cypress resin. The cicadas croaked on and on as both scanned the old northwards-winding track to Dardania for signs of movement. They hid like that for hours, the shade becoming hot, their mouths dry and their tempers fraying.

Diomedes scratched madly at his crotch again. 'Damned war brides,' he cursed.

'Yes, how dare they,' Odysseus said with a derisive sideways look.

Diomedes scowled. 'Hold on, don't get all high and mighty with me. What about you and your "morning swim", eh? Bet you and the dolphins get really close, eh? I bet that-'

'Shh!' Odysseus hissed.

Something was emerging through the heat haze in the north: sunburnt heads, crooks, bleating sheep. He saw how – as before – there was a core of families wearing clothes made from the same tribal hides, headbands dyed with the same shade of madder red. But walking with then were men from different places wearing different garments of wool, some with just kilts and others with shawls. Some with sandals and some with Hittite-style boots. These ones must have joined the trek to Troy along the way, the group building like a rolling dustball. He watched them as they passed the cypress wood, breath held.

'Go!' he hissed at last.

He and Diomedes hurried out from their hiding spot and joined onto the back of the group. As soon as they caught up, both slowed to put on a tired walk, using their crooks like old men. Nobody challenged them and only a few even noticed them. One, a boy carrying a recently born lamb, smiled at the two. 'Soon we will be in mighty Troy. There we will be safe,' he said in a tongue Odysseus recognised.

As the lad turned away, Odysseus felt a hot streak of shame, for his every action now would put that boy and his kinsfolk in great danger. He closed his eyes for a moment as he walked. *Win the war. End this as quickly as possible. If blood is the price then let it be sparing.*

As they went, Odysseus noticed the sheep growing agitated, bleating and refusing to obey their herders. A moment later, he felt something under the soles of his feet. He glanced down, seeing the few strands of grass around his ankles shaking, blurred, hundreds of tiny cracks appearing in the baked earth. Now the other herders began muttering in unease. A sound rose, like the distant thunder of galloping horses. 'Another tremor,' he whispered looking all around at the shivering countryside. The ground jolted twice, like a bucking steed, and his heart climbed into his mouth. But as gently as could be, the tremor passed, just like the others. *No, not like the others,* he mused. *That one was stronger, sharper*. It made him wonder where it might lead, and question just how invincible Troy's walls really were.

Soon, they were on their way again. They crested the Silver Ridge, and here the agitated shepherds at once saw the safety of Troy and the danger of the Ahhiyawan encampment on Thorn Hill. They broke into a shamble towards the former, shouting up to the sentries on the walls. The small hatch hinged into the Dardanian gates swung open. Herders and sheep hopped inside – though a few stubborn animals trailing behind were left out there, the hatch clicking shut once more. The Trojan sentries eyed every newcomer, but none recognised the bloated face of Odysseus or the shaggy, unkempt Diomedes.

Inside, a Trojan Guardian guided the newcomers uphill towards the city's heart. Odysseus walked with his head down. With furtive glances, he noticed how shabby these lower wards were. The famous wide streets were pitted with holes and sprouting with weeds. Many homes were cracked and dilapidated and lean-tos had been erected here, there and everywhere. A dog – more like a cage of bones wrapped in skin, came hobbling alongside them, sniffing madly at one of the sheep. Next it took a great interest in the pungent reek emanating from Diomedes' loincloth. With a swish of his crook, the big Tirynean sent the dog scampering away.

'Easy now,' Odysseus whispered to his bullish companion.

Diomedes grumbled, glancing around as they climbed the Scaean Way. 'I never thought I would be entering Troy armed only with a crook.'

'It's already gotten you further than a spear or a ladder or one of those lumbering battering rams. Anyway, stay quiet,' he said, glancing ahead, 'we're being taken up to the citadel.'

The mighty doors of the Scaean Gate lay open, and the shepherds trickled inside. Odysseus glanced around the citadel shiftily. Many times he had sat at the door of his stinking hut on the plain, gazing up at this shining acropolis, imagining untold wealth and beauty. And so it was: halls banded in gold and silver, tall marble pillars gleaming in the sunlight, tumbling rooftop gardens, wide paved streets polished and undamaged. Even the air smelt sweet, the steady hot wind carrying the scent of perfumes and cooking spices from the cool, shady halls. The palace, the storehouses and most of the temples seemed to be unguarded. But, infuriatingly, the one place that mattered was flanked by two watchful Guardians.

'It's in there?' Diomedes mused.

'Aye,' Odysseus whispered, eyeing the dominant temple to their right, the doors pinned open with bronze arrow bolts.

Diomedes stroked his chin as he eyed the two guards there. 'I *could* use my fists to knock that pair out. But getting in, taking the thing, then getting out again?' He shook his head. 'You've overstretched yourself with this one, Island King.'

'That's the trouble with you, Diomedes. Always looking for the direct route to victory.'

Diomedes shrugged. 'It's served me well so far. Besides, I see no other options. I think you'll have to admit you've failed here. That silver ring is mine.'

'Is it?' Odysseus said.

Diomedes frowned. 'Yes, it is. Why are you looking so smug?' He fished in his pouch to pull the ring out. 'Look, I'll put it on my finger to remind you of my…' he fell silent, staring at the ring in his hand. Copper – nearly worthless. 'No,' he drawled. 'You gave me a *silver* ring.'

'Hmm,' Odysseus mused, flashing his own hand, the third finger glinting silver below the knuckle. 'You mean this one?'

'How… you cheating swine!' Diomedes said, his voice rising.

'Shhh!' Odysseus elbowed his comrade as a few shepherds nearby turned to look. 'Lest we are caught and roasted like swine for Priam's feast tonight.'

'But how, and *why* did you do that?' Diomedes whispered.

'I thought you might need convincing – that the eyes can be deceived. We *will* get inside that temple.'

Diomedes glanced around. 'I never mistook you for an optimist. Look around you, there are many pairs of eyes upon us. If we take one step away from this group of stinking herders, we're dead.'

'I agree. Many *are* watching,' Odysseus said, glancing around those on the grounds and up at the many faces looking on from the balconies and roof terraces. 'Including our friend.'

***

Hattu strolled around the rooftop of Antenor's villa, the Helm of Troy clasped under one arm as he surveyed the lower city defences. All seemed correct with the new sentry system he had organised along those walls and turrets. A changing watch pattern was essential, for then the enemy – and the Shadow – would have little chance of understanding and exploiting it. Yet so few men. Too few. The second treasure ship had been gone for so long now that people had stopped talking about whether it might return with allies in tow. Some even speculated that the Shadow had convinced the captain of this ship to sail off and stay away.

Hattu did not believe this, but then he could not be certain about anything in relation to the hidden traitor. He thought over his latest theory with increasing doubt: Paris? No, Paris could not be the enemy helper. It was too dark and uncomfortable to be true. Yet all other possibilities so far had been ruled out. This was the only one remaining. In his mind's eye, it glared like a silver ingot in the sand. Burning, searing. Until yesterday, he had not spoken a word of his theory to anyone. Then, last night as he and Antenor ate a meal of bacon, eggs and bread, he had revealed his thoughts. At first, the elder had laughed, spluttering into his mountain tea. Soon, the laughter faded and he turned pale, realising Hattu was serious. The old man rose shakily, first locking the villa doors and shutters lest anyone else be listening in, then went on to protest and debate skilfully in Paris' defence, almost backing Hattu into a place where he was sure he had made a mistake. But Hattu came back with a flurry of irrefutable coincidences and strange behaviours that once again painted a dark picture of the crown prince.

'But Paris is… he *is* Troy now, her future, everything,' Antenor had argued at the last. 'In the spring, he swore an oath to protect her before the entire royal court.'

'I could swear that I was a crow,' Hattu had replied impassively. 'It wouldn't mean I could fly.'

In the end, it was Antenor who relented, sagging into a disconsolate silence, unable to finish his meal.

Hattu's head pounded sharply. Turning away from the roof's edge, he eyed Antenor's hammock. He had always envied the old man for having the stillness and sense to take regular naps there. Perhaps now was the time to follow the elder's example, he mused. So he clunked the helmet down on the trestle table beside the hammock, and slid his leather bag from his shoulder and put it there too. Sinking into the hammock with a deep sigh, he beheld the blue dome of sky over Troy. Andor was circling high up there and he found that watching her helped clear his mind. The pain seeped away from his head and he sighed again. *Best not fall asleep*, he told himself. Yet watching Andor up in the cloudless blue, wheeling, banking, drew him into a trance. One hand flopped loosely from the hammock-side, his eyes slid shut and he began drifting down, down, down…

*He found himself walking in a meadow of graves. A field of dark red soil, sprouting with weeds and tomb markers of Trojans and allies. So many of them he could not count. There were five great tombstones near the centre… and a creature perched upon one like a dragon – Ishtar, wings folded, head dipped, eyes moving to follow his path. Her twin lions lay in the darkness behind the giant stones, betrayed only by their low growls.*

*He approached carefully. Closer, he saw that the five great stones were not tomb markers at all, but the tablets from the Scaean Gate. Four bore stark cracks across their surfaces, only the one upon which Ishtar sat remained intact.*

*'Time runs short for Troy, King Hattu,' she whispered.*

*Hattu's eyes widened as he saw cracks spidering across the stone upon which she rested. Her lips spread in a fang smile as the stone began to break apart with a series of rhythmic clunks.*

He blinked awake. The dream noises of the breaking stone became something else…

Footsteps... padding urgently across the rooftop towards him.

He cranked both eyes open. A tall, dark figure rose over him. Flailing, he almost fell from the hammock. 'By all the Gods!' he croaked. '*Tuhkanti*? Where did you come from?'

'From the stairs, about an hour ago, not long after you fell asleep,' Tudha replied.

Hattu, rising to his feet, noticed the torn look on Tudha's face: resentment, simmering like that ever since the night battle; and the way his eyes darted every few moments to the trestle table – at Hattu's leather bag, and his confiscated iron sword. 'You have come to demand your blade again?' he said.

'I fought well in the chariot during the night attack. Tell me I did not,' Tudha said confidently.

Hattu regarded him for a time. 'You fought well. But you could fight one thousand future battles well and it would still not change the past.'

'Hatenzuwa,' Tudha said, his jaw stiffening. 'Always Hatenzuwa.'

'You wrote that chapter. Now you must live with it, *Tuhkanti*.'

Tudha glared at him. 'You cannot even say my name, can you?'

'From the moment I walked into that shrine, it has felt like fire on my tongue.'

Tudha laughed coldly. 'For years before that you have only called me *Tuhkanti*. It has nothing to do with the shrine.'

Hattu lifted the sword bag and slung it over one shoulder, cupping the helm of Troy under the other arm. 'I can never trust you with the iron sword – that blade from which I had to clean my cousin's blood, and that of her… her *baby*,' he paused, galled at having said it aloud, horror-struck at the image of the tot's corpse, cleaved almost in half. 'Do you ever wonder what the child might have grown to become?'

'I… I… ' Tudha stammered, then fell silent with a shake of the head.

'You can't even talk about it, can you? With one sword stroke you destroyed that babe's future… and forever tarnished your own, *Tuhkanti.*'

The two stepped apart. Tudha, chest rising and falling sharply, eyes red and wet, cast a hand towards the roof's edge. 'I did not come for my damned sword. I came only to tell you that more herdsmen have come in from the north.'

Hattu heard it then: bleating and voices from street level.

He brushed past Tudha and strode to the roof's edge. The latest gang of grubby refugee families were forming in a cluster down on the citadel grounds. What a patchwork they were. Two in particular caught his eye: one taller than the rest with a wiry nest of hair; and the short one beside him with a face that looked like it had watched a chariot race from underneath. 'More flocks will help provide milk and wool,' he murmured to himself, 'but we need men of the sword.'

He descended the stairs to the citadel grounds, Tudha reluctantly following in his wake. The babble of voices was chaotic, guards trying to organise and calm the newcomers, animals skipping to and fro and babies crying. King Priam and Queen Hekabe emerged from the palace and wandered amongst the shepherds, trying to reassure them that they would be safe here. Prince Deiphobus and the priests came out too to greet them. Scamandrios organised trays of bread to be brought out. Helen and Cassandra were there too, organising the servants and handing people drinks. From a balcony, Paris looked down on it all, his face dark, as if the newcomers had spoiled his day. He remained there for a moment only before slipping away inside with a swish of his cloak.

'There aren't enough free houses here for this lot,' Dagon said, arriving by Hattu and Tudha's sides.

'Then we'll build some more shacks,' Hattu replied. He spotted a mother and baby amongst the herders, both emaciated and the mother swaying on her feet with weakness. 'Bring bread and water here,' he called, stepping over to guide the woman towards a patch of shade where she might sit. 'Rest here. I will bring you-'

*'FIRE!'*

The cry echoed across the citadel at the same time as an acrid waft of smoke. All heads switched towards the sound. Hattu's eyes sharpened on the tendrils of blackness crawling from one lane – near the royal armoury. The slave boy who had shouted skidded out from the lane and fell onto his knees, retching, pointing back down the lane. 'Fire,' he croaked again.

Voices exploded in alarm, calling for water, footsteps clattering to and fro, buckets being passed from the drinking fonts and troughs, on down the lane. Guardians shambled down from the battlements to help.

Hattu entered the lane and edged towards the blaze, holding up an arm to shield his face from the ferocious wall of orange gushing from the wide armoury doorway. The hairs on his forearm shrivelled up and the skin stung. He saw spears and huge stockpiles of arrows in there, ablaze. Bronze shields buckling and warping, leather boots and more basic helmets turning black. The water carriers hurled their burdens into the fire. Someone shoved a bucket into his free hand and he tossed its contents upon the flames too. The fire sizzled and spat, enraged, flames licking out like angry tongues towards the nearby timber beams of the Temple of Apollo. If that caught light then old Antenor's house and the palace itself would be next and the rest would go up quickly after. 'More water,' Hattu roared over his shoulder.

***

'The fire is spreading,' the shouts continued and the chaos intensified. 'We need more help!'

Odysseus watched, carefully, until the two Guardians standing by the mighty Palladium temple peeled away from their stations, rushing to the scene of the disaster.

'Stay here, give me a signal if those two come back,' Odysseus said, then melted into the shadows of the Palladium's entrance like a gentle breath of wind. Inside, the shouting and chaos faded to a muffled echo. He padded up to the silver altar and beheld the smooth-worn likeness of Athena. With little fuss, he picked it up and placed it in his pouch. It almost hurt his pride that stealing the famous talisman of Troy was so straightforward. The reaction, when the people discovered its disappearance, was bound to be more memorable. The statue was the last – and, some said, the strongest – of their five prophecies of protection.

Emerging outside and into the cacophony of confusion and scudding black smoke, he spotted and nodded discreetly to the one who had lit the blaze, then sought out and found Diomedes. The pair peeled away back out of the citadel and down onto Troy's lower city streets again. 'We did it,' Odysseus hissed, opening a flap of his shepherd robe and showing Diomedes the Palladium statuette.

Diomedes frowned. 'Is that it?' he moaned. 'We did all this for... a piece of wood? I still don't understand.'

'Is a crown just a hunk of metal? Is a palace but a stack of stone?' Odysseus sniped, tapping his temple. 'It's not about what it *is*, it's about what is *means.*'

'If you say so, Island King,' Diomedes rumbled in amusement. 'I'll be happy so long as I can hear the Trojans weeping with despair when they look upon the empty space it once sat.'

Odysseus grinned. 'Not empty. Well, not quite. I left something behind.'

***

Dagon and two others hurled a fresh trough of water. It foamed across the blackened ruins, and the sad, mangled and charred ruins of military equipment, Troy's central reserve. Plumes of smoke still oozed from the charred timbers, but at least the flames were out. The citadel had been saved.

Hattu gasped for breath, exhausted, skin soaked with sweat and stained black with smoke. Dagon threw down the empty trough and sank to his knees, broken by the effort. Tudha, hair plastered to his face and the hem of his tunic burnt, helped the Hittite Chariot Master back to his feet. All around the ruined arms warehouse hundreds of Trojans stared at the black mess. Yet worse was to come.

A Guardian – one of those who had helped quell the fire and had subsequently hurried back to his post – reappeared at the armoury ruins. Hattu squinted, confused by the way the man was walking – as if he had been shot in the leg with an arrow. His feet dragged, and his face was sagging, horrified. Slowly, all noticed his odd gait.

'That's one of the Palladium guards,' Dagon whispered.

'Forgive me,' the guard said weakly. Drawing his sword, jaw lolling, he then turned the tip upon his breastbone and – with one horrible jolt – dropped to his knees. The pommel hit the flagstones first, then his weight came down upon the tip. The bronze plating of his armour screeched and gave, the skin, bone and gristle of his chest crunched and crackled, then the blade sliced swiftly through his heart. With a wet sigh, he knelt like that, arms sliding free of the sword handle, blood pitter-pattering from his dead lips.

Laocoon and Chryses, the chief priests, shared a ghastly look. Together, they approached the Palladium Temple. There, by the doorway, the second Guardian had nicked his own throat and sat slumped in death, grey in the face, armour soaked in the crimson of his own blood.

Hattu followed the priests inside, his ears ringing at the madness of all this, a crowd following.

He stared at the silver altar. Priam and Deiphobus too. Hekabe, Helen and Cassandra arrived together, clutching each other as if afraid to look upon the silver pedestal.

Empty. The Palladium was gone. The final prophecy had been blown away like dust. Hattu thought of the dream from moments ago, saw in his mind's eye Ishtar launching into flight, the prophecy stone collapsing to rubble under her.

'This means the end for us,' Chryses the Priest wailed. His voice carried all around the Palladium Temple and no doubt sailed outside and over the city too.

Priam, hair loose and hanging in greasy tangles, looked from the empty altar to Hattu, his face hangdog, his eyes distant.

Laocoon dropped his hippocampus staff, fell to all-fours and erupted in a series of ceremonial wails, clawing at his face. Prince Scamandrios arrived, face white when they saw that the spreading news was true. That was when Paris entered. When he saw what had happened, his strut became a stagger. He fell to one knee and wept.

'What happened here?' Dagon whispered, arriving by his side.

Hattu shook his head, numb. He stalked around the altar, dumbstruck. In the shadows at its rear, he noticed something that nobody else had: a tiny blue vial. He stopped to pick it up and examined the insignia on the front: an Ithacan hunting bow. Odysseus' voice echoed in his mind: *It is men, not Gods, who break walls.* His mind whirled crazily, then realisation struck him like a hammer. 'The shepherds,' he croaked.

'What?' Dagon said.

Hattu barged past him and outside, squinting into the bright sunshine. The herdsmen still stood in that nervous cluster. But two were conspicuously absent: the tall one with the wiry hair and the smaller one with the bloated face. 'They're gone,' he croaked to Dagon, who followed him out. 'Two of them were Ahhiyawans in disguise.'

'Then the idol is still in the city,' Dagon replied. 'Remember,

Priam's Guardians aren't letting a soul outside these days.' His face fell. 'Except…'

The two sped to the Scaean Gate. 'Where are they?' Hattu demanded of the sentry there. 'Two of the herdsmen, one tall, one-'

'One bloated and bruised, aye,' the guard finished for him, then jabbed a thumb through the open gates. 'They left while everyone was fighting the blaze. Going back outside to shepherd in the stragglers from their flock, they said.'

Hattu stared downhill to the lower city's Dardanian Gate. It was too late: the guards there were shutting the hatch door and the two shepherds – tiny dots from this distance – who had left through it were already outside the city. They were moving towards the knot of sheep still out there. Hattu and Dagon watched, for a heartbeat wishing it all to be a mistake, wishing that the two out there would simply wave their sheep into the city.

Instead, the herder pair ran on past the sheep, on towards the enemy encampment on Thorn Hill. One of the pair lifted something high, and a mighty cry arose from the Locrian camp sentries. 'The Palladium of Troy!' they cried with glee. 'It is ours… *ours!*'

The cry echoed across Troy. Weeping spread across the city.

Hattu and Dagon stumbled back into the citadel grounds, stunned. Dagon sat by the blue sphinx, head in hands, while Hattu paced to and fro, his thoughts spinning and twisting. A short while later, a dull *thunk* sounded from outside the Scaean Gate as the stonemason smashed the fifth and final prophecy tablet there.

'The fire was a distraction. A perfect one,' Hattu growled.

Dagon looked up, paling. 'That shepherd pair could not have started it. They were present when the shout went up. I am sure of it.'

Hattu halted, swivelling on the ball of one foot. The pair looked at one another for a moment, a horrible realisation rising within. 'The Shadow started the blaze,' he hissed.

'Who… who is this damned Shadow?' Dagon snarled.

Hattu wrung his hands through his hair, his head pounding. He shot a furtive look at the Palladium Temple's doorway. Inside knelt the Crown Prince of Troy, his tears spotting on the floor. Paris had disappeared from the scene before the fire gone up. *Surely not?* He told himself again. But what had started as a vague notion now grew horns and a tail of thorns, real and fierce.

He tore his gaze from Paris to look once again at Odysseus' vial.

Was this meant in fact for the Trojan Crown Prince as some kind of reward? He turned it over to examine it, and when he saw the rough Ahhiyawan script etched on the base, he instantly knew it was not.

*For Sirtaya,* it read.

# CHAPTER 18

## POSEIDON'S HERD

Time passed, the nights balmy, the days hot. One sweltering afternoon, Odysseus sat in the doorway of his hut, tending to a rabbit roasting on a spit. A horrible sucking noise sounded beside him. It was Kalchas the augur, on his haunches, sucking undercooked rabbit meat from a bone. Bloody, fatty juices ran down the long twin braids of his white beard, staining the hair pink and yellow. 'Your knuckles are white as milk,' he remarked, eyeing the statuette clutched in Odysseus' hands. 'You haven't set that thing down in days.'

Odysseus dropped his gaze to stare at the Palladium. He traced the tips of his stubby fingers over its smooth-worn surface. At first great moans of dismay had arisen from Troy's streets as word had spread about the statue's disappearance. Then Trojans had climbed to their roofs to watch in horror as Diomedes had paraded the stolen idol out here. Even better, some allied groups within the city had gathered near the locked gates, demanding they be allowed to leave.

*Why should we stay here now that the Gods of Troy have deserted us?* one wailed.

*To stay here is to die,* another boomed.

The effect did not last. Priam appeared on the Scaean turret's high roof, a speck of white and purple. The Trojan King's proclamations were desperate, but effective. *Stay, stay and shield the city. Stay and you will have your share of her wealth. You will see, you will see!*

Wagons had rocked out from the citadel gates and through the lower city streets, carrying hastily gathered up silvers and trinkets. Trojan Guardians tossed these to the wayward allies. One by one, the unsettled groups stood down, rejoining the more steadfast allies. The people of Troy gained heart at the sight by this.

*I might as well have stolen a horse bit*, he grumped, thumping the idol down.

'You said that once they found out their idol had been taken, all order would break down, that they would begin to desert the city,' a gruff voice grunted, stirring Odysseus back to the present. This time it was Diomedes, buffing his cyclops shield nearby. 'You said they would be melting with fear.'

'They should be, for my father's shade stalks them,' said young Neoptolemus, resting his weight on Achilles' spear.

Menelaus, leaning against Odysseus' hut, pointed at the Palladium. 'Island King, it has been seven days since you claimed that ugly statuette. We need another plan.' He glanced to the nearby royal hut of Agamemnon. From within, the *Wanax's* low drunken singing sailed out. Slaves moved around inside, taking drinks and food to the sozzled Lord of Mycenae.

'Oh, and you think the drunkard in there will have any better ideas?' Diomedes said with a snort of amusement. 'Even when he was sober his words were meaningless, like the wind.'

'Agamemnon is our *Wanax*,' Odysseus chided his comrade. 'He roused us to this war and remains our leader.'

'He is a sot,' said Neoptolemus.

'He is my brother,' Menelaus growled at the youthful one.

'Only you and old Nestor bother to wait for his commands now,' Diomedes argued on Neoptolemus' side.

'He still controls the camp,' Menelaus said, stretching a little taller, twisting to face Diomedes and Neoptolemus, planting one hand on the hilt of his sword. 'Unless you're planning to change that?'

'Nobody's talking about a coup,' Kalchas intervened, rising from his haunches. 'But Odysseus here is clearly the one with the ideas now.' He placed a calming hand on Menelaus' chest. 'If you want Helen back, if you want Troy, you'll listen to him.'

Menelaus' bottom lip curled a little, and he folded his hands together over the bronze buckle of his belt and sighed. 'Very well then. So what next, Island King?'

Sensing all eyes falling upon him, Odysseus speared a little rabbit meat from the spit with the end of his knife and chewed on the salty and satisfying morsel. All the time he gazed over Troy wistfully. He had seen old men on Ithaca look out to sea with that same moody, contemplative look, and they always seemed sage-like, heavy with wisdom. But the truth was that he was absolutely bereft of ideas. People called him a trickster because of one or two famous ruses from the past. They assumed he had some well of knowledge which he could draw upon to solve any problem. Right now, the well was bone-dry.

And that was when he saw it all in his mind's eye. A minor detail that the spy within Troy had told him. A ploy that no city could withstand.

He looked up and smiled at them all smugly. 'Gather round...'

***

Hattu held the vial back for a moment, reticent to place it in Kelenus' palm.

'I thought you said it would help relieve him of pain?' the healer said, confused.

Hattu eyed the tiny vessel again, the Ithacan bow etched on its surface. Odysseus' gift, apparently. A potion that would relieve poor Sirtaya of pain, or so the Island King had claimed. It had taken him all these days since the armoury fire to bring the vial to the healer's house. At first he had looked at the thing with contempt, for it brought back long-buried memories of Volca the Sherden's cruel trick with a vial like this – one that promised to contain a cure but turned out to be poison. But the more he thought back over his chats with the Island King, the surer he became that although Odysseus was many things – an ambitious warrior, a trickster, an enemy of Troy – he was not a wicked person. Certainly not a Volca.

'He... he doesn't have long, King Hattu,' Kelenus urged. 'A moon at best. If this potion makes that short time easier, then surely it is best he has it?'

A surge of sadness rose through Hattu's throat. At last he placed the vial in the healer's palm.

'I'll give him some now,' the ruddy healer smiled, shuffling back inside his house.

Hattu slumped down on the bench outside, resting his back on the vine-clad wall. Shins aching again, he kicked off his boots and flexed and clenched his toes. The kittens hopped up onto the bench to frolic by his side. He tickled their bellies while looking down towards the Thymbran Gatehouse, seeing Dagon and Tudha there. *Tudha*, he thought with a sigh. The two had barely spoken since their fiery words on the day the Palladium was stolen.

He noticed that Prince Aeneas was at the gatehouse too. The Dardanian had always seemed uncomplicated and dismissive of princely pleasures. Him and men like Kelenus, *they* were Troy… not the greedy hoarders around Priam's table. And Priam… was he any different? It felt like a knife in his chest to think that way for the first time in his life. During times past, all in Troy had enjoyed riches and luxury – feasts would be spread across the lower city and the citadel alike. It had been easy for Priam to shine in those days – in the complete absence of adversity. Yes, he had excelled amidst the storm of battle at Kadesh. There, he had served as one of the chief allies and a fine advisor to the Hittite high command. But here, here in his home, in Troy's darkest days when he was at the helm, Priam's flaws were being blown bare by the wind of war.

What of his son and heir, Paris? Paris, the Shadow? No, it could not be, he told himself over and over. How to prove or even speak such an accusation aloud? Why would Paris do such a thing? Bring war upon his home then aid the enemy in their efforts? Perhaps during the visit to Sparta long ago when he had fled with Helen, he had been brought in on the plan for war and promised some share of the bounty? Horrible thoughts.

He glanced across the dusty bowl of the lower city then up to the citadel. The contrast was no longer as stark as it had once been. Finally, the higher wards had been forced to feed the beast of war. The lesser halls and shrines – those at the edges of the citadel – were webbed with ropes and crusted with scaffolds. Sweating, bare-backed men climbed and crawled, their chisels and hammers *tink-tink-tinking* to strip away silver chasings and inlaid jewels. With a series of arhythmic, ugly thuds, these treasures were dropped into deep, wheeled chests. These were not bound for a new treasure ship in search of reinforcements, but for distribution amongst the more wayward allies already present, to buy their ongoing loyalty in light of the grievous loss of the Palladium. The bronze and copper, meanwhile, would be hastily fashioned into crude armour to replace some of the stores lost in the armoury fire. The highest parts of the citadel still gleamed, golden and glorious, like an island, but the tide of deprivation was rising around it.

The scuff of Kelenus' feet scattered his thoughts. 'It worked?' he asked boyishly.

Kelenus gave him a sympathetic smile but also a shake of the head.

'Not that I can see. If it does help, it will likely take time.'

'He… he doesn't have time.'

Kelenus simply patted him on the shoulder. 'Come back tomorrow.'

The following day, he was on his way to Kelenus' house when a shout from the Bay Gate defences distracted him. Aeneas and Dagon were up there, beckoning him.

'It started this morning,' Aeneas muttered as he reached them, shielding his eyes from the sun and gesturing out to the Scamander plain.

Hattu peered at the strange goings-on. Lumbering ox wagons moved from the elm woods in the south, crossed the Scamander ford and passed through the enemy crescent camp, then ambled on along the banks, heading downstream to a kink in the river near the Bay of Troy. There, Odysseus stood on top of an upturned wagon, waving his arms and directing the wagons to the riverside. A huge number of enemy soldiers were there, bare backed and sweating, unloading the cargo from each new wagon – sawn elm trunks. Hundreds upon hundreds of them. Diomedes seemed to be Odysseus' second in command in this initiative, swearing at and threatening those who were too slow. With a series of splashes and curses, they dumped the first shipment of logs into the river. It would be some time before they were finished, but Hattu already knew what the Island King was doing. 'They're trying to divert the river,' he said quietly.

'Aye,' agreed Dagon. 'Turning it south, by the looks of it.'

'Why?' Aeneas spluttered. 'What harm does that do us and what good does it do them? They can't flood the city, for it is too high. They can't cut us off from anywhere we are not already cut off from.'

'I agree,' Hattu said. Yet he could not help but feel a twinge of anxiety – a sense that there was a third possibility. He glanced over his shoulder into the lower city, and at one building there in particular. *Surely not?*

Two days later, the river diversion was complete, the waterway veering sharply south before curving into the Bay of Troy at another point. The original stretch of riverbed lay dry and cracked, like an old tongue. In the deepest section lay a dark hole. A cavity that plunged into the earth to Gods knew where. Though Hattu had a horrible feeling that *he* knew.

For two more days he studied the goings-on in the city: women washing clothes at troughs, men ladling water into cups and drawing bucketloads for their animals, birds pecking at the foaming fountains.

The clay channels that fed these watering points all emanated from one place: the Apollonian Springhouse. The lone source of water within Troy's walls. He remembered the day they had been tracking Aeneas inside the springhouse, how he had noticed the water was that same shade of yellow as the Scamander. Now he understood where the dried-out cavity in the river led to. Now he understood Odysseus' game.

The first shouts echoed over the lower city. 'Apollo deserts us, the springhouse has run dry!'

Hattu closed his eyes. Troy might endure the ongoing hunger for moons. But thirst would end the city much faster. How could Odysseus have known about the riverbed cavity, let alone that it was the source of the Apollonian Spring? How could he have known… but for the Shadow of Troy. Hattu looked up to the citadel, seeing a gleaming figure up there. Prince Paris, watching everything with an impassive look.

*It cannot be,* he prayed. *Surely it cannot be.*

The Wind of Wilusa sighed, offering no answers.

Soon after, the royals, the elders, the priests and the nobles gathered at the steps outside Priam's palace in an impromptu and panicked council, all bleating about the dry spring. Priam was nowhere to be seen, nor was Paris. Instead, Prince Scamandrios tried to calm them all, waving his hands downwards for quiet. 'The troughs are still full, and there are three cisterns here in the citadel. We will have to ration what we have until the winter rains come, but it can be done.'

Hattu eyed the three small stone-lined reservoirs. There was no way they would stretch until the winter. He considered raising this point, only for the others on the palace steps to rise in a discordant squabble. In no mood to shout over that din, he swallowed the words on his tongue. So, with a swoosh of his green cloak, he stomped off to the one place he hoped there might be some good news.

***

'It's working,' said the ruddy-faced Kelenus, beckoning him in. 'He's stirring, and the pain *is* easing.'

It was the perfect tonic. Hattu went inside, the kittens hopping along with him.

'He was none too pleased to find out that Tekka and I had trimmed his fingernails… or talons or whatever they were,' said Kelenus. 'But apart from that, he is lucid and happy. It will make his final days more pleasant. You owe a debt to whoever gave you that vial.'

Hattu smiled wryly at this.

There on the bed at the back of the house was Sirtaya, sitting up. It was the first time he had seen the Egyptian awake since that night attack when Achilles had fallen. His skin hung from his bones like old rags, but his face lit up like a boy's when the kittens leapt onto the bed to attack his tuft beard. 'You are a fearsome monster. Yes you *are!*' he whispered as one of the kittens play fought with his fingers, chewing madly on them until another one bit its tail and the third leapt upon its back.

Sirtaya realised he had a visitor. When his and Hattu's eyes met, there was a gladness and a sadness there at the same time. 'Master Hattu,' he said, his thin old face wrinkling into a smile. Sensing their need for privacy, Kelenus shuffled off to the other room where his wife was busy making broth.

'Old friend,' Hattu replied, sitting by the bed. 'Is there anything I can do for you?'

Sirtaya slowly shook his head. They did not say much for a time, both stroking the kittens, enjoying the calmness of the slow dusk, the coming of darkness. Through the window, they watched the sun dipping into the bay, casting a road of gold across the water, all the way here to Troy. 'Kelenus tells me you have something on your mind. Something you wish to tell me?'

Sirtaya smiled. 'No. Nothing.'

Hattu cocked an eyebrow. 'Come on; nothing? You know you can tell me anything. We shared our darkest moments together in the bowels of the Well of Silence.'

Sirtaya shrugged. 'Kelenus must have been mistaken. Or perhaps I was feverish and jabbering nonsense.'

Hattu sighed, stroking one of the kittens' heads. 'Did my heir come to see you this morning?'

'He did. Like every morning. I heard everything he was saying to me, even though it must have seemed to him like I was asleep.'

Hattu thought of his wayward protégé. He could not stop another sigh escaping his lips.

'Seems like *you* have something you want to say to *me*, Master Hattu,' Sirtaya said quietly.

Hattu looked away. He could not bring himself to ask what he wanted to ask, for fear of the answer. After a time, he found the courage: 'I have trained him to be immaculate in every respect as a future king must be. Yet he can't even talk about what he did. Always he goes on the offensive – so much anger.' He parted his hands, palms up. 'How can there be any hope for him if he cannot even speak of what he did, let alone regret or repent? Is he destined to become another Urhi-Teshub? A monster? I loved Zanduhepa like a sister. Her death killed a part of me. Her child's death even more. That it was my heir who did it…' he stopped and shook his head, choked for a moment.

Sirtaya let out a long, slow sigh. His gaze grew distant, set on the horizon. 'You know, Master Hattu, there is one abiding memory of my life back in Egypt: it was of that day before I set out to bring Pharaoh's message to the Hittite court – the last time I was ever in my homeland.'

Hattu felt a sudden rush of guilt. 'If I could fight back time itself, I would. I would stand between you and my father. I would stop him from throwing you into the Well of Silence.'

Sirtaya smiled at the image. 'I doubt it. Your father did not suffer protests from anyone. You could not have prevented my incarceration. Even if you had, it would have meant that we would never have met. That would have been truly sad.' He patted Hattu's hand in reassurance. 'Now let me tell you the story: I was standing on the threshold of my estate in the emmer wheat lands near Memphis, set to leave. I looked back and saw my wife, busy badgering her attendants in the gardens. She knew I was looking at her but she didn't look at me. Back when we first met, she and I were deeply in love. But as the years passed, we began to squabble like cats. We grew used to it after a time. It just… became our way. So much so that I almost did not recognise the spellbound young pair we had once been. That day, standing at the edge of my estate, I… I chewed and swallowed the words I wanted to say to her, to remind her that – inside – we were still that young couple. Of course, I said nothing, left, and never returned.' He turned his gaze to Hattu. 'You should speak to Tudha. You never know if it might be your last chance.'

'I speak to him every day,' Hattu said with a nervous laugh.

Sirtaya smiled. 'I mean the other words,' he said softly, 'the ones that so often go unspoken.'

Hattu felt a pang of nerves at the idea – a sudden tightening of that invisible, kingly armour. If the goal was to understand Tudha's version of what had gone on at the forest rebellion, then there were other ways, surely. He eyed Sirtaya's gnarled feet, poking from the bottom of the blanket, remembering the many times the Egyptian and a young Tudha had gone gambolling along the Ambar River. Inseparable they had been.

The Egyptian was his closest confidante. 'He must have spoken about Hatenzuwa to you, Sirtaya? He tells you everything.'

Sirtaya gazed into space. 'He used to. But he and I have spent little time together in the past year. I do not know what went on in those forest lands.'

Hattu took Sirtaya's bony hands in his. 'Do you still believe in him? Is there still hope for my heir?'

Sirtaya interlocked his fingers with Hattu's. 'You know my past, King Hattu, and I know yours. Every man has within him the weeds of evil and the buds of virtue. There is always hope, always danger. That is all I can say. For the answers you seek, *you* must speak to him.'

'I have tried. But the *Tuhkanti* is stubborn and-'

'His name is Tudha,' Sirtaya cut him off with a solemn stare, 'not *Tuhkanti.* Speak to him for once not as a king to his heir, but as a father to his son. Honestly, openly. You asked if there was anything you could do for me. This is it.'

Hattu gulped a few times, nodding. Tonight, he thought. There was another ill-conceived citadel feast planned. There, perhaps, he could speak to Tudha. He glanced to the window, hearing a scrape of sandals outside. Kelenus and his wife were ambling downhill to feed the two goats they kept in a byre there.

Hattu heard the gentlest tap of liquid hitting something. A tear, spotting on the blanket. Sirtaya's tear. 'Sirtaya?'

'Now, I must speak of the other matter,' the Egyptian said. He squeezed Hattu's hand feebly. 'You see, I *did* have something I wanted to tell you. We are completely alone now and so I can speak freely. That night at the quarrel over Achilles' body, when Glaucus of Lukka died in the struggle.'

'Achilles' last victim,' Hattu mourned.

'If only it were so,' Sirtaya said. 'Achilles was dead even before Glaucus arrived on the scene.'

'Then who…' Hattu started.

'Paris. Prince Paris killed him.'

Hattu stared at the Egyptian. The words were like a nail, pinning his theory about Paris to a wall. Glaucus, leader of the Lukkans since Sarpedon's demise. The Lukkans, Troy's staunchest ally.

'He and his closest Guardians speared him down then made up the lie about Achilles. I could not speak those words in earshot of any Trojan,' Sirtaya whispered, looking towards the window and the byre.

'You know as well as I do that it would cause deep distress and division. And if the remaining Lukkan soldiers found out, no amount of gold or silver could keep them here in Troy.'

Hattu's eyes darted. He grabbed Sirtaya's hand with both of his, kissing it. 'Old friend, please, tell me exactly what happened. I must be sure.'

Sirtaya nodded. 'It started when Paris and Glaucus quarrelled over what was to happen to Achilles' body. It was just heated words at first, and then…' he stopped, his face slackening.

'Sirtaya?'

A faint sound passed through the house then, a low hum.

Sirtaya's face changed, turning white, his eyes widening like moons. 'By the Gods of the Black Land, no,' he croaked.

'What is it?' Hattu said, feeling the chair under him shaking, and the frame of the bed too. Stacked plates in the other room chattered.

'I felt more soft tremors in my many days of unconsciousness,' he said, 'but I thought they were part of my feverish dreams.' The plates clanked noisily now, and dust puffed here and there from the ceiling. 'This… this is no normal quake, Master Hattu.'

Hattu's blood ran cold. 'It will pass, it *will* pass,' he tried to reassure the Egyptian, squeezing his hand. At that moment, the house juddered violently. The plates in the other room pitched out and smashed. From the byre, Kelenus wailed and his wife screamed. From elsewhere outside a clatter of falling stone sounded, horses whinnied in terror and soldiers cried to one another. Hattu – breath trapped in his lungs – looked up and around. For an instant it seemed like it was over. Then, with a thunderclap of noise, the world jolted madly to one side then the other.

He scooped Sirtaya up in his arms and ran through plunging chunks of plaster and dust. Coughing and retching he staggered onto the street, seeing families everywhere scrambling from their homes likewise, plumes of dust shooting up everywhere as these lower city abodes shifted and sagged. Another judder sent him stumbling. Kelenus steadied him and took Sirtaya from him. Another jolt like the slap of a God's hand sent everyone on the streets of Troy staggering.

He glanced in every direction: the Scamander was alive, bursting with geysers of muddy water, foaming and lashing the banks; overhead, screaming flocks of storks sped from their nests and in every direction away from Troy and the Scamander plain. The few goats and sheep in the city bleated in panic, throwing themselves to their sides. He looked finally to Sirtaya, barely conscious in Kelenus' arms, and recalled the Egyptian's story about the old man in the Well of Silence who had taught him to read the shaking earth.

*The rivers will boil. The birds will scatter. The herds will lie down... and the cities of men will fall.*

A sonorous *boom!* sounded from Troy's edge. With a shiver of horror, he turned his gaze to the lower city walls: the jagged-tooth merlons were toppling away from the battlements, and the entire run of those defences wobbled horribly as it they were a sheet of linen moving in a breeze.

Poseidon's herd was cantering no more. This was a stampede.

Hattu broke into a sprint downhill, fuelled by a pulse of dread. As he sped past a low-walled barrack house, he screamed at the startled soldiers in and around there: 'Every man to the city's edge!'

***

The Scamander belched and spewed. Ahhiyawan huts and tents crumpled. A pot boiling on a fire shook and fell, the broth seeping into the earth. Nearby, an upright stack of spears toppled over with a clatter and a clang.

Odysseus staggered through this, the cup in his hand falling to the ground, his unblinking eyes fixed on Troy. The curtain wall of the lower city rippled and bulged like a ribbon of stone as the earth bucked and spasmed wildly. He knew that this was not at all like the frequent tremors of these parts. He had never felt fear such as this.

Fear.

And opportunity.

A quake that could bring down walls…

'To arms,' he croaked. It was the sound a frog with a sore throat might make, barely audible. Clearing his throat he tried again. '*TO ARMS!*' he screamed.

Diomedes swung round from the spectacle of the river, gawping at Troy. Nestor, watching the camp and the city of Troy shaking crazily, muttered some fearful oath to the Gods. Neoptolemus was for once timid, pale with fear.

That was when a great *crack!* emanated from the lower city walls, the noise shuddering across the Scamander plain. All eyes fell upon the dark, jagged fissure that sped down from the tip of the outer defences, spearing right through the base of ashlar blocks too. Merlons toppled outwards, stone fell away here and there.

'Troy is breached. To arms!' Diomedes howled too now, he, Menelaus, Nestor and every other seeing what Odysseus had seen.

Ahhiyawan soldiers tossed away half-eaten food, threw on helms and snatched spears from racks. As they gathered in an unruly mass outside their camp, facing Troy, three more such cracks appeared in the walls, and one up on the citadel defences too. All eyes stared as the cracks grew wider. Wide enough for a slender man to edge through… wider still.

*Yes...* Odysseus cried inwardly, imagining the gaps opening like a palace door, the city streets being presented to the Ahhiyawan army at last. Victory… then home! In his mind's eye he saw the shores of Ithaca, saw his palace, his wife and boy. *Yes!*

But there the breaches stopped growing. Narrow, awkward, not wide enough to attack. The quake began to soften.

*No!*

***

As the quake eased, Hattu and Dagon led the defenders up onto the battlements and directed squadrons to guard the narrow fissures, just in case any invaders might try to squeeze through. He saw them out there, arrayed in their masses, ready, eyes hungrily watching Troy's fortifications. As the quake faded to nothing, his eyes met Odysseus'. *Not today, Island King,* he mouthed.

All around him, the defenders rose in a chorus of giddy, delirious laughter and cheering. 'What are you standing around out there for? Troy's walls cannot be broken, you fools!' They whistled and jeered and mocked the Ahhiyawans, some bowmen and slingers loosing at the would-be attackers, all missiles falling a few strides shy of them. With curses and gestures of their own, the Ahhiyawans slunk back towards their crescent camp.

'Save your arrows and stones,' Hattu snarled. The shooting stopped but the cheering continued all around. But in amongst it all, he heard different sounds: gasps of horror and dismay from some defenders. He saw one such, gawping back into the city. A coldness rose through him as he turned and saw it for himself: the walls had ridden the quake and remained intact apart from a few narrow fissures, but the sea of less solidly-constructed houses across the lower town had been devastated. Closely-packed and often abutting, these warrens of homes lay in semi-ruins, more than half of the abodes had collapsed, some on fire. Every single ward was like this, plumes of dust rising from the wreckage like spirits, the high Trojan wind spreading it across the sky in dirty streaks. The remaining soldiers' celebrations fell away as they all realised what had happened.

In place of those triumphal sounds, mothers wailed and babies screamed, dogs howled and men cried out in anguish. Groups of bony Trojan citizens began scrambling over the wrecked homes, digging crazily with their bare hands to rescue buried loved ones. Bloody limbs and stained rags of clothing jutted from the collapsed houses.

Hattu staggered down from the walls to street level.

'Gods, Hattu,' Dagon croaked. 'I have never known a tremor like it.'

'Sirtaya?' a voice called from nearby. A voice was tight with anguish.

Hattu moved instinctively towards the sound.

When he found Tudha, it took him a moment to realise that the heap of rubble upon which his heir crouched was the remains of Kelenus' house. Kelenus was standing nearby, red-eyed, holding his weeping wife Tekka to his chest. The kittens cowered under an upturned wicker basket nearby. He noticed that Tudha's fingers were bloody, the nails broken from frantic digging. 'Where is Sirtaya?' Hattu asked.

Kelenus' eyes shone with tears and his lips trembled. 'He… he went back inside. The kittens were hiding under the bed, you see. He said there was no use in them perishing when he only had a short time left.' Hattu heard a tired old sigh, not realising it was his own, and felt hot tears strain and sting behind his eyes.

'He can't be dead!' Tudha said, starting to dig again.

Hattu and Dagon clambered onto the rubble and began digging too. But soon the men around them stopped, exhausted, the wreckage too deep and heavy. When Hattu stopped, Dagon stopped too. The Chariot Master, who had never let a day pass without griping or arguing with the Egyptian, closed his eyes slowly, a lone tear stealing down his dusty cheek.

But Tudha carried on, on all fours, madly shifting great chunks of mud-brick and rock.

Hattu felt a need to console him, yet the kingly armour was choking now, binding the emotions within where they had been caged for many years. To take one step closer and place a hand on Tudha's shoulder felt like a journey of one thousand strides.

Eventually, it was Dagon who wrapped an arm around Tudha, guiding him to his feet. 'It is too late, *Tuhkanti*. He is gone.'

***

A blur of days passed. The dead were recovered from the ruins of the collapsed lower town houses and prepared for burning. Rubble from the toppled homes was ferried by dusty, thirsty and gaunt townsfolk to the fissures in the lower walls and tipped into the narrow gaps to crudely repair the defences. The cracks in the citadel's soaring fortifications required more than just rubble, and so marble slabs were prized from the royal streets and fountains were smashed down into chunks to seal up those breaches.

Three nights after the earth shook, small funeral fires burned all around Troy's lower town. One small group gathered near the ruins of Kelenus' house. Dagon and Hattu piled up small logs of spruce and pine, then Tudha and Aeneas brought Sirtaya's body – washed and groomed – on a stretcher and placed it atop the pyre. The Egyptian's face was puckered with death but at peace.

Shaking, Tudha touched a torch to the kindling, then the four stood back to observe. As the Egyptian's body became a silhouette in the heart of the flames, Hattu stared into the past, remembering the strange paths that had brought Sirtaya and him together as firm friends. Grief tore at his throat and pounded at the centre of his chest. *Walk tall through the Field of Reeds, old friend,* he mouthed, unable to speak.

Behind him, he heard a rustle of activity. He glanced over his shoulder to see Tudha, now rummaging in Sirtaya's leather bag. He produced from it his iron sword and held the blade up, turning it to admire the workmanship. Hattu's grief vanished, replaced by a stark unease. This was the first time Tudha had held the sword in over a year… since Hatenzuwa.

'*Tuhkanti*,' he burred. 'What are you doing?'

Baring the blade, Tudha walked towards Hattu, his scarred face hard… then brushed past him. Quietly, he added his sword to the flames. Stepping back he said simply: 'He deserves to rest with honour.'

'Aye,' Hattu said quietly, his fears retreating. 'Aye, he does.'

They watched as the iron blackened along with the Egyptian's bones. Apt, for a man who had been unbendingly loyal. High above, Andor circled, keening mournfully.

# CHAPTER 19

## THE ARROWS OF HERAKLES

The sun glared down on the dusty channels that once carried water through Troy. Thirst had brought a strange silence over the streets. A slow, silent procession of people lined up to receive their water ration each day – a ladle of brackish liquid in the morning and again at night, with a third noonday ladle for the soldiers on watch during that hottest period.

Hattu sat in the shade of the Palladium temple, his head throbbing with thirst. He heard the dull scrape of a bucket and looked up, the Guardians at the cistern looked ashen-faced. He read their lips. *Nothing left,* one said. Another at the second cistern said the same. The men at the third had to work to draw full buckets from it, so low were the waters within.

'King Hattu,' a voice croaked. It was Prince Scamandrios, beckoning him from the palace doorway.

Inside the palace the air was cool and fresh, but he noticed how some of the furniture and ornaments were gone – given to the allies to keep them onside, he guessed. He came to the megaron to see that the other notables of Troy had already gathered – many with cracked lips and dark pouches under the eyes. Priam was there on his throne, listless and withered. It was Paris who spoke for him, walking to and fro at the front of the throne plinth. Hattu watched him with a dark glower.

'It seems that we do not have enough water to make it to winter after all,' he said with a derisive look at Scamandrios. 'My father is unsure what to do, so it falls upon me to decide. If we are to find fresh water then we must, it seems, break the curfew he imposed.'

Murmurs rose.

Hattu's eyes narrowed.

'The two rivers are closely watched by the enemy; thus, we cannot draw fresh supplies there. The next nearest source of fresh water is on Tenedos Isle.'

The murmurs rose to a low babble.

'Down at the wharf, we have three seaworthy ships left. The enemy encirclement does not prevent us from reaching them. Thus, I will lead a force which will set sail to Tenedos and fill as many skins and barrels from the island's streams as we can carry. It should be enough to replenish the cisterns. Perhaps enough to see us through to winter.'

Hattu noticed a group of ten Guardians were standing to one side. Picked men, by the look of it. Skorpios amongst them.

'Prince Aeneas, I need you to come with me,' Paris said.

Aeneas dutifully stepped to join the ten.

Paris' eyes slid round to meet Hattu's. '*Labarna*, you too, and bring your Chariot Master.'

Hattu did not reply for a moment. Just long enough to gauge Paris. The crown prince's eyes were gleaming. What was going on behind them? 'As you wish,' he said, joining the party.

***

A short time later, the Bay Gates creaked open, with archers lining the western defences lest the enemy try to intercept the mission. The party hurried outside, assisted by teams of sailors carrying the skins and barrels to be filled. They were at sea within the hour, unmolested.

The lead Trojan battleship was first to ship oars and hoist sail – the purple and cream linen sheet thundering in the wind, bulging like a puffed-out chest. While a few sailors clambered around on the spar, securing the rigging, the rest took the opportunity to fish. They caught sackloads of tunny and one older sailor even pulled in a swordfish – all of which could be salted and rationed out once back in Troy. The old fellow bragged and bloviated about his catch to the extent that the others began jeering him. Oblivious to all this, one overenthusiastic young sailor drew his rod back over his shoulder, failed to hear the strangled yelp behind him, then cast off with all his might. The older sailor behind turned pale, staring down at his bleeding groin – the kilt ripped through, his scrotum too, both testicles dangling free. He turned his volcanic glare upon the back of the young one who had ripped his parts open, before stomping forward in a rage, cursing and swearing. The young one swung round to the noise, confused, accidentally poking the older one in the eye with his fishing rod. Temporarily blinded, scrotum sliced open, enraged, the older man retreated to the ship's healer, while his fellow sailors hooted with laughter.

Hattu stood at the rail on the other edge of the boat, his face and hair wet with briny spray. The coolness of it was wonderful, and he longed to lick the moisture from his lips but knew it would slake only a fool's thirst. He watched as Tenedos Isle rose to prominence in the south, it's steep, thickly-wooded hills veined with plunging waterfalls and the cliffs spotted with nesting seabirds, all stark against the cobalt sea and pastel-blue sky. A mountain rose further inland, the peak ringed with brilliant white cloud. At the war's outset, the people of Tenedos had fled the island to take shelter in Troy. Their king, Tenes, had died early in the conflict, and now there were only a few dozen of them left. When Hattu asked them for guidance about the deserted island – its danger areas, what kind of predatory wildlife lived there, where the hidden rocks lay under the coastal waters – most were uncertain. Only the few older ones remembered well enough to advise. *Stay clear of the deep woods,* one warned, *make shore at the white bay, take water from the streams that run downhill to that beach and be away.* He eyed the shadowy woods once more with new suspicion. Once again, he glanced along the deck at Paris, standing at the prow, one foot on the rail, his purple cape flaring in the wind. His suspicions began to multiply.

'I know you better than you know yourself,' Dagon muttered, arriving beside him. 'You're watching him as if he was the plague walking. What's going on?'

Hattu did not speak for a time. To say it aloud again would feel like spitting poison in the air. He still felt guilty for having upset old Antenor so much. But what other option did he have? 'It's him, Dagon,' he said in a whisper. 'He is the man we have been seeking all this time.' He looked at his oldest friend. 'Paris is the Shadow.'

Dagon stayed locked in a sideways look, stunned.

'It makes little sense, but all the pieces fit. I didn't believe it myself until Sirtaya told me just before the ruinous tremor: Glaucus did not die to Achilles' sword. Paris killed him, needlessly.'

Dumbstruck, Dagon hung his head low, taking it all in. 'If he is trying to sabotage his own city… then why is he right now sailing to gather water to save her?'

Hattu eyed the looming cliffs and hills of Tenedos again. 'I have a dreadful feeling that this island might hold the answer.'

The trio of boats came round on Tenedos' southern edge and shipped oars as they slipped into a calm sandy cove, blinding white in the sunlight. With a hiss of shingle, the hulls beached. Hattu leapt down, padded across the beach, and eyed the belt of bluffs lining the cove. Three waterfalls toppled over the edge, hurtling down like white pillars, plunging into pools at the base before snaking across the beach towards the shore. Iridescent spray wafted from the falls in mesmerizing shapes.

Dagon crouched by one of the snaking beach streams, eyeing the clear currents. 'Are my eyes deceiving me, or is this going to be as easy as it looks?'

Around them, the sailors laughed, hurrying to the foaming pools at the base of the waterfalls with their skins and barrels. The old sailor splashed into the waters first, squatting to dunk his freshly-sutured scrotum into the cold currents, a look of extreme bliss rising across his face. The rest stood under the falls, drenching themselves and whooping, washing their bodies and opening their mouths to drink as they did so. Paris watched on from a short distance, hands clasped behind his back.

Hattu stepped towards the nearest fall, enticed by the idea of soaking himself in the chilly waters.

Just then, one of the workers retched, spitting. 'Urgh!' He staggered out from the fall, wiping at his mouth. 'The water is bad.'

'Argh,' another did the same, then the rest. Even those at the other two falls.

Hattu held out a hand to catch a little of the fall then stepped back. Sniffing at it was enough. He had been on hunts around Hattusa often enough to know the scent of polluted water.

'Is there a problem?' Paris asked.

'An animal has died, somewhere upstream,' Hattu replied. 'See how the three falls are relatively close? It is a fork from one stream, coming from that high mountain.'

'Hmm,' Paris said. 'We are expected back before sunset. Those bluffs are high, and we don't know how far upstream we will have to go.'

Hattu tried to read Paris' eyes again. Once more they were bright, calculating… but giving nothing away. 'All we have to do is find and shift the corpse, then the water will run clean. It only requires a small party. The sailors can wait here.'

'We cannot return to Troy without water,' Aeneas agreed. 'We have to go inland.'

Paris regarded the bluffs once more, then raised a hand and snapped his fingers. 'Skorpios, you and your men stay here to guard the ships. I will venture upstream with the *Labarna* and my cousin to deal with this dead thing in the water. Sailors, you stay by the falls and begin filling the barrels as soon as the waters run clean.'

As he swished past to pick up a few provisions, Hattu stared at his back. From sceptic to advocate in a few breaths. *Have I just been hoodwinked?* he wondered.

Paris, Dagon, Aeneas and Hattu set off shortly after. Behind a tangle of thorns, they found a cliff path and picked their way up it and onto the bluff tops. There, the three streams emerged from the dense wall of spruce. The fork was somewhere within the forest, he realised. The words of the islander he had consulted crackled in his mind.

*Stay clear of the deep woods.*

Hattu led the way into the trees. It was cool under the canopy of branches, the air spiced with the scent of spruce and their every step accompanied by the *crunch* of fallen needles.

Soon, they reached the fork, but no sign of the dead animal. So, on they went up the banks of this source stream. All the way, Hattu watched from the corners of his eyes. Something just didn't feel right about this. An hour passed and he began to fret about how deep in the wilderness they were. All around him, insects clicked, birds chattered and squawked and every so often small rodents scampered and scurried.

A hand clamped on his shoulder. Paris' hand. The hand that had slain Glaucus.

'Look, *Labarna.* Movement.'

Hattu followed the outstretched finger of his other hand. Up ahead, something was stirring by the stream side. Hattu waved for them all to sink to their haunches. With shallow breaths he watched the thing. It was agitated, moving jerkily, but partly masked behind a screen of ferns. Finally, the fawn emerged with a grunt, trotting to the stream side and away again, bleating and grunting once more. Hattu sighed, now seeing the body of a mother doe in the waters. He rose, approaching, letting the fawn run off. The doe's body was badly decomposed, ribbons of grey maggoty meat trailing from the cadaver and flies buzzing all around. The stench was overpowering.

'Someone, take the back legs,' he sighed, grabbing hold of the front limbs.

With some effort, he and Dagon dragged the doe's body clear of the water and far enough away from the banks that it would not leak into the currents.

'The waters will run clear now,' he said to Paris. 'The sailors at the beach will already be filling-'

'Hattu,' Dagon hissed, cutting him off.

Hattu twisted to his friend, crouching by the doe's body. He was holding something in a rag, something plucked from the deer's corpse. An arrow head. 'I thought this island was deserted?' Dagon said, examining and sniffing the arrowhead. 'There's some kind of substance on the metal too.'

All of Hattu's senses sharpened at that moment. He saw something move far off, deep in the canopy of shadows. It was pure instinct that saved him, as he grabbed and flashed up one of his swords, deflecting the red-tailed arrow that had been whizzing towards him. With a *clang* the shaft spun crazily up into the air. As if a swarm of wasps was coming for them, more arrows shot out of the blackness. But Aeneas and Dagon were swift, swinging their shields round from their backs to catch those aimed at them, and clustering around Paris and Hattu.

'Back, back downstream, *go!*' Hattu roared. Like a tortoise, they backstepped away from the direction of attack. Arrows whacked against the two shields in volleys. In the gaps in between Aeneas lowered his shield to shoot back. One of these shafts elicited a pained groan from the shadows. That was when they emerged. A dozen bowmen, led by a limping man with long hair, bald on top, shaking his fist.

'That was my brother you just killed, Aeneas!' he raged.

'Philoctetes?' Aeneas gasped.

'Who?'

'An Ahhiyawan king who never made the war. They said he was bitten by a snake and his wound grew so purulent and stinking that Agamemnon put him to shore on an island and left him there.'

'I think we've found which island,' Dagon said glibly.

'Keep the shields tight,' Aeneas impelled in panting breaths as they went. 'Philoctetes is an expert shot and… and he smears his arrowheads in some filthy poison… claims they are the arrows of Herakles and the poison is the Hydra's blood.'

The small group hurried back downstream with Philoctetes and his archers ranging in pursuit. Arrows whizzed and hummed past them, sending splinters of spruce bark spraying into the air. The cool, dark woods changed then, stripes of sunlight breaking through. A few heartbeats later and they were back at the forest's edge and full, blinding sunlight. Hattu saw the top of the cliff path and knew they were doomed if they tried to slow down to navigate its awkward descent. His eyes slid along the bluff edge to the point where the nearest stream vanished over the precipice. 'Jump!' he cried.

With a gasp for breath he propelled himself over, praying, feeling the sudden roar of air in his ears as he plummeted, seeing the pool at the waterfall's base far below and much smaller than he had remembered it… growing larger, larger. With an almighty *boom!* he was underwater, deafened, hair and cloak entangling him like weeds, his lungs burning. Silent arrows sped down into and through the waters like darting fish, leaving trails of bubbles in their wake. With a surge of his legs and arms, he clawed his way up and burst clear of the surface, gasping for air. Panicked, babbling sailors sped over to help him to the edge of the pool at the waterfall's base. They already had Aeneas and Dagon and Paris, helping them back to the shoreline and the boats. The arrows of Philoctetes and his mob continued to batter down around them as they fled. Hattu climbed aboard the flagship and fell to his knees, panting, dripping wet. As the ships hastily put to sea, he saw the Ahhiyawan bowman Philoctetes and his band making hand gestures and whistling and jeering from the blufftop.

The sea wind quickly dried him out. A sailor approached and handed him a cup brimful of water. 'Drink, *Labarna*,' the man said with a smile. 'We filled all of our barrels and skins. And Prince Paris' wound does not look too bad.'

Hattu, gulping down the water, the sweet cold water, gagged. 'Wound? What wound?'

He looked along the deck to see the crown prince sitting on the edge of a crate, the ship's healer examining the red-tailed arrow that jutted from Paris' shoulder – the one Hattu had deflected. Paris was laughing and making light of it as the healer eased the shaft free, then applied some paste to the wound.

Dagon sat next to Hattu. When the sailor had given him a cup too then left them alone, he said: 'That arrow was not meant for Paris. It was meant for you.'

'Aye,' Hattu said, 'And I think that's why the doe was dumped in the river, why we were led – no *lured* – into the woods.'

'By Paris?' Dagon murmured.'

'Aye, and those archers knew we were coming. I was supposed to die there, you and Aeneas too, probably. We were never supposed to succeed in taking water.'

As the boats cut north, fighting against the currents and the headwind, Hattu noticed that the scene around Paris had changed. Now he was leaning forward, elbows on knees, head hanging like a drunk about to be sick. His skin had turned white as the shore they had beached upon. The healer was now wide-eyed and anxious, muttering to sailors nearby. Skorpios looked on with a scowl.

Hattu rose, approaching Paris. He halted a step away, seeing the dark grey lesion the arrow had made. That was grim looking enough – like month-old meat – but the dark, jagged lines emanating from the wound were far more sinister.

As they came round towards the Bay of Troy, Paris began to moan with pain. The healer helped him to lie down on the deck, revealing his face – the handsome visage warped and puffed up. Now his limbs began to swell grotesquely, the flesh straining at the edges of his armour, the extremities an angry, shiny red. 'Help me,' he croaked, his tongue fat and black. A pair of Guardians unbuckled his armour, and when it fell away he issued a huge groan of relief as his bloated trunk expanded.

The boat docked at the wharf, and the Guardians carried the groaning Paris on a stretcher through the Bay Gate. Hattu and Dagon followed the party, and they could hear Paris muttering deliriously now. 'Take me to Mount Ida, to the nymphs who live there. They can ease this pain.'

A commotion arose all round Troy's streets, the starving, thirsty masses gathering around the stretcher bearers as they hurried uphill to the Healers' House. A party rushed down from the citadel to meet them: King Priam, Queen Hekabe, Helen and Andromache. Priam shambled to a halt, barely recognizing his son. Queen Hekabe staggered and fell. Helen stared at the distended mass that was her lover, her face turning whiter than milk.

On the doorstep of the Healers' House, and with a violent shudder, Paris took his last breath.

'Noooo,' Hekabe shrieked.

Hattu, numb at all that had happened in such a short space of time, stared at the dead crown prince. It all echoed through his head: Prince Paris killed Glaucus of Lukka, sabotaged the embassy at the outset of the war; poisoned the springhouse well, betrayed young Prince Troilus to the enemy, stole the Thymbran Gate keys; betrayed the river camp, poisoned Hektor, signalled for the enemy night attack, set the armoury ablaze, advised the enemy to divert the river and necessitate the mission to Tenedos. Paris, behind it all.

'The Shadow is no more,' Dagon whispered. 'The trap he and the enemy arranged to dispatch you ended up destroying him.'

Hattu looked around the weeping masses, Paris' parents and siblings amongst them. 'We should let his secret die with him,' he replied, 'and be thankful that the threat within Troy is lifted.'

# CHAPTER 20

## THE FOOL OF ITHACA

At the same time as the cisterns were replenished, Prince Paris' body was washed, oiled, groomed and dressed. At dusk, great crowds gathered up on the citadel grounds to sing and lament as he became ashes. That very same night – while Paris' body still smouldered – Helen and Prince Deiphobus were wed.

They sat upon a makeshift plinth, face to face, she veiled, he holding a silver cup. Chryses lifted his sun tiara from his bald head and held it towards the sky, chanting and calling upon the Gods to witness their joining. Young men played lyres and girls carried pots of burning sweet resin around the plinth. Priestesses draped strings of flowers over the couple, then Deiphobus lifted Helen's veil and offered her the cup. Both drank then placed their wet lips together. Not a soul watching – their faces still stained with tears for the dead Paris – cheered or made any note of joy. Soon, a sombre dance began, with pipes droning, flutes sighing. There was no feast, just weak wine, small loaves of bread and the few baked fish caught on the Tenedos expedition. This fare was passed around to fill unsmiling mouths, for the famine had well and truly reached the citadel now.

Hattu sat on a stone bench by the Temple of Apollo. Shadows of passing dancers swept across him, tall against the temple's sides – scarred and bare now that the bronze and silver had been twisted and prized away. He gazed at the cinders rising from the funeral pyre. The stack was composed mainly of furniture gathered from the palace – so short had firewood become. His eyes fell to the blackened shape that remained of Paris. It was impossible to escape the deep sense of sadness all around, but there was a certain comfort in that the traitor within Troy – whatever his motives – was dead. The man who had brought this war upon Troy and then done so many terrible things to make it worse was no more.

Andor pecked at a small pile of grain he had poured onto the bench for her from his ration pouch. Dagon, Tudha and Aeneas sat slumped nearby, watching the wedding dance with empty eyes. The tradition was well known in Hittite lands and here too: when a husband perished, it was his brother's duty to wed and protect the widow. But given all *this* widow had been through, it just seemed wrong. Had Menelaus not been so hungry to punish her, tonight might have been the time to send Helen back to him. It would have been no embarrassment to Paris now that he walked the Dark Earth. It might not have ended the war, but it would surely have softened the moods of the Ahhiyawans… made them less ruthless if they finally broke this city and ran free around its streets. *If?* he mused with a growing sense of doom, looking around the weary citadel, the hotchpotch of soldiery and the bereft royalty.

He noticed Princess Cassandra – sitting on the ground nearby like a slave, knees hugged to her chest, disinterested in the dance. 'My condolences for your loss,' he said to her.

She touched her breastbone, gulping. 'It hurts in a way I cannot explain. First little Troilus, then Polydorus, then Hektor, now Paris. I find the part of me that once loved my fallen brothers is no longer there, as if it died with them.' She took a deep breath, tears quivering on her lower eyelids. 'It matters not, for we all hurtle towards the same fate, regardless…'

Hattu thought of her strange demeanour ever since he had arrived at Troy, then of that night when she had come to him, when they had both shared a similar dream. *I saw a great shadow, looming over our city. A wretched thing, with eyes of blood, a tongue of bronze and a mane of fire. A giant stallion of war that some great dark spirit might ride. Around its hooves, Troy lay in ruins.*

Since the ruinous earth tremor, he had hoped that her dream and his of the skeleton horse had been premonitions of that rampant charge of Poseidon's steeds. A threat been and gone. 'You are… still having that dream, Majesty?' he said, the words low.

She gulped gently, hesitant for a time before nodding reluctantly. 'Once more that *thing* was stampeding over Troy's ashes. Except this time on its back sat a rider.'

'Who?' he whispered, leaning closer to her.

She took a moment before rolling her eyes up to meet his. She gripped his hands. 'It was you, King Hattu.'

Hattu recoiled, staring as she rose and fled inside the Temple of Apollo. Confused and unsettled, he stared at the temple's dark entrance, wondering whether he should go after her. As soon as he rose to do so, a clanking of bronze sounded by his side.

Two Guardians flanked Prince Deiphobus. Dressed in soft white and purple robes, he was smiling broadly for once, his receding curls oiled and combed back from his face. He cradled the silver wedding cup in the fingers of one hand. 'King Hattu, do not leave,' he said, offering Hattu the cup. 'All have drunk from the joining vessel. You should as well.'

Hattu took the vessel. 'I must say it is difficult to recognise you wearing that thing.'

'The crown prince's robe?'

'The smile.'

Deiphobus laughed. There was a coldness to it.

'You do not mourn the loss of Paris as keenly as the others,' Hattu said. 'Nor, I noticed, did you cry for Hektor.'

Deiphobus shrugged. 'One is told to love his brothers and his country, but not in what order. I love Troy, and the Gods of Troy have seen fit to clear the path before me so that I may be the new crown prince and sit upon the throne once my father passes. More, I have the hand of the fairest woman in the world, and the honour of leading Troy to victory. I have always believed I should have been Father's chosen son and heir.'

Hattu wanted to ask the usually surly prince what might have been, had he given his all for his brothers rather than sulking and grousing about their stations. Instead, he sipped at the wine, warm and fruity on his tongue. Quarter-bowing in respect, he handed the cup back. 'I wish nothing but the best for you and your new bride, Majesty,' he said. He noticed something then: Deiphobus' eyes glancing over at the bench where Hattu had been sitting… and where the Helm of Troy rested. A desirous look. He understood Deiphobus fully now: a man never satisfied with his lot, ambitious to a fault. Now he coveted the post of High Commander to go with his position as crown prince – a dual role only ever held once before, by Hektor.

With deliberate care, Hattu stepped over to scoop the helm up underarm. 'And, as appointed by your father, I will continue to marshal the city defences watchfully.' With a bow, he turned away from Deiphobus, sensing the man's smile turn into a scowl again.

He made his way back to the bench. Dagon and Aeneas had upped and left, leaving Tudha there, alone, flexing the fingers of one hand endlessly, gently stroking Andor with the other. His silver eyes stared through his hanging veil of hair, gazing at nothing.

It was time, Hattu realised, to fulfil his final promise to Sirtaya. *You must speak to Tudha now. Honestly, openly. For once not as a king to his heir, but as a father to his son.*

He sat. Both said nothing for a time. Thoughts rose into his mind like skeletal hands from the grave: of the rebellion, the bloody forest shrine, Zanduhepa and her baby slaughtered. *Where to begin?* he mused miserably. Old habits rose and he considered asking his heir to give a report on the watch or to detail the stock of arms and supplies. But in his mind's eye he saw Sirtaya on his death bed, felt the Egyptian squeezing his hand. *As a father to his son...*

'Sirtaya was dear to me.'

This seemed to catch Tudha by surprise. He twisted a little towards Hattu.

'He would not want you to grieve,' Hattu continued quietly. 'He was in great pain, and he died saving the kittens. A selfless act that probably spared him a handful more days of agony.'

'Him and those damned kittens,' Tudha said with an awkward laugh.

The sound made Hattu smile. 'I knew him first when I was a boy and he was an enemy of the Hittite world. Then I met him next in the depths of the earth, when both of us were forgotten prisoners. Friendship springs from the most unexpected of circumstances.'

'It does,' Tudha said with a twitch of a smile that quickly fell. 'He was my only friend.'

'What about Aeneas?' Hattu asked, glancing over to the wine bench where the Dardanian Prince was busy filling cups.

'He and I get along well,' he replied. 'Best of all, he does not judge me. He says that the man who has not made a mistake has made nothing.' He held Hattu's gaze now. 'Wouldn't you agree?'

As if sensing a change of mood, Andor waddled between the two like a mediator.

'I have made enough mistakes of my own,' Hattu answered, looking over at the cinders of Paris' funeral pyre. 'Each felt like a burden of glowing rock on my back... until I found the courage to talk about things.' He looked slowly back at his son. 'Before the earth shook, on that last day of his life, Sirtaya held me to a promise: that you and I should talk.' He took in a deep breath, spreading his palms, gesturing for Tudha to speak next.

Tudha nodded a few times, gazing into space. 'And we have,' he replied at last. His eyes rolled round to meet Hattu's. 'Unless… there is something else you wish to ask me?'

The question hit Hattu like an unexpected jab. A burning need rose within him. To pose the infernal question: *Hatenzuwa! Tell me what happened there. Tell me why! Why did you kill Zanduhepa? And her baby? Why? Why!* He fought the urge to speak those words aloud in the way he had seen Dagon struggling to break colts in the chariot fields. It had to come from Tudha willingly. They stared at one another. Beads of sweat patrolled down Hattu's back and his tongue grew hot with the need to demand answers. Silently, he shook his head.

'Then I shall bid you goodnight,' Tudha said, rising.

Hattu sighed, dropping his head into his hands.

Aeneas, arriving back at the bench with bread and two small cups of watered wine, shot a look at the departing Tudha and deduced what was going on. 'He snarled at me earlier for breathing too noisily,' he said with a weak chuckle, offering Hattu a cup. 'I think it is his way of mourning for Sirtaya.'

Hattu took and swigged at the drink – harsher than the joining wine. 'It may well be, but he has been like this with me for a long, long time now.'

'Since…'

'Aye,' Hattu replied quickly, so Aeneas didn't have to mention the name of the infernal forest land where it had all begun.

The pair took a stroll around the edge of the wedding dance. Hattu glanced over the rag-tag of soldiery in the citadel, unsettled by the lack of numbers. They halted at the Scaean Gate, open and with a perfect view across the lower city. Holding Troy would be one challenge, but driving off the enemy, breaking these chains of famine and deprivation was another entirely. Out there in the countryside the enemy camp – a crescent of torchlight – smirked at Troy like a wrathful god.

'The Ahhiyawans remain strong, despite rampant plague, despite all their losses, despite the quarrels within their tent city,' said Aeneas. 'It seems that Agamemnon simply will not give up,' he sighed. 'Can he not see for himself? The city is no longer a prize. What drives him like this?'

'He does not seek plunder and treasure,' Hattu replied. 'The prize he pursues is redemption. A prize he will never have.'

'I don't understand?' Aeneas said.

Hattu looked at the Dardanian Prince. He was intelligent, and would comprehend the sorry tale of Agamemnon's daughter well enough. But what good would it do to share the depressing story, he mused. 'It matters not. Agamemnon is no longer the greatest concern. It is the Ithacan who motivates and organises their armies now.'

'Odysseus?'

'Aye,' Hattu said. 'For ten years Troy has endured Agamemnon's blunt attacks. Now, the Island King's every move will be misleading, every attack lateral. It was he who stole the Palladium, he who diverted the river, he who helped arrange the ambush on Tenedos. And he has only just begun.'

'The man fights a battle of wits,' Aeneas said, biting his bottom lip in frustration.

Hattu stared out at the crescent camp with Aeneas. *Aye*, he thought, *and he is winning.*

***

Odysseus sat on a log at the edge of the crescent camp, sipping slowly on a water skin, gazing up at the glow of torchlight from the acropolis of Troy. The self-inflicted bruises and cuts around his eyes and nose still smarted. All for nothing. Taking the Palladium statuette had neither wrecked Trojan morale nor stirred Ahhiyawan spirits to new and great heights. Nor, he thought with a chuckle, had it suddenly started shooting lightning at the Trojan defenders – as Neoptolemus had hoped it might. Diverting the Scamander had been back-breaking work, but the Trojans had found a way to draw fresh water – and the attempt to ambush the Tenedos expedition had been thwarted. Even the shaking earth – the work of the Gods – had failed to breach Troy. *Still* he and his countrymen remained encamped on this wretched plain. All the while he thought of the reports from the new Ahhiyawan soldiers who had arrived last moon.

*The wandering hordes descended from the north like locusts, and their boats landed in droves at the same time. They pulled down the village pickets and butchered the people so they might feed their many mouths from those villages' paltry stores. Town after town has fallen like this.*

He thought of his chat with Hattu on the sand, the Hittite King's words coming back to him. *I came to offer Agamemnon a chance to end this war peaceably...*

The gruff laughter of Diomedes and Menelaus split the night air behind him, and it reminded him that the multitudes here, whether led by him or by Agamemnon, were lost in this madness too. There could be no amicable end to this.

His eyes swept over Troy again and again. Maybe the war could not be ended with words as Hattu had hoped, but perhaps it could be quick? All he needed was a way in. The shore tunnel had been in-filled. The gates were stolidly barred. The walls were cracked and listing but standing nonetheless.

His eyes ran up and down the defences once more. The western section was as always tempting, lower and less sound in its construction – vulnerable to a siege machine. But the slope, the damned slope, meant getting a device up there would be beyond the ram-makers in the camp. Even if they could get a device up that slope to those walls then break into the lower city, were it to make it up to the citadel and its sacred Scaean Gate… what then? For those obnoxiously well-crafted citadel defences would laugh at the Ahhiyawan rams. Even his erstwhile hope that Mardukal the Assyrian siege master could build something to outwit those ramparts now seemed doubtful. For surely no hulk of timber on wheels could. In any case, Agamemnon and many others would never accept the arrival of an Assyrian to win them the war. Most would rather see Mardukal arrive and fail. Something about the that absurdity snagged in his mind.

Behind him, two swords struck together in mock-battle. Yet Odysseus heard nothing of the drunken laughter and storytelling going on around the display, for his thoughts were drifting, back through the years… to his childhood.

*Everyone knew the strongman of Ithaca. He was fast, powerful, the best at everything. He spent his days at the exercise field and his nights in the bayside tavern, enjoying the adoring looks of women and the envious gazes of men. He owned just two things: a fine villa and a silver sword of great value – a blade so great that nobody possessed enough riches to buy it. This meant he had little spare wealth with which to buy or barter for other things. 'I have a home but can't even afford a damned slave!' he would groan, teeth wet with wine.*

*One day a beggar came to the tavern, and challenged the strongman to a contest of strength and speed: to bring a gannet's egg from the cliffs at the isle's northern edge. If he won, the beggar wanted the strongman's silver-hilted sword. If he lost, he would surrender himself as a slave to the eternal service of the strongman. 'First one to pop the egg in this here vessel,' the beggar had said, planting a clay cup on the table, the sides marked with a Gorgon head. The strongman had roared himself hoarse with laughter at first, and so too did the crowds who hung around his sides, fawning over him. It was only later that he noticed the beggar was still there at the end of the table, waiting for an answer.*

*The contest had taken place the next day. The strongman turned up near the cliffs, applauded by the gathered crowds but suffering a pounding head and a dry mouth from all the wine. It made little difference, for although the beggar lurched quickly over to the base of the cliff, he could not climb more than a few steps up the rock without sliding down gracelessly, his tunic riding up to unveil his bare and unwashed buttocks. The strongman whimpered with laughter at this, taking his time to stretch and drink plenty of water. When he set to the climb, he was like a spider. When he reached the top, all the onlookers cheered as he held aloft a pale egg like a trophy. Down he came and just as skilfully too, past the scratched, shaking and grumpy beggar who had not managed to climb more than his own height.*

*'I should have known I was no match for you,' the beggar sighed.*

*The crowds followed the laughing strongman back into the tavern, singing and cheering. He planted the egg on the table and began draining the celebratory wine cups planted before him. 'Hold on,' he slurred after a time, 'where's my new slave got to?'*

*'Slave? Oh I don't think so,' the beggar answered calmly. All looked to the scrawny man at the end of the table, all watching agog as he lifted the egg and placed it carefully in the gorgon cup. 'I'll have your sword now,' he grinned.*

*'No, I won,' the strongman complained.*

*'No, you assumed you had won,' the beggar corrected him.*

*The strongman wailed and complained, but none could dispute the beggar had been the one to place the egg in the cup, fulfilling the bet.*

*'I know a good merchant from Egypt,' said the beggar. 'He will be able to sell your sword. With the proceeds, I will buy from you your house. I will allow you to continue to live in it, of course... for I will need a slave.'*

*There had been a moment of stunned silence, then the most thunderous round of laughter and applause as the crowds congregated around the beggar, drifting away from the strongman... thereafter known as the fool of Ithaca.*

Slowly, Odysseus rose from the log and took a final swig of water. He walked through the camp, acknowledging the salutes and throaty shouts of the soldiery. Arriving at Agamemnon's hut, the guards there simply stepped aside, neither any longer bothering to wait for Agamemnon's permission to let him in. Inside it reeked of stale nepenthe wine. Agamemnon sat in a weak bubble of tallow candle light, a stinking heap on his throne. His robes were stained with stew slops and his eyes were black-ringed with drunken stupor and lack of sleep.

'*Wanax,*' Odysseus said, 'I have a plan…'

# CHAPTER 21

## EYES OF BLOOD

Hattu and Dagon walked the lower city wall circuit as they did most mornings, with Andor wheeling overhead. At this early hour, the heat was tolerable, and the sun's glare softer. They passed a small squadron of ten soldiers, who straightened and saluted the pair as they passed. One of them was a child, face stained with smoke, wearing the dented armour his dead father had fought in. There was a woman with them too – not an Amazon, but a grey-haired Trojan widow, wearing a tattered leather helmet that had once belonged to her husband. She held a spear and a crude wooden shield made from broken-down furniture and wore a granite look of defiance. He noticed that the squadron was gathered nearby a brazier upon which a scrawny joint of meat crackled and spat. Hattu knew there were no livestock left in the city. He recalled the mocking gossip of one wine-supping nobleman: *They're like vermin down in the slums, living in rubble... even eating dogs!*

He swept his gaze up towards the citadel. The joke was turning on those rich types. The high villas up there were now but dull and grey stone and chipped remnants of colour, the precious metals stripped away to pay the more restless of the allies. Even the columns of speckled blue and green marble were coated in dust, neglected, cracked thanks to the earth tremor. Likewise those upper city defences teetered at awkward angles, sporting dark fractures, partly-fallen battlements and listing towers. Only the very highest residences – those immediately beside Priam's palace – remained relatively untouched. But how long before the invisible beast of war began chewing at that last islet of health?

At least, he thought, remembering Paris' smouldering corpse, the Shadow of Troy was dead and gone. Now they were fighting only on one front – albeit a huge and imbalanced one. He and Dagon had yet again reorganised what remained of the Trojan Army in the last few weeks, establishing new squadrons and assigning each to watch a section of these outer walls. Each squadron was of one origin: either Trojan, Dardanian, Lukkan, Elamite, Amazon, Masan, Thracian or from the Seha Riverland while the eighty-seven surviving Guardians functioned as a central reserve. The Guardians needed a new commander, now that Paris was gone. King Priam, mute and disinterested, had delegated the matter to Deiphobus. Deiphobus had dithered and delegated to Hattu. Hattu had appraised the Guardians briefly but carefully, selecting a lantern-jawed fellow named Polydamas – an old war mastiff whom he remembered from Kadesh, and one not associated with any of the grim acts some of the other Guardians had committed. Polydamas now came to him every few hours with reports on supplies and developments in enemy activity.

The pair halted at the Thymbran Gatehouse, resting their palms on the merlons to gaze out over the Scamander Plain and the Ahhiyawan crescent camp. Andor landed on the parapet beside them, chirping as she surveyed the land with them. Hattu spotted stretcher bearers carrying plague dead to an area behind the camp for burning. The champion-kings sat around the shadows at the sides of their huts, dressed in rags, overly-lean, hiding from the sun. Polydamas had earlier witnessed one minor enemy king selling his golden helm to another in exchange for meat. Hungry and plague-ridden, yet still they remained here, obstinate and determined to see Troy burn.

His smoke-grey eye ached and he noticed something: a smudge on the southern sky, far beyond the crescent camp, the Scamander and the Borean Hills… somewhere out at sea. Gulls massing, circling, moving slowly. Following something.

'What's this?' Dagon cooed.

'A ship, heading to the city of boats,' Hattu guessed.

'There have been no new arrivals for some time,' said Dagon, his voice tight with suspicion.

*More reinforcements?* Hattu lamented inwardly. How much more heavily could the odds be stacked? A notion arose and cavorted through his thoughts like a dancing spectre: that he and his party might slip out of Troy, somehow, and be gone from this place before the inevitable came – back home to the sides of those who mattered. Unconsciously, he brought the goat figurine from his purse, stroking it with the pad of his thumb. Feeling a streak of guilt, he glanced sidelong at Dagon, and saw how he toyed with his silver horse pendant, likewise lost in his own thoughts of distant family. The two shared a look, each understanding the other's anguish. There were doubtless many more trapped in the city who were tormented with the idea of escape.

Dagon tucked his horse pendant inside the collar of his robe. 'Thank the Gods we are more resolute than Chryses, eh?' he said.

Hattu put his goat figurine away likewise, thinking of the rotund Priest of Apollo. A dry laugh tumbled from his lips. 'Chryses. The wretched bastard. He made good his escape alright,' he said glibly, 'right out of Troy and all the way to the Dark Earth.'

The apparently fat, slow-moving priest had one night stolen a sackload of what remained in Priam's treasure vault. Next, he had sneaked onto the citadel's northern walls, thrown a rope over the side and rappelled his way down the gnarly limestone bluff that overlooked the Bay of Troy. Impressive, until he had lost his footing and his grip on the rope. The Guardians spotted his fat corpse the next day, hanging like a wet garment over the spar of one of the rotting, disused galleys by the wharf side. The golden rings and bracelets from his treasure sack lay scattered across the dock and the sands, winking and glittering in the sunlight. This was enough to tempt a few sentries to break curfew and rush from the Bay Gate's hatch door and down to the waterside to try to reclaim the riches. A party of Ahhiyawans hiding behind rocks nearby had rushed out to slay these guards. They took the treasure for themselves – or as much of it as they could pick up under a light rain of arrows from Troy's walls, before tossing torches upon the remaining seaworthy ships and fleeing.

Dagon laughed bitterly, a sound that slid into a heavy sigh. 'Why did we come here, Hattu?'

'To fulfil the oath of the Hittite Empire, as Troy's overlord and protector.'

'That's not what we spoke of on the wagon when we were on the road. We spoke of comrades, brothers. But some of the things we've seen here… '

Hattu thought of the atrocities witnessed during this struggle. Poison, rape, murder, torture, unforgivable greed, desecration of corpses. Those were things he had always attributed to 'the enemy', but in these few months at Troy, they had been shared sins. He looked over the lower city and the starving huddles, then up at the citadel grounds and its elites. Yes, the people of Troy wore unique clothes and spoke a dissimilar tongue to the Ahhiyawans, but were they truly different? Was there any kingdom, including the Empire of the Hittites, that had not sunk into the depths of depravity at some point? 'The enemy… is the war,' he said quietly.

Dagon said nothing for a moment, then nodded slowly. 'Always has been. In the Kaskan lands, at Kadesh, in the struggle for the Hittite throne.'

'I've realised since I came here that this war must be the last,' said Hattu.

'The last? Do you truly believe that?'

'It must be our ambition,' Hattu replied.

When Polydamas ascended the steps onto the gatehouse walkway to relieve the watch, saluting Hattu and Dagon, the pair left the walls and returned to their billets.

Back at Antenor's villa, Hattu and the elder enjoyed a pot of mountain tea and a chat about times past. The themes of war and home arose again and again. When he could no longer keep his eyelids open he retired to his bedchamber, lay down and drifted into a slumber, thinking again of his loved ones.

*Ishtar walked through a sunny meadow, leading a blue-dun mare by the reins. She came to him, handed him the tethers and said one word. 'Go…'*

*Entranced, he mounted the steed and heeled it into a trot. He did not look backwards to the land he was leaving, for all that mattered was what lay ahead. 'Home,' he whispered as the fresh meadow breeze brushed at his face. Through hills and fields he rode, until finally, he came to the familiar highlands of Hattusa. On a wooded tor stood Puduhepa and Ruhepa, smiling and glassy-eyed, with Kurunta standing confidently by their side, protective and watchful.*

*'My loves,' Hattu called to them.*

*Closer, closer…*

*But the beast reared up, screaming demonically. Hattu clung to the beast's neck lest he fall, only to find not skin and hair but an empty cage of bones. A skeleton horse with a mane of flames and empty eye sockets that drooled blood. It bucked and thrashed. All around it the sky turned the colour of mud, and the ground black and shining wet. Dark imitations of men rose from this inky mire, milling, screaming, clawing at one another, pulling one another's limbs and bodies apart. Hattu clung to the skeleton steed as it charged round and round through this nightmare.*

He woke, shaking. The images took an age to fade from his mind. Even then, all he could think of was Cassandra's vision: *I saw the rider. It was you, King Hattu.*

Groaning, he slid his legs from the bed. His body was damp with sweat from the balmy night. More, an infernal pounding noise sailed in through the shutters. With a croak, a stretch and a gulp of water from a bowl near his bed, he rose and belted on his kilt to step outside the villa. The noise was not from these high wards, but from somewhere beyond. So he climbed onto the roof of the Scaean Tower, edging round the giant beacon bell to take it all in. The early sun dazzled on every surface, making the lower city a maze of bright roofs and shadowy lanes, and the crescent camp a serrated sea of shabby tents as always. The noise was coming from there. 'Hammers,' he realised, now hearing the discordant rhythm of men at work in different cycles.

'It started at first light,' Aeneas said. The Dardanian Prince was sitting with one leg folded over the parapet, sharpening arrowheads.

Tudha was there too, Andor on his shoulder. 'They're building something,' he said tersely without looking at Hattu. Still flinty and cold, the vertical scar on his face now fully healed and like a line of ice.

'More rams,' Dagon suggested, arriving behind Hattu, pointing to the spot in the enemy camp where men were scurrying to and fro. 'That section there is where their engineers live. It was the same when they built their first fleet of devices.'

Aeneas seemed to relax a little. 'You think it's more rams? That just means more kindling for us to collect once they have foundered at our walls! Perhaps the great Odysseus has finally run out of ideas.'

Hattu watched the men at work. In the glare of the sun, it was hard to see exactly what they were doing. He, Dagon and Aeneas shared a small loaf of bread as they watched while Tudha sat in surly silence nearby, glaring out at the enemy camp. As the sun rose to its zenith, the heat haze made a puzzle out of the engineers' works. Only when a tall pole rose, then another with it, and a third set horizontally to join and brace the first two, did Hattu's concerns begin to rise. 'A scaffold,' he murmured.

'They're building something different,' Dagon agreed, 'something big.'

Throughout it all there was a strange voice in the air, the tone sharp and intimidating, but the words masked by the constant northerly wind. It was coming from behind the screen of scaffold, and every command seemed to be directing the rhythm of the workers.

Hours passed like this, hammers tapping constantly and saws rasping away, the strange voice issuing orders. Yet the scaffold and draped hides concealed the enemy works annoyingly well. Eventually, Tudha batted the parapet with one hand. 'What is it? Gods, this is infuriating! More torturous than any nightmare I can remember.'

'That is the only power Odysseus holds over us,' Hattu said. 'This show of industry might be his latest ruse – nothing more than sights and sounds to cause us to dream up the most terrible conclusions, to second-guess ourselves. To drive us mad with terror.' Yet for all the confidence of his words, he sensed it was more than a mere show.

Days slid past. One day, exhausted by the sheer tension of watching, waiting, Hattu wondered if he was going mad. He slid down to sitting, back to the parapet, body coated in its thin shade, leaving Tudha, Aeneas and Dagon to observe the strange works. He massaged his temples and rubbed his eyes with balled fists. In his mind he heard many chattering voices of people present and long dead: Kurunta One-eye berating him for sitting down on duty; his father scorning him for not being able to see the latest enemy ploy; Pudu and Ruhepa weeping and begging him to come home. And then he heard another voice. Real this time. The voice out there, directing the works. He realised the Wind of Wilusa had fallen still for the first time in an age, and now he could hear the lungfuls of instruction, the accent trilling and refined... but not in the Ahhiyawan tongue.

'Who is that?' Aeneas muttered.

Hattu's eyes pinged open. He shuffled onto his knees and turned back to the parapet, staring out at the enemy works again.

On the voice went. Hattu now recalled his days of youth in old Ruba's scribal classroom.

'He's speaking… Akkadian,' Tudha said, getting there first. 'With an Assyrian twang.'

Dagon dropped his drinking skin. 'What?'

Aeneas squinted. 'Assyrians, here? Have you had too much sun?'

'He's right,' Hattu said. 'Listen.' All fell quiet, hearing the continued babble. Every line was followed by a low murmur of another voice translating into the Ahhiyawan tongue. Hattu stood tall now, recalling what he and Dagon had seen a few days ago – signs of a new boat arriving at the enemy ship camp. The continued bleating of the voice sent his mind spinning. He had heard it before, he realised, years ago in the halls of Ashur during a diplomatic visit to Assyria. A shiver shuddered up his spine, horrible in the sapping heat as he remembered what he had heard in Agamemnon's hut that very first day he had arrived at this war.

*If we can finally bring our army to the foot of Troy's walls then what better man to show us how to break them apart than Mardukal?*

'Mardukal… Odysseus has brought Mardukal here.'

'Mardukal?' Aeneas scowled.

'An Assyrian siege general,' Hattu said. His head swam and throbbed. How long had these works been going on? How long might it take Mardukal to produce something that even Troy's walls could not withstand? *Damn you, Odysseus,* he cursed silently towards the enemy camp.

Commander Polydamas, standing near enough to hear, said: 'Assyrian, eh? Well, Troy's walls might not be as tall as some of those out in his lands,' he looked up and around the defences, 'but they are of stronger foundation, thicker too, aye?'

Hattu, Dagon, Aeneas and Tudha shared looks. Hattu wanted to reply confidently, but knew he could not. He thought of Mardukal's reputation. The Breaker of Walls. The Leveller of Cities. 'I must speak with King Priam,' he said tersely. 'Dagon, you have command of the walls.'

He descended into the citadel in a blur, striding over to and inside the palace, the two Guardians there parting. The megaron throne hall was a different place now. Statues of the Trojan Gods stared down on him, the paint flaking and chipped. The walls, once striped with purple drapes, were bare; the bright patterns and hunting scenes painted upon them looked bald and pale without those sumptuous cloths, the room more echoey, less meaningful. The fineries and furniture had long since gone for firewood, repairs, and to make new arrows and crude board shields. There were no other guards inside, so sparse was the Trojan manpower. Upon the throne at the hall's end sat a lonely figure.

'King of Troy!' Hattu called out. The words echoed and bounced down the long hall. Priam did not stir or reply. As Hattu approached, he saw in Priam a reflection of Agamemnon. Staring at the floor. Broken by loss and regret. 'Majesty, the situation has changed.'

Priam's eyes swam lazily up to regard Hattu. 'Ah, *Labarna*, you have arrived at last?' He smiled eerily, shuffling and rising from the royal seat, spreading his arms high and wide to an audience of ghosts. 'The Great King of the Hittites is here with his endless ranks. Troy is saved!' he croaked with a strange trill that was both joyous and sorrowful at once.

'Majesty?' Hattu said sharply, cocking his head to one side.

Priam whumped back down on his throne, laughing gently now, muttering away to himself. 'We will organise the battalions of Troy tomorrow. Hektor and Paris will work with you like the prongs of Poseidon's trident.'

Hattu did well to disguise his unease.

'With your twenty thousand men, the battle will be swift,' Priam clapped and rubbed his hands together weakly. 'But that is for tomorrow. On this glorious night… we must feast!'

Hattu glanced to the high windows of the hall, streaming with daylight.

'The feast will begin soon,' Hekabe spoke calmly, appearing from the side of the hall. She climbed the plinth steps and enclosed Priam's hands in hers, then planted a kiss on his forehead. Her face was beatific and loving, until she turned away from her husband and descended the stairs towards Hattu, and then her features fell like a stone. 'Walk with me,' she said quietly, guiding him back down the hall.

'King Priam is not himself,' Hattu opened.

'He has grown ever more witless with grief since the night of Paris' funeral. I awoke that night to find the bed empty by my side. I searched the palace for him.' She paused and gulped. 'I found him on his knees… hovering over the tip of his own sword.'

Hattu's heart plunged.

'The people of Troy cannot see him for what he has become,' Hekabe fretted. 'It would be the end.'

'You should stay with him,' Hattu said, looking back at the slumped Priam. 'But you should know that things have taken a grave turn. The Ahhiyawans have brought a great Assyrian siege general to their ranks. A man named Mardukal. He is famed for his ability to crack open cities and-'

'Can you hold the walls, King Hattu?' she asked plainly.

Hattu felt his lips move, wondered if he could let a lie slide from them.

'If you think you cannot then you must tell me now… give me a chance to lead the innocents of my city to safety.'

'There is no way out, My Queen. The enemy have all of the outer gates covered, the Springhouse passageway is in-filled and the boats at the wharf are all charred, sunken ruins.'

'*Labarna!*' A cry reverberated down the throne hall.

Hattu and Hekabe's heads snapped towards the doors. Commander Polydamas was there with two Guardians, beckoning madly.

Hattu grabbed Hekabe's hands. 'Stay here, stay with Priam.'

With that, he strode to the door, breaking into a run halfway when he saw the look on Polydamas' old face: moon-eyed, streaked with sweat. 'They… they're coming. *It's* coming.'

'It? What is *it*?'

The floor shivered then as, somewhere outside, horns moaned – first low like angry bulls, then high like trumpeting elephants. Again and again, curdling the air. Hattu and Polydamas scrambled outside, loping to the Scaean Tower and flitting up the steps. 'It's a monstrosity. It's taller than a tree…' Polydamas wailed behind him as they went.

Bursting onto the Scaean turret roof, Hattu slammed against the outer parapet to rejoin Tudha, Dagon and Aeneas. His eyes swept across the Scamander plain and the crescent camp: the Ahhiyawans were at arms in a great mass. The troops up in the Thorn Hill camp on the Silver Ridge had come down to join them. Then his gaze locked onto the site of the secretive works. The final poles of the scaffold were being tugged away, revealing all.

Hattu's heart pumped so hard in his chest he thought it might smash through his ribs. The device was truly gargantuan: a ram-house the size of a barrack fort – the bronze-capped log peeking from within many times the girth and length of those used before – all resting on four huge solid wooden wheels. Stretching upwards from the front of the ramming house was a 'neck' – a war tower, capped with a 'head' decorated to look like that of a nightmarish battle horse, with eyes painted bright crimson as if leaking blood, a mane of scarlet cloth and orange ribbons that rippled and flailed like flames, and a gaping mouth, from which lolled a long, solid bronze pole, tipped with a vicious siege hook. The whole thing was draped heavily in hide sheets – like flaps of decaying skin.

He glanced sideways along the defences to see the black-robed Cassandra, transfixed by the thing. Her nightmare was alive. All apart from one thing: *he* was not the rider of this siege horse. Instead, it was the silk-robed Assyrian, Mardukal, standing on a covered platform upon the battle-horse's back surrounded by a dense pack of Locrian archers. He screeched over the ongoing chorus of keening horns. 'Go forth, mighty stallion. Tear proud Troy's walls asunder. Carve open their treasure vaults and crush the Trojans like ants!'

With an angry whine of bronze and groan of timber, the horse rocked forward on its wheels, driven by teams of men inside the ram house and helped by others swarming around its base.

'Hattu,' Dagon croaked. 'That thing…'

'I know,' Hattu replied. Both had fought in the east. Both had seen Assyrian 'siege horses' like these, and what they could do. Neither had seen one as colossal as this. Andor circled out there above the swaying device, shrieking madly.

'*Forward!*' the Ahhiyawan warrior kings boomed, spurring the tide of infantry forth too.

Hattu's eyes darted across the mass advance and its gargantuan centrepiece. All coming straight for Troy. For the Thymbran Gates, he thought. Those fortified doors had weathered everything until now. But could they possibly withstand this monstrous thing? Yes, they can hold… *will* hold, he told himself.

That was when Mardukal shrieked some new order, and the horse groaned, veering away at an angle towards the Bay of Troy. Like a murmuration of starlings the soldiers folded in behind it. His eyes crept along the path the horse was taking. 'The slope… the western walls,' he burred. 'It's going for the weak section.'

'Even Troy's weakest points are strong enough to resist any war engine,' Prince Deiphobus said confidently, arriving beside the others.

'You do not know Mardukal,' Dagon countered.

'Commander,' Hattu said to Polydamas, 'organise a skeleton guard up here to watch the citadel, then send every other man down to the western walls to join me there. Dagon, Prince Aeneas, with me.' He halted for an instant, seeing Tudha left standing alone. There was no time for deliberations, every man was needed. '*Tuhkanti*, you too.'

They tumbled from the citadel and sped down the Scaean Way, breaking right and along the wide street that led to the western defences. Cats and dogs scattered from his path and the people gawped.

They sprinted up the stone steps onto the battlements of the old, thin section of walls adjoining the Bay Gate. The few sentries posted there were riveted by the enemy movements. 'They can't bring that thing up here, can they?' one sentry asked, his voice almost childlike.

Hattu glanced along the sweeping walkway of Troy's lower city walls: so many defenders were strung along that great length while the enemy was coming here to this one point. It was what he had demanded of them, to stand at their posts and never leave them. Now, everything had changed. He cupped his hands to his mouth and bawled: 'All soldiers to the western walls!' Dagon waved his arms, echoing the order, and Tudha took a triton horn from a hook on the battlements and blew five short hard notes. The squadrons all along the distant sections of the walls now swarmed towards these western defences.

The archers arrived first – Aeneas' Dardanians and three squadrons of Thracians. 'Bowmen,' Hattu demanded, 'loose at will.' The gathering marksmen rattled into place, falling to one knee, nocking, drawing, bows creaking. With a whistle and thrum, shafts leapt up and plunged down upon the encroaching Ahhiyawan mass. They raised shields and wide wicker screens to catch many of these arrows, but still groans and grunts rang out. Men of every country fell – Spartans, Mycenaeans, Cretans, Tiryneans, Ithacans and more. In reply, the packed mob of Locrian marksmen on the siege horse's back nocked, drew and loosed as one, sending a shower of arrows back at the western walls, concentrated upon the Amazon squadron just arriving there. The volley was lethal, wiping out dozens and injuring many more of that small band of warrior-women.

As the horse reached the southwestern edge of Troy and rocked round to face up the western slope, Hattu saw the thing in its true proportions. The head was taller than Troy's outer walls. But it was the wheels that would be the decisive factor. He crouched between two merlons, peeking out as arrows whizzed past him, one scuffing against the mud-brick defences and sending a puff of loam-coloured dust into the air. The front wheels were well-designed, broad so as to spread what was the surely terrific weight of the thing evenly across the ground. But between the wooden horse and Troy lay the ditch, and those wheels were simply not big enough to span that furrow. His eyes narrowed, staring at the loose earth near the ditch edge, already crumbling as the horse approached. His heart slowed, his fingers clenched into fists, as if grabbing hold of the hopes that the device would founder and pitch over, grabbing hold and clinging on desperately.

'Drop timbers,' Mardukal screeched.

Somewhere on the siege device, an axe *thocked*, ropes whizzed, and then two huge panels of strapped wood toppled forward from the horse's shoulders, like a drawbridge descending. As the two walkways whumped down to span the ditch, Hattu's stomach twisted tight and his hopes evaporated. He felt like a fool for daring to dream that Mardukal, the Smasher of Walls, would have designed this without getting it exactly right. The horse swayed forth; the plank walkways strained... but the device rocked safely on over to the far side of the ditch. All the while, Mardukal's archers showered the western defences constantly, keeping the Trojan archer squadrons there at bay, allowing the Ahhiyawan footsoldiers to flood across the twin walkways in the horse's wake.

Hattu could see the Assyrian siege general clearly now, his long dark curls and beard billowing in the breeze, his blue silk gown fluttering. His eyes and teeth flashed white as he spotted Hattu and cried to the defenders. 'So it is true: the *Labarna* of the Hittites is here, trapped with all the other Trojan rats.' He pointed a ring-encrusted finger at Hattu. 'You have some history with my Assyrian kinsmen, King Hattu. Many scores to be settled. Remember Saruc the torturer? Before he perished, Saruc taught me his methods. I know how to boil a man's head for days on end, while keeping him alive. I have a crushing device here with me – a heavy metal wheel – that I can expertly and slowly drive across a man's body, crushing him piece by piece.'

Hattu heard men around him gasping in horror. He felt the same fears sink into him like fangs of fire. But he strained to fend them off, to keep his mind clear. The horse had to be beaten. He thought of the smaller rams that had tried to attack before. Those that had tried to climb this rough and steep western slope had foundered, and this siege horse was at the very foot of that climb. He watched the siege horse's wheels turn, mouthing words of prayer, visualising them slipping on scree, the whole thing driving itself into a hopeless rut... but the wheels did not slip, the serrated rims biting confidently into the earth and the whole thing rising uphill steadily, side on to Troy's defences. The trench had been bridged. The slope would not stop it. The enemy was coming for these decrepit walls. Suddenly, Hattu felt acutely aware of the fact that he was wearing nothing but kilt and cloak. He snatched a Trojan bronze sword from a rack, that would have to do – no time to don armour, he realised, for the horse was only a short way from reaching the Bay Gates. One last hope, he realised – the thing that had beaten the rams that had tried to batter down the Thymbran Gate. *Fire!*

'Masturi,' Hattu roared, seeing the Seha Riverland King hurrying along the battlements, arriving at the western walls. He and his men were closest to the siege machine. 'Light your arrows, rain fire on that thing.' Within moments, the Seha Riverlanders had blazing shafts nocked and aimed.

'Loose!' Hattu bellowed.

Every Trojan watched as the fiery barrage sped down upon the ascending siege horse. These arrows whacked into the hides and timbers. The flames crept upwards like hungry tongues. Mardukal's face flagged from within his covered platform. 'Now, the resin pots,' Hattu yelled. A dozen clay pots were hurled at the siege horse. They exploded against its sides, the black resin splashing, staining the thing's hide-covered flanks. With a burst of blinding orange, the sticky filth caught light.

Hattu's eyes widened…

'Yes…' Aeneas hissed by his side.

…and then the flames sloughed from the thing like water separating from oil. The blazing resin slapped onto the ground in burning piles, engulfing a few handfuls of enemy troops down there, but leaving the siege horse undamaged.

The next waft of the warm breeze brought with it a sharp stink. Hattu's nose wrinkled, seeing the glistening wetness of the hides. Mardukal's laughter rang out over Troy.

'Vinegar,' Aeneas croaked. 'He's soaked the hides in vinegar.'

Hattu beat a fist against the parapet, confounded.

Dagon scuttled over beside him, a bow in hand, moving low to stay within the protection of the crenelations. He risked a look over then ducked down again when a sling bullet blasted away the top of the merlon. 'Hattu, we need to hold that monstrosity back. If it reaches these gates….'

Hattu's mind spun crazily. What other arrows remained in the quiver? 'Bring the bee hives,' he said.

'And the heated sand,' Dagon agreed. The Chariot Master sped away, calling some Lukkans with him as he hurried back down into the city and to the nearest armoury.

'Masturi,' Hattu called to the Seha Riverland king.

Masturi ducked under a speeding arrow, then crouched beside Hattu just as the siege horse's horrific head juddered up level with the gatehouse battlements then rose above, casting its shadow down across them. 'That thing…'

'I know. Listen, we're going to try everything to hold it back,' he paused, thinking of Hekabe's plea, 'but I need you to prepare for the worst.'

Masturi's face sagged.

'The streets of the lower city are packed with people – starving, weak. If the Ahhiyawans break inside, those families will be killed like sheep. But the enemy have put everything into this assault on the Bay Gate. The Dardanian Gate over on the far side of the city and the Silver Ridge beyond are clear. Take a band of men, herd the lower city people to the eastern wards and be ready… *if* this gate falls, take them out through the Dardanian Gate, into the countryside and into hiding.

'But you need me here. You need every man here,' Masturi complained as, beside them, a kneeling Trojan archer rose a fraction to shoot, only to be hit in the throat by an enemy sling bullet that threw him back from the walls in a shower of blood that soaked the pair and all nearby.

Hattu grabbed his forearm. 'I need you to do this, friend. Why are we here, if not to save the families of Troy?'

Masturi sucked in a breath, nodding, his chest swelling. 'Aye, it will be done,' he said, then backed towards the steps and flitted down into the city streets, calling a band of his Riverlanders with him.

The siege horse rocked and swayed up the final stretch of the slope, then bent round to face Troy's weakest and oldest entry point, hundreds of warriors vying to lend their shoulder to the efforts of the crew driving the thing.

'Raze these gates,' Mardukal screamed, 'raze them to dust!' The enemy masses exploded in a feverish roar, parting to allow the horse to sway closer to the Bay Gate. Only a handful of strides shy.

At just that moment, Dagon and the Lukkans came back with three pots of glowing sand and a stretcher loaded with bee hives.

'Up, up!' Hattu cried, rising from behind the merlons, waving every other up likewise. 'Hold them back, with everything.' He and Dagon moved onto the Bay Gate walkway and helped throw consignments of heated sand over the parapet. This whumped down on the extra warriors helping push the thing. A horrible chorus of screaming and sizzling arose and many fell away. The horse slowed for a moment – only for hundreds more men to take the place of the fallen ones. Once more the siege horse swayed towards the gates. The Lukkans threw down the hives now, and chaos erupted once more, men running in fright or rolling on the ground screaming, plagued by angry bees. Yet more soldiers came to take their place. Aeneas marshalled the archers into a constant rain of arrows, felling many more enemy soldiers… yet on the horse came.

'Bring arrows, spears, rocks, everything,' Hattu called over his shoulder to the men in the streets who were ferrying weapons and armaments to the defenders. That was when the bronze 'tongue' of the siege horse struck out. It was more like the tongue of a gecko – a great hooked bronze blade that stabbed forth onto the parapet, striking and casting away three Thracians as if they were flies. Screaming, they plunged to their deaths in the streets below.

Hattu saw within the horse's mouth the team of men holding this siege hook. He saw the bloodshot eyes and grinning yellow teeth, heard their grunts as they levered the hook up sharply to one side, bringing the pole sweeping along the merlons with a *rat-tat-tat* sound, the hook streaking across the battlement walkway at chest height, clearing the defences of men. It ripped two Lukkans apart and was coming straight for Tudha. Hattu elbowed his heir to one side and then dived under the hook end.

Now the pole slowed and retracted, the hook end catching on one merlon.

'Puuuuull!' someone cried from within the mouth.

*Crunch!* The hook jerked backwards this time, ripping away the merlon and pulling structural timbers with it. Dust ballooned up over Hattu and the defenders, blinding, choking. There was a strange and short hiatus until it cleared. Hattu blinked at the huge gap in the teeth of the defences… and then the hook struck forth again, this time gouging into the walkway itself, ripping, shredding through the baked mud, hauling away the struts and posts. Hundreds of cracks sped across the narrow battlement. Hattu felt the whole thing shift under his feet. One crack began to widen and darken. He felt the parapet listing, heard the compromised timbers within groaning… 'Get off the walkway,' he croaked.

'But *Labarna*, the siege horse ram will reach the gates if we don't stay up here to resist it.'

'*Get off the walkway,*' Hattu roared, shouldering the one who had spoken towards the nearest of the two flanking turrets, shoving Tudha and Dagon too. Weapons were cast down as men darted towards this turret and the other. The hook smashed down on the spot where Hattu had been standing, destroying the defences there. As they bowled into the thin shell of safety within the turret room, the entire structure shuddered wildly. From behind them, a great thunderous moan rose as the gatehouse walkway disintegrated, the terrible sound punctuated by the shrill screams of a Lukkan trio who were too slow.

In the shade and cool of the turret interior, all shot looks at one another, all knowing what was coming. The defences had been cleared of men and smashed away. Only the gates themselves stood in the horse's way.

'Rammers… heave!' Mardukal cried gleefully.

Another moment of strange silence and stillness, and then…

*Crash!*

The turret shuddered crazily, dust spewing and fragments of mud plaster toppling down around them.

*Crash!*

This time with the sound of splintering wood. The Bay Gate's locking bar.

Hattu met Dagon's eyes. He knew his oldest friend was thinking the same thing: *The gate will not hold. The lower city is doomed.*

'Outside,' he barked to all in the turret. They funnelled down the narrow stairwell and spilled out into the harsh light of the afternoon, just in time for the next strike of the mighty ram.

*Crash!*

A cloud of splinters showered them, and the bronze-capped tip of the ram pierced a small hole through the gates, like the finger of a sadistic killer pointing at its next victim. The gates were buckling either side of this clear breach. They had two more strikes, Hattu knew, maybe three, and the Bay Gates would be gone. He glanced down the streets behind and either side of him: no sign of the huddled families. They were gone from the city, safe – Masturi had done his job. The main avenues aside, the streets of Troy were tight and maze-like. In the moons spent here, he had often considered how he might marshal a defence within that labyrinth should it come to it: archers hiding on roofs; men springing from doorways to ambush the enemy; dead-end traps. But the numbers were far too few to contemplate that now, and the siege horse would be headed to one place and one place only.

'Fall back to the citadel,' he roared.

*Crash!*

The gates bulged inwards, every plank part-shredded now.

'Move, get back!' Dagon howled to the men spilling out from the opposite gate turret and those draining down the stairs from the abutting walls.

'Pull back!' Aeneas cried, reinforcing the order.

Trojans, Lukkans, Dardanians, Thracians, Seha Riverlanders and smatterings of Elamites, injured Amazons and Masans staggered down the broad street that led towards the Scaean Way, choking on the dust blowing from the collapsed gatehouse walkway, shielding their eyes from it, their armour dull with it. Arrows and slingshot arced down from outside, catching many in the back. They tumbled and fell with dull grunts, blood spraying.

*Crash!*

This time it was like thunder rolling from faraway and passing right overhead. Hattu glanced back, seeing the gates burst open then fall from their hinges in pieces, utterly ruined. In the void where the gates and the walkway had been, the demonic siege horse stood like a gloating giant, red eyes blazing in the sunlight, fiery mane whipping in the hot wind, glaring along the way at the fleeing defenders. Around its base, the armies of Ahhiyawa broiled like a sea of glinting bronze, their cheering rolling into the city like breakers on a shore. Hattu felt time slow as the enemy kings led the surge through the breach: Diomedes, Agamemnon, Neoptolemus and old Nestor. No Odysseus or Menelaus in this front line. Behind them came the masses of men who had waited ten years for this chance to storm Troy.

He noticed something then: most were grubby, pitted with plague scars, spotted with shiny boils and gaunt with hunger. Even the kings – once like golden lions – looked like jackals now; dull, dented and scruffy versions of their former selves. Old Nestor's feather headdress was tangled and many quills were broken. Neoptolemus' bright armour was dull and dented, badly repaired. Diomedes moved with a limp, his shield ragged around the edges and the painted cyclops emblem all but scratched off. The banners and battle totems they carried were threadbare. Desperate men. Dangerous men. So many of them.

'Move!' he cried, pushing and shoving those defenders who lagged, lending an arm to one Amazon with an arrow in her thigh. The noise of the pursuing enemy grew and echoed in and out of the lanes either side of the street, coming at them from every side, overtaking them and coming at them from ahead as if they were surrounded. The grinding of the siege horse's wooden wheels moving over the Bay Gate rubble and then on the flagstones reverberated through the city, sending horrible shivers up through each running man. Arrows skidded and skated around their heels, falling just short.

'Uphill, come on,' Dagon rasped, standing at the junction with the sloping Scaean Way, waving all up towards the citadel.

As soon as Hattu made that turn, the wall of noise from the invader fell away, the houses and temples on the Scaean Way shielding them from it. He craned his head up to keep the Scaean Gate in his line of sight, seeing Prince Deiphobus there on the high defences, face pale with shock. Commander Polydamas was by the open gate, urging the remnants of their army uphill, helping the first to arrive inside.

In a stupor of fatigue, he stumbled into the citadel, hearing the dull, other-worldly shouts and gasps of the rest as they flooded inside too. With a groan of timber and bronze, the mighty Scaean Gates slammed shut behind him, and a bar of bronze-strapped oak as wide as a pillar thump down to secure them. It echoed around the citadel like the final clunk of a stone lid sealing a tomb.

# CHAPTER 22

## THE CHILDREN OF APOLLO

Hattu slumped by the blue sphinx, exhausted. When a hand thrust a cup in his direction, he took it and drank like a madman, emptying the last third over his face. The water was ice cold, shocking him outside and in. Dagon and Tudha were beside him, doubled over, panting. Prince Deiphobus paced nearby, taking snippets of information from everyone, wringing his hands through his hair, his purple cloak swishing with his every nervous change of direction. The confidence he had displayed upon becoming Crown Prince of Troy was nowhere to be seen.

'The citadel is sealed. All gates are closed,' a Trojan Guardian bawled from somewhere.

'And they must not open, not for anyone,' Deiphobus croaked.

'Aye,' Hattu agreed. 'The Ahhiyawans may have the lower city, but the citadel must be like a shell now. We have not the numbers to sally or even risk a diversionary assault.'

Deiphobus approached Hattu and sank onto his haunches, lowering his voice. 'These gates will hold, won't they… against that *thing?*' For all he was a hulking man, he sounded like a frightened boy, his voice reed-thin.

Hattu stared past Deiphobus, to the Scaean Gates. The afternoon sun was winking just above the defences there. They were tall, he reckoned. Taller than the Bay Gates by a half. Thicker and heavier too, and with chunky straps of bronze on the age-blackened timbers making the whole thing one solid screen. But that ram, and the hook, and the sheer numbers out there…

Before he could answer Deiphobus, a Guardian shouted: 'They've reached the Scaean Way!'

The cacophonous din of the invaders rose again, clear and sharp, the noise tumbling uphill and crawling up and over the walls, echoing above the citadel like a screaming gale.

'Every soldier up to the defences,' Hattu said, rising to his feet, his knees and swollen ankles cracking horribly as he did so. Many of those bearing arms were lower city folk, he realised, fathers and young men. While Masturi had led their families out of Troy and to safety, these ones had stayed behind, bold and defiant, offering their lives for their sacred city. Nearby, he noticed that there were others without spears or swords or even clubs or tools of any sort. The nobles, he realised. The elites and the templefolk – standing shy of the Scaean Gate area as if it were beneath them to get involved.

Easier to teach a cat to sing than to coerce these ones to take up arms and stand with the rest, he realised. Spotting Commander Polydamas, he growled so he and the elites would hear. 'Commander, put every non-combatant to work. Have them bring out furniture, supply sacks, waste, even the statues of the Gods, and pile it all up to bolster the Scaean Gates.'

'What about the other two gatehouses?' Polydamas asked, flashing looks at the Apollonian Gate and the Thunder Gate.

'The streets leading up to them are too narrow for that siege horse to navigate, and the enemy troops have no ladders or secondary rams with which to assault those entrances. They mean to attack the Scaean Gate only. But put a squadron of men on those other gates just in case some of the Ahhiyawans bring grappling hooks and ropes.'

'It will be done, *Labarna,*' Polydamas affirmed again. 'You, you,' he barked at his Guardians, relaying the order. He clicked his fingers to a third. 'And you, bring the *Labarna* his armour.'

A moment later and a pair of Guardians were helping Hattu into his bronze jacket. He clipped on his swordbelts and cloak, took a spear from a rack, planted Hektor's helmet on his head, then climbed the stairs to the Scaean defences, Tudha, Dagon, Aeneas and Polydamas following in his wake.

As the group emerged onto the Scaean defences, Hattu regarded the Trojan force arrayed along those battlements. Apart from the allied warriors, it was once again mainly inhabitants from the lower city: pockets of men, boys and women, wounded and grubby; their shaking hands holding crude spears and cudgels; their bodies strapped with panels of timber in lieu of armour; their eyes heavy with fear and doubt.

As the approaching Ahhiyawans roared some discordant song of battle, throaty and menacing, he sensed the plummeting mood in the same way one can almost taste a thunderstorm in the air before it begins. He had known moments like this so many times before. They needed careful and confident words, a show of poise and assurance. A leader. But King Priam was adrift. His chief sons, Hektor and Paris, were dead – one a traitor anyway.

Who was left? Prince Deiphobus cut a confident figure in court or at feasts, desirous of Hattu's command, but here and now in the face of adversity he was a trembling wreck, watching on nervously from the doorway leading into the Scaean Tower stairwell. Scamandrios too – even though he was up here and armed – was meek and quiet. Priam's other sons – dozens of them by many concubines – were down at street level with the other elites, being herded by Polydamas in the effort to barricade the gates. In any case, they were a mish-mash of callow and timid types, poor speakers or drunken braggarts. He spotted Hekabe, Helen, Andromache and Cassandra watching from the palace balcony, but it was not for them to rouse the scant remains of the army of Troy.

When the defenders realised Hattu had arrived on the gatehouse battlements, a moment of silence fell, the summer wind whistling around them. So many faces, all twisted with fear and a morsel of hope that he could save them, despite the overwhelming odds. This was what it had come down to – this last stand, this final chance. If they were to have even a pale hope, he realised, they had to believe.

'Defenders of Troy,' he boomed, striding along behind them, all heads turning, watching him in awe. 'For ten years, you have known fear, hardship, hunger. So many of you have lost loved ones to this struggle. And nothing... *nothing* cuts deeper than loss.' He paused, feeling old, buried emotions rise within him. He fought them back down, caging it all within. 'It casts upon one's heart an eternal night, an endless winter.'

A groan of timbers sounded from the Scaean Way as the great siege horse swayed confidently uphill, the tide of Ahhiyawans jostling and jeering around it, packing out the wide street.

'But, every winter passes, every night ends. Yet only *you* can conjure the dawn.' He pointed at the nearest soldier – an older man from the lower city slums – then ran his finger round to point at them all. 'So think of all those dear to you who have fallen. Take strength from the love you once shared. I ask you, Children of Apollo: In this moment of darkness, stand tall and blaze golden like your archer-god.' The wind blasted his silver hair back as he drew his twin iron blades and held them high. 'Stand with me… for Troy!'

The defenders seemed to quiver for a moment. Hattu saw tears in the eyes of some, then a sea of fists pumped into the air with a rasping, desperate swell of cheering.

Just as his confidence began to swell, another strange surge of noise pierced the air. Shouting, somewhere down at the base of the citadel walls. Outside.

Hattu glanced down to the ground below these gates. Nothing. He ran his eyes eastwards, following the base of the acropolis defences, and felt his heart turn to ice and fall through his body. 'Masturi?' he croaked.

There, at the Apollonian Gate, the Seha Riverland King was with a small knot of his kinsmen, struggling to control a huge rabble of Trojans – some of the starving families of the lower city. They clamoured and beat their fists on the minor gate's barred timbers, wailing and pleading for them to be thrown open. The healers, Kelenus and his wife Tekka, were amongst them. The lone squadron of Guardians posted to watch that gate were doing nothing but gazing down upon them. The defenders up here with Hattu – some seeing family members amongst the group out there – began to murmur in distress.

Masturi spotted Hattu up on the Scaean defences. 'I'm sorry, King Hattu,' he cried, his voice echoing against the huge citadel walls. 'Most fled outside through the Dardanian Gate and into the countryside as you wished, but some were too afraid to risk it. They were afraid that the Ahhiyawans might be waiting out there. So they broke away and came flooding up here.'

From the base of the mazy lane leading up to the Apollonian Gate, a burst of noise erupted. Neoptolemus and the white-horned Myrmidons came swarming into view – a splinter force, but a deadly one. They raced uphill towards Masturi and the mass of many hundreds of Trojan citizens, who exploded in a swell of nightmarish screams. Masturi and his small knot of men turned to face the oncoming Myrmidons, putting themselves between the Trojan people and the enemy elites, hopelessly outnumbered. 'King Hattu?' Masturi cried, shooting ashen-faced glances back to Hattu and the Trojan soldiery on the Scaean defences.

'Open the Apollonian Gate!' Hattu cried across to the squadron manning the Apollonian gatehouse. His shout came in unison with scores of others around him who realised what was happening. Polydamas roared at his charges too. The squadron commander on the Apollonian Gates gazed across the walltops, past those shouting, past Hattu and Polydamas, straight at Prince Deiphobus as if he was the only man who mattered.

Deiphobus, trembling, shook his head. 'Keep those gates closed,' he wailed to the squadron.

'What are you doing?' Hattu roared at him.

'We cannot open the gates now. You said it yourself, King Hattu, we simply cannot.'

'Your people out there are going to be slaughtered like sheep if you do not,' Tudha snarled at him.

Deiphobus wrung his hands together, still shaking his head. 'Too risky… too risky. What if the attackers g-g-get inside?'

Hattu grabbed him by the collars of his purple cloak, towering a head above. 'By the God of Thunder, open those damned gates *now*, or I will throw you from these walls!'

The latest Crown Prince of Troy's lips flapped a few times, then he pursed them defiantly.

With a smash of bronze and ripping of blades carving through living meat, the Myrmidons butchered the Seha Riverlanders. From the corner of Hattu's disbelieving eye, he saw his old comrade, Masturi, being driven onto his knees on the end of Neoptolemus' spear. Six other Myrmidons lanced down into the kneeling hero, driving him to the ground, and then all of them trampled across the corpse and sliced into the families of Troy. Spurts of red leapt high, staining the Apollonian Gates. Kelenus and Tekka fell. Babies screamed and mothers howled in distress while old men tried to fight the Myrmidons with bare fists. The screaming did not last long. Soon, the throaty victory shouts of Neoptolemus and his men rose in its place, their white horns dripping red, their shells of armour glistening wet, the steam from the wounds of the ripped-open dead rising around them.

One defender near Hattu, having just witnessed his wife's slaying, sank to his knees, staring, his spear falling from his hand. Hattu saw another vomit and another weeping, tearing at his hair. The shell of morale built up by his speech now lay in pieces.

'They died so that the royal and noble lines of Troy might live on,' a weak voice spoke, snapping Hattu from his stupor. He realised he was still holding Deiphobus by the collar. The Trojan prince licked his dry lips and continued: 'Is that not a worthwhile price to p-p-pay?'

With shaking hands, Hattu shoved Deiphobus away. The crown prince flailed across the battlements and landed on his backside, tumbling head over foot and becoming entangled in his purple cloak.

'I had no ch-ch-choice,' he protested.

Hattu turned his back on the man and his bleating excuses. He gripped the battlements and beheld the horrors coming for this gate: the mighty siege horse, the red eyes and swishing mane, the lolling and devilish bronze hook tongue, the band of archers on its back protecting Mardukal, the many thousands of Ahhiyawans helping to push it up towards this, the final bastion of Troy. Closer and closer. The enemy kings moved in a slow walk behind these front lines, eyes eagerly combing the thin force up on the Scaean defences. Down in the citadel ground behind him, Hattu heard the clunk and clatter of things being heaped behind the gates. He heard voices of complaint too, seeing from the corner of his eye Laocoon the priest clinging onto his silver chest and gilded plates while Lukkans and Elamites tried to pull the things free to add to the makeshift barricade.

'Loose!' Aeneas bawled, pulling Hattu's attentions to back to the defenders up here with him. Every Trojan and allied archer on the citadel walls bent their bow skywards and together let fly a storm of shafts plunged down upon the Scaean Way. The battering of bronze tips onto shields and wicker screens sounded like a hard rain, scored with wet thuds where they found their way between, piercing necks and faces and limbs. Ahhiyawans screamed and fell in their hundreds. Another volley, another massacre. Over and over, thinning them but never by enough. The horse rocked on uphill, pricked with ever more arrows now, yet undamaged, closer and closer. Moments away now. The head was almost as tall as the huge gates, the red eyes glaring up at the Scaean walkway menacingly. Extra men flooded inside the ground level ram house for the final push, and Hattu saw flashes of those stationed inside the head getting ready to operate the bronze hook.

He heard the many murmurs around him, all asking the same question *how to stop the siege horse?* His mind flashed with crazed ideas, nonsensical, laughable… and then one which seemed less insane than the rest. The horse's lower jaw was constructed solidly of oak planks, but the upper jaw and 'skull' comprised of a lighter wood and leather canopy – strong enough only to withstand missiles, he reckoned. He glanced sideways to the Scaean Tower. Up there on its roof, a level higher than this gatehouse, the bronze bell of Troy hung – tall as a man.

The same bell that had initiated the beacon call for help to the Hittite Empire. The call that had for so long gone unanswered. He shouted over to Commander Polydamas: 'That thing. Can it be moved?'

'*Labarna?*' Polydamas said, perplexed. 'The bell? Why would-'

'*Can* it be moved?' Hattu demanded once again.

'It is huge, and heavy,' the commander began to protest.

'Good. Bring it down to this level, and the rope upon which it hangs.'

Polydamas' lips flapped as if to protest further, but Hattu gave him a look that made him think twice. 'Men, with me,' the commander called to a pair of Guardians, the trio speeding off and up the stairs.

'Rear up, mighty steed,' Mardukal crowed, throwing his hands aloft. 'Kick down this last door of Troy. Let us capture the Hittite *Labarna* and then roll his head towards the feet of King Priam. Yes, Priam! Are you listening? We will wring your body of blood in front of what family you have left. Your organs will burst one by one, and in the hottest of agonies, you will finally slip away, defeated, broken, humiliated.'

'Pull the battlements away!' a commander bawled from within the horse's head.

Hattu's eyes widened like moons as he saw the great bronze hook lurch upwards and come hacking down for the gatehouse parapet as it had done at the Bay Gate. He leapt to one side as it smashed down into the spot where he had been, decapitating a merlon. The hook then juddered sideways, the sharp tip ripping through the ribs of an old man and batting four of Aeneas' Dardanians away. Hattu hacked down at the bronze pole, but even his iron blades could do no more than notch the arm-thick rod. The pole slowed and halted, then suddenly skittered back the way it had come, mowing down a boy-soldier and a clutch of Elamites, tearing the spine from one like a needle picking out a thread. Blood wafted like a fine mist across the gatehouse. 'Heeeave!' The men inside the horse's mouth groaned with effort and hauled the pole back in, the hook catching against the base of the decapitated merlon and pulling away a huge chunk of the battlement. Seven defenders fell with it. The thing would clear the parapet or reduce it to rubble like the Bay Gate in no time, Hattu realised, seeing the hook retract. It would come again in moments.

Just then, a dull rumble of bronze on stone sounded, as Polydamas and his two red-faced guardians clunked the giant bronze bell down at the base of the steps leading up to the Scaean Tower roof. With a groan, they lifted it again, bringing the piece before Hattu and setting it down there on the parapet. The rope tied to the loop at the top of the bell was thick as his arm, long and trailing. He looked around those nearest, all gawping, confused. So little time, how to explain his plan…

'You tie, I'll push,' said Dagon, his eyes sparkling with that razor-intelligence that had kept him and Hattu alive through so many battles past.

Tudha sized up the bell. 'You'll need my weight too,' he said with a confident burr.

Dagon and Tudha crouched, facing the parapet, their backs resting against the bell. Hattu snatched up the loose end of the bell rope, fumbling madly to tie a loop. His fingers felt numb and tangled. First, he tied a useless knot that slackened instantly.

'Heeeave!' the bronze hook officer boomed again from within the horse's mouth. It shot out again like a boxer's jab, blasting through another merlon a few paces from Hattu and the bell and sending the triangular piece of mud-brick and a Trojan Guardian shooting into the citadel grounds like giant sling bullets. Hattu's heart thundered, hands shaking as he tried again to tie a knot in the rope's end. Again… it fell slack.

'Drag!' the hook commander screamed in a frenzy. The hook tensed and began sweeping along the battlements once more, harrowing up dust and clumps of mud brick from the flat walkway with a metallic whine. Hattu saw it coming for him, set to smash through him then slash across Dagon and Tudha also.

With a flash of energy, he yanked the third attempt at a knot tight, tossed the looped end of the rope over the onrushing hook, then threw himself back from it all with a shout of: 'Push!'

As the hook end hurtled towards them, Dagon and Tudha planted their feet against the parapet for purchase, then shoved hard until the bronze bell plunged from the inner edge of the battlements like a giant anchor. The looped end of the rope suddenly yanked down on the hook and, with a *bang!* the other end of bronze pole came bursting free of the siege horse's head, sending the leathers and timbers of the 'muzzle' and the members of the hook team up into the air like tossed petals, shrieking. The hook commander came shooting into the Trojan citadel, flying straight into the side of the palace right next to the balcony where Hekabe, Helen, Andromache and Cassandra watched. The great bell slammed to the ground, smashing the flagstones to pieces and tolling ominously. An instant later, the dislocated bronze pole plunged down and cartwheeled across the citadel, coming to a rest when it struck against the blue marble sphinx, dashing off its fine face.

A moment of strange silence ensued. The siege horse was now a grim parody of itself: the ram house body was intact, but the head had a ragged cleft in it, running from between its eyes to its mouth where the hook had been wrenched free. All across the gatehouse, a mighty roar of defiance rose like a storm wind, the defenders beating their spears and swords against their shields, shouting oaths and spitting down at the Ahhiyawan masses. But the glory was short lived.

'Put your shoulders to the ram. Smash the gates!' Mardukal cried from outside.

*Crash!* the ram set to work.

*Crash!*

The Scaean Gates shuddered and settled with every strike, the feeble barricade of furniture down below crumbling away. Arrows and sling bullets skated and whizzed up from the Ahhiyawans and the defenders rained a desperate barrage down in reply. Trojan dead lay amongst the ankles of the living, and every so often bodies would fall lifelessly or screaming backwards into the citadel grounds. Outside, many hundreds of the enemy lay speared or with heads caved in by rocks, dead or twitching in pools of their own blood, but still so many of them. Too many. And the ram was intact, and on it swung.

*Crash!*

'It won't be long now, Prince Hattu,' Mardukal crooned from the horse's back. 'Tell King Priam he'd best open his own neck now... quickly!' he said this with a playful yap.

A deranged laughter rose from nearby on the battlements. Prince Deiphobus sat, back propped against the parapet and turned away from battle, legs splayed, palms upturned, hooting with glee as he looked at his empty hands. 'Where are you, Hektor, Paris? This game is not like the ones we used to play when we were young. Come out from wherever you are hiding.'

Chilled by the sight, seeing defenders near their crown prince waver and gulp, Hattu snapped at Commander Polydamas. 'Shut him up!'

*Crash!*

'The gates are cracking!' came a wail from below.

*Crash!*

'The hinges are buckling!'

*Crash!*

Hattu's head pounded in time with the ram. If, *when* the gates gave, the defenders were too few to hope to tackle the Ahhiyawan swarm. They might flee through the two other citadel gates, but they would quickly be run down and slaughtered by the eager enemy. The Springhouse passage was deeply packed with rubble now – it would take days to dig it out. No way out.

'Aeneas,' he grabbed the Dardanian Prince. 'Is there any other way?'

'King Hattu?'

'Another passage, a secret gate?'

Aeneas' eyes changed shape, a sadness in there, a realisation that Troy's latest battle leader had run out of ideas like all the others. 'There is no way out, *Labarna.*' He glanced back into the citadel, to the niche beside the broken sphinx where his father, wife and young son were cowering.

*Crash! Crunch!*

Tudha shook him by one shoulder, his face wracked with tension. 'There *is* another route under this citadel. I've seen it. Slaves entering and leaving a cave mouth behind the palace several times a day, carrying *pithoi.*

'Ha!' a manic hoot of laughter pealed across the defences. Prince Deiphobus, still sitting like a bored man, swung his head to face them. 'Your boy means to lead you into your grave. The passage behind the palace leads into a cavern where we store olive oil. One way in, one way out. Think again!'

Hattu stared at the man, angry at first, but then he felt something else arise within him. He remembered that first day they had arrived in Troy. Climbing the Scaean Way. The running lad with the clay jar…

Dagon's gaze met his. Tudha's eyes widened. Just like with the bell, all three shared the same moment of epiphany.

Hattu glanced once more at the siege horse, then to Commander Polydamas, seizing him by the shoulders. 'Take every spare man, woman and child to that cave. Empty it of every pot it contains.'

'It is pointless, *Labarna,* the cave has no other way out as our crown prince says, and it is not big enough for us to hide in.'

'For the sake of your family and the people of this city, go to the cave,' Hattu burred. 'Bring… the pots… *here.* As many as you can.'

Polydamas backed away, terrified by Hattu's menacing glower. He spun away, calling a group of men with him, descended into the citadel and shouted for others to join him.

*Crash! Crunch! Snap!*

'We need more time. Go down to ground level,' he commanded Dagon and Tudha. 'Use the bronze siege hook to bolster the gates.'

The pair were on their way in a blink.

*Crash! Crunch! Groan!*

Hattu craned round to look across the citadel. Polydamas' team were streaming behind the palace. The commander himself emerged again first, hauling a stoppered clay pot as large as a boy, waddling, so great was its weight. Dozens more followed in his wake. Up on the palace balcony, Hekabe, Cassandra, Helen and Andromache peeled away and soon emerged from the ground floor doors to join the effort.

When Polydamas emerged up on the Scaean Gatehouse roof, he almost tripped and pitched over back into the city. Hattu grabbed the pot before it hit the walkway and shattered, then placed a steadying hand on Polydamas' shoulder. 'Do as I do,' he said, meeting the old commander's eyes and moving towards a broken section of the parapet.

With a groan, Hattu heaved the pot out through the gap. His heart pumped once, then a dull clunk sounded below and the curses of the enemy who had been struck by the clay jar. Hattu risked edging his head out to look down. One man lay unconscious, the thing having broken over him, and some around him spat and swore, wiping olive oil from their bodies.

Polydamas took the next jar that was brought up and hurled it out likewise.

Mardukal threw his head back and laughed. 'They run short of arrows and rocks. The end grows near!' Diomedes and Neoptolemus pumped their silver and gilt spears aloft, roaring like bears, and the rest of the masses joined in. They hurled a new storm of missiles up at the defenders. One struck Commander Polydamas in the shoulder, wounding him grievously, yet on he worked to lift the next jar. 'Now I understand,' he growled through a battle grin.

'More!' Hattu cried, ushering the next three pairs of men who brought the jars to the battlements. They heaved them out, one after another, and the clatter and unctuous splash of oil became like a pulsing heartbeat.

*Crash!* the battering ram swung again, this time with the moan of bending bronze as the hook pole now serving as a locking bar began to yield.

*Smash! Smash! Smash!* the jars fell like giant hailstones now. Dozens upon dozens of them.

Dagon and Tudha arrived back up on the walkway beside him, bringing another pot of oil each for good measure.

'Ha, I told you: no way out from that cave,' Prince Deiphobus warbled, demented.

Hattu threw a hard jab at his chin, knocking him out cold. Then he gripped the parapet's edge, panting, heart thumping. His eyes drank in the chaos below: the waiting plunderers now slithered and slipped in the slick mess of oil, their confident clamour changing into a chorus of yelps and curses. More, the ram had missed a beat. 'Heave!' Mardukal demanded. The strain of the ram cradle's leathers sounded... but no subsequent *Crash!* as the ramhead swung and missed by a stride or so. The oil, crawling freely down the Scaean Way in thick folds, had found its way underneath the horse's solid wooden wheels. The monstrous device was sliding back from the gates.

'Forward!' Mardukal raged.

The ram team strained and pushed, only for their feet to slide away under them, and when a tranche of them on one side fell, the siege horse slid askew, moving calmly back from the gates to clunk against the side of a nobleman's house a short way down the slope, coming to a rest.

'Loose, with everything!' Aeneas cried. Now a thunderous volley of arrows, slingshot, rocks, spears and chunks of smashed defences were hurled down on the sprawling, disordered mess of men, slipping like newborns. The barrage was devastating – crushing and piercing bodies of soldiers who could barely bring their shields to bear. 'Again!' Hattu roared.

*Thrum! Whack!* Most of Neoptolemus' Myrmidons – nigh-on invincible throughout the war – were mowed down. A huge chunk of parapet, listing already, was pushed free by two Lukkans. It sailed down and pulverised several dozen Spartans. Another volley of missiles tore through hundreds more Ahhiyawans.

All the while, Mardukal was ranting to the soldiery from the siege horse's back. 'Push, push! Get this ram back to the gates.' Diomedes and Neoptolemus put their shoulders to the effort. For a moment, it seemed to be working... until Andor sped down and raked her talons across Mardukal's face. He stumbled to the edge of the siege horse's back and fell to the ground behind it. A moment later, Diomedes and Neoptolemus slipped in the oil and the siege horse slithered backwards again. The grounded and dazed Mardukal screamed as a serrated rear wheel of the device ground across his legs and then – with a staccato series of crunching sounds – pulped his pelvis, then his stomach, chest and finally his head, killing him horribly in just the way he had threatened to dispatch Hattu.

'What're the chances?' Dagon smiled wickedly.

The siege horse slid another few strides down the slope, drifting even further askew like a punch-drunk boxer until it was side-on to the Scaean Gate.

'Loose!' Aeneas bellowed again.

Hattu watched as hundreds more invaders pitched over, groaning. His heart pounded, not daring to believe what his eyes were seeing. Mardukal the famous siege master was dead, his wooden horse thwarted. The huge federated army of Ahhiyawa was beginning to break and run from the endless assault from above. It was that moment that the red veil of battle truly dropped, and Hattu once again saw them for what they really were – desperate men who had just seen their best and only chance of getting into Troy snatched away. Ten years of their lives sacrificed. For nothing.

The gradual retreat became a mass withdrawal. Order and leadership disintegrated. Only Diomedes raged and called after his men, yet they continued to scatter, some even throwing away their weapons. He saw four Pylians turn upon their king, old Nestor, and try to bludgeon his skull in. The old king somehow fought them off and fled on foot, balding head streaked with blood, his fine griffin cape in filthy tatters. The four who had attacked him clambered aboard Nestor's chariot and whipped the horses into a clumsy gallop away back to the broken Bay Gates, out onto the Scamander Plain. The rest of the Ahhiyawan army fled like this, spilling across the plain. Some halted at the crescent camp, perhaps minded to re-establish lines there or simply to loot their kings' supplies, but many more charged on to the south, fording the river, surging up over the Borean Hills and vanishing down towards the camp of ships. The minority who had considered halting at the crescent camp now fled that way too, nerve gone.

Hattu, Tudha and Dagon looked at one another, sweating, panting. The old war hound, Polydamas, watched them go with a final sigh, then slid to the ground, succumbing to his wounds.

Deiphobus stirred now and rose groggily. He stepped over

Polydamas' corpse to gaze at the retreat, then erupted in crazy laughter. 'The war is over!'

***

An hour later, in the pink light of dusk, a partially repaired Destroyer chariot limped across the Scamander Plain, over the tattered ruins of the deserted crescent camp. Dagon steered it carefully, eyes watchful as they crossed the river. He slowed to a halt at the foot of the Borean Hills and stepped down from the vehicle. Silently, Hattu and Aeneas disembarked with him. The trio climbed the Borean Hills on foot. At the crest of the hills they halted, gazing down upon the ragged, churned sands and shell of old dilapidated huts. All but a handful of the black boats had departed, and those last few were now being hauled into the waters. They watched until every single one was gone, the last one vanishing into the sunset haze.

'Deiphobus – arsehole that he is – was right,' Aeneas remarked. 'The war is finished. Victory is Troy's.'

Hattu stared into the sea haze, then across the abandoned beach camp, then over his shoulder across the Scamander Plain and to the hazy, stained ruin that was Troy, thinking over all he had witnessed here in this wretched summer. He fought the urge to weep.

# CHAPTER 23

## THE GLORY OF TROY

Pipes skirled into the night sky and voices soared in all manner of celebratory songs and chatter. Noblemen and their families danced in a great circle, hand-in-hand, whirling around the torchlit citadel, their laughter rising in drunken shrieks. In dark corners, garlanded Trojan Guardians rutted with women – slaves and noble wives alike. At the centre of the celebrations, beside the palace, a painted acrobat spun and leapt to the rumble of drums and whistle of flutes, jumping through fiery hoops before landing in a vat of wine. Applause exploded from the highest born of Troy, seated at tables and benches all around the display. They jabbered, clacked cups, laughing uproariously. Slaves hurried to and fro with kraters of wine, platters of freshly-baked bread and hunks of salted meats and stewed fruits.

'Troy, eternal Troy!' slurred Laocoon, his mouth stained with wine as he stepped up onto his stool and held his arms high and wide. 'For ten summers you have weathered the storm of the Ahhiyawans and suffered terrible deprivations.'

Hattu sat at a table near the back holding a goblet of water. He watched as the priest's wide sleeves slid down his outstretched arms, revealing his silver bracelets. Hanging from a golden chain around his neck was a fire-red carnelian stone the size of an apple, caged in filigree.

'Yes… such deprivations,' Dagon muttered mordantly, sipping on his own drink then pushing the cup away. 'And where did this food suddenly appear from? Could it not have been shared with the lower city families before now? People starved to death down there.'

Hattu looked at the faces in these upper city revellers. These were not the real people of Troy, he realised. These were the very highest of the palace elites – the ones who had kept closely-guarded stores of food while the majority starved. The ones who had breezed around the citadel in soft robes and slippers, glittering with personal jewels, while the masses had endured the raw reality of the war. The ones who had been absent from the walls in that final battle. He glanced to the stained citadel defences, where allies and poorer soldiers had given their lives today to keep the enemy out – to save these elites. Beyond the walls, all was quiet. The lower city was deserted now, the streets dark and strewn with rubble mounds and innumerable battle corpses. He heard Andor flaring her wings and turned to see Tudha feeding the eagle on the table nearest. His face was blank, staring. A look Hattu knew well – a soldier's gaze. Perhaps now – with the war finally concluded – he and his heir might find a way to speak more openly and honestly. Yet try as he might, he could not find the words.

A clay wine vase fell and smashed. Hattu glanced over to see Prince Deiphobus at the heart of the celebrations, now red-faced and roaring with laughter. Brash and bold – everything he was not during the Scaean Gate siege. Given the choice of saving the poor, starving ones who were begging for their lives at the Apollonian Gate or letting them die to save his own skin, Deiphobus had chosen dreadfully. Then there was Prince Scamandrios, dancing a jig to a flute player's tune; he had neither shone nor sinned, but that in itself was a crime for a man born with everything at his disposal. King Priam sat in a grand chair at the main table, slumped, hair tangled and greasy, silver circlet askew, eyes gazing through the acrobat show, lips wet with drool. How many times over those ten years might he have chosen differently, more wisely? Had the war bent and twisted these once-noble people out of shape… or had the struggle peeled away their masks, revealing them for what they truly were. *What sharper mirror is there,* Hattu thought, *than that of adversity?*

Hekabe sat by Priam's side, smoothing his palm. On his other side sat Cassandra. The priests had given her the calming potion again, by the looks of it, for her head lolled and her lips were slack. Andromache at least had the decency to forgo wine and remain solemn. She had become a diminished figure since Hektor's death, nursing young Astyanax quietly, speaking rarely. And then there was Helen. Of all the burdens of war, hers was surely the greatest. It had all begun when Paris winged her away from Sparta. The ten years that had followed had been like a harrow cutting across this warm, windy corner of the world, destroying an ancient way of life, burying the oldest family lines, desecrating the natural beauty of the Wilusan meadows, turning the golden hill that was once Troy into this smashed and ugly shell of drunken dogs.

A tramping of boots sounded nearby. '*Labarna,*' said the young Elamite who had taken Memnon's place as leader of their contingent. He even wore Memnon's leopardskin and spiked golden crown. Of the two thousand coal-skinned men who had arrived at Troy, less than eighty remained. They each held sacks of provisions, and their spears like walking poles. 'It has been an honour to serve with you. Perhaps in future, we will fight alongside one another again?'

Hattu smiled wryly. 'If I could ask the Gods one thing, my friend, it would be that we never again need to array our spears like this. May the spirits of the way be kind to you on your journey home.' He took a small clay token from his purse, marked with his personal seal, and flicked it with his thumb. The Elamite caught the piece. 'If you pass any Hittite towns on your path, show them that. It will guarantee you shelter, food, fresh clothes and supplies for your men.'

'May Jabru, greatest of all Gods of Elam, be with you, My Sun,' he said with a bow. They left through the Scaean Gate hatch – still operational. The gates themselves were still buckled and crudely barred shut by the badly-bent bronze pole ripped from the siege horse.

Hattu watched them go. The small pocket of surviving Amazons had departed for home earlier, as had the Seha Riverlanders and Lukkans, the Thracians and Masans and the tiny bands of local villagers and islanders. In fact, he realised, of all the allies it was just his own party and Aeneas' Dardanians who remained in Troy. The thought made him feel wearier than ever – like a drunk who realises he is the last man in the tavern and the night is over. And what a wretched night! His legs and feet were swollen badly, and his back raged with knots and strains.

Just then, a bunch of drunk Trojans opened the gate hatch and danced in a chain out onto the dark Scaean Way, weaving and laughing around the strewn bodies.

Hattu's nose wrinkled in distaste. 'We should leave the Trojans to their celebrations,' he mused, glancing over at Antenor's villa, thinking of the soft bed and the comfort of the hounds dozing around him. 'Turn in. Prepare for tomorrow.'

Dagon looked up, looking like a five year old for a moment. 'Home?' he said.

Tudha rose in his seat too, as if someone had whispered the name of a ghost.

There were other plans for tomorrow – to go down to the Scamander and hack away the log dam, allowing the waters to flow once more along their original course and quench the dry Apollonian Springhouse. But these soft-handed Trojan elites could do that, Hattu decided. All that mattered now was that one word Dagon had uttered. 'Home,' Hattu agreed, lifting the small wooden goat figurine from his pouch and kissing it, 'to see our loved ones.' *Pudu, Ruhepa, Kurunta,* he mouthed softly, his eyes wet in the torchlight.

Tudha's eyes met his, and the young man's lips flickered with the beginnings of a smile. Yet there was a strange reluctance written on his face.

The three rose and edged around the crazed, drunken festivities – now nobles and royal cousins were dancing and stamping on the tables, and one woman had stripped naked for the entertainment of all the others.

Hattu caught Aeneas' eye. The Dardanian Prince, sitting back from the royal table with his wife, boy and quivering old father, gave a look in reply that perfectly summed up his feelings on things. 'It was all worth it,' Aeneas said glibly, gesturing to the shrieking crowds, 'for this, eh?'

Hattu smiled wryly and shook his head, gesturing to Aeneas' family. 'For *them.*'

Aeneas raised his cup, untouched so far, to that.

The trio slipped from the festival area and arrived near the smashed blue sphinx. Set to go to their respective billets, Hattu turned to Dagon and Tudha to wish them goodnight.

'You fought well today, old friend,' he offered to Dagon. Next, he looked to Tudha. 'You were not supposed to be here, *Tuhkanti*...'

Tudha straightened, his jaw stiffening.

'...but you fought expertly also, and I was glad of your presence over this summer.'

Tudha's defences slackened just a fraction.

'Until tomorrow,' Hattu finished.

Hattu and Dagon turned in different directions to head to their quarters.

But Tudha did not. 'What does tomorrow hold for me?' he said.

Hattu twisted back to his heir. 'As I said... we go home.'

'Home... to be your true heir once more? Whom you trust wholly?'

Hattu hesitated, and Tudha pounced upon the moment.

'I can see in your eyes the answer, and that you are afraid to say it,'

Tudha said, his voice gentle, flat. 'So maybe the truth will help you…'

'The truth?' Hattu said quietly.

Tudha held his gaze for a time before answering: 'I killed Aunt Zanduhepa.'

The words were like a boxer's blow to Hattu's ears. A ringing sound rose within his head.

Dagon, watching this, paled.

'You wanted me to speak of what went on at the forest shrine, to admit what I did, and now I have. I killed her. Not one of my men. Me. And it was no accident.'

Hattu's eyes slid closed. He shook as if it were winter. All this time he had harboured a tiny hope that it had all been a mistake. That it had been another who had cut poor Zanduhepa down. No… it had been his heir.

'Now you know what I am,' Tudha continued. 'And so I ask of you: forgive me… or send me away. If you do not think I deserve to be your successor then I would rather you choose a new heir whom you trust… and exile me as you did Urhi-Teshub.'

Hattu sensed time passing like slow droplets of cold rainwater, knowing his next words had to be well chosen. 'Forgive you?' he said in little more than a whisper. The notion tumbled through his mind like a madman flailing through a dense forest. It was all he had wanted since the rebellion, to forgive, but he couldn't – not while he did not understand. 'First, you must answer one last question: why?' His eyes slid open, his gaze affixing Tudha. 'If you are to be *Tuhkanti* and future *Labarna,* it is your duty to explain. *Why* did you do it?'

Tudha backed away from him, shaking his head with a miserable smile. 'That… I can never answer,' he said in a low drawl. With a swish of his black cloak, he swung and stormed away towards his billet.

Hattu stared at his heir's back, sagging.

Dagon planted a hand on his shoulder in reassurance. 'He is exhausted. We all are. In the morning it will be different.'

Hattu shook his head slowly. 'He is lost to me now. I can feel it. I have failed him. I have failed our empire. I sent him to the northern woods and in doing so created a murderer... another Urhi-Teshub.'

'This is no time for such talk,' Dagon implored him, guiding him round towards Antenor's villa. 'Rest!'

Dejectedly, he nodded. The thought of his bed was like a hook, and so he dragged his weary feet that way. When he heard Andor's cry from somewhere behind, he clicked his tongue and, without looking back, shot out one arm for her to glide in and land upon. But she did not come. She cried again. Next came a mighty chattering of wood scraping against flagstones. A whine of bronze hinges.

Hattu halted, turning to look back towards the celebrations, a horrible tingle rising on the back of his neck. It took a moment to comprehend what he was seeing. Some of the drunk Trojans who had danced through the hatch door were back inside. The bronze pole was gone from the Scaean Gate, and they were dragging the listing gates open. Outside, the light cast by the torches of the citadel faded into utter blackness. Hattu stared into the inky nothingness, a corpse's breath rolling across his back and scalp as he heard something out there… then saw movement. Something giant, swaying. More of the drunk ones emerged from the darkness first, grunting, pulling on ropes. Hattu stared, dumbstruck, as the torchlight gradually revealed what they were dragging.

The siege horse with its manic broken face, body bloodstained and arrow-pricked, edged up and through the arch of the Scaean Gate. The oil on the street outside had thinned and drained away, apparently.

'What are they doing?' Dagon croaked, halted like Hattu, staring.

The two numbly watched as the siege horse was brought before the royal tables. All those enjoying the festivities gawped up, shrieking in fright at first, dropping cups and swaying back from the towering monstrosity. But the shrieks became wild laughter as they realised the last desperate gambit of the Ahhiyawans was here before them now, broken and helpless like a sacrificial cow. Now they shrieked in theatrical horror. Men pelted the thing with food. Women took to springing around it, hands linked, singing mocking songs.

Two more of the drunks who had ventured outside pushed a shaking, blood-stained man into and across the citadel grounds. 'We found an injured Ahhiyawan out there too,' they jeered. The crowds roared in cold laughter and tossed their drinks over the enemy fighter, who slumped to his knees in utter defeat.

Hattu recognised his face from one of the battles. A vicious and skilled soldier.

His head rolled back and he wept to the skies. 'I am Sinon, son of Aesimus. Spare me this shame. Kill me.' He stretched his neck. 'Kill me or give me a sword and let me fight you all!'

Laughter exploded all around at this.

Laocoon staggered forward, tipped his wine over Sinon's head, then approached the horse. Taking a torch from its holder on a wall, he grabbed one of the hide flaps on the horse's side, feeling then sniffing it. His eyes bulged and he smiled feverishly. 'The vinegar has dried off. It will go up like a pyre!'

'Put your torch down, Priest,' Prince Deiphobus slurred, staggering out to stand between Laocoon and the horse, swaying on his feet. 'The Ahhiyawans made monuments of the armour they stripped from Trojan dead. Well this is *my* monument to their failure. You will not burn it down.'

'Burn it!' cried many voices joyously as if their latest crown prince had not spoken. 'Tie Sinon to it and burn it!'

'Keep it – for one hundred days of celebration at least,' another argued. Others rumbled in support of this idea.

'Let the fires turn the sky bright as noon!' Laocoon brayed on.

Old Antenor – one of the only ones who had steadfastly refused wine – stepped over to Deiphobus' side to protest at Laocoon as well. 'Think! If you put that giant thing to the torch, the rest of the citadel could easily catch light,' he pleaded, exasperated. 'Now is not the time to be starting great fires. We are all imbibed and delirious with our victory. But let us not act rashly. Come morning, we can have the thing taken down to the plain and dismantled, for I dare say we will need the timber for pyres,' he finished sombrely, gesturing towards the open gates where the closest of the strewn dead out there were just visible at the edges of the citadel torchlight.

The rest of the elders rumbled in agreement with this, drumming their canes on the ground. So too did many of the older citizens. Yet others protested, blood hot with wine. Quickly, arguments broke out. Soon, it was a cacophony of squabbling. Priam's old eyes slid up and down, regarding the crippled siege horse as if it was a vengeful God. Hekabe was shouting, trying to bring calm to the masses. Aeneas was there on the edge of the quarrel, his face lined with confusion.

Hattu and Dagon waded into this heated gathering.

'Who gave the order to bring this in?' Hattu barked.

Deiphobus swung round on one heel, hiccupping, the whites of his mud-coloured eyes shot with blood. 'I did. King Hattu. You see, the war is over. Your station as High Commander is revoked. You'll deliver Hektor's helm to my chambers.' Another hiccup as he swung to face Laocoon. 'And you, Priest of Poseidon, set down that torch.'

Laocoon clutched the burning torch as if it was a child. 'Never. That monstrosity must burn!'

Deiphobus clicked his tongue and, like hounds responding to their master, four Guardians came over to stand with him. At the same time, Laocoon's templefolk gathered with him, unarmed, but plentiful. Antenor tore at his hair in despair. 'Now is not the time to quarrel, people of Troy,' he lamented.

'Father! Have your priest step away,' Deiphobus brayed across the crowd towards Priam. But Priam remained listless and silent.

Arguments exploded again, Laocoon remonstrating, torch in hand, accusing Prince Deiphobus of being a worm, Deiphobus' spittle spraying as he recited all of Laocoon's failings during the ten year siege. Now the lumps of food and cups of wine were thrown between Trojans. Threats became swinging arms and wagging fingers. Old Antenor staggered away from this, head shaking in dismay as he retreated to his villa.

Amidst it all, Queen Hekabe saw Hattu. She clambered up onto the royal table and swept her hands out as if parting the sea of noise. 'Let the *Labarna* speak,' she cried. When the quarrelling went on, she stooped, picked up two plates and smashed them together, the shards flying everywhere, stunning everyone. All the squabbling voices faded. 'The Great King of the Hittites thwarted the siege, broke this giant wooden device. It is his right to judge what should happen to this, this… *horse* of Troy.'

'Mother, I-' Deiphobus began to protest.

'Shut that wine-stained mouth of yours,' she howled. 'I suckled you and endured your capricious moods all these years. All I asked of you in return was respect. So still your tongue!' She turned her eyes on Laocoon. 'And you, you old meddler. Set down that torch or I will stuff it down your throat.'

With the chief agitators tamed, the many ruddy torchlit faces now turned to Hattu, eyes wide in fear and respect. They parted to make a corridor, inviting his approach.

Hattu stepped up to the siege horse. A rife stink of dried blood wafted from it. He could see strips of human skin plastered to the hide sheath with blood and the filth of battle. He stepped past the thing's open rear and peered into the hollow guts of the ram house. Edging inside, he gagged at the odour of sweat and blood trapped in that closed space. Pulling the edge of his cloak up and over his mouth and nose, he went deeper inside. The battering ram hung in its leather cradle. The walls were solid, crafted of pine panels. Expert design by Mardukal, he conceded, running a hand along the panelling. Just then, clipped voices arose again from outside. The unrest was brewing again, rapidly.

'Well, what say you, *Labarna?*' one man demanded as he stepped back out again. 'Burn it or keep it?' pressed another.

As he stepped back outside, more voices rasped at him, demanding a verdict. Hattu looked up at the horse's giant, cleft face gazing madly into the night, uplit by the torches. Andor landed up there and padded around, pecking at the structure. *Burn it. Be rid of the gory symbol of the war,* he decided inwardly.

He twisted to look over the Trojan masses. Only one amongst them wasn't staring back at him. One who had to be consulted.

'What say you, Majesty?'

Deiphobus made to reply, then flinched as he realised Hattu was not addressing him but the one seated behind him. Princess Cassandra.

She looked up, her head swaying, her eyes hooded with the temple potion. 'Not… there,' she groaned in a stupor. 'He wasn't… there.'

'I don't understand,' Hattu frowned.

'Nor do we,' Deiphobus said with a forced laugh. He snapped his fingers at the long-robed Servants of Apollo, who scurried over. 'Take her back to the Temple,' he demanded.

'Wait,' Hattu said as one of the templefolk tilted a cup of the potion to her lips. 'What say you, seeress?' he asked Cassandra.

'He wasn't there,' she repeated.

'Ignore her,' Deiphobus snapped. The potion slipped down Cassandra's throat and her head fell slack. The two templefolk lifted her from her seat and carried her away.

Hattu recoiled. 'Ignore her? Have you learned nothing? She sees what is to come.'

Deiphobus shook his head with a supercilious smile. 'Ah, King Hattu. You too have been charmed by her ramblings? Most are, at first. Her words are misleading and dangerous, best ignored.'

'They are the words of the Gods,' Hattu snarled. He raised his voice so all could hear. 'Did you know that she foresaw Paris' affair with Helen? That she had visions of young Prince Troilus' death at Thymbra? Of Hektor's demise? Nobody here listened. Tonight, she wanted to tell us something and again you sealed her lips with some wretched potion.'

'My mother asked *you* to make a decision about the horse, King Hattu,' Deiphobus said with a smirk. 'Are you going to keep her waiting?'

Hattu swung away from Deiphobus, seething. He looked the horse up and down again. 'This thing must burn. But the elders are right – it would be madness to burn it here with so many houses close. So we should take it down onto the plain, and burn it there.'

'Come morning, it will be so, King Hattu,' Deiphobus burbled and bowed mockingly, over-confident with so much wine in his veins. 'But tonight, it will remain as my monument of victory. All of you, raise your cups and gaze up at our marvellous trophy. For the glory of Troy!' he yelled.

'For the glory of Troy!' many hundreds echoed. The celebrations exploded back into life. People threw garlands up and over the siege horse. Some even climbed upon its back, where Mardukal had been standing during the battle, and danced drunken jigs, their feet drumming on the timbers. A group dragged the injured Sinon to the base of the device and tied him there tightly, pouring more wine over his lolling head and pelting him with food.

Hattu stalked away back towards Antenor's house, head shaking, teeth gritted.

'What in the Dark Earth was all that about?' Dagon whispered, shadowing him.

'Hubris, power games between the princes and priests and... everything we once pretended was not part of Troy. *Golden* Troy,' he said with a mocking twang. 'Effortlessly rich and prosperous, where every man, woman and child drinks milk and eats bread and honey until their belly grows fat. Where no man is wronged, where no voice goes unheard.'

Dagon planted a hand on his shoulder. 'Think only of this: it is over. Tomorrow... we can go home.'

'Home,' He sighed, the word enough to dampen his anger. Placing a hand on Dagon's shoulder in return, he bid goodnight to his oldest friend and the two parted. As Hattu stalked away back towards Antenor's house, he began planning inwardly how he would rise at first light tomorrow and leave this sorry place. Even the Gods could not make him remain a moment longer. All that mattered now was the dawn. The chance to go home. The chance to put this horrible summer behind him.

***

Antenor had turned in already, but had prepared him some mountain tea, leaving a cup of it by Hattu's bedside. He sat on his bed and held the warm drink, enjoying its scent. Taking the goat figurine from his purse, he closed his eyes and kissed it once more, thinking of the sweet pleasure that awaited once they reached home: Pudu and Ruhepa, in his arms. He thought of Kurunta too. All would be well once he was back with them. All but one matter. Tudha.

A pang of sadness passed through him as he realised that this summer had finally laid bare to him the stark truth: Tudha was a killer, unrepentant. No remorse for Zanduhepa and her baby. Not even an explanation. His heir was a monster. Going home would not change that.

Dejected once more, he took a sip of tea before he sank back onto the bed, fully-dressed. He slept like a corpse, falling through a black well of infinity, weightless and silent…

*She came from nowhere, grabbing him in her talons, soaring through a screaming gale, riven with stinging bullets of hail and snow. Fighting madly to free himself from her cage of claws, he saw that the blackness was black no more. Far below, a gloomy countryside stretched. A winter sea lapping against a deserted shoreline. A bay where galleys lay submerged and rotting. A long silvery ridge, and at its bluff end stood a blackened, tumbledown ruin.*

*He felt a surge of triumph swell within him. 'You were wrong, Goddess. Wrong!' he growled, looking up through her claws at her mighty body and huge, outstretched wings. 'Troy stands, her attackers are vanquished.'*

*Ishtar gazed down at him, smiling. 'Ah, the wild words of a man who has lived in the cage of Troy for too long. Look upon the ruin below, and weep. I show you nothing but that which is to come.'*

*'It cannot be and will not be.'*

*'It is exactly as you see it. More, Great King of the Hittites, it will be you who does this to Troy... you.'*

*'Never. I swore as my father did before me and his father before him that Troy would always stand strong, the pillar at the west of the Hittite Empire, the bastion of-'*

*'But that was before you came here...' she cut him off with a feral confidence. 'Your heart understands, even if your mind has yet to accept it.' She wheeled around, spiralling down towards the ruined foundations of the acropolis. 'Wake, Hattu. Wake and see for yourself.' She released*

*him from her grip, sending him shooting down towards the rubble like a sling bullet. He threw up his hands in terror, the wind screaming in his ears.*

He woke with a gasp, shaking, his body bathed in sweat in the choking night heat. Groaning, he sat up, rubbing his temples, gazing around the wood-panelled darkness of Antenor's home. His head boomed like a war drum – as if he had been drinking bad wine. Crickets chirped from beyond the shutters. Through a crack, he saw that the celebrations had burnt themselves out: the torches had all been doused, and Trojans lay here and there, snoring, wine skins clutched to chests or discarded nearby. He saw only two Guardians on watch: one of them was up on the walls, still swigging away at a wine cup; the other – the wretched Skorpios – stood watch near Sinon the Ahhiyawan, who sagged in his tight bonds at the foot of the siege horse, unconscious and awaiting death the next day. He examined the sky, hoping there might be streaks of pre-dawn in the east, for that would mean he could rise and set off for home. But it was still black as resin, pricked by stars and sliced by the waning, coppery moon. He had only been asleep for a few hours, he realised. With a sigh, he reached down to the floor beside the bed to stroke the pile of hounds there. Their coats were smooth and warm, pleasant to the touch. A slight whimper sounded. He just about made out the shape of one young hound, unsettled, breathing heavily.

'What's wrong, boy?' Hattu croaked.

The dog whimpered again. Hattu stroked its neck until he fell asleep again.

When he woke next, the young hound was still like the others. Blinking, rubbing his eyes, he sat up. Now his head swam crazily. He slid from the bed and crept over to the shutters to peer out from the cracks. It was *still* night. Shafts of grey moonlight striped the citadel. The Guardian on the walls now lay slumped in a drunken stupor. Skorpios was no longer out there. His gaze drifted to the severed ropes at the base of the horse. It took a moment for him to realise what he was staring at, and what it meant.

The enemy soldier, Sinon, was gone.

A horrid shiver burst across his skin as he remembered Sinon's bloodthirstiness during battle. Now the man was roaming in the citadel with all Troy asleep. One word pealed through his head: *Danger!*

He backed away from the shutters, mind flashing with all manner of thoughts. 'Up,' he said in the direction of the dogs – they would be first to sniff out or chase off the escaped Ahhiyawan. None of them moved. He reached down to rouse the young dog gently. This time its body was cold. Cold as stone. So too the others. Hattu choked, stepping back from the dead animals. He saw froth at their mouths. Poisoned. Sinon was at large.

A lightning-flash of fear struck through him. If the dogs had been poisoned, then what about… 'Antenor,' he gasped. He fumbled on his sword crossbands over his bare chest. 'Antenor?' he called in a weak whisper as he stumbled from his chamber, the swimming sensation in his head growing thicker. He rested his weight in the doorway of the second bedchamber where the elder slept. The bed lay disturbed but empty. 'Antenor?' he called again, fearful of attracting Sinon's attention.

He edged into each of the villa's rooms with caution – in case the Ahhiyawan was waiting in there to spring upon him – and searched. Every room was a jumble of shadows, but no sign of Antenor. He came to the scullery. Empty too. His fears for the old man began to spiral out of control, and then he noticed something. Under the shelves of herb jars, a drawer lay open. In it was a small, dark ring. Hattu lifted it, squinting, confused at the strange shape of it. How could it be?

He stumbled through to the villa's entrance, seeking a shaft of moonlight so he could see it clearly. He padded out into the night air and saw that it was what he thought it was. Aeneas' thumb ring. Or at least a perfect copy of it.

Swaying on his feet, punch-drunk now, he lifted his eyes to regard the villa. 'It was you,' he croaked in a weak whisper. 'All of it. All this time, it was you. You are the Shadow of Troy.'

Antenor emerged from the darkness at the side of his house, seeing what Hattu held and smiling affably. 'Ah, Aeneas' ring. Well, you had to find out at some point.'

'Then Paris-' Hattu croaked.

'Was merely a bitter son,' Antenor finished for him. 'He was meant to die on Tenedos with you and all the others. Still, his jealous antics provided a welcome distraction, allowing me to do the things I had to do. I told you the day you arrived here: I'm a merchant, always have been – I get my thrills from brokering the sharpest deals. I wanted Troy to win this war. I really did. Yes, I secretly helped the Ahhiyawans from time to time when it suited me and when they rewarded me appropriately, and I helped Troy often enough too. But I was sure Troy would win in the end… and then you arrived here with nothing but a broken old chariot master, a hunched Egyptian and a boy. From that moment on, I knew that Troy was doomed to fall, so it was up to me to make the deal that would ensure that I survived it.'

Hattu clutched at his pounding head. The fragments of conspiracy that had so far only clumsily knitted into place on the shoulders of Prince Paris now broke apart and settled on Antenor instead. 'You sabotaged the embassy that preceded the war, polluted the springhouse well, betrayed young Prince Troilus to the enemy. You locked the Thymbran Gate, betrayed the river camp, poisoned Hektor… then tried to point the finger of blame at Aeneas. You killed Theron the slave and signalled for the night attack to begin. You set the armoury ablaze, conspired with the enemy to divert the river and deny the city water,' the words came in a confused, endless breath.

'Come now, I am an old man. I didn't do all of those things,' he smiled. The smile slid into a sneer. 'I had help.'

Hattu noticed his glance towards a smaller villa across the way. Skorpios' house. There was something different about it. Pinned above the doorway, Hattu realised, was a panther's pelt. He shook his head, turning back to Antenor. 'You cut Sinon free. You… you poisoned your own hounds?'

The elder nodded gently. 'Else they would have barked and made a commotion when I came out to do this,' he said as he unfurled a panther skin of his own and calmly hung it beside his villa door. 'Oh, I poisoned your tea also, but evidently you did not drink enough of it.' He sucked air in through his teeth. 'I was being kind to you, you know. The poison would have been a gentler death.'

'Gentler?' Hattu said. 'Gentler than wha-' He froze, his eyes rolling to one side, to the siege horse's ram house… to the shadows crawling out from behind the panels within. One shadow landed in a crouch. Odysseus' eyes met his. It was like that moment during a hunt, when deer and tracker sense one another.

Hattu's heart pounded. Now he understood what Cassandra had meant. *He wasn't there… Odysseus was not present during the battle!* Yet all the time as arrows and spears flew, he *had* been present, concealed in the horse's structure, waiting… for this moment. Hattu's chest swelled with breath to shout… when a hand grabbed his tail of hair from behind and yanked his head back, then a cold blade pressed against his throat.

'Menelaus, wait,' Odysseus whispered to this other. The Ithacan King scurried out from the ram house, holding up a flat palm to the one behind Hattu. The knife at Hattu's throat eased a little, but it was still a death grip.

Six other men emerged from the panelled walls of the ram house, where they had lain hidden since the end of the siege.

Odysseus came to stand before Hattu.

'*This* was your ruse,' Hattu hissed. 'You knew the Assyrian horse would not break the citadel gates.'

'I knew you would believe Mardukal's reputation and fear that the horse could not be beaten. I also knew that *you* would be the one to thwart it,' Odysseus replied. 'I never wanted Mardukal to come here. Nobody did. But we had tried everything else. *Everything*. You foiled us at every turn. In the end, I used Mardukal… to distract you, to give you an illusion of victory.'

'What do you mean? The war is over. We saw your ships sail from the Bay of Boreas and… ' he fell silent, feeling like a fool. It had been many, many years since anyone had tricked him like this. 'How far away are they?'

Odysseus smiled with one edge of his mouth. 'The ships wait behind Tenedos Isle. They will make land and be here before well before dawn comes.'

Hattu saw a figure stealing up onto the citadel walls. The "wounded" enemy soldier, Sinon, now moving like a cat. The Ahhiyawan took a bow from his back, held one of his arrows over a low-burning brazier then aimed skywards, sending the fire signal high into the night. The blade at his throat pressed closer, breaking skin, runnels of blood trickling down his neck. 'One word, and I'll cut through to your spine,' Menelaus hissed from behind with a waft of bear's breath.

Odysseus once again raised a placatory palm towards the Spartan King, then returned his gaze to Hattu.

'Why delay my death?' Hattu growled. 'If what you say is true then every soul left in Troy will be dead by morning.'

Odysseus shrugged. 'It doesn't need to be that way.'

Hattu frowned, then from the corner of his eye noticed the panther skin newly installed above Antenor's door. He almost laughed as he understood what it meant now. 'Ah, so your soldiers will pass by any houses with animal pelts above the threshold? The treacherous elder will live. Good for him.'

Odysseus glanced at the panther skin and smirked. 'No, he is just a self-serving rat. Forget about him. Listen to me. The people left in this city do not need to die or fall into slavery tonight.'

'You cast more illusions, Island King?' Hattu sneered. 'Cut my neck open now, or I will cry out with every drop of breath in my lungs.'

Odysseus shook his head mournfully. 'And then the soldiers in this citadel will rouse and butcher me and my small band. After that? The Trojans will go on to barricade the citadel gates, to man the walls with what defenders they have left. The Ahhiyawan ships will return and the plague-ridden armies will pour through the lower city to besiege this height once more. The war will shamble on. How many more years? Your son and that wolf of a chariot driver will be trapped in here throughout it all. In the end, your wife and probably mine too will be widows and our children fatherless.'

Hattu's heart pulsed with anguish. 'Tormenting a man before he dies? I thought better of you, Island King. Now get on with it!' he snarled, pushing his neck against Menelaus' knife.

'I am trying to tell you that there is another way,' Odysseus said. 'Go, rouse those on this broken hill. Tell them they must leave with you. Use whatever story you must. Do not reveal that we are here for they must not raise a general panic. We will stay hidden. Take them from Troy before our ships come back. Let this vile war *end*.'

'I came here to save Troy. You ask me to abandon her?' Hattu croaked. All at once, Cassandra's dreams flooded his thoughts, tangling with those of Ishtar – of him harming Troy, riding the demonic horse. It felt as if the Goddess was speaking through Odysseus' lips.

'Let Agamemnon have this half-ruined hovel of brick and wood. The houses and halls are not what matter. Do you remember when we spoke, down in the bay?' His eyes were full, pleading. 'You begged me to let you speak with our *Wanax* in order to bring this war to a close. I helped you then. Now it is me begging you to take this chance to end the war. A real, bloodless chance. Please, help me.'

The words reached deep inside Hattu's chest.

'And I have not forgotten what you told me that day by the Scamander side,' continued Odysseus. 'The balance of power. The danger of collapse. I will make it my duty to push Agamemnon into treaty discussions with you Hittites. Already he thinks this way after your talk with him.'

Hattu's head dipped as, from the deep vaults of memory, his father's words boomed, strong and resonant. *Troy is the western pillar of the Hittite Empire and the Hittite lands are the great bulwark that shields Troy from the east. We are one, we live to protect each other – as it has been for over four hundred years…*

What felt like an age passed. Then…

'Forgive me,' he said quietly to the spirits of his father and his ancestors. 'Troy must be forsaken if those left within are to be saved.' He looked up and met Odysseus' eyes again with a slow, solemn nod.

Odysseus sighed. He gave Menelaus a look, and – with a dog's growl – the Spartan King removed the blade from Hattu's neck.

Hattu rose, touching the bloody, light cut there.

'You do not have long, an hour at best.' Odysseus said. 'Do not waste a moment.'

***

In a daze, Hattu shambled around the streets of the citadel. Stupefied, crawling with guilty horror at his choice, he stumbled when his hip bumped a pithoi jar. The empty vase rocked a few times then fell, the clay crumpling mutedly. For an instant, he felt sure he was going to vomit with fright, that it would waken all Trojans and send them into a state of panic… but when the shards of clay settled, there was nothing. Just the trill of crickets and the gentle hum of the warm wind.

His mind tumbled over it all. *Wake a few, tell them there is some important matter but that I cannot explain it until I have led them away from Troy. Have them gently rouse the others. Usher them all outside and to safety. Let the Ahhiyawans have the husk city.*

Entering the palace, he crept along the corridor of royal bedchambers. He took the goat figurine in one hand, clutching it nervously as a reminder of home, the prize that awaited tomorrow if he acted swiftly in the remainder of this night. Who to waken first? Prince Deiphobus? He reached for the door handle, then stopped. Deiphobus would not leave quietly or without making an argument of it. On through the palace he went. To wake Andromache first, perhaps? No, little Astyanax would begin crying and that would be no good. Scamandrios then. No, he changed his mind again. Time was running out. Aeneas, it had to be Aeneas – and then straight to Dagon and Tudha's billets. He swung on his heel, set on heading for the Dardanian's quarters... and froze.

Queen Hekabe stood at the end of the corridor: formidable, lips thin, eyes accusing. 'I watched you,' she said, voice tremulous. 'I watched you out there. I saw you with others by the siege horse. In the darkness, I assumed they were our men.' She raised a knife, pointing it at him like an accusing finger. 'Then I heard their whispers... saw the fire arrow. Tell me it is not as it looks? The enemy *are* gone, aren't they?'

Hattu considered lying to this proud matriarch, but he held her in too much esteem. Quietly, he shook his head.

Hekabe's face drained of colour. 'So you were the spy. You were the Shadow all along. *You!* Why have you turned upon Troy. You... our greatest hope?'

'No, my Queen. Antenor was behind it all – the poisonings, the deceptions, the sabotage, the-'

'Yet in Troy's darkest hour it is you, King Hattu, who fails her. It is your shadow that stretches over the city. *Yours!*' she wailed, striding for him with the knife.

He shook his head madly. 'No. I do this *for* Troy. For what is left of her, for the people – just as you asked me to before the enemy attacked,' he appealed. Hekabe halted a stride away, her hand and the knife shaking. 'There is little time to explain. Rouse Priam and your children. Waken them quietly and gather down by the Dardanian Gate.'

She backed away now, shaking her head, brandishing the knife as if she expected Hattu to attack her. 'Oh, I will rouse my people,' she said, her chest swelling to scream. Before Hattu could even draw breath to beg her not to, something hissed along the corridor from behind him and whacked into Hekabe's stomach. She gagged and fell, bleeding and winded, clutching the arrow.

Just as Hattu swung to face the one who had shot her, a fire-hardened club smashed against his temple. He fell like a stack of wooden blocks, the goat figurine rolling from his twitching hand. Skorpios, bearing club and bow, smirked down at him.

Antenor appeared too and stepped over the fallen pair. 'Apologies, Mother of Troy, but I can't have you raising the alarm and bringing this place to arms. And you, King Hattu. I like you, but not as much as I like the terms I have agreed with Agamemnon – and he wants to capture Troy with everyone still in it.'

Hattu reached towards the goat figurine. The club whooshed down again. White light filled his skull, throwing him into utter blackness.

# CHAPTER 24

## THE FINAL PYRE

Sick to his core, Tudha took up a bronze sword, spear and bow from the corner of the archer compound storehouse. Next, he loaded a few small loaves into his leather bag, threw it over his shoulder then left his billet. He glanced over the rooftops in the direction of the Scaean Gate, to which he was headed.

The night would pass, morning would arrive, then his father would find that his heir had made the decision for him. His plan was rough, to say the least: to head south along the coast and take ship. To where he did not know – only that he would recognise his new home when he found it. A place where he would not be burdened by the past. A place where he could bury the truth forever.

Crickets chirruped around the quiet citadel grounds as he picked his way from the archer compound and past the Royal Palace. He could not resist a last glance in there. The great doorway yawned like a mouth, the moonlit strip of red-tiled floor like a long tongue. Beyond lay a corridor. There was so little light reaching that passageway that he should not have been able to see a thing, yet he did. Something glinting on the floor. Intrigued, he stepped inside, across the megaron – careful to walk softly lest the echoes of his footsteps waken anyone.

Entering the adjoining corridor, he sank to one knee, reached down to pick up the figurine. Ruhepa's goat. The symbol of love between Father and daughter. For a time, Tudha stared at the piece, at once longing for things to have been different, and confused as to why it was here. Another question arose then: why were the tiles around it wet. He touched a hand to the wetness, then examined his fingertips.

Blood.

*Father?* he mouthed.

Long shadows crawled across the floor from behind him. Horned men.

He rose, turning slowly to face the band creeping towards him. Men who should not have been here. Men who should have been consigned to his nightmares of this war. Four of them: Myrmidons and Spartans. They edged towards him, grinning, spears and swords trained, herding him down the winding corridor and towards its dead end. When three more joined the four, Tudha stopped retreating, set his feet wide apart, drew his spear in one hand and his Trojan sword in the other. The truth, it seemed, would die right here.

***

Numb, silent. Then a ringing in his ears. Hekabe's words, echoing distantly: *You are the Shadow of Troy, King Hattu. You!*

He prized his eyelids open, feeling lightning streak through his head as he tried to focus. He touched a hand to his temple – wet with blood. Glancing around him he saw that he was alone in a dark palace side room. He gasped a few times, sitting up to rest his back against the wall. It only took a few moments before he remembered the urgency of what he had been trying to do. Shambling to his feet and over to the blurry outline of a door, he clawed weakly at the handle.

Locked.

Panic began to spin crazily within him. He stared at the handle, confused as to why it was turning even after he had let go of it. With a *click*, the door opened. A young Guardian stood there, sighing, staring absently through him… then whumped face down into the room, an axe lodged between his shoulders. Aghast, he stepped past the dead man and into the palace corridor where he had been knocked unconscious: but no sign of Hekabe, Skorpios, or Antenor. All seemed blindingly bright and, still deafened, he could make sense of nothing. Then he felt the floor shake in a rapid rhythm. Something coming for him. Closer, closer…

It was nightmarish: the white stallion, a supreme specimen from the herds of Troy, came galloping along the palace corridor, mane ablaze, eyes bulging in terror, two Mycenaean arrows quivering in its neck. He threw himself tight to the corridor wall as the beast stormed past. With a sharp rush of breath, all senses came back to him at that moment. The screaming. Roaring flames. The stink of burning cloth and hair. The discordant *clang* of bronze from every direction. The dull grunts and cries of surprise. Horses whinnying, goats bleating in panic. Dogs howling and crying. The earth-shaking *crash* of falling masonry. With a wet gurgle, a body plummeted down onto the floor of the megaron hall at the corridor's end, having plunged from a mezzanine in there. Prince Deiphobus. Blood pulsed from the spear hole in his throat in great black gouts. A moment later, King Menelaus of Sparta leapt down beside the doomed prince and took out a knife. Snarling like a wolf, he sliced off Deiphobus' nose and ears, his face and the curling white horns on his helmet darkening with blood spray.

Three Guardians rushed Menelaus only for a pounce of Spartan warriors to charge them first, bowling them over and butchering them. Hattu, legs like stone, head swimming, staggered a few steps down the corridor towards the scene, as if he could possibly fight them. They did not see him, and rampaged off down another passageway before he could reach the megaron and the body of Deiphobus.

Hattu stared at the prince's corpse, until a clattering wave of battle echoed in from the hall's open main doors. Out there, the citadel grounds shone bright as day. He staggered to the doorway, resting on the stone pillar to gasp in more short, sharp breaths, gazing out in confusion. It was not day at all. The inky sky and sea of stars remained... but Troy was engulfed in flames. The Palladium Temple was a mountain of fire, ripping and roaring in the Wind of Wilusa. All around it the guard houses, the villas and the storerooms blazed and belched black smoke. In the weltering air of the streets between the burning buildings, Ahhiyawans swarmed, leaping upon dazed, terrified Trojan soldiers and people alike. Shekelesh and Locrians clambered up ancient statues and rocked, using their body weight to bring the sacred icons toppling down to smash across the citadel flagstones in tiny pieces and explosions of dust. Marauding Tiryneans speared down into the backs of fleeing noblemen and their families. Diomedes dragged a tanner around by the hair, throwing him like a toy, slashing at the man's sons when they tried to intervene. Neoptolemus and his Myrmidons hacked like harvesters into a knot of cowering priests, then forced their way into the Temple of Apollo. More and more of the invaders flooded in through the Scaean Gate. Then there was Helen, walking through this, shaking, face streaked with tears, King Menelaus a stride behind, like an executioner, one hand on his sword pommel, his face strained with humiliation. Andor circled above all of this, keening madly.

Hattu gazed around, horrified. *Dagon... Tudha...*

'Bring the progeny of Hektor to the roof…' a voice pealed above it all.

Hattu staggered fully outside and craned his neck to look up, barely noticing the arrows and thrown spears whizzing past him from many directions. Kalchas the Ahhiyawan battle-augur stood up on the palace roof, arms wide. Two grinning Sherden fighters brought a bundle of rags to the edge, while a third held a hysterical Andromache, making her watch, She struggled in vain, reaching out for the bundle. 'Astyanax, no, please, noooo,'

'…and cast him to his doom,' Kalchas bleated.

Andromache shrieked in horror as the two Sherden hurled the baby boy from the roof's edge. The babe screamed as he fell three storeys. Hattu swung away before the child landed on the flagstones. But the horror was not over: the Myrmidons emerged from the temple of Apollo, dragging King Priam with them. 'The old bastard claims sanctuary under the eyes of the archer god,' one crowed, kicking Priam in the small of the back, sending the King of Troy flailing onto his knees before Neoptolemus. The son of Achilles grinned, stalking round Priam, drawing his sword… then sheathing it again.

Hattu, fading in and out of consciousness, slumped beside a toppled statue of Poseidon, wondering if this was the moment when the massacre would slow and stop. That was when Neoptolemus stepped over to the remains of baby Astyanax. He lifted the child's corpse by the ankles, slung the body over his shoulder like a sack… then swished it down like a cudgel upon the back of the floundering Priam's head. Hattu threw up, seeing only a blur of the horrific scene. Priam screamed and wept as Neoptolemus bludgeoned him with the ragged remains of his grandson, then the rest of the Myrmidons speared him to death in a frenzy. Neoptolemus stepped back from the spraying blood, then called up to the palace roof where Andromache was on her knees, shaking, staring at her worst nightmares incarnate. 'Bring me Hektor's widow,' he shouted to Kalchas. 'I claim her as my own.' He was no sooner finished making his demands when he stretched out an arm to catch a running girl and the boy she was escorting. Princess Polyxena and young Polites. 'More royalty, eh?' he purred, seeing the purple on their collars. He sniffed at Polyxena's hair. 'You will live through tonight… and tomorrow, we will cut open your neck at the mound where my father is buried.' She shuddered, paling with fright, a dark urine stain appearing below the waist of her gown. Neoptolemus wrenched the boy from her and shoved him onto all fours in front of his Myrmidons, 'As for the boy… get rid of him.' The warriors encircled the weeping boy and quickly the weeping ended.

Hattu stumbled through this, stunned.

He barely recognized the torn halves of a body that a group of Cretans paraded on top of spears. Then he saw the face. Skorpios, agog in death.

'We made a deal! See, see my home, see the panther skin?' a familiar voice appealed nearby. Antenor, on his knees, begged another Cretan warrior. 'I am to be spared. I helped you!'

'Thank you, old fool,' the Cretan laughed, then brought the club thundering down on Antenor's head, breaking his skull like an egg, sending brain and blood spraying in chunks. Antenor's body quivered madly then flopped to one side.

'Ha!' Diomedes barked, slitting the throat of Laocoon the priest, letting the spasming body slide down his red-soaked armour. 'And I will have the bride of Priam,' he laughed, reaching towards the wrist of a woman shambling away nearby, clutching a stomach wound.

*Hekabe,* Hattu mouthed, unable to help.

But another stepped in, grabbing Hekabe before Diomedes could. 'Too slow, old comrade,' Odysseus said, standing between Diomedes and the Queen of Troy.

Diomedes rose like a lion preparing to fight its ground, but Odysseus, much the shorter, stood his too. 'You overestimate your station, old one,' Diomedes growled, then twisted to shout to someone nearby. '*Wanax,* judge this matter for us.'

Hattu barely recognised Agamemnon, drawn, gaunt of face and at the same time bloated around the middle, his wine-sack of a belly protruding from below his bronze cuirass and his hair a dry, tousled mess. The Great King of Ahhiyawa stared at his quarrelling warrior kings. 'Odysseus will have the Queen of Troy,' he said quietly, barely audible over the discordant din of the slaughter going on all around. Diomedes turned away with a roar, beheading a fleeing man in rage.

Just then, a flurry of screaming erupted from the innards of the burning Palladium Temple. Cassandra, clutching her torn-open robes, lurched from the blaze, her nose broken and bleeding, her thighs streaked with smoke stains and scratch marks. The weasel-like King of Locris came speeding out after her, kiltless and erect, eyes wild with lust. Agamemnon's eyes followed this uncompleted rape, the woman and her pursuer coming this way. With a swish of one arm, the enemy *Wanax* brought his sword hilt round to flatten the face of the Locrian King, knocking him out cold. He caught Cassandra's arm and pulled her to him. She screamed at first, but then he unbuckled his cloak and lent it to her to cover her nakedness.

Hattu, stunned by Agamemnon's unexpected display of virtue amidst this sea of slaughter, did not notice a Shekel pirate closing in on him. The man, wearing a rope of severed hands around his neck, came speeding over and slashed down with his sickle sword. It was all Hattu could do to flail clear, yet the curved blade caught him on the back of the thigh, scoring deep. The pain was like the touch of a white hot smith's poker. He heard a twisted scream without realising it was his own. Blood sheeted down his leg.

'Ha!' the Shekel cried. 'Tonight I will cut off the hands of the *Labarna* himself.' He whirled his sword in his hand. Two more Shekelesh approached to join the first, the three pacing menacingly towards Hattu.

Hattu staggered backwards, dragging his wounded leg, still shaking, half-blinded and sick from the earlier blow to his temple. He could not fight these men, he knew. The only place close enough to flee to was the Palladium Temple. The place was ablaze, but he was in no position to choose. He half-staggered, half-crawled in through the fiery doorway, over the blood and flesh of the slain, leaving a trail of his own blood behind him.

The temple was empty, echoing with the dissonant cries of plunder and the angry crackle of the blaze on the outside. Cinders fell from the ceiling like a silent, searing rain all around him. His legs began to give way. He came to the silver altar where once the Palladium statuette had been, and slid helplessly down to sit with his back against it, legs trembling and splayed out, the wounded one dark with blood.

The pursuing Shekelesh three entered the temple, hooting with laughter, then spread out like claws, ready to rush him.

He tried to reach for his twin blades but his arms were shaking madly. Troy had fallen and now all would fall with her. At the last, only one thing mattered to him. 'Ishtar, hear me, he croaked. 'Let my boy escape this massacre… let him see his mother and sister again.' Every word that fell from his tongue felt like chunks of that invisible kingly armour dropping away. 'Let him know the love I have denied him. I have been a fool all this time.'

The central Shekel with the ring of severed hands stepped over and took Hattu's wrist, smirking as he lined up for a clean cut. 'These hands will fetch a fortune at the shore markets back on my island,' he purred. The second held his spear ready for a killing strike to the chest. Hattu closed his eyes.

A whirring noise sliced through the air. Hattu blinked his eyes open. An Egyptian throwing stick hurtled through the temple and smashed into the face of the first Shekel. The man spasmed and fell, dead.

Tudha, in the doorway of the burning temple, hurled a spear into the belly of the second Shekel. The third tried to rush him, only for Tudha to feint, duck and hack through the small of the man's back with his bronze sword, nearly halving him.

'Father,' Tudha gasped, rushing over to Hattu, falling to his knees. He held up the bloodstained goat figurine. 'I found this in the palace. For a moment I thought… ' he could not finish the sentence. 'I should never have stormed off like that earlier. I said I could never tell you why I did what I did but… but… ' again he began to falter.

Hattu beheld his heir, smoke and bloodstained. He had been a mere boy when despatched north to deal with the rebellion. A boy who wasn't ready. The blame was as much his as it was Tudha's. 'I forgive you, Tudha,' he said, the words toppling out unexpectedly. 'Tudha, for that is your name… not *Tuhkanti.*' In his mind's eye he saw the face of Sirtaya, smiling, then fading away forever. 'For the things you did at Hatenzuwa, I forgive you, and I do not need to know why. I have done many dark things in my time, yet never have you judged me.'

Tudha's face crumpled with emotion, his eyes wet with tears. It was a look Hattu had not seen in many moons.

'I love you, my son. Outside the court and away from the battlefield, I am clumsy with my words but let the Gods hear me tell you at least this once that I love you.' He took Tudha's hand firmly. 'Now leave me – I am finished. Go. Swear to me you will reach home. Promise me you will look after your mother and your sister.' He shoved Tudha's hand away, like a charioteer cutting the reins and letting his horse run free.

Tudha did not move. 'The things that happened at Hatenzuwa. I did them because… because Ishtar gave me a choice.'

Hattu's blood turned to ice crystals. He shook his head slowly, disbelievingly. 'Why do you say this? She haunts me,' he patted his chest, 'not you… *me.*'

Tudha looked at him sadly. 'You, and your father before you… and now me too.'

Hattu heard the Goddess' wintry laugh echo in the caverns of his mind.

'Two nights before it happened, we camped at the shrine. Zanduhepa fed us and had our garments cleaned. The next night, we moved on and camped in the woods. That was when Ishtar came to me. In a dream – a dream more vivid than life. She showed me two futures…'

Hattu's stomach twisted into knots.

'She showed me one vision of Aunt Zanduhepa informing the rebels, giving them seals stolen from the bags of my men. The rebels using the seals to infiltrate Hattusa… then their swords flashing in the Hall of the Sun and in the palace.' He paused, shuddering. 'Mother and Ruhepa l-lying dead while they danced around the bodies. Then she showed me a second future, in which it was me who stood over Zanduhepa's corpse. Me, fated to become a hated murderer and outcast.'

Hattu's skin crept. He understood the bittersweet fruits Ishtar offered only too well: two paths, both horrid, the responsibility and choice a curse. He tried to push Tudha's descriptions from his mind, only for the remembered and real images of the stone forest shrine to slide into his mind's eye instead. Zanduhepa, and the little bundle in her arms. 'But… but the baby? It did not have to perish, surely?'

Tudha shook his head slowly, choking on tears.

Hattu squeezed his shoulder with a deep sigh. 'You do not have to tell me.'

'I do,' Tudha quivered. His lips moved with no sound for a time, as if he had lost the power of speech. Then: 'Zanduhepa did it. She… she used the babe – her own child – as an offering. A s-sacrifice to the Forest Spirits so that they might aid the rebellion.'

An unintelligible, strangled sound leapt from Hattu's throat.

Tudha gulped hard. 'We stormed the shrine in the midst of the ceremony. She had cut off the head of a snake, then slain her own child. I had intended only to arrest her, but when I saw what she had done… I killed her in a rage.'

Hattu's head spun madly.

'I did not want you to know, Father. The troop of soldiers with me that day said you had endured enough evil, betrayal and madness in your life already, and that the truth might destroy you. Ishtar taunted me with more dreams of you throwing yourself from the mountains. I thought it better for you to think that your son was errant and rash, than to know that you had been betrayed by your beloved cousin.'

Hattu sighed, a long exhalation that seemed to empty him, his head tilting back to rest against the altar.

'I tried to do what was right, Father,' Tudha appealed. 'I tried, I trie-'

His words crumbled when Hattu wrapped his arms around him and drew him into an embrace. 'The Goddess presents no painless paths, yet you chose the selfless route to save your mother and sister,' he replied in a tearful whisper into his son's ear. 'I am sorry for doubting you all this time.' He raised one hand to his chest, finding the bronze buckle holding his leather crossbands in place and flicking it loose. The twin baldrics slid from his arms, the iron sword hilts glinting. He guided the bands onto Tudha's arms.

Tudha jolted with a caged sob.

'Take these swords,' Hattu said. 'Know that they belonged to a legend before me, and do all you can to become a legend in your own right.'

Tudha buckled on the crossbands.

Hattu sighed back against the altar. 'Now go…'

An instant later he jolted with pain as something clamped violently around his wounded thigh. Tudha was wrenching at a strip of cloth, tightening it around the top of the leg. It felt as though it would bite the limb off, so tight it was. 'What are you doing?'

Wordlessly, Tudha hauled him to his feet, looping an arm around his shoulder, supporting the weight of his wounded leg and guiding him towards the temple doors.

'You can't make it out of here with me like this!' Hattu protested.

On Tudha went, ignoring him.

Outside, the carnage had intensified. A Spartan spotted and ran towards the pair, screaming with battle rage. Until a charioteer's whip lashed across the man's eyes. He went down screaming. Dagon stumbled over, armed with the whip and a shield. 'I thought you were both dead,' he panted.

'Down!' a voice roared – Aeneas, bow nocked and drawn. The three ducked as best they could. Aeneas loosed an arrow that flew like a hawk and took the creeping Mycenaean killer behind them in the neck. 'Troy is finished,' Aeneas panted, joining them. 'Come with me. My family and a small group of men are waiting down in the lower city, by the Dardanian

Gate.'

They hobbled and fought their way across the tangle of bodies, swerving around pockets of fighting and slaughter, braving opaque clouds of black smoke within which any number of horrors might be lurking. Coughing and retching, they veered towards the acropolis' broken and wide-open Scaean Gate, Hattu saw the heads of many Ahhiyawans twist towards them like hounds on the scent, faces wet with the blood of the murdered. Diomedes' face scrunched up in a gleeful rictus as he stabbed out his sword like a finger. 'The Hittites and the Dardanian Prince. Kill them!'

Hattu's small group broke into a hopeless, loping flight as swarms of Myrmidons, Spartans, Mycenaeans, Locrians, Pylians and Tiryneans converged on them. Andor swooped from the smoke-stained night sky, talons bared, but failed to slow the chasers.

'We can't outrun them,' Dagon gasped.

'Give me a sword, a spear,' Hattu panted to his small group. 'Give me a weapon then go on. Leave me to delay them.' He wriggled free of Tudha and Dagon's supporting arms, grabbing a spear and sword from a dead soldier and using one as a crutch and the other as a weapon. 'I will hold them back so you may escape.'

'Don't be a fool,' Aeneas cried.

'Hattu, no,' Dagon gasped.

'Go,' Hattu snarled at them, his voice slurred from blood loss. 'My time is over!'

'Father, no!' Tudha cried. 'You are the *Labarna,* the Sun incarnate.'

Hattu looked his boy in the eye. 'You will succeed me and be a better king than I. A better person than I. You have shown that much to me in the summer gone and with what you told me tonight.'

Turning to face the onrushing Ahhiyawans, shaking with fatigue, he held up the sword. An instant later, Dagon, Aeneas and Tudha stepped up by his side, defying his commands.

'And you have shown me, Father, that I have much still to learn,' said Tudha. His son was different now, pregnant with energy, an aura about him, his eyes and face brighter. Maybe it was the addition of the twin swords jutting from behind his shoulder blades. Or perhaps the removal of that burden of truth he had been carrying all this time. 'Only beside you can I become a good king for our people. I will not leave you here.' With that, he stepped proud of the others, unsheathed both iron blades and clashed them together. Sparks flew. 'Tarhunda, God of

Thunder, hear me!' Tudha cried, tears of defiance rolling down his cheeks.

Diomedes slowed, booming with laughter at this, his men closing in around the four laughing also… but then a new and terrible sound exploded across the acropolis: a mighty rumble of splitting stone, a gravelly boom like thunder…

Diomedes' animal smirk faded then, his eyes growing wide and darting around the smoky heavens, his throat lump shooting up and down in a deep gulp. The men with him cowered too, suddenly robbed of their confidence. 'The Thunder God of the Hittites… *is* here!' one wailed.

And then the true source of the noise, the Palladium Temple, that mighty and final pyre of the Trojan War, collapsed. The near wall came crashing down on top of the enemy like a fiery hammer. Mud brick exploded, ashlar blocks bounced crazily, pulverising scores of Diomedes' men, blazing timbers burnt many more. A thick wall of smoke and dust spouted up from this. Through it, Hattu saw Diomedes backing away, face ashen, gawping.

Tudha struck his swords together once more in a fresh shower of sparks, then pointed one at Diomedes. 'If we ever meet again, King of Tiryns, I will make you pay for the crimes you have committed in this war.'

'Come, Son,' Hattu pleaded. As they hobbled away together, gazing around the devastated, blazing wreck of Troy, golden Troy, he mouthed to the burning ruins: *Forgive me.*

In a blur, they stumbled out via the Scaean Gate and down through the dark, deserted lower city. Eumedes, the son of Commander Dolon, emerged from the shadows by the Dardanian Gate. Two Guardians were with him. They shielded an old fellow and a boy. Aeneas' father and son. 'Papa!' the lad yelped, rushing to hug Aeneas.

'Where is my wife? Where is Kreousa?' Aeneas asked, head switching from side to side, stricken with panic.

'She must have fled earlier,' Eumedes replied. 'There were some others who came down here before I arrived.'

Aeneas nodded hurriedly. 'Aye, she must… she must.'

The group stumbled out into the dark night, hobbling across the Scamander Plain. Hattu slipped in and out of consciousness as they went, Dagon and Tudha taking his weight. A few times he heard Aeneas demanding skins of honeyed water and felt the rough hands of others forcing him to drink. The sweet potion brought him round a little. As they floundered through the wild wheat fields upriver from the city, the stink of smoke and the sounds of pillage began to fade behind them. In their place rose the sounds of the countryside: wolves howling and owls hooting. Andor glided low alongside them like a scout. They splashed across an old Scamander ford near Thymbra and halted on the far banks, dropping to their knees to take on more water. Hattu drained an entire skin of it.

'We will take refuge on the slopes of Mount Ida,' Aeneas declared, pointing to the dark outline of the massif further south. 'We will be safe there. Any others who have escaped Troy will know to gather there also. Kreousa too,' he said staring back at the city, his face twitching with anxiety. 'She will meet us there.'

Hattu was gazing back at the angry glow in the north with him, face wrought with lines. The glassy Bay of Troy glowed an evil red, reflecting the blaze. A deep, primal cry echoed somewhere inside him, for he knew then that neither he nor any other Hittite would ever know or set foot inside Troy again. The golden city was gone. 'This is not how it was supposed to be,' he croaked. He thought of the King of Troy, in better times. 'I am sorry, Priam, old friend,' he whispered.

'After seeing what they did to Astyanax,' Aeneas seethed, 'King Priam would have been glad to die.'

'Hekabe, Cassandra, Andromache…' Hattu continued.

'The women,' Aeneas shook his head sombrely. 'They cannot be saved now. At least they will keep their lives, albeit as concubines or loom workers in the halls of the Ahhiyawan Kings.'

'Father,' said Tudha. 'The four tablets I have marked throughout the summer. I left all but one behind.' He brought out a clay slab, marked with tiny and incredibly neat wedge-shaped markings. 'It records only that which happened after the death of Hektor up until the celebrations last night.'

Hattu took the slab, gazing over the writing. Some of the things on there were vague and tinted with a heroic edge. Some of them were brutally honest. The cruel tricks, the horrible deaths, the deprivations, the greed. One thing was not on there: his choice tonight.

*You are the Shadow of Troy, King Hattu. You!*

He thought back to the moment, with Menelaus' knife at his neck, and wondered if he had done the right thing. One shout was all it would have taken – to raise the alarm, to give Troy a chance to organise her defences. Instead, he had chased the impossible, believing he could persuade the Trojans – after ten years of defending their city with everything they had – to quietly file out of their ancient home before the enemy came to take it for themselves. He lifted the slab with two hands and cast it down onto a riverside boulder. It exploded into many pieces which washed away in the current. Tudha and Dagon stared at him, aghast. 'I have no wish to recall this last summer, have you?' his son and oldest friend understood, slowly, neither disagreeing. 'No Hittite will sing of what went on here. Troy is gone. Let us allow her remains to lie in peace.'

'I never thought I would see the place in flames,' Dagon said softly, a tear rolling down his cheek, painting a pale line against the grime there. Wiping his face dry, he asked Hattu: 'The great pillar of the west has fallen. What now for our empire… or what is left of it?'

But it was Tudha who answered: 'We can only pray to the Gods that the Ahhiyawans are content with their plunder. In case they are not, I will marshal what forces we have back at Hattusa as best I can in case they try to encroach upon our heartlands.'

'It need not come to swords,' Hattu added. 'As soon as we reach home, we must despatch messengers to the Ahhiyawan palaces to propose talks. A treaty.' He looked from the blazing city to the darkness of the western horizon. It wasn't the Ahhiyawans that were the greatest danger now. They had spent themselves in the taking of Troy. He thought back over all he and Odysseus had discussed: the tales of tribal mass migrations, warrior nomads, vast pirate fleets out that way, roving eastwards. A huge and troubling unknown. 'We will treat with the Ahhiyawans. We will bring stability to these parts once more. No more war. Those who fell here must be the last to die in battle like this.' He closed his eyes, willing it to be so.

Yet from the blackness behind his eyelids, he saw Tudha, older, crouched like a warrior, watchful. Ishtar appeared before his son, swaying towards him with her twin lions prowling at her sides. From the blackness behind her, terrible sounds rose. Strange echoes of the future. Sounds of stampeding hooves, of clashing bronze, of utter devastation, visions of dark smoke crawling across the lands like panthers' paws, surrounding Tudha on all sides. Over it all, the Goddess sang the final two lines of her sour song:

*And the time will come, as all times must,*
*when the world will shake, and fall to dust…*

# EPILOGUE

## LATE SUMMER 1258 BC

The wind blew westwards and the lion-emblazoned sails of the Mycenaean fleet thundered, stark against the blue dome of sky. The squall whipped the green waters of the Aegean into a field of frothy peaks, sending spume and iridescent mist across the boats. Agamemnon walked the decks of his flagship for the hundredth time that morning, the briny spray dampening his lined and haggard face and stubbled jaw. He ran one hand along the ship's scarred rail, recalling every sword blow and arrow strike that had made these very marks. It seemed hard to believe that it had been ten summers since last this vessel had been afloat. Ten years on chocks in the sandy Bay of Boreas on the now faraway shores of Troy. The truth of it brought an aching sadness pressing down on top of his heart. *Ten years?* The meaning of time had deserted him during the war.

These last two days, since leaving the eastern shores, had been the first in months in which he had not touched wine or nepenthe, had not gone to sleep in a drunken haze nor woken and begun drinking before rising from his bed. There was a cold, fresh clarity about everything now. A spring of energy in his muscles and a sharpness of thought that reminded him of childhood. But it also threw into sharp relief the things that had been done in the toppling of Priam's city.

He heard the tap-tapping of a reed stylus against clay. His royal scribe stood, face wet from the sea spray, long curls of hair flapping, writing madly. '*Wanax*,' the young man said brightly. 'I have written almost all of the story as you tasked me to. What about Penthesilea the Amazon?'

He thought of the lioness warrior. A legend. Even her defeat was legendary, and it had happened under his watch. 'Be sure to mention that she is, *was*, a daughter of Ares.'

The scribe tapped away, tongue poking out. He looked up again. 'What about the Hittite Emperor?'

Agamemnon's mouth opened to reply, then shrank again. His mind drifted to the chat he had shared with the tall, silver-haired Hattu. Some claimed he too was of divine parentage – the Son of Ishtar, they said. Agamemnon had realised that day in the hut that he was just a man, albeit a sharp and incredible one, and so too was his heir. More, Hattu had outfoxed his army at every turn except the very last. There was not much about the Hittite presence at Troy that could be committed to clay that would not make him or his Ahhiyawan confederation sound like fools. 'Do not bother with him,' Agamemnon said, waving a nonchalant hand.

The scribe raised an eyebrow, but dutifully kept his stylus at bay.

'And Mardukal too, make no mention of him. When the bards sing of our victory in years to come, they must sing not of Hittites or Assyrians, but of the men I wisely picked for this expedition. It was the engineer, Epeius, who built the siege horse, and Odysseus who devised the ruse of hiding within it.'

'Very good, *Wanax*,' the scribe bowed, backing away, stylus woodpeckering away again.

Agamemnon strolled along the deck. He noticed one of his war prizes, Cassandra, standing at the prow wrapped in blankets, her hair dancing in the wind. 'You should retire to the aft cabin, Princess,' he called to her, seeing that her blankets were soaked through, 'take shelter from the wind and wetness.'

She looked back at him almost coquettishly. 'Oh, that doesn't matter,' she said.

'I've seen brutes of men scoff at the spray only to fall ill with fever,' he replied, joining her at the prow.

'But we are almost across the sea, are we not?' she asked.

Agamemnon peered west, seeing more of the small rocky islands ahead, and a great ethereal rampart of mountains on the horizon. 'We will be on the shores of the Argolid come noon, and soon after we will reach my city, Mycenae!' he said, sucking in a breath through his nostrils. 'You can smell the land now, eh? The air in Mycenae tastes different,' he said. 'Sweet with the scent of pine and oleander petals.'

'When I was a girl, the Bay of Boreas used to smell of fresh bread and baking fish,' Cassandra said. 'Rosewater too, and incense and spices of every colour. It was Troy's market bay, you see, before you came.'

Agamemnon felt the need to shuffle and straighten. He did recall the landing at Troy well enough, even after all this time. The beach had been a patchwork of hastily adapted stalls, pens and skiffs – thrown over and dug into the sand as makeshift defences. The Trojans had organised a stout defence of the bay. But then the first of the ships had crunched up onto the shores. The struggle on the sands was frantic but balanced… until Achilles' boat landed. Agamemnon closed his eyes. 'You are right. The place stank of blood, sweat, sheep and shit from the moment we arrived.'

'Many died on that beach, yes?' she asked.

He thought of the landing battle, and the terrible day when Hektor had nearly overwhelmed the city of ships. 'Aye,' he mumbled. 'Why do you ask?'

'It makes me wonder: hundreds of years from now, when the bones of those buried there are ground down into tiny fragments and mixed in with the sand, will anyone remember them?' A strand of soaked hair blew across her face, sticking there. 'When they come to the ruins of Troy, and see the dark streaks on the plain where the soil is infused with ashes, will they know that they look upon the remains of my brothers and my people?' She gently brushed the wet lock of hair away. 'Or was it all for nothing?'

He slid his thumbs into his belt and rocked back on his heels with a low laugh, flicking his head towards the scribe. 'My Lady, people will speak of my victory for evermore,' he said with a confidence he didn't feel. He thought back to his early excuses for the conflict. 'Not only did I avert war in my own lands, but also I broke the trade stranglehold. Troy had cornered all sea commerce for herself. The tolls your father demanded of passing ships were extortionate, the punishments for non-payment brutal. I have dismantled that cartel. Now traders will be able to move freely and fill their own coffers instead of Priam's. More, I will not apologise for taking my fair share of his treasure from the city vaults.'

Cassandra smiled at him like a mother to a naïve child. 'Yes, my father was greedy, even if he did not believe it of himself. But his wealth ensured stability. All those who lived along the coastline from Wilusa to Lukka knew that Troy was the guardian of the western shores, with the means to summon the Hittite Empire and to hire many mercenaries. And that's what he used his treasure for, in the end.' She nodded her head towards the five sorry sacks tied near the base of the mast. 'That which you found in the vaults was but the scrapings of what there once was. You have won far less than you spent, King of Mycenae. I see before me a victor with a thin treasure and an old man's face.'

He felt a flare of anger within him. Princess or not, she was now his and she would obey him! But he caught his temper before it spun out of control. The time for anger was over, he thought, sighing deeply. 'I have not yet apologised for the behaviour of my men on the night of Troy's fall.' His voice cracked a little as he said this, his mind flashing with images of the Locrian King loping after her, having ravaged her once already in the sacred Palladium Temple.

'You saved me from your animal underling,' said Cassandra. 'I harbour no anger against you. But the Goddess Athena...' she said, shaking her head slowly with a tight smile.

Just then, the sail snapped and bulged in a fresh squall. Agamemnon looked up and around, seeing his crew and those of the other boats suddenly taken by surprise, men struggling to adjust the rigging. A shout came from somewhere off to the north. One of his warships was passing close to an islet – a rocky fang bereft of greenery apart from one defiant mulberry tree on the stony peak. The waters foamed, gurgled and slapped against the island's steep sides. 'Wreckage,' the man shouted, waving. Another used an oar to fish out a soaked heraldic cloth, baring the image of a deer. 'The ships of Locris were dashed against these rocks.'

Cassandra smiled on.

Agamemnon's heart thumped. It seemed that Pallas Athena had taken her revenge for the sacrilegious rape at her altar. But was she finished? He glanced around the seven Mycenaean galleys with his flagship. Apart from that, the sea was empty. The Ahhiyawans had departed from Troy in a giant fleet, just the way they had arrived. But a storm had separated them. His brother Menelaus' fleet had not been seen since. Odysseus' boats too had vanished. And the flotilla of the Locrians. At first, he had assumed they were all simply more than a day adrift. Now he wondered, spotting a bloated corpse bobbing near the Locrian wreckage, if they had met a fate like this. He gulped and looked around once more, fearing the Goddess' wrath.

But the winds were kind, and soon the flagship drew into a quiet cove, gliding across the calm turquoise waters to the Mycenaean harbour. The timbers of the ship clunked gently against the wooden jetty. Agamemnon was the first to disembark. He spread his arms wide, fears dissipating, eyes sliding shut as he breathed in the sweet air. A round tower of stone loomed nearby – a lookout post and billet for his Watchmen of the Coast. But so relieved to be off the ship was he that he did not even notice the absence of any Mycenaean guards there.

'I'm home!' he purred.

***

The Mycenaeans trekked inland, sweating and panting. The heat grew intense as they passed through a tight creek, the cicadas chattering away in the sparse greenery by the trackside. Hawks watched from high eyries, intrigued by these 'strangers' and the crunching of their boots echoing up through the corridor. Agamemnon enjoyed the noise, and it took him a moment to realise why: because it sounded as if there were many warriors with him, just as there had been all those years ago when the army set out towards Aulis and the great mustering of the kingdoms. *When Iphigenia was still alive*, he thought, overwhelmed by sadness. A glance over his shoulder showed the truth. Less than two hundred warriors were coming home. More than one thousand wives, parents and children would weep tonight.

They emerged from the creek then rounded a wooded hill to emerge onto the great, sun-splashed plain of the Argolid. Agamemnon, blinded by the sun, remembered it as he had left it: a wide green landscape of wheat fields and pastures, running all the way from the coast to the high golden mountain overlooking it all, upon which the city of Mycenae sat like a stony overlord. Then the dazzling trickery of the sunlight faded, and he began to see it for real. He blinked a few times, confused.

The valley was as golden and dry as the creek. No carpet of shimmering green crop, no roving herds of sheep or goats. No lowing of oxen or barking of farm dogs, nor the whisper and rustle of wheat being sheafed. He slowed, stepping from the trackside and to a small field that he had personally granted to a local man named Erimes. Stooping, he picked up a handful of the earth. It was like powder, utterly parched. In one corner of the allotment lay a pile of desiccated timbers. Beside it rose a small tomb mound and two even smaller ones beside it – the graves of a woman and her children. He gazed past this smallholding, seeing the many others lying derelict and barren like it. Near the heart of the plain, the stone villas of the richer men were stained black and some tumbledown or with their roofs caved in, drifts of dust lying against the walls. 'What happened here?' he croaked, the song of the cicadas growing mocking, maddening.

A goat bleated by way of reply, almost causing Agamemnon to spring from his boots. He swung to see an ancient man – a cage of bones wrapped in thin leather, walking with a stick, ushering the goat to one side. His eyes were clouded. 'Please,' he said, 'do not take my last animal from me. I have nothing else left.'

Agamemnon squinted, stepping over to the fellow. 'Erimes?' he said, not quite believing that this could be the vital man he had granted land to.

Erimes' face changed, as if overcome with fright. 'Have I passed across the River?' he whispered. 'I must have, surely, if the shades of the dead speak to me?'

Agamemnon felt a stark shiver race up his spine. He took the old man's hands in his and lifted them to his face. 'I am no shade. It is your king who speaks.'

Erimes squinted as if he could see again, his fingers feeling Agamemnon's features. '*Wanax?* By all the Gods… where have you been?'

'At war,' Agamemnon said with a triumphant laugh. 'The greatest war ever fought.'

Yet none of his men laughed, nor did Erimes.

'War? The last we heard of you was some years ago, several summers after you had set sail to conquer Troy. We long ago assumed you were dead.' Suddenly he recoiled. 'Hold on. Surely you do not mean you have been at Troy all this time?'

Agamemnon swallowed a spike of offence. This old man had suffered plenty already. 'Come to my halls tonight,' he said, flicking a finger up at the fortified palace-city of Mycenae, 'I will regale you all with my tales of our victory.'

Erimes looked unimpressed. 'There are not many people here for you to entertain, *Wanax.*'

An arid, hot breeze passed over the valley then, casting up a few puffs of tumbleweed across the desiccated valley. Agamemnon tried to remember how long it had been since he had last received a clear and direct communication from his homeland. *Three summers? More?* 'What has happened to my kingdom?'

Erimes sagged. 'Pestilence at first. A poor crop. Then the earth shuddered in a way it never has done before.' He pointed in the direction of a furrow that wended its way from the mountains near the city and on across the valley towards the coast. 'It broke the land like a god's axe. The river drained into the darkness and never returned. The drought then took the land in its waterless claws and wrung the soil dry. What once was green and fertile is now parched and barren. It seems many of the other green vales of Ahhiyawa have suffered similar fates. Nearby Tiryns and Argos, faraway Pylos and Sparta too.' He shrugged. 'I tried to tend my plot as best I could. For those first few years I believed you would return. Others, however, began rioting. They tried a few times to storm the high city to break into the royal grain silo, but the guard contingent you left behind were ruthless in despatching them. Most of those who survived fled. That,' he said with a rattling sigh, 'was when *they* came.'

'They?'

Erimes shook his old head slowly and sadly. 'The tribes of the distant west. The Sherden, the Shekelesh and many others. They, upon whom we once looked upon as opportunistic brigands, now move in great waves from their faraway homelands – tens of thousands of warriors and many more families – driven by the same storm of earth tremors and relentless drought. They come not to raid, but to claim for themselves these lands. They are crude, bloodthirsty peoples.'

Agamemnon planted a hand on Erimes' shoulder. 'I ask you again to come to my hall tonight. Spread the word to what farmers and herdsmen remain in the Argolid that their king has returned home. I will feed you well, and I will assure you of a better future. After all, we bring home the riches of Troy!' he took one of the treasure sacks from the soldier carrying them and shook it. The sack was light and the sound it made was pathetic. 'Mycenae will flourish again,' he insisted. 'So too will the cities of our fellow Ahhiyawans. Soon we will send boats back to broken Troy to colonise the land for ourselves.' He stopped to think of what King Hattu had alluded to and what Odysseus had implored him to do – to seek stability and treaty in his lands and on the shores they had won. It made some sense now, after ten years of war. An age of truce, perhaps, in which he could enjoy his spoils and his reputation – a time when his expanded dominion and that of the Hittites could be equal neighbours. 'Soon… we will rule the lands here and make permanent homes on the coasts across the sea. We will be a great power to match the others of this world!'

Erimes gave him a sad smile and a look with those blind eyes that seemed to see deep inside him. 'Until tonight, *Wanax,*' he said quietly.

Agamemnon and his soldiers climbed the tightly-snaking path up towards the walled city of Mycenae, the afternoon sun fierce on their backs. When they reached the mountain top, the moaning wind furrowed pleasantly through Agamemnon's sweat-soaked hair. He felt weary, but forced himself to strut confidently towards the Lion Gate – the huge stone entrance into the fortified city. The sun winked and blinked behind the massive defences. His eyes drank in the sight of the carved lions prowling above the lintel stone… so much so that he almost tripped over the huge bar of broken limestone lying before the gate. He stared down at the immense block, then up at the hole in the defences where it had once been. Now he noticed that all along the city wall, pieces were missing like this, and one section lay sloughed away and strewn down the mountainside. Weeds and bright pink cyclamen sprouted from the gaps.

'The earthquake,' he said over his shoulder to the nearest of his men. 'How long ago did Erimes say it happened?'

'This damage looks years old, *Wanax*,' said the man. 'Anyway, earthquake or not… where are the sentries?'

Unnerved, they entered Mycenae. The palatial city he had left behind had gone to seed. The gardens were a sprawling mess of vines and piles of decaying vegetation. The guardhouse lay in semi-ruin like the villas down on the plain, and the stonework was criss-crossed with the tell-tale marks of spears. At least the palace itself was still in one piece, he mused. Waiting there for him was the woman he had not seen nor lain with for more than ten years.

'Clytemnestra,' he whispered, eyes welling up.

She gazed down at him from the stone porch, her face wide with disbelief, as if she had seen a god walking. She stumbled as she descended the few steps towards him, grabbing the bannister to balance. 'Agamemnon… you… you are alive?'

He slid his arms around her and wept. 'I am home, my love. I am home.'

***

Come late afternoon, he slid into a sunken stone pool laced with sweet oils and surrounded by burning incense cones. Groans of pain and pleasure slid from his lips as he sank in up to his neck, the warm waters grabbing hold of every rock-hard muscle and knot in his weary body. Ten years since he had enjoyed such a pleasure. He sank under the surface and let his breath escape in a slow trickle of bubbles. In that watery netherworld, everything seemed to float away from him – the burden of his excess weight and the troubling news he had returned to. For those few moments, he remembered what life had been like, before the war. Before Aulis. When she was still alive. *Iphigenia,* he mouthed quietly, a bubble escaping his lips and rising to the surface. There, then gone, just like his beloved daughter – now just bleached bones in her barrow tomb at Aulis.

Rising from the water, he swept his hair back from his face, the plink-plonk of condensation droplets from the painted ceiling falling into the pool and echoing around the bath chamber. He gazed from the open end of the chamber, down over the small city and across the arid sun washed valley far-below. Much to do. Many problems to rectify.

He turned to look through the doorway into his royal megaron – 'The Hall of Lions'. His throne – polished of Trojan sand and dust and reinstalled there by his small troop of men – overlooked four brightly painted pillars and an empty hearth. Princess Cassandra was there, kneeling quietly by the hearth, waiting. Waiting for what? He wondered. 'Princess,' he called to her. 'Seeress!' he tried again. 'Come, join me, tell me what the future holds.'

She looked up and at him, her face sombre. 'There is not much more to tell, My Lord.'

Bemused, he sank against the poolside and closed his eyes.

A short time later the water rippled, otherwise he would not have known that his wife had joined him in the pool. Naked, beautiful, she glided over, pressing herself to him. He felt a frantic surging in his loins – something he had curiously never truly experienced despite all the war-brides of which he had his choice at Troy. Briseis had been taken from Achilles purely to put the man in his place. Nobody knew that he had been flaccid that night when he tried to lie with her. Achilles' prize had gone unspoiled.

Clytemnestra slid herself onto him and began to slide expertly up and down, caressing his manhood. He felt himself charging towards a climax, along with a sudden embarrassment at the quickness of it. 'My love,' he said, taking her face in his hands, trying to slow her, 'we must speak.'

'About the land? The soldiers? The wreckage?' she gasped, writhing faster and faster. 'Later, my love… later.'

'About Iphigenia,' he said. The bath chamber fell silent and still as a tomb. 'You… you will have heard about what happened?'

She fell still, slid from him and drifted backwards to the far end of the pool. 'I bathed her on the night before she was supposed to wed Achilles… and I washed her once again, on the empty shores at Aulis, after your fleet had departed. I washed out her neck wound and finished digging her barrow myself.'

'It was a great mistake,' Agamemnon pleaded. 'The madness of war.' He raised a hand, spraying water droplets as he gestured towards the open end of the chamber and the baking countryside. 'I foresaw the troubles brewing in the many thronerooms of Ahhiyawa. I knew that if I did not unite them for war then they would start fighting against one another. I did it for our land. I did it for us… I…'

Clytemnestra nodded. But not at him. The one who had crept into the bath chamber behind Agamemnon reached down from the pool's edge to grab his chin with one hand, then pressed a small surgeon's hook to the side of his neck. He gawped up at the smirking man.

'Aegisthus?' he yelped.

'I was the king of Mycenae before you took the kingdom for yourself,' Aegisthus said calmly. 'Now I will be so once again. Thank you for returning the throne.'

'Guards!' Agamemnon howled.

Aegisthus hooted with laughter, the hook tight against Agamemnon's pulsing jugular.

'The few soldiers you brought back did well to survive the war at Troy,' Clytemnestra said, 'but by now they are all dead.'

A clashing and clattering sounded from somewhere deep inside the palace, coming closer. Agamemnon looked across the pool at Clytemnestra. 'My love?' he rasped. 'What is this?' He watched, dumbfounded, as she rose from the waters, sleek and wet, to sit down on a bench by the door, smiling, naked. Beyond the door, Cassandra still knelt out there in the megaron by the hearth, but her head was bowed, her robes dark red with her own blood. His stomach twisted sharply.

'I slit your Trojan whore's neck just as you had our daughter's throat cut,' Clytemnestra said in a low burr. 'Mycenae is mine now… ours.' Her eyes rolled up to Aegisthus. 'Kill him.'

'Wait,' Agamemnon pleaded. 'Spare me. You need me. The land is in disarray. We need to arrange a permanent coalition of the Ahhiyawan kingdoms, then we need to treat with the Hittites. These things must happen if we are to defend our country against the roving bands of the west.'

She threw her head back and laughed long and loud. 'The western warriors? How do you think I managed to keep control of this place after the great quake?'

At just that moment, the shrieking, clattering and smashing from somewhere else in the palace spilled into the Hall of Lions. Agamemnon's heart almost burst from his chest when he saw one of his warriors stumbling into view. He filled his lungs to shout for help, when a trident burst through the man's chest. The killer – a horn-helmed Sherden – kicked the body from the end of the weapon and let loose a horrific shriek, head sweeping from side to side as he searched for more victims, while dozens more of those pirates sped into and scurried across the megaron, eager for blood.

One rushed into the bath chamber as if to continue the rampage, then slowed and sank to one knee before Clytemnestra. 'We have dealt with all of the returning troops, as you commanded, My Lady. They will present no threat to the rule of the true king,' he finished with a bow to Aegisthus.

'My love, what have you done?' Agamemnon croaked.

'Only that which you have driven me too,' she replied. Her eyes met Aegisthus'. The hook at Agamemnon's throat jerked backwards, tearing out and snapping his jugular like the root of a weed. Blood spurted from the wound. Clutching at the deep gash, he thrashed and staggered, the strength pouring out of him. Finally, he sagged onto his back, sinking down into the darkening waters, seeing with the last moments of light his wife and her usurping lover walking hand in hand from the bath chamber, then more of the shrieking Sherden entering, standing by the edges of the pool to stare down at his sinking body.

The lead Sherden watched and waited until Clytemnestra and Aegisthus were gone. 'So it is true,' he drawled to his tribal comrades. 'Across the sea, the city of Troy lies in ruin, the lands undefended and ripe for plunder. And the doorway to the great empire beyond lies wide open. Spread word to the tribes and the ships. We must gather as one. Our future lies in the east.'

As one, they raised their spears and tridents '*Haaa!*'

THE END

**The *Empires of Bronze* series CONCLUDES with 'THE DARK EARTH'**

*The time will come, as all times must, when the world will shake, and fall to dust…*

1237 BC: It is an age of panic. The great empires are in disarray – ravaged by endless drought, shaken by ferocious earthquakes and starved of precious tin. Some say the Gods have abandoned mankind.
When Tudha ascends the Hittite throne, the burden of stabilising the realm falls upon his shoulders. Despite his valiant endeavours, things continue to disintegrate; allies become foes, lethal plots arise, and enemy battle horns echo across Hittite lands.

Yet this is nothing compared to the colossal, insidious shadow emerging from the west. Crawling unseen towards Tudha's collapsing Hittite world comes a force unlike any ever witnessed; an immeasurable swarm of outlanders, driven by the cruel whip of nature, spreading fire and destruction: the Sea Peoples.

Every age must end. The measure of a man is how he chooses to face it.

***Empires of Bronze: The Dark Earth*** is available at all good online stores!

# AUTHOR'S NOTE

The Trojan War is so fundamental and foundational to the history of Western civilization that this project was, to put it mildly, a daunting prospect. Homer's *Iliad* is a revered text, and serves not only as our poetic reference to the war we think happened at Troy some 3,200 years ago, but also as the only source of substantial detail about that conflict. Now, just about every word of that last sentence could quite rightly be challenged from many angles, and so I will start by outlining my four main assumptions upon which *The Shadow of Troy* was based:

Firstly, Troy *was* a very real city. In the Hittite world, it was known as Taruisa, the major settlement in the vassal region of Wilusa. In the world of the Ahhiyawans (Homer's Achaeans or Greeks), it was known as Troia, and the region as Ilios. It doesn't take a philologist to spot the similarity in the names. Take the Ahhiyawan region name 'Ilios', add the Hittite-style 'w' prefix and 'sa' suffix and you'll see what I mean – same goes if you add the 'sa' suffix alone to Troia. As for the location of the city: the ruins lie at Hisarlik in northwestern Turkey.

Secondly, there *was* a war over Troy in the Late Bronze Age. In fact, there were probably several. The clincher here is the existence of a very real Hittite tablet sent from Great King Hattusilis III (our hero, Hattu) to an unnamed Ahhiyawan Great King. It talks of a military clash between the Ahhiyawans and the Hittite Empire over the territory of Troy:

*"Now as we have come to an agreement on Wilusa over which we went to war."* – excerpt from 'the Tawagalawa letter'.

Thirdly, while the Trojan War has been 'dated' to various decades around the end of the Bronze Age, with estimates spanning 1260-1180 BC, I believe that the war from which the legend derives occurred in the earlier part of that range. My rationale is threefold: the tablet from which the above quote comes from – thought to have been sent in 1250 BC – refers to a past conflict, which means the ten years war must have begun in 1260 BC or earlier; the VIh layer of the Troy ruins, carbon-dated to around 1260 BC, sports the distinctively huge sloping/beetling walls and towers that fit the tale of *The Iliad*; finally, the VIh layer also shows evidence of warfare and destruction at that time.

Troy has been depicted in countless works of art as a golden city of palaces and orchards, and most often Aegean Greek in style. This is understandable as the rich imagery of *The Iliad* is based on an Ahhiyawan or Greek viewpoint. Historically, the city of Troy was almost certainly much more of a cosmopolitan hub – a Singapore of the Bronze Age, a crossroads between east and west, north and south. The city's markets and in particular her trade ports would have been constantly clogged with merchants – from Mycenae, Egypt, Babylon… even tin traders from distant Britannia! Underneath this current of passing trade, the people of Troy were more likely to have been culturally Anatolian. The practices detailed in *The Iliad* – such as Hektor's funeral ritual with the cleaning and burial of his bones, plus his brother Deiphobus' immediate marriage to the widowed Helen – are very strikingly Anatolian and specifically Hittite customs. Despite some of the Iron Age anachronisms that creep into *The Iliad's* verses in places (such as the use of chariots as no more than 'battle taxis'), this stands out as an irrefutable Bronze Age truth.

The army of Troy was another thing which would have distinguished the Trojans from their Ahhiyawan attackers. Agamemnon's forces – from the mountainous regions of Greece – appear to have been largely composed of spear and sword infantry with a small number of elite royal chariots. In contrast, the Trojan military would have been trained on the sweeping plains of Anatolia – perfect country for archery and horse breeding – and would have comprised more of both bowmen and chariots. As depicted, the gathered Trojan allies would indeed have spoken a fair mix of languages. As Homer says:

*Armies of allies crowd the mighty city of Priam, true, but they speak a thousand different tongues, fighters gathered here from all ends of the realm.* – excerpt from *The Iliad.*

Tablets and engravings most often reveal clues as to the core cultural leanings of ancient peoples – their customs and appearances and so on. Infuriatingly, despite all the excavations at and around Troy, we have only ever uncovered one piece of writing. It was a seal, tellingly marked with Luwian (Hittite) text.

So the Trojans were probably culturally close to their Anatolian neighbours in the Hittite Empire. We know for certain that they were vassals to the Hittite Throne. This all brings me to the open question I posed at the end of the previous book in the series: in Troy's moment of great peril, surrounded by the armies of Agamemnon, where were the

Hittites – their overlords and protectors?

The big problem is that *The Iliad* does not mention the Hittites. Not even a passing reference to them. This is akin to Latvia and Estonia going to war and nobody ever mentioning Russia. However, *The Iliad* covers just a few months in the 10th and final year of the war, ending with Hektor's funeral. The things that happened between then and the actual end of the war – the coming of the Amazons and the Elamites, the deaths of Paris and Achilles, the horse, the sacking of the city and more – survive only in the tantalising fragments of the subsequent six ancient texts that make up what is known as *The Epic Cycle*. Regardless, as fragmentary as those texts may be, none of them mention the Hittites either!

What's going on there? One theory is that the Hittite Empire had collapsed by the time of the Trojan War. This doesn't really hold water, as the Ahhiyawan world collapsed at roughly the same time as the Hittite world, so if the Hittites were gone, then so too must be Agamemnon and his lot, and how could there be a Trojan War then? Even if the end of the Hittite Empire preceded the fall of Ahhiyawa by several years, one would expect there to be at least an echo of the Hittites in *The Iliad.*

Most likely, I think, we are looking too hard and too literally at the *Epic Cycle* texts for a mention of the Hittites. After all, the name 'Hittite' didn't actually exist in the time of Hattu. He and his people knew themselves as 'The People of the Land of Hatti'. More, Egypt knew them as 'The Khetti'. And that's where one theory arises: *Odyssey,* the tale of Odysseus' tumultuous and circuitous voyage home, contains a passage of exposition about the war which mentions the arrival of a force known as 'The Keteioi' as reinforcements to the Trojan effort. They turned up in the final year of the war and became Troy's last hope following the death of Hektor. Could these Keteioi be the Hittites? It is a frustratingly flimsy deduction but intriguing nonetheless. Certainly, it seems more plausible at least than other wilder theories – that the Amazons were in fact the Hittites (owing to their long, dark 'feminine' hair and shaved chins), or that a minor Trojan ally, the Halizones, were the Hittites.

There, then, is my fourth major assumption: that the Hittites *were* at the Trojan War in some capacity. Hattu had only recently claimed the Hittite throne from Urhi-Teshub, though perhaps letting his nephew live was a huge mistake. Many of the vassal kingdoms, sensing that the exile might be on the brink of returning in an effort to reclaim the throne – bringing war and retribution with him – wavered in their loyalty to

Hattu's rule. Hattu was also plagued by jibes of illegitimacy from mocking foreign rulers. The Great King of Assyria – a rival empire – sent neither envoys nor gifts to Hattu's coronation ceremony, and went as far as to label him as 'A substitute for the real Hittite King'. Hattu – without an army – had no option but to seek treaty and stability with any region who would have it. The greatest agreement of this kind was that which he struck with Ramesses II of Egypt. He and his erstwhile and mighty enemy agreed what is known as 'The Eternal Treaty' or 'The Silver Treaty', which laid out the conditions of a defensive alliance between the Hittites and the Egyptians. This effectively mitigated the huge threat posed by Assyria, and – in my take on things – allowed Hattu to tend to the long unanswered call for help from Troy. His efforts there, although speculative, occur at a watershed period in his life. Following the years about which you have just read, Hattu withdrew from his previous incarnation as a battle leader into a shell of introspection. He wrote many texts, known as 'The Apologies', detailing his failings and regrets, and took up the role of a diplomat-king. His son, Tudha, rose to the fore of the Hittite army in his place. And that army, patchwork and unprepared as it might be, would be needed…

My first draft of this tale was something of a slavish regurgitation of *The Iliad*. Every cut to the hand, every turn of weather and all the most famous poetic lines were in there. So… I tore it up and started again. My goal, you see, was never to recount the tale that Homer has already told so well. I wanted to get under the skin of the legend, to understand how things might have been in the pauses between the verses of *The Iliad*; to match up the historicity of the Hittite tablets and the excavated finds against the poetry. I have thus opted to omit and truncate many events and minor characters from *The Iliad* in order for this book to be the story I wanted it to be. I have also kept the tale largely secular, even though the cast hold deeply-spiritual views and believe in their very vivid dreams. In the space freed up by these omissions, I have written of guerrilla warfare, treachery, plausible numbers of soldiers on both sides, the trauma of such a brutal war on the individuals involved (I urge you to find and gaze upon the painting 'Ulysses and the sirens' by Herbert Draper, which captures this theme with haunting perfection), the possible origins of the huge trenches found by excavators along Troy's southern edge and the speculative mercenary involvement of an Assyrian siege general in the building of the famous horse of Troy.

The Trojan Horse is iconic and legendary, yet – as previously mentioned – it is only mentioned in passing in *Odyssey*, which tortures us with just a single line:

*A single horse captured Troy.*

We have no firm idea what this 'horse' actually was. Theories are wide and varied: that it was a wooden gift which the Trojans pulled into their city only for the enemy hiding inside the belly to drop out and throw open the gates; or a chariot wing of some sort that charged inside the city; or that Helen herself *was* the horse in the form of a spy; or that it was a ship (ships were known as 'horses of the sea'); or that it was an earthquake that pulled down Troy's defences (the God Poseidon was thought to be the Lord of Earthquakes). There are various other theories, but the one makes most sense to me as a historian is that the horse was a siege device. Later writers Pausanius and Pliny the Elder were both convinced that this was the case, the former stating:

*Anyone who doesn't think the Trojans utterly stupid will have realized that the horse as really an engineer's device for breaking down the walls.*

Assyrian siege technology in this age was unsurpassed, and their engineers were adept at designing and constructing city-taking devices. More, these were often named after animals – The Assyrian Horse, the Wild Ass, The Wooden One-Horned Animal. Tablets depict the first of these as a ram shed with a 'neck and head', the head containing a drill bit used to pick apart walls. Even if an Assyrian hadn't been present at the Trojan War, the siege technology could have made its way there. My take on it all was a twist on the gift theory, making it a seemingly abandoned super-siege engine as opposed to an apparent tribute.

The title of the story "The Shadow of Troy" can be interpreted several ways – most literally as the traitor, but also metaphorically as the shadow that the war-tangled city casts over Hattu's world – compelling him to march to Troy's aid and fulfil the long neglected oath. Equally, it touches upon the shadowy future that the Goddess Ishtar predicts will follow Troy's demise.

So that's my take on the history and the fiction. This is my twentieth novel. Had I written of the Trojan war any earlier, it might have been a simple war story. Now, I hope it is what I waited for: a tale of legend and history, of the futility of war, of fathers and sons.

Regardless of how you choose to interpret the legendary story – as a poetic symbol or as a historical record – the outcome of the tale is a sorry one: the Trojans lost everything; Priam's line was wiped out and his city was never the same again. Worse, the conquering armies soon discovered that their victory was fleeting, for their realm across the sea quickly fell into the dust of history too, consumed by a storm of migrating masses. Next in the path of that storm lay the land of the Hittites…

Yours faithfully,
Gordon Doherty
www.gordondoherty.co.uk

P.S. If you enjoyed the story, please spread the word. My books live or die by word of mouth, so tell your friends or – even better – leave a short review on Amazon or Goodreads. Anything you can do in this vein would be very much appreciated.

**Connect with me!** I always enjoy chatting with my readers. Get in touch or sign up for my newsletter at: www.gordondoherty.co.uk

The *Empires of Bronze* saga CONCLUDES with…

EMPIRES OF BRONZE

# THE DARK EARTH

LATE WINTER 1237 BC

The heavens growled, flickering with veins of lightning. Tudha rolled his silver eyes skywards. A fine mist-rain, cold as death, settled on his broad face, causing the white line of scar running from forehead to chin to ache. Why, he thought, did the Thunder God choose to speak now? Where were these rains in the many months past when the crops had failed?

'Prince Tudha, I beg of you, *please!*'

Tudha dropped his gaze slowly to the kneeling man: his upper lip was bloody and swollen, his chest heaving from the effort of the skirmish just lost. The sixty or so captives with him were equally wretched. Gaunt cheeks, rotten teeth. Worst of all, they were not bandits or raiders from abroad. These men were Hittites. His own people. The minor town of Lalanda had long been a place of brothers, inherently loyal to the Grey Throne. Then the thin herds around the capital had started to go missing during the night. The animal tracks all led back here.

'Did you think about the hungry people of Hattusa?' Tudha replied, the rain on his lips puffing as he spoke, his jet-black collar length hair quivering. 'Those who went without milk and meat because of what you did?'

'We took only what we needed for our families,' the man pleaded. 'Twelve sheep and seven goa-*argh!*' he flailed forwards, landing on his face in the mud. A cloaked officer stood behind him, haft end of his spear trained for a second jab at the downed man's back. 'You dare to lie to your prince?' raged Heshni, Tudha's half-brother and commander of the royal guard. '*Hundreds* of animals disappeared.'

The grounded man rose on his elbows, blinking and spitting mud. 'No, we, we did not-' he fell silent when Heshni swivelled the spear to train the bronze tip on his throat. At the same time, Heshni's elite *Mesedi* soldiers pressed their spears and swords to the necks of the other kneeling ones. 'Just give the word, my prince,' Heshni said, looking to Tudha.

The thunder crackled overhead, and Tudha felt a spike of fury that these people had forced this choice upon him. He glared down at the ringleader, hoping to see some glint of defiance or malice. But there was nothing. The man's eyes were like a mirror. For a moment they were just two Hittites on this bleak, wintry plain. He re-appraised the swelling on the man's muddy lip. A battle injury… or was it? An idea came to him then. 'Take their weapons,' he said quietly. 'Let them go.'

Heshni snorted. 'What?'

'They are plague-carriers,' Tudha said. 'See the lesion on this one's face?'

Heshni shuffled back a step, aghast. So did the other soldiers.

'We can't take them as slaves, and killing them will most likely infect you too,' Tudha explained.

'We can't just let them go,' Heshni protested. 'They stole from your father when they took those animals.'

Tudha did not repeat his decision. Instead he turned to the captured ones. 'Rise. Go back to your homes.'

The muddy-faced man rose to his feet, trembling. Gingerly, he and his band of men edged from the ring of soldiers, struck dumb and shambling, back towards the bare hills and the track that led to the town of Lalanda. Tudha could not help but notice a few dark looks between the Mesedi. They did not approve of his choice, apparently. 'Be ready to march,' he ordered them, 'we must return to the capital.'

Come noonday, the sky remained sullen, and now the mist-rain had turned to snow that settled in white streaks across the gloomy steppe. Tudha held onto the leatherbound rail of his silver-painted battle chariot as it rumbled northwards, a stiff and bitter wind buffeting him and the hunched old driver by his side. Heshni and his young driver rode abreast in a second war-car, while the bronze-shelled Mesedi contingent jogged behind. Tudha glanced over his shoulder at the train of bodyguards. There had been a time in the past when the Mesedi had numbered in their hundreds. All had perished in the civil war during Tudha's infant years. These few dozen were the first of a new era, trained in the old way. Heshni noticed him regarding his corps and bumped a fist against his chest armour. 'We are your shield, *Tuhkanti*,' he said, beaming with pride.

Tudha smiled back. As he turned to face forwards again, he noticed from the corner of his eye one of the jogging bodyguards: a bull-necked colossus with three pigtails of hair swishing in his wake. Had the man been… staring at him? It was not unusual for the soldiers to gaze at him – for he was *Tuhkanti,* heir to the realm. But this felt different, the look had been baleful. Furtively, he snatched another quick look back. The pigtailed warrior was looking dead-ahead now, but his face was still a picture of menace.

Ill at ease, he turned his eyes forwards once more. In this age of poverty and hunger, there had been much disgruntlement amongst the ranks. Talk even of sedition. Amongst the people too. Traitors and claimants everywhere, King Hattu often moaned. Tudha had not begun to recognise the signs for himself until the last few years: the clandestine meetings of nobles in dark corners of the capital; the sly looks and signals between cliques from the temples and the guilds. Twice in the last hot season cutthroats had been caught trying to break into the palace. Who had sponsored them, nobody knew – for both were shot through with arrows before they could be questioned. 'Cattle thieves are the least of our problems,' he muttered to himself.

Hearing this, his chariot driver's old face creased with a wry and poorly-disguised grin. Dagon had a reputation for reading people like a clay tablet.

'Something to say about my decision, Master Dagon?' he snapped. 'I suppose you think I should have ordered those men back there executed too?'

Dagon turned his white-haired head a little towards Tudha, his face riddled with age-lines and scars. 'You asked me to drive you on this mission, Prince Tudha, not to advise you.'

'That's funny, Old Horse, because it looks like you have some sparkling advice hidden behind your lips.'

Dagon cocked an eyebrow.

Tudha sighed. 'Forgive me. My temper is foul.'

'Understandable,' Dagon said, his voice dropping like the sails of a ship on a windless sea. 'Your father's condition is… worrying.'

Tudha heard the men jogging behind them chatting about the very same matter. 'King Hattu will step forth from the acropolis one day soon,' a veteran proclaimed, 'and he will stamp his foot on the earth, and all these troubles will be gone.'

'I have only ever seen the *Labarna* at the holy festivals,' replied a younger one. 'They say when he takes up weapon and wears armour his eyes become like those of an eagle and his teeth like those of a lion. Is it true?'

'No,' said a third. 'He is far greater than that.'

Their voices rose in a baritone doggerel as they went:

*'Lord of the storm, master of battle,*
*Enemies weep when they see Great King Hattu,*
*Bright as the sun, heartbeat like thunder,*
*Speed of the wind, strength of Tarhunda…'*

The song was stirring, but the truth was very different, Tudha knew. His father had not been a warrior for many years. Some said he had never been the same from the moment he ousted his murderous nephew Urhi-Teshub from the Hittite throne. The decline had truly begun later, in the moons after they had returned home from the war at Troy – a clash that seemed to have broken something inside the Hittite King. Yes, there had been battles after that, but more and more his father had retreated into a shell of introspection, languishing in the draughty halls of the palace, talking to himself, weeping while he wrote his memoirs. Hundreds upon hundreds of clay tablets Hattu had authored, each detailing a chapter of his past. He had forbidden anyone to set eyes upon the words.

'Last moon, before he became bedridden,' said Tudha, 'I went to Father's writing room. It was empty.'

Dagon rattled with a wry laugh. 'For once.'

'I read his tablets. The things that happened when you were both young. The training at the Fields of Bronze – before they fell into ruin. The battle for the Lost North. The plot of the Volca the Sherden. Is it true?'

Dagon stared ahead, a sadness in his eyes. 'All of it.'

Tudha shook his head slowly. 'The soldiers sing of heroism. I saw none of that in those texts. They grow ever more plaintive – tales of tragedy, betrayal and loss. All through the desert clash at Kadesh, and then the civil war. He even writes of his guilt about deposing Urhi-Teshub, and asks the Gods to watch over his nephew in his exile in the Egyptian deserts. So much remorse. And then I read his account of the Trojan War…'

Dagon and he shared a look. Both remembered the moments after the city's fall, when Hattu had taken the adolescent Tudha's clay slab – his eye-witness account of the struggle – and smashed it to pieces, declaring that it was best forgotten forever. 'He came back into the room then, saw me reading it. It was as if he had caught me opening a grave. He stormed across the room to snatch the tablet from me and, once again, smashed it to smithereens.'

Dagon smiled forlornly. 'He must have written and rewritten the tale of Troy a thousand times now. Every time, he bakes the tablet in the kilns, then destroys it immediately.'

'Why?'

'Maybe he has no wish to remember it, yet a compulsion to write it out – to try to understand it all.' Dagon sighed. 'I would give anything to see him in there writing again. He looks so weak lying in his bed.'

News had spread far and wide of the king's condition. Many covetous and powerful Hittite and foreign eyes now watched the Grey Throne and its ailing incumbent, wondering when it might next change hands, recognising the dawn of a game of power. It was an age of doubt.

'He will recover,' Tudha said, drumming the words into the air as if to make them true.

Dagon said nothing. Tudha noticed a watery sheen in the old man's eyes. Perhaps it was the bitter wind? Certainly, he had only once witnessed the old Chariot Master cry. The night he and his beloved wife Nirni had lain down to sleep together, their daughter Wiyani safely tucked up in the neighbouring room. He had risen in the hours of darkness to shuffle outside to the latrine. During those moments, the earth had shaken, and the house had collapsed upon his wife and girl. Tudha had led the rescue team, digging frantically for hours in the darkness. Dagon had been the one to call the dig to a halt, his face wet with tears. The moons of grief that followed had visibly aged him, bringing on his stoop.

'I always value your advice, Master Dagon. Always. Tell me what was on your mind about the captives back there?'

With a wry look, Dagon flicked his head back in the direction of Lalanda. 'Those men. They were no plague-victims. I saw you deal the one at the front the injury that burst his lip. Besides,' he tapped the pockmarks on his own cheeks, 'I know what real plague scars look like.'

'Aye. The only plague they carried was hunger, and does that not trouble us all these days?' said Tudha. 'Yes, they sinned by stealing from the herds, but what good would it do to bring them back to Hattusa in chains. How would we feed them?' he shrugged. 'To kill them? No, I have seen enough blood.'

Dagon stared into the blizzard as if seeing an old enemy out there in the murk. 'And yet the blood keeps coming.'

The old man's words sent a shiver through Tudha.

'*Tuhkanti,*' Heshni called out, his chariot wheels scraping as the vehicle peeled wide of the track. He was pointing to a sheltered col overlooking the road. 'The light is failing. This spot will make a good campsite for the night.'

***

Darkness fell and the blizzard hissed over the col. The Hittite soldiers hunkered down around a fire, pinching their hands for heat. Tudha moved around the edges, thanking each man by name for their swiftness in tracking down the cattle rustlers. It was a technique King Hattu had taught him – to show them that they were more than just soldiers, to forge a bond. He spotted the granite-faced one again, and realised that – to his shame – he didn't know this man's name. The mountain of muscle sat in just his leather kilt – no cloak for warmth – re-braiding his three pigtails.

'What's your name, soldier?'

The man looked up, sour at the interruption. 'Skarpi.'

Tudha noticed how he seemed detached from the others. A loner. 'You did well today. I will not forget your part in things.'

'Hmm,' the man said, then turned back to his braiding.

Bemused, Tudha left him to it rather than make an issue of his demeanour. Yet as he strolled away, he was certain – *certain* – that the man's eyes were burning into his back.

'My prince,' Heshni called from the edge of the camp, beckoning Tudha over, shooting concerned looks past him and towards the spot where Skarpi was seated.

'Who is that man?' Tudha asked quietly as he neared his half-brother.

'Skarpi? A nobody – son of a prostitute, some say. Lucky to be part of the Mesedi.' Heshni eyed the surly soldier again sceptically, then beckoned Tudha towards the edge of the col. 'Come, I wanted to show you something. Lights.'

'Lights?'

'I saw a torch, out there in the night, shining damply in the murk,' Heshni explained, guiding Tudha forward, round the base of the col and down a loose track. Outside the lee of their camp, the storm roared, casting their long hair and cloaks horizontal. 'I think the cattle thieves have doubled back,' Heshni shouted to be heard in the scream of the blizzard. 'They mean to steal from you again.'

'Could they be so foolish?' Tudha said, the snow stinging his bare arms and face. He could see nothing out there. 'Where are these lights?'

'There, look,' Heshni said, pointing into the whiteout. He stepped aside to allow Tudha past to see for himself.

Tudha stared hard, but could see nothing except speeding white snow and darkness beyond. 'I see no lights, and even if I could, I cannot believe that those men would risk their necks again. They knew how close they came to death today.'

'If only you were so wise,' Heshni purred from behind, the words underscored by the zing of a sword being plucked from its sheath.

Tudha swung on his heel, horrified by the sight of his half-brother, rising over him, teeth gritted in a snarl, blade plunging down towards his chest. Blood erupted, hot and stinking. Tudha fell to his back, coughing, retching. Snow and blood all around.

Yet no pain. No wound.

Shaking with fright, he saw Heshni still towering there, his sword frozen mid swing… his neck stump spurting blood. The severed head spun through the air and tumbled through the snow. Finally, the headless body whumped face-first into the snow, dead.

Skarpi stood there holding a bloody sword, sneering at the corpse of his former commander. 'I overheard him last night, talking about his plan. He led you to this place specifically. He had it all planned out.'

Tudha stared at the corpse, at Skarpi and then to the glow of firelight from the col where the main group were, just out of sight. 'Wait... talking? Talking with whom?'

'Two veterans were in on it with him. They planned to kill you then strike at your father.'

'Give me your spear,' Tudha said, his voice flat and emotionless. 'Point them out to me.'

Skarpi nodded sombrely. Together, the pair stomped back round to the fire. All the way, Tudha heard old Dagon's words echo in his mind.

*And yet the blood keeps coming.*

***

The next day, the Hittite band marched homewards. Tudha stood, head bowed, at the rail of the silver-painted chariot as it cut across the blizzard. Thunder cracked and rumbled, tormenting him with memories of last night.

'He may have been your half-brother, but in the end he was nothing,' Dagon tried to console him again.

Tudha glanced over to Heshni's chariot, adjacent, in the cabin of which the driver rode alone. Equally, two of the Mesedi were now gone. The executions had been swift and wordless, Skarpi beheading one and Tudha running the other through. Although shocked, none of the others had questioned the killings, and word quickly spread amongst them of Heshni's betrayal. 'The age of the Mesedi has passed,' he said quietly. 'During the civil war, the Golden Spearmen became seditious, and now so too have the Mesedi. I will speak to Father about it as soon as we are home. These men will be posted back to the regular divisions from which they came.' He looked over his shoulder at the colossus, Skarpi, face like granite, his trio of braided tails swishing as he ran. 'Of them all I trusted him the least. He will be the one I keep by my side.'

'I will be your eyes and ears also,' Dagon said. 'Your father's too.'

Tudha nodded gently in appreciation. Yet for all that, he could not shake the feeling that, just as the two Mesedi had been working for Heshni... Heshni might have been working for another. Someone higher in either station, power... or ambition.

'*Tuhkanti,* beware!' Skarpi bawled.

Jolting, Tudha dropped into a crouch in the chariot cabin, eyes sweeping the land for some incoming brigand attack. There was nothing out there. Then, an almighty *screech!* split the air from above. He cranked his head back to stare upwards: a great bird was spiralling down from the thunderous snow clouds. An eagle, he realised… fighting with its prey. Dagon slowed the chariot and Skarpi and his soldiers slowed too. All gawped at the tussle overhead.

'It is the spirit of Andor,' one of Skarpi's spearmen croaked in awe.

Tudha felt a strange shiver pass through him. His father had once kept an eagle, named Andor, as a companion for many years, and falcons before that. Some said that in battle the two were one, the king becoming man and eagle.

Now Tudha could see that it was certainly not the long-dead Andor. He could also see what this eagle was fighting with: a small bundle of grey fur. With a shriek and a howl, the plummeting pair parted, the eagle speeding off up into the sky again, dropping its prey. Instinctively, Tudha reached out to catch the hoary thing. A wolf cub; tiny and weighing almost nothing. Whimpering, bleeding and shivering, the cub nuzzled into the crook of his arm. Tudha looked up to see the eagle vanishing into the dark mass of snow clouds, as if leaving the world behind.

All around him, Skarpi and the other Mesedi gawped, paling, whispering in disbelief. Even Dagon drew back from him in the chariot cabin, struck dumb with amazement at what he had just witnessed. The small marching column ground to a halt.

Tudha felt his heart pounding harder and harder, a terrible sense of dread building within. What was this, if not the most profound of portents? Angered by the spiralling feeling that he was losing control of everything, he roared to them: 'Onwards. We are but hours from home.'

Soon, the chariots rolled onto a high plateau. A bolt of lightning shuddered across the sky, illuminating Hattusa. Tudha beheld the mighty Sphinx Rampart – a grand, sloping limestone bastion that shielded the capital's southern approaches, its central gate flanked by a pair of menacing winged sphinxes. On the whaleback hillside within these defences soared an army of temples – majestic structures of shining black stone, bronze statues, pearl-studded doors and fluttering ribbons. Through it all cut a glorious new avenue known as the Thunder Road. *I will write my own legend in stone,* he mouthed the mantra that had driven him to build this new, lofty ward. King Hattu had granted him all he required, and he had set about the task with zeal. The Temple Plateau, as the district was known, had almost doubled the size of the capital, making it a worthy peer to Pharaoh's Memphis or the Assyrian capital of Ashur.

Just then, the bundle he held in his left arm shuffled and whimpered. The cub, now wrapped in his black cloak for warmth, licked at the talon slashes on its shoulder. 'Sleep, little one. The animal healers in the city will tend to your cuts.' He knew not why he felt he had to care for this wild thing, only that he must.

The brumal wind keened again, as if driving them back from the Hittite capital. Only as the sound faded, did Tudha hear the other noise, shuddering through the storm.

*Clang!*

He straightened up a little in the cabin. Dagon too.

'Why does the great bell ring?' Skarpi asked through chattering teeth, behind them.

Tudha felt the blood in his veins turn cold as he saw, up there in the lee of the Sphinx Gate, a small figure, head hanging in grief: the Great Queen of the Hittites, Puduhepa. *Mother?* he mouthed. He knew what had happened. He had known – in truth – from the moment the eagle vanished into the heavens.

He wetted his lips and croaked: 'Because my father has become a god.'

Hope you enjoyed the sample! **Empires of Bronze: The Dark Earth** is available now at all good online stores.

# GLOSSARY

*Arzana House;* A tavern, usually outside the city walls. Men would go here for food, music, prostitutes and wrestling. Soldiers particularly favoured these places. There is evidence that Hittite princes would be taken there for cultic festivals and for puberty rites/inductions.

*Danna;* A measure of distance, somewhere between a kilometre and a mile.

*Hippocampus;* Mythological creature with the upper body of a horse with the lower body of a fish.

*Hurkeler;* A sexual deviant – one who performs an act of *hurkel* with an animal. The Hittites believed bestiality was a sin punishable by death… unless it was committed with a horse, in which case it was perfectly alright.

*Ishtar;* The Goddess of Love and War. Also known as Shauska, Inanna and many other names. She was infamous for her deceitful promises.

*Kerosia;* the Ahhiyawan council of elders.

*Labarna;* The Great King and High Priest of the Hittite Empire. Steward of the Gods. Also known as 'My Sun'.

*Lyarri*; Possible Trojan/Anatolian equivalent of the sun god Apollo.

*Megaron;* The largest room in a palatial building in the Aegean region, with four columns built around an open hearth, supporting the ceiling.

*Namra;* Prisoners of war who formed a big part of Bronze Age war booty. They would often be put to work in their captor's crop fields so that native men could be freed up to serve as soldiers. Sometimes the namra themselves were integrated en-masse into the Hittite army.

*Sarruma;* Hittite God of the Mountains.

*Syrinx;* Ancient pan pipes.

*Tarhunda;* Hittite God of the Storm, spouse of the Sun Goddess Arinniti and principal male deity of the Hittite pantheon.

*Tuhkanti;* The Tuhkanti was 'the second commander' and intended heir to the Hittite throne. Usually a son of the king.

*Wanax;* The highest king or military leader in Helladic-era (Late Bronze Age) Greece

Name Alterations

| **Person Name in Story** | **Person Name in History** |
|---|---|
| Hattu | Hattusili III |
| Muwa | Muwatalli II |
| Colta | Kikkuli (Means 'Colt' in Hurrian) |
| Sirtaya, the Egyptian envoy | Zirtaya |

If you enjoyed *Empires of Bronze: The Shadow of Troy*, why not try:

***Legionary*, by Gordon Doherty**

*The Roman Empire is crumbling, and a shadow looms in the east...*
376 AD: the Eastern Roman Empire is alone against the tide of barbarians swelling on her borders. Emperor Valens juggles the paltry border defences to stave off invasion from the Goths north of the Danube. Meanwhile, in Constantinople, a pact between faith and politics spawns a lethal plot that will bring the dark and massive hordes from the east crashing down on these struggling borders.
The fates conspire to see Numerius Vitellius Pavo, enslaved as a boy after the death of his legionary father, thrust into the limitanei, the border legions, just before they are sent to recapture the long-lost eastern Kingdom of Bosporus. He is cast into the jaws of this plot, so twisted that the survival of the entire Roman world hangs in the balance…

***Strategos: Born in the Borderlands*, by Gordon Doherty**

*When the falcon has flown, the mountain lion will charge from the east, and all Byzantium will quake. Only one man can save the empire . . . the Haga!*
1046 AD. The Byzantine Empire teeters on the brink of all-out war with the Seljuk Sultanate. In the borderlands of Eastern Anatolia, a land riven with bloodshed and doubt, young Apion's life is shattered in one swift and brutal Seljuk night raid. Only the benevolence of Mansur, a Seljuk farmer, offers him a second chance of happiness.
Yet a hunger for revenge burns in Apion's soul, and he is drawn down a dark path that leads him right into the heart of a conflict that will echo through the ages.

***Rise of Emperors: Sons of Rome*, by Gordon Doherty & Simon Turney**

*Four Emperors. Two Friends. One Destiny.*

As twilight descends on the 3rd century AD, the Roman Empire is but a shadow of its former self. Decades of usurping emperors, splinter kingdoms and savage wars have left the people beleaguered, the armies weary and the future uncertain. And into this chaos Emperor Diocletian steps, reforming the succession to allow for not one emperor to rule the world, but four.

Meanwhile, two boys share a chance meeting in the great city of Treverorum as Diocletian's dream is announced to the imperial court. Throughout the years that follow, they share heartbreak and glory as that dream sours and the empire endures an era of tyranny and dread. Their lives are inextricably linked, their destinies ever-converging as they rise through Rome's savage stations, to the zenith of empire. For Constantine and Maxentius, the purple robes beckon...

Printed in Great Britain
by Amazon

27528501R00249